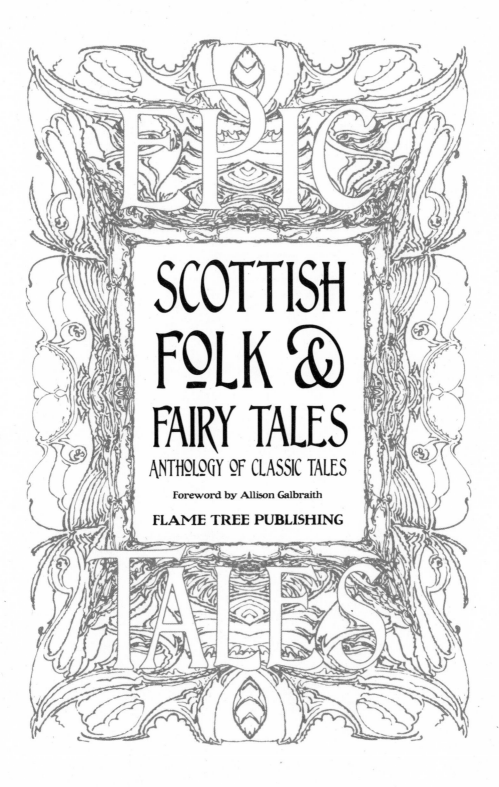

EPIC

SCOTTISH FOLK & FAIRY TALES

ANTHOLOGY OF CLASSIC TALES

Foreword by Allison Galbraith

FLAME TREE PUBLISHING

TALES

This is a FLAME TREE Book

Publisher & Creative Director: Nick Wells
Editorial Director: Catherine Taylor
Editorial Assistant: Jocelyn Pontes

Publisher's Note: Due to the historical nature of the classic text, we're aware
that there may be some language used which has the potential to cause offence
to the modern reader. However, wishing overall to preserve the integrity of the
text, rather than imposing contemporary sensibilities, we have left it unaltered.

FLAME TREE PUBLISHING
6 Melbray Mews, Fulham,
London SW6 3NS, United Kingdom
www.flametreepublishing.com

First published 2023

Copyright © 2023 Flame Tree Publishing Ltd

23 25 27 26 24
1 3 5 7 9 10 8 6 4 2

ISBN: 978-1-80417-590-3
Special ISBN: 978-1-80417-342-8

The cover image is created by Flame Tree Studio based on artwork by
Slava Gerj, Gabor Ruszkai and Arthur Rackham. Internal decorations are
courtesy Shutterstock.com and the following artists: ReVelStockArt,
Bourbon-88 and Karlionau (story headers).

A copy of the CIP data for this book is available from the British Library.

Printed and bound in China

EPIC

SCOTTISH FOLK & FAIRY TALES

ANTHOLOGY OF CLASSIC TALES

Foreword by Allison Galbraith

FLAME TREE PUBLISHING

TALES

Contents

TALES OF MAGIC & FAIRY FOLK

SPIRITS, MONSTERS & GHOSTLY TALES

ANIMALS & FABLES

Foreword

SCOTTISH LEGENDS, FOLKLORE AND FAIRY TALES are among the most enigmatic and intriguing worldwide. This collection offers a broad selection of traditional stories from every genre of Scottish mythology. Folklorists initially gathered them in the 19th and early 20th centuries, like John Francis Campbell of Islay, who, inspired by the Brothers Grimm, set out to save his local Highland folktales. He recorded hundreds of tales, mostly told in the Gaelic language, later translated into English. Campbell believed Scotland had a rich source of folktales because of Celtic and Nordic influences on its culture. The localised tales contain ghosts, giants, witches, fairies and fantastical creatures. The hero sagas of Fionn MacCumhail (Finn McCool) are also translated straight from Gaelic storytellers. Some are historical legends, stories of clans, battles, jealousy, betrayals, bravery, lovers, wild scenery and even wilder weather. They are told as true stories, rooted firmly in time, place and history, but containing the magical elements of folklore and supernatural surprises.

Some of the stories are versions of popular Grimms' Fairy Tales, like 'Gold Tree and Silver Tree', which is similar to Snow White; and 'The Sharp Grey Sheep' and 'Nippit Fit and Clippit Fit', both different versions of Cinderella. These Scottish variants are infused with local folk customs and supernatural beasts, making them raw, earthy and timeless. The language of the stories transports you to the fireside of a farm kitchen or to the great hall of an ancient castle, where you find yourself listening to a gifted grandmother or talented bard telling the most thrilling tales you've ever heard.

Neil Gaiman said of folktales and legends, "They give us the collective knowledge of humanity." A folktale can connect us to our ancestors and humanity's collective experience. This connection leads to a greater understanding of the present, helping us make sense of the times we live in. Humans crave experiences. The rich and diverse tales in this collection offer a myriad of adventures. Within the tales are many pearls of wisdom, showing us what it means to survive, overcome hardship and thrive in the world. The characters in these stories set out on quests and demonstrate every kind of virtue and vice known to humankind. The kind-hearted and thoughtful characters achieve happier lives than the wicked and greedy ones. These messages of how to live well and succeed in life resonate as profoundly with us now as they did with listeners long ago. They are often about the experiences of ordinary people, containing our fears and nightmares, but also our hopes and joys – these tales of adventure offer us a toolkit for resilience.

As well as descriptions of fantastical beings like Brownies, Selkies, Bogles, Kelpies and Mermaids, some tales relate to features of the land, like the story behind the origin of Loch Ness. The accounts of Saint Columba are fascinating, dating from the 6th century. They describe the remains of Druidical circles in Ardnamurchan and folk customs carried out in a cave in the Hebrides. Stories from the Borders include tales of the wizard Michael Scott, Thomas the Rhymer, and Canonbie Dick. They are set in locations popular with visitors, like Rhymer's Tower in Earlston, in the Eildon Hills, where Canonbie Dick meets King Arthur and his sleeping knights, still waiting under the hills to wake and save Britain from disaster. The story of the Dwarfie Stone from Orkney resonates with a Game of Thrones-style plot, filled with irreverent skulduggery from a cast of colourful characters.

We are all storytellers; our cultures live, breathe and evolve through the stories we tell. These legends, folk and fairy tales have lasted through generations because they contain everything that makes us feel alive, shudder, and laugh equally. They offer romanticism, glamour, nightmares, horror, reality and escapism. The stories are essential because they mirror our inner fears and desires. Humanity plays out within these pages (and other worlds of monsters and spirits). Still, you will surely come back from each story wiser and refreshed.

Allison Galbraith

Publisher's Note

MANY OF THE STORIES presented here were written down just as they were orally told more than a century ago. The work done by the authors to preserve the folklore of Scotland was largely conducted in the late nineteenth-century, and it often entailed transcribing and translating the words of native Gaelic-speakers throughout the country and from numerous walks of life. There is occasional variation in spellings and names, demonstrating the diversity within traditional folk culture that can often exist across a country or region. Some stories are derived from Celtic sources, indicating the influence that the Celts had on the development of culture in Scotland. This collection aims to provide a broad cross section of tales that demonstrate the evolution of folklore in Scotland, and the various influences that have shaped it over the centuries.

EPIC

SCOTTISH FOLK & FAIRY TALES

ANTHOLOGY OF CLASSIC TALES

Foreword by Allison Galbraith

FLAME TREE PUBLISHING

TALES

Scottish Folk & Fairy Tales

Introduction

THIS IS A BOOK of folk and fairy tales gathered from storytelling traditions across the Scottish islands, western and northern, and the mainland. When a princess cooks porridge for a crowd of 'wee peerie folk' (Orkney fairies), we realize how deeply local these stories are, reminders of the deep-rooted folk traditions of Scottish culture. At the same time, we quickly see how they are full of echoes and whispers, those gleanings of international myths, fairy tales and legends; a jealous stepmother asks the trout in a well, rather than a magic mirror, who is the most beautiful of all ('Gold-Tree and Silver-Tree'). A global storehouse of richly adaptable story patterns and protagonists are sieved through the specificities of Scottish culture, language and history. The grains of stories that fall through are distinctive, strange and beautiful in their 'eldritch' (a unique Scots word meaning uncanny or enchanted) powers.

Intuitively, we might think we know already the 'stuff' of such tales. It might comprise lost glass slippers, princesses, forests, witches, wolves or gingerbread houses, while the very notion of a folk tale evokes storyworlds of raw, earthy and timeless energy. As Angela Carter, godmother of the modern fairy tale, has remarked:

When we hear the formula 'Once upon a time', or any of its variants, we know in advance that what we are about to hear isn't going to pretend to be true. Mother Goose may tell lies, but [...] she is going to entertain you, to help you pass the time. In the hands of folklorists and traditional narrative scholars inclined to classification, this material is meticulously defined. Broadly speaking, a folk tale is an anonymous narrative transmitted through informal oral traditions [...]. Folk narrative embraces a diversity of kinds and forms, ranging from proverbs, riddles, sayings and anecdotes to legends, myths and Märchen (the German term commonly used to describe a tale characterized by elements of wonder and magic). A great many of the tales here belong to this last group. Some are studded with flickers of well-known fairy tales such as Cinderella and Bluebeard. Others reveal the influence of the classical myth [...].

What is a Fairy Tale?

It is worth noting how thorny (in scholarly terms) the definition of 'fairy tale' easily becomes. Although there has always been continued, busy traffic between oral and literary cultures, the term itself is derived from the French *contes des fées* (literally, tales of the fairies), drawn from the earliest printed collections of magical, marvellous tales published by women in seventeenth-century France. This 'book' tradition nurtured the development of the classical Western fairy tale canon, first introduced to eighteenth-century readers in Britain through popular chapbooks (cheaply produced pamphlets distributed at fairs and marketplaces by travelling pedlars). In a famous piece of fairy tale history Jacob and Wilhelm Grimm, two brothers from Hanau in Germany, moulded the genre into a book suitable for all the household, the *Kinder- und Hausmärchen*, 1812, 1815. The work was reprinted throughout the nineteenth century and thereafter, ensuring that fairy stories would come to haunt the threshold between so-called 'children's' and 'adult' literature – the stuff of our nightmares as well as our dreams.

Unsurprisingly, given the development of psychoanalysis at the turn of the century, the material of fairy tale and myth was strewn through the dreams and stories of 'patients' who told their inner lives to analysts. In so doing they helped to articulate insights into the unconscious realm of an individual (in the work of Sigmund Freud) or a collective culture (in that of Carl Jung). Every fairy tale which is retold or reimagined holds a mirror up to its own culture. It provides an endlessly creative looking glass which shows us our desires, longings and fears.

A Diverse Cauldron of Tales

Another group of stories in our volume can be classed as 'legendary', with the implication of truthfulness or verisimilitude attached. These include stories of how a particular location (or fish, as in one tale) acquired its name, or stories associated with specific, often deeply resonant or emotive historical events and figures (such as the eighteenth-century Jacobite Wars and the fate of Charles Stuart, Bonnie Prince Charlie). Tales about clans and clan lore are a strong feature of many of these traditional stories, reflecting the enduring power of clan-based society in the Highlands. Another tale draws from the life of the medieval alchemist and legendary wizard Michael Scot, practitioner of the diabolic arts. This wonderfully compressed account of his life leads the reader from the manufacture of the 'ropes' which take Scot 'to the back of the moon' to the intriguing battle between raven and dove for custody of his soul.

There are also stories which feature accounts of saints. The tale of Saint Columba (or Colum Cille in Irish), for example, fuses the historical, the legendary and the marvellous by drawing on oral traditions of the saint's wonder-workings that reach back to the early Middle Ages. Our collection also contains stories that belong to the great medieval Irish Gaelic cycles and sagas, in particular those featuring the heroic deeds of Fionn mac Cumhaill. The sea channel between Ireland and Scotland proved a rich carrier of oral legend and lore, washing tales of Celtic warrior-heroes and the old kings of Ireland onto western Scottish shores.

In another distinctive grouping of tales, animals are the chief protagonists. Stories about 'talking beasts' are found in the earliest storytelling cultures and myths. Animals who spoke and behaved like humans appeared in the short moral narratives of the classical fabulist called Aesop; some of the first printed, popular tale collections were imitations and reinventions of Aesopian fables. This genre gifted to the world such characters as the roguish Reynard the Fox, with his admirable guile and wit. Scottish tradition absorbed these stories with particular skill and ease. The animal stories in this volume occupy the rich threshold between parable, fable, fairy and folk tales. A bittersweet vein of satire runs through the narrative of 'The Fox and the Wolf', for example – the account of a friendship soured by the arrival of a pot of butter from Ireland.

Then there are the tales in this collection that derive from other oral folk traditions, such as ballads, now turned into prose narratives. Here we find the stories of Thomas the Rhymer, Lowland Scotland's most famous fairy communicant. Scottish folk and fairy tales therefore spring out of a diverse, fluid and metamorphic cultural world.

Haunted Imaginations: Scotland and the Supernatural

Stories of spirit worlds and magic permeate every culture – but do they take particular shape and form when distilled through the imaginations of Scottish writers? There is in many ways a deep-rooted association between the idea of 'Scotland' and the idea of the 'fantastic'. Such a connection ranges from medieval poetry, with its incarnations of devils and fairies and the uncanny realms of ballad tradition, through James Macpherson's notorious Ossian tales in the eighteenth century and their portrayal of an ancient, mystical Highland culture which enchanted Europe, to the attempts of the earliest critics of Scottish literature to fashion a distinctive national tradition around the idea of a pervasive 'otherworldly' dimension.

Tradition and folk culture have constituted the deep-rooted historical heart of Scottish literature, providing an endless pool of 'auld warld stories' [old world stories], in the phrase of James Hogg (creator of the demonic Gothic novel, *The Private Memoirs and Confessions of a Justified Sinner*). Through the centuries Scottish writers have made striking and powerful interventions into the genres of Gothic fiction, ghost story, fairy tale, horror, crime noir and their contemporary reimaginings. J.M. Barrie is well-known, indeed well-loved, by many for his fairy play *Peter Pan* – yet that, too, draws on a darker realm of fairy belief from Scottish folklore, cutting through its Edwardian escapism with a swathe of folkloric malevolence.

A Map of Storytelling

Many of the stories collected here are associated with particular regions and places – for example, Argyllshire, Islay, Barra, the Scottish Borders – and often, in the detail of their imaginative fabric, allude to a specific hill or loch, the site of a battle or haunting. This geographical diversity maps out the cultural and linguistic diversity of the country's storytelling heritage. Although this volume contains stories translated into English, they are drawn from the Gaelic-speaking culture of the Highlands and islands and its Irish inheritance, the Orkney and Shetland Islands, with their own dialect traditions and close ties to Scandinavia, and the Lowland regions (especially the Borders), its story culture rooted in the languages of both Scots and English.

While a shared imaginative currency permeates all these tales, we should be mindful that each place, each language, bears its own social and political history. Gaelic and the culture of the *Gàidhealtachd*, for example, were subject to oppression and persecution, especially in the wake of the nineteenth-century Highland Clearances. And the broad imaginative arc of these stories bears witness to profound historical changes in Scotland's national identity – from its status as the independent medieval kingdom of Alba to a country which lost its political sovereignty in the wake of the Union of the Crowns (1603) and the Union of Parliaments (1707).

And yet, as well as recognizing difference and diversity in the provenance of these tales, we should acknowledge their socially cohesive role, binding together communities of tellers and listeners. This is a vital part, for example, of the heritage and identity of Traveller communities in Scotland. In Gaelic culture, the *cèilidh* or neighbourhood gathering was a place for sharing story materials among folk of all ages. Traditional storytelling united generations (Robert Burns, Walter Scott and James Hogg wrote tenderly of the tales and ballads they had heard in childhood from nursemaids and grandparents) and often unfolded against a background of work: spinning, carding, fishing, harvesting. These marvellous stories were also the stuff of everyday life.

Foraging for Stories

How, then, did these spoken tales find their way into print? This metamorphosis was largely enabled by the endeavours of nineteenth-century folklorists, antiquarians and collectors. In turn they were influenced by a European-wide, Romantic movement driven by the desire to preserve the fragile and vanishing oral folk heritage of national and regional cultures. In the Scottish Borders the twenty-one-year-old Walter Scott set out on horseback to collect songs and ballads from local people, resulting in the publication of the famous *Minstrelsy of the Scottish Border*. In the Highlands and Islands John Francis Campbell of Islay (Iain Òg Ile), immersed in Gaelic culture from childhood, began to collect local stories in 1847. This became a lifelong and systematic enterprise through his friendship with Sir George Webb Dasent, a collector of Norse folk tales who was influenced by Jacob Grimm. Along with a small team, Campbell collected material from storytellers across the region – restoring visibility and importance to Gaelic culture and transforming collection practice in the process – in his landmark, four-volume publication, *Tales of the West Highlands*. Many of the stories in this book come from Campbell's work.

A Weave of Story Patterns

Behind the printed versions of these stories, then, are the voices of the oral tellers who first recounted them. In the stories themselves, we may become aware of yet another storyteller – not the 'invisible', anonymous teller of tradition, but a figure who appears at the end, wryly commenting (see 'they left me sitting here' in 'The Girl and the Dead Man'). Usually, though, the story unfurls without storyteller comment in a world of bare factuality where strange and often shockingly violent things happen, delivered at a compelling pace. In a few stories characters themselves are storytellers, for example the tale of 'Conall Cra Bhuidhe', in which the king must tell stories in order to deliver his three sons from a deathly fate. The gift of storytelling literally has life-giving powers – as it famously does in the story of Scheherazade and her courageous eloquence from the ancient and medieval Middle Eastern folk tale collection, *One Thousand and One Nights*.

These sharp, linear narratives always proceed towards resolution, frequently driven by the quest or task which their protagonist(s) must undertake. Some tales are very brief;

others may be more complex and interwoven with multiple episodes, as if one story 'gives birth' to another. We find this elaborate narrative architecture in many of the heroic tales and in those that entail a series of quests or challenges for the hero, or heroine, to undertake. In the midst of such busy, incident-filled narrative, we notice how the number three acquires a magical, talismanic quality.

Such familiar recurrent patterns and weaves of repetition constitute a collection of recognizable, recurring narratives. Known in folk tale scholarship as 'tale types', they are identified by an international classificatory system known as the ATU Index (or Aarne–Thompson–Uther Index, after the folklorists who devised it). Traditional folk and fairy tales create worlds which, as the Russian scholar Vladimir Propp famously argued, offer up familiar, stylized protagonists and scenarios. Their character arcs are supposedly predictable and formulaic, with the protagonists facing first danger and challenge, then success and resolution. This surefast folk tale paradigm is described by another well-known scholar, Tzvetan Todorov, as the movement from equilibrium to disruption – which always, ultimately, returns to equilibrium.

All this alerts us to reassuring structures of symmetry and consistency in these tales, and to an awareness of characters and events as pieces to be moved to infinite variation on the storyteller's chessboard. Despite this, however, each tale still generates its own emotional push and pull. Heroes and heroines from across the social spectrum reveal desires and vulnerabilities that foster our sympathy and care. Repeated numbers, quests and tasks weave their own incantatory spell:

> *She had besides, of nuts as she broke, of needles as she lost, of thimbles as she pierced, of thread as she used, of candles as she burned, a bed of green silk over her, a bed of green silk under her, sleeping by day and watching by night.* ('The Girl and the Dead Man')

Even in bare narrative worlds, where only the outer shell of action and events seems foremost, there is always room for images and symbols whose beauty and strangeness resist explanation:

> *they filled for her a glass of wine [...] a flame went up out of the glass, and a golden pigeon and a silver pigeon sprung out of it.* ('The Battle of the Birds')

Magical Worlds and the Realm of the Fairies

Magic is the enabling and transformative power of folk and fairy tales the world over. Supernatural agency resides in words and objects: a rhyme, a name, an egg, a sword, even a cockleshell which serves as a boat for an Otherworld journey. However, the fairies and witches, monsters and demons of these story types have their own cultural particularity. The tales in this volume depict spirit worlds which are diverse and heterogenous, teeming with beings, creatures and occult powers that belong to the universe of traditional Scottish folk belief.

Perhaps the most active and dangerous magical activity across these tales comes from the fairies – the *daoine sìth* or 'people of peace'. In the late seventeenth century Scotland had its own fairy chronicler in the figure of Robert Kirk, a minister and Gaelic scholar from Perthshire. His treatise, *The Secret Commonwealth*, was a radical fusion of folkloric, religious and scientific thought, describing the uncanny proximity of fairy and human realms. As both Kirk's work and these stories attest, the world of the Scottish *fae* is wholly unlike anything we might know from Victorian ethereality or even contemporary culture's ideas of the fairy world. These fairies can be malevolent, capricious and vengeful. They steal human children and leave ancient changelings in their place; they wound cattle; punish the disobedient; or lure the curious into a fairy realm with a tricksy temporality. Such creatures have a Gothic and macabre tinge, like the fairy woman who steals a kettle only to return it each day with 'flesh and bones' in it, then sets her fairy hell-hounds on the husband who neglects his sacred duty to her; or the demonic goblin figures of 'The Elfin Knight'; or the Gruagach, the scarily hirstute goblin linked to the wild man of the forest. Yet they can also bestow gifts on humans if they choose; Thomas the Rhymer learns prophecy and poetry.

The space of fairyland in these tales is often portrayed as a beautiful realm, filled with music (in one tale the fairies dance furiously to 'a tiny set of bagpipes'), colour and carnivalesque revelry. It is often a sensual, erotically charged world too, with a tricky temporality. The Fairy Queen possesses distinctive power in Scottish lore. Riding at the helm of the fairy host, she enchants the Rhymer, for instance, by her iconic beauty. Yet even this proves to be duplicitous as she shape-shifts into a 'hag' on their journey.

Active at particular times of the year, fairies frequently reside in caverns, caves and hills, or within enchanted fairy rings imprinted on the earth. In that sense Scottish fairies are strongly associated with the green world, with the energy and earthiness of nature. Fairies, along with other kindred spirits, have long been associated with the natural world – their powers linked to sacred places or wells, to various herbs, plants and animals, or reflected in the green fabrics of their clothes and shoes. But at the same time they also share in its fragility, and many of these stories suggest that the last of the fairies has been seen, or their dwelling-place has disappeared.

For the most part in these stories, the fairy world exists outside the moral universe of Christian values, though many of them make evocative use of religious imagery and symbols. For instance the Rhymer at first mistakes the Fairy Queen for the Virgin Mary, while in 'The Elfin Knight' Earl St Clair is protected from fairy *glamour* (the archaic Scots term for 'enchantment') by carrying the sign of the cross with him. The utterance of a holy word can 'unspell' an enchantment; another story invokes the belief of fairies as fallen angels. These tales make incarnate a vital world of living folk belief which, in the historical reality of early modern Scotland, ran the tragic and deadly risk of witchcraft charges.

The Dead and the Demonic

The rituals of life and death underpin the heart of folk and fairy tales, so it is no surprise that a number of these stories are preoccupied with in-between, liminal realms and the spirits who reside there. The destructive, life-devouring energies of the Cailleach, a powerful winter crone goddess, play havoc with the life cycles of the forest. Unquiet landscapes contain spirits and creatures, while ghosts refuse to settle (in one tale even fighting between themselves). The world of the dead can intrude into the living in matter-of-fact, quotidian ways. The heroine of 'The Girl and the Dead Man' is tasked with watching over a corpse who is 'under spells', while in the grisly, corporeal tale of 'The Death Bree' [broth], the dead are the useful source of remedies and charms. A kind of deadpan folk-Gothic is at play in such tales.

Other tales summon occult and diabolic powers for a variety of purposes. Drawing on long-established folk and literary representations of women and witchcraft in Scottish culture, the brilliant 'Witch of Fife', based on a ballad by James Hogg, shows how the nocturnal satanic trafficking of east-coast women – including trips to Norway and Lapland to feast with 'witches and elves [...] Fairies, and Mermaids of the North [...] Warlocks, and Brownies, and Pixies' – subverts gender hierarchies in comic yet radical fashion. Occult knowledge offers women joyful liberation from the oppressive strictures of domestic and social life.

The Powers of Nature

In these stories fairies and other creatures belong to water as much as to earth and woods – to seas and lochs, pools and wells. Here we encounter vengeful water spirits, sea maidens who bargain for human children, kelpies intent on drowning unguarded humans and the terrifying loch monster, the *uile-bhéist*. Then there are stories about selkies – beings who are half-human, half-seal – in an enduringly powerful Celtic reimagining of a body of European mermaid and siren lore. In one tale, set on Unst, the most northerly of the Shetland Islands, the marriage between a selkie and the man who stole her sealskin can only ever be temporary. In a moving twist of fate, her own child accidentally discovers her skin. Their return of it to her means abandonment of family – but she resumes her form with joy and returns to her own kind in the sea for all eternity. Within the compass of this folk tale is a prescient ecological fable to leave nature alone.

In this volume we come across landscapes which are both entirely natural and organic yet simultaneously *un*natural – sheltering spirits and creatures with the constant potential to be awakened into uncanny life. Nature in all its forms is a vital and dynamic feature of fairy and folk tales. Usually a healing, creative and instructive presence, it can nevertheless dispense curses as well as blessings, and certain creatures can be the instruments and means of diabolic work.

These tales give distinctive imaginative and symbolic life to trees, plants and animals. They are populated by ravens, dogs, snakes, otters, falcons, cats, frogs who speak rhymes, little birds who cry warnings and 'invisible horses of wind'. The forest and the greenwood are home to wild dogs and enchanted deer as well as to wild men and crones. Animals teach, collaborate with and are sources of wisdom for the human protagonists whom they meet. Acts of kindness and generosity ensure that messages, gifts and rewards are brought to fairy-tale heroes and heroines. These tales suggest how mutual compassion, honour and respect between humans and wild things keep the world in balance.

Rebel Women

On one level, fairy and folk tales portray a world of gender and family governed by 'conservative' structures. Women are seen as emblems of beauty and marriageability, as well as the bearers of future heirs. The trinity of maidens, mothers and crones prevails – but in these stories the latter category encompasses not only wise women and healers but also older women, whose bodies are often treated with shocking violence. Successful marriage, with the expectation of love, riches and inevitable procreation, is the approved destiny for the majority of folk and fairy-tale heroines.

However, the apparently immutable framework of that conventional ideology only holds so far in some of these Scottish stories. We find gestures of wonderful resistance: heroines worthy of Angela Carter and other feminist fairy-tale revisionists show strength, courage and ingenuity as they outwit predatory giants or evade jealous stepmothers who seek to do them harm. In 'The Battle of the Birds' the heroine employs an extraordinary range of ingenious tricks to help the hero (her eventual husband) evade capture, such as swiftly weaving a ladder for a tree five hundred feet tall. In order to climb the 'hill of poison', assailable only by wearing horseshoes on hand and feet, a heroine swiftly becomes expert in the craft of smithing ('The Tale of the Hoodie').

Strikingly, there is room for sisterly solidarity as well as the traditional fairy-tale rivalry which locks women (sisters, stepsisters, mothers and (step)daughters, as well as young females in general) into eternal destructive battles for competition. In 'Gold Tree and Silver Tree', for instance, the potential rival of 'the Other Princess' for the hero's love heals and saves the legitimate bride; her selfless act is rewarded in a happy ending which sees a kind of ménage-à-trois triumphantly subvert a patriarchal and heterosexual ending. In 'Peerifool' the youngest sister heroically rescues her older siblings from the clutches of an evil giant; she brings them back to life but, horrified by their bruises and wounds, swiftly and elegantly contrives the brutal despatch of their oppressor. Male violence and cruelty are again challenged and ultimately destroyed in the story of 'The Widow and her Daughters', which recasts the misogynistic horror of the Bluebeard narrative – these women are survivors, and agents of their own destinies. Time and again the heroines of these anonymous tales from Scottish oral tradition show resilience, resistance and creativity in the face of oppression. In so doing they reveal a striking difference from many of their more passive, confined and victimized counterparts in the classic European fairy-tale tradition.

* * *

Though drawn from deep wells of heritage, memory and community these tales of the old magic still speak to us now, if we let them – they survive for a reason. Storytelling is a living tradition in Scotland today and the traditional arts are flourishing for new generations. Though some of the tales' frames of reference might make them seem strange and remote from our own concerns, they also celebrate enduring attributes such as kindness, trust and courage, as well as the powers of love and imagination. In the interconnectedness of the worlds they depict – human, natural, spirit – these stories can still teach us things. They re-enchant through the optimism at their heart, making room for healing, restoration and justice. And there is always the promise that at the end of 'great hardships' lies the 'realm of gladness' (Conall Cra Bhuidhe), and that intriguing flickers of wonder exist in the everyday.

Dr. Sarah Dunnigan

HEROIC MYTHOLOGY

Introduction

BATTLES JOINED; giants slain; perilous journeys and princesses won. Such is the stuff of heroic legend in every culture. Generally, though, the folk tradition has looked for something more than military prowess and derring-do. The Scottish tradition is certainly no exception. As the stories of Conall and others show, heroes have been valued not just for their courage but for their quick-wittedness; or for the quieter foresight the hooded crow shows in 'The Hoodie and the Fox'. Heroic mythology frequently touches on the macabre ('The Poor Brother and the Rich') and the mysterious ('A Puzzle'; 'Canonbie Dick and Thomas of Ercildoune').

Ultimately, though, these stories have in common an upbeat estimation of human resourcefulness: our capacity to prevail, whatever the difficulties we face, when we summon up all our intelligence and resolve.

Conall Cra Bhuidhe

CONALL CRA BHUIDHE WAS a sturdy tenant in Eirinn: he had four sons. There was at that time a king over every fifth of Eirinn. It fell out for the children of the king that was near Conall, that they themselves and the children of Conall came to blows. The children of Conall got the upper hand, and they killed the king's big son. The king sent a message for Conall, and he said to him – "Oh, Conall! what made thy sons go to spring on my sons till my big son was killed by thy children? but I see that though I follow thee revengefully, I shall not be much the better for it, and I will now set a thing before thee, and if thou wilt do it, I will not follow thee with revenge. If thou thyself, and thy sons, will get for me the brown horse of the king of Lochlann, thou shalt get the souls of thy sons." "Why," said Conall, "should not I do the pleasure of the king, though there should be no souls of my sons in dread at all. Hard is the matter thou requirest of me, but I will lose my own life, and the life of my sons, or else I will do the pleasure of the king."

After these words Conall left the king, and he went home: when he got home he was under much trouble and perplexity. When he went to lie down he told his wife the thing the king had set before him. His wife took much sorrow that he was obliged to part from herself, while she knew not if she should see him more. "Oh, Conall," said. she, "why didst not thou let the king do his own pleasure to thy sons, rather than be going now, while I know not if ever I shall see thee more?" When he rose on the morrow, he set himself and his four sons in order, and they took their journey towards Lochlann, and they made no stop but (were) tearing ocean till they reached it. When they reached Lochlann they did not know what they should do. Said the old man to his sons – "stop ye, and we will seek out the house of the king's miller."

When they went into the house of the king's miller, the man asked them to stop there for the night. Conall told the miller that his own children and the children of the king had fallen out, and that his children had killed the king's son, and there was nothing that would please the king but that he should get the brown horse of the king of Lochlann. "If thou wilt do me a kindness, and wilt put me in a way to get him, for certain I will pay thee for it." "The thing is silly that thou art come to seek," said the miller; "for the king has laid his mind on him so greatly that thou wilt not get him in any way unless thou steal him; but if thou thyself canst make out a way, I will hide thy secret." "This, I am thinking," said Conall, "since thou art working every day for the king, that thou and thy gillies should put myself and my sons into five sacks of bran." "The plan that came into thy head is not bad," said the miller. The miller spoke to his gillies, and he said to them to do this, and they put them in five sacks. The king's gillies came to seek the bran, and they took the five sacks with them, and they emptied them before the horses. The servants locked the door, and they went away.

When they rose to lay hand on the brown horse, said Conall, "You shall not do that. It is hard to get out of this; let us make for ourselves five hiding holes, so that if they perceive us we may go in hiding." They made the holes, then they laid hands on the horse. The horse was pretty well unbroken, and he set to making a terrible noise through the stable.

The king perceived him. He heard the noise. "It must be that that was my brown horse," said he to his gillies; "try what is wrong with him."

The servants went out, and when Conall and his sons perceived them coming they went into the hiding holes. The servants looked amongst the horses, and they did not find anything wrong; and they returned and they told this to the king, and the king said to them that if nothing was wrong that they should go to their places of rest. When the gillies had time to be gone, Conall and his sons laid the next hand on the horse. If the noise was great that he made before, the noise he made now was seven times greater. The king sent a message for his gillies again, and said for certain there was something troubling the brown horse. "Go and look well about him." The servants went out, and they went to their hiding holes. The servants rummaged well, and did not find a thing. They returned and they told this. "That is marvellous for me," said the king: "go you to lie down again, and if I perceive it again I will go out myself." When Conall and his sons perceived that the gillies were gone, they laid hands again on the horse, and one of them caught him, and if the noise that the horse made on the two former times was great, he made more this time.

"Be this from me," said the king; "it must be that some one is troubling my brown horse." He sounded the bell hastily, and when his waiting man came to him, he said to him to set the stable gillies on foot that something was wrong with the horse. The gillies came, and the king went with them. When Conall and his sons perceived the following coming they went to the hiding holes. The king was a wary man, and he saw where the horses were making a noise. "Be clever," said the king, "there are men within the stable, and let us get them somehow." The king followed the tracks of the men, and he found them. Every man was acquainted with Conall, for he was a valued tenant by the king of Eirinn, and when the king brought them up out of the holes he said, "Oh, Conall art thou here?" "I am, O king, without question, and necessity made me come. I am under thy pardon, and under thine honour, and under thy grace." He told how it happened to him, and that he had to get the brown horse for the king of Eirinn, or that his son was to be put to death. "I knew that I should not get him by asking, and I was going to steal him." "Yes, Conall, it is well enough, but come in," said the king. He desired his look-out men to set a watch on the sons of Conall, and to give them meat. And a double watch was set that night on the sons of Conall. "Now, O Conall," said the king, "wert thou ever in a harder place than to be seeing thy lot of sons hanged tomorrow? But thou didst set it to my goodness and to my grace, and that it was necessity brought it on thee, and I must not hang thee. Tell me any case in which thou wert as hard as this, and if thou tellest that, thou shalt get the soul of thy youngest son with thee." "I will tell a case as hard in which I was," said Conall.

"I was a young lad, and my father had much land, and he had parks of year-old cows, and one of them had just calved, and my father told me to bring her home. I took with me a laddie, and we found the cow, and we took her with us. There fell a shower of snow. We went into the herd's bothy, and we took the cow and the calf in with us, and we were letting the shower (pass) from us. What came in but one cat and ten, and one great one-eyed fox-coloured cat as head bard over them. When they came in, in very deed I myself had no liking for their company. 'Strike up with you,' said the head bard, I why should we be still? and sing a cronan to Conall Cra-Bhui.' I was amazed that my name was known to the cats themselves. When they had sung the cronan, said the head bard, 'Now, O Conall, pay the reward of the cronan that the cats have sung to thee.' 'Well then,' said I myself, 'I have no reward whatsoever for you, unless you should go down and take that calf.' No sooner said I the word than the two cats and ten went down to attack the calf, and, in very deed, he did not last them long. 'Play up with you, why should you be silent? Make a cronan to Conall Cra-Bhui,' said the head bard. Certainly I had no liking at all for the cronan, but up came the one cat and ten, and if they did not sing me a cronan then and there! 'Pay them now their reward,' said the great fox-coloured cat. 'I am tired myself of yourselves and your rewards,' said I. 'I have no reward for you unless you take that cow down there.' They betook themselves to the cow, and indeed she did not stand them out for long.

"'Why will you be silent? Go up and sing a cronan to Conall Cra-Bhui,' said the head bard. And surely, oh, king, I had no care for them or for their cronan, for I began to see that they were not good comrades. When they had sung me the cronan. they betook themselves down where the head bard was. 'Pay now their reward,' said the head bard; and for sure, oh, king, I had no reward for them; and I said to them, 'I have no reward for you, unless you will take that, laddie with you and make use of him.' When the boy heard this he took himself out, and the cats after him. And surely, oh, king, there was 'striongan' and catterwauling between them. When they took themselves out, I took out at a turf window that was at the back of the house. I took myself off as hard as I might into the wood. I was swift enough and strong at that time; and when I felt the rustling 'toirm' of the cats after me I climbed into as high a tree as I saw in the place, and (one) that was close in the top; and I hid myself as well as I might. The cats began to search for me through the wood, and they were not finding me; and when they were tired, each one said to the other that they would turn back. 'But,' said the one-eyed fox-coloured cat that was commander-in-chief over them, 'you saw him not with your two eyes, and though I have but one eye, there's the rascal up in the top of the tree.' When he had said that, one of them went up in the tree, and as he was coming where I was, I drew a weapon that I had and I killed him. 'Be this from me!' said the one-eyed one – 'I must not be losing my company thus; gather round the root of the tree and dig about it, and let down that extortioner to earth.' On this they gathered about her (the tree), and they dug about her root, and the first branching root that they cut, she gave a shiver to fall, and I myself gave a shout, and it was not to be wondered at. There was in the neighbourhood of the wood a priest, and he had ten men with him delving, and he said, 'There is a shout of extremity and I must not be without replying to it.' And the wisest of the men said, 'Let it alone till we hear it again.' The cats began, and they began wildly, and they broke the next root; and I myself gave the next shout, and in very deed it was not weak. 'Certainly,' said the priest, 'it is a man in extremity – let us move.' They were setting themselves in order for moving. And the cats arose on the tree, and they broke the third root, and the tree fell on her elbow. I gave the third shout. The stalwart men hasted, and when they saw how the cats served the tree, they began at them with the spades; and they themselves and the cats began at each other, till they were killed altogether – the men and the cats. And surely, oh king, I did not move till I saw the last one of them falling. I came home. And there's for thee the hardest case in which I ever was; and it seems to me that tearing by the cats were harder than hanging tomorrow by the king of Lochlann."

"Oh! Conall," said the king, "thou art full of words. Thou hast freed the soul of thy son with thy tale; and if thou tellest me a harder case than thy three sons to be hanged tomorrow, thou wilt get thy second youngest son with thee, and then thou wilt have two sons."

"Well then," said Conall, "on condition that thou dost that, I was in a harder case than to be in thy power in prison tonight." "Let's hear," said the king. – "I was there," said Conall, "as a young lad, and I went out hunting, and my father's land was beside the sea, and it was rough with rocks, caves, and geos. When I was going on the top of the shore, I saw as if there were a smoke coming up between two rocks, and I began to look what might be the meaning of the smoke coming up there. When I was looking, what should I do but fall; and the place was so full of manure, that neither bone nor skin was broken. I knew not how I should get out of this. I was not looking before me, but I was looking over head the way I came – and the day will never come that I could get up there. It was terrible for me to be there till I should die. I heard a great clattering 'tuarneileis' coming, and what was there but a great giant and two dozen of goats with him, and a buck at their head. And when the giant had tied the goats, he came up and he said to me, 'Hao O! Conall, it's long since my knife is rusting in my pouch waiting for thy tender flesh.' 'Och!' said I, 'it's not much thou wilt be bettered by me, though thou should'st tear me asunder; I will make but one meal for thee. But I see that thou art one-eyed. I am a good leech, and I will give thee the sight of the other eye.' The giant went and he drew the great caldron on the site of the fire. I myself was telling him how he should heat the water, so that I should give its sight to the other eye. I got heather and I made a rubber of it, and I set him upright in the caldron. I began at the eye that was well, pretending to him that I would give its sight to the other one, till I left them as bad as each other; and surely it was easier to spoil the one that was well than to give sight to the other.

"When he 'saw' that he could not see a glimpse, and when I myself said to him that I would get out in spite of him, he gave that spring out of the water, and he stood in the mouth of the cave, and he said that he would have revenge for the sight of his eye. I had but to stay there crouched the length of the night, holding in my breath in such a way that he might not feel where I was.

"When he felt the birds calling in the morning, and knew that the day was, he said – 'Art thou sleeping? Awake and let out my lot of goats.' I killed the buck. He cried, 'I will not believe that thou art not killing my buck.' 'I am not,' said I, 'but the ropes are so tight that I take long to loose them.' I let out one of the goats, and he was caressing her, and he said to her, 'There thou art thou shaggy, hairy white goat, and thou seest me, but I see thee not.' I was letting them out by the way of one and one, as I flayed the buck, and before the last one was out I had him flayed bag wise. Then I went and I put my legs in place of his legs, and my hands in place of his fore legs, and my head in place of his head, and the horns on top of my head, so that the brute might think that it was the buck. I went out. When I was going out the giant laid his hand on me, and he said, 'There thou art thou pretty buck; thou seest me, but I see thee not.' When I myself got out, and I saw the world about me, surely, oh, king! joy was on me. When I was out and had shaken the skin off me, I said to the brute, 'I am out now in spite of thee.' 'Aha!' said he, 'hast thou done this to me. Since thou were so stalwart that thou hast got out, I will give thee a ring that I have here, and keep the ring, and it will do thee good.' 'I will not take the ring from thee,' said I, 'but throw it, and I will take it with me.' He threw the ring on the flat ground, I went myself and I lifted the ring, and I put it on my finger. When he said me then. 'Is the ring fitting thee?' I said to him, 'It is.' He said, 'Where art thou ring?' And the ring said, 'I am here.' The brute went and he betook himself towards where the ring was speaking, and now I saw that I was in a harder case than ever I was. I drew a dirk. I cut the finger off from me, and I threw it from me as far as I could out on the loch, and there was a great depth in the place. He shouted, 'Where art thou, ring?' And the ring said, 'I am here,' though it was on the ground of ocean. He gave a spring after the ring, and out he went in the sea. And I was as pleased here when

I saw him drowning, as though thou shouldst let my own life and the life of my two sons with me, and not lay any more trouble on me.

"When the giant was drowned I went in, and I took with me all he had of gold and silver, and I went home, and surely great joy was on my people when I arrived. And as a sign for thee, look thou, the finger is off me."

"Yes, indeed, Conall, thou art wordy and wise," said the king. "I see thy finger is off. Thou hast freed thy two sons, but tell me a case in which thou ever wert that is harder than to be looking on thy two sons being hanged tomorrow, and thou wilt get the soul of thy second eldest son with thee."

"Then went my father," said Conall, "and he got me a wife, and I was married. I went to hunt. I was going beside the sea, and I saw an island over in the midst of the loch, and I came there where a boat was with a rope before her and a rope behind her, and many precious things within her. I looked myself on the boat to see how I might get part of them. I put in the one foot, and the other foot was on the ground, and when I raised my head what was it but the boat over in the middle of the loch, and she never stopped till she reached the island. When I went out of the boat the boat returned where she was before. I did not know now what I should do. The place was without meat or clothing, without the appearance of a house on it. I raised out on the top of a hill. I came to a glen; I saw in it, at the bottom of a chasm, a woman who had got a child, and the child was naked on her knee, and a knife in her hand. She would attempt to put the knife in the throat of the babe, and the babe would begin to laugh in her face, and she would begin to cry, and she would throw the knife behind her. I thought to myself that I was near my foe and far from my friends, and I called to the woman, 'What art thou doing here?' And she said to me, 'What brought thee here?' I told her myself word upon word how I came. 'Well then,' said she, 'it was so I came also.' She showed me to the place where I should come in where she was. I went in, and I said to her, 'What was in fault that thou wert putting the knife on the neck of the child.' 'It is that he must be cooked for the giant who is here, or else no more of my world will be before me.' I went up steps of stairs, and I saw a chamber full of stripped corpses. I took a lump out of the corpse that was whitest, and I tied a string to the child's foot, and a string to the lump, and I put the lump in his mouth, and when it went in his throat he would give a stretch to his leg, and he would take it out of his throat, but with the length of the thread he could not take it out of his mouth. I cast the child into a basket of down, and I asked her to cook the corpse for the giant in place of the child. 'How can I do that?' said she, 'when he has count of the corpses.' 'Do thou as I ask thee, and I will strip myself, and I will go amongst the corpses, and then he will have the same count,' said I. She did as I asked her. We put the corpse in the great caldron, but we could not put on the lid. When he was coming home I stripped myself, and I went amongst the corpses. He came home, and she served up the corpse on a great platter, and when he ate it he was complaining that he found it too tough for a child.

"'I did as thou asked me,' said she. 'Thou hadst count of the corpses thyself, and go up now and count them.' He counted them and he had them. 'I see one of a white body there,' said he. 'I will lie down a while and I will have him when I wake.'

When he rose he went up and gripped me, and I never was in such a case as when he was hauling me down the stair with my head after me. He threw me into the caldron, and he lifted the lid and he put the lid into the caldron. And now I was sure I would scald before I could get out of that. As fortune favoured me, the brute slept beside the caldron. There I was scalded by the bottom of the caldron. When she perceived that he was asleep, she set her mouth quietly to the hole that was in the lid, and she said to me 'was I alive.' I said I was. I put up my head, and the brute's forefinger was so large, that my head went through easily. Everything was coming easily with me till I began to bring up my hips. I left the skin of my hips about the mouth of the hole, and I came out. When I got out of the caldron I knew not what to do; and she said to me that there was no weapon that would kill him but his own weapon. I began to draw his spear, and every breath that he would draw I would think I would be down his throat, and when his breath came out I was back again just as far. But with every ill that befell me I got the spear loosed from him. Then I was as one under a bundle of straw in a great wind, for I could not manage the spear. And it was fearful to look on the brute, who had but one eye in the midst of his face; and it was not agreeable for the like of me to attack him. I drew the dart as best I could, and I set it in his eye. When he felt this he gave his head a lift, and he struck the other end of the dart on the top of the cave, and it went through to the back of his head. And he fell cold dead where he was; and thou mayest be sure, oh king, that joy was on me. I myself and the woman went out on clear ground, and we passed the night there. I went and got the boat with which I came, and she was no way lightened, and took the woman and the child over on dry land; and I returned home."

The king's mother was putting on a fire at this time, and listening to Conall telling the tale about the child. "Is it thou," said she, "that were there?" "Well then," said he, "'twas I." "Och! och!" said she, "'twas I that was there, and the king is the child whose life thou didst save; and it is to thee that life thanks might be given." Then they took great joy.

The king said, "Oh Conall, thou camest through great hardships. And now the brown horse is thine, and his sack full of the most precious things that are in my treasury."

They lay down that night, and if it was early that Conall rose, it was earlier than that that the queen was on foot making ready. He got the brown horse and his sack full of gold and silver and stones of great price, and then Conall and his four sons went away, and they returned home to the Erin realm of gladness. He left the gold and silver in his house, and he went with the horse to the king. They were good friends evermore. He returned home to his wife, and they set in order a feast; and that was the feast, oh son and brother!

The Tale of Conal Cròbhi

THERE WAS A KING over England once, and he had three sons, and they went to France to get learning, and when they came back home they said to their father that they would go to see what order was in the kingdom since they went away; and that was the first place to which they went, to the house of a man of the king's tenants, by name Conal Cròbhi.

Conal Cròbhi had everything that was better than another waiting for them; meat of each meat, and draughts of each drink. When they were satisfied, and the time came for them to lie down, the king's big son said –

"This is the rule that we have since we came home – the goodwife must wait on me, and the maid must wait on my middle brother, and the guidman's daughter on my young brother." But this did not please Conal Cròbhi at all, and he said – "I won't say much about the maid and the daughter, but I am not willing to part from my wife, but I will go out and ask themselves about this matter;" and out he went, and he locked the door behind him, and he told his gillie that the three best horses that were in the stable were to be ready without delay; and he and his wife went on one, his gillie and his daughter on another, and his son and the maid on the third horse, and they went where the king was to tell the insult his set of sons had given them.

The king's watchful gillie was looking out whom he should see coming. He called out that he was seeing three double riders coming. Said the king, "Ha! hah! This is Conal Cròbhi coming, and he has my three sons under cess, but if they are, I will not be." When Conal Cròbhi came the king would not give him a hearing. Then Conal Cròbhi said, when he got no answer, "I will make thy kingdom worse than it is," and he went away, and he began robbing and lifting spoil.

The king said that he would give any reward to any man that would make out the place where Conal Cròbhi was taking his dwelling.

The king's swift rider said, that if he could get a day and a year he would find out where he was. He took thus a day and a year seeking for him, but if he took it he saw no sight of Conal Cròbhi. On his way home he sat on a pretty yellow brow, and he saw a thin smoke in the midst of the tribute wood.

Conal Cròbhi had a watching gillie looking whom he should see coming. He went in and he said that he saw the likeness of the swift rider coming. "Ha, ha!" said Conal Cròbhi, "the poor man is sent away to exile as I went myself."

Conal Cròbhi had his hands spread waiting for him, and he got his choice of meat and drink, and warm water for his feet, and a soft bed for his limbs. He was but a short time lying when Conal Cròbhi cried, "Art thou asleep, swift rider?" "I am not," said he. At the end of a while again he cried, "Art thou asleep?" He said he was not. He cried again the third time, but there was no answer. Then Conal Cròbhi cried, "On your soles! all within, this is no crouching time. The following will be on us presently." The watchman of Conal Cròbhi was shouting that he was seeing the king's three sons coming, and a great company along with them. He had of arms but one black rusty sword. Conal Cròbhi began at them, and he did not leave a man alive there but the king's three sons, and he tied them and took them in, and he laid on them the binding of the three smalls, straitly and painfully and he threw them into the peat corner, and he said to his wife to make meat speedily, that he was going to do a work whose like he never did before. "What is that, my man!" said she. "Going to take the heads off the king's three sons." He brought up the big one and set his head on the block, and he raised the axe. "Don't, don't," said he, "and I will take thy part in right or unright for ever." Then he took the middle one, he set his head on the block and he raised the axe. "Don't, don't," said he, "and I will take with thee in right or unright for ever." Then he brought up the young one, and he did the very same to him. "Don't, don't," said he, "and I will take with thee, in right or unright for ever." Then he went, himself and the king's three sons, where the king was.

The watching gillies of the king were looking out when they should see the company coming with the head of Conal Cròbhi. Then one called out that he was seeing the likeness of the king's three sons coming, and Conal Cròbhi before them.

"Ha, ha!" said the king, "Conal Cròbhi is coming, and he has my three sons under cess, but if they are I won't be." He would give no answer to Conal Cròbhi, but that he should be hanged on a gallows in the early morning of the morrow's day.

Now, the gallows was set up and Conal Cròbhi was about to be hanged, but the king's big son cried, "I will go in his place." The king's middle son cried, "I will go in his place;" and the king's young son cried, "I will go in his place." Then the king took contempt for his set of sons. Then said Conal Cròbhi, "We will make a big ship, and we will go steal the three black white-faced stallions that the king of Eirinn has, and we will make the kingdom of Sasunn as rich as it ever was." When the ship was ready, her prow went to sea and her stern to shore, and they hoisted the chequered flapping sails against the tall tough masts; there was no mast unbent, nor sail untorn, and the brown buckies of the strand were glagid-ing on her floor. They reached the "Paileas" of the King of Eirinn. They went into the stable, but when Conal Cròbhi would lay a hand on the black white-faced stallions, the stallions would let out a screech. The King of Eirinn cried, "Be out lads; someone is troubling the stallions." They went out and they tried down and up, but they saw no man. There was an old hogshead in the lower end of the stable, and Conal Cròbhi and the king's three sons were hiding themselves in the hogshead. When they went out Conal laid hands on the stallion and the stallion let out a screech, and so they did three times, and at the third turn, one of those who were in the party said, that they did not look in the hogshead. Then they returned and they found the king's three sons and Conal in it. They were taken in to the king. "Ha, ha, thou hoary wretch," said the king, "many a mischief thou didst before thou thoughtest to come and steal my three black stallions."

The binding of the three smalls, straitly and painfully, was put on Conal Cròbhi, and he was thrown into the peat corner, and the king's three sons were taken up a stair. When the men who were above had filled themselves full of meat and drink, it was then that the king thought of sending word down for Conal Cròbhi to tell a tale. 'Twas no run for the king's big son, but a leap down to fetch him. Said the king, "Come up here, thou hoary wretch, and tell us a tale." "I will tell that," said he, "if I get the worth of its telling; and it is not my own head nor the head of one of the company." "Thou wilt get that," said the king. "Tost! hush! over there, and let us hear the tale of Conal Cròbhi."

"As a young lad I was fishing on a day beside a river, and a great ship came past me. They said to me would I go as 'pilot' to go to Rome. I said that I would do it; and of every place as we reached it, they would ask, was that Rome? and I would say that it was not, and I did not know where in the great world Rome was.

"We came at last to an island that was there, we went on shore, and I went to take a walk about the island, and when I returned back the ship was gone. There I was, left by myself, and I did not know what to do. I was going past a house that was there, and I saw a woman crying. I asked what woe was on her; she told me that the heiress of this island had died six weeks ago, and that they were waiting for a brother of hers who was away from the town, but that she was to be buried this day.

"They were gathering to the burying, and I was amongst them when they put her down in the grave; they put a bag of gold under her head, and a bag of silver under her feet. I said to myself, that were better mine; that it was of no use at all to her. When the night came I turned back to the grave. When I had dug up the grave, and when I was coming up with the gold and the silver I caught hold of the stone that was on the mouth of the grave, the stone fell down and I was there along with the dead carlin. By thy hand, oh, King of Eirinn! and by my hand, though free, if I was not in a harder case along with the carlin than I am here under thy compassion, with a hope to get off."

"Ha! ha! thou hoary wretch, thou camest out of that, but thou wilt not go out of this."

"Give me now the worth of my ursgeul," said Conal.

"What is that?" said the king.

"It is that the big son of the King of Sasunn, and the big daughter of the King of Eirinn, should be married to each other, and one of the black white-faced stallions a tocher for them."

"Thou shalt get that," said the king.

Conal Cròbhi was seized, the binding of the three smalls laid on him straitly and painfully, and he was thrown into the peat corner; and a wedding of twenty days and twenty nights was made for the young couple. When they were tired then of eating and drinking, the king said that it were better to send for the hoary wretch, and that he should tell them how he had got out of the grave.

'Twas no run, but a leap for the king's middle son to go to fetch him; he was sure he would get a marriage for himself as he had got for his brother. He went down and he brought him up.

Said the king, "Come up and tell to us how thou gottest out of the grave." "I will tell that," said Conal Cròbhi, "if I get the worth of telling it; and it is not my own head, nor the head of one that is in the company." "Thou shalt get that," said the king.

"I was there till the day. The brother of the heiress came home, and he must see a sight of his sister; and when they were digging the grave I cried out, oh! catch me by the hand; and the man that would not wait for his bow he would not wait for his sword, as they called that the worst one was there; and I was as swift as one of themselves. Then I was there about the island, not knowing what side I should go. Then I came across three young lads, and they were casting lots. I asked them what they were doing thus. They said, what was my business what they were doing? 'Hud! hud!' said I myself. 'You will tell me what you are doing.' Well, then, said they, a great giant took away our sister. We are casting lots which of us shall go, down into this hole to seek her. I cast lots with them, and there was but that the next lot fell on myself to go down to seek her. They let me down in a creel. There was the very prettiest woman I ever saw, and she was winding golden thread off a silver windle. Oh! said she to myself, how didst thou come here? I came down here to seek thee; thy three brothers are waiting for thee at the mouth of the hole, and you will send down the creel tomorrow to fetch me. If I be living, 'tis well, and if I be not, there's no help for it. I was but a short time there when I heard thunder and noise coming with the giant. I did not know where I should go to hide myself; but I saw a heap of gold and silver on the other side of the giant's cave. I thought there was no place whatsoever that was better for me to hide in than amidst the gold. The giant came with a dead carlin trailing to each of his shoe-ties. He looked down, and he looked up, and when he did not see her before him, he let out a great howl of crying, and he gave the carlins a little singe through the fire and he ate them. Then the giant did not know what would best keep wearying from him, but he thought that he would go and count his lot of gold and silver; then he was but a short time when he set his hand on my own head. 'Wretch!' said the giant, I many a bad thing didst thou ever before thou thoughtest to come to take away the pretty woman that I had; I have no need of thee tonight, but 'tis thou shalt polish my teeth early tomorrow.' The brute was tired, and he slept after eating the carlins; I saw a great flesh stake beside the fire. I put the iron spit in the very middle of the fire till it was red. The giant was in his heavy sleep, and his mouth open, and he was snoring and blowing. I took the red spit out of the fire and I put it down in the giant's mouth; he took a sudden spring to the further side of the cave, and he struck the end of the spit against the wall, and it went right out through him. I caught the giant's big sword, and with one stroke I struck the head off him.

On the morrow's day the creel came down to fetch myself; but I thought I would fill it with the gold and silver of the giant; and when it was in the midst of the hole, with the weight of the gold and silver, the tie broke. I fell down amidst stones, and bushes, and brambles; and by thy hand, oh, King of Eirinn! and by my hand, though free, I was in a harder case than I am tonight, under thy clemency, with the hope of getting out."

"Ah! thou hoary wretch, thou camest out of that, but thou wilt not go out of this," said the king.

"Give me now the worth of my ursgeul."

"What's that?" said the king.

"It is the middle son of the King of Sasunn, and the middle daughter of the King of Eirinn to be married to each other, and one of the black white-faced stallions as tocher."

"That will happen," said the king.

Conal Cròbhi was caught and bound with three slender ends, and tossed into the peat corner; and a wedding of twenty nights and twenty days was made for the young couple, there and then.

When they were tired of eating and drinking, the king said they had better bring Conal Cròbhi up, till he should tell how he got up out of the giant's cave. 'Twas no run, but a spring for the king's young son to go down to fetch him; he was sure he would get a "match" for him, as he got for the rest.

"Come up here, thou hoary wretch," said the king, and tell us how thou gottest out of the giant's cave."

"I will tell that if I get the worth of telling; and it is not my own head, nor the head of one in the company." "Thou wilt get that," said the king. "Tost! silence over there, and let us listen to the sgeulachd of Conal Cròbhi," said the king.

"Well! I was there below wandering backwards and forwards; I was going past a house that was there, and I saw a woman there, and she had a child in one hand and a knife in the other hand, and she was lamenting and crying. I cried myself to her, 'Hold on thy hand, woman, what art thou going to do?' 'Oh!' said she, 'I am here with three giants, and they ordered my pretty babe to be dead, and cooked for them, when they should come home to dinner.' 'I see,' said I, 'three hanged men on a gallows yonder, and we will take down one of them; I will go up in the place of one of them, and thou wilt make him ready in place of the babe.' And when the giants came home to dinner, one of them would say, 'This is the flesh of the babe;' and another would say, 'It is not.' One of them said that he would go to fetch a steak out of one of those who were on the gallows, and that he would see whether it was the flesh of the babe he was eating. I myself was the first that met them; and by thy hand, oh, King of Eirinn, and by my hand, were it free, if I was not in a somewhat harder case, when the steak was coming out of me, than I am tonight under thy mercy, with a hope to get out."

"Thou hoary wretch, thou camest out of that, but thou wilt not come out of this," said the king.

"Give me now the reward of my ursgeul?"

"Thou wilt get that," said the king.

"My reward is, the young son of the King of Sasunn, and the young daughter of the King of Eirinn, to be married, and one of the black stallions as tocher."

There was catching of Conal Cròbhi, and binding him with the three slender ends, straitly and painfully, and throwing him down into the peat corner; and there was a wedding made, twenty nights and twenty days for the young pair. When they were tired eating and drinking, the king said that it were best to bring up that hoary wretch to tell how he came off the gallows. Then they brought myself up.

"Come up hither, thou hoary wretch, and tell us how thou gottest off the gallows." "I will tell that," said I myself, "if I get a good reward." "Thou wilt get that," said the king.

"Well! when the giants took their dinner, they were tired and they fell asleep. When I saw this, I came down, and the woman gave me a great flaming sword of light that one of the giants had; and I was not long throwing the heads off the giants. Then I myself, and the woman were here, not knowing how we should get up out of the giant's cave. We went to the farther end of the cave, and then we followed a narrow road through a rock, till we came to light, and to the giant's 'biorlinn' of ships. What should I think, but that I would turn back and load the biorlinn with the gold and silver of the giant; and just so I did. I went with the biorlinn under sail till I reached an island that I did not know. The ship, and the woman, and the babe were taken from me, and I was left there to come home as best I might. I got home once more to Sasunn, though I am here tonight."

Then a woman, who was lying in the chamber, cried out, "Oh, king, catch hold of this man; I was the woman that was there, and thou wert the babe." It was here that value was put on Conal Cròbhi; and the king gave him the biorlinn full of the giant's gold and silver, and he made the kingdom of Sasunn as rich as it ever was before.

The Tale of Connal

THERE WAS A KING over Eirinn once, who was named King Cruachan, and he had a son who was called Connal MacRigh Cruachan. The mother of Connal died, and his father married another woman. She was for finishing Connal, so that the kingdom might belong to her own posterity. He had a foster mother, and it was in the house of his foster mother that he made his home. He and his eldest brother were right fond of each other; and the mother was vexed because Connal was so fond of her big son. There was a bishop in the place, and he died; and he desired that his gold and silver should be placed along with him in the grave. Connal was at the bishop's burying, and he saw a great bag of gold being placed at the bishop's head, and a bag of silver at his feet, in the grave. Connal said to his five foster brothers, that they would go in search of the bishop's gold; and when they reached the grave, Connal asked them which they would rather; go down into the grave, or hold up the flagstone. They said that they would hold up the flag. Connal went down; and whatever the squealing was that they heard, they let go the flag and they took to their soles home. Here he was, in the grave on top of the bishop. When the five foster brothers reached the house, their mother was somewhat more sorrowful for Connal than she would have been for the five. At the end of seven mornings, there went a company of young lads to take the gold out of the bishop's grave, and when they reached the grave they threw the flag to the side of the further wall; Connal stirred below, and when he stirred they went, and they left each arm and dress they had. Connal arose, and he took with him the gold, and arms and dress, and he reached his foster mother with them. They were all merry and lighthearted as long as the gold and silver lasted.

There was a great giant near the place, who had a great deal of gold and silver in the foot of a rock; and he was promising a bag of gold to any being that would go down in a creel. Many were lost in this way; when the giant would let them down, and they would fill the creel, the giant would not let down the creel more till they died in the hole.

On a day of days, Connal met with the giant, and he promised him a bag of gold, for that he should go down in the hole to fill a creel with the gold. Connal went down, and the giant was letting him down with a rope; Connal filled the giant's creel with the gold, but the giant did not let down the creel to fetch Connal, and Connal was in the cave amongst the dead men and the gold.

When it beat the giant to get another man who would go down in the hole, he sent his own son down into the hole, and the sword of light in his lap, so that he might see before him.

When the young giant reached the ground of the cave, and when Connal saw him he caught the sword of light, and he took off the head of the young giant. Then Connal put gold in the bottom of the creel, and he put gold over him; and then he hid in the midst of the creel, and he gave a pull at the rope. The giant drew the creel, and when he did not see his son, he threw the creel over the top of his head. Connal leaped out of the creel, and the black back of the giant's head (being) towards him, he laid a swift hand on the sword of light, and he took the head off the giant. Then he betook himself to his foster mother's house with the creel of gold and the giant's sword of light.

After this, he went one day to hunt on Sliamh na leirge. He was going forwards till he went into a great cave. He saw, at the upper part of the cave, a fine fair woman, who was thrusting the flesh stake at a big lump of a baby; and every thrust she would give the spit, the babe would give a laugh, and she would begin to weep. Connal spoke, and he said, "Woman, what ails thee at the child without reason?" "Oh," said she, "since thou art an able man thyself, kill the baby and set it on this stake, till I roast it for the giant." He caught hold of the baby, and he put a plaid that he had on about the babe, and he hid the baby at the side of the cave.

There were a great many dead bodies at the side of the cave, and he set one of them on the stake, and the woman was roasting it.

Then was heard underground trembling and thunder coming, and he would rather that he was out. Here he sprang in the place of the corpse that was at the fire, in the very midst of the bodies. The giant came, and he asked, "Was the roast ready?" He began to eat, and he said, "Fiu fau hoagrich; it's no wonder that thy own flesh is tough; it is tough on thy brat."

When the giant had eaten that one, he went to count the bodies; and the way he had of counting them was, to catch hold of them by the two smalls of the leg, and to toss them past the top of his head; and he counted them back and forwards thus three or four times, and as he found Connal somewhat heavier, and that he was soft and fat, he took that slice out of him from the back of his head to his groin. He roasted this at the fire, and he ate it, and then he fell asleep. Connal winked to the woman to set the flesh stake in the fire. She did this, and when the spit grew white after it was red, he thrust the spit through the giant's heart, and the giant was dead.

Then Connal went and he set the woman on her path homewards, and then he went home himself. His stepmother sent him and her own son to steal the white-faced horse from the King of Italy, "Eadailt". And they went together to steal the white-faced horse, and every time they would lay hand on him, the white-faced horse would let out an *ialt* (neigh). A "company" came out, and they were caught. The binding of the three smalls was laid on them straitly and painfully. "Thou big red man," said the king, "wert thou ever in so hard a case as that?" "A little tightening for me, and a loosening for my comrade, and I will tell thee that," said Connal.

The Queen of the Eadailt was beholding Connal.

Then Connal said:

> *"Seven morns so sadly mine,*
> *As I dwelt on the bishop's top,*
> *That visit was longest for me,*
> *Though I was the strongest myself.*
> *At the end of the seventh morn*
> *An opening grave was seen,*
> *And I would be up before*
> *The one that was soonest down.*
> *They thought I was a dead man,*
> *As I rose from the mould of earth*
> *At the first of the harsh bursting*
> *They left their arms and their dresses,*
> *I gave the leap of the nimble one,*
> *As I was naked and bare.*
> *'Twas sad for the, a vagabond,*
> *To enjoy the bishop's gold."*

"Tighten well, and right well," said the king; "it was not in one good place that he ever was; great is the ill he has done." Then he was tightened somewhat tighter, and somewhat tighter, and the king said, "Thou great red man, wert thou ever in a harder case than that?" "Tighten myself, and let a little slack with this one beside me, and I will tell thee that."

They did that. "I was," said he,

> *"Nine morns in the cave of gold;*
> *My meat was the body of bones,*
> *Sinews of feet and hands.*
> *At the end of the ninth morn*
> *A descending creel was seen;*
> *Then I caught hold on the creel,*
> *And laid gold above and below;*
> *I made my hiding within the creel,*
> *I took with me the glaive of light,*
> *The luckiest turn that I did."*

They gave him the next tightening, and the king asked him, "Wert thou ever in case, or extremity, as hard as that?" "A little tightening for myself, and a slack for my comrade, and I will tell thee that."

They did this.

"On a day on Sliabh na leirge,
As I went into a cave,
I saw a smooth, fair, mother-eyed wife,
Thrusting the stake for the flesh
At a young unreasoning child. 'Then,' said I,
'What causes thy grief, oh wife,
At that unreasoning child?'
'Though he's tender and comely,' said she,
'Set this baby at the fire.'
Then I caught hold on the boy,
And wrapped my 'maundal' around;
Then I brought up the great big corpse
That was up in the front of the heap;
Then I heard, Turstar, Tarstar, and Turaraich,
The very earth mingling together
But when it was his to be fallen
Into the soundest of sleep,
There fell, by myself, the forest fiend.
I drew back the stake of the roast,
And I thrust it into his maw."

There was the Queen, and she was listening to each thing that Connal suffered and said; and when she heard this, she sprang and cut each binding that was on Connal and on his comrade; and she said, "I am the woman that was there," and to the king, "thou art the son that was yonder."

Connal married the king's daughter, and together they rode the white-faced horse home; and there I left them.

Conall

THERE WAS AN OLD KING before now in Erin, and a sister of his, whose name was Maobh, had three sons. The eldest of them was Ferghus, the middlemost Lagh an Laidh, and the youngest one Conall.

He thought he would make an heir of the eldest one, Ferghus. He gave him the schooling of the son of a king and a 'ridere,' and when he was satisfied with school and learning he brought him home to the palace. Now they were in the palace.

Said the king, "I have passed this year well; the end of the year is coming now, and trouble and care are coming on with it."

"What trouble or care is coming on thee?" said the young man. "The vassals of the country are coming to reckon with me today." "Thou hast no need to be in trouble. It is proclaimed that I am the young heir, and it is set down in papers and in letters in each end of the realm. I will build a fine castle in front of the palace for thee. I will get carpenters, and stonemasons, and smiths to build that castle."

"Is that thy thought, son of my sister?" said the king. "Thou hadst neither claim nor right to the realm unless I myself had chosen to give it to thee with my own free will. Thou wilt not see thyself handling Erin till I go first under the mould."

"There will be a day of battle and combat before I let this go on," said the young man.

He went away, and he sailed to Alba. A message was sent up to the king of Alba that the young king of Erin was come to Alba to see him. He was taken up on the deadly points. Meat was set in the place for eating; drink in the place for drinking; and music in the place for hearing; and they were plying the feast and the company.

"Oh! young king of Erin," said the king of Alba, "it was not without the beginning of some matter that thou art come to Alba."

"I should not wish to let out the knowledge of my matter till I should first know whether I may get it."

"Anything I have thou gettest it, for if I were seeking help, perhaps I would go to thee to get it."

"There came a word with trouble between me and my mother's brother. It was proclaimed out that I was king of Erin; and he said to me that I should have nothing to do with anything till a clod should first go on him. I wish to stand my right, and to get help from thee."

"I will give thee that," said the king; "three hundred swift heroes, three hundred brave heroes, three hundred full heroes; and that is not bad helping."

"I am without a chief over them, and I am as ill off as I was before; but I have another small request, and if I might get it, I would wish to let it out."

"Anything I have that I can part from, thou shalt get it," said the king; "but the thing I have not, I cannot give it to thee. Let out thy speech, and thou shalt have it."

"It is Boinne Breat, thy son, at their head."

"My torture to thee! had I not promised him to thee, thou hadst not got him. But there were not born in Alba, nor in Erin, nor in Sassun, nor in any one place (those) who would gain victory over my son if they keep to fair play. If my son does not come back as be went, the word of an Eriannach is never again to be taken, for it is by treachery he will be overcome."

They went away on the morrow, and they sailed to the king of Sassun. A message went up to the king of Sassun that the young king of Erin had come to the place. The king of Sassun took out to meet him. He was taken up on the deadly points; music was raised, and lament laid down in the palace of the king of Sassun; meat was set in the place for eating; drink in the place for drinking; music in the place of hearing; and they were plying the feast and the company with joy and pleasure of mind.

"Oh! young king of Erin," said the king of Sassun, "it is not without the end of a matter that thou art come here."

"I got the schooling of the son of a king and a ridere. My mother's brother took me home. He began to speak about the vassals of the country and the people of the realm; that care and trouble were on him; and that he had rather the end of the year had not come at all. Said I to him, 'I will build thee a palace, so that thou shalt have but to wash thy face, and stretch thy feet in thy shoes.' Said he, 'My sister's son, thou hadst no right to the realm, and thou gettest it not till a clod goes on me, in spite of everything.' Said I, 'There will be a day of battle and combat between thee and me, before the matter is so.' I went away; I took my ship; I took a skipper with me; and I sailed to Alba. I reached Alba, and I got three hundred swift heroes, three hundred brave heroes, and three hundred full heroes; now I am come to thee to see what help thou wilt give me."

"I will give thee as many more, and a hero at their head," said the king of Sassun.

They went away, and they sailed to Erin. They went on shore on a crag in Erin, and the name of Carrig Fhearghuis is on that rock still. He reached the king. "Brother of my mother, art thou now ready?" – "Well, then, Fhearghuis, though I said that, I thought thou wouldst not take anger; but I have not gathered my lot of people yet." – "That is no answer for me. Thou hast Erin under thy rule. I am here with my men, and I have neither place, nor meat, nor drink for them."

"Oo!" said the king, "the storehouses of Erin are open beneath thee, and I will go away and gather my people."

He went away. He went all round Erin. He came to a place which they called 'An t' Iubhar' (Newry). There was but one man in Iubhar, who was called Goibhlean Gobba (Goivlan Smith). He thought to go in, for thirst was on him; and that he would quench his thirst, and breathe a while. He went in. There was within but the smith's daughter. She brought him a chair in which he might sit. He asked for a drink. The smith's daughter did not know what she should do, for the smith had but one cow, which was called the Glas Ghoibhlean (Grey Goivlan), with the vessel he had for the milk of the cow; three times in the day it would go beneath the cow; three times in the day thirst would be on him; and he would drink the vessel each time, and unless the daughter had the vessel full she was not to get off. She was afraid, when the king asked for a drink, that unless she had the vessel full her head would be taken off. It was so that she thought the vessel should be set before the king at all hazards. She brought down the vessel, and she set it before him. He drank a draught; he took out the fourth part, and he left three quarters in it. "I would rather you should take it out altogether than leave it. My father has made an oath that unless I have the vessel full, I have but to die."

"Well, then," said the king, "it is a spell of my spells to leave the vessel as full as it was before."

He set the vessel on the board, he struck his palm on it, and he struck off as much as was above the milk, and the vessel was full; and before he went away, the girl was his own.

"Now, thou art going, oh king of Erin, and I am shamed; what wilt thou leave with me?"

"I would give thee a thousand of each hue, a thousand of each kind, a thousand of each creature."

"What should I do with that, for I wilt not find salt in Erin to salt them?"

"I would give thee glens and high moors to feed them from year to year."

"What should I do with that? for if Fearghus should kill you, he will take it from me, unless I have it with writing, and a drop of blood to bind it."

"I am in haste this night, but go tomorrow to the camp to Croc Maol Nam Muc," said the king; and he left his blessing with her.

Her father came.

"Far from thee – far from thee be it, my daughter! I think that a stranger has been to see thee here this day."

"How dost thou know that?"

"Thou hadst a maiden's slow eyelash when I went out; thou hast the brisk eyelash of a wife now."

"Whom wouldst thou rather had been here?"

"I never saw the man I would rather be here than the king of Erin."

"Well, it was he; he left me a thousand of each hue, a thousand of each kind, a thousand of each creature.

"'What,' said I, 'shall I do with them, as I cannot get in Erin as much salt as will salt them?'

"Said he, 'I would give thee glens and high moors to feed them from year to year.'

"'What shall I do if Fearghus should kill you? I will not get them.'

"He said, 'I should have writing and a drop of his own blood to bind it.'"

They slept that night as they were. If it was early that the day came, it was earlier that the smith arose. "Come, daughter, and let us be going." She went, herself and the smith, and they reached the king in his camp.

"Wert thou not in the Iubhar yesterday?" said the smith to the king, "I was; and hast thou mind of thy words to the girl?"

"I have; but the battle will not be till tomorrow. I will give thee, as I said, to the girl; but leave her."

The smith got that, and he went away.

That night, when she had slept a while, she awoke, for she had seen a dream. "Art thou waking?"

"I am; what wilt thou with me? I saw a dream there: a shoot of fir growing from the heart of the king, one from my own heart, and they were twining about each other." "That is our babe son." They slept, and it was not long till she saw the next dream.

"Art thou waking, king of Erin?" "I am; what wilt thou with me?" "I saw another dream. Fearghus, coming down, and taking the head and the neck out of me."

"That is, Fearghus killing me, and taking out my head and neck."

She slept again, and she saw another dream.

"Art thou sleeping, king of Erin?"

"I am not; what wilt thou with me now?

"I saw Erin, from side to side, and from end to end, covered with sheaves of barley and oats. There came a blast of wind from the east, from the west, from the north; every tree was swept away, and no more of them were seen."

"Fearghus will kill me, and he will take the head and neck out of me. As quickly as ever thou didst (anything), seize my set of arms, and keep them. A baby boy is begotten between thee and me. Thou shalt suckle and nurse him, and thou shalt set him in order. Keep the arms. When thou seest that he has speech, and can help himself, thou shalt send him away through the world a wandering, till he find out who he is. He will get to be king over Erin; his son will be king over Erin; his grandson will be king over Erin. His race will be kings over Erin till it reaches the ninth knee. A child will be born from that one. A farmer will come in with a fish; he will cook the fish; a bone will stick in his throat, and he will be choked."

Maobh, the king's sister, the mother of Fearghus, had two other sons, and the battle was to be on the morrow. Lagh an Laidh and Conall; and Lagh an Laidh was the eldest.

"Whether," said Lagh an Laidh, "shall we be with our mother's brother or with Fearghus?"

"I know not. If our mother's brother wins, and we are with Fearghus, it is a stone in our shoe for ever; but if Fearghus wins, he will turn his back to us, because we were on the other side."

"Well, then, it is not thus it shall be; but be thou with Fearghus, and I will be with our mother's brother."

"It shall not be so; we will leave it to our mother."

"Were I a man," said Maobh, "I would set the field with my own brother."

"Well, then, I will be with Fearghus," said Lagh an Laidh, "and be thou with Fearghus, oh Conall!"

Fearghus went to Fionn; he blessed him in calm, soft words. Fionn blessed him in better words; and if no better, they were no worse.

"I heard that there was a day of battle and combat between thyself and thy mother's brother," said he.

"That is to be, and I came to you for help."

"It is but bold for me to go against thy mother's brother, since it was on his land that I got my keep. If thy mother's brother should win, we shall get neither furrow nor clod of the land of Erin as long as we live. I will do thus. I will not strike a blow with thee, and I will not strike a blow against thee."

Fearghus went home on the morrow, and they set in order for the battle. The king's company was on one side, and the company of Fearghus on the other. Fearghus had no Gaisgich heroes but Boinne Breat and his company. The great Saxon hero and his company, and Lagh an Laidh. Boinne Breat drew out to the skirt of the company; he put on his harness of battle and hard combat. He set his silken netted coat above his surety shirt; a booming shield on his left side; how many deaths were in his tanned sheath!

He strode out on the stern steps like a sudden blaze; each pace he put from him was less than a hill, and greater than a knoll on the mountain side. He turned on them, cloven and cringing. Three ranks would he drive of them, dashing them from their shields, to their blood and their flesh in the skies. Would he not leave one to tell the tale, or report bad news; to put in a land of holes or a shelf of rock. There was one little one-eyed russet man, one-eyed, and on one knee and one handed. "Thou shalt not be to tell a tale of me;" he went and he took his head off. Then Boinne Breat shunned the fight, and he took his armour off.

"Go down, Fearghus, and take off the head of thy mother's brother, or I will take it off."

Fearghus went down, he caught hold of his mother's brother, and he took his head off. The smith's daughter went to the arms, and she took them with her.

Lagh an Laidh kept on his armour. When he saw Fearghus going to take off the head of his mother's brother, he took a frenzy. Lagh and Laidh went about the hill to try if he could see Boinne Breat, who was unarmed. Boinne Breat thought that man was drunk with battle. He thought that he would turn on the other side of the hill to try if he could come to his own place. Lagh an Laidh turned on the other side against him. He thought to turn again to try if the battle frenzy would abate. The third time he said he would not turn for all who were in Albuin, or Eirinn, or Sassun. "It is strange thou, man, that wert with me throughout the battle, to be against me?" "I will not believe but that thou hast taken the drunkenness of battle," said Boinne Breat.

"I am quite beside myself."

"Well, then," said he, "though I am unarmed, and thou under arms, remember that thou art no more to me than what I can hold between these two fingers."

"I will not be a traiter to thee, there behind thee are three of the best heroes in Albuin, or Eirinn, or Sassun."

He gave a turn to see the three heroes, and when he turned Lagh an Laigh struck off his head.

"My torture," said Fearghus, "I had rather my own head were there. An Eireannach is not to be taken at his word as long as a man shall live. It is a stone in thy shoe every day for ever, and a pinch of the land of Eirinn thou shalt not have."

Lagh and Laidh went away and he went to the mountain. He made a castle for himself there, and he stayed in it.

The smith's daughter came on well till she bore a babe-son. She gave him the name of Conal Mac Righ Eirinn. She nourished him well, and right well. When speech came and he could walk well, she took him with her on a wet misty day to the mountain amongst high moors and forests. She left him there astray to make out a way for himself, and she went home.

He did not know in the world what he should do, as he did not know where to go, but he found a finger of a road. He followed the road. What should he see but a little hut at the evening of the day at the wayside. He went into the hut: there was no man within: he let himself down at the fire-side. There he was till a woman came at the end of the night, and she had six sheep. She saw a great slip of a man beside the fire, who seemed to be a fool. She took great wonder when she saw him, and she said that he had better go out of that, and go down to the king's house, and that he would get something amongst the servants in the kitchen. He said he would not go, but if she would give him something that he might eat, that he would go to herd the sheep for herself. What should be the name of the woman but Caomhag Gentle. "If I thought that, I would give thee meat and drink," said she. On the morrow he went away with the sheep. "I have not a bite of grass for them," said she, "but a road; and thou shalt keep them at the edge of the road, and thou shalt not let them off it."

At the time of night he came home with them; on the morrow he went away with the sheep. There were near to the place where he was with them three fields of wheat that belonged to three gentlemen. The sheep were wearing him out. He went and he levelled the dyke, and he let them in from one to the other till they had eaten the three fields. On a day of days, the three gentlemen gathered. When they came, he had let the fields be eaten by the sheep.

"Who art thou? Thou hast eaten the fields?"

"It was not I that ate them at all; it was the sheep that ate them."

"We will not be talking to him at all; he is but a fool. We will reach Caomhag to see if the sheep are hers."

They reached Caomhag. They took her with them to the court. This was the first court that Fearghus had made after he got the crown.

The kings had a heritage at that time. When they did not know how to split justice properly, the judgment-seat would begin to kick, and the king's neck would take a twist when he did not do justice as he ought.

"I can make nothing of it," said the king, "but that they should have the tooth that did the damage."

The judgment-seat would begin to kick, and the king's neck took a turn. "Come here one of you and loose me; try if you can do justice better than that." Though there were thousands within, none would go in the king's place. They would not give the king such bad respect, as that any one of them would go before him.

"Is there a man that will loose me?"

"There is not, unless the herd of Caomhag himself will loose thee."

Caomhag's herd was set down.

"Loose for me, my little hero, and do justice as it should (be done), and let me out of this."

"(Nor) right nor justice will I do before I get something that I may eat."

Then he got something which he ate.

"What justice didst thou do thyself?" said he.

"I did but (doom) the tooth that did the damage to be theirs."

"What was in the way that thou didst not give death to Caomhag? This is what I would do: Caomhag has six sheep, and though the six sheep were taken from her, they would not pay the gentlemen. Caomhag will have six lambs, the gentlemen shall have the six lambs, and she herself shall have the sheep to keep."

The turn went out of the king's neck. He went away, and they did not ask who he was, and he got no skaith.

There was another gentleman, and he had a horse, and he sent him to a smithy to be shod. The smith had a young son and a nurse under the child. What should it be but a fine day, and it was without that the horse was being shod, and she never saw a horse shod before; and she went out to see the shoeing of the horse. She sat opposite to the horse, and he took the nail and the shoe, and he did not hit the hoof with the nail but he put it in the flesh, and the horse struck the child, and drove the cup of his head off. They had but to go to justice again to the king, and the justice the king made for them was, that the leg should be taken off the horse. The judgment-seat began to kick again, and the king's neck took a twist. The herd of Caomhag was there, and they asked him to loose the king. He said that he would not do a thing till he should first get something to eat.

He got that. He went where the king was.

"What law didst thou make?"

"The leg to be taken off the horse?"

"That will not pay the smith. Send hither to me the groom that broke the horse, and the gentleman to whom he belongs. Send over here the smith and the nurse."

The gentleman and the groom came.

"Well then, my gentleman, didst thou make this groom break this horse as he should?"

The groom said that he had done that as well as he knew (how to do it).

"No more could be asked of thee. Well, smith, didst thou give an order to the nurse to stay within without coming out of her chamber?"

"I did not give it," said the smith, "but (she might do) as she chose herself."

"My gentleman," said he, "since thou art best kept, I will put a third of the Eiric of the smith's son on thee, and another third on the smith himself, because he did not measure the nail before he put it to use, and another third on the nurse and the groom because she did not stay within in her chamber, and in case he left some word or other untaught to the horse."

The gentleman went away and the smith; the judgment-seat stopped, and she hadn't a kick; the turn came out of the king's neck, and they let him go as usual.

Said the king – "If he has travelled over the universe and the world, there is a drop of king's blood in that lad; he could not split the law so well as that if it were not in him. Let the three best heroes I have go, and let them bring me his head."

They went after him. He gave a glance from him and what should he see coming but they. They came where he was. "Where are you going?" – "We are going to kill thyself. The king sent us to thee."

"Well, then, that was but a word that came into his mouth, and it is not worth your while to kill me."

"He is but a fool," said they.

"Since he sent you to kill me, why don't you kill me?"

"Wilt thou thyself kill thyself, my little hero?" said they.

"How shall I kill myself?"

"Here's for thee a sword and strike it on thee about the neck, and cast the head off thyself," said they.

He seized on the sword, and gave it a twirl in his fist. "Fall to killing thyself, my little hero."

"Begone," said he, "and return home, and do not hide from the king that you did not kill me."

"Well, then, give me the sword," said one of them.

"I will not give it; there are not in Erin as many as will take it from my fist," said he.

They went and they returned home. As he was going by himself, he said, "I was not born without a mother, and I was not begotten without a father. I have no mind (of) ever coming to Erin, and I know that it was in Erin I was born. I will not leave a house in which there is smoke or fire in Erin till I know who (am)."

He went to the Iubhar. What was it but a fine warm day. Whom did he see but his mother washing. He was coming to a sort of understanding, so that he was thinking that it was his mother who was there. He went and he went behind her, and he put his hand on her breast. "Indeed," said he, "a, foster son of thy right breast am I." She gave her head a toss. "Thy like of a tarlaid drudge, I never had as a son or a foster son."– "My left hand is behind thy head, and a sword in my right hand, and I will strike off thy head unless thou tell me who I am." – "Still be thy hand, Conall, son of the king of Erin."

"I knew myself I was that, and that there was a drop of the blood of a king's son in me; but who killed my father?"

Fearghus killed him; and a loss as great as thy father was slain on the same day – that was Boinne Breat, son of the king of Alba."

"Who slew Boinne Breat?" – "It is a brother of Fearghus, whom they call Lagh an Laidh." And where is that man dwelling?

He could not get a bit on the land of Erin when once he had slain Boinne Breat; he went to the hills, and he made him a 'còs' in the forest, amongst 'uille biaste,' monsters, and untamed creatures."

"Who kept my father's arms?" – "It is I."

"Go fetch them, and bring them hither to me." She brought them.

He went and put the arms on him, and they became him as well as though they had been made for himself.

"I eat not a bit, and I drink not a draught, and I make no stop but this night, until I reach where that man is, wheresoever he may be."

He passed that night where he was. In the morning, on the morrow he went away; he went on till there was black upon his soles and holes in his shoes. The white clouds of day were going, and the black clouds of night coming, and without his finding a place of staying or rest for him. There he saw a great wood. He made a 'còs,' in one of the trees above in which he might stay that night. In the morning, on the morrow he cast a glance from him. What should he see but the very uile bheist, whose like was never seen under the sun, stretched without clothing, without foot coverings, or head covering, hair and beard gone over him. He thought, though he should go down, that he could not do for him. He put an arrow in a 'crois,' and he fired at him. He struck him with it on the right fore-arm, and the one who was below gave a start. "Move not a sinew of thy sinews, nor a vein of thy veins, nor a bit of thy flesh, nor a hair of thy locks, till thou promise to see me a king over Erin, or I will send down of slender oaken darts enough to sew thee to the earth." The uile bheist did not give him yielding for that. He went and he fired again, and he struck him in the left fore-arm. "Did I not tell thee before, not to stir a vein of thy veins nor a bit of thy flesh, nor a hair of thy locks till thou shouldst promise to see me king over Erin." – "Come down then, and I will see thyself or myself that before this time tomorrow night." He came down.

"If I had known that it was thy like of a drudge that should dictate thus to me, I would not do it for thee for anything; but since I promised thee I will do it, and we will be going."

They went to the palace of the king. They shouted Battle or Combat to be sent out, or else the head of Fearghus, or himself a captive.

Battle and combat they should get, and not his head at all, and they could not get himself a captive.

There were sent out four hundred swift heroes, four hundred full heroes, and four hundred strong heroes.

They began at them. The one could not put from the other's hand as they were killed.

They shouted battle or combat again, or else the head of Fearghus to be sent out, or himself a captive.

"It is battle and combat thou shalt have, and not at all my head, and no more shalt thou get myself a captive."

There were sent out twelve hundred swift heroes, twelve hundred full heroes, and twelve hundred stout heroes.

The one could not put from the other's hand as they killed of them.

They shouted battle and combat, or else the head of Fearghus, or himself a captive.

Battle and combat they should have, and not the head of Fearghus at all, nor himself a captive.

There were sent out four hundred score to them. The one could not put from the other as they killed.

They shouted battle and combat.

"Those who are without," said Fearghus, "are so hard (to please) that they will take but my head, and unless they get (it) they will kill all there are in Erin and myself after them. Take one of you a head from one of those who were slain, and when Lagh an Laidh comes and asks my head, or myself a captive, give it to him, and he will think it is my head."

The head was given to Lagh an Laidh. He went where Conall was with it.

"What hast thou there?" said Conall.

"The head of Fearghus."

"That is not the head of Fearghus yet. I saw him a shorter (time) than thyself, but turn and bring hither to me the head of Fearghus."

Lagh an Laidh returned.

Let another go to meet him in the king's stead, and say that it is his head he shall get, not himself a captive.

This one went to meet Lagh an Laidh. He seized him and took the head out of his neck. He reached Conall. "What hast thou there?" – "The head of Fearghus."

"That is not the head of Fearghus yet; turn and bring to me the head of Fearghus."

Lagh an Laidh returned.

"The one who is without is so watchful, and the other is so blind, that there is no man in Erin but they will kill unless they get. myself."

"Where art thou going, Lagh an Laidh?" said Fearghus.

"I am going to seek thy head, or thyself as a captive."

"It's my head thou shalt get, and not myself as a captive; but what kindness art thou giving thy brother?"

"The kindness that thou gavest thyself to me, I will give it to thee."

He took the head out of his neck, and he took it with him. He came where Conall was.

"What hast thou there?" – "The head of Fearghus." – "It is not." – "Truly it is." – "Let me see it."

He gave it to him. He drew it, and he struck him with it, and he made two heads of the one. Then they began at each other.

They would make a bog on the rock, and a rock on the bog. In the place where the least they would sink, they would sink to the knees, in the place where the most they would sink, they would sink to the eyes.

Conall thought it would be ill for him to fall after he had got so near the matter.

He drew his sword, and he threw the head off Lagh an Laidh.

"Now I am king over Erin, as I myself had a right to be."

He took his mother and her father from the Iubhar, and took them to the palace; and his race were in it till the ninth knee. The last one was choked, as a babe, with a splinter of bone that went crosswise into his throat, and another tribe came in on Eirinn.

The Feen

THE FEEN WERE ONCE, and their hunting failed, and they did not know what they should do. They were going about strands and shores gathering limpets, and to try if they should fall in with a pigeon or a plover. They were holding counsel together how they should go to get game. They reached a hill, and sleep came on them. What should Fionn see but a dream. That it was at yon crag of rock that he would be, the longest night that came or will come; that he would be driven backwards till he should set his back to the crag of rock. He gave a spring out of his sleep. He struck his foot on Diarmid's mouth, and he drove out three of his teeth. Diarmid caught hold of the foot of Fionn, and he drove an ounce of blood from every nail he had. "Ud! what didst thou to me?" – "What didst thou thyself to me?" – "Be not angry, thou son of my sister. When I tell thee the reason, thou wilt not take it ill." – "What reason?" – "I saw a dream that at yonder crag I would pass the hardest night I ever passed; that I should be driven backwards till I should set my back to the crag, and there was no getting off from there." "What's our fear! Who should frighten us! Who will come!" "I fear, as we are in straits just now, that if this lasts we may become useless." They went and they cast lots who should go and who should stay.

The Feen altogether wished to go. Fionn was not willing to go, for fear the place should be taken out before they should come (back). "I will not go," said Fionn. "Whether thou goest or stayest, we will go," said they.

The rest went, but Fionn did not go. They stopped, on the night when they went, at the root of a tree; they made a booth, and they began to play at cards. Said Fionn, when the rest were gone, "I put him from amongst heroes and warriors any man that will follow me out." They followed after Fionn. They saw a light before them, and they went forward where the light was. Who were here but the others playing at cards, and some asleep; and it was a fine frosty night. Fionn hailed them so stately and bravely. When they heard the speaking of Fionn, those who were laid down tried to rise, and the hair was stuck to the ground. They were pleased to see their master. Pleasant to have a stray hunting night. They went home. Going past a place where they used to house, they saw a house. They asked what house was that. They told them there was the house of a hunter. They reached the house, and there was but a woman within, the wife of the fine green kirtle. She said to them, "Fionn, son of Cumal, thou art welcome here." They went in. There were seven doors to the house. Fionn asked his gillies to sit in the seven doors. They did that. Fionn and his company sat on the one side of the house to breathe. The woman went out. When she came in, she said, "Fionn, son of Cumal, it is long since I was wishing thy welfare, but its little I can do for thee tonight. The son of the king of the people of Danan is coming here, with his eight hundred full heroes, this night." "Yonder side of the house be theirs, and this side ours, unless there come men of Eirinn." Then they came, and they sat within. "You will not let a man on our side," said Fionn, "unless there comes one that belongs to our own company." The woman came in again, saying, "The middle son of the king of the people of Danan is coming, and his five hundred brave heroes with him." They came, and more of them staid without on a knoll. She came in again, saying, "The youngest son of the king of the people of Danan is coming, and his five hundred swift heroes with him." She came in again, saying, "That Gallaidh was coming, and five hundred full heroes." – "This side of the house be ours, and that be theirs, unless there come of the men of Eirinn." The people of Danan made seven ranks of themselves, and the fourth part of them could not cram in. They were still without a word. There came a gillie home with a boar that had found death from leanness and without a good seeming, and he throws that in front of Fionn with an insult. One of Fionn's gillies caught hold of him, and he tied his four smalls, and threw him below the board, and they spat on him. "Loose me, and let me stand up; I was not in fault, though it was I that did it, and I will bring thee to a boar as good as thou ever ate." – "I will do that," said Fionn; "but though thou shouldst travel the five-fifths of Eirinn, unless thou comest before the day comes, I will catch thee." They loosed him; he went away, and gillies with him. They were not long when they got a good boar. They came with it, and they cooked it, and they were eating it. "A bad provider of flesh art thou," said Gallaidh to Fionn. "Thou shalt not have that any longer to say;" and the jawbone was in his hand. He raised the bone, and he killed seven men from every row of the people of Danan, and this made them stop. Then a gillie came home, and the black dog of the people of Danan with him, seeking a battle of dogs. Every one of them had a pack of dogs, and a dozen in every pack. The first one of them went and slipped the first dozen. The black dog killed the dozen; he killed them by the way of dozen and dozen, till there was left but Bran in loneliness. Said Fionn to Conan, "Let slip Bran, and, unless Bran makes it out, we are done." He loosed him. The two dogs began at each other. It was not long till Bran began to take driving; they took fear when they saw that; but what was on Bran but a venomous claw. There was a golden shoe on the claw of Venom, and they had not taken off the shoe. Bran was looking at Conan, and now Conan took off the shoe; and now he went to meet the black dog again; and at the third "spoch" he struck on him; he took his throat out. Then he took the heart and the liver out of his chest. The dog took out to the knoll; he knew that foes were there. He began at them. A message came in to Fionn that the dog was doing much harm to the people without. "Come," said Fionn to one of the gillies, "and check the dog." The gillie went out, and (was) together with the dog; a message came in that the gillie was working worse than the dog. From man to man they went out till Fionn was left within alone. The Feen killed the people of Danan altogether. The lads of the Feen went out altogether, and they did not remember that they had left Fionn within. When the children of the king saw that the rest were gone, they said that they would get the head of Fionn and his heart. They began at him, and they drove him backwards till he reached a crag of rock. At the end of the house he set his back to it, and he was keeping them off. Now he remembered the dream. He was tightly tried. Fionn had the "Ord Fianna," and when he was in extremity it would sound of itself, and it would be heard in the five-fifths of Eirinn. The gillies heard it; they gathered and returned. He was alive, and he was no more. They raised him on the point of their spears: he got better. They killed the sons of the king, and all that were alive of the people, and they got the chase as it ever was.

The Poor Brother and the Rich

THERE WAS A POOR BROTHER and a rich brother before now. The work that the poor one had, was to be at drains; he hired a gillie, and they had nothing with their mealtime but to take it without sauce. "Hadn't we better," said the gillie, "steal a cow of thy brother's lot?" They went and they did this.

The rich brother was taking a notion that it was they who stole his cow; and he did not know in what way he could contrive to find out if it were they who stole her. He went and he put his mother-in-law in a kist, and he came to seek room for the kist in his brother's house; he put bread and cheese with the crone in the kist; and there was a hole in it, in order that she might find out everything. The gillie found out that the crone was in the kist; he wetted sacks and put them on top of the kist; the water was streaming out of the sacks on the crone, and she was not hearing a word. He went, in the night, where the crone was, and he said to her, "Was she hearing?" "I am not," said she." "Art thou eating a few?" "I am not." "Give me a piece of the cheese, and I will cut it for thee." He cut the cheese, and he stuffed it into her throat till she was choked. The kist was taken home, and the dead crone in it. They buried the crone, and they laid out but little on her.

In the night, said the poor man's gillie to his master, "Is it not lamentable that such and such linen should go with the crone to the cell, while the children are so much in want of shirts?" He went, and he took a spade with him, and he reached the church-yard. He dug the grave, and he took the crone from the coffin; he took off her the tais dress, he threw her on his back, and he came to the house of the rich brother; he went in with her, and he placed her seated at the fireside, and the tongs between her two feet. When the maid servant rose in the morning, she fell in a faint when she saw the crone before her. The rich brother thrashed his wife because of her mother saying, "that she was about to bring him to bare ruin." He went to the house of his poor brother and told that the crone had come home. "Ah ha!" said the gillie, "because thou didst not spend enough on her living, thou wilt spend it on her dead; I saw the like of this before; thou must lay out a good deal on her."

They bought a good lot of things for the funeral, and they left the one half of it in the house of the poor brother and they buried the crone again. "Is it not lamentable," said the poor brother's gillie to his master, "that such a lot of linen should go on the crone, while thou art so much in want of a shirt thyself?" He went to the cell that night again, he raised the crone, he took off her the tais clothes, and he took her with him on his back; he went into the house of the rich brother, as was usual, and be set the crone standing at the end of the dresser, with her claw full of seeds from the dish of sowens, as if she were eating it. When the man of the house saw her back in the morning, he thrashed his wife soundly, because of her mother. He went then to the house of his poor brother, and he told that the crone had come home again. "Aha!" said the gillie, "because thou didst not spend money on her living, thou wilt spend it on her dead; I saw the like of this before." "Go thou, then, and lay out a good deal on her, for I am tired of her," said the man. He bought a good lot for the crone's funeral, and he took the one half to his master's house. They buried the crone. In the night, said the gillie to his master, "Is it not lamentable that such linen should go with the crone to the cell, while I myself am in such want of a shirt."He took himself to the cell, he raised the crone, he took off her the tais dress, he put her on top of him, and he reached the rich brother's house. He did not get in this journey, so he went with her to the stable, and he tied her on top of a year-old colt. When they rose in the morning, they were well pleased when they did not see the crone before them. He was going from home; he went out to the stable, and he took the mare with him; but he never perceived that the crone was on top of the year-old. When he went away on top of the mare, after him went the year-old with the crone clattering on top of him. He turned back when he saw the crone, and he was like to kill his wife this time. He went to his brother's house and he told that the crone had come back again.

"As thou didst not spend money on her living," said the gillie, "thou must spend it on her dead."

"Go and lay out as thou wilt on her," said he to the gillie, "but keep her away."

He went this time and he bought a good lot for the crone's funeral, and he invited every one in the place.

They buried the crone again; and the poor brother was as wealthy as the other, by reason of the funerals.

A Puzzle

THERE WAS A CUSTOM ONCE through the Gældom, when a man would die, that the whole people of the place would gather together to the house in which the dead man was – Tigh aire faire (the shealing of watching), and they would be at drinking, and singing, and telling tales, till the white day should come.

At this time they were gathered together in the house of watching, and there was a man in this house, and when the tale went about, he had neither tale nor song, and as he had not, he was put out at the door. When he was put out he stood at the end of the barn; he was afraid to go farther. He was but a short time standing when he saw nine, dressed in red garments, going past, and shortly after that he saw other nine going past in green dresses; shortly after this he saw other nine going past in blue dresses. A while after that came a horse, and a woman and a man on him. Said the woman to the man, "I will go to speak to that man who is there at the end of the barn." She asked him what he was doing standing there? He told her? "Sawest thou any man going past since the night fell?" said she. He said that he had; he told her all he had seen. "Thou sawest all that went past since the night fell," said she. "Well then," said she, "the first nine thou sawest, these were brothers of my father, and the second nine brothers of my mother, and the third nine, these were my own sons, and they are altogether sons to that man who is on the horse. That is my husband; and there is no law in Eirinn, nor in Alaba, nor in Sasunn that can find fault with us. Go thou in, and I myself will not believe but that a puzzle is on them till day;" and she went and she left him.

The Two Shepherds

THERE WERE OUT BETWEEN LOCHABER and Baideanach two shepherds who were neighbours to each other, and the one would often be going to see the other. One was on the east side of a river, and another on the west. The one who was on the west side of the river came to the house of the one who was on the east of it on an evening visit. He staid till it was pretty late, and then he wished to go home. "It is time to go home," said he. "It is not that which thou shalt do, but thou shalt stay tonight," said the other, "since it is so long in the night." "I will not stay at all events; if I were over the river I don't care more."

The houseman had a pretty strong son, and he said, "I will go with thee, and I will set thee over the river, but thou hadst better stay." – "I will not stay at all events." – "If thou wilt not stay I will go with thee." The son of the houseman called a dog which he had herding. The dog went with him. When he set the man on the other side of the river, the man said to him, "Be returning now, I am far in thy debt." The strong lad returned, and the dog with him. When he reached the river as he was returning back home, he was thinking whether he should take the stepping-stones, or put off his foot-clothes and take below. He put off his foot-clothes for fear of taking the stepping-stones, and when he was over there in the river, the dog that was with him leaped at the back of his head. He threw her off him; she leaped again; he did the same thing. When he was on the other side of the river, he put his hand on his head, and there was not a bit of a bonnet on it. He was saying, whether should he return to seek the bonnet, or should he go home without it. "It's disgusting for me to return home without my bonnet; I will return over yet to the place where I put my foot-clothes off me; I doubt it is there that I left it." So he returned to the other side of the river. He saw a right big man seated where he had been, and his own bonnet in his hand. He caught hold of the bonnet, and he took it from him. "What business hast thou there with that? – It is mine, and thou hadst no business to take it from me, though thou hast got it." Over the river then they went, without a word for each other, fiercely, hatingly. When they went over, then, on the river, the big man put his hand under the arm of the shepherd, and he began to drag the lad down to a loch that was there, against his will and against his strength. They stood front to front, bravely, firmly on either side. In spite of the strength of the shepherd's son, the big man was about to conquer. It was so that the shepherd's son thought of putting his hand about an oak tree that was in the place. The big man was striving to take him with him, and the tree was bending and twisting. At last the tree was loosening in the earth. She loosened all but one of her roots. At the time when the last root of the tree slipped, the cocks that were about the wood crowed. The shepherd's son understood that when he heard the cocks crowing that it was on the short side of day. When they heard between them the cocks crowing, the big man said, "Thou has stood well, and thou hadst need, or thy bonnet had been dear for thee." The big man left him, and they never more noticed a thing near the river.

Thomas of the Thumb

THERE WAS ONE BEFORE NOW whose name was Tómas na h òrdaig, and he was no bigger than the thumb of a stalwart man. Tómas went once to take a walk, and there came a coarse shower of hailstones, and Tómas went in under a dock leaf; and there came a great drove of cattle past, and there was a great brindled bull amongst them, and he was eating about the docken, and he ate Tómas of the Thumb. His mother and his father missed him, and they went to seek him. They were going past the brindled bull, and quoth Tómas na h òrdaig,

> *"Ye are there a seeking me,*
> *Through smooth places, and moss places;*
> *And here am I a lonely one,*
> *Within the brindled bull."*

Then they killed the brindled bull, and they sought Tómas na h òrdaig amongst the paunches and entrails of the bull, but they threw away the great gut in which he was.

There came a carlin the way, and she took the great gut, and as she was going along she went over a bog.

Tómas said something to her, and the old wife threw away the great gut from her in a fright.

There came a fox the way, and he took with him the gut, and Tómas shouted "Bies taileù! the fox. Bis taileù! the fox."

Then the dogs ran after the fox, and they caught him, and they ate him and though they ate the gut they did not touch Tómas na h òrdaig.

Tómas went home, where his mother and his father were, and he it was indeed that had the queer story for them.

The Story of the Lay of the Great Fool

THERE WERE TWO BROTHERS ONCE in Eirinn, and one of them was a king and the other a 'ridire.' They were both married. On the knight there was a track (that is, the knight had children), and there were no children at all to the king. It was a source of insult to the knight and his lot of sons, that the king should have the realm at all. The thing that happened was, that they gathered armies, both of them, on each side. On the day of the battle that they gave, the knight and his three sons were slain.

The wife of the knight was heavy, and the king sent word that if she were to have a babe son to slay him, but that if it were a baby daughter to keep her alive, and keep her. It was a lad that she had, and there was a kitchen wench within who had a love son. Braomall was her name, and Domhnull was the name of her son.

When the son of the knight was born, this one fled with the two, the knight's son and her own son. They were being fed at the cost of the knight's wife. She was there on a day, and for fear they should be hungry, she went to a town land to seek food for them. They were hungry, and she was not coming, and they saw three deer coming towards the bothy. The knight's son was where the other was, and he asked what creatures were there. He told him there were creatures on which there was meat and clothing.

"If we were the better for it I would catch them," said he.

He ran and he caught the three deer, and they were before his 'muime' when she came. She flayed them, and they ate, and she made a dress for him of the deer's hides. Thus they were in a good way till the deer failed, and hunger came upon them again, and she went again to the town land. There came a great horse that belonged to the king – a wild horse – to the place where they were. He asked of Donald what beast was that.

"That is a beast on which sport is done, one is upon him riding him."

"If we were the better for him I would catch him," said he.

"Thou ill-conditioned tatterdemalion! to catch that beast! It would discomfit any man in the realm to catch him." He did not bear any more chatter, but he came round about, and he struck his fist on Donald, and he drove his brains out. He put an oaken skewer through his ear, and he hung him up against the door of the bothy. "Be there thou fifty beyond the worst," said he.

Then he stretched out after the horse, and the hides were trailing behind him. He caught the horse, and he mounted him; and the horse that had never borne to see a man, he betook himself to the stable for fear. His father's brother had got a son by another wife. When he saw the palace he went up with wonder to look at the palace of his father's brother.

His muime never had called him anything but 'the great fool' and 'Creud orm.' When he perceived the son of his father's brother playing shinty, he went where he was, and, "Creud orm," said he.

"Who art thou," said the king's son – "of the gentles or ungentles of the realm, that has the like of that speech?"

"I am the great fool, the son of the knight's wife, the nursling of the nurse, and the foster-brother of Donald the nurse's son, going to do folly for myself, and if need were, it is I that could make a fool of thee also."

"Thou ill-conditioned tatterdemalion! make a fool of me?" said the king's son.

He put over the fist and he drove the brain out of him. "Be there, then, thou fifty over worse, as is Donald the nurse's son, with an oaken skewer through his ear."

He went in where the king was. "Creud orm," said he.

"Who art thou," said the king – "of the gentles or ungentles of the realm, that hast such a speech?"

"I am the great fool, the son of the knight's wife, the nursling of the nurse, and the foster-brother of the nurse's son, going to make folly for myself, and if need were, it is I that could make a fool of thee also."

"Well, then, it is not thou that made me that, but my counsellor, on the day that I slew thy father, and did not slay thy mother."

Then the king went with him. Every one, then, that he fell in with in the town, they were going with him, and that was their blessing, "Creud orm."

There was a splendid woman in the realm, and there was a great 'Fachnach,' that had taken her away. The people thought, if they could bring him to the presence of this woman, that be would set his head upon her, and that he would let the people away; that it was likely they would come between himself and the Fachach, and that the Fachach would kill him. That time he was an utter fool.

The Hoodie and the Fox

THE HOODIE AND THE FOX were good at early rising, and they laid a wager with each other, for which should soonest get up in the morning. The hoodie went into a tree top, and she slept; and the fox staid at the foot of the tree, looking aloft (to see) when the day would come. As soon as he perceived the day he cried,

"Sê-n-lAbAn-ê." (It is bright day.)

The hoodie had never stirred all the night, and then she awoke with the cry, and she answered, "SAd-o-bê-ê, SAd-o-bê-ê." It's long since it was. Then the fox lost the wager and the hoodie won.

The Reason Why the Dallag (Dog-Fish) is Called the King's Fish

THAT BUT THAT THE KING of Lochlann should come to the King of Eirinn to be a while along with him.

The King of Lochlann and Fionn went on a day to fish, and they had a little boat, and they had no man but themselves.

They spent the greatest part of the day fishing, and they did not get a thing.

Then there laid a beast on (the hook of) Fionn, and he fell to fishing, so that he put the hook into him. He took in the fish; and what fish was it but a dog-fish. The hook of the King of Lochlann was in her maw, under the hook of Fionn, and the hook of Fionn was in the outer mouth. Then the King of Lochlann fell to at taking out the dog-fish, since it was his hook that was farthest down in her. They fell to arguing with each other, and Fionn would not yield a bit till they should go to law.

Then they went to land with the boat, and they went to law, and the law made (over) the fish to Fionn; and that there should be a fine laid upon the King of Lochlann, since he had not felt the fish when first it struck him.

With the rage that the King of Lochlann took he went home to Lochlann, and he told to his muime and his oide (his foster parents) how it had happened.

The Muilearteach was his muime, and the Smith of Songs, who was married to her, was his foster-father.

She said that it was she who would bring out the recompense for that.

Then she came till she reached Eirinn, and the King of Lochlann with her, and the Smith of Songs.

The Dallag was never said after that but the king's fish.

Canonbie Dick and Thomas of Ercildoune

IT CHANCED, LONG YEARS AGO, that a certain horse-dealer lived in the South of Scotland, near the Border, not very far from Longtown. He was known as Canonbie Dick; and as he went up and down the country, he almost always had a long string of horses behind him, which he bought at one fair and sold at another, generally managing to turn a good big penny by the transaction.

He was a very fearless man, not easily daunted; and the people who knew him used to say that if Canonbie Dick dare not attempt a thing, no one else need be asked to do it.

One evening, as he was returning from a fair at some distance from his home with a pair of horses which he had not succeeded in selling, he was riding over Bowden Moor, which lies to the west of the Eildon Hills. These hills are, as all men know, the scene of some of the most famous of Thomas the Rhymer's prophecies; and also, so men say, they are the sleeping-place of King Arthur and his Knights, who rest under the three high peaks, waiting for the mystic call that shall awake them.

But little recked the horse-dealer of Arthur and his Knights, nor yet of Thomas the Rhymer. He was riding along at a snail's pace, thinking over the bargains which he had made at the fair that day, and wondering when he was likely to dispose of his two remaining horses.

All at once he was startled by the approach of a venerable man, with white hair and an old-world dress, who seemed almost to start out of the ground, so suddenly did he make his appearance.

When they met, the stranger stopped, and, to Canonbie Dick's great amazement, asked him for how much he would be willing to part with his horses.

The wily horse-dealer thought that he saw a chance of driving a good bargain, for the stranger looked a man of some consequence; so he named a good round sum.

The old man tried to bargain with him; but when he found that he had not much chance of succeeding – for no one ever did succeed in inducing Canonbie Dick to sell a horse for a less sum than he named for it at first – he agreed to buy the animals, and, pulling a bag of gold from the pocket of his queerly cut breeches, he began to count out the price.

As he did so, Canonbie Dick got another shock of surprise, for the gold that the stranger gave him was not the gold that was in use at the time, but was fashioned into Unicorns, and Bonnet-pieces, and other ancient coins, which would be of no use to the horse-dealer in his everyday transactions. But it was good, pure gold; and he took it gladly, for he knew that he was selling his horses at about half as much again as they were worth. "So," thought he to himself, "surely I cannot be the loser in the long run."

Then the two parted, but not before the old man had commissioned Dick to get him other good horses at the same price, the only stipulation he made being that Dick should always bring them to the same spot, after dark, and that he should always come alone.

And, as time went on, the horse-dealer found that he had indeed met a good customer.

For, whenever he came across a suitable horse, he had only to lead it over Bowden Moor after dark, and he was sure to meet the mysterious, white-headed stranger, who always paid him for the animal in old-fashioned golden pieces.

And he might have been selling horses to him yet, for aught I know, had it not been for his one failing.

Canonbie Dick was apt to get very thirsty, and his ordinary customers, knowing this, took care always to provide him with something to drink. The old man never did so; he paid down his money and led away his horses, and there was an end of the matter.

But one night, Dick, being even more thirsty than usual, and feeling sure that his mysterious friend must live somewhere in the neighbourhood, seeing that he was always wandering about the hillside when everyone else was asleep, hinted that he would be very glad to go home with him and have a little refreshment.

"He would need to be a brave man who asks to go home with me," returned the stranger; "but, if thou wilt, thou canst follow me. Only, remember this – if thy courage fail thee at that which thou wilt behold, thou wilt rue it all thy life."

Canonbie Dick laughed long and loud. "My courage hath never failed me yet," he cried. "Beshrew me if I will let it fail now. So lead on, old man, and I will follow."

Without a word the stranger turned and began to ascend a narrow path which led to a curious hillock, which from its shape, was called by the country-folk the 'Lucken Hare.'

It was supposed to be a great haunt of Witches; and, as a rule, nobody passed that way after dark, if they could possibly help it.

Canonbie Dick was not afraid of Witches, however, so he followed his guide with a bold step up the hillside; but it must be confessed that he felt a little startled when he saw him turn down what seemed to be an entrance to a cavern, especially as he never remembered having seen any opening in the hillside there before.

He paused for a moment, looking round him in perplexity, wondering where he was being taken; and his conductor glanced at him scornfully.

"You can go back if you will," he said. "I warned thee thou wert going on a journey that would try thy courage to the uttermost." There was a jeering note in his voice that touched Dick's pride.

"Who said that I was afraid?" he retorted. "I was just taking note of where this passage stands on the hillside, so as to know it another time."

The stranger shrugged his shoulders. "Time enough to look for it when thou wouldst visit it again," he said. And then he pursued his way, with Dick following closely at his heels.

After the first yard or two they were enveloped in thick darkness, and the horse-dealer would have been sore put to it to keep near his guide had not the latter held out his hand for him to grasp. But after a little space a faint glimmering of light began to appear, which grew clearer and clearer, until at last they found themselves in an enormous cavern lit by flaming torches, which were stuck here and there in sconces in the rocky walls, and which, although they served to give light enough to see by, yet threw such ghostly shadows on the floor that they only seemed to intensify the gloom that hung over the vast apartment.

And the curious thing about this mysterious cave was that, along one side of it, ran a long row of horse stalls, just like what one would find in a stable, and in each stall stood a coal-black charger, saddled and bridled, as if ready for the fray; and on the straw, by every horse's side, lay the gallant figure of a knight, clad from head to foot in coal-black armour, with a drawn sword in his mailed hand.

But not a horse moved, not a chain rattled. Knights and steeds alike were silent and motionless, looking exactly as if some strange enchantment had been thrown over them, and they had been suddenly turned into black marble.

There was something so awesome in the still, cold figures and in the unearthly silence that brooded over everything that Canonbie Dick, reckless and daring though he was, felt his courage waning and his knees beginning to shake under him.

In spite of these feelings, however, he followed the old man up the hall to the far end of it, where there was a table of ancient workmanship, on which was placed a glittering sword and a curiously wrought hunting-horn.

When they reached this table the stranger turned to him, and said, with great dignity, "Thou hast heard, good man, of Thomas of Ercildoune – Thomas the Rhymer, as men call him – he who went to dwell for a time with the Queen of Fairy-land, and from her received the Gifts of Truth and Prophecy?"

Canonbie Dick nodded; for as the wonderful Soothsayer's name fell on his ears, his heart sank within him and his tongue seemed to cleave to the roof of his mouth. If he had been brought there to parley with Thomas the Rhymer, then had he laid himself open to all the eldrich Powers of Darkness.

"I that speak to thee am he," went on the white-haired stranger. "And I have permitted thee thus to have thy desire and follow me hither in order that I may try of what stuff thou art made. Before thee lies a Horn and a Sword. He that will sound the one, or draw the other, shall, if his courage fail not, be King over the whole of Britain. I, Thomas the Rhymer, have spoken it, and, as thou knowest, my tongue cannot lie. But list ye, the outcome of it all depends on thy bravery; and it will be a light task, or a heavy, according as thou layest hand on Sword or Horn first."

Now Dick was more versed in giving blows than in making music, and his first impulse was to seize the Sword, then, come what might, he had something in his hand to defend himself with. But just as he was about to lift it the thought struck him that, if the place were full of spirits, as he felt sure that it must be, this action of him might be taken to mean defiance, and might cause them to band themselves together against him.

So, changing his mind, he picked up the Horn with a trembling hand, and blew a blast upon it, which, however, was so weak and feeble that it could scarce be heard at the other end of the hall.

The result that followed was enough to appal the stoutest heart. Thunder rolled in crashing peals through the immense hall. The charmed Knights and their horses woke in an instant from their enchanted sleep. The Knights sprang to their feet and seized their swords, brandishing them round their heads, while their great black chargers stamped, and snorted, and ground their bits, as if eager to escape from their stalls. And where a moment before all had been stillness and silence, there was now a scene of wild din and excitement.

Now was the time for Canonbie Dick to play the man. If he had done so all the rest of his life might have been different.

But his courage failed him, and he lost his chance. Terrified at seeing so many threatening faces turned towards him, he dropped the Horn and made one weak, undecided effort to pick up the Sword.

But, ere he could do so, a mysterious voice sounded from somewhere in the hall, and these were the words that it uttered:

"Woe to the coward, that ever he was born,
Who did not draw the Sword before he blew the Horn."

And, before Dick knew what he was about, a perfect whirlwind of cold, raw air tore through the cavern, carrying the luckless horse-dealer along with it; and, hurrying him along the narrow passage through which he had entered, dashed him down outside on a bank of loose stones and shale. He fell right to the bottom, and was found, with little life left in him, next morning, by some shepherds, to whom he had just strength enough left to whisper the story of his weird and fearful adventure.

Gold-Tree and Silver-Tree

IN BYGONE DAYS THERE LIVED a little Princess named Gold-Tree, and she was one of the prettiest children in the whole world.

Although her mother was dead, she had a very happy life, for her father loved her dearly, and thought that nothing was too much trouble so long as it gave his little daughter pleasure. But by and by he married again, and then the little Princess's sorrows began.

For his new wife, whose name, curious to say, was Silver-Tree, was very beautiful, but she was also very jealous, and she made herself quite miserable for fear that, some day, she should meet someone who was better looking than she was herself.

When she found that her step-daughter was so very pretty, she took a dislike to her at once, and was always looking at her and wondering if people would think her prettier than she was. And because, in her heart of hearts, she was afraid that they would do so, she was very unkind indeed to the poor girl.

At last, one day, when Princess Gold-Tree was quite grown up, the two ladies went for a walk to a little well which lay, all surrounded by trees, in the middle of a deep glen.

Now the water in this well was so clear that everyone who looked into it saw his face reflected on the surface; and the proud Queen loved to come and peep into its depths, so that she could see her own picture mirrored in the water.

But today, as she was looking in, what should she see but a little trout, which was swimming quietly backwards and forwards not very far from the surface.

"Troutie, troutie, answer me this one question," said the Queen. "Am not I the most beautiful woman in the world?"

"No, indeed, you are not," replied the trout promptly, jumping out of the water, as he spoke, in order to swallow a fly.

"Who is the most beautiful woman, then?" asked the disappointed Queen, for she had expected a far different answer.

"Thy step-daughter, the Princess Gold-Tree, without a doubt," said the little fish; then, frightened by the black look that came upon the jealous Queen's face, he dived to the bottom of the well.

It was no wonder that he did so, for the Queen's expression was not pleasant to look at, as she darted an angry glance at her fair young step-daughter, who was busy picking flowers some little distance away.

Indeed, she was so annoyed at the thought that anyone should say that the girl was prettier than she was, that she quite lost her self-control; and when she reached home she went up, in a violent passion, to her room, and threw herself on the bed, declaring that she felt very ill indeed.

It was in vain that Princess Gold-Tree asked her what the matter was, and if she could do anything for her. She would not let the poor girl touch her, but pushed her away as if she had been some evil thing. So at last the Princess had to leave her alone, and go out of the apartment, feeling very sad indeed.

By and by the King came home from his hunting, and he at once asked for the Queen. He was told that she had been seized with sudden illness, and that she was lying on her bed in her own room, and that no one, not even the Court Physician, who had been hastily summoned, could make out what was wrong with her.

In great anxiety – for he really loved her – the King went up to her bedside, and asked the Queen how she felt, and if there was anything that he could do to relieve her.

"Yes, there is one thing that thou couldst do," she answered harshly, "but I know full well that, even although it is the only thing that will cure me, thou wilt not do it."

"Nay," said the King, "I deserve better words at thy mouth than these; for thou knowest that I would give thee aught thou carest to ask, even if it be the half of my Kingdom."

"Then give me thy daughter's heart to eat," cried the Queen, "for unless I can obtain that, I will die, and that speedily."

She spoke so wildly, and looked at him in such a strange fashion, that the poor King really thought that her brain was turned, and he was at his wits' end what to do. He left the room, and paced up and down the corridor in great distress, until at last he remembered that that very morning the son of a great King had arrived from a country far over the sea, asking for his daughter's hand in marriage.

"Here is a way out of the difficulty," he said to himself. "This marriage pleaseth me well, and I will have it celebrated at once. Then, when my daughter is safe out of the country, I will send a lad up the hillside, and he shall kill a he-goat, and I will have its heart prepared and dressed, and send it up to my wife. Perhaps the sight of it will cure her of this madness."

So he had the strange Prince summoned before him, and told him how the Queen had taken a sudden illness that had wrought on her brain, and had caused her to take a dislike to the Princess, and how it seemed as if it would be a good thing if, with the maiden's consent, the marriage could take place at once, so that the Queen might be left alone to recover from her strange malady.

Now the Prince was delighted to gain his bride so easily, and the Princess was glad to escape from her step-mother's hatred, so the marriage took place at once, and the newly wedded pair set off across the sea for the Prince's country.

Then the King sent a lad up the hillside to kill a he-goat; and when it was killed he gave orders that its heart should be dressed and cooked, and sent to the Queen's apartment on a silver dish. And the wicked woman tasted it, believing it to be the heart of her step-daughter; and when she had done so, she rose from her bed and went about the Castle looking as well and hearty as ever.

I am glad to be able to tell you that the marriage of Princess Gold-Tree, which had come about in such a hurry, turned out to be a great success; for the Prince whom she had wedded was rich, and great, and powerful, and he loved her dearly, and she was as happy as the day was long.

So things went peacefully on for a year. Queen Silver-Tree was satisfied and contented, because she thought that her step-daughter was dead; while all the time the Princess was happy and prosperous in her new home.

But at the end of the year it chanced that the Queen went once more to the well in the little glen, in order to see her face reflected in the water.

And it chanced also that the same little trout was swimming backwards and forwards, just as he had done the year before. And the foolish Queen determined to have a better answer to her question this time than she had last.

"Troutie, troutie," she whispered, leaning over the edge of the well, "am not I the most beautiful woman in the world?"

"By my troth, thou art not," answered the trout, in his very straightforward way.

"Who is the most beautiful woman, then?" asked the Queen, her face growing pale at the thought that she had yet another rival.

"Why, your Majesty's step-daughter, the Princess Gold-Tree, to be sure," answered the trout.

The Queen threw back her head with a sigh of relief. "Well, at any rate, people cannot admire her now," she said, "for it is a year since she died. I ate her heart for my supper."

"Art thou sure of that, your Majesty?" asked the trout, with a twinkle in his eye. "Methinks it is but a year since she married the gallant young Prince who came from abroad to seek her hand, and returned with him to his own country."

When the Queen heard these words she turned quite cold with rage, for she knew that her husband had deceived her; and she rose from her knees and went straight home to the Palace, and, hiding her anger as best she could, she asked him if he would give orders to have the Long Ship made ready, as she wished to go and visit her dear step-daughter, for it was such a very long time since she had seen her.

The King was somewhat surprised at her request, but he was only too glad to think that she had got over her hatred towards his daughter, and he gave orders that the Long Ship should be made ready at once.

Soon it was speeding over the water, its prow turned in the direction of the land where the Princess lived, steered by the Queen herself; for she knew the course that the boat ought to take, and she was in such haste to be at her journey's end that she would allow no one else to take the helm.

Now it chanced that Princess Gold-Tree was alone that day, for her husband had gone a-hunting. And as she looked out of one of the Castle windows she saw a boat coming sailing over the sea towards the landing place. She recognised it as her father's Long Ship, and she guessed only too well whom it carried on board.

She was almost beside herself with terror at the thought, for she knew that it was for no good purpose that Queen Silver-Tree had taken the trouble to set out to visit her, and she felt that she would have given almost anything she possessed if her husband had but been at home. In her distress she hurried into the servants' hall.

"Oh, what shall I do, what shall I do?" she cried, "for I see my father's Long Ship coming over the sea, and I know that my step-mother is on board. And if she hath a chance she will kill me, for she hateth me more than anything else upon earth."

Now the servants worshipped the ground that their young Mistress trod on, for she was always kind and considerate to them, and when they saw how frightened she was, and heard her piteous words, they crowded round her, as if to shield her from any harm that threatened her.

"Do not be afraid, your Highness," they cried; "we will defend thee with our very lives if need be. But in case thy Lady Step-Mother should have the power to throw any evil spell over thee, we will lock thee in the great Mullioned Chamber, then she cannot get nigh thee at all."

Now the Mullioned Chamber was a strong-room, which was in a part of the castle all by itself, and its door was so thick that no one could possibly break through it; and the Princess knew that if she were once inside the room, with its stout oaken door between her and her step-mother, she would be perfectly safe from any mischief that that wicked woman could devise.

So she consented to her faithful servants' suggestion, and allowed them to lock her in the Mullioned Chamber.

So it came to pass that when Queen Silver-Tree arrived at the great door of the Castle, and commanded the lackey who opened it to take her to his Royal Mistress, he told her, with a low bow, that that was impossible, because the Princess was locked in the strong-room of the Castle, and could not get out, because no one knew where the key was.

(Which was quite true, for the old butler had tied it round the neck of the Prince's favourite sheep-dog, and had sent him away to the hills to seek his master.)

"Take me to the door of the apartment," commanded the Queen. "At least I can speak to my dear daughter through it." And the lackey, who did not see what harm could possibly come from this, did as he was bid.

"If the key is really lost, and thou canst not come out to welcome me, dear Gold-Tree," said the deceitful Queen, "at least put thy little finger through the keyhole that I may kiss it."

The Princess did so, never dreaming that evil could come to her through such a simple action. But it did. For instead of kissing the tiny finger, her step-mother stabbed it with a poisoned needle, and, so deadly was the poison, that, before she could utter a single cry, the poor Princess fell, as one dead, on the floor.

When she heard the fall, a smile of satisfaction crept over Queen Silver-Tree's face. "Now I can say that I am the handsomest woman in the world," she whispered; and she went back to the lackey who stood waiting at the end of the passage, and told him that she had said all that she had to say to her daughter, and that now she must return home.

So the man attended her to the boat with all due ceremony, and she set sail for her own country; and no one in the Castle knew that any harm had befallen their dear Mistress until the Prince came home from his hunting with the key of the Mullioned Chamber, which he had taken from his sheep-dog's neck, in his hand.

He laughed when he heard the story of Queen Silver-Tree's visit, and told the servants that they had done well; then he ran upstairs to open the door and release his wife.

But what was his horror and dismay, when he did so, to find her lying dead at his feet on the floor.

He was nearly beside himself with rage and grief; and, because he knew that a deadly poison such as Queen Silver-Tree had used would preserve the Princess's body so that it had no need of burial, he had it laid on a silken couch and left in the Mullioned Chamber, so that he could go and look at it whenever he pleased.

He was so terribly lonely, however, that in a little time he married again, and his second wife was just as sweet and as good as the first one had been. This new wife was very happy, there was only one little thing that caused her any trouble at all, and she was too sensible to let it make her miserable.

That one thing was that there was one room in the Castle – a room which stood at the end of a passage by itself – which she could never enter, as her husband always carried the key. And as, when she asked him the reason of this, he always made an excuse of some kind, she made up her mind that she would not seem as if she did not trust him, so she asked no more questions about the matter.

But one day the Prince chanced to leave the door unlocked, and as he had never told her not to do so, she went in, and there she saw Princess Gold-Tree lying on the silken couch, looking as if she were asleep.

"Is she dead, or is she only sleeping?" she said to herself, and she went up to the couch and looked closely at the Princess. And there, sticking in her little finger, she discovered a curiously shaped needle.

"There hath been evil work here," she thought to herself. "If that needle be not poisoned, then I know naught of medicine." And, being skilled in leechcraft, she drew it carefully out.

In a moment Princess Gold-Tree opened her eyes and sat up, and presently she had recovered sufficiently to tell the Other Princess the whole story.

Now, if her step-mother had been jealous, the Other Princess was not jealous at all; for, when she heard all that had happened, she clapped her little hands, crying, "Oh, how glad the Prince will be; for although he hath married again, I know that he loves thee best."

That night the Prince came home from hunting looking very tired and sad, for what his second wife had said was quite true. Although he loved her very much, he was always mourning in his heart for his first dear love, Princess Gold-Tree.

"How sad thou art!" exclaimed his wife, going out to meet him. "Is there nothing that I can do to bring a smile to thy face?"

"Nothing," answered the Prince wearily, laying down his bow, for he was too heart-sore even to pretend to be gay.

"Except to give thee back Gold-Tree," said his wife mischievously. "And that can I do. Thou wilt find her alive and well in the Mullioned Chamber."

Without a word the Prince ran upstairs, and, sure enough, there was his dear Gold-Tree, sitting on the couch ready to welcome him.

He was so overjoyed to see her that he threw his arms round her neck and kissed her over and over again, quite forgetting his poor second wife, who had followed him upstairs, and who now stood watching the meeting that she had brought about.

She did not seem to be sorry for herself, however. "I always knew that thy heart yearned after Princess Gold-Tree," she said. "And it is but right that it should be so. For she was thy first love, and, since she hath come to life again, I will go back to mine own people."

"No, indeed thou wilt not," answered the Prince, "for it is thou who hast brought me this joy. Thou wilt stay with us, and we shall all three live happily together. And Gold-Tree and thee will become great friends."

And so it came to pass. For Princess Gold-Tree and the Other Princess soon became like sisters, and loved each other as if they had been brought up together all their lives.

In this manner another year passed away, and one evening, in the old country, Queen Silver-Tree went, as she had done before, to look at her face in the water of the little well in the glen.

And, as had happened twice before, the trout was there. "Troutie, troutie," she whispered, "am not I the most beautiful woman in the world?"

"By my troth, thou art not," answered the trout, as he had answered on the two previous occasions.

"And who dost thou say is the most beautiful woman now?" asked the Queen, her voice trembling with rage and vexation.

"I have given her name to thee these two years back," answered the trout. "The Princess Gold-Tree, of course."

"But she is dead," laughed the Queen. "I am sure of it this time, for it is just a year since I stabbed her little finger with a poisoned needle, and I heard her fall down dead on the floor."

"I would not be so sure of that," answered the trout, and without saying another word he dived straight down to the bottom of the well.

After hearing his mysterious words the Queen could not rest, and at last she asked her husband to have the Long Ship prepared once more, so that she could go and see her step-daughter.

The King gave the order gladly; and it all happened as it had happened before.

She steered the Ship over the sea with her own hands, and when it was approaching the land it was seen and recognised by Princess Gold-Tree.

The Prince was out hunting, and the Princess ran, in great terror, to her friend, the Other Princess, who was upstairs in her chamber.

"Oh, what shall I do, what shall I do?" she cried, "for I see my father's Long Ship coming, and I know that my cruel step-mother is on board, and she will try to kill me, as she tried to kill me before.

"Oh! come, let us escape to the hills."

"Not at all," replied the Other Princess, throwing her arms round the trembling Gold-Tree. "I am not afraid of thy Lady Step-Mother. Come with me, and we will go down to the sea shore to greet her."

So they both went down to the edge of the water, and when Queen Silver-Tree saw her step-daughter coming she pretended to be very glad, and sprang out of the boat and ran to meet her, and held out a silver goblet full of wine for her to drink.

"'Tis rare wine from the East," she said, "and therefore very precious. I brought a flagon with me, so that we might pledge each other in a loving cup."

Princess Gold-Tree, who was ever gentle and courteous, would have stretched out her hand for the cup, had not the Other Princess stepped between her and her step-mother.

"Nay, Madam," she said gravely, looking the Queen straight in the face; "it is the custom in this land for the one who offers a loving cup to drink from it first herself."

"I will follow the custom gladly," answered the Queen, and she raised the goblet to her mouth. But the Other Princess, who was watching for closely, noticed that she did not allow the wine that it contained to touch her lips. So she stepped forward and, as if by accident, struck the bottom of the goblet with her shoulder. Part of its contents flew into the Queen's face, and part, before she could shut her mouth, went down her throat.

So, because of her wickedness, she was, as the Good Book says, caught in her own net. For she had made the wine so poisonous that, almost before she had swallowed it, she fell dead at the two Princesses' feet.

No one was sorry for her, for she really deserved her fate; and they buried her hastily in a lonely piece of ground, and very soon everybody had forgotten all about her.

As for Princess Gold-Tree, she lived happily and peacefully with her husband and her friend for the remainder of her life.

The Three Widows

THERE WERE THREE WIDOWS, and every one of them had a son apiece. Dòmhnull was the name of the son of one of them.

Dòmhnull had four stots, and the rest had but two each. They were always scolding, saying that he had more grass than they had themselves. On a night of the nights they went to the fold, and they seized on the stots of Dòmhnull and they killed them. When Dòmhnull rose and went out in the morning to see the stots, he found them dead.

He flayed the stots, and he salted them, and he took one of the hides with him to the big town to sell. The way was so long, that the night came on him before he reached the big town. He went into a wood and he put the hide about his head. There came a heap of birds, and they lighted on the hide; he put out his hand and he seized on one of them. About the brightening of day he went away; he betook himself to the house of a gentleman.

The gentleman came to the door, and he asked what he had there in his oxter. He said that he had a soothsayer. "What divination will he be doing?"

"He will be doing every sort of divination," said Dòmhnull. "Make him do divination," said the gentleman.

He went and he wrung him, and the bird gave a ran. "What is he saying?" said the gentleman. "He says that thou hast a wish to buy him, and that thou wilt give two hundred pounds Saxon for him," said Dòmhnull. "Well, surely! – it is true, doubtless; and if I were thinking that he would do divination, I would give that for him," said the gentleman.

So now the gentleman bought the bird from Dòmhnull, and he gave him two hundred pounds Saxon for him.

"Try that thou do not sell him to any man, and that there is no knowing that I might not come myself to seek him yet. I would not give him to thee for three thousand pounds Saxon were it not that I am in extremity."

Dòmhnull went home, and the bird did not do a pinch of divination ever after.

When he took his meat he began at counting the money. Who were looking at him but those who killed the stots. They came in.

"Ah, Dòmhnull," said they, "How didst thou get all the money that is there?"

"I got it as you may get it too. It's I that am pleased that you killed the stots for me," said be. "Kill you your own stots and flay them, and take with you' the hides to the big town, and be shouting, 'Who will buy a stot's hide,' and you will get plenty of money."

They killed the stots, and they flayed them. They took with them the hides to the big town, and they began at shouting, "Who will buy a stot's hide." They were at that work the length of the day; and when the people of the big town were tired making sport of them, they returned home. Now they did not know what they should do. They were vexed because of the stots that were killed. They saw the mother of Dòmhnull going to the well, and they seized on her and they choked her.

When Dòmhnull was taking sorrow, so long was his mother coming, he looked out to try if he could see her. He reached the well, and he found her dead there. He did not know what he should do. Then he took her with him home. On the morrow he arrayed her in the best clothes she had, and he took her to the big town. He walked up to the king's house with her on the top of him. When he came to the king's house he met with a large well. He went and he stuck the stick into the bank of the well, and he set her standing with her chest on the stick. He reached the door and he struck at it, and the maidservant came down.

"Say to the king," said he, "that there is a respectable woman yonder, and that she has business with him."

The maidservant told that to the king. "Say to him to say to her to come over," said the king.

"The king is asking thee to say to her to come over," said the maidservant to Dòmhnull.

"I won't go there; go there thyself; I am tired enough."

The maid went up, and she told the king that not a bit of the man would go there. "Go there thyself," said the king.

"If she will not answer thee," said Dòmhnull to the maidservant, "thou shalt push her; she is deaf."

The maidservant reached where she was. "Good woman," said the maidservant to her, "the king is asking yourself to come over." She took no notice. She pushed her and she said not a word. Dòmhnull was seeing how it was without.

"Draw the stick from her chest," said Dòmhnull; "it's asleep she is."

She drew the stick from her chest, and there she went head foremost into the well. Then he shouted out, "Oh my cattle! my cattle! my mother drowned in the well! What shall I do this day?" Then he struck his two palms against each other, and there was no howl he gave that could not be heard at three miles' distance.

The king came out. "Oh, my lad, never give it voice for ever, and I will pay for thy mother. How much wilt thou be asking for thy mother?"

"Five hundred pounds Saxon," said Dòmhnull.

"Thou shalt get that within the minute," said the king.

Dòmhnull got the five hundred Saxon pounds. He went where his mother was; he took the clothes off that were on her, and he threw her into the well.

He came home, and he was counting the money. They came – the two – where he was, to see if he should be lamenting his mother. They put a question to him – "Where had he got all the money that was there?"

"I got it," said he, "where you may get it if you yourselves should choose."

"How shall we get it?"

"Kill you your mothers, and take them with you on top of you, and take them about the big town, and be shouting, 'Who will buy old dead carlins?' and you get your fortunes."

When they heard that they went home, and each one of them began upon his mother with a stone in a stocking till he killed her.

They went on the morrow to the big town. They began at shouting, "Who will buy old carlins dead?" And there was no man who would buy that.

When the people of the big town were tired making sport of them, they set the dogs at them home.

When they came home that night they laid down and they slept. On the morrow, when they rose, they went where Dòmhnull was, and they seized on him and they put him into a barrel. They went with it to reel it down from a peak of rock. They were thus, and they had time about carrying it. The one said to the other, "Since the way was so long, and the day so hot, that they should go in to take a dram." They went in, and they left him in the barrel on the great road without. He heard a 'Tristrich' coming, and who was there but the shepherd, and a hundred sheep with him. He came down, and he began to play a 'trump' (Jew's harp) which he had in the barrel. The shepherd struck a stroke of his stick on a barrel. "Who's in here?" said he. "It's me," said Dòmhnull. "What art thou doing in it?" said the shepherd. "I am making a fortune in it," said Dòmhnull, "and no man ever saw such a place with gold and silver. I have just filled a thousand purses here, and the fortune is nearly made." "It's a pity," said the shepherd, "that thou shouldest not let myself in a while."

"I won't let thee. It is much that would make me."

"And wilt thou let me in? Mightest thou not let me in for one minute, and mightest thou not have enough thyself nevertheless?"

"By the books, poor man, since thou art needful, I will not let thee in. (Do) thou thyself drive the head out of the barrel and come here; but thou shalt not get (leave) to be long in it," said Dòmhnull.

The shepherd took the head out of the barrel, and he came out; he seized on the shepherd by the two shanks, and he set him head foremost in the barrel.

"There is neither silver nor gold here," said the shepherd.

"Thou wilt not see a thing till the head goes on the barrel," said Dòmhnull.

"Oh, I don't see a shadow in here," said he.

"If thou seest not, so be it with thee," said Dòmhnull.

Dòmhnull went and he put on the plaid that the shepherd had, and when he put on the plaid the dog followed him. Then they came out and they seized the barrel, and they raised it on their shoulders. They went away with it.

The shepherd would say at the end of every minute, "It's me that's in it – it's me that's in it." "Oh, it's thou, roguey! belike it's thou?"

They reached the peak of the rock, and they let down the barrel with the rock and shepherd in its inside.

When they returned, whom did they see but Dòmhnull, with his plaid and his dog, and his hundred of sheep with him in a park.

They went over to him.

"Oh, Dòmhnull," said they, "how gottest thou to come hither?"

"I got as you might get if you would try it. After that I had reached the world over yonder, they said to me that I had plenty of time for going over there, and they set me over here, and a hundred sheep with me to make money for myself."

"And would they give the like of that to us if we should go there?" said they.

"They would give (that.) It's they that would give," said Dòmhnull.

"(By) what means shall we get going there?" said they.

"Exactly the very means by which you yourselves sent me there," said he.

They went and they took with them two barrels to set themselves into up above.

When they reached the place one of them went into one of the barrels, and the other sent him down with the rock. That one gave a roar below, and his brains just after going out with the blow he got.

The other one asked Dòmhnull. what he was saying?

"He is shouting. 'Cattle and sheep, wealth and profit,'" said Dòmhnull.

"Down with me, down with me!" said the other one.

He did not stay to go into the barrel. He cut a caper down, and the brains went out of him.

Dòmhnull went home, and he had the land to himself.

The King of Lochlin's Three Daughters

THERE WAS A KING OVER LOCHLIN, once upon a time, who had a leash of daughters; they went out (on) a day to take a walk; and there came three giants, and they took with them the daughters of the king, and there was no knowing where they had gone. Then the king sent word for the sheanachy, and he asked him if he knew where his lot of daughters had gone. The sheanachy said to the king that three giants had taken them with them, and they were in the earth down below by them, and there was no way to get them but by making a ship that would sail on sea and land; and so it was that the king set out an order: anyone who would build a ship that would sail on sea and on land, that he should get the king's big daughter to marry. There was a widow there who had a leash of sons; and the eldest said to his mother on a day that was there, "Cook for me a bannock, and roast a cock; I am going away to cut wood, and to build a ship that will go to seek the daughters of the king." His mother said to him, "Which is better with thee, the big bannock with my cursing, or a little bannock with my blessing?" "Give me a big bannock, it will be small enough before I build a ship." He got a bannock and he went away. He arrived where there was a great wood and a river, and there he sat at the side of the river to take the bannock. A great Uruisg came out of the river, and she asked a part of the bannock. He said that he would not give her a morsel, that it was little enough for himself. He began cutting the wood, and every tree he cut would be on foot again; and so he was till the night came.

When the night came, he went home mournful, tearful, blind sorrowful. His mother asked, "How went it with thee today, son?" He said, "It went but black ill; every tree I would cut would be on foot again." A day or two after this the middle brother said that he himself would go; and he asked his mother to cook him a cake and roast him a cock; and in the very way as happened to his eldest brother, so it happened to him. The mother said the very same thing to the young one; and *he* took the little bannock. The Uruisg came, and she asked a part of the cake and the cock. He said to her that she should get that. When the Uruisg had eaten her own share of the cake and of the cock, she said to him that she knew what had brought him there as well as he himself, but he was to go home; but to be sure to meet her there at the end of a day and year; and that the ship would be ready at the end.

It was thus it happened: At the end of a day and a year the widow's young son went, and he found that the Uruisg had the ship floating on the river, fully equipped. He went away then with the ship, and a leash of gentlemen, as great as were in the kingdom, that were to marry the daughters of the king. They were but a short time sailing when they saw a man drinking a river that was there. He asked him, "What art thou doing there?" "I am drinking up this river." "Thou hadst better come with me, and I will give thee meat and wages, and better work than that." "I will do that," said he. They had not gone far forward, when they saw a man eating a stot in a park. "What art thou doing there?" said he.

"I am here going to eat all the stots in this park."

"Thou hadst better go with me, and thou wilt get work, and wages better than raw flesh." "I will do that," said he. They went but a short distance when they saw another man with his ear to the earth. "What art thou doing there?" said he. "I am here hearing the grass coming through earth." "Go with me, and thou wilt get meat, and better wages than to be there with thy ear to the earth." They were thus sailing back and forwards, when the man who was listening said that this was the place in which were the king's daughters and the giants. The widow's son, and the three that had fallen in with them, were let down in a creel in a great hole that was there. They reached the house of the big giant. "Ha! ha!" said he, the giant, "I knew well what thou art seeking here. Thou art seeking the king's daughter, but thou wilt not get that, unless thou hast a man that wilt drink as much water as I." He set the man who was drinking the river to hold drinking against the giant; and before he was half satisfied the giant burst. Then they went where the second giant was. "Ho, both! ha, hath!" said the giant, "I know well what sent thee here; thou art seeking the king's daughter; but thou shalt not get her, if thou hast not a man who will eat as much flesh as I." He set the man who was eating the stot to hold the eating of flesh against the giant; but before he was half satisfied the giant burst. Then he went where the third giant was. "Haio!" said the giant, "I know what set thee here; but thou wilt not get the king's daughter, by any means, unless thou stayest a day and a year by me a sgalag" (slave, servant). "I will do that," said he; and he sent up in the basket, first the three men, and then the king's daughters. The three great men were waiting at the mouth of the hole till they should come up, and they went with them where the king was; and they told the king that they themselves had done all the daring deeds that there were.

When the end of a day and a year had come, he said to the giant that he was going. The giant said that he had an eagle that would set him up to the top of the hole. The giant set the eagle away with him, and five stots and ten for a meal for her; but the eagle went not half-way up through the hole when she had eaten the stots, and she returned back again.

Then the giant said to him, "Thou must remain by me another day and year, and then I will send thee away." When the end of this year came, he sent the eagle away with him, and ten stots and twenty. They went this time well further on than they went before, but she ate the stots and she turned back. "Thou must," said the giant, "stay by me another year, and then I will send thee away." The end of this year came, and the giant sent them away, and three score of stots for the eagle's meat; and when they were at the mouth of the hole the stots were expended, and she was going to turn back; but he took a steak out of his own thigh, and he gave this to the eagle, and with one spring she was on the surface of the earth.

At the time of parting the eagle gave him a whistle, and she said to him, "Any hard lot that comes on thee, whistle and I will be at thy side." He did not allow his foot to stop, or empty a puddle out of his shoe, till he reached the king's big town. He went where there was a smith who was in the town, and he asked the smith if he was in want of a gillie to blow the bellows. The smith said that he was. He was but a short time by the smith, when the king's big daughter sent word for the smith. "I am hearing," said she, "that thou art the best smith in the town; but if thou dost not make for me a golden crown, like the golden crown that I had when I was by the giant, the head shall be taken off thee." The smith came home sorrowfully, lamentably; and his wife asked him his news from the king's house. "There is but poor news," said the smith; "the king's daughter is asking that a golden crown shall be made for her, like the crown that she had when she was under the earth by the giant; but what do I know what likeness was on the crown that the giant had." The bellows-blowing gillie said, "Let not that set thee thinking; get thou for me enough of gold, and I will not be long making the crown."

The smith got of gold as he asked, with the king's order. The gillie went into the smithy, and he shut the door; and he began to splinter the gold asunder, and to throw it out of the window. Each one that came the way was gathering the gold, that the bellows lad was hurling out. Here, then, he blew the whistle, and in the twinkling of an eye the eagle came. "Go," said he to the eagle, "and bring here the golden crown that is above the big giant's door." The eagle went, and she was not long on the way, and the crown (was) with her. He gave the crown to the smith. The smith went so merrily, cheerily with the crown where the king's daughter was. "Well then," said she, "if I did not know that it could not be done, I would not believe that this is not the crown I had when I was with the big giant." The king's middle daughter said to the smith, "Thou wilt lose the head if thou dost not make for me a silver crown, like the one I had when I was by the giant." The smith took himself home in misery, but his wife went to meet him, expecting great news and flattery; but so it was, that the gillie said that he would make a silver crown if he could get enough of silver. The smith got plenty of silver with the king's order. The gillie went, and he did as he did before. He whistled: the eagle came. "Go," said he, "and bring hither here to me, the silver crown that the king's middle daughter had when she was by the giant."

The eagle went, and she was not long on the journey with the silver crown. The smith went merrily, cheerily, with the silver crown to the king's daughter. "Well, then," said she, "it is marvellously like the crown I had when I was by the giant." The king's young daughter said to the smith that he should make a copper crown for her, like the copper crown she had when she was by the giant. The smith now was taking courage, and he went home much more pleasantly this turn. The gillie began to splinter the copper, and to throw it out of each door and window; and now they were from each end of the town gathering the copper, as they were gathering the silver and gold. He blew the whistle, and the eagle was at his side.

"Go back," said he, "and bring here hither to me the copper crown that the king's young daughter had when she was by the giant," The eagle went, and she was not long going and coming. He gave the crown to the smith. The smith went merrily, cheerily, and he gave it to the king's young daughter. "Well, then!" said she, "I would not believe that this was not the very crown that I had when I was by the giant underground, if there were a way of getting it." Here the king said to the smith, that he must tell him where he had learned crown-making, "for I did not know that the like of thee was in the kingdom." "Well, then," said the smith, "with your leave, oh king, it was not I who made the crowns, but the gillie I have blowing the bellows." "I must see thy gillie," said the king, "till he makes a crown for myself."

The king ordered four horses in a coach, and that they should go to seek the smith's gillie; and when the coach came to the smithy, the smith's gillie was smutty and dirty, blowing the bellows. The horse gillies came, and they asked for the man who was going to look on the king. The smith said, "That was he yonder, blowing the bellows." "Oov! oov!" said they; and they (set) to catch him, and throw him head-foremost into the coach, as if they had a dog.

They went not far on their journey when he blew the whistle. The eagle was at his side. "If ever thou didst good for me take me out of this, and fill it full of stones," said he. The eagle did this. The king was out waiting on the coach; and when the king opened the door of the coach, he was like to be dead with the stones bouncing on top of him. There was catching of the horse gillies, and hanging them for giving such an affront to the king.

Here the king sent other gillies with a coach and when they reached the smithy – "Oov! oov!" said they. "Is this the black thing the king sent us to seek?" They caught him, and they cast him into the coach as if they had a turf peat. But they went not far on their way when he blew the whistle, and the eagle was at his side; and he said to her, "Take me out of this, and fill it with every dirt thou canst get." When the coach reached the king's palace, the king went to open the door. Each dirt and rubbish fell about the king's head. Then the king was in a great rage, and he ordered the horse gillies to be hanged immediately. Here the king sent his own confidential servant away; and when he reached the smithy, he caught the black bellows-blowing gillie by the hand. "The king," said he, "sent me to seek thee. Thou hadst better clean a little of the coal off thy face." The gillie did this; he cleaned himself well, and right well; and the king's servant caught him by the hand, and he put him into the coach. They were but a short time going, when he blew the whistle. The eagle came; and he asked her to bring the gold and silver dress that was by the big giant here without delay, and the eagle was not long going and coming with the dress. He arrayed himself with the giant's dress. And when they came to the king's palace, the king came, and he opened the door of the coach, and there was the very finest man the king ever saw. The king took him in, and he told the king how it happened to him from first to last. The three great men who were going to marry the king's daughters were hanged, and the king's big daughter was given him to marry; and they made them a wedding the length of twenty nights and twenty days; and I left them dancing, and I know not but that they are cutting capers on the floor till the day of today.

Bailie Lunnain

THERE WERE AT SOME TIME of the world two brothers in one farm, and they were very great friends, and they had each a son; and one of the brothers died, and he left his brother guardian. When the lad was near to be grown up, he was keeping the farm for his mother almost as well as his father could have done. One night he saw a dream in his sleep, the most beautiful lady that there was in the world, and he dreamed of her three times, and he resolved to marry her and no other woman in the world; and he would not stay in the farm, and he grew pale, and his father's brother could not think what ailed him; and he was always asking him what was wrong with him. "Well, never mind," one day he said, "brother of my father, I have seen a dream, the most beautiful woman that there is in the world, and I will marry no other but she; and I will now go out and search for her over the whole world till I find her."

Said the uncle, "Son of my brother, I have a hundred pounds; I will give them to thee, and go; and when that is spent come back to me, and I will give thee another hundred."

So the lad took the hundred pounds, and he went to France, and then he went to Spain, and all over the world, but he could not find the lady he had seen in his sleep.

At last he came to London, and he had spent all his money, and his clothes were worn, and he did not know what he should do for a night's lodging.

Well, as he was wandering about the streets, whom should he see but a quiet-looking respectable old woman; and he spoke to her; and, from less to more, he told her all that had happened to him; and she was well pleased to see a countryman, and she said,

"I, too, am a Highland woman, though I am in this town." And she took him to a small house that she had, and she gave him meat and clothes.

And she said, "Go out now and take a walk; maybe thou mayest see here in one day what thou mightest not see in a year."

On the next day he was out taking a walk about the town, and he saw a woman at a window, and he knew her at once, for she was the lady he had seen in his sleep, and he went back to the old woman.

"How went it with thee this day, Gael?" said she.

"It went well," said he. "Oh, I have seen the lady I saw in my sleep," said he. And he told her all about it.

Then the old woman asked about the house and the street; and when she knew – "Thou hast seen her," said she. "That is all thou wilt see of her. That is the daughter of the Bailie of London; but I am her foster mother, and I would be right glad if she would marry a countryman of my own. Now, do thou go out on the morrow, and I will give thee fine highland clothes, and thou wilt find the lady walking in such a street: herself and three maidens of company will go out together; and do thou tread on her gown; and when she turns round to see what is the matter, do thou speak to her."

Well, the lad did this. He went out and he found the lady, and he set his foot on her dress, and the gown rent from the band; and when she turned round he said, "I am asking you much grace – it was an accident."

"It was not your fault; it was the fault of the dressmaker that made the dress so long," said she.

And she looked at him; and when she saw how handsome he was, she said, "Will you be so kind as to come home with me to my father's house and take something?"

So the lad went and sat down, and before she asked him anything she set down wine before him and said, "Quicker is a drink than a tale."

When he had taken that, he began and he told her all that happened, and how he had seen her in his sleep, and when, and she was well pleased.

"And I saw thee in my sleep on the same night," said she.

He went away that day, and the old woman that he was lodging with asked him how he had got on, and he told her everything that had happened; and she went to the Bailie's daughter, and told her all the good she could think of about the young lad; and after that he was often at the Bailie's house; and at last the daughter said she would marry him. "But I fear that will not do," said she. "Go home for a year, and when thou comest back I will contrive to marry thee," said she, "for it is the law of this country that no one must be married unless the Bailie himself gives her by the hand to her bridegroom," said she; and she left blessing with him.

Well, the lad went away as the girl said, and he was putting everything in order at home; and he told his father's brother all that had happened to him; but when the year was nearly out he set off for London again, and he had the second hundred with him, and some good oatmeal cakes.

On the road, whom should he meet but a Sassanach gentleman who was going the same road, and they began to talk.

"Where art thou going?" said the Saxon.

"Well, I am going to London," said he. "When I was there last I set a net in a street, and I am going to see if it is as I left it. If it is well I will take it with me; if not, I will leave it."

"Well," said the other, "that is but a silly thing. How can lintseed be as thou hast left it? It must be grown up and trodden down by ducks and geese, and eaten by hens long ago. I am going to London, too; but I am going to marry the Bailie's daughter."

Well, they walked on together, and at long last the Saxon began to get hungry, and he had no food with him, and there was no house near; and he said to the other, "Wilt thou give me some of thy food?"

"Well," said the Gael, "I have but poor food-oaten bread; I will give you some if you will take it; but if I were a gentleman like you I would never travel without my own mother."

"How can I travel with my mother?" said the Saxon. "She is dead and buried long ago, and rotting in the earth; if not, why should I take her with me?"

And he took the oat cake and ate it, and they went on their way.

They had not gone far when a heavy shower came on, and the Gael had a rough plaid about him, but the Saxon had none; and he said to the other,

"Wilt thou lend me thy plaid?"

"I will lend you a part of it," said the Gael, "but if I were a gentleman like you, I would never travel without my house, and I would not be indebted to anyone for favours."

"Thou art a fool," said the Saxon; "my house is four storeys high. How could any man carry a house that is four storeys high about with him?"

But he wrapped the end of the Highlander's plaid about his shoulders, and they went on.

Well, they had not gone far till they came to a small river, and the water was deep after the rain, and there was no bridge, and in those days bridges were not so plentiful as they are now; and the Saxon would not wet his feet, so he said to the Highlander,

"Wilt thou carry me over?"

"Well," said the Gael, "I don't mind if I do; but if I were a gentleman like you, I would never travel without my own bridge, and I would not be in any man's debt for favours."

"Thou art a silly fellow," said the Saxon. "How can any man travel about with a bridge that is made of stone and lime? Thou art but a 'burraidh,' and weighs as much as a house?"

But he got on the back of his fellow-traveller nevertheless, and they travelled on till they got to London. Then the Saxon went to the house of the Bailie, and the other went to the little house of his old countrywoman, who was the foster-mother of the Bailie's daughter.

Well, the Saxon gentleman began to tell the Bailie all that had happened to him by the way; and he said –

"I met with a Gael by the way, and he was a perfect fool – the greatest booby that man ever saw. He told me that he had sown lint here a year ago in a street, and that he was coming to fetch it, if he should find it as he left it, but that if he did not, he would leave it; and how should he find that after a year? He told me I should never travel without my mother, and my house, and my bridge; and how could a man travel with all these things? But though he was nothing but a fool, he was a good-natured fellow, for he gave me some of his food, and lent me a bit of his plaid, and he carried me over a river."

"I know not but he was as wise as the man that was speaking to him," said the Bailie; for he was a wise man. "I'll tell you what he meant," said he.

"Well, I will shew that he was a fool as great as ever was seen," said the Saxon.

"He has left a girl in this town," said the Bailie, "and he is come to see if she is in the same mind as she was when he left her; if so, he will take her with him, if not, he will leave her; and he has set a net," said he. "Your mother nourished you, and a gentleman like you should have his own nourishment with him. He meant that you should not be dependent on him. It was the booby that was with him," said the Bailie. "A gentleman like you should have his own shelter, and your house is your shelter when you are at home. A bridge is made for crossing a river, and a man should always be able to do that without help; and the man was right, and he was no fool, but a smart lad, and I should like to see him," said the Bailie; "and I would go to fetch him if I knew where he was," said he.

Well, the next day the Bailie went to the house where the lad was, and he asked him to come home to his dinner; and the lad came, and he told the Bailie that he had understood all that had been said.

"Now," said he, "as it is the law that no man may be married here unless the Bailie gives him the bride by the hand, will you be so kind as to give me the girl that I have come to marry, if she is in the same mind? I will have everything ready."

And the Bailie said, "I will do that, my smart lad; tomorrow, or whenever thou dost choose. I would go farther than that for such a smart boy," said he.

"Well, I will be ready at such a house tomorrow," said the lad; and he went away to the foster-mother's house.

When the morrow came, the Bailie's daughter disguised herself, and she went to the house of the foster-mother, and the Gael had got a churchman there; and the Bailie came in, and he took his own daughter by the hand; but she would not give her hand to the lad.

"Give thy hand, girl," said the Bailie. "It is an honour for thee to marry such a smart lad." And he gave her to him, and they were married according to law.

Then the Bailie went home, and he was to give his daughter by the hand to the Saxon gentleman that day; but the daughter was not to be found; and he was a widower, and she was keeping the house for him, and they could not find her anywhere.

"Well," said the Bailie, "I will lay a wager that Gael has got her, after all." And the Gael came in with the daughter, and he told them everything just as it had happened, from beginning to the end, and how he had plenty in his own country.

And the Bailie said, "Well, since I myself have given thee my daughter by the hand, it is a marriage, and I am glad that she has got a smart lad like thee for a husband."

And they made a wedding that lasted a year and a day, and they lived happily ever after, and if they have not died since then they are alive yet.

The Slim Swarthy Champion

THERE WAS A POOR MAN dwelling in Ard na h-Uamh, and a son was born to him, and he gave him school and learning till he was fourteen years of age. When he was fourteen years of age, he said to his father,

"Father, it is time for me to be doing for myself, if thou wouldst give me a fishing-rod and a basket."

The poor man found every chance till he got a fishing-rod and a basket for him. When he got the fishing-rod and the basket, he went round about Loch na h-Àirde, and took down (by) Loch Thorabais; and after he had fished Loch Thorabais closely, he came to Loch Port an Eilean; and after he had fished Loch Port an Eilean before him, he took out by Loch Allallaidh. He stayed the night in Aird Eileastraidh, and every trout he had he left with a poor woman that was there.

On the morrow he thought that he would rise out, and that he would betake himself to Eirinn. He came to the garden of Aird Inneasdail, and he plucked with him sixteen apples, and then he came to Mull of Otha. He threw an apple out into the sea, and he gave a step on it; he threw the next one, and he gave a step on it; he threw thus one after one, until he came to the sixteenth, and the sixteenth took him on shore in Eirinn.

When he was on shore he shook his ears, and he thought that it was in no sorry place he would stay.

> He moved as sea heaps from sea heaps,
> And as playballs from playballs –
> As a furious winter wind
> So swiftly, sprucely, cheerily,
> Right proudly,
> Through glens and high-tops,
> And no stop made he
> Until he came
> To city and court of O'Domhnuill.
> He gave a cheery, light leap
> O'er top and turret
> Of court and city
> Of O'Domhnuill.

O'Domhnuill took much anger and rage that such an unseemly ill stripling should come into his court, while he had a doorkeeper for his town.

"I will not believe," said the Champion, "but that thou art taking anger and rage, O'Domhnuill."

"Well, then, I am," said O'Domhnuill, "if I did but know at whom I should let it out."

"My good man," said the Champion, "coming in was no easier for me than going out again would be."

"Thou goest not out," said O'Domhnuill, "until thou tellest me from whence thou camest."

> "I came from hurry-skurry,
> From the end of endless spring.
> From the loved swanny glen –
> A night in Islay and a night in Man,
> A night on cold watching cairns.
> On the face of a mountain

In the Scotch king's town
Was I born.
A soiled, sorry Champion am I,
Though I happened upon this town."

"What," said O'Domhnuill, "canst thou do, oh Champion? Surely, with all the distance thou hast travelled, thou canst do something."

"I was once," said he, "that I could play a harp."

"Well, then," said O'Domhnuill, "it is I myself that have got the best harpers in the five-fifths of Eirinn, or in the bridge of the first of the people, such as Ruairidh O'Cridheagan, Tormaid O'Giollagan, and Thaog O'Chuthag."

"Let's hear them playing," said the Champion.

"They could play tunes and 'uirt' and 'orgain',
Trampling things, tightened strings,
Warriors, heroes, and ghosts on their feet.
Ghosts and spectres, illness and fever,
They'd set in sound lasting sleep
The whole great world,
With the sweetness of the calming tunes
That the harpers could play."

The music did not please the Champion. He caught the harps, and he crushed them under his feet, and he set them on the fire, and made himself a warming, and a sound warming at them.

O'Domhnuill took much lofty rage that a man had come into his court who should do the like of this to the harps.

"My good man, I will not believe that thou art not taking anger," said the Champion.

"Well, then, I am, if I did but know at whom I should let it out."

"Back, my good man; it was no easier for me to break thy harps than to make them whole again," said the Champion.

"I will give anything to have them made whole again," said O'Domhnuill.

"For two times five marks I will make thy harps as good as they were before," said the Champion.

"Thou shalt get that," said O'Domhnuill.

O'Domhnuill gave him the marks, and he seized on the fill of his two palms of the ashes, and he made a harp for Ruairidh O'Cridheagan; and one for Tormaid O'Giollagan; and one for Thaog O'Chuthag; and a great choral harp for himself.

"Let's hear thy music," said O'Domhnuill.

"Thou shalt hear that, my good man," said the Champion.

The Champion began to play, and och! but he was the boy behind the harp.

"He could play tunes, and 'uirt' and 'orgain',
Trampling things, tightened strings,
Warriors, heroes, and ghosts on their feet,
Ghosts and souls, and sickness and fever,

That would set in sound lasting sleep
The whole great world
With the sweetness of the calming tunes
That the champion could play."

"Thou art melodious, oh Champion!" said O'Domhnuill.

When the harpers heard the Champion playing, they betook themselves to another chamber, and though he had followed on, still they had not come to the fore.

O'Domhnuill went away, and he sent a bidding to meat to the Champion.

"Tell the good man that he will not have that much to gloom on me when I go at mid-day tomorrow," said the Champion.

O'Domhnuill took much proud rage that such a man should come into his court, and that he would not take meat from him. He sent up a fringed shirt, and a storm mantle.

"Where is this going?" said the Champion.

"To thee, oh Champion," said they.

"Say you to the good man that he will not have so much as that to gloom on me when I go at mid-day tomorrow," said the Champion.

O'Domhnuill took much anger and rage that such a man had come into his court and would not either take meat or dress from him. He sent up five hundred Galloglachs to watch the Champion, so that O'Domhnuill might not be affronted by his going out by any way but by the door.

"Where are you going?" said the Champion.

"To watch thee, Champion, so that thou shouldst not go to affront O'Domhnuill, and not to let thee out but as thou shouldst," said they.

"Lie down there," said the Champion, "and I will let you know when I am going."

They took his advice, and they lay down beside him, and when the dawn broke, the Champion went into his garments.

"Where are my watchers, for I am going?" said the Champion.

"If thou shouldst stir," said the great Galloglach, "I would make a sharp sour shrinking for thee with this plough-board in my hand."

The Champion leaped on the point of his pins, and he went over top and turret of court and city of O'Domhnuill.

The Galloglach threw the plough-board that was in his hand, and he slew four and twenty persons of the very people of O'Domhnuill.

Whom should the Champion meet, but the tracking lad of O'Domhnuill, and he said to him –

"Here's for thee a little sour grey weed, and go in and rub it to the mouths of those whom it killed and bring them alive again, and earn for thyself twenty calving cows, and look behind thee when thou partest from me, whom thou shalt see coming."

When the tracking lad did this he saw no being coming, but he saw the Champion thirteen miles on the other side of Luimneach (Limerick).

He moved as sea-heaps o' sea-heaps,
And as playballs o' playballs.
As a furious winter wind
So swiftly, sprucely, cheerily,

Right proudly,
Through glens and high tops,
And he made no stop
Until he reached
MacSeathain, the Southern Earl.

He struck in the door. Said MacSeathain, the southern Earl, "Who's that in the door?"

"I am Duradan o' Duradan, Dust of Dust," said the Champion.

"Let in Dust of Dust," said MacSeathain, the southern Earl; "no being must be in my door without getting in."

They let him in.

"What couldst thou do, Duradan o' Duradan?" said the southern Earl.

"I was on a time, and I could play a juggle," said he.

"Well, then, it is I myself that have the best juggler in the five-fifths of Eirinn, or the bridge of the first of the people, as is Taog Bratach Mac a Cheallaich, rascally Toag, the son of Concealment."

They got up the juggler.

"What," said the southern Earl, "is the trick that thou canst do, Dust of Dust?"

"Well, I was on a time that I could bob my ear off my cheek," said he.

The Champion went and he takes the ear off the cheek.

Said rascally Taog, the son of Concealment: "I could do that myself."

He went and he took down his ear, and up he could not bring it! but the Champion put up his own ear as it was before.

The Earl took much anger and rage that the ear should be off his juggler.

"For five merks twice over," said the Champion, "I would set the ear as it was before."

He got the five merks twice over, and he put the ear on the juggler as it was before.

"I see," said the Earl, "that the juggling of this night is with thee."

Rascally Taog went away; and though they should have staid there the length of the night, he would not have come near them.

Then the Champion went and he set a great ladder up against the moon, and in one place of it he put a hound and a hare, and in another place of it he put a carl and a girl. A while after that he opened first where he had put the hound and the hare, and the hound was eating the hare; he struck him a stroke of the edge of his palm, and cast his head off. Then he opened again where were the carl and the girl, and the carl was kissing the girl. He struck him a stroke of the edge of his palm, and he cast his head off.

"I would not for much," said the Earl, "that a hound and a carl should be killed at my court.

"Give five merks twice over for each one of them, and I will put the heads on them," said the Champion.

"Thou shalt get that," said the southern Earl.

He got the five merks twice over, and he put the head on the hound and the carl as they were before; and though they should be alive till now, the hound would not have touched a hare, nor the carl a girl, for fear their heads should be taken off.

On the morrow, after their meat in the morning, he went hunting with the Earl. When they were amongst the wood, they heard a loud voice in a knoll (or a bush).

"Be this from me," said Dust of Dust, "I must go to see the foot of the carl MacCeochd." He went out –

> And moved as sea-heaps o' sea-heaps,
> And as playballs o' playballs;
> As a furious winter wind –
> So swiftly, sprucely, cheerily,
> Right proudly,
> Through glens and high tops,
> And no stop made he
> Until he reached
> The house of the Carl MacCeochd.

He struck at the door. "Who's that?" said the carl MacCeochd.

"I," said he, "am the leech's lad."

"Well," said the carl, "many a bad black leech is coming, and they are not doing a bit of good to me."

Give word to the carl that unless he will not let me in, I will be going," said the Champion.

"Let in the leech's lad; perhaps he is the one in whom is my help," said the carl MacCeochd.

They let him in.

"Rise up, carl MacCeochd, thou art free from thy sores," said the Champion.

Carl MacCeochd arose up, and there was not a man in Eirinn swifter or stronger than he.

"Lie down, carl MacCeochd, thou art full of sores," said the Champion.

The carl MacCeochd lay down, and he was worse than he ever was.

"Thou didst ill," said the carl MacCeochd, "to heal me and spoil me again."

"Thou man here," said the Champion, "I was but shewing thee that I could heal thee."

"I have," said the carl MacCeochd, "but the one daughter in the world, and thou shalt get her and half of all I have, and all my share when I go way, and heal my leg."

"It shall not be so, but send word for every leech that thou hast had, that I might get talking with them," said the leech's lad.

They sent word by running lads through the five-fifths of Eirinn for the leeches that were waiting on the carl, and they came, all thinking that they would get pay, and when they came riding to the house of the carl, the Champion went out and he said to them,

"What made you spoil the leg of the carl MacCeochd, and set himself thus?"

"Well then," said they, "if we were to raise the worth of our drugs, without coming to the worth of our trouble, we would not leave him the worth of his shoe in the world.

Said the leech's lad, "I will lay you a wager, and that is the full of my cap of gold, to be set at the end of yonder dale, and that there are none in Eirinn that will be at it sooner than the carl MacCeochd."

He set the cap full of gold at the end of the dale, and the leeches laid the wager that they could never be.

He went in where the carl MacCeochd was, and he said to him,

"Arise, carl MacCeochd, thou art whole of sores, I have laid a wager on thee."

The earl got up whole and healthy, and he went out, and he was at three springs at the cap of gold, and he left the leeches far behind.

Then the leeches only asked that they might get their lives. Promise of that they got not (but) the leech's lad got in order.

He snatched his holly in his fist, and he seized the grey hand plane that was on the after side of his haunch, and he took under them, over them, through and amongst them; and left no man to tell a tale, or earn bad tidings, that he did not kill.

When the carl was healed he sent word for the nobles and for the great gentles of Eirinn to the wedding of his daughter and the Champion, and they were gathering out of each quarter.

"What company is there?" said the leeches' lad.

"There is the company of thine own wedding, and they are gathering from each half and each side," said the carl MacCeochd.

"Be this from me!" said he; "O'Conachar of Sligo has a year's service against me," and he put a year's delay on the wedding.

> Out he went as Voorveel o Voorveel
> And as Veerevuil o Veerevuill,
> As a furious winter wind,
> So swiftly, sprucely, cheerily,
> Right proudly,
> Through glens and high tops.
> And no stop did he make
> Till he struck in the door
> Of Conachar of Sligo.

"Who's that?" said O'Conachar of Sligo.

"I," said he, "Goodherd."

"Let in Goodherd," said O'Conachar of Sligo, for great is my need of him here." They let him in.

"What couldst thou do here?" said O'Conachar.

"I am hearing," said he, to O'Conachar of Sligo, "that the chase is upon thee. If thou wilt keep out the chase, I will keep in the spoil," said Goodherd.

"What wages wilt thou take?" said O'Conachar of Sligo.

"The wage I will take is that thou shouldst not make half cups with me till the end of a day and year," said Goodherd.

O'Conachar made this covenant with him, and the herdsman went to herd.

The chase broke in on O'Conachar of Sligo, and they betook themselves to where the herdsman was, to lift the spoil. When the herdsman saw that they had broken in, he took the holly in his fist, and seized the grey hand-plane that was on the after side of his haunch, and left no man to tell a tale, or earn bad tidings, that he did not kill. He went into a herd's bothy, and he (was) hot, and he saw O'Conachar Sligheach just done drinking a boyne of milk and water.

"Witness, gods and men, that thou hast broken thy promise," said Goodherd.

"That fill is no better than another fill," said O'Conachar Sligheach.

"That selfsame fill thou didst promise to me," said Goodherd.

He took anger at O'Conachar Sligheach, and he went away, and he reached the house of the carl MacCeochd. The daughter of the earl made him a drink of green apples and warm milk, and he was choked.

And I left them, and they gave me butter on a cinder, porridge kail in a creel, and paper shoes; and they sent me away with a big gun bullet, on a road of glass, till they left me sitting here within.

The Ridere (Knight) of Riddles

THERE WAS A KING ONCE, and he married a great lady, and she departed on the birth of her first son. And a little after this the king married another one, and he had a son by this one too. The two lads were growing up. Then it struck in the queen's head that it was not her son who would come into the kingdom; and she set it before her that she would poison the eldest son. And so she sent advice to the cook that they would put poison in the drink of the heir; but as luck was in it, so it was that the youngest brother heard them, and he said to his brother not to take the draught, nor to drink it at all; and so he did. But the queen wondered that the lad was not dead; and she thought that there was not enough of poison in the drink, and she asked the cook to put more in the drink on this night. It was thus they did: and when the cook made up the drink, she said that he would not be long alive after this draught. But his brother heard this also, and he told this likewise. The eldest thought he would put the draught into a little bottle, and he said to his brother – "If I stay in this house I have no doubt she will do for me some way or other, and the quicker I leave the house the better. I will take the world for my pillow, and there is no knowing what fortune will be on me." His brother said that he would go with him, and they took themselves off to the stable, and they put saddles on two horses and they took their soles out of that.

They had not gone very far from the house when the eldest one said – "There is no knowing if poison was in the drink at all, though we went away. Try it in the horse's ear and we shall see." The horse went not far when he fell. "That was only a rattle-bones of a horse at all events," said the eldest one, and together they got up on the one horse, and so they went forwards. "But," said he, "I can scarce believe that there is any poison in the drink, let's try it on this horse." That he did, and they went not far when the horse fell cold dead. They thought to take the hide off him, and that it would keep them warm on this night for it was close at hand. In the morning when they woke they saw twelve ravens coming and lighting on the carcase of the horse, and they were not long there when they fell over dead.

They went and lifted the ravens, and they took them with them, and the first town they reached they gave the ravens to a baker, and they asked him to make a dozen pies of the ravens. They took the pies with them, and they went on their journey. About the mouth of night, and when they were in a great thick wood that was there, there came four and twenty robbers out of the wood, and they said to them to deliver their purses; but they said that they had no purse, but that they had a little food which they were carrying with them. "Good is even meat!" and the robbers began to eat it, but they had not eaten too boldly when they fell hither and thither. When they saw that the robbers were dead, they ransacked their pockets, and they got much gold and silver on the robbers. They went forward till they reached the Knight of Riddles.

The house of the Knight of Riddles was in the finest place in that country, and if his house was pretty, it was his daughter was pretty indeed. Her like was not on the surface of the world altogether; so handsome was she, and no one would get her to marry but the man who would put a question to this knight that he could not solve. The chaps thought that they would go and they would try to put a question to him; and the youngest one was to stand in place of gillie to his eldest brother. They reached the house of the Knight of Riddles with this question – "One killed two, and two killed twelve, and twelve killed four and twenty, and two got out of it;" and they were to be in great majesty and high honour till he should solve the riddle.

They were thus a while with the Ridere, but on a day of days came one of the knight's daughter's maidens of company to the gillie, and asked him to tell her the question. He took her plaid from her and let her go, but he did not tell her, and so did the twelve maidens, day after day, and he said to the last one that no creature had the answer to the riddle but his master down below. No matter! The gillie told his master each thing as it happened. But one day after this came the knight's daughter to the eldest brother, and she was so fine, and she asked him to tell her the question. And now there was no refusing her, and so it was that he told her, but he kept her plaid. And the Knight of Riddles sent for him, and he solved the riddle. And he said that he had two choices: to lose his head, or to be let go in a crazy boat without food or drink, without oar or scoop. The chap spoke and he said – "I have another question to put to thee before all these things happen." "Say on," said the knight. "Myself and my gillie were on a day in the forest shooting. My gillie fired at a hare, and she fell, and he took her skin off, and let her go; and so he did to twelve, he took their skins off and let them go. And at last came a great fine hare, and I myself fired at her, and I took her skin off and I let her go." "Indeed thy riddle is not hard to solve, my lad," said the knight. And so the lad got the knight's daughter to wife, and they made a great hearty wedding that lasted a day and a year. The youngest one went home now that his brother had got so well on his way, and the eldest brother gave him every right over the kingdom that was at home.

There were near the march of the kingdom of the Knight of Riddles three giants, and they were always murdering and slaying some of the knight's people, and taking the spoil from them. On a day of days the Knight of Riddles said to his son-in-law, that if the spirit of a man were in him, he would go to kill the giants, as they were always bringing such losses on the country. And thus it was, he went and he met the giants, and he came home with the three giants' heads, and he threw them at the knight's feet. "Thou art an able lad doubtless, and thy name hereafter is the Hero of the White Shield." The name of the Hero of the White Shield went far and near.

The brother of the Hero of the White Shield was exceedingly strong and clever, and without knowing what the Hero of the White Shield was, he thought he would try a trick with him. The Hero of the White Shield was now dwelling on the lands of the Giants, and the knight's daughter with him. His brother came and he asked to make a comhrag (fight as a bull) with him. The men began at each other, and they took to wrestling from morning till evening. At last and at length, when they were tired, weak, and given up, the Hero of the White Shield jumped over a great rampart, and he asked him to meet him in the morning. This leap put the other to shame, and he said to him, "Well may it be that thou wilt not be so supple about this time tomorrow." The young brother now went to a poor little bothy that was near to the house of the Hero of the White Shield tired and drowsy, and in the morning they dared the fight again. And the Hero of the White Shield began to go back, till he went backwards into a river. "There must be some of my blood in thee before that was done to me." "Of what blood art thou?" said the youngest. "'Tis I am son of Ardan, great King of the Albann." "'Tis I am thy brother." It was now they knew each other. They gave luck and welcome to each other, and the Hero of the White Shield now took him into the palace, and she it was that was pleased to see him – the knight's daughter. He stayed a while with them, and after that he thought that he would go home to his own kingdom; and when he was going past a great palace that was there he saw twelve men playing at shinny over against the palace. He thought he would go for a while and play shinny with them; but they were not long playing shinny when they fell out, and the weakest of them caught him and he shook him as he would a child. He thought it was no use for him to lift a hand amongst these twelve worthies, and he asked them to whom they were sons. They said they were children of the one father, the brother of the Hero of the White Shield, but that no one of them had the same mother. "I am your father," said he; and he asked them if their mothers were all alive. They said that they were. He went with them till he found the mothers, and when they were all for going, he took home with him the twelve wives and the twelve sons; and I don't know but that his seed are kings on Alba till this very day.

Maghach Colgar

FIONN MAC CUMHAILL was in Eirinn, and the king of Lochlann in Lochlann. The king of Lochlann sent Maghach Colgar to Fionn to be taught. The king of the Sealg sent to him his own son, whom they called Innsridh Macrigh nan Sealg. They were of age, six years (and) ten. Then they were in Erin with Fionn, and Fionn taught Maghach, son of the king of Lochlann, every learning he had.

There came a message from the king of Lochlann, that he was in the sickness of death for leaving the world; and that the Maghach must go home to be ready for his crowning. Maghach went away, and the chase failed with the Feinn, and they did not know what they should do.

Maghach wrote a letter to Fionn from Lochlann to Eirinn: "I heard that the chase failed with you in Eirinn. I have burghs on sea, and I have burghs on shore; I have food for a day and a year in every burgh of these – the meat thou thinkest not of, and the drink thou thinkest not of; come thou hither thyself and thy set of Fiantachan. The keep of a day and a year is on thy head."

Fionn got the letter, and he opened it. "He is pitiable who would not do a good thing in the beginning of youth; he might get a good share of it again in the beginning of his age. Here is a letter came from my foster-son from Lochlann that he has burghs on sea and burghs on shore, food for a day and a year in every one of them – the drink that we can think of, and the drink that we do not think of; the meat we can think of, and the meat that we do not think of – and it is best for us to be going."

"Whom shall we leave," said Fiachaire MacFhinn (the trier son of Fionn) his son, "to keep the darlings and little sons of Eireann."

"I will stay," said Fiachaire MacFhinn.

"I will stay," said Diarmid O'Duibhne, his sister's son.

"I will stay," said Innsridh Macrigh nan Sealg, his foster-son.

"I will stay," said Cath Conan Mac Mhic Con.

"We will stay now," said they – the four.

"Thou art going, my father," said Fiachere, "and it is as well for thee to stay; how then shall we get word how it befalls thee in Lochlainn?"

"I will strike the Ord Fiannt (hammer of Fiant) in Lochlainn, and it will be known by the blow I strike in Lochlainn, or in Eirinn, how we shall be."

Fionn and his company went, they reached Lochlainn. Maghach Colgar, son of the king of Lochlainn, went before to meet them.

"Hail to thee, my foster father," said Maghach.

"Hail to thyself, my foster-son," said Fionn.

"There is the business I had with thee; I heard that the chase had failed in Eirinn, and it was not well with me to let you die without meat. I have burghs on sea and burghs on shore, and food for a day and year in every one of them, and which kind wouldst thou rather choose?"

"It is on shore I used to always be, and it is not on sea; and I will take some on shore," said Fionn.

They went into one of them. There was a door opposite to every day in the year on the house; every sort of drink and meat within it. They sat on chairs; they caught every man hold of a fork and of a knife, they gave a glance from them, and what should they see in the "araich" (great half-ruined building), but not a hole open but frozen rime. They gave themselves that lift to rise. The chairs stuck to the earth. They themselves stuck to the chairs. Their hands stuck to the knives, and there was no way of rising out of that.

It was day about that Fiachaire MacFhinn and Innsridh MacRigh nan Sealg were going to keep the chase, and Diarmid O'Duibhne and Conan were going on the other day. On their returning back, what should they hear but a blow of the hammer of Fionn being struck in Lochlainn.

"If he has wandered the universe and the world, my foster-father is in pledge of his body and soul."

Fiachaire MacFhinn and Innsridh MacRigh nan Sealg went from Eirinn, and they reached Lochlainn.

"Who is that without on the burgh?"

"I am," said Fiachaire MacFhinn and Innsridh MacRigh nan Sealg.

"Who is there on the place of combat?"

"There are two hundred score of the 'Greugachaibh' (Greeks) come out and great Iall at their head coming to seek my head to be his at his great meal tomorrow."

Fiachaire MacFhinn and Innsridh MacRigh nan Sealg went and they reached the place of combat.

"Where are ye going?" said Fiachaire MacFhinn.

"We are going to seek the head of Mac Cumhaill to be ours at our great meal tomorrow."

"It is often that man's head might be sought and be on my own breast at early morning."

"Close up," said Iall, "and leave way for the people."

"There is a small delay on that," said Fiachaire.

Fiachaire, son of Fhinn, pressed out on the one end of them. Innsridh, son of the king of the Sealg, began in the other end, till the two glaves clashed against each other. They returned, and they reached the burgh.

Co aig a bha 'n càth grannda
A bha air an àth chomhrag
An diugh? "With whom was the hideous fight
That was on the battle-place
today?"
said Fionn.

"With me," said Fiachaire, "and with the son of the king of the Sealg."

"How was my foster-son off there?"

"Man upon man," said Fiachaire. "And if he had not another man, he had lacked none."

"Over the field, to my foster-son," said Fionn, "and his bones but soft yet! but mind the place of combat. Yonder are three hundred score of the Greeks coming out seeking my head to be theirs at their great meal tomorrow."

Fiachaire MacFhinn, and Innsridh MacRigh nan Sealg went, and they reached the place of combat.

"Where are you going?" said Fiachaire MacFhinn.

"Going to seek the head of Mac Cumhaill to be ours at our great meal tomorrow."

"It's often that very man's head might be sought, and be on my own breast at early morning."

"Close up and leave way for the people."

"There is still a small delay on that."

Fiachaire began in the one end of the company, and Innsridh MacRigh nan Sealg in the other, till the two glaves clashed on each other. They returned to the burgh.

"Who is that?" said Fionn.

"I am Fiachaire, thy son, and Innsridh, son of the king of the Sealg, thy foster son,

> *"With whom was the hideous fight*
> *That was on the battle place*
> *Today.*

"It was with me and with three hundred score of Greeks."

"Mind the place of battle; there are four hundred score of the Greeks, and a great warrior at their head coming to seek my head to be theirs at their great meal tomorrow."

They went and they reached the place of battle.

"Where are you going?" said Fiachaire MacFhinn to the Greeks.

"Going to seek the head of Mac Cumhaill, to be ours at our great meal tomorrow."

"It's often that man's head might be sought, and be on my own breast at early morning."

"Close up from the way, and leave way for the people."

"There is a small delay on that yet."

He himself and Innsridh MacRigh nan Sealg began at them till they had killed every man of them, and till the two glaves clashed on each other. They returned home, and they reached the burgh.

"Who's that without?" said Fionn.

"I am Fiachaire, thy son, and Innsridh, son of the king of the Sealg, thy foster-son,

"With whom was the hideous fight
That was at the battle place
Today.

"It was with me and so many of the Greeks."

"How was my foster-son off there?"

"Man upon man, and if there had been no one besides, he had lacked none."

"Mind the place of battle. There are twice as many as came out, a good and heedless warrior at their head, coming to seek my head, to be theirs at their great meal tomorrow."

They reached the place of battle; and when they reached it, there came not a man of the people.

"I won't believe," said Fiachaire MacFhinn, "that there are not remnants of meat in a place whence such bands are coming. Hunger is on myself, and that we ate but a morsel since we ate it in Eirinn. And come thou, Innsridh, and reach the place where they were. They will not know man from another man, and try if thou canst get scraps of bread, and of cheese, and of flesh, that thou wilt bring to us; and I myself will stay to keep the people, in case that they should come unawares."

"Well, then, I know not the place. I know not the way," said Innsridh, son of the king of Sealg, "but go thyself and I will stay."

Fiachaire went, and Innsridh staid, and what should they do but come unawares.

"Where are ye going?" said Innsridh.

"Going to seek the head of Mac Cumhaill, to be ours at our great meal tomorrow."

"It is often that man's head might be sought, and be on my own breast at early morning."

"Close up, and leave way for the people."

"There is a small delay on that yet." Innsridh began at them, and he left not one alone.

"What good did it do thee to slay the people, and that I will kill thee," said the great warrior at their head.

"If I had come out, from my meat and from my warmth, from my warmth and from my fire, thou shouldst not kill me." He and the warrior began at each other. They would make a bog of the crag, and a crag of the bog, in the place where the least they would sink they would sink to the knees, in the place that the most they would sink they would sink to the eyes. The great warrior gave a sweep with his glave, and he cut the head off Innsridh MacRigh nan Sealg.

Fiachaire came. The warrior met him, and with him was the head of Innsridh.

Said Fiachaire to the great warrior, "What thing hast thou there?"

"I have here the head of Mac Cumhail."

"Hand it to me."

He reached him the head. Fiachaire gave a kiss to the mouth, and a kiss to the back of the head.

"Dost thou know to whom thou gavest it?" said Fiachaire to the warrior.

"I do not," said he. "It well became the body on which it was before."

He went and he drew back the head, and strikes it on the warrior's head while he was speaking, and makes one head of the two. He went and he reached (the place) where Fionn was again.

"Who is that without?" said Fionn.

"I am Fiachaire, thy son,

> *"With whom was the hideous fight*
> *That was at the battle place*
> *Today.*

"It was with Innsridh, thy foster-son, and with the Greeks."

"How is my foster-son from that?"

"He is dead without a soul. Thy foster-son killed the Greeks first, and the great Greek killed him afterwards, and then I killed the great Greek."

"Mind the place of combat. There is Maghach, son of the king of Lochlann, and everyone that was in the Greek burgh with him."

He went and he reached the place of combat.

"Thou art there, Fiachaire?" said Maghach Colgar.

"I am."

"Let hither thy father's head, and I will give thee a free bridge in Lochlainn."

"My father gave thee school and teaching, and every kind of 'draochd' (Magic) he had, and though he taught that, thou wouldst take the head off him now, and with that thou shalt not get my father's head, until thou gettest my own head first."

Fiachaire began at the people, and he killed every man of the people.

"Thou has killed the people," said Maghach, "and I will kill thee."

They began at each other.

They would make a bog of the crag, and a crag of the bog, in the place where the least they would sink they would sink to the knees; in the place where the most they would sink, they would sink to the eyes. On a time of the times the spear of Mhaghach struck Fiachaire, and he gave a roar. What time should he give the roar but when Diarmid was turning step from the chase in Eirinn.

"If he has travelled the universe and the world," said Diarmid, "the spear of the Maghach is endured by Fiachaire."

"Wailing be on thee," said Conan. "Cast thy spear and hit thy foe."

"If I cast my spear, I know not but I may kill my own man."

"If it were a yellow-haired woman, well wouldst thou aim at her."

"Wailing be on thee now; urge me no longer."

He shook the spear, and struck under the shield.

"Who would come on me from behind in the evening, that would not come on me from the front in the morning?" said Maghach.

"'Tis I would come on thee," said Diarmid, "early and late, and at noon."

"What good is that to thee," said Maghach, "and that I will take the head off Fiachaire before thou comest."

"If thou takest the head off him," said Diarmid, "I will take off thy head when I reach thee."

Diarmid reached Lochlann. Maghach took the head off Fiachaire. Diarmid took the head off the Maghach. Diarmid reached Fionn.

"Who's that without?" said Fionn.

"It is I, Diarmid,

*"With whom was the hideous fight
That was on the battle place
Today.*

"It was with so many of the Greeks, and with the Maghach, son of the king of Lochlann, and with Fiachaire, thy son; Fiachaire killed all the Greeks, Maghach killed Fiachaire, and then I killed Maghach."

"Though Maghach killed Fiachaire, why didst thou kill Maghach, and not let him have his life? But mind the place of combat, and all that are in the burghs of the Greeks coming out together."

"Whether wouldst thou rather, Cath Conan, go with me or stay here?"

"I would rather go with thee."

They went, and when they reached the place of combat, no man met them. They reached where they were; they sat there, and what should Cath Conan do but fall asleep, they were so long coming out. It was not long after that till they began to come, and the doors to open. There was a door before every day in the year on every burgh, so that they burst forth all together about the head of Diarmid. Diarmid began at them, and with the sound of the glaves and return of the men, Cath Conan awoke, and he began thrusting his sword in the middle of the leg of Diarmid. Then Diarmid felt a tickling in the middle of his leg. He cast a glance from him, and what should he see but Cath Conan working with his own sword.

"Wailing be on thee, Cath Conan," said Diarmid; "pass by thy own man and hit thy foe, for it is as well for thee to thrust it into yonder bundle as to be cramming it into my leg. Do not thou plague me now till I hit my foe!"

They killed every man of the people.

They thought of those who were in the burgh, and they without food; each one of them took with him the full of his napkin, and his breast, and his pouches.

"Who's that without?" said Fionn.

"I am Diarmid, thy sister's son."

"How are the Greeks?"

"Every man of them is dead, without a soul."

"Oh, come and bring hither to me a deliverance of food."

"Though I should give thee food, how shouldst thou eat it, and thou there and thee bound?"

He had no way of giving them food, but to make a hole in the burgh above them, and let the food down to them.

"What is there to loose thee from that?" said Diarmid.

"Well, that is hard to get," said Fionn; "and it is not every man that will get it; and it is not to be got at all."

"Tell thou me," said Diarmid, "and I will get it."

"I know that thou wilt subdue the world till thou gettest it; and my healing is not to be got, nor my loosing from this, but with the one thing."

"What thing is it that thou shouldst not tell it to me, and that I might get it?"

"The three daughters of a king, whom they call King Gil; the daughters are in a castle in the midst of an anchorage, without maid, without 'sgalag' (servant), without a living man but themselves. To get them, and to wring every drop of blood that is in them out on plates and in cups; to take every drop of blood out of them, and to leave them as white as linen."

Diarmid went, and he was going till there were holes in his shoes and black on his soles, the white clouds of day going, and the black clouds of night coming, without finding a place to stay or rest in. He reached the anchorage, and he put the small end of his spear under his chest, and he cut a leap, and he was in the castle that night. On the morrow he returned, and he took with him two on the one shoulder and one on the other shoulder; he put the small end of his spear under his chest, and at the first spring he was on shore. He reached Fionn; he took the girls to him; he wrung every drop of blood that was in every one of them out at the finger ends of her feet and hands; he put a black cloth above them, and he began to spill the blood on those who were within, and everyone as he spilt the blood on him, he would rise and go. The blood failed, and everyone was loosed but one, whom they called Conan.

"Art thou about to leave me here, oh Diarmid?"

"Wailing be on thee; the blood has failed."

"If I were a fine yellow-haired woman, it's well thou wouldst aim at me?"

"If thy skin stick to thyself, or thy bones to thy flesh, I will take thee out."

He caught him by the hand and he got him loose, but that his skin stuck to the seat, and the skin of his soles to the earth. "It were well now," said they, "if the children of the good king were alive, but they should be buried under the earth." They went where they were, and they found them laughing and fondling each other, and alive. Diarmid went, and took them with him on the shower top of his shoulder, and he left them in the castle as they were before, and they all came home to Eirinn.

The Knight of the Red Shield

THERE WAS BEFORE NOW a king of Eirinn, and he went himself, and his people, and his warriors, and his nobles, and his great gentles, to the hill of hunting and game. They sat on a hillock coloured green colour, where the sun would rise early, and where she would set late. Said the one of swifter mouth than the rest:

"Who now in the four brown quarters of the universe would have the heart to put an affront and disgrace on the King of Eirinn, and he in the midst of the people, and the warriors, great gentles, and nobles of his own realm?"

"Are ye not silly," said the king; "he might come, one who should put an affront and disgrace on me, and that ye could not pluck the worst hair in his beard out of it."

It was thus it was. They saw the shadow of a shower coming from the western airt, and going to the eastern airt and a rider of a black filly coming cheerily after it.

As it were a warrior on the mountain shore,
As a star over sparklings,
As a great sea over little pools,

As a smith's smithy coal
Being quenched at the river side;
So would seem the men and women of the world beside him,
In figure, in shape, in form, and in visage.

Then he spoke to them in the understanding, quieting, truly wise words of real knowledge; and before there was any more talk between them, he put over the fist and he struck the king between the mouth and the nose, and he drove out three of his teeth, and he caught them in his fist, and he put them in his pouch, and he went away.

"Did not I say to you," said the king, "that one might come who should put an affront and disgrace on me, and that you could not pluck the worst hair in his beard out of it!"

Then his big son, the Knight of the Cairn, swore that he wouldn't eat meat, and that he wouldn't drink draught, and that he would not hearken to music, until he should take off the warrior that struck the fist on the king, the head that designed to do it.

"Well," said the Knight of the Sword, the very same for me, until I take the hand that struck the fist on the king from off the shoulder.

There was one man with them there in the company, whose name was Mac an Earraich uaine ri Gaisge, The Son of the Green Spring by Valour. "The very same for me," said he, "until I take out of the warrior who struck the fist on the king, the heart that thought on doing it."

"Thou nasty creature!" said the Knight of the Cairn, "what should bring thee with us? When we should go to valour, thou wouldst turn to weakness; thou wouldst find death in boggy moss, or in rifts of rock, or in a land of holes, or in the shadow of a wall, or in some place."

"Be that as it will, but I will go," said the Son of the Green Spring by Valour.

The king's two sons went away. Glance that the Knight of the Cairn gave behind him, he sees the Son of the Green Spring by Valour following them.

"What," said the Knight of the Cairn to the Knight of the Sword, "shall we do to him?"

"Do," said the Knight of the Sword, "sweep his head off."

"Well," said the Knight of the Cairn, "we will not do that; but there is a great crag of stone up here, and we will bind him to it."

"I am willing to do that same," said the other.

They bound him to the crag of stone to leave him till he should die, and they went away. Glance that the Knight of the Cairn gave behind him again, he sees him coming and the crag upon him.

"Dost thou not see that one coming again, and the crag upon him!" said the Knight of the Cairn to the Knight of the Sword. "What shall we do to him?"

"It is to sweep the head off him, and not let him (come) further," said the Knight of the Sword.

"We will not do that," said the Knight of the Cairn; but we will turn back and loose the crag off him. It is but a sorry matter for two full heroes like us; though he should be with us, he will make a man to polish a shield, or blow a fire heap or something."

They loosed him, and they let him come with them. Then they went down to the shore; then they got the ship, which was called An Iubhrach Brallach, The Speckled Barge.

They put her out, and they gave her prow to sea, and her stern to shore.
They hoisted the speckled, flapping, bare-topped sails
Up against the tall, tough, splintery masts.

They had a pleasant little breeze as they might choose themselves,
Would bring heather from the hill, leaf from grove, willow from its roots,
Would put thatch of the houses in furrows of the ridges.
The day that neither the son nor the father could do it,
That same was neither little nor much for them,
But using it and taking it as it might come,
The sea plunging and surging,
The red sea the blue sea lashing
And striking hither and thither about her planks.
The whorled dun whelk that was down on the ground of the ocean,
Would give a snag on her gunwale and crack on her floor,
She would cut a slender oaten straw with the excellence of her going.

They gave three days driving her thus. "I myself am growing tired of this," said the Knight of the Cairn to the Knight of the Sword, "It seems to me time to get news from the mast."

"Thou thyself are the most greatly beloved here, oh Knight of the Cairn, and shew that thou wilt have honour going up; and if thou goest not up, we will have the more sport with thee," said the Son of the Green Spring by Valour.

Up went the Knight of the Cairn with a rush, and he fell down clatter in a faint on the deck of the ship.

"It is ill thou hast done," said the Knight of the Sword.

"Let us see if thyself be better and if thou be better, it will be shewn that thou wilt have more will to go on; or else we will have the more sport with thee," said the Son of the Green Spring by Valour.

Up went the Knight of the Sword, and before he had reached but half the mast, he began squealing and squealing, and he could neither go up nor come down.

"Thou hast done as thou wert asked; and thou hast shewed that thou hadst the more respect for going up; and now thou canst not go up, neither canst thou come down! No warrior was I nor half a warrior, and the esteem of a warrior was not mine at the time of leaving; I was to find death in boggy moss, or in rifts of rock, or in the shade of a wall, or in some place; and it were no effort for me to bring news from the mast."

"Thou great hero!" said the Knight of the Cairn, "try it."

"A great hero am I this day, but not when leaving the town," said the Son of the Green Spring by Valour.

He measured a spring from the ends of his spear to the points of his toes, and he was up in the cross-trees in a twinkling.

"What art thou seeing?" said the Knight of the Cairn.

"It is too big for a crow, and it is too little for land," said he.

"Stay, as thou hast to try if thou canst know what it is," said they to him; and he stayed so for a while.

"What art thou seeing now?" said they to him.

"It is an island and a hoop of fire about it, flaming at either end; and I think that there is not one warrior in the great world that will go over the fire," said he.

"Unless two heroes such as we go over it," said they.

"I think that it was easier for you to bring news from the mast than to go in there," said he.

"It is no reproach!" said the Knight of the Cairn.

"It is not; it is truth," said the Son of the Green Spring by Valour.

They reached the windward side of the fire, and they went on shore; and they drew the speckled barge up her own seven lengths on grey grass, with her mouth under her, where the scholars of a big town could neither make ridicule, scoffing, or mockery of her. They blew up a fire heap, and they gave three days and three nights resting their weariness.

At the end of the three days they began at sharpening their arms.

"I," said the Knight of the Cairn, "am getting tired of this; it seems to me time to get news from the isle."

"Thou art thyself the most greatly beloved here," said the Son of the Green Spring by Valour, "and go the first and try what is the best news that thou canst bring to us."

The Knight of the Cairn went and he reached the fire; and he tried to leap over it, and down he went into it to his knees, and he turned back, and there was not a slender hair or skin between his knees and his ankles, that was not in a crumpled fold about the mouth of the shoes.

"He's bad, he's bad," said the Knight of the Sword.

"Let us see if thou art better thyself," said the Son of the Green Spring by Valour. "Shew that thou wilt have the greater honour going on, or else we will have the more sport with thee."

The Knight of the Sword went, and he reached the fire; and he tried to leap over it, and down he went into it to the thick end of the thigh; and he turned back, and there was no slender hair or skin between the thick end of the thigh and the ankle that was not in a crumpled fold about the mouth of the shoes.

"Well," said the Son of the Green Spring by Valour, "no warrior was I leaving the town, in your esteem; and if I had my choice of arms and armour of all that there are in the great world, it were no effort for me to bring news from the isle."

"If we had that thou shouldst have it," said the Knight of the Cairn.

"Knight of the Cairn, thine own arms and armour are the second that I would rather be mine (of all) in the great world, although thou thyself art not the second best warrior in it," said the Son of the Green Spring by Valour.

"It is my own arms and array that are easiest to get," said the Knight of the Cairn, "and thou shalt have them; but I should like that thou wouldst be so good as to tell me what other arms or array are better than mine."

"There are the arms and array of the Great Son of the sons of the universe, who struck the fist on thy father," said the Son of the Green Spring by Valour.

The Knight of the Cairn put off his arms and array; and the Son of the Green Spring by Valour went into his arms and his array.

He went into his harness of battle and hard combat,
As was a shirt of smooth yellow silk and gauze stretched on his breast;
His coat, his kindly coat, above the kindly covering;
His boss covered; hindering sharp-pointed shield on his left hand,
His head-dress a helm of hard combat,
To cover his crown and his head top,
To go in the front of the fray and the fray long-lasting,
His heroes hard slasher in his right hand,
A sharp surety knife against his waist.

He raised himself up to the top of the shore; and there was no turf he would cast behind his heels, that was not as deep as a turf that the bread-covering tree would cast when deepest it would be ploughing. He reached the circle of fire; he leaped from the points of his spear to the points of his toes over the fire.

Then there was the very finest isle that ever was seen from the beginning of the universe to the end of eternity; he went up about the island, and he saw a yellow bare hill in the midst. He raised himself up against the hill; there was a treasure of a woman sitting on the hill, and a great youth with his head on her knee, and asleep. He spoke to her in instructed, eloquent, true, wise, soft maiden words of true knowledge. She answered in like words; and if they were no better, they were not a whit worse, for the time.

"A man of thy seeming is a treasure for me; and if I had a right to thee, thou shouldst not leave the island," said the little treasure.

"If a man of my seeming were a treasure for thee, thou wouldst tell me what were waking for that youth," said the Son of the Green Spring by Valour.

"It is to take off the point of his little finger," said she.

He laid a hand on the sharp surety knife that was against his waist, and he took the little finger off him from the root. That made the youth neither shrink nor stir.

"Tell me what is waking for the youth, or else there are two oft whom I will take the heads, thyself and the youth," said the Son of the Green Spring by Valour.

"Waking for him," said she, "is a thing that thou canst not do, nor any one warrior in the great world, but the warrior of the red shield, of whom it was in the prophecies that he should come to this island, and strike yonder crag of stone on this man in the rock of his chest; and he is unbaptized till he does that."

He heard this that such was in the prophecy for him, and he unnamed. A fist upon manhood, a fist upon strengthening, and a fist upon power went into him. He raised the crag in his two hands, and he struck it on the youth in the rock of his chest. The one who was asleep gave a slow stare of his two eyes and he looked at him.

"Aha!" said the one who was asleep, "hast thou come, warrior of the Red Shield. It is this day that thou has the name; thou wilt not stand long to me."

"Two thirds of thy fear be on thyself, and one on me," said the Warrior of the Red Shield; "thou wilt not stand long to me."

In each other's grips they went, and they were hard belabouring each other till the mouth of dusk and lateness was. The Warrior of the Red Shield thought that he was far from his friends and near his foe; he gave him that little light lift, and he struck him against the earth; the thumb of his foot gave a warning to the root of his ear, and he swept the head off him.

"Though it be I who have done this, it was not I who promised it," said he.

He took the hand off him from the shoulder, and he took the heart from his chest, and he took the head off the neck; he put his hand in the dead warrior's pouch, and he found three teeth of an old horse in it, and with the hurry took them for the king's teeth, and he took them with him; and he went to a tuft of wood, and he gathered a withy, and he tied on it the hand and the heart and the head.

"Whether wouldst thou rather stay here on this island by thyself, or go with me?" said he to the little treasure.

"I would rather go with thee thyself, than with all the men of earth's mould together," said the little treasure.

He raised her with him on the shower top of his shoulders, and on the burden (bearing) part of his back, and he went to the fire. He sprang over with the little treasure upon him. He sees the Knight of the Cairn and the Knight of the Sword coming to meet him, rage and fury in their eyes.

"What great warrior," said they, "was that after thee there, and returned when he saw two heroes like us?"

"Here's for you," said he, "this little treasure of a woman, and the three teeth of your father; and the head, and hand, and heart of the one who struck the fist on him. Make a little stay and I will return, and I will not leave a shred of a tale in the island."

He went away back; and at the end of a while he cast an eye behind him, and he sees them and the speckled barge playing him ocean hiding.

"Death wrappings upon yourselves!" said he, "a tempest of blood about your eyes, the ghost of your hanging be upon you! to leave me in an island by myself, without the seed of Adam in it, and that I should not know this night what I shall do."

He went forward about the island, and was seeing neither house nor tower in any place, low or high. At last he saw an old castle in the lower ground of the island, and he took (his way) towards it. He saw three youths coming heavily, wearily, tired, to the castle. He spoke to them in instructed, eloquent, true, wise words of true wisdom. They spoke in return in like words.

They came in words of the olden time on each other; and who were here but his three true foster brothers. They went in right good pleasure of mind to the big town.

> They raised up music and laid down woe;
> There were soft drunken draughts
> And harsh, stammering drinks,
> Tranquil, easy toasts
> Between himself and his foster brethren,
> Music between fiddles, with which would sleep
> Wounded men and travailing women
> Withering away for ever; with the sound of that music
> Which was ever continuing sweetly that night.

They went to lie down. In the morning of the morrow he arose right well pleased, and he took his meat. What should he hear but the gliogarsaich, clashing of arms and men going into their array. Who were these but his foster brethren.

"Where are you going?" said he to them.

"We are from the end of a day and a year in this island," said they, "holding battle against MacDorcha MacDoilleir, the Son of Darkness Son of Dimness, and a hundred of his people: and every one we kill today they will be alive tomorrow. Spells are on us that we may not leave this for ever until we kill them."

"I will go with you this day; you will be the better for me," said he.

"Spells are on us," said they, "that no man may go with us unless he goes there alone."

"Stay you within this day, and I will go there by myself," said he.

He went away, and he hit upon the people of the Son of Darkness Son of Dimness, and he did not leave a head on a trunk of theirs.

He hit upon MacDorcha MacDoilleir himself, and MacDorcha MacDoilleir said to him, "Art thou here, Warrior of the Red Shield?"

"I am," said the Warrior of the Red Shield.

"Well then," said MacDorcha MacDoilleir, "thou wilt not stand long for me."

In each other's grips they went, and were hard belabouring each other till the mouth of dusk and lateness was. At last the Knight of the Red Shield gave that cheery little light lift to the Son of Darkness Son of Dimness, and he put him under, and he cast the head off him.

Now there was MacDorcha MacDoilleir dead, and his thirteen sons; and the battle of a hundred on the hand of each one of them.

Then he was spoilt and torn so much that he could not leave the battlefield; and he did but let himself down, laid amongst the dead the length of the day. There was a great strand under him down below; and what should he hear but the sea coming as a blazing brand of fire, as a destroying serpent, as a bellowing bull; he looked from him, and what saw he coming on shore on the midst of the strand, but a great toothy carlin, whose like was never seen. There was the tooth that was longer than a staff in her fist, and the one that was shorter than a stocking wire in her lap. She came up to the battlefield, and there were two between her and him. She put her finger in their mouths, and she brought them alive; and they rose up whole as best they ever were. She reached him and she put her finger in his mouth, and he snapped it off her from the joint. She struck him a blow of the point of her foot, and she cast him over seven ridges.

"Thou pert little wretch," said she, "thou art the last I will next-live in the battlefield."

The carlin went over another, and he was above her; he did not know how he should put an end to the carlin; he thought of throwing the short spear that her son had at her, and if the head should fall off her that was well. He threw the spear, and he drove the head off the carlin. Then he was stretched on the battlefield, blood and sinews and flesh in pain, but that he had whole bones. What should he see but a musical harper about the field.

"What art thou seeking?" said he to the harper.

"I am sure thou art wearied," said the harper; "come up and set thy head on this little hillock and sleep."

He went up and he laid down; he drew a snore, pretending that he was asleep, and on his soles he was brisk, swift, and active.

"Thou art dreaming," said the harper.

"I am," said he.

"What sawest thou?" said the harper.

"A musical harper," he said, "drawing a rusty old sword to take off my head."

Then he seized the harper, and he drove the brain in fiery shivers through the back of his head.

Then he was under spells that he should not kill a musical harper for ever, but with his own harp.

Then he heard weeping about the field. "Who is that?" said he.

"Here are thy three true foster brothers, seeking thee from place to place today," said they.

"I am stretched here," said he, "blood and sinews, and bones in torture."

"If we had the little vessel of balsam that the great carlin has, the mother of MacDorcha MacDoilleir, we would not be long in healing thee," said they.

"She is dead herself up there," said he, "and she has nothing that ye may not get."

"We are out of her spells forever," said they.

They brought down the little vessel of balsam, and they washed and bathed him with the thing that was in the vessel; then he arose up as whole and healthy as he ever was. He went home with them, and they passed the night in great pleasure.

They went out the next day in great pleasure to play at shinty. He went against the three, and he would drive a half hail down, and a half hail up, in against them.

They perceived the Great Son of the Sons of the World coming to the town; that was their true foster brother also. They went out where he was, and they said to him –

"Man of my love, avoid us and the town this day."

"What is the cause?" said he.

"The Knight of the Red Shield is within, and it is thou he is seeking," said they.

"Go you home, and say to him to go away and to flee, or else that I will take the head off him," said the Great Son of the Sons of the Universe.

Though this was in secret the Knight of the Red Shield perceived it; and he went out on the other side of the house, and he struck a shield blow, and a fight kindling.

The great warrior went out after him, and they began at each other.

> There was no trick that is done by shield man or skiff man,
> Or with cheater's dice box,
> Or with organ of the monks,
> That the heroes could not do
> As was the trick of Cleiteam, trick of Oigeam,
> The apple of the juggler throwing it and catching it
> Into each other's laps
> Frightfully, furiously,
> Bloodily, groaning, hurtfully.
> Mind's desire! umpire's choice!
> They would drive three red sparks of fire from their armour,
> Driving from the shield wall, and flesh
> Of their breasts and tender bodies,
> As they hardly belaboured each other.

"Art thou not silly, Warrior of the Red Shield, when thou art holding wrestling and had battle against me?" said Macabh Mhacaibh an Domhain.

"How is this?" said the hero of the Red Shield.

"It is, that there is no warrior in the great world that will kill me till I am struck above the covering of the trews," said Macabh Mor.

"The victory blessing of that be thine, telling it to me! If thou hadst told me that a long time ago, it is long since I had swept the head off thee," said the Warrior of the Red Shield.

"There is in that more than thou canst do; the king's three teeth are in my pouch, and try if it be that thou will take them out," said Macabh Mor.

When the Warrior of the Red Shield heard where the death of Macabh Mor was, he had two blows given for the blow, two thrusts for the thrust, two stabs for the stab; and the third was into the earth, till he had dug a hole; then he sprung backwards. The great warrior sprung towards him, and he did not notice the hole, and he went down into it to the covering of the trews. Then he reached him, and he cast off his head. He put his hand in his pouch, and he found the king's three teeth in it, and he took them with him and he reached the castle.

"Make a way for me for leaving this island," said he to his foster brethren, "as soon as you can."

"We have no way," said they, "by which thou canst leave it; but stay with us forever, and thou shalt not want for meat or drink."

"The matter shall not be so; but unless you make a way for letting me go, I will take the heads and necks out of you," said he.

"A coracle that thy foster mother and thy foster father had, is here; and we will send it with thee till thou goest on shore in Eirinn. The side that thou settest her prow she will go with thee, and she will return back again by herself; here are three pigeons for thee, and they will keep company with thee on the way," said his foster brothers to him.

He set the coracle out, and he sat in her, and he made no stop, no stay, till he went on shore in Eirinn. He turned her prow outwards; and if she was swift coming, she was swifter returning. He let away the three pigeons, as he left the strange country; and he was sorry that he had led them away, so beautiful was the music that they had.

There was a great river between him and the king's house. When he reached the river, he saw a hoary man coming with all his might, and shouting, "Oh, gentleman, stay yonder until I take you over on my back, in case you should wet yourself."

"Poor man, it seems as if thou wert a porter on the river," said he.

"It is (so)," said the hoary old man.

"And what set thee there?" said he.

"I will tell you that," said the hoary old man; "a big warrior struck a fist on the King of Eirinn, and he drove out three of his teeth, and his two sons went to take out vengeance; there went with them a foolish little young boy that was son to me; and when they went to manhood, he went to faintness. It was but sorry vengeance for them to set me as porter on the river for it."

"Poor man," said he, "that is no reproach; before I leave the town thou wilt be well."

He seized him, and he lifted him with him: and he set him sitting in the chair against the king's shoulder.

"Thou art but a saucy man that came to the town; thou hast set that old carl sitting at my father's shoulder; and thou shalt not get it with thee," said the Knight of the Cairn, as he rose and seized him.

"By my hand, and by my two hands' redemption, it were as well for thee to seize Cnoc Leothaid as to seize me," said the Warrior of the Red Shield to him, as he threw him down against the earth.

He laid on him the binding of the three smalls, straitly and painfully. He struck him a blow of the point of his foot, and he cast him over the seven highest spars that were in the court, under the drippings of the lamps, and under the feet of the big dogs; and he did the very same to the Knight of the Sword; and the little treasure gave a laugh.

"Death wrappings be upon thyself said the king to her. "Thou art from a year's end meat companion, and drink companion for me, and I never saw smile or laugh being made by thee, until my two sons are being disgraced."

"Oh, king," said she, "I have knowledge of my own reason."

"What, oh king, is the screeching and screaming that I am hearing since I came to the town? I never got time to ask till now," said the hero of the Red Shield.

"My sons have three horses' teeth, driving them into my head, since the beginning of a year, with a hammer, until my head has gone through other with heartbreak and torment, and pain," said the king.

"What wouldst thou give to a man that would put thy own teeth into thy head, without hurt, without pain?" said he.

"Half my state so long as I may be alive, and my state altogether when I may go," said the king.

He asked for a can of water, and he put the teeth into the water.

"Drink a draught," said he to the king.

The king drank a draught, and his own teeth went into his head, firmly and strongly, quite as well as they ever were, and every one in her own place.

"Aha!" said the king, "I am at rest. It is thou that didst the valiant deeds; and it was not my set of sons!"

"It is he," said the little treasure to the king, "that could do the valiant deeds; and it was not thy set of shambling sons, that would be stretched as seaweed seekers when he was gone to heroism."

"I will not eat meat, and I will not drink draught," said the king, "until I see my two sons being burnt tomorrow. I will send some to seek faggots of grey oak for burning them."

On the morning of the morrow, who was earliest on his knee at the king's bed, but the Warrior of the Red Shield.

"Rise from that, warrior; what single thing mightest thou be asking that thou shouldst not get?" said the king.

"The thing I am asking is, that thy two sons should be let go; I cannot be in any one place where I may see them spoiled," said he. "It were better to do bird and fool clipping to them, and to let them go."

The king was pleased to do that. Bird and fool clipping was done to them. They were put out of their place, and dogs and big town vagabonds after them.

The little treasure and the Warrior of the Red Shield married, and agreed. A great wedding was made, that lasted a day and a year; and the last day of it was as good as the first day.

Maol a Chliobain

THERE WAS A WIDOW ERE NOW, and she had three daughters; and they said to her that they would go to seek their fortune. She baked three bannocks. She said to the big one, "Whether dost thou like best the half and my blessing, or the big half and my curse?" "I like best," said she, "the big half and thy curse." She said to the middle one, "Whether dost thou like best the big half and my curse, or the little half and my blessing?" "I like best," said she, "the big half and thy curse." She said to the little one, "Whether dost thou like best the big half and my curse, or the little half and my blessing?" "I like best the little half and thy blessing." This pleased her mother, and she gave her the two other halves also. They went away, but the two eldest did not want the youngest to be with them, and they tied her to a rock of stone. They went on, but her mother's blessing came and freed her. And when they looked behind them, whom did they see but her with the rock on top of her. They let her alone a turn of a while, till they reached a peat stack, and they tied her to the peat stack. They went on a bit (but her mother's blessing came and freed her), and they looked behind them, and whom did they see but her coming, and the peat stack on the top of her. They let her alone a turn of a while, till they reached a tree, and they tied her to the tree. They went on a bit (but her mother's blessing came and freed her), and when they looked behind them, whom did they see but her, and the tree on top of her.

They saw it was no good to be at her; they loosed her, and let her (come) with them. They were going till night came on them. They saw a light a long way from them; and though a long way from them, it was not long that they were in reaching it. They went in. What was this but a giant's house! They asked to stop the night. They got that, and they were put to bed with the three daughters of the giant. (The giant came home, and he said, "The smell of the foreign girls is within.") There were twists of amber knobs about the necks of the giant's daughters, and strings of horsehair about their necks. They all slept, but Maol a Chliobain did not sleep. Through the night a thirst came on the giant. He called to his bald, rough-skinned gillie to bring him water. The rough-skinned gillie said that there was not a drop within. Kill," said he, "one of the strange girls, and bring to me her blood." How will I know them?" said the bald, rough-skinned gillie. "There are twists of knobs of amber about the necks of my daughters, and twists of horsehair about the necks of the rest."

Maol a Chliobain heard the giant, and as quick as she could she put the strings of horsehair that were about her own neck and about the necks of her sisters about the necks of the giant's daughters; and the knobs that were about the necks of the giant's daughters about her own neck and about the necks of her sisters; and she laid down so quietly. The bald, rough-skinned gillie came, and he killed one of the daughters of the giant, and he took the blood to him. He asked for more to be brought him. He killed the next. He asked for more; and he killed the third one.

Maol a Chliobain awoke her sisters, and she took them with her on top of her, and she took to going. (She took with her a golden cloth that was on the bed, and it called out.)

The giant perceived her, and he followed her. The sparks of fire that she was putting out of the stones with her heels, they were striking the giant on the chin; and the sparks of fire that the giant was bringing out of the stones with the points of his feet, they were striking Maol a Chliobain in the back of the head. It is this was their going till they reached a river. (She plucked a hair out of her head and made a bridge of it, and she run over the river, and the giant could not follow her.) Maol a Chliobain leaped the river, but the river the giant could not leap.

"Thou art over there, Maol a Chliobain." "I am, though it is hard for thee." "Thou killedst my three bald brown daughters." "I killed them, though it is hard for thee." "And when wilt thou come again?" "I will come when my business brings me."

They went on forward till they reached the house of a farmer. The farmer had three sons. They told how it happened to them. Said the farmer to Maol a Chliobain, "I will give my eldest son to thy eldest sister, and get for me the fine comb of gold, and the coarse comb of silver that the giant has." "It will cost thee no more," said Maol a Chliobain.

She went away; she reached the house of the giant; she got in unknown; she took with her the combs, and out she went. The giant perceived her, and after her he was till they reached the river. She leaped the river, but the river the giant could not leap. "Thou art over there, Maol a Chliobain." "I am, though it is hard for thee." "Thou killedst my three bald brown daughters." "I killed them, though it is hard for thee." "Thou stolest my fine comb of gold, and my coarse comb of silver." "I stole them, though it is hard for thee." "When wilt thou come again?" "I will come when my business brings me."

She gave the combs to the farmer, and her big sister and the farmer's big son married. "I will give my middle son to thy middle sister, and get me the giant's glave of light." "It will cost thee no more," said Maol a Chliobain. She went away, and she reached the giant's house; she went up to the top of a tree that was above the giant's well. In the night came the bald rough-skinned gillie with the sword of light to fetch water. When he bent to raise the water, Maol a Chliobain came down and she pushed him down in the well and she drowned him, and she took with her the glave of light.

The giant followed her till she reached the river; she leaped the river, and the giant could not follow her. "Thou art over there, Maol a Chliobain." "I am, if it is hard for thee." "Thou killedst my three bald brown daughters." "I killed, though it is hard for thee." "Thou stolest my fine comb of gold, and my coarse comb of silver." "I stole, though it is hard for thee." "Thou killedst my bald rough-skinned gillie." "I killed, though it is hard for thee." "Thou stolest my glave of light." "I stole, though it is hard for thee." "When wilt thou come again?" "I will come when my business brings me." She reached the house of the farmer with the glave of light; and her middle sister and the middle son of the farmer married. "I will give thyself my youngest son," said the farmer, "and bring me a buck that the giant has." "It will cost thee no more," said Maol a Chliobain. She went away, and she reached the house of the giant; but when she had hold of the buck, the giant caught her. "What," said the giant, "wouldst thou do to me? If I had done as much harm to thee as thou hast done to me, I would make thee burst thyself with milk porridge; I would then put thee in a pock! I would hang thee to the roof-tree; I would set fire under thee; and I would set on thee with clubs till thou shouldst fall as a faggot of withered sticks on the floor." The giant made milk porridge, and he made her drink it. She put the milk porridge about her mouth and face, and she laid over as if she were dead. The giant put her in a pock, and he hung her to the roof-tree; and he went away, himself and his men, to get wood to the forest. The giant's mother was within. When the giant was gone, Maol a Chliobain began – "'Tis I am in the light! 'Tis I am in the city of gold!" "Wilt thou let me in?" said the carlin. "I will not let thee in." At last she let down the pock. She put in the carlin, cat, and calf, and cream-dish. She took with her the buck and she went away. When the giant came with his men, himself and his men began at the bag with the clubs. The carlin was calling, "'Tis myself that's in it." "I know that thyself is in it," would the giant say, as he laid on to the pock. The pock came down as a faggot of sticks, and what was in it but his mother. When the giant saw how it was, he took after Maol a Chliobain; he followed her till she reached the river. Maol a Chliobain leaped the river, and the giant could not leap it. "Thou art over there, Maol a Chliobain." "I am, though it is hard for thee." "Thou killedst my three bald brown daughters." "I killed, though it is hard for thee." "Thou stolest my golden comb and my silver comb." "I stole, though it is hard for thee." "Thou killedst my bald rough-skinned gillie." "I killed, though it is hard for thee." "Thou stolest my glave of light." "I stole, though it is hard for thee." "Thou killedst my mother." "I killed, though it is hard for thee." "Thou stolest my buck." "I stole, though it is hard for thee." "When wilt thou come again?" "I will come when my business brings me." "If thou wert over here, and I yonder," said the giant, "what wouldst thou do to follow me?" "I would stick myself down, and I would drink till I should dry the river." The giant stuck himself down, and he drank till he burst. Maol a Chliobain and the farmer's youngest son married.

The Barra Widow's Son

THERE WAS A POOR WIDOW IN BARRA, and she had a babe of a son, and Iain was his name. She would be going to the strand to gather shellfish to feed herself and her babe. When she was on the strand on a day, what did she see but a vessel on the west of Barra. Three of those who were on board put out a boat, and they were not long coming on shore.

She went to the shore and she emptied out the shellfish beside her. The master of the vessel put a question to her, "What thing was that?" She said that it was strand shellfish the food that she had. "What little fair lad is this?" – "A son of mine." – "Give him to me and I will give thee gold and silver, and he will get schooling and teaching, and he will be better off than to be here with thee." – "I had rather suffer death than give the child away." – "Thou art silly. The child and thyself will be well off if thou lettest him (go) with me." With the love of the money she said that she would give him the child. "Come hither, lads, go on board; here's for you the key. Open a press in the cabin, and you will bring me hither a box that you will find in it." They went away, they did that, and they came. He caught the box, he opened it, he emptied it with a gush (or into her skirt), and he did not count it all, and he took the child with him.

She staid as she was, and when she saw the child going on board she would have given all she ever saw that she had him. He sailed away, and he went to England. He gave schooling and teaching to the boy till he was eighteen years on the vessel. It was Iain Albanach the boy was called at first, he gave him the name of Iain Mac a Maighstir (John, master's son), because he himself was master of the vessel. The "*owner*" of the vessel had seven ships on sea, and seven shops on shore – each one going to her own shop with her cargo. It happened to the seven ships to be at home together. The *owner* took with him the seven skippers to the house. "I am growing heavy and aged," said he; "you are there seven masters; I had none altogether that I would rather than thou. I am without a man of clan though I am married; I know not with whom I will leave my goods, and I have a great share; there was none I would rather give it to than thee, but that thou art without clan as I am myself." "I," said the skipper, "have a son eighteen years of age in the ship, who has never been let out of her at all." – "Is not that wonderful for me, and that I did not hear of it!" – "Many a thing might the like of me have, and not tell it to you." – "Go and bring him down hither to me that I may see him." He went and he brought him down, and he set him in order. "Is this thy son?" – "It is," said the skipper. "Whether wouldst thou rather stay with me, or go with thy father on the sea as thou wert before, and that I should make thee an heir for ever. Well then, it was ever at sea that I was raised, and I never got much on shore from my youth; so at sea I would rather be; but as you are determined to keep me, let me stay with yourself."

"I have seven shops on shore, and thou must take thy hand in the seven shops. There are clerks at every one of the shops," said he. "No one of them will hold bad opinion of himself that he is not as good as I. If you insist that I take them, I will take the seventh one of them."

He took the seventh one of the shops, and the first day of his going in he sent word through the town, the thing that was before a pound would be at fifteen shillings; so that everything in the shop was down, and the shop was empty before the ships came. He (the owner) went in, he counted his money, and he said that the shop was empty. "It is not wonderful though it were, when the thing that was before a pound is let down to fifteen shillings." – "And, My oide, are you taking that ill? Do you not see that I would put out all in the shop seven times before they could put it out once?" – "With that thou must take the rest in hand, and let them out so." Then he took the rest in hand, and he was a master above the other clerks. When the ships came the shops altogether were empty. Then his master said, "Whether wouldst thou rather be master over the shops or go with one of the seven ships? Thou wilt get thy choice of the seven ships." – "It is at sea I was ever raised and I will take a ship." He got a ship. "Come, send hither here to me the seven skippers." The seven skippers came. "Now," said he to the six skippers that were going with Iain, "Iain is going with you, you will set three ships before and three behind, and he will be in the middle, and unless you bring him whole hither to me, there is but to seize you and hang you." – "Well, then, my adopted father," said Iain, "that is not right. The ships are going together, a storm may come and drive us from each other; let each do as best he may." The ships went, they sailed, and it was a cargo of coal that Iain put in his own. There came on them a great day of storm. They were driven from each other. Where did Iain sail but to Turkey. He took anchorage in Turkey at early day, and he thought to go on shore to take a walk. He was going before him walking; he saw two out of their shirts working, and as though they had two iron flails. What had they but a man's corpse! "What are you doing to the corpse?" – "It was a Christian; we had eight marks against him, and since he did not pay us while he was alive, we will take it out of his corpse with the flails." – "Well then, leave him with me and I will pay you the eight marks." He seized him, he took him from them, he paid them, and he put mould and earth on him. It was soon for him to return till he should see more of the land of the Turk. He went on a bit and what should he see there but a great crowd of men together. He took over where they were. What did he see but a gaping red fire of a great hot fire, and a woman stripped between the fire and them. "What," said he, "are you doing here?" "There are," said they, "two Christian women that the great Turk got; they were caught on the ocean; he has had them from the end of eight years. This one was promising him that she would marry him every year: when the time came to marry him she would not marry him a bit. He ordered herself and the woman that was with her to be burnt. One of them was burnt, and this one is as yet unburnt."

"I will give you a good lot of silver and gold if you will leave her with me, and you may say to him that you burnt her." They looked at each other. They said that he would get that. He went and he took her with him on board, and he clothed her in cloth and linen.

"Now," said she, "thou hast saved my life for me; thou must take care of thyself in this place. Thou shalt go up now to yonder change-house. The man of the inn will put a question to thee what cargo thou hast. Say thou a cargo of coal. He will say that would be well worth selling in the place where thou art. Say thou it is for selling it that thou art come; what offer will he make for it. He will say, tomorrow at six o'clock there would be a *waggon* of gold going down, and a waggon of coal coming up, so that the ship might be kept in the same *trim*, till six o'clock on the next night. Say thou that thou wilt take that; but unless thou art watchful they will come in the night when every man is asleep, with muskets and pistols; they will set the ship on the ground; they will kill every man, and they will take the gold with them."

He went to the man of the inn, and agreed with him as she had taught him. They began on the morrow, in the morning, to put down the gold, and take up the coal. The skipper had a man standing looking out that the vessel should be in trim. When the coal was out, and the ship was as heavy with the gold as she was with the coal; and when he was on shore, she got an order for the sailors to take her advice till he should come. "Put up," said she, "the sails, and draw the anchors. Put a rope on shore." They did that. He came on board; the ship sailed away through the night; they heard a shot, but they were out, and they never caught them more.

They sailed till they reached England. Three ships had returned, and the three skippers were in prison till Iain should come back. Iain went up and he reached his adopted father. The gold was taken on shore, and the old man had two thirds and Iain a third. He got chambers for the woman, where she should not be troubled.

"Art thou thinking that thou wilt go yet?" said the woman to him. "I am thinking that I have enough of the world with that same." – "Thou wentest before for thine own will, if thou wouldst be so good as to go now with my will." – "I will do that." – "Come to that shop without; take from it a coat, and a brigis, and a waistcoat; try if thou canst got a cargo of herring and thou shalt go with it to Spain. When the cargo is in, come where I am before thou goest."

When he got the cargo on board he went where she was. "Hast thou got the cargo on board?" – "I have got it."

"There is a dress here, and the first Sunday after thou hast reached Spain thou wilt put it on, and thou wilt go to the church with it. Here is a whistle, and a ring, and a book. Let there be a horse and a servant with thee. Thou shalt put the ring on thy finger; let the book be in thine hand; thou wilt see in the church three seats, two twisted chairs of gold, and a chair of silver. Thou shalt take hold of the book and be reading it, and the first man that goes out of the church be thou out. Wait not for man alive, unless the King or the Queen meet thee."

He sailed till he reached Spain; he took anchorage, and he went up to the change-house. He asked for a dinner to be set in order. The dinner was set on the board. They went about to seek him. A trencher was set on the board, and a cover on it, and the housewife said to him – "There is meat and drink enough on the board before you, take enough, but do not lift the cover that is on the top of the trencher." She drew the door with her. He began at his dinner. He thought to himself, though it were its fill of gold that were in the trencher, or a fill of "daoimean", nothing ever went on board that he might not pay. He lifted the cover of the trencher, and what was on the trencher but a couple of herring. "If this be the thing she was hiding from me she need not," and he ate one herring and the one side of the other. When the housewife saw that the herring was eaten – "Mo chreach mhor! my great ruin," said she; "how it has fallen out! Was I never a day that I could not keep the people of the realm till today?" – "What has befallen thee?" – "It is, that I never was a day that I might not put a herring before them till today." – "What wouldst thou give for a barrel of herrings?" – "Twenty Saxon pounds." – "What wouldst thou give for a ship load?" – "That is a thing that I could not buy." – "Well, then, I will give thee two hundred herring for the two herring, and I wish the ship were away and the herrings sold."

On the first Sunday he got a horse with a bridle and saddle, and a gillie. He went to the church; he saw the three chairs. The queen sat on the right hand of the king, and he himself sat on the left; he took the book out of his pocket, and he began reading.

It was not on the sermon that the king's looks were, nor the queen's, but raining tears. When the sermon skailed he went out. There were three nobles after him, shouting that the king had a matter for him. He would not return. He betook himself to the change-house that night. He staid as he was till the next Sunday, and he went to sermon; he would not stay for anyone, and he returned to the change-house. The third Sunday he went to the church. In the middle of the sermon the king and queen came out; they stood at each side of the (bridle) rein. When the king saw him coming out he let go the rein; he took his hat off to the ground, and he made manners at him. "By your leave; you needn't make such manners at me. It is I that should make them to yourself." – "If it were your will that you should go with me to the palace to take dinner." – "Ud! Ud! it is a man below you with whom I would go to dinner." They reached the palace. Food was set in the place of eating, drink in the place of drinking, music in the place of hearing. They were plying the feast and the company with joy and gladness, because they had hopes that they would get news of their daughter. "Oh, skipper of the ship," said the queen, hide not from me a thing that I am going to ask thee." Anything that I have that I can tell I will not hide it from you." "And hide not from me that a woman's hand set that dress about your back, your coat, your brigis, and your waistcoat, and gave you the ring about your finger, and the book that was in your hand, and the whistle that you were playing." "I will not hide it.

With a woman's right hand every whit of them was reached to me." "And where didst thou find her? 'Tis a daughter of mine that is there." "I know not to whom she is daughter. I found her in Turkey about to be burned in a great gaping fire." "Sawest thou a woman along with her?" "I did not see her; she was burned before I arrived. I bought her with gold and silver. I took her with me, and I have got her in a chamber in England." "The king had a great general," said the queen, "and what should he do but fall in love with her. Her father was asking her to marry him, and she would not marry him. She went away herself and the daughter of her father's brother with a vessel, to try if he would forget her. They went over to Turkey; the Turk caught them, and we had not hope to see her alive for ever."

If it be your pleasure, and that you yourself are willing, I will set a ship with you to seek her; you will get herself to marry, half the realm so long as the king lives, and the whole realm when he is dead." "I scorn to do that; but send a ship and a skipper away, and I will take her home; and if that be her own will, perhaps I will not be against it."

A ship was made ready; what should the general do but pay a lad to have him taken on board unknown to the skipper; he got himself hidden in a barrel. They sailed far; short time they were in reaching England. They took her on board, and they sailed back for Spain. In the midst of the sea, on a fine day, he and she came up on deck, and what should he see but an island beyond him; it was pretty calm at the time. "Lads, take me to the island for a while to hunt, till there comes on us the likeness of a breeze." "We will." They set him on shore on the island; when they left him on the island the boat returned. When the general saw that he was on the island, he promised more wages to the skipper and to the crew, for that they should leave him there; and they left Iain on the island.

When she perceived that they had left Iain on the island, she went mad, and they were forced to bind her. They sailed to Spain. They sent word to the king that his daughter had grown silly, as it seemed, for the loss of the form of her husband and lover. The king betook himself to sorrow, to black melancholy, and to woe, and to heart-breaking, because of what had arisen; and (because) he had but her of son or daughter.

Iain was in the island, hair and beard grown over him; the hair of his head down between his two shoulders, his shoes worn to pulp, without a thread of clothes on that was not gone to rags; without a bite of flesh on him, his bones but sticking together.

On a night of nights, what should he hear but the rowing of a boat coming to the island. "Art thou there, Iain Albanich?" said the one in the boat. Though he was, he answered not. He would rather find death at the side of a hill than be killed.

"I know that thou hearest me, and answer; it is just as well for thee to answer me, as that I should go up and take thee down by force." He went, and he took himself down. "Art thou willing to go out of the island?" "Well, then, I am; it is I that am that, if I could get myself taken out of it." "What wouldst thou give to a man that would take thee out of this?" "There was a time when I might give something to a man that would take me out of this; but today I have not a thing." "Wouldst thou give one half of thy wife to a man that would take thee out of this?" "I have not that." "I do not say if thou hadst, that thou wouldst give her away." "I would give her." "Wouldst thou give half thy children to a man that would take thee out of this?" "I would give them." "Down hither; sit in the stern of the boat." He sat in the stern of the boat. "Whether wouldst thou rather go to England or Spain?" "To Spain." He went with him, and before the day came he was in Spain.

He went up to the change-house; the housewife knew him in a moment. "Is this Iain!" said she. "It is the sheath of all that there was of him that is here."

"Poorly has it befallen thee!" said she. She went and she sent a message to a barber's booth, and he was cleansed; and word to a tailor's booth, and clothes were got for him; she sent word to a shoemaker's booth, and shoes were got for him. On the morrow when he was properly cleansed and arrayed, he went to the palace of the king, and he played the whistle. When the king's daughter heard the whistle she gave a spring, and she broke the third part of the cord that bound her. They asked her to keep still, and they tied more cords on her. On the morrow he gave a blast on the whistle, and she broke two parts of all that were on her. On the third day when she heard his whistle, she broke three quarters; on the fourth day she broke what was on her altogether. She rose and she went out to meet him, and there never was a woman more sane than she. Word was sent up to the king of Spain, that there never was a girl more sane than she; and that the bodily presence of her husband and lover had come to her.

A coach was sent to fetch Iain; the king and his great gentles were with him; he was taken up on the deadly points. Music was raised, and lament laid down; meat was set in the place of eating, drink in the place of drinking, music in the place for hearing; a cheery, hearty, jolly wedding was made. Iain got one half of the realm; after the king's death he got it altogether. The general was seized; he was torn amongst horses; he was burned amongst fires; and the ashes were let fly with the wind.

After the death of the king and queen, Iain was king over Spain. Three sons were born to him. On a night he heard a knocking in the door. "The asker is come," said he. Who was there but the very man that took him out of the island. "Art thou for keeping thy promise?" said the one who came. "I am," said Iain. "Thine own be thy realm, and thy children and my blessing! Dost thou remember when thou didst pay eight merks for the corpse of a man in Turkey; that was my body; health be thine; thou wilt see me no more.

The Son of the Scottish Yeoman who Stole the Bishop's Horse and Daughter, and the Bishop Himself

THERE WAS ONCE A SCOTTISH YEOMAN who had three sons. When the youngest of them came to be of age to fellow a profession, he set apart three hundred marks for each of them. The youngest son asked that his portion might be given to himself, as he was going away to seek his fortune. He went to the great city of London. He was for a time there, and what was he doing but learning to be a gentleman's servant? He at last set about finding a master. He heard that the chief magistrate (provost) of London wanted a servant. He applied to him, they agreed, and he entered his service. The chief magistrate was in the habit of going every day in the week to meet the Archbishop of London in a particular place. The servant attended his master, for he always went out along with him. When they had broken up their meeting on one occasion, they returned homewards, and the servant said to his master by the way,

"That is a good brown horse of the bishop's," said he, "with your leave, master."

"Yes, my man," said the master, "he has the best horse in London."

"What think you," said the servant, "would he take for the horse, if he were to sell it?"

"Oh! you fool," said his master, "I thought you were a sensible fellow; many a man has tried to buy that horse, and it has defied them as yet."

"I'll return and try," said he.

His master returned along with him to see what would happen. This was on a Thursday. The young man asked the bishop, would he sell the horse? The bishop became amazed and angry, and said he did not expect that he could buy it.

"But what beast could you, or any man have," said the young man, "that might not be bought?"

"Senseless fellow," said the bishop; "how foolish you are I go away home, you shan't buy my horse."

"What will you wager," said the young man, "that I won't have the horse by this time tomorrow?"

"Is it my horse you mean?" said the bishop.

"Yes, your horse," said the young man. "What will you wager that I don't steal it?"

"I'll wager five hundred merks," said the bishop, "that you don't."

"Then," said the young man, "I have only one pound, but I'll wager that, and my head besides, that I do."

"Agreed," said the bishop.

"Observe," said the young man, "that I have wagered my head and the pound with you, and if I steal the horse he will be my own property."

"That he will, assuredly," said the chief magistrate.

"I agree to that," said the bishop.

They returned home that night.

"Poor fellow," said the chief magistrate to his servant by the way, "I am very well satisfied with you since I got you. I am not willing to lose you now. You are foolish. The bishop will take care that neither you nor any other man will steal the horse. He'll have him watched."

When night came, the young man started, and set to work; he went to the bishop's house. What did he find out there, but that they had the horse in a room, and men along with it, who were busy eating and drinking. He looked about him, and soon saw that he would require another clever fellow along with him. In looking about, who does he find but one of the loose fellows about the town.

"If you go along with me for a little time," said he, I will give you something for your pains."

"I'll do that," said the other.

He set off, and at the first start both he and his man reached the hangman of the city.

"Can you tell me," said he to the hangman, "where I can get a dead man?"

"Yes," said the hangman, "there was a man hanged this very day, after midday."

"If you go and get him for me," said the young man, "I'll give you something for your pains."

The hangman agreed, and went away with him to where the body was.

"Do you know now," said the young man, "where I can get a long stout rope?"

"Yes," said the hangman, "the rope that hanged the man is here quite convenient; you'll get it."

They set off with the body, both himself and his man.

They reached the bishop's house. He said to his man when they had reached –

"Stay you here and take charge of this, until I get up on the top of the house."

He put both his mouth and his ear to the chimney in order to discover where the men were, as they were now speaking loud from having drunk so much. He discovered where they were.

"Place the end of the rope," said he to his man, "round the dead man's neck, and throw the other end up to me."

He dragged the dead man up to the top of the chimney. The men in the room began to hear the rubbish in the chimney falling down. He let the body down by degrees, until at last he saw the bright light of the watchmen falling on the dead man's feet.

"See," said they, "what is this? Oh, the Scottish thief, what a shift! He preferred dying in this way to losing his head. He has destroyed himself."

Down from the chimney came the young man in haste. In he went into the very middle of the men, and as the horse was led out by the door, his hand was the first to seize the bridle. He went with the horse to the stable, and said to them that they might now go and sleep, that they were safe enough.

"Now," said he to the other man, "I believe you to be a clever fellow; be at hand here tomorrow evening, and I will see you again."

He paid him at the same time, and the man was much pleased. He, himself, returned to his master's stable with the bishop's brown horse. He went to rest, and though the daylight came early, earlier than that did his master come to his door.

"I wouldn't grudge my pains," said he, if my poor Scotsman were here before me today."

"I am here, good master," said he, "and the bishop's brown horse beside me."

"Well done, my man," said his master, "you're a clever fellow. I had a high opinion of you before; I think much more of you now."

They prepared this day, too, to go and visit the bishop. It was Friday.

"Now," said the servant, "I left home without a horse, yesterday, but I won't leave in the same way today."

"Well, my man," said his master, "as you have got the horse, I'll give you a saddle."

So they set off this day again to meet the bishop, his master and himself riding their horses. They saw the bishop coming to meet them, apparently mad. When they came close together they observed that the bishop rode another horse, by no means so good as his own. The bishop and chief magistrate met with salutations. The bishop turned to the chief magistrate's servant –

"Scroundel," said he, "and thorough thief!"

"You can't call me worse," said the other. "I don't know that you can call me that justly; for, you know, I told you what I was to do. Without more words, pay me my five hundred merks."

This had to be done, though not very willingly.

"What would you now say," says the lad, "if I were to steal your daughter tonight?"

"My daughter, you worthless fellow," said the bishop; "you shan't steal my daughter."

"I'll wager five hundred merks and the brown horse," said the lad, "that I'll steal her."

"I'll wager ten hundred merks that you don't," said the bishop.

The wager was laid. The lad and his master went home. "Young man," said his master, "I thought well of you at one time, but you have done a foolish thing now, just when you had made yourself all right."

"Never mind, good master," said he, "I'll make the attempt at any rate."

When night came, the chief magistrate's servant set off for the bishop's house. When he reached, he saw a gentleman coming out at the door.

"Oh," said he to the gentleman, "what is this going on at the bishop's house tonight?"

"A great and important matter," said the gentleman; "a rascally Scotsman who is threatening to steal the bishop's daughter, but I can tell you neither he nor any other man will steal her; she is well guarded."

"Oh, I'm sure of that," said the lad, and turned away. "There is a man in England, however," said he to himself, "who must try it."

He set off, and reached the king's tailors. He asked them whether they had any dresses ready for great people?

"No," said the tailor, "but a dress I have for the king's daughter and one for her maid of honour."

"What," said the chief magistrate's servant, "will you take for the use of these, for a couple of hours?"

"Oh," said the tailor, "I fear I dare not give them to you."

"Don't be in the least afraid," said the lad, "I'll pay you, and I'll return the two dresses without any injury or loss. You'll get a hundred merks," said he.

The tailor coveted so large a sum, and so he gave them to him. He returned, and found his man of the former night. They went to a private place, and got themselves fitted out in the dresses got from the tailor. When this was done as well as they could, they came to the bishop's door. Before he arrived at the door he found out that when any of the royal family came to the bishop's house they didn't knock, but rubbed the bottom of the door with the point of the foot. He came to the door, and rubbed. There was a doorkeeper at the door that night, and he ran and told the bishop.

"There is some one of the royal family at the door," said he.

"No," said the bishop, "there is not. It's the thief of a Scotsman that is there."

The doorkeeper looked through the key-hole, and saw the appearance of two ladies who stood there. He went to his master and told him so. His master went to the door that he might see for himself. He who was outside would give another and another rub to the door, at the same time abusing the bishop for his folly. The bishop looked, and recognized the voice of the king's daughter at the door. The door is quickly opened, and the bishop bows low to the lady. The king's daughter began immediately to chide the bishop for laying any wager respecting his daughter, saying that he was much blamed for what he had done.

"It was very wrong of you," said she, "to have done it without my knowledge, and you would not have required to have made such a stir or been so foolish as all this."

"You will excuse me," said the bishop.

"I can't excuse you," she said.

In to the chamber he led the king's daughter, in which his own daughter was, and persons watching her. She was in the middle of the chamber, sitting on a chair, and the others sitting all around.

Said the king's daughter to her, "My dear, your father is a very foolish man to place you in such great danger; for if he had given me notice, and placed you under my care, any man who might venture to approach you would assuredly not only be hanged, but burned alive. Go," said she to the bishop, "to bed, and dismiss this large company, lest men laugh at you."

He told the company that they might now go to rest, that the queen's daughter and her maid of honour would take charge of his daughter. When the queen's daughter had seen them all away, she said to the daughter of the bishop, "Come along with me, my dear, to the king's palace."

He led her out, and then he had the brown horse all ready, and as soon as the Scotsman got her to where the horse stood, he threw off the dress he wore, in a dark place. He put a different dress above his own, and mounted the horse. The other man is sent home with the dresses to the tailor. He paid the man, and told him to meet him there next night. He leaped on the brown horse at the bishop's house, and off he rode to the house of his master. Early as daylight came, earlier came his master to the stable. He had the bishop's daughter in his bed. He wakened when he heard his master.

"I wouldn't grudge my pains," said the latter, "if my poor Scotsman were here before me today."

"Eh, and so I am," said the lad, "and the bishop's daughter along with me here."

"Oh," said he, "I always thought well of you, but now I think more of you than ever."

This was Saturday. He and his master had to go and meet the bishop this day also. The bishop and chief magistrate met as usual. If the bishop looked angry the former day, he looked much angrier this day. The chief magistrate's servant rode on his horse and saddle behind his master. When he came near the bishop he could only call him "thief" and "scoundrel."

"You may shut your mouth," said he; "you cannot say that to me with justice. Send across here my five hundred merks. He paid the money. He was abusing the other.

"Oh man," said he, "give up your abuse; I'll lay you the ten hundred merks that I'll steal yourself tonight."

"That you steal me, you worthless fellow," said the bishop. "You shan't be allowed."

He wagered the ten hundred merks.

"I'll get these ten hundred merks back again," said the bishop, "but I'll lay you fifteen hundred merks that you don't steal me."

The chief magistrate fixed the bargain for them. The lad and his master went home.

"My man," said the master, "I have always thought well of you till now; you will now lose the money you gained, and you can't steal the man."

"I have no fear of that," said the servant.

When night came he set off, and got to the house of the bishop. Then he thought he would go where he could find the fishermen of the city, in order to see what might be seen with them. When he reached the fishermen he asked them whether they had any fresh-killed salmon? They said they had. He said to them –

"If you skin so many of them for me I will give you such and such a sum of money, or as much as will be just and right."

The fishermen said they would do as he wished, and they did so. They gave him as many fish skins as he thought would make him a cloak of the length and breadth he wished. He then went to the tailors. He said to the tailors, would they make him a dress of the fish skins by twelve o'clock at night, and that they should be paid for it. They told him what sum they would take. They took the young man's measure and began the dress. The dress was ready by twelve o'clock. They could not work any longer as the Sunday was coming in. He left with the dress, and when he found himself a short way from the bishop's church he put it on. He had got a key to open the church and he went in. He at once went to the pulpit. The doorkeeper casting an eye in on an occasion, while a great watch was kept over the bishop, he went and said there was a light in the church.

"A light," said his master, "go and see what light it is." It was past twelve o'clock by this time.

"Oh," said the doorkeeper, coming back, "there is a man preaching in it."

The bishop drew out his time-piece, and he saw that it was the beginning of the Sunday. He went running to the church. When he saw the brightness that was in the church, and all the movements of the man that was preaching, he was seized with fear. He opened the door a little and put in his head that he might see what he was like. There was not a language under the stars that the man in the pulpit was not taking a while of. When he came to the languages which the bishop understood, he began to denounce the bishop as a man who had lost his senses. In the bishop ran, and down he is on his knees before the pulpit. There he began to pray, and when he saw the brightness that was about the pulpit, he took to heart the things that were said to him. At length he said to him, if he would promise sincere repentance, and go along with him, he would grant him forgiveness. The bishop promised him that he would.

"Come with me till I have a little time of you," said he.

"I will," said the bishop, "though thou shouldst ask me to leave the world."

He went along with him, and the young man walked before him. They reached the stable of the chief magistrate. He got a seat for the bishop, and he kept him sitting. He sat down himself. They required no light, for the servant's clothes were shining bright where they were. He was then expounding to the bishop in some languages which he could understand, and in others which he could not. He went on in that way until it was time for his master to come in the morning. When the time drew near, he threw off the dress, bent down and hid it, for it was near daylight. The bishop was now silent, and the chief magistrate came.

"I wouldn't grudge my pains," said he, "if I had my poor Scotsman here before me today."

"Eh, so I am here," said he, "and the bishop along with me."

"Hey, my man," says his master, "you have done well."

"Oh, you infamous scoundrel," said the bishop, "is it thus you have got the better of me?"

"I'll tell you what it is," said the chief magistrate, "you had better be civil to him. Don't abuse him. He has got your daughter, your horse, and your money, and as for yourself, you know that he cannot support you, so it is best for you to support him. Take himself and your daughter along with you and make them a respectable wedding." The young man left and went home with the bishop, and he and the bishop's daughter were lawfully married, and the father shewed him kindness. I left them there.

The Tale of the Soldier

THERE WAS AN OLD SOLDIER ONCE, and he left the army. He went to the top of a hill that was at the upper end of the town land, and he said –

"Well, may it be that the mischief may come and take me with him on his back, the next time that I come again in sight of this town."

Then he was walking till he came to the house of a gentleman that was there; John asked the gentleman if he would get leave to stay in his house that night. "Well, then," said the gentleman, "since thou art an old soldier, and hast the look of a man of courage, without dread or fear in thy face, there is a castle at the side of yonder wood, and thou mayest stay in it till day. Thou shalt have a pipe and baccy, a cogie full of whisky, and a bible to read."

When John got his supper, he took himself to the castle: he set on a great fire, and when a while of the night had come, there came two tawny women in, and a dead man's kist between them. They threw it at the fireside, and they sprang out. John arose, and with the heel of his foot he drove out its end, and he dragged out an old hoary bodach, and he set him sitting in the great chair; he gave him a pipe and baccy, and a cogie of whisky, but the bodach let them fall on the floor. "Poor man," said John, "the cold is on thee." John laid himself stretched in the bed, and he left the bodach to toast himself at the fireside; but about the crowing of the cock he went away.

The gentleman came well early in the morning.

"What rest didst thou find, John?"

"Good rest," said John. "Thy father was not the man that would frighten me."

"Right, good John, thou shalt have two hundred '*pund*', and lie tonight in the castle."

"I am the man that will do that," said John; and that night it was the very like. There came three tawny women, and a dead man's kist with them amongst them. They threw it up to the side of the fireplace, and they took their soles out (of that).

John arose, and with the heel of his foot he broke the head of the kist, and he dragged out of it the old hoary man; and as he did the night before he set him sitting in the big chair, and gave him pipe and baccy, and he let them fall. "Oh! poor man," said John, "cold is on thee." Then he gave him a cogie of drink, and he let that fall also. "Oh! poor man, thou art cold."

The bodach went as he did the night before; "but," said John to himself, "if I stay here this night, and that thou shouldst come, thou shalt pay my pipe and baccy, and my cogie of drink."

The gentleman came early enough in the morning, and he asked, "What rest didst thou find last night, John?" "Good rest," said John, "it was not the hoary bodach, thy father, that would put fear on me."

"Och!" said the gentleman, "if thou stayest tonight thou shalt have three hundred '*pund.*'"

"It's a bargain," said John.

When it was a while of the night there came four tawny women, and a dead man's kist with them amongst them; and they let that down at the side of John.

John arose, and he drew his foot and he drove the head out of the kist, and he dragged out the old hoary man and he set him in the big chair. He reached him the pipe and the baccy, the cup and the drink, but the old man let them fall, and they were broken.

"Och," said John, "before thou goest this night thou shalt pay me all thou hast broken;" but word there came not from the head of the bodach. Then John took the belt of his "abersgaic," and he tied the bodach to his side, and he took him with him to bed. When the heath-cock crowed, the bodach asked him to let him go.

"Pay what thou hast broken first," said John. "I will tell thee, then," said the old man, "there is a cellar of drink under, below me, in which there is plenty of drink, tobacco, and pipes; there is another little chamber beside the cellar, in which there is a caldron full of gold; and under the threshold of the big door there is a crocky full of silver. Thou sawest the women that came with me tonight?"

"I saw," said John.

"Well, there thou hast four women from whom I took the cows, and they in extremity; they are going with me every night thus, punishing me; but go thou and tell my son how I am being wearied out. Let him go and pay the cows, and let him not be heavy on the poor. Thou thyself and he may divide the gold and silver between you, and marry thyself my old girl; but mind, give plenty of gold of what is left to the poor, on whom I was too hard, and I will find rest in the world of worlds."

The gentleman came, and John told him as I have told thee, but John would not marry the old girl of the hoary bodach.

At the end of a day or two John would not stay longer; he filled his pockets full of the gold, and he asked the gentleman to give plenty of gold to the poor. He reached the house, but he was wearying at home, and he had rather be back with the regiment. He took himself off on a day of days, and he reached the hill above the town from which he went away; but who should come to him but the Mischief.

"Hoth! hoth! John, thou hast come back?"

"Hoth! on thyself," quoth John, "I came; who art thou?"

"I am the Mischief; the man to whom thou gavest thyself when thou was here last."

"Ai! ai!" said John, "it's long since I heard tell of thee, but I never saw thee before. There is glamour on my eyes, I will not believe that it is thou at all; but make a snake of thyself, and I will believe thee."

The Mischief did this.

"Make now a lion of roaring."

The Mischief did this.

"Spit fire now seven miles behind thee, and seven miles before thee."

The Mischief did this.

Well," said John, "since I am to be a servant with thee, come into my 'abersgaic,' and I will carry thee; but thou must not come out till I ask thee, or else the bargain's broke."

The Mischief promised, and he did this.

"Now," said John, "I am going to see a brother of mine that is in the regiment, but keep thou quiet."

So now, John went into the town; and one yonder and one here, would cry, "There is John the 'desairtair'."

There was gripping of John, and a court held on him; and so it was that he was to be hanged about mid-day on the morrow, and John asked no favour but to be floored with a bullet.

The Coirneal said, "Since he was an old soldier, and in the army so long, that he should have his asking."

On the morrow when John was to be shot, and the soldiers foursome round all about him, "What is that they are saying?" said the Mischief. "Let me amongst them and I wont be long scattering them."

"Cuist! cuist!" said John.

"What's that speaking to thee?" said the Coirneal.

"Oh! it's but a white mouse," said John.

"Black or white," said the Coirneal, "don't thou let her out of the 'abersgaic' and thou shalt have a letter of loosing, and let's see thee no more."

John went away, and in the mouth of night he went into a barn where there were twelve men threshing.

"Oh! lads," said John, "here's for you my old abersgaic, and take a while threshing it, it is so hard that it is taking the skin off my back."

They took as much as two hours of the watch at the abersgaic with the twelve flails; and at last every blow they gave it, it would leap to the top of the barn, and it was casting one of the threshers now and again on his back. When they saw that, they asked him to be out of that, himself and his abersgaic; they would not believe but that the Mischief was in it.

Then he went on his journey, and he went into a smithy where there were twelve smiths striking their great hammers.

"Here's for you, lads, an old abersgaic, and I will give you half-a-crown, and take a while at it with the twelve great hammers; it is so hard that it is taking the skin off my back."

But that was fun for the smiths; it was good sport for them the abersgaic of the soldier; but every "sgailc" it got, it was bounding to the top of the smithy. "Go out of this, thyself and it," said they; "we will not believe but that the 'Bramman' is in it."

So then John went on and the Mischief on his back, and he reached a great furnace that was there.

"Where art thou going now, John?" said the Mischief.

"Patience a little, and thou'lt see that," said John.

"Let me out," said the Mischief, "and I will never put trouble on thee in this world."

"Nor in the next?" said John.

"That's it," said the Mischief.

"Stop then," said John, "till thou get a smoke;" and so saying, John cast the abersgaic and the Donas into the middle of the furnace, and himself and the furnace went as a green flame of fire to the skies.

Mac-a-Rusgaich

THERE WAS (AT) SOME TIME A TENANT, and he was right bad to his servants, and there was a pranky man who was called Gille Neumh Mac-a-Rusgaich (holy lad son of Skinner), and he heard tell of him, and he went to the fair, and he took a straw in his mouth, to shew that he was for taking service.

The dour tenant came the way, and he asked Mac-a-Rusgaich if he would take service; and Mac-a-Rusgaich said that he would take it if he could find a good master; and Mac-a-Rusgaich said,

"What shall I have to do if I take with thee?"

And the dour tenant said, "Thou wilt have to herd the mountain moor."

And Mac-a-Rusgaich said, "I will do that."

And the tenant said, "And thou wilt have to hold the plough."

And Mac-a-Rusgaich said, "I will do that."

"And thou wilt have ever so many other matters to do."

And Mac-a-Rusgaich said, "Will these matters be hard to do?"

And the other said, "They will not be (so), I will but ask thee to do the thing that thou art able to do but I will put into the covenant that if thou dost not answer, thou must pay me two wages."

And Mac-a-Rusgaich said, "I will put into the covenant, if thou askest me to do anything but the thing which I am able to do, thou must give me two wages."

And they agreed about that.

And the dour tenant said, "I am putting it into the covenant that if either one of us takes the rue, that a thong shall be taken out of his skin, from the back of his head to his heel."

And Mac-a-Rusgaich said, "Mind that thou hast said that, old carle."

And he took service with the hard tenant, and he went home to him.

The first work that Mac-a-Rusgaich was bidden to do, was to go to the moss to cast peats, and Mac-a-Rusgaich asked for his morning meal before he should go, so that he need not come for it, and he got as much meat as they used to allow the servants at one meal, and he ate that; and he asked for his dinner, so that he need no stop at mid-day, and he got the allowance which there was for dinner, and he ate that; and he asked for his supper, so that he need not come home at night, and they gave him that, and he ate that; and he went where his master was, and he asked him,

"What are thy servants wont to do after their supper?"

And his master said to him, "It is their wont to put off their clothes and go to lie down."

And Mac-a-Rusgaich went where his bed was, and he put off his clothes, and he went to lie down.

The mistress went where the man of the town (the master) was and she asked him, "What sort of a servant he had got there, that he had eaten three meals at one meal, and had gone to lie down?" And the master went where Mac-a-Rusgaich was, and he said to him,

"Why art thou not at work?"

And Mac-a-Rusgaich said, "It is that thou thyself saidst to me that it was thy servants' wont, when they had got their supper, to put off their clothes and go to lie down."

And the master said, "And why didst thou eat the three meals together?"

And Mac-a-Rusgaich said, "It is that the three meals were little enough to make a man content."

And the master said, "Get up and go to thy work."

And Mac-a-Rusgaich said, "I will get up, but I must get meat as I need, or my work will accord. I am but to do as I am able. See! art thou taking the rue, old carle?"

"I am not, I am not," said the carle, and Mac-a-Rusgaich got his meat better after that.

And there was another day and the carle asked Mac-a-Rusgaich to go to hold the plough in a dale that was down from the house, and Mac-a-Rusgaich went away, and he reached (the place) where the plough was, and he caught the stilts in his hands and there he stood.

And his master came where he was, and his master said to him.

"Why art thou not making the red land?" And Mac-a-Rusgaich said, "It is not my bargain to make a thraive, but to hold the plough; and thou seest that I am not letting her go away."

And his master said, "Adversity and calamities be upon thee!"

And Mac-a-Rusgaich said, "Adversity and calamities be on thyself, old carle! Art thou taking the rue of the bargain that thou madest?"

"Oh! I am not, I am not," said the old carle.

"But if thou wilt give me another reward for it, I will make a ploughing," said Mac-a-Rusgaich.

"Oh, I will give, I will give it!" said the carle; and they made a bargain about the thraive.

And there was a day, and the hard tenant asked Mac-a-Rusgaich to go to the mountain moor to look if he could see anything wrong, and Mac-a-Rusgaich went up to the mountain. And when he saw his own time he came home, and his master asked him,

"Was each thing right in the mountain?" and Mac-a-Rusgaich said,

"The mountain himself was all right."

And the hard tenant said, "That is not what I am asking; but were the neighbours' cattle on their own side?"

And Mac-a-Rusgaich said, "If they were they were, and if they were, not let-a-be. It is my bargain to herd the mountain, and I will keep the mountain where it is."

And the carle said, "Adversity and calamities be upon thee, thou boy!"

And he said, "Adversity and calamities be on thyself, old carle! Art thou taking the rue that thou hast made such a bargain?"

"I am not, I am not!" said the dour tenant; "I will give thee another reward for herding the cattle."

And Mac-a-Rusgaich said, "If I get another reward, I will take in hand if I see the neighbours' cattle on thy ground that I will turn them back, and if I see thy cattle on the neighbours' ground I will turn them back to thine own ground; but though some of them should be lost, I will not take in hand to find them; but if thou askest me to go to seek them, I will go, and if I get them I will bring them home."

And the dour tenant had for it but to agree with Mac-a-Rusgaich, and to give Mac-a-Rusgaich another reward for herding his cattle.

Next day the carle himself went to the hill, and he could not see his heifers; he sought for them, but could not find them. He went home, and be said to Mac-a-Rusgaich,

"Thou must go thyself to search for the heifers, Mac-a-Rusgaich, I could not find them this day; and go thou to search for them, and search for them until thou find them."

And Mac-a-Rusgaich said, "And where shall I go to seek them?"

The old carle said, "Go and search for them in the places where thou thinkest that they are; and search for them in places where thou dost not suppose them to be."

Mac-a-Rusgaich said, "Well, then, I will do that."

The old carte went into the house; and Mac-a-Rusgaich got a ladder, and set it up against the house; he went up upon the house, and he began at pulling the thatch off the house, and throwing it down. And before the carle came out again, the thatch was about to be all but a very little off the house, and the rafters bare; and Mac-a-Rusgaich was pulling the rest and throwing it down.

The old carle said, "Adversity and calamity be upon thee, boy; what made thee take the thatch off the louse in that way?"

Mac-a-Rusgaich said, "It is because that I am searching for the heifers in the thatch of the house."

The old carle said, "How art thou seeking the heifers in the thatch of the house, where thou art sure that they are not?"

Mac-a-Rusgaich said, "Because thou thyself saidst to me to search for them in places where I thought that they were; and also in places where I did not suppose them to be; and there is no place where I have less notion that they might be in than in the thatch of the house."

And the carle said, "Adversity and calamity be upon thee, lad."

Mac-a-Rusgaich said, "Adversity and calamity be upon thyself, old carle; art thou taking the rue that thou desiredst me to search for the heifers in places where I did not suppose them to be?"

"I am not, I am not," said the carle. "Go now and seek them in places where it is likely that they may be."

"I will do so," said Mac-a-Rusgaich; and Mac-a-Rusgaich went to seek the heifers, and he found them, and brought them home.

Then his master desired Mac-a-Rusgaich to go to put the thatch on the house, and to make the house as water-tight to keep out rain as he was able. Mac-a-Rusgaich did so, and they were pleasant for a while after that.

The dour tenant was going to a wedding, and he asked Mac-a-Rusgaich when the evening should come, to put a saddle on the horse, and to go to the house of the wedding to take him home; and he said to him –

"When it is near the twelfth hour, cast an ox eye on the side where I am, and I will know that it is near the time to go home."

"I will do that," said Mac-a-Rusgaich.

When the tenant went to the wedding, Mac-a-Rusgaich went to put the stots into the fang, and he took a knife and took their eyes out, and he put the eyes in his pocket: and when the night came, Mac-a-Rusgaich put the saddle on the horse, and he went to the wedding house to seek his master, and he reached the wedding house, and he went into the company, and he sat till it was near upon the twelfth hour.

And then he began at throwing the eye of a stot at the carle at the end of each while, and at last the old carle noticed him, and he said to him,

"What art thou doing?"

And Mac-a-Rusgaich said, "I am casting an ox-eye on the side that thou art, for that it is now near upon the twelfth hour."

And the old carle said, "Dost thou think thyself that thou hast gone to take the eyes out of the stots?"

And Mac-a-Rusgaich said, "It is not thinking it I am at all; I am sure of it. Thou didst ask me thyself to cast an ox eye the side thou mightest be when it was near upon the twelfth hour, and how could I do that unless I should have taken the eyes out of the stots?"

And the tenant said, "Adversity and calamities be upon thee, thou boy."

And Mac-a-Rusgaich said, "Adversity and calamities on thyself, old carle! Art thou taking the rue that thou didst ask me to do it?

"I am not, I am not!" said the carle; and they went home together, and there was no more about it that night.

And the end of a day or two after, his master asked Mac-a-Rusgaich to go up to the gates at the top and make a sheep footpath.

"I will do that," said Mac-a-Rusgaich; and he went, and he put the sheep into the fang, and he cut their feet off, and he made a stair with the sheeps' legs, and he went back where his master was, and his master said to him,

"Didst thou that?"

And Mac-a-Rusgaich said, "I did. Thou mayest go thyself and see."

And the master went to see the sheep footpath that Mac-a-Rusgaich had made, and when he arrived and saw the sheeps' legs in the path, he went into a rage, and he said, "Adversity and calamities be upon thee, boy; what made thee cut the legs off the sheep?"

And Mac-a-Rusgaich said, "Didst thou not ask me thyself to make a sheep footpath; and how should I make a sheep footpath unless I should cut the legs off the sheep? See! Art thou taking the rue that thou didst ask me to do it, old carle?"

"I am not, I am not!" said his master.

"What have I to do again?" said Mac-a-Rusgaich.

"It is," said his master, "to clean and to wash the horses and the stable, both without and within."

And Mac-a-Rusgaich went and he cleaned out the stable, and he washed the walls on the outside, and he washed the stable on the inside; he washed the horses, and he killed them, and he took their insides out of them, and he washed their insides, and he went where his master was, and he asked him what he was to do again; and his master said to him to put the horses in what concerned them (harness) in the plough, and to take a while at ploughing.

Mac-a-Rusgaich said, "The horses won't answer me."

"What ails them?" said his master.

"They won't walk for me," said Mac-a-Rusgaich.

"Go and try them," said his master.

And Mac-a-Rusgaich went where the horses were, and he put a morsel of one of them into his mouth, and he went back where his master was, and he said, "They have but a bad taste."

"What art thou saying?" said his master.

The master went where his horses were, and when he saw them, and the inside taken out of them, and washed and cleaned, he said, "What is the reason of this?"

"It is," said Mac-a-Rusgaich, "that thou thyself didst ask me to clean and to wash both the horses and the stable both without and within, and I did that. Art thou taking the rue?" said Mac-a-Rusgaich.

"I had rather that I had never seen thee," said the master.

"Well, then," said Mac-a-Rusgaich, "thou must give me three wages, or else a thong of thy skin shall be taken from the back of thy head down to thy heel."

The dour tenant said that he had rather the thong to be taken out of his skin, from the back of his head to his heel, than give the money to a filthy clown like Mac-a-Rusgaich.

And according to law the dour tenant was tied, and a broad thong taken from the back of his head down his back. And he cried out that he had rather give even the money away than that the thong should be cut any longer; and he paid the money, and he was forced to be a while under the leeches, and he was a dour man no longer.

After that Mac-a-Rusgaich was set to be a servant to a giant that was bad to his servants.

Mac-a-Rusgaich reached the giant, and he said, "Thy servant is come."

The giant said, "If thou be servant to me, thou must keep even work with me, or else I will break thy bones as fine as meal."

Said Mac-a-Rusgaich, "What if I beat thee?"

"If thou beatest me," said the giant, "thou shalt have like wages."

"What are we going to do, then?" said Mac-a-Rusgaich.

"It is (this)," said the giant; "we will go to bring home faggots."

And they went and they reached the wood, and the giant began to gather every root that was thicker than the rest, and Mac-a-Rusgaich began to gather every top that was slenderer than the others.

The giant looked and he said, "What art thou doing so?"

And Mac-a-Rusgaich said, "I am for that we should take the whole wood with us instead of leaving a part of it useless behind us."

Said the giant, "We are long enough at this work; we will take home these burdens, but we will get other work again."

The next work they went to was to cut a swathe; and the giant asked Mac-a-Rusgaich to go first. Mac-a-Rusgaich would mow the swathe, and he began and he went round about short on the inner side, and the giant had to go a longer round on the outside of him.

"What art thou doing so?" said the giant.

"I," said Mac-a-Rusgaich, "am for that we should mow the park at one cut instead of turning back every time we cut the swathe, and we shall have no time lost at all."

The giant saw that his cut would be much longer than the cut of Mac-a-Rusgaich, and he said, "We are long enough at this work, we will go to another work. We will go and we will thresh the corn."

And they went to thresh the corn, and they got the flails, and they began to work. And when the giant would strike the sheaf, he would make it spring over the baulk (rafter), and when Mac-a-Rusgaich would strike it, it would lie down on the floor.

He would strike, and Mac-a-Rusgaich would say to the giant,

"Thou art not half hitting it. Wilt thou not make it crouch as I am doing?"

But the stronger the giant struck, the higher leaped the sheaf, and Mac-a-Rusgaich was laughing at him; and the giant said,

"We are long enough at this work; I will try thee in another way. We will go and try which of us can cast a stone strongest in the face of a crag that is beyond the fall."

"I am willing," said Mac-a-Rusgaich; and the giant went and he gathered the hardest stones he could find. And Mac-a-Rusgaich went and he got clay, and he rolled it into little round balls, and they went to the side of the fall.

The giant threw a stone at the face of the crag, and the stone went in splinters, and he said to Mac-a-Rusgaich, "Do that, boy."

Mac-a-Rusgaich threw a *dudan*, lump of the clay, and it stuck in the face of the crag, and he said to the giant, "Do that, old carl."

And the giant would throw as strongly as he could, but the more pith the giant would send with the stone he would throw, the smaller it would break. And Mac-a-Rusgaich would throw another little ball of the clay, and he would say,

"Thou art not half throwing it. Wilt thou not make the stone stick in the crag as I am doing?"

And the giant said, "We are long enough at this work; we will go and take our dinner, and then we will see which of us can best throw the stone of force (putting stone)."

"I am willing," said Mac-a-Rusgaich, and they went home.

They began at their dinner, and the giant said to Mac-a-Rusgaich, "Unless thou eatest of bread and cheese as much as I eat, a thong shall be taken out of thy skin, from the back of thy head to thy heel."

"Make seven of it," said Mac-a-Rusgaich, "on covenant that seven thongs shall be taken out of thy skin, from the back of thy head to thy heel, unless thou eatest as much as I eat."

"Try thee, then," said the giant.

"Stop then till I get a drink," said Mac-a-Rusgaich, and he went out to get a drink, and he got a leathern bag, and he put the bag between his shirt and his skin, and he went in where the giant was, and he said to the giant, "Try thee now."

The two began to eat the bread and the cheese, and Mac-a-Rusgaich was putting the bread and the cheese into the bag that he had in under his shirt, but at last the giant said,

"It is better to cease than burst."

"It is better even to burst than to leave good meat," said Mac-a-Rusgaich.

"I will cease," said the giant.

"The seven thongs shall be taken from the back of thy head to thy heel," said Mac-a-Rusgaich.

"I will try thee yet," said the giant.

"Thou hast thy two choices," said Mac-a-Rusgaich.

The giant got curds and cream, and he filled a cup for himself and another cup for Mac-a-Rusgaich.

"Let's try who of us is best now," said the giant.

"It's not long till that is seen," said Mac-a-Rusgaich. "Let's try who can soonest drink what is in the cup."

And Mac-a-Rusgaich drank his fill, and he put the rest in the bag, and he was done before the giant.

And he said to the giant, "Thou art behind."

The giant looked at him, and he said, "Ceasing is better than bursting."

"Better is bursting itself than to leave good meat," said Mac-a-Rusgaich.

We will go out and try which of us can throw the stone of force the furthest, before we do more," said the giant.

"I am willing," said Mac-a-Rusgaich. And they went out where the stone was, but the giant was so full that he could not stoop to lift it.

"Lift that stone and throw it," said the giant.

"The honour of beginning the beginning is to be thine own," said Mac-a-Rusgaich.

The giant tried to lift the stone, but he could not stoop. Mac-a-Rusgaich tried to stoop, and he said,

"Such a belly as this shall not be hindering me," and he drew a knife from a sheath that was at his side, and he put the knife in the bag that was in front of him, and he let out all that was within, and he said, "There is more room without than within," and he lifted the stone and threw it, and he said to the giant, "Do that."

"Canst thou not throw it further than that?" said the giant.

"Thou hast not thrown it as far as that same," said Mac-a-Rusgaich.

"Over here thy knife!" said the giant.

Mac-a-Rusgaich reached his knife to the giant. The giant took the knife, and he stabbed the knife into his belly, and he let out the meat; and the giant fell to earth, and Mac-a-Rusgaich laughed at him, and the giant found death.

Mac-a-Rusgaich went in to the giant's house, and he got his gold and silver, then he was rich, and then he went home fully pleased.

Fearachur Leigh

NOW FARQUHAR WAS ONE TIME a drover in the Reay country, and he went from Glen Gollich to England, to sell cattle; and the staff that he had in his hand was hazel (caltuinn). One day a doctor met him. "What's that," said he, "that ye have got in y'r hand?" "It is a staff of hazel." "And where did ye cut that?" "In Glen Gollig: north, in Lord Reay's country." "Do ye mind the place and the tree?" "That do I." "Could ye get the tree?" "Easy." "Well, I will give ye gold more than ye can lift, if ye will go back there and bring me a wand of that hazel tree; and take this bottle and bring me something more, and I will give you as much gold again. Watch at the hole at the foot, and put the bottle to it; let the six serpents go that come out first, and put the seventh one into the bottle, and tell no man, but come back straight with it here."

So Farquhar went back to the hazel glen, and when he had cut some boughs off the tree he looked about for the hole that the doctor had spoken of. And what should come out but six serpents, brown and barred like adders. These he let go, and clapped the bottle to the hole's mouth, to see would any more come out. By and by a white snake came rolling through. Farquhar had him in the bottle in a minute, tied him down, and hurried back to England with him.

The doctor gave him siller enough to buy the Reay country, but asked him to stay and help him with the white snake. They lit a fire with the hazel sticks, and put the snake into a pot to boil. The doctor bid Farquhar watch it, and not let any one touch it, and not to let the steam escape, "for fear," he said, "folk might know what they were at."

He wrapped up paper round the pot lid, but he had not made all straight when the water began to boil, and the steam began to come out at one place.

Well, Farquhar saw this, and thought he would push the paper down round the thing; so he put his finger to the bit, and then his finger into his mouth, for it was wet with the bree.

Lo! he knew everything, and the eyes of his mind were opened. "I will keep it quiet though," said he to himself.

Presently the doctor came back, and took the pot from the fire. He lifted the lid, and, dipping his finger in the steam drops, he sucked it; but the virtue had gone out of it, and it was no more than water to him.

"Who has done this!" he cried, and he saw in Farquhar's face that it was he. "Since you have taken the bree of it, take the flesh too," he said in a rage, and threw the pot at him – (ma dh' ol thu 'n sugh ith an fheoil). Now Farquhar had become allwise, and he set up as a doctor, and there was no secret bid from him, and nothing that he could not cure.

He went from place to place and healed men, and so they called him Farquhar Leigheach (the healer). Now he heard that the king was sick, and he went to the city of the king to know what would ail him. "It was his knee," said all the folk, "and he has many doctors, and pays them all greatly; and whiles they can give him relief, but not for long, and then it is worse than ever with him, and you may hear him roar and cry with the pain that is in his knee, in the bones of it." One day Farquhar walked up and down before the king's house. And he cried –

"An daol dubh ris a chnamh gheal." (The black beetle to the white bone.)

And the people looked at him, and said that the strange man from the Reay country was through-other.

The next day Farquhar stood at the gate and cried, "The black beetle to the white bone!" and the king sent to know who it was that cried outside, and what was his business. The man, they said, was a stranger, and men called him the Physician. So the king, who was wild with pain, called him in; and Farquhar stood before the king, and aye, "The black beetle to the white bone!" said he. And so it was proved. The doctors, to keep the king ill, and get their money, put at whiles a black beetle into the wound in the knee, and the beast was eating the bone and his flesh, and made him cry day and night. Then the doctors took it out again, for fear he should die; and when he was better they put it back again. This Farquhar knew by the serpent's wisdom that he had, when he laid his finger under his teeth; and the king was cured, and had all his doctors hung.

Then the king said that he would give Farquhar lands or gold, or whatever he asked. Then Farquhar asked to have the king's daughter, and all the isles that the sea runs round, from point of Storr to Stromness in the Orkneys; so the king gave him a grant of all the isles. But Farquhar the physician never came to be Farquhar the king, for he had an ill-wisher that poisoned him, and he died.

The Fair Gruagach, Son of the King of Eirinn

THE FAIR CHIEF, SON OF THE KING OF EIRINN, went away with his great company to hold court, and keep company with him. A woman met him, whom they called the Dame of the Fine Green Kirtle; she asked him to sit a while to play at the cards; and they sat to play the cards, and the Fair Chief drove the game against the Dame of the Fine Green Kirtle.

"Ask the fruit of the game," said the Wife of the Fine Green Kirtle.

"I think that thou hast not got a fruit; I know not of it," said the Fair Chief, son of the King of Eirinn.

"On the morrow be thou here, and I will meet thee," said the Dame of the Fine green Kirtle.

"I will be (here)," said the Fair Chief.

On the morrow he met her, and they began at the cards, and she won the game.

Ask the fruit of the game," said the Fair Chief.

"I," said the Dame of the Fine Green Kirtle, "am laying thee under spells, and under crosses, under holy herdsmen of quiet travelling, wandering women, the little calf, most feeble and powerless, to take thy head and thine ear and thy wearing of life from off thee, if thou takest rest by night or day; where thou takest thy breakfast that thou take not thy dinner, and where thou takest thy dinner that thou take not thy supper, in whatsoever place thou be, until thou findest out in what place I may be under the four brown quarters of the world."

She took a napkin from her pocket, and she shook it, and there was no knowing what side she had taken, or whence she came.

He went home heavily-minded, black sorrowfully; he put his elbow on the board, and his hand under his cheek, and he let out a sigh.

"What is it that ails thee, son?" said the king of Eirinn; "Is it under spells that thou art? But notice them not; I will raise thy spells off thee. I have a smithy on shore, and ships on sea; so long as gold or silver lasts me, stock or dwelling, I will set it to thy losing till I raise these spells off thee."

"Thou shalt not set them," said he; "and, father, thou art high-minded. Thou wouldst set that away from thyself, and thou wilt lose all that might be there. Thou wilt not raise the spells; thy kingdom will go to want and to poverty, and that will not raise the spells; and thou wilt lose thy lot of men; but keep thou thy lot of Men by thyself, and if I go I shall but lose myself."

So it was in the morning of the morrow's day he went away without dog, without man, without calf, without child.

He was going, and going, and journeying; there was blackening on his soles, and holes in his shoes; the black clouds of night coming, and the bright, quiet clouds of the day going away, and without his finding a place of staying, or rest for him. He spent a week from end to end without seeing house or castle, or any one thing. He was grown sick; sleepless, restless, meatless, drinkless, walking all the week. He gave a glance from him, and what should he see but a castle. He took towards it, and round about it, and there was not so much as an auger hole in the house. His "dudam" and his "dadam" fell with trouble and wandering, and he turned back, heavily-minded, black sorrowfully. He was taking up before him, and what should he hear behind him but a shout.

"Fair Chief, son of the king of Eirinn, return: there is the feast of a day and year awaiting thee; the meat thou thinkest not (of), and the drink thou thinkest not of; the meat thou thinkest on, and the drink thou thinkest on," and he returned.

There was a door for every day in the year in the house; and there was a window for every day in the year in it. It was a great marvel for him, the house that he himself had gone round about, and without so much as an auger hole in it, that door and window should be in it for every day in the year when he came back.

He took in to it. Meat was set in its place for using, drink in its place of drinking, music in its place for hearing, and they were plying the feast and the company with solace and pleasure of mind, himself and the fine damsel that cried after him in the palace.

A bed was made for him in the castle, with pillows, with a hollow in the middle; warm water was put on his feet, and he went to lie down. When he rose up in the morning, the board was set over with each meat that was best; and he was thus for a time without his feeling the time pass by.

She stood in the door. "Fair Chief, son of the king of Eirinn, in what state dost thou find thyself, or how art thou?" said the damsel of the castle.

"I am well," said he.

"Dost thou know at what time thou camest here?" said she.

"I think I shall complete a week, if I be here this day," said he.

"A quarter is just out today," said she. "Thy meat, thy drink, or thy bed will not grow a bit the worse than they are till it pleases thyself to return home."

There he was by himself till he was thinking that he had a month out. At this time she stood in the door.

"Yes! Fair Chief, how dost thou find thyself this day?" said she.

"Right well," said he.

"In what mind dost thou find thyself?" said she.

"I will tell thee that," said he; "if my two hands could reach yonder peaked hill, that I would set it on yon other bluff hill."

"Dost thou know at what time thou camest hither?" said she.

"I am thinking that I have completed a month here," said he.

"The end of the two years is out just this day," said she.

"I will not believe that the man ever came on the surface of the world that would gain victory of myself in strength or lightness," said he.

"Thou art silly," said she; "there is a little band here which they call An Fhinn, the Feen, and they will get victory of thee. The man never came of whom they would not get victory."

"Morsel I will not eat, draught I will not drink, sleep there will not come on my eye, till I reach where they are, and I know who they are," said he.

"Fair Chief be not so silly, and let that lightness pass from thy head; stay as thou art, for I know thou wilt return," said she.

"I will not make stay by night or day, until I reach them," said he.

"The day is soft and misty," said she, "and thou art setting it before thee that thou wilt go. The Feen are in such a place, and they have a net fishing trout. Thou shalt go over where they are. Thou wilt see the Feen on one side, and Fionn alone on the other side. Thou shalt go where he is, and thou shalt bless him. Fionn will bless thee in the same way; thou shalt ask service from him; he will say that he has no service for thee, now that the Feen are strong enough, and he will not put a man out. He will say, 'What name is upon thee?' Thou shalt answer, the name thou didst never hide, An Gruagach ban Mac Righ Eireann. Fionn will say then, 'Though I should not want of a man, why should I not give service to the son of thy father.' Be not high minded amongst the Feeantan. Come now, and thou shalt have a napkin that is here, and thou shalt say to Fionn, whether thou be alive or dead to put thee in it when comes its need."

He went away, and he reached the (place) where the Feen were; he saw them there fishing trout, the rest on the one side, and Fionn on the other side alone. He went where Fionn was, and he blessed him. Fionn blessed him in words that were no worse.

"I heard that there were such men, and I came to you to seek hire from you," said the Fair Chief.

"Well, then, I have no need of a man at the time," said Fionn. "What name is upon thee?"

"My name I never hid. The Gruagach Ban, son of the king of Eireann," said he.

"Bad! bad! for all the ill luck that befel me! where I got my nourishment young, and my dwelling for my old age; who should get service unless thy father's son should get it; but be not high minded amongst the Feentan," said Fionn. "Come hither and catch the end of the net, and drag it along with me."

He began dragging the net with the Feen. He cast an eye above him, and what should he see but a deer.

"Were it not better for the like of you, such swift, strong, light, young men to be hunting yonder deer, than to be fishing any one pert trout that is here, and that a morsel of fish or a mouthful of juice will not satisfy you rather than yonder creature up above you a morsel of whose flesh, and a mouthful of whose broth will suffice you," said the Fair Chief, son of the king of Eirinn.

"If yonder beast is good, we are seven times tired of him," said Fionn, "and we know him well enough."

Well, I heard myself that there was one man of you called Luathas (Swiftness) that could catch the swift March wind, and the swift March wind could not catch him," said the Fair Chief.

"Since it is thy first request, we will send to seek him," said Fionn.

He was sent for, and Caoilte came. The Fair Chief shouted to him.

"There is the matter I have for thee," said the Gruagach, "to run the deer that I saw yonder above."

"The Fair Chief came amongst our company this day, and his advice may be taken the first day. He gave a glance from him, and he saw a deer standing above us; he said it was better for our like of swift, strong, light men to be hunting the deer, than to be fishing any one pert trout that is here; and thou Caoilte go and chase the deer."

"Well, then, many is the day that I have given to chasing him, and it is little I have for it but my grief that I never got a hold of him," said Caoilte.

Caoilte went away, and he took to speed.

"How will Caoilte be when he is at his full speed?" said the Fair Chief.

"There will be three heads on Caoilte when he is at his full speed," said Fionn.

"And how many heads will there be on the deer?" said the Chief.

"There will be seven heads on him when he is at full swiftness," said Fionn.

"What distance has he before he reaches the end of his journey?" said the Chief.

"It is seven glens and seven hills, and seven summer seats," said Fionn; "he has that to make before he reaches a place of rest."

"Let us take a hand at dragging the net," said the Chief.

The Fair Chief gave a glance from him, and he said to Fionn, "Een, son of Cumhail, put thy finger under thy knowledge tooth, to see what distance Caoilte is from the deer."

Fionn put his finger under his knowledge tooth. "There are two heads on Caoilte, and on the deer there are but two heads yet," said Fionn.

"How much distance have they put past?" said the Fair Chief.

"Two glens and two hills; they have five unpassed still," said Fionn.

"Let us take a hand at fishing the trout," said the Fair Chief.

When they had been working a while, the Fair Chief gave a glance from him. "Fionn, son of Cumal," said he, "put thy finger under thy knowledge tooth to see what distance Caoilte is from the deer."

"There are three heads on Caoilte, and four heads on the deer, and Caoilte is at full speed," said Fionn.

"How many glens and hills and summer seats are before them?" said the Chief.

"There are four behind them, and three before them," said Fionn.

"Let us take a hand at fishing the trout," said the Fair Chief.

They took a while at fishing the trout.

"Fionn, son of Cumal," said the Chief, "what distance is still before the deer before he reaches the end of his journey?"

"One glen and one hill, and one summer seat," said Fionn.

He threw the net from him, and he took to speed. He would catch the swift March wind, and the swift March wind could not catch him, till he caught Caoilte; he took past him, and he left his blessing with him. Going over by the ford of Sruth Ruadh, the deer gave a spring – the Fair Chief gave the next spring, and he caught the deer by the hinder shank, and the deer gave a roar, and the Carlin cried –

"Who seized the beast of my love?"

"It is I," said the Fair Chief, "the son of the king of Eirinn."

"Oh, Gruagach ban, son of the king of Eirinn, let him go," said the Carlin.

"I will not let (him go); he is my own beast now," said the Gruagach.

"Give me the full of my fist of his bristles, or a handful of his food, or a mouthful of his broth, or a morsel of his flesh," said the Carlin.

"Any one share thou gettest not," said he.

"The Feen are coming," said she, "and Fionn at their head, and there shall not be one of them that I do not bind back to back."

"Do that," said he, "but I am going away."

He went away, and he took the deer with him, and he was taking on before him till the Feen met him.

"Een, son of Cumal, keep that," said he, as he left the deer with Fionn.

Fionn, son of Cumal, sat at the deer, and the Fair Chief went away. He reached the smithy of the seven and twenty smiths. He took out three iron hoops out of it for every man that was in the Feen (Fhinn); he took with him a hand hammer, and he put three hoops about the head of every man that was in the Feen, and he tightened them with the hammer.

The Carlin came out, and let out a great screech.

"Een, son of Cumal, let hither to me the creature of my love."

The highest hoop that was on the Feeantan burst with the screech. She came out the second time, and she let out the next yell, and the second hoop burst. (Was not the Carlin terrible!) She went home, and she was not long within when she came the third time, and she let out the third yell, and the third hoop burst. She went and she betook herself to a wood; she twisted a withy from the wood; she took it with her; she went over, and she bound every man of the Feeantaichean back to back, but Fionn.

The Fair Chief laid his hand on the deer, and he flayed it. He took out the gaorr, and every bit of the inside; he cut a turf, and he buried them under the earth. He set a caldron in order, and be put the deer in the caldron, and fire at it to cook it.

"Een, son of Cumal," said the fair Chief, "whether wouldst thou rather go to fight the Carlin, or stay to boil the caldron?"

"Well, then," said Fionn, "the caldron is hard enough to boil. If there be a morsel of the flesh uncooked, the deer will get up as he was before; and if a drop of the broth goes into the fire, he will arise as he was before. I would rather stay and boil the caldron."

The Carlin came. "Een, son of Cumal," said she, "give me my fist full of bristles, or a squeeze of my fist of gaorr, or else a morsel of his flesh, or else a gulp of the broth."

"I myself did not do a thing about it, and with that I have no order to give it away," said Fionn.

Here then the Fair Chief and the Carlin began at each other; they would make a bog on the rock and a rock on the bog. In the place where the least they would sink, they would sink to the knees; in the place where the most they would sink, they would sink to the eyes.

"Art thou satisfied with the sport, Een, son of Cumal?" said the Fair Chief.

"It is long since I was satiated with that," said Fionn.

"There will be a chance to return it now," said the Chief.

He seized the Carlin, and he struck her a blow of his foot in the crook of the hough, and he felled her.

"Een, son of Cumal, shall I take her head off?" said the Chief.

"I don't know," said Fionn.

"Een, son of Cumal," said she, "I am laying thee under crosses, and under spells, and under holy herdsman of quiet travelling, wandering woman, the little calf, most powerless, most uncouth, to take thy head and thine ear, and thy life's wearing off, unless thou be as a husband, three hours before the day comes, with the wife of the Tree Lion."

"I," said the Fair Chief, "am laying thee under crosses and under spells, under holy herdsman of quiet travelling, wandering woman, the little calf most powerless and most uncouth, to take thy head and thine ear, and thy life's wearing off, unless thou be with a foot on either side of the ford of Struth Ruadh, and every drop of the water flowing through thee."

He arose, and he let her stand up.

"Raise thy spells from off me, and I will raise them from off him," said the Carlin. "Neither will I lift nor lay down, but so; howsoever we may be, thou comest not."

The fair Chief went and he took off the caldron; he seized a fork and a knife, and he put the fork into the deer; he seized the knife and he cut a morsel out of it, and he ate it. He caught a turf, and cut it, and he laid that on the mouth of the caldron.

"Een, son of Cumal, it is time for us to be going," said he; "art thou good at horsemanship?"

"I could hit upon it," said Fionn.

He caught hold of a rod, and he gave it to Fionn. "Strike that on me," said he.

Fionn struck the rod on him and made him a brown ambler.

"Now, get on top of me," said the Chief. Fionn got on him.

"Be pretty watchful; I am at thee."

He gave that spring and he went past nine ridges, and Fionn stood on him. "She" gave the next spring and "she" went past nine other ridges and Fionn stood fast on "her." He took to speed. He would catch the swift March wind, and the swift March wind could not catch him.

"There is a little town down here," said the ambler, "and go down and take with thee three stoups of wine and three wheaten loaves, and thou shalt give me a stoup of wine and a wheaten loaf, and thou shalt comb me against the hair, and with the hair."

Fionn got that and they reached the wall of the Tree Lion.

"Come on the ground, Een, son of Cumal, and give me a stoup of wine and a wheaten loaf."

Fionn came down and he gave him a stoup of wine and a wheaten loaf.

"Comb me now against the hair, and comb me with the hair."

He did that.

"Take care of thyself," said the ambler.

Then "she" leaped, and she put a third of the wall below her, and there were two-thirds above, and she returned.

"Give me another stoup of wine and another wheaten loaf, and comb me against the hair, and comb me with the hair."

He did that.

"Take care of thyself, for I am for thee now," said the ambler.

She took the second spring, and she put two-thirds of the wall below her, and there was a third over her head, and she returned.

"Give me another stoup of wine and a wheaten loaf, and comb me against the hair, and with the hair."

He did that.

"Take care of thyself, for I am for thee now," said she.

She took a spring, and she was on the top of the wall.

"The matter is well before thee, Een," said the ambler, "the Tree Lion is from home."

He went home. My Chief, and all hail! were before him: meat and drink were set before him; he rested that night, and he was with the wife of the Tree Lion three hours before the day.

So early as his eye saw the day, earlier than that he arose, and he reached the ambler, the Gruagach Ban, and they went away.

Said the Fair Chief, "The Tree Lion is from home; anything that passed she will not hide; he is coming after us, and he will not remember his book of witchcraft; and since he does not remember the book of witchcraft, it will go with me against him; but if he should remember the book, the people of the world could not withstand him. He has every draochd magic, and he will spring as a bull when be comes, and I will spring as a bull before him, and the first blow I give him, I will lay his head on his side, and I will make him roar. Then he will spring as an aiseal (ass), and I will spring as an ass before him, and the first thrust I give him I will take a mouthful out of him, between flesh and hide as it may be. Then he will spring as a hawk in the heavens; I will spring as a hawk in the wood, and the first stroke I give him, I will take his heart and his liver out. I will come down afterwards, and thou shalt seize that napkin yonder, and thou shalt put me in the napkin, and thou shalt cut a turf, and thou shalt put the napkin under the earth, and thou shalt stand upon it. Then the wife of the Tree Lion will come, and thou standing on the top of the turf, and I under thy feet; and she with the book of witchcraft on her back in a hay band, and she will say – Een, son of Cumal, man that never told a lie, tell me who of the people of the world killed my comrade, and thou shalt say I know not above the earth who killed thy comrade. She will go away and take to speed with her weeping cry."

When they were on forward a short distance, whom saw they coming but the Tree Lion.

He became a bull; the Fair chief became a bull before him, and the first blow he struck him he laid his head on his side, and the Tree Lion gave out a roar. Then he sprung as an ass, the Fair Chief sprung as an ass before him, and at the first rush he gave towards him he took a mouthful between flesh and skin. The Tree Lion then sprang as a hawk in the heavens, the Fair Chief sprang as a hawk in the wood, and he took the heart and liver out of him. The Fair Chief fell down afterwards, Fionn seized him and he put him into the napkin, and he cut a turf, and he put the napkin under the earth, and the turf upon it, and he stood on the turf. The wife of the Tree Lion came, and the book of witchcraft was on her back in a hay band.

"Een, son of Cumal, man that never told a lie, who killed my comrade?"

"I know not above the earth, who killed thy comrade," said Fionn.

And she went away in her weeping cry, and she betook herself to distance.

He caught hold of the Fair Chief and he lifted him with him, and he reached the castle in which was the dame of the Fine Green Kirtle. He reached her that into her hand. She went down with it, and she was not long down when she came up where he was.

"Een, son of Cumal, the Gruagach Ban, son of the king of Eirinn, is asking for thee."

"That is the news I like best of all I ever heard, that the Fair Chief is asking for me," said Fionn.

She set meat and drink before them, and they would not eat a morsel nor drink a drop till they should eat their share of the deer with the rest at Sruth Ruaidh.

They reached (the place) where the Een were bound, and they loosed every single one of them, and they were hungry enough. The Fair Chief set the deer before them, and they left of the deer thrice as much as they ate.

"I should go to tell my tale," said the Fair Chief. He reached the carlin at the ford of Sruth Ruaidh, and he began to tell the tale how it befel him. Every tale he would tell her she would begin to rise; every time she would begin to rise he would seize her, and he would crush her bones, and he would break them until he told his lot of tales to her.

When he had told them he returned, and he reached the Een back again.

Fionn went with him to the Castle of the Dame of the Fine Green Kirtle.

"Blessing be with thee, Een, son of Cumal," said the Fair Chief, son of the king of Eirinn, "I have found all I sought – a sight of each matter and of each thing, and now I will be returning home to the palace of my own father."

"It is thus thou art about to leave me, after each thing I have done for thee; thou wilt take another one, and I shall be left alone."

"Is that what thou sayest?" said he. "If I thought that might be done, I never saw of married women or maidens that I would take rather than thee, but I will not make wedding or marrying here with thee, but thou shalt do to the palace of my father with me."

They went to the palace of his father, himself and the Dame of the Fine Green Kirtle, and Fionn. A churchman was got, and the Fair Chief and the dame of the Fine Green Kirtle married. A hearty, jolly, joyful wedding was made for them; music was raised and lament laid down; meat was set in the place for using, and drink in the place for drinking, and music in the place for hearing, and they were plying the feast and the company until that wedding was kept up for a day and a year, with solace and pleasure of mind.

The Rider of Grianaig, and Iain the Soldier's Son

THE KNIGHT OF GRIANAIG had three daughters, such that their like were not to be found or to be seen in any place. There came a beast from the ocean and she took them with her, and there was no knowledge what way they had taken, nor where they might be sought.

There was a soldier in the town, and he had three sons, and at the time of Christmas they were playing at shinny, and the youngest said that they should go and that they should drive a hale on the lawn of the knight of Grianaig. The rest said that they should not go; that the knight would not be pleased; that that would be bringing the loss of his children to his mind, and laying sorrow upon him. "Let that be as it pleases," said Iain, the youngest son, "but we will go there and we will drive a hale; I am careless of the knight of Grianaig, let him be well pleased or angry."

They went to play shinny, and Iain won three hales from his brethren. The knight put his head out of a window, and he saw them playing at shinny, and he took great wrath that anyone had the heart to play shinny on his lawn – a thing that was bringing the loss of his children to his mind, and putting contempt upon him. Said he to his wife, "Who is so impudent as to be playing shinny on my ground, and bringing the loss of my children to my mind? Let them be brought here in an instant that punishment may be done upon them." The three lads were brought to the presence of the knight, and they were fine lads.

"What made you," said the knight, "go and play shinny upon my ground and bring the loss of my children to my mind? you must suffer pain for it."

"It is not thus it shall be," said Iain; "but since it befell us to come wrong upon thee, thou hadst best make us a dwelling of a ship, and we will go to seek thy daughters, and if they are under the leeward, or the windward, or under the four brown boundaries of the deep, we will find them out before there comes the end of a day and year, and we will bring them back to Grianaig."

"Though thou be the youngest, it is in thy head that the best counsel is, let that be made for you."

Wrights were got and a ship was made in seven days. They put in meat and drink as they might need for the journey. They gave her front to sea and her stern to land, and they went away, and in seven days they reached a white sandy strand, and when they went on shore there were six men and ten at work in the face of a rock blasting, with a foreman over them.

"What place is here?" said the skipper.

"Here is the place where are the children of the knight of Grianaig; they are to be married to three giants."

"What means are there to get where they are?"

"There are no means but to go up in this creel against the face of the rock."

The eldest son went into the creel, and when he was up at the half of the rock, there came a stumpy black raven, and he began upon him with his claws, and his wings till he almost left him blind and deaf. He had but to turn back.

The second one went into the creel, and when he was up half the way, there came the stumpy black raven, and he began upon him, and he had for it but to return back as did the other one.

At last Iain went into the creel. When he was up half the way there came the stumpy black raven, and he began upon him, and he belaboured him about the face.

"Up with me quickly!" said he, "before I be blinded here."

He was set up to the top of the rock. When he was up the raven came where he was, and he said to him:

"Wilt thou give me a quid of tobacco?"

"Thou high-priced rogue! little claim hast thou on me for giving that to thee."

"Never thou mind that, I will be a good friend to thee. Now thou shalt go to the house of the big giant, and thou wilt see the knight's daughter sewing, and her thimble wet with tears."

He went on before him till he reached the house of the giant. He went in. The knight's daughter was sewing.

"What brought thee here?" said she.

"What brought thyself into it that I might not come into it?"

"I was brought here in spite of me."

"I know that. Where is the giant?"

"He is in the hunting hill."

"What means to get him home?"

"To shake yonder battle-chain without, and there is no one in the leeward, or in the windward, or in the four brown boundaries of the deep, who will hold battle against him, but young Iain the soldier's son, from Albainn, and he is but sixteen years of age, and he is too young to go to battle against the giant."

"There is many a one in Albainn as strong as Iain the soldier's son, though the soldier were with him."

Out he went. He gave a haul at the chain, and he did not take a turn out of it, and he went on his knee. He rose up, he gave the next shake at the chain, and he broke a link in it. The giant heard it in the hunting hill.

"Aha!" said he, "who could move my battle-chain but young Iain the soldier's son from Albainn? And he is but sixteen years of age; he is too young yet."

The giant put the game on a withy, and home he came.

"Art thou young Iain the soldier's son, from Albainn?"

"Not I."

"Who art thou in the leeward, or in the windward, or in the four brown boundaries of the deep, that could move my battle-chain, but young Iain the soldier's son, from Albainn?"

"There is many a one in Albainn as strong as young Iain the soldier's son, though the soldier should be with him."

"I have got that in the prophesyings."

"Never thou mind what thou hast got in the prophesyings."

"In what way wouldst thou rather try thyself?"

"When I and my mother used to be falling out with each other, and I might wish to get my own will, it was in tight wrestling ties we used to try; and one time she used to get the better, and two times she used not."

They seized each other, and they had hard hugs, and the giant put Iain on his knee.

"I see," said Iain, "that thou art the stronger." "It is known that I am," said the giant.

They went before each other again. They were twisting and hauling each other. Iain struck a foot on the giant in the ankle, and he put him on the thews of his back under him on the ground. He wished that the raven were at him.

The stumpy black raven came, and he fell upon the giant about the face and about the ears with his claws and with his wings until he blinded him, and he deafened him.

"Hast thou got a nail of arms that will take the head off the monster?"

"I have not."

"Put thy hand under my right wing, and thou wilt find a small sharp knife which I have for gathering briar-buds, and take the head off him."

He put his hand under the raven's right wing and he found the knife, and he took the head off the giant.

"Now Iain, thou shalt go in where is the big daughter of the knight of Grianaig, and she will be asking thee to return and not to go farther; but do not thou give heed, but go on, and thou wilt reach the middle daughter; and thou shalt give me a quid of tobacco."

"I will give that to thee indeed; well hast thou earned it. Thou shalt have half of all I have."

"I will not. There's many a long day to Bealtain."

"The fortune will not let me be here till Bealtain."

"Thou hast knowledge of what has passed, but thou hast no knowledge of what is before thee; get warm water, clean thyself in it; thou wilt find a vessel of balsam above the door, rub it in thy skin, and go to bed by thyself and thou wilt be whole and wholesome tomorrow, and tomorrow thou shalt go on to the house of the next one."

He went in and he did as the raven asked him. He went to bed that night, and he was whole and wholesome in the morning when he arose.

"It is better for thee," said the knight's big daughter, "not to go further, and not to put thyself in more danger; there is plenty of gold and silver here, and we will take it with us and we will return."

"I will not do that," said he; "I will take (the road) on my front."

He went forwards till he came to the house where was the middle daughter of the knight of Grianaig. He went in and she was seated sewing, and she (was) weeping, and her thimble wet with her tears.

"What brought thee here?"

"What brought thyself into it that I might not come into it?"

"I was brought in spite of me."

"I have knowledge of that. What set thee weeping?"

"I have but one night till I must be married to the giant."

"Where is the giant?"

"He is in the hunting hill."

"What means to get him home?"

"To shake that battle-chain without at the side of the house, and he is not in the leeward nor in the windward, nor in the four brown boundaries of the deep, who is as much as can shake it, but young Iain the soldier's son, from Albainn, and he is too young yet, he is but sixteen years of age."

"There are men in Albainn as strong as young Iain the soldier's son, though the soldier should be with him."

He went out, and he gave a haul at the chain, and he came upon his two knees. He rose up and gave the next haul at it, and he broke three links in it.

The giant heard that in the hunting hill.

"Aha!" said he, and he put the game on a withy on his shoulder, and home he came.

"Who could move my battle-chain but young Iain the soldier's son from Albainn? And he is too young yet; he is but sixteen years of age."

"There are men in Albainn as strong as young Iain the soldier's son, though the soldier should be with him."

"We have got that in the prophesyings."

"I care not what is in your prophesyings."

"In what way wouldst thou rather try thyself?"

"In hard hugs of wrestling."

They seized each other and the giant put him on his two knees.

"Thine is my life," said Iain, "thou art stronger than I. Let's try another turn."

They tried each other again, and Iain struck his heel on the giant in the ankle, and he set him on the thews of his back on the ground.

"Raven!" said he, "a flapping of thine were good now."

The raven came, and he blinded and deafened the giant, giving it to him with his beak, and with his claws, and with his wings.

"Hast thou a nail of a weapon?"

"I have not."

"Put thy hand under my right wing, and thou wilt find there a small sharp knife that I have for gathering briar-buds, and take the head off him."

He put his hand under the root of the raven's right wing, and he found the knife, and he took the head off the giant.

"Now thou shalt go in and clean thyself with warm water, thou wilt find the vessel of balsam, thou shalt rub it upon thyself, thou shalt go to bed, and thou wilt be whole and wholesome tomorrow. This one will be certainly more cunning and more mouthing than was the one before, asking thee to return and not to go further; but give thou no heed to her. And thou shalt give me a quid of tobacco."

"I will give it indeed; thou art worthy of it."

He went in and he did as the raven asked him. When he got up on the morrow's morning he was whole and wholesome.

"Thou hadst better," said the knight's middle daughter, "return, and not put thyself in more danger; there is plenty of gold and of silver here."

"I will not do that; I will go forward."

He went forward till he came to the house in which was the little daughter of the knight; he went in and he saw her sewing, and her thimble wet with tears.

"What brought thee here?"

"What brought thyself into it that I might not come into it?"

"I was brought into it in spite of me."

"I know that."

"Art thou young Iain the soldier's son, from Albainn?"

"I am; what is the reason that thou art weeping?"

"I have but this night of delay without marrying the giant."

"Where is he?"

"He is in the hunting hill."

"What means to bring him home?"

"To shake that battle-chain without."

He went out, and he gave a shake at the chain and down he came on his hurdies.

He rose again, and he gave it the next shake, and he broke four links in it, and he made a great rattling noise. The giant heard that in the hunting hill; he put the withy of game on his shoulder.

"Who in the leeward, or in the windward, or in the four brown boundaries of the deep, could shake my battle-chain but young Iain the soldier's son, from Albainn? And if it be he, my two brothers are dead before this."

He came home in his might, making the earth tremble before him and behind him.

"Art thou young Iain the soldier's son?"

"Not I."

"Who art thou in the leeward, or in the windward, or in the four brown boundaries of the deep, that could shake my battle-chain but young Iain the soldier's son, from Albainn? and he is too young yet, he is but sixteen years of age."

"Is there not many a one in Albainn as strong as young Iain the soldier's son, though the soldier were with him?"

"It is not in our prophesyings."

"I care not what is in your prophesyings."

"In what way wouldst thou like thy trial?"

"Tight wrestling ties."

They seized each other and the giant set him on his haunches.

"Let me go; thine is my life."

They caught each other again; he struck his heel on the giant in the ankle, and he laid him on the shower top of his shoulder, and on the thews of his back on the ground.

"Stumpy black raven, if thou wert here now!"

No sooner said he the word than the raven came. He belaboured the giant about the face, and the eyes, and the ears, with his beak, and with his claws and with his wings.

"Hast thou a nail of a weapon?"

"I have not."

"Put thy hand under the root of my right wing and thou wilt find a small sharp knife that I have for gathering whortleberries, and take his head off."

He did that.

"Now," said the raven, "take rest as thou didst last night, and when thou returnest with the three daughters of the knight, to the cut (edge) of the rock, thou shalt go down first thyself, and they shall go down after thee; and thou shalt give me a quid of tobacco."

"I will give it; thou hast well deserved it; here it is for thee altogether."

"I will but take a quid; there is many a long day to Bealtain."

"The fortune will not let me be here till Bealtain."

Thou hast knowledge of what is behind thee, but thou hast no knowledge what is before thee."

On the morrow they set in order asses, and on their backs they put the gold and the silver that the giants had, and he himself and the three daughters of the knight reached the edge of the rock: when they reached the edge of the rock, for fear giddiness should come over any of the girls, he sent them down one after one in the creel. There were three caps of gold on them, made up finely with "daoimean" (diamond); caps that were made in the Roimh (Rome), and such that their like were not to be found in the universe. He kept up the cap that was on the youngest. He was waiting and waiting, and though he should be waiting still the creel would not come up to fetch him. The rest went on board, and away they went till they reached Grianaig.

He was left there, and without a way in his power to get out of the place. The raven came where he was.

"Thou didst not take my counsel?"

"I did not take it; if I had taken it I should not be as I am."

"There is no help for it, Iain. The one that will not take counsel will take combat. Thou shalt give me a quid of tobacco."

"I will give it."

"Thou shalt reach the giant's house, and thou shalt stay there this night."

"Wilt thou not stay with me thyself to keep off my dullness?"

"I will not stay; it is not suitable for me."

On the morrow came the raven where he was.

"Thou shalt now go to the giant's stable, and if thou art quick and active, there is a steed there, and sea or shore is all one to her, and that may take thee out of these straits."

They went together and they came to the stable, a stable of stone, dug into a rock, and a door of stone to it. The door was slamming without ceasing, backwards and forwards, from early day to night, and from night to day.

"Thou must now watch," said the raven, "and take a chance, and try if thou canst make out to go in when it is open, without its getting a hold of thee."

"Thou hadst best try first, since thou art best acquainted."

"It will be as well."

The raven gave a bob and a hop and in he went, but the door took a feather out of the root of his wing, and he screeched.

"Poor Iain, if thou couldst get in with as little pain as I, I would not complain."

Iain took a run back and a run forward, he took a spring to go in, the door caught him, and it took half his hurdies off. Iain cried out, and he fell cold dead on the floor of the stable. The raven lifted him, and he carried him on the points of his wings, out of the stable to the giant's house. He laid him on a board on his mouth and nose, he went out and he gathered plants, and he made ointments that he set upon him, and in ten days he was as well as ever he was.

He went out to take a walk and the raven went with him.

"Now, Iain, thou shalt take my counsel. Thou shalt not take wonder of any one thing that thou mayest see about the island, and thou shalt give me a quid of tobacco."

He was walking about the island, and going through a glen; he saw three full heroes stretched on their backs, a spear upon the breast of every man of them, and he in lasting sound sleep, and a bath of sweat.

"It seems to me that this is pitiable. What harm to lift the spears from off them?"

He went and he loosed the spears from off them. The heroes awoke, and they rose up.

"Witness fortune and men, that thou art young Iain the soldier's son, from Albainn, and it is as spells upon thee to go with us through the southern end of this island past the cave of the black fisherman."

He went away himself and the three full heroes. They saw a slender smoke (coming) out of a cave. They went to the cave. One of the heroes went in, and when he went in there was a hag there seated, and the tooth that was the least in her mouth would make a knitting pin in her lap, a staff in her hand, and a stirring stick for the embers. There was a turn of her nails about her elbows, and a twist of her hoary hair about her toes, and she was not joyous to look upon.

She seized upon a magic club, she struck him, and she made him a bare crag of stone. The others that were without were wondering why he was not returning.

"Go in," said Iain to another one, "and look what is keeping thy comrade."

He went in, and the carlin did to him as she did to the other. The third went in, and she did to him as she did to the rest. Iain went in last. There was a great red-skulled cat there, and she put a barrow full of red ashes about her fur so as to blind and deafen him. He struck the point of his foot on her and drove the brain out of her. He turned to the carlin.

"Don't, Iain! These men are under spells, and in order to put the spells off them thou must go to the island of big women and take a bottle of the living water out of it, and when thou rubbest it upon them the spells will go and they will come alive."

Iain turned back under black melancholy.

"Thou didst not take my counsel," said the raven, "and thou hast brought more trouble upon thyself. Thou shalt go to lie down this night, and when thou risest tomorrow thou shalt take with thee the steed, and shalt give her meat and drink. Sea or land is all one to her, and when thou reachest the island of big women sixteen stable lads will meet thee, and they will all be for giving food to the steed, and for putting her in for thee, but do not thou let them. Say that thou wilt thyself give her meat and drink. When thou leavest her in the stable, every one of the sixteen will put a turn in the key, but thou shalt put a turn against every turn that they put in it. Thou shalt give me a quid of tobacco."

"I will indeed."

He went to rest that night, and in the morning he set the steed in order, and he went away. He gave her front to sea and her back to shore, and she went in her might till they reached the island of big women. When he went on shore sixteen stable lads met him and every one of them asked to set her in and feed her.

"I myself will put her in, and I will take care of her; I will not give her to anyone."

He put her in, and when he came out every man put a turn in the key, and he put a turn against every turn that they put into it. The steed said to him that they would be offering him every sort of drink, but that he should not take any drink from them but whey and water. He went in and every sort of drink was being put round about there, and they were offering each kind to him, but he would not take a drop of any drink but whey and water. They were drinking and drinking, till they fell stretched about the board.

The steed asked him before she parted from him that he should take care and not sleep, and to take his chance for coming away. When they slept he came out from the chamber; and he heard the very sweetest music that ever was heard. He went on, and he heard in another place music much sweeter. He came to the side of a stair and he heard music sweeter and sweeter, and he fell asleep.

The steed broke out of the stable, and she came where he was, and she struck him a kick, and she awoke him.

"Thou didst not take my counsel," said she, "and there is no knowing now if thou canst get thy matter with thee, or if thou canst not get it."

He arose with sorrow; he seized upon a sword of light that was in a corner of the chamber, and be took out the sixteen beads. He reached the well, he filled a bottle and he returned. The steed met him, and be set her front to sea and her back to shore, and he returned to the other island. The raven met him.

"Thou shalt go and stable the steed, and thou shalt go to lie down this night; and tomorrow thou shalt go and bring the heroes alive, and thou shalt slay the carlin, and be not so foolish tomorrow as thou wert before now."

"Wilt thou not come with me tonight to drive off my dullness from me?"

"I will not come; it will not answer for me."

On the morning he reached the cave – "Failte dhuit, all hail to thee, Iain," said the carlin; "failte dhuit's, all hail to thee, but cha shlainte dhuit, not health to thee."

He shook the water on the men and they rose up alive, and he struck his palm on the carlin and scattered the brains out of her. They betook themselves out, and they went to the southern end of the island. They saw the black fisherman there working at his tricks. He drew his palm, and he struck him, and he scattered the brains out of him, and he took the heroes home to the southern end of the island. The raven came where he was.

"Now thou shalt go home, and thou shalt take with thee the steed to which sea and shore are alike. The three daughters of the knight are to have a wedding, two to be married to thy two brothers, and the other to the chief that was over the men at the rock. Thou shalt leave the cap with me, and thou wilt have but to think of me when thou hast need of it, and I will be at thee."

"If anyone asks thee from whence thou camest, say that thou camest out from behind thee; and if he say to thee, where art thou going? say that thou art going before thee."

He mounted upon the steed, and he gave her front to sea, and her back to shore, and away he was, and no stop nor stay was made with him till he reached the old church in Grianaig, and there was a grass meadow, and a well of water, and a bush of rushes, and he got off the steed.

"Now," said the steed, "thou shalt take a sword and thou shalt take the head off me."

"I will not take it indeed; it would be sad for me to do it, and it would not be my thanks."

"Thou must do it. In me there is a young girl under spells, and the spells will not be off me till the head is taken off me. I myself and the raven were courting; he in his young lad, and I in my young girl, and the giants laid draoidheachd magic upon us, and they made a raven of him and a steed of me."

He drew his sword, he turned his back, and he took the head off her with a scutching blow, and he left the head and the carcass there. He went on forwards and a carlin met him.

"From whence didst thou come?" said she.

"I am from behind me."

"Whither art thou going?

"I am going before me."

"That is the answer of a castle man."

"An answer that is pretty answerable for an impudent carlin such as thou art."

He went in with her and he asked a drink, and he got that.

"Where is thy man?"

"He is at the house of the knight seeking gold and silver that will make a cap for the knight's young daughter, such as her sisters have; and the like of the caps are not to be found in Albainn."

The smith came home.

"What's trade to thee, lad?"

"I am a smith."

"That is good, and that thou shouldst help me to make a cap for the knight's young daughter, and she going to marry."

"Dost thou not know that thou canst not make that?"

"It must be tried; unless I make it I shall be hanged tomorrow; here thou hadst best make it."

"Lock me into the smithy, keep the gold and silver, and I will have the cap for thee in the morning."

The smith locked him in. He wished the raven to be with him. The raven came, he broke in through the window, and the cap was with him.

"Thou shalt take the head off me now."

"It were sorrow for me to do that, and it would not be my thanks."

"Thou must do it. A young lad under spells am I, and they will not be off me till the head comes off me."

He drew his sword, and he scutched his head off, and that was not hard to do. In the morning the smith came in, and he gave him the cap, and he fell asleep. There came in a noble-looking youth with brown hair, and he awoke him.

"I," said he, "am the raven, and the spells are off me now."

He walked down with him where he had left the dead steed, and a young woman met them there, as lovely as eye ever saw.

"I," said she, "am the steed, and the spells are off me now."

The smith went with the cap to the house of the knight. The servant maid betook herself to the knight's young daughter, and she said that there was the cap which the smith had made. She looked at the cap.

"He never made that cap. Say to the lying rogue to bring hither the man that made him the cap, or else that he shall be hanged without delay."

The smith went and he got the man that gave him the cap, and when she saw him she took great joy. The matter was cleared up. Iain and the knight's young daughter married, and backs were turned on the rest, and they could not get the other sisters. They were driven away through the town with stick swords and straw shoulder-belts.

Diarmaid and Grainne

FIONN WAS GOING TO MARRY GRAINNE, the daughter of the king of Carmag in Eirinn. The nobles and great gentles of the Feinne were gathered to the wedding. A great feast was made, and the feast lasted seven days and seven nights; and when the feast was past, their own feast was made for the hounds. Diarmaid was a truly fine man, and there was a ball seirc, a love spot, on his face, and he used to keep his cap always down on the beauty spot; for any woman that might chance to see the ball seirc, she would be in love with him. The dogs fell out roughly, and the heroes of the Feinn went to drive them from each other, and when Diarmaid was driving the dogs apart, he gave a lift to the cap, and Grainne saw the ball seirc and she was in heavy love for Diarmaid.

She told it to Diarmaid, and she said to him, "Thou shalt run away with me."

"I will not do that," said Diarmaid.

"I am leaving it on thee as a wish; and as spells that thou go with me."

"I will not go with thee; I will not take thee in softness, and I will not take thee in hardness, I will not take thee without, and I will not take thee within; I will not take thee on horseback, and I will not take thee on foot," said he; and he went away in displeasure, and he went to a place apart, and he put up a house there, and he took his dwelling in it.

On a morning that there was, who cried out in the door but Grainne, "Art thou within, Diarmaid?"

"I am."

"Come out and go with me now."

"Did I not say to thee already that I would not take thee on thy feet, and that I would not take thee on a horse, that I would not take thee without, and that I would not take thee within, and that I would not have anything to do with thee."

She was between the two sides of the door, on a buck goat. "I am not without, I am not within, I am not on foot, and I am not on a horse; and thou must go with me," said she.

"There is no place to which we may go that Fionn will not find us out when he puts his hand under his tooth of knowledge, and he will kill me for going with thee!"

"We will go to Carraig, and there are so many Carraigs that he will not know in which we may be." They went to Carraig an Daimh (the stag's crag).

Fionn took great wrath when he perceived that his wife had gone away, and he went to search for her. They went over to Ceantire, and no stop went on their foot, nor stay on their step, till they reached Carraig an Daimh in Ceantire, near to Cille Charmaig. Diarmaid was a good carpenter, and he used to be at making dishes, and at fishing, and Grainne used to be going about selling the dishes, and they had beds apart.

On a day that there was there came a great sprawling old man the way, who was called Ciofach Mac a Ghoill, and he sat, and he was playing at dinnsirean (wedges). Grainne took a liking for the old earl, and they laid a scheme together that they would kill Diarmaid. Diarmaid was working at dishes. The old man laid hands on him, and he turned against the old man, and they went into each other's grips. The old man was pretty strong, but at last Diarmaid put him under. She caught hold of the knife and she put it into the thigh of Diarmaid. Diarmaid left them, and he was going from hole to hole, and he was but just alive, and he was gone under hair and under beard. He came the way of the Carraig and a fish with him, and he asked leave to roast it. He got a cogie of water in which he might dip his fingers, while he was roasting it. Now there would be the taste of honey or anything which Diarmaid might touch with his finger, and he was dipping his fingers into the cogie. Grainne took a morsel out of the fish and she perceived the taste of honey upon it. To attack Diarmaid went Ciofach, and they were in each other's grips for a turn of a while, but at last Diarmaid killed Ciofach, and away he went, and he fled, and he went over Loch a Chaisteil.

When Grainne saw that Ciofach was dead she followed Diarmaid, and about the break of day, she came to the strand, and there was a heron screaming. Diarmaid was up in the face of the mountain, and said Grainne –

> "It is early the heron cries,
> On the heap above Sliabh gaoil.
> Oh Diarmaid O Duibhne to whom love I gave,
> What is the cause of the heron's cry?
> "Oh Ghrainne, daughter of Carmaig of Steeds,
> That never took a step aright,
> It seems that before she gave the cry
> Her foot had stuck to a frozen slab.

"Wouldst thou eat bread and flesh, Diarmaid?"

"Needful were I of it if I had it."

"Here I will give it to thee; where is a knife will cut it?"

"Search the sheath in which thou didst put it last," said Diarmaid.

The knife was in Diarmaid ever since she had put it into him, and he would not take it out. Grainne drew out the knife, and that was the greatest shame that she ever took, drawing the knife out of Diarmaid.

Fear was on Diarmaid that the Fheinn would find them out, and they went on forwards to Gleann Eilg.

They went up the side of a burn that was there, and took their dwelling there, and they had beds apart.

Diarmaid was making dishes, and the shavings which he was making were going down with the burn to the strand.

The Fiantan were hunting along the foot of the strand, and they were on the track of a venomous boar that was discomfiting them. Fionn took notice of the shavings at the foot of the burn.

"These," said he, "are the shaving of Diarmaid."

"They are not; he is not alive," said they.

"Indeed," said Fionn, "they are. We will shout Foghaid (a hunting cry), and in any one place in which he may be, he is sworn to it that he must answer."

Diarmaid heard the Foghaid.

"That is the Foghaid of the Fiantan; I must answer."

"Answer not the cry, oh Diarmaid, it is but a lying cry."

Diarmaid answered the shout, and he went down to the strand. It was set before Diarmaid to hunt the boar. Diarmaid roused the boar from Bein Eidin to Bein Tuirc.

> While drawing down the long mountain,
> The brute was bringing Diarmaid to straits.
> His tempered blades were twisted
> Like withered rushy plaits.

Diarmaid gave a draw at the slasher that Lon Mac Liobhain made, and he put it in under the armpit and he killed the boar.

This was no revenge for Fionn yet over Diarmaid. There was a mole on the sole of the foot of Diarmaid, and if one of the bristles should go into it, it would bring his death.

Said Fionn –

"Oh Diarmaid, measure the boar, how many feet from his snout to his heel?"

Diarmaid measured the boar.

"Sixteen feet of measure true."

"Measure the boar against the hair."

He measured the boar against the hair; one of the bristles went into the mole and he fell.

Fionn took sorrow for him when he fell. "What would make thee better, Diarmaid?"

"If I could get a draught of water from the palms of Fionn I would be better."

Fionn went for the water, and when he thought on Grainne he would spill the water, and when he would think of Diarmid, he would take sorrow, and he would take it with him; but Diarmaid was dead before Fionn returned.

They walked up the side of the burn till they came to where Grainne was; they went in; they saw two beds, and they understood that Diarmaid was guiltless. The Fheinn were exceedingly sorrowful about what had befallen. They burned

Grainne, daughter of Carmaig of steeds
That never took a step aright,
In a faggot of grey oak.

Guaigean Ladhrach 'S Loirean Spagach

THERE WAS AT SOME TIME a king in Albainn whose name was Cumhall, and he had a great dog that used to watch the herds. When the cattle were sent out, the dog would lead them to a place where there might be good grass; and the dog would herd them there for the day, and in the evening he would bring them home.

There were certain people dwelling near to the king's house, and they had one son, and they used to send the son on matters to the king's house every evening. There was one beautiful sunny evening, and the boy was going to the king's house on a matter, and he had a ball and a shinny, and he was playing shinny forwards on the way to the king's house. A dog met him, and the dog began to play with the ball; he would lift it in his mouth and run with it. At last the boy struck a blow on the ball while it was in the dog's mouth, and he drove the ball down the dog's throat; he stuffed it down with the shank of the shinny, and he choked the dog; and since he had choked the dog, he himself had to go and keep the king's cattle instead of the dog. He had to drive out the cattle in the morning, to drive them to good grass, and to stay and to herd them all day, for fear they should be stolen, and to bring them home in the evening, as the dog used to do. So since he killed the dog, and since it was in the place of the king's dog that he was, it was "Cu Chumhail" (Cual's dog) that they used to say to him; and afterwards they altered the name to "Cuthullain."

On a day of the days, Cuchullin put out the cattle, and be drove them to a plain that was there, and he was herding them; and he saw a giant who was so big that he thought he could see the lift between his legs, coming to the side where he was, and driving a great ox before him; and there were two great horns on the ox, and their points were backwards instead of being forwards. The giant came forward with the ox where Cuchullin was, and he said,

"I am going to take a while of sleep here, and if thou seest any other man of the giants coming after me, awaken me. It may be that I will not easily be wakened, but waken thou me if thou canst."

"What is waking to thee?" said Cuchullin.

"It is," said the giant, "to take the biggest stone thou canst find and strike me on the chest with it, and that will wake me."

The giant lay and slept, and his snoring was as loud as thunder. But sleep was not long for him, till Cuchullin saw another giant coming, who was so big that he thought he could see the lift between his legs.

Cuchullin ran and he began to awaken the first giant that came, but waken he would not. Cuchullin was shoving him, but his wakening could not be done; but at last he lifted a great stone, and he struck the giant in the chest with it. The giant awoke, and he rose up sitting, and he said, "Is there another giant coming?"

"There is; yonder he is," said Cuchullin, as he held his forefinger towards him.

The giant struck his two palms on each other, and he said, "Ach, he is!" and he sprang on his feet.

The other giant came forwards, and he said, "Yes, Ghuaigean làdhraich, thou hast stolen my ox."

"I did not steal it, Loirean Spàgaich," said he, "I took it with me in the sight of every man as my own."

Shamble Shanks seized one horn of the ox to take it with him, and Crumple Toes seized the other. Shamble Shanks gave a swift jerk at the horn which he had in his hand, and he took it off the bone; he threw it from him with all his strength, and he drove it into the earth, point foremost, and it went down into the earth to the root. Then he seized the bone, and the two hauled at the ox to drag it from each other.

At last the head of the ox split, and the ox tore asunder down through his very middle to the root of the tail. Then they threw the ox from them, and they began at wrestling; and that was the wrestling! There was no knowing which of them was the stronger.

Cuchullin came to bring aid to Crumple Toes; he could not reach up aloft to give a blow to Shamble Shanks with a sword which he had, but he began to cut at the back of his legs to try to make a stair up the back of the giant's legs, up which he might climb to give him a blow of his sword.

Shamble Shanks felt something picking the back of his legs, and he put down his hand and he threw Cuchullin away; and where should Cuchullin go but foot foremost into the horn of the ox, and oat of the horn he could not come. But at that time that Shamble Shanks was throwing Cuchullin away, Crumple Toes got a chance at him, and Shamble Shanks was levelled, and Crumple Toes got him killed.

When that was done he looked about for Cuchullin, but he could not see him; and he shouted, "Where art thou now, thou little hero that wert helping me?"

Quoth Cuchullin, "I am here in the horn of the ox."

The giant went to try to take him out, but he could not put his hand far enough down into the horn; but at last he straddled his legs, and he drove his hand down into the horn, and he got hold of Cuchullin between his two fingers, and he brought him up. Cuchullin went home with the cattle at the going down of the sun, and I heard no more of the tale.

The Story of Conall Gulban

Part I

THERE WAS AT SOME TIME a young king in Eirinn, and when he came to man's estate the high counsellors of the realm were counselling him to marry; but he himself was inclined to go to foreign countries first, so that he might get more knowledge, and that he might be more instructed how the realm should be regulated; and he put each thing in order for matters to be arranged till he should come back. He staid there a while till he had got every learning that he thought he could get in that realm. Then he left Greece and he went "do'n Fheadailte," to Italy to get more learning. When he was in that country he made acquaintance with the young king of "an Iubhair," and they were good comrades together; and when they had got every learning that they had to get in Italy, they thought of going home.

The young king of the Iubhar gave an invitation to the young king of Eirinn that he should go to the realm of the Iubhar, and that he should stay a while there with him. The young king of Eirinn went with him, and they were together in the fortress of Iubhar for a while, at sports and hunting.

The king of Iubhar had a sister who was exceedingly handsome; she was "stuama beusach," modest and gentle in her ways, and she was right (well) instructed. The young king of Eirinn fell in love with her, and she fell in love with the young king of Eirinn, and he was willing to marry her, and she was willing to marry him, and the king of Iubhar was willing that the wedding should go on; but the young king of Eirinn went home first, and he gathered together the high counsellors of the realm, and he told them what he desired to do; and the high counsellors of the realm of Eirinn counselled their king to marry the sister of the kin, of Iubhar.

The king of Eirinn went back and he married the king's sister; and the king of the Iubhar and the king of Eirinn made "co-cheanghal", a league, together. If straits, or hardships, or extremity, or anything counter should come upon either, the other was to go to his aid.

When they had settled each thing as it should be, the two kings gave each other a blessing and the king of Eirinn and his queen went home to Eirinn.

At the end of a little more than a year after that they had a young son, and they gave him Eobhan as a name. Good care was taken of him, as should be of a king's son. At the end of a little more than a year after that they had another son, and they gave him Claidhean as a name. Care was taken of this one as had been taken of his brother; and at more than a year after that they had another son, and they gave him Conall as a name, and care was taken of him as had been taken of the two others.

They were coming on well, and at the fitting time a teacher was got for them. When they had got about as much learning as the teacher could give them, they were one day out at play, and the king and the queen were going past them, and they were looking at their children (clann).

Said the queen, "This is well, and well enough, but more than this must be done for the children yet. I think that we ought to send them to Gruagach Bhein Eidinn to learn feats and heroes' activity (luth ghaisge), and that there is not in the sixteen realms another that is as good as the Gruagach of Beinn Eidinn.

The king agreed with her, and word was sent for the Gruagach. He came, and Eobhan and Claidhean were sent with him to Bein Eidinn to learn feats and activity, and what thing soever besides the Gruagach could teach them.

They thought that Conall was too young to send him there at that time. When Eobhan and Claidhean were about a year by the Gruagach, he came with them to their father's house; they were sent back again, and the Gruagach was giving every learning to the king's children. He took them with him one day aloft up Beinn Eidinn, and when they were on high about half the mountain, the king's children saw a round brown stone, and as if it were set aside from other stones. They asked what was the reason of that stone being set aside so, rather than all the other stones on the mountain. The Gruagach said to them that the name of that stone was "Clach nan gaisgeach," the stone of the heroes.

Anyone that could lift that stone till he could place the wind between it and earth, that he was a hero.

Eobhan went to try to lift the stone; he put his arms about it, and he lifted it up to his knees; Claidhean seized the stone, and he put the wind between it and earth.

Said the Gruagach to them, "Ye are but young and tender yet, be not spoiling yourselves with things that are too weighty for you. Stop till the end of a year after this and you will be stronger for it than you are now."

The Gruagach took them home and taught them feats and activity, and at the end of a year he took them again up the mountain. Eobhan and Claidhean went to the stone; Eobhan lifted it to his shoulder top, and set it down; Claidhean lifted the stone up to his lap, and the Gruagach said to them, "There is neither want of strength nor learning with you; I will give you over to your father."

At the end of a few days after that, the Gruagach went home to the king's house, and he gave them to their father; and he said that the king's sons were the strongest and the best taught that there were in the sixteen realms. The king gave thanks and reward to the Gruagach, and he sent Conall with him.

The Gruagach began to teach Conall to do tricks and feats, and Conall pleased him well; and on a day he took Conall with him up the face of Beinn Eidinn, and they reached the place where the round brown stone was. Conall noticed it, and he asked as his brothers had done; and the Gruagach said as he said before. Conall put his hands about the stone, and he put the wind between it and earth; and they went home, and he was with the Gruagach getting more knowledge.

The next year after that they went up Beinn Eidinn where the round brown stone was. Conall thought that he would try if he was (na bu mhurraiche) stronger to lift the heroes' stone. He caught the stone, and he raised it on the top of the shoulder, and on the faggot gathering place of his back, and he carried it aloft to the top of Beinn Eidinn, and down to the bottom of Beinn Eidinn, and back again; and he left it where he found it.

And the Gruagach said to him, "Ach! thou hast enough of strength, if thou hast enough of swiftness."

The Gruagach shewed Conall a black thorn bush that was a short way from them, and he said, "If thou canst give me a blow with that black thorn bush yonder, before I reach the top of the mountain, I may cease giving thee instructions," and the Gruagach ran up the hill.

Conall sprang to the bush; he thought it would take too much time to cut it with his sword, and he pulled it out of the root, and he ran after the Gruagach with it, and before he was but a short way up the mountain, Conall was at his back striking him about the backs of his knees with the black thorn bush.

The Gruagach said, "I will stop giving thee instructions, and I will go home and I will give thee up to thy father."

The Gruagach wished to go home with Conall, but Conall was not willing till he should get every knowledge that the Gruagach could give him; and he was with him after that more than a year, and after that they went home.

The king asked the Gruagach how Conall had taken up his learning. "It is so," said the Gruagach, "that Conall is the man that is the strongest and best taught in the sixteen realms, and if he gets days, he will increase that heroism yet."

The king gave full reward and thanks to the Gruagach for the care he had taken of his son. The Gruagach gave thanks to the king for the reward he had given him. They gave each other a blessing, and the Gruagach and the king's sons gave each other a blessing, and the Gruagach went home, and he was fully pleased.

The young King of Eirinn and the king of Laidheann were comrades, and fond of each other; and they used to go to the green mound to the side of Beinn Euadain to seek pastime and pleasure of mind.

The King of Eirinn had three sons, and the King of Laidheann one daughter; and the youngest son that the King of Eirinn had was Conall. On a day, as they were on the green mound at the side of Beinn Eudain, they saw the seeming of a shower gathering in the heart of the north-western airt, and a rider of a black filly coming from about the shower; and he took (his way) to the green mound where were the King of Eirinn and the King of Laidheann, and he blessed the men, and he inquired of them. The King of Eirinn asked what he came about; and he said that he was going to make a request to the King of Eirinn, if it were so that he might get it. The King of Eirinn said that he should get it if it should be in his power to give it to him.

"Give me a loan of a day and a year of Conall thy son."

"I myself promised that to thee," said the King of Eirinn; "and unless I had promised thou shouldst not got him."

He took Conall with him. Now the King of Eirinn went home; he laid down music, and raised up woe, lamenting his son; he laid vows on himself that he would not stand on the green mound till a day and a year should run out. There then he was at home, heavy and sad, till a day and a year had run.

At the end of a day and year he went to the green mound at the side of Beinn Eudain. There he was a while at the green mound, and he was not seeing a man coming, and he was not seeing a horseman coming, and he was under sorrow and under grief. In the same air of the heaven, in the mouth of the evening he saw the same shower coming, and a man upon a black filly in it, and a man behind him. He went to the green mound where the man was coming, and he saw the King of Laidheann.

"How dost thou find thyself, King of Eirinn?"

"I myself am but middling."

"What is it that lays trouble on thee, King of Eirinn?"

"There is enough that puts trouble upon me. There came a man a year from yesterday that took from me my son; he promised to be with me this day, and I cannot see his likeness coming, himself or my son."

"Wouldst thou know thy son if thou shouldst see him?"

"I think I should know him for all the time he has been away."

"There is thy son for thee then," said the lad who came.

"Oh, it is not; he is unlike my son; so great a change as might come over my son, such a change as that could not come over him since he went away."

"He is all thou hast for thy son."

"Oh, you are my father, surely," said Conall.

"Thanks be to thee, king of the chiefs and the mighty! that Conall has come," said the King of Eirinn; "I am pleased that my son has come. Anyone thing that thou settest before me for bringing my son home, thou shalt get it, and my blessing."

"I will not take anything but thy blessing; and if I got thy blessing I am paid enough."

He got the blessing of the King of Eirinn, and they parted; and the King of Eirinn and his children went home.

After the sons of the King of Eirinn had gotten their learning, they themselves, and the king and the queen, were in the fortress; and they were full of rejoicing with music and joy, when there came a messenger to them from the King of Iubhar, telling that the Turcaich were at war with him to take the land from him; and that the realm of Iubhar was sore beset by the Turks; that they were (lionar nearthmhor 's borb) numerous, powerful, and proud (ra gharg), right fierce, merciless without kindliness, and that there were things incomprehensible about them; though they were slain today they would be alive tomorrow, and they would come forward to hold battle on the next day, as fierce and furious as they ever were; and the messenger was entreating the King of Eirinn to go to help the King of Iubhar, according to his words and his covenants. The King of Eirinn must go to help the King of the Iubhar, because of the heavy vows: if strife, danger, straits, or any hardship should come against the one king, that the other king was to go to help him.

They put on them forgoing; and when they had put on them for going away, they sent away a ship with provisions and with arms. There went away right good ships loaded with each thing they might require – noble ships indeed. The King of Eirinn and the King of Laidheann gave out an order that every man in the kingdom should gather to go.

The King of Eirinn asked, "Is there any man about to stay to keep the wives and sons of Eirinn, till the King of Eirinn come back? Oh, thou, my eldest son, stay thou to keep the kingdom of Eirinn for thy father, and thine is the third part of it for his life, and at his death."

"Thou seemest light-minded to me, my father," said the eldest son, "when thou speakest such idle talk; I would rather hold one day of battle and combat against the great Turk, than that I should have the kingdom of Eirinn altogether."

"There is no help for it," said the king. "But thou, middlemost son, stay thou to keep the kingdom of Eirinn for thy father, and thine is the half for his life, and at his death."

"Do not speak, my father, of such a silly thing! What strong love should you have yourself for going, that I might not have?"

"There is no help for it," said the King of Eirinn.

"Oh, Conall," said the king, "thou that hast ever earned my blessing, and that never deserved my curse, stay thou to keep the wives and sons of Eirinn for thy father until he himself returns home again, and thou shalt have the realm of Eirinn altogether for thyself, for my life, and at my death."

"Well then, father, I will stay for thy blessing, and not for the realm of Eirinn, though the like of that might be."

The king thought that Conall was too young for the realm to be trusted to him; he gathered his high counsellors and he took their counsel about it. The counsellors said that Conall was surely too young, but that was (faillinn a bha daonan a dol am feobhas) a failing that was always bettering; though he was young, that he would always be growing older; and that as Eobhan and Claidhean would not stay, that it was best to trust the realm to Conall.

Then here went the great nobles of Eirinn, and they put on them for going to sail to the realm of the Tuirc, themselves and the company of the King of Laidhean altogether.

They went away, and Conall went along with them to the shore; he and his father and his brothers gave a blessing to each other; and the King of Eirinn and his two sons, Eobhan and Claidhean, went on board of a ship, and they hoisted the speckled flapping sails up against the tall tough masts; and they sailed the ship fiulpande fiullande. Sailing about the sandy ocean, where the biggest beast eats the beast that is least, and the beast that is least is fleeing and hiding as best he may; and the ship would split a hard oat seed in the midst of the sea, so well would she steer; and so she was as long as she was in the sight of Conall.

And Conall was heavy and dull when his father and brothers left him, and he sat down on the shore and he slept; and the wakening he got was the one wave sweeping him out, and the other wave washing him in against the shore.

Conall got up swiftly, and he said to himself, "Is this the first exploit I have done! It is no wonder my father should say I was too young to take care of the realm, since I cannot take care of myself."

He went home and he took better care of himself after that.

There was not a man left in the realm of Eirinn but Conall; and there was not left a man in the realm of Laidheann, but the daughter of the King of Laidheann, and five hundred soldiers to guard her.

Anna Diucalas, daughter of the King of Laidheann, was the name of that woman, the very drop of woman's blood that was the most beautiful of all that ever stood on leather of cow or horse. Her father left her in his castle, with five hundred soldiers to keep her; and she had no man with her in Laidheann but the soldiers, and Conall was by himself in the realm of Eirinn.

Then sorrow struck Conall, and melancholy that he should stay in the realm of Eirinn by himself; that he himself was better than the people altogether, though they had gone away. He thought that there was nothing that would take his care and his sorrow from off him better, than to go to the side of Beinn Eudainn to the green mound. He went, and he reached the green mound; he laid his face downwards on the hillock, and he thought that there was no one thing that would suit himself better, than that he should find his match of a woman. Then he gave a glance from him, and what should he see but a raven sitting on a heap of snow; and he set it before him that he would not take a wife forever, but one whose head should be as black as the raven, and her face as fair as the snow, and her cheeks as red as blood. Such a woman was not to be found, but the one that the King of Laidheann left within in his castle, and it would not be easy to get to her, for all the soldiers that her father left to keep her; but he thought that he could reach her.

He went away, and there went no stop on his foot nor rest on his head, till he reached the castle in which was the daughter of the King of Laidheann.

He took (his burden) upon him, and he went on board of a skiff, and he rowed till he came on shore on the land of the King of Laidheann. He did not know the road, but he took a tale from every traveller and walker that he fell in with, and when he came near to the dun of the king of Laidheann, he came to a small strait. There was a ferry boat on the strait, but the boat was on the further side of the narrows. He stood a little while looking at its breadth; at last he put his palm on the point of the spear, and the shaft in the sea, he gave his rounded spring, and he was over.

Then here he was on a great top that was there, and he was looking below beneath him, and he saw the very finest castle (luchairt) that ever was seen from the beginning of the universe to the end of eternity, and a great wall at the back of the fortress, and iron spikes within a foot of each other, about and around it; and a man's head upon every spike but the one spike. Fear struck him, and he fell a shaking. He thought that it was his own head that would go on the headless spike.

The dun was guarded by nine ranks of soldiers. There were nine warriors (curaidhnean) at the back of the soldiers that were as mighty as the nine ranks of soldiers. There were behind the warriors six heroes (gasgaich) that were as mighty as the nine warriors and the nine ranks of soldiers. There were behind these six heroes three full heroes (Ian gasgaich) that were as mighty as all that were outside of them; and there was one great man behind these three, that was as mighty as the whole of the people that there were altogether, and many a man tried to take out Ann Iuchdaris, but no man of them went away alive.

He came to near about the soldiers, and he asked leave to go in, and that he would leave the woman as she was before.

"I perceive," said one of them, "that thou art a beggar that was in the land of Eirinn; what worth would the king of Laidheann have if he should come and find his daughter shamed by any one coward of Eirinn."

"I will not be long asking a way from you," said Conall.

Conall looked at the men who were guarding the dun; he went a sweep round about with ears that were sharp to hear, and eyes rolling to see. A glance that he gave aloft to the dun he saw an open window, and Breast of Light on the inner side of the window combing her hair. Conall stood a little while gazing at her, but at last he put his palm on the point of hip, spear, he gave his rounded spring, and he was in at the window beside Breast of Light.

"Who is he this youth that sprang so roundly in at the window to see me?" said she.

"There is one that has come to take thee away," said Conall.

Breast of Light gave a laugh, and she said, "Sawest thou the soldiers that were guarding the dun?"

"I saw them," said he; "they let me in, and they will let me out."

She gave another laugh, and she said, "Many a one has tried to take me out from this, but none has done it yet, and they lost their luck at the end; my counsel to thee is that thou try it not."

Conall put his hand about her very waist; he raised her in his oxter; he took her out to the rank of soldiers; he put his palm on the point of his spear, and he leaped over their heads; he ran so swiftly that they could not see that it was Breast of Light that he had, and when he was out of sight of the dun he set her on the ground.

Breast of Light heaved a heavy sigh from her breast. "What is the meaning of thy sigh?" said Conall.

"It is," said she, "that there came many a one to seek me, and that suffered death for my sake, and that it is (gealtair) the coward of the great world that took me away."

"I little thought that the very coward of Eirinn that should take me out, who staid at home from cowardice in the realm of Eirinn, and that my own father should leave five hundred warriors to watch me, without one drop of blood taken from one of them."

"How dost thou make that out?" said Conall.

"It is," said she, "that though there were many men about the dun, fear would not let thee tell the sorriest of them who took away Breast of Light, nor to what side she was taken."

Said Conall – "Give me thy three royal words, and thy three baptismal vows, that thou wilt not move from that, and I will still go and tell it to them."

"I will do that," said she.

Conall turned back to the dun, and nothing in the world, in the way of arms, did he fall in with but one horse's jaw which he found in the road; and when he arrived he asked them what they would do to a man that should take away Breast of Light.

"It is this," said they, "to drive off his head and set it on a spike."

Conall looked under them, over them, through, and before them, for the one of the biggest knob and slenderest shanks, and he caught hold of the slenderest shanked and biggest knobbed man, and with the head of that one he drove the brains out of the rest, and the brains of that one with the other's heads. Then he drew his sword, and he began on the nine warriors, and he slew them, and he killed the six heroes that were at their back, and the three full heroes that were behind these, and then he had but the big man. Conall struck him a slap, and drove his eye out on his cheek; he levelled him and stripped his clothes off, and he left no one to tell a tale or wear out bad news, but the one to whom he played the clipping of a bird and a fool, and though there should be ten tongues of a true wise bard in that man's head, it is telling his own exploits, and those of his men that he would be; the plight that the youth who had come to the town had made of them.

He asked him where was the king of Laidheann, and the big man said that he was in the hunting hill with his court and his following (dheadhachail) of men and beasts.

Said Conall to him, "I lay it on thee as disgrace and contempt (tair agus tailceas) that thou must go stripped as thou art to tell to the king of Laidheann that Conall Guilbeanach came, the son of the king of Eirinn, and that he has taken away his daughter Breast of Light."

When the big man understood that he was to have his life along with him, he ran in great leaps, and in a rough trot, like a venomous snake, or a deadly dragon; he would catch the swift March wind that was before him, but the swift March wind that was after him could not catch him. The King of Laidheann saw him coming, and he said, "What evil has befallen the dun this day, when the big man is coming thus stark naked to us?" They sat down, and he came.

Said the king, "Tell us thy tale, big man."

"That which I have is the tale of hate, that there came Conall Guilbeanach, son of the King of Eirinn, and slew all that there were of men to guard the dun, and it was not my own might or my own valour that rescued me rather than the sorriest that was there, but that he laid it on me as disgrace and reproach that I should go thus naked to tell it to my king, to tell him that there came Conall Guilbeanach, son of the King of Eirinn, and he has taken away Breast of Light, thy daughter."

"Much good may it do him then," said the King of Laidheann. "If it is a hero like that who has taken her away, he will keep her better than I could keep her, and my anger will not go after her."

Conall returned, and he reached the woman after he had finished the hosts.

"Come now," said he to Breast of Light, daughter of the King of Laidheann, "and walk with me; and unless thou hadst given me the spiteful talk that thou gavest, the company would be alive before thy father, and since thou gavest it thou shalt walk thyself. Let thy foot be even with mine."

She rose well-pleased, and she went away with him; they reached the narrows, they put out the ferry boat, and they crossed the strait. Conall had neither steed, horse, nor harness to take Breast of Light on, and she had to take to her feet.

When they reached where Conall had left the currach they put the boat on the brine, and they rowed over the ocean. They came to land at the lower side of Bein Eidin, in Eirinn. They came out of the boat, and they went on forward.

They reached the green mound at the foot of Bein Eidin.

Conall told Breast of Light that he had a failing, every time that he did any deed of valour he must sleep before he could do brave deeds again.

"There now, I will lay my head in thy lap."

"Thou shalt not, for fear thou shouldst fall asleep."

"And if I do, wilt thou not waken me?"

"What manner of waking is thine?"

"Thou shalt cast me greatly hither and thither, and if that will not rouse me, thou shalt take the breadth of a penny piece of flesh and hide from the top of my head. If that will not wake me, thou shalt seize on yonder great slab of a stone, and thou shalt strike me between the mouth and nose, and if that will not rouse me thou mayest let me be."

He laid his head in her lap, and in a little instant be fell asleep.

He was not long asleep when she saw a great vessel sailing in the ocean. Each path was crooked, and each road was level for her, till she came to the green mound at the side of Bein Eidin.

There was in the ship but one great man, and he would make rudder in her stern, cable in her prow, tackle in her middle, each rope that was loose he would tie, and each rope that was fast he would loose, and the front of each rope that was on board was towards him, till he came on shore at the shoulder of Bein and Mae – Eidin. He came in with the ship at the foot of Bein Nair Eidin, and the big man leapt on shore; he caught hold of the prow of the ship, and he hauled her her own nine lengths and nine breadths up upon green grass, where the force of foes could not move her out without feet following behind them.

He came where Breast of Light was, and Conall asleep, with his head on her knee. He gazed at Breast of Light, and she said,

"What side is before thee for choice? Or where art thou going?

"Well, they were telling me that Breast of Light, daughter of the King of Laidheann, was the finest woman in the world, and I was going to seek her for myself."

"That is hard enough to get," said she. "She is in yonder castle, with five hundred soldiers for her guard, that her father left there."

"Well," said he, "though she were brighter than the sun, and more lovely than the moon, past thee I will not go."

"Well, thou seemest silly to me to think of taking me with thee instead of that woman, and that I am not worthy to go and untie her shoe."

"Be that as it will, thou shalt go with me."

I know that it is thou by thy beauty, Breast of Light, daughter of the king of Laidheann."

"Thou hast the wishing knowledge of me," said she.

"I am not she, but a farmer's daughter, and this is my brother; he lost the flock this day, and he was running after them backwards and forwards throughout Bein Eudain, and now he is tired and taking a while of sleep."

"Be that as it will," said he, "there is a mirror in my ship, and the mirror will not rise up for any woman in the world, but for "Uchd Soluisd," daughter of the King of Laidheann. If the mirror rises for thee, I will take thee with me, and if it does not I will leave thee there."

He went to the mirror, and fear would not let her cut off the little finger, and she could not awaken Conall. The man looked in the mirror, and the mirror rose up for her, and he went back where she was.

Said the big one, "I will be surer than that of my matter before I go further." He plucked the blade of Conall from the sheath, and it was full of blood. "Ha!" said he, "I am right enough in my guess. Waken thy champion, and we will try with swift wrestling, might of hands, and hardness of blades, which of us has best right to have thee."

"Who art thou?" said Breast of Light.

"I," said the big man, "am Mac-a-Moir MacRigh Sorcha. It is in pursuit of thee I came."

"Wilt thou not waken my companion," said she.

He went, and he felt him from the points of the thumbs of his feet till he went out at the top of his head. "I cannot rouse the man myself; I like him as well asleep as awake."

Breast of Light got up, and she began to rock (a chriothnachadh) Conall hither and thither, but he would not take waking.

Said Mac-a-Moir, "Unless thou wakest him thou must go with me and leave him in his sleep."

Said she, "Give thou to me before I go with thee thy three royal words and thy three baptismal vows that thou wilt not seek me as wife or as sweetheart till the end of a day and a year after this, to give Conall time to come in my pursuit."

Mac-a-Moir gave his three royal words and his three baptismal vows to Breast of Light, that she should be a maiden till the end of a day and a year, to give time to Conall to come in pursuit of her, if he had so much courage. Breast of Light took the sword of Conall from the sheath, and she wrote on the sword how it had fallen out. She took the ring from off the finger of Conall, and she put her own ring on his finger in its stead, and put Conall's ring on her own finger, and she went away with Mac-a Moir, and they left Conall in his sleep.

He took the woman with him on his shoulder and he went to the ship. He shoved out the ship and he gave her prow to sea, and her stern to shore; he hoisted the flapping white sails against the mast, tall and enduring, that would not leave yard unbent, sail untorn, running the seas, ploochkanaiche plachkanaiche, blue clouds of Lochlanach, the little buckie that was seven years on the sea, clattering on her floor with the excellence of the lad's steering.

When Conall awoke on the green mound he had but himself, a shorn one and bare alone. Glance that he gave from him, what should he see but herds that the king of Eirinn and Laidheann had left, dancing for joy on the point of their spears. He thought that they were mocking him for what had befallen him. He went to kill the one with the other's head, and there was such a (sgrann) grim look upon him that the little herds were fleeing out of his way.

He said to one of them, "What fleeing is on the little herds of Bein Eidin before me this day, as if they were mad – are ye mocking me for what has befallen me?"

"We are not," said they; "it was grievous to us (to see) how it befell thee."

"What, my fine fellow, did you see happening to me?"

Said the little herd, "Thou art more like one who is mad than any one of us. If thou hadst seen the rinsing, and the sifting, and the riddling (an luasgadh, an cathadh, 'as an creanacadh) that they had at thee down at the foot of the hill, thou wouldst not have much esteem for thyself. I saw," said the little herd, "the one who was with thee putting a ring on thy finger."

Conall looked, and it was the ring of Breast of Light that was on his finger.

Said the little herd, "I saw her writing something on thy sword, and putting it into the sheath."

Conall drew his sword, and he read, "There came Mac-a-Moir, the king of Sorcha, and took me away, Breast of Light; I am to be free for a year and a day in his house waiting for thee, if thou hast so much courage as to come in pursuit of me."

Conall put his sword into its sheath, and he gave three royal words.

"I lay it on myself as spells and as crosses, that stopping by night, and staying by day, is not for me, till I find the woman. Where I take my supper, that I will not take my dinner, and that there is no place into which I go that I will not leave the fruit of my hand there to boot, and the son that is unborn he shall hear of it, and the son that is unbegotten he shall hear tell of it."

Said the little herd to him, "There came a ship to shore at the port down there. The shipmen (sgiobe) went to the hostelry, and if thou be able enough thou mayest be away with the ship before they come back."

Conall went away, and he went on board of the ship, and he was out of sight with her before the mariners missed him.

He gave her prow to sea, and her stern to shore, helm in her stern, rope in her prow, that each road was smooth, and crooked each path, till he went into the realm of Lochlann at a place which was called Cath nam peileirn (Battle of bullets), but he did not know himself where he was.

He leaped on shore, and he seized the prow of the ship, and he pulled her up on dry land, her own nine lengths and nine breadths, where the foeman's might could not take her out without feet following behind.

The lads of the realm of Lochlann were playing shinny on a plain, and Gealbhan Greadhna, the son of the King of Lochlann, working amongst them.

He did not know who they were, but he went to where they were, and it was the Prince of Lochlann and his two scholars, and ten over a score; and the Prince of Lochlann was alone, driving the goals against the whole of the two-and-thirty scholars.

Conall stood singing "iolla" to them, and the ball came to the side where he was; Conall struck a kick on the ball, and he drove it out on the goal boundary against the Prince of Lochlann. The Prince came where he was, and he said, "Thou, man, that came upon us from off the ocean, it were little enough that would make me take the head off thee, that we might have it as a ball to kick about the field, since thou wert so impudent as to kick the ball. Thou must bold a goal of shinny against me and against the two-and-thirty scholars. If thou get the victory thou shalt be free; if we conquer thee, every one of us will hit thee a blow on the head with his shinny."

"Well," said Conall, "I don't know who thou art, great man, but it seems to me that thy judgment is evil. If every one of you were to give me a knock on the head, you would leave my head a soft mass. I have no shinny that I can play with."

"Thou shalt have a shinny," said Gealbhan Greadhna.

Conall gave a look round about, and he saw a crooked stick of elder growing in the face of a bank. He gave a leap thither and plucked it out by the root, and he sliced it with his sword and made a shinny of it.

Then Conall had got a shinny, and he himself and Gealbhan Greadhna went to play.

Two halves were made of the company, and the ball was let out in the midst. On a time of the times Conall got a chance at the ball; he struck it a stroke of his foot, and a blow of his palm and a blow of his shinny, and he drove it home.

"Thou wert impudent," said Gealbhan Greadhna, "to drive the game against me or against my share of the people."

"That is well said by thee, good lad! Thou shalt get two shares (earrann) of the band with thee, and I will take one share."

"And what wilt thou say if it goes against thee?"

"If it goes against me with fair play there is no help for it, but if it goes against me otherwise I may say what I choose."

Then divisions were made of the company, and Gealbhan Greadhna had two divisions and Conall one. The ball was let out in the midst, and if it was let out Conall got a chance at it, and he struck it a stroke of his foot, and a blow of his palm, and a blow of his shinny, and he drove it in.

"Thou wert impudent," said Gealbhan Greadhna a second time, "to go to drive the game against me."

"Good lad, that is well from thee! But thou shalt get the whole company the third time, and what wilt thou say if it goes against thee?"

"If it goes by fair play I cannot say a jot; if not, I may say my pleasure."

The ball was let go, and if so, Conall got a chance at it, and be all alone; and he struck it a stroke of his foot, and a blow of his palm, and a blow of his shinny, and he drove it in.

"Thou wert impudent," said Gealbhan Greadhna, "to go and drive it against me the third time."

"That is well from thee, good lad, but thou shalt not say that to me, nor to another man after me," and he struck him a blow of his shinny and knocked his brains out.

He looked (taireal) contemptuously at them; he threw his shinny from him, and he went from them.

He was going on, and he saw a little man coming laughing towards him.

"What is the meaning of thy laughing at me?" said Conall.

Said the little man, "It is that I am in a cheery mood at seeing a man of my country."

"Who art thou," said Conall, "that art a countryman of mine?"

"I," said the little man, "am Duanach MacDraodh (songster, son of magic), the son of a prophet from Eirinn. "Wilt thou then take me as a servant, lad?"

"I will not take thee," said Conall. "I have no way (of keeping) myself here without word of a gillie. What realm is this in which I am here?"

"Thou art," said Duanach, "in the realm of Lochlann."

Conall went on, and Duanach with him, and he saw a great town before him.

"What town is there, Duanach?" said Conall.

"That," said Duanach, "is the great town of the realm of Lochlann."

They went on and they saw a big house on a high place.

"What big house is yonder, Duanach?"

"That," said Duanach, "is the big house of the King of Lochlann;" and they went on.

They saw another house on a high place.

"What pointed house is there, Duanach?" said Conall.

"That is the house of the Tamhasg, the best warriors that are in the realm of Lochlann," said Duanach.

"I heard my grandfather speaking about the Tamhaisg, but I have never seen them; I will go to see them," said Conall.

"It were not my counsel to thee," said Duanach.

On he went to the palace of the King of Lochlann (bhuail e beum sgeithe) and he clashed his shield, battle or else combat to be sent to him, or else Breast of Light, the daughter of the King of Laidheann.

That was the thing he should get, battle and combat, and not Breast of Light, daughter of the King of Laidheann, for she was not there to give him; but he should get no fighting at that time of night, but he should get (fardoch) lodging in the house of the amhuish, where there were eighteen hundred amhuish and eighteen score; but he would get battle in the morrow's morning, when the first of the day should come.

'Twas no run for the lad, but a spring, and he would take no better than the place he was to get. He went, and he went in, and there was none of the amhuish within that did not grin. When he saw that they had made a grin, he himself made two.

"What was the meaning of your grinning at us?" said the amhuish.

What was the meaning of your grinning at me?" said Conall.

Said they, "Our grinning at thee meant that thy fresh royal blood will be ours to quench our thirst, and thy fresh royal flesh to polish our teeth."

And said Conall, "The meaning of my grinning is, that I will look out for the one with the biggest knob and slenderest shanks, and knock out the brains of the rest with that one, and his brains with the knobs of the rest.

Every one of them arose, and he went to the door, and he put a stake of wood against the door. He rose up himself, and he put two against it so tightly that the others fell.

"What reason had he to do that?" said they.

"What reason had you to go and do it?" said he. "It were a sorry matter for me though I should put two there, when you yourselves put one there each, every one that is within."

"Well, we will tell thee," said they, "what reason we had for that: we have never seen coming here (one), a gulp of whose blood, or a morsel of whose flesh could reach us, but thou thyself, except one other man, and he fled from us; and now everyone is doubting the other, in case thou shouldst flee."

"That was the thing that made me do it myself likewise, since I have got yourselves so close as you are." Then he went and he began upon them. "I feared to be chasing you from hole to hole, and from hill to hill, and I did that." Then he gazed at them, from one to two, and he seized on the one of the slenderest shanks and the fattest head; he drove upon the rest, sliochd! slachd! till he had killed every one of them; and he had not a jot of the one with whom he was working at them, but what was in his hands of the shanks.

He killed every man of them, and though he was such a youth as he was, he was exhausted. Then he began redding up the dwelling (reitach na h-araich) that was there, to clean it for himself that night. Then he put them out in a heap altogether, and he let himself (drop) stretched out on one of the beds that was within.

There came a dream (Bruaduil) to him then, and he said to him, "Rise, oh Conall, and the chase about to be upon thee."

He let that pass, and he gave it no heed, for he was exhausted.

He came the second journey, and he said to him, "Conall, wilt thou not arise, and that the chase is about to be upon thee?"

He let that pass, and he gave it no heed; but the third time he came to him, he said, "Conall art thou about to give heed to me at all! and that thy life is about to be awanting to thee."

He arose and he looked out at the door, and he saw a hundred carts, and a hundred horses, and a hundred carters, coming with food to the amhuish; supposing that they had done for the youth that went amongst them the night before; and a piper playing music behind them, with joy and pleasure of mind.

They were coming past a single bridge, and the bridge was pretty large; and when Conall saw that they were together (cruin round) on the bridge, he reached the bridge, and he put each cart, and each horse, and each carter, over the bridge into the river; and he drowned the men.

There was one little bent crooked man here with them behind the rest.

"My heart is warming to thee with the thought that it is thou, Conall Gulban MacNiall Naonallaich, the name of a hero was on his hand a hundred years ere he was born."

"Thou hast but what thou hast of knowledge, and the share that thou hast not, thou wilt not have this day," said Conall Gulban.

He went away, and he reached the palace of the King of Lochlann; and he clashed his shield, battle or else combat to be given to him, or else Breast of Light, daughter of the King of Laidheann.

That was the thing which he should have, battle and combat; and not Breast of Light, for she was not there to give him.

So he went back and he slept again.

Word reached the young king of Lochlann, that the big man who came off the ocean had gone to the house of the "Tamhasg;" that they had set a combat, and that the "Tamhasgan" had been slain. The young king of Lochlann ordered four of the best warriors that were in his realm, that they should up to the house of the Tamhasg, and take off the head of the big man that that had come off the ocean, and to bring it up to him before he should sit down to his dinner.

The warriors went, and they found Duanach there, and they railed at him for going with the big man that came out of the outer land, for they did not know who he was.

"And why," said Duanach, "should I not go with the man of my own country? But it you knew it, I am as tired of him as you are yourselves. He has given me much to do; see you I have just made a heap of corpses, a heap of clothes, and a heap of the arms of the Tamhasg; and you have for it but to lift them along with you."

"It is not for that we came," said they, "but to slay him, and to take his head to the young king of Lochlann before he sits to dine. Who is he?" said they.

"He is," said Duanach, "one of the sons of the king of Eirinn."

"The young King of Lochlann has sent us to take his head off," said they.

"If you kill one of the children of the King of Eirinn in his sleep you will regret it enough afterwards," said Duanach.

"What regret will there be?" said they.

"There is this," said Duanach. "There will be no son to woman, there will be no calf to cow, no grass nor braird shall grow in the realm of Lochlann, till the end of seven years, if ye kill one of the clan of the King of Eirinn in his sleep, and go and tell that to the young King of Lochlann."

They went back, and they told what Duanach had said.

The young King of Lochlann said that they should go back, and do as he had bidden them, and that they should not heed the lies of Duanach. The four warriors went again to the house of the Tamhasg, and they said to Duanach,

"We have come again to take the head off the son of the King of Eirinn."

And Duanach said, "He is yonder then, over there, for you, in his sleep; but take good heed to yourselves, unless your swords are sharp enough to take off his head at the first blow, all that is in your bodies is to be pitied after that; he will not leave one of you alive, and he will bring (sgrios) ruin on the realm."

Each of them stretched his sword to Duanach, and Duanach said that their swords were not sharp enough, that they should go out to the Tamhasg stone to sharpen them. They went out, and they were sharpening their swords on the smooth grinding-stone of the Tamhasg, and Conall began to dream (again).

It seemed to him that he was going on a road that went through the midst of a gloomy wood, and it seemed to him that he saw four lions before him, two on the upper side of the rood, and two on the lower side, and they were gnashing their teeth, and switching their tails, making ready to spring upon him, and it seemed to him that it was easier for the lions that were on the upper side of the road to leap down, than it was for the lions that were on the lower side to leap up; and it was better for him to slay those that were on the tipper side first, and he gave a cheery spring to be at them; and he sprang aloft through his sleep, and he struck his head against a tie beam (sail shuimear) that was across above him in the house of the Tamhasgan, and he drove as much as the breadth of a half-crown piece of the skin off the top of his head, and then he was aroused, and he said to Duanach,

"I myself was dreaming, Duanach," and he told him his dream.

And Duanach said, "Thy dream is a dainty to read. Go thou out to the stone of the Tamhasg, and thou wilt see the four best warriors that the King of Lochlann has, two on each side of the stone round about it, sharpening their swords to take off thy head."

Conall went out with his blade in his hand, and he took off their heads, and he left two heads on each side of the stone of the Tamhasg and he came in where Duanach was, and he said, I am yet without food since I came to the realm of Lochlann, and I feel in myself that I am growing weak."

And Duanach said, "I wilt get thee food if thou wilt take my counsel, and that is, that thou shouldst go to court the sister of the King of Lochlann, and I myself will go to redd the way for thee.

There were three great warriors in the king's palace in search of the daughter of the King of Lochlann, and they sent word for the one who was the most valiant of them to go to combat the youth that had come to the town. This one came, and the Amhus Ormanach was his name, and he and Conall were to try each other. They went and they began the battle, Conall and the Avas Ormanach. The daughter of the King of Lochlann came to the door, and she shouted for Duanachd Acha Draohd.

"I am here," said Duanach.

"Well, then, if thou art, it is but little care thou hast for me. Many calving cattle and heifers gave my father to thy father, though thou art not going down, and standing behind the Avas Ormanach, and giving him the urging of a true wise bard to hasten the head of the wretch to me for my dinner, for I have a great thirst for it."

"Faire! faire! watch, oh queen," said Duanach; "if thou hadst quicker asked it, thou hadst not got it slower."

Away went Duanach down, and it was not on the side of the Avas Ormanach he began, but on the side of Conall. "Thou hast not told it to me for certain, yet if it be thou, when thou art not hastening thine hand, and making heavy thy blow! And to let slip that wretch that ought to be in a land of holes, or in crannies of rock, or in otter's cairns! Though thou shouldst fall here for slowness or slackness, there would neither be wife nor sweetheart crying for thee, and that is not the like of what would befall him."

Conall thought that it was in good purpose the man was for him, and not in evil purpose; he put his sword under the sword of the Avas Ormanach, and he cast it to the skies, and then he himself gave a spring on his back, and he levelled him on the ground, and then he began to take his head off.

"Still be thy hand, O Conall," said Duanach Acha Draodh, "make him the binding of the three smalls there, until he gives thee his oaths under the edge of his set of arms, that there is no stroke he will strike for ever against thee."

"I have not got strings enough to bind him," said Conall.

"That is not my case," said Duanach. "I have of cords what will bind back-to-back all that are in the realm of Lochlann altogether."

Duanach gave the cords to Conall, and Conall bound the Avas Ormanach. He gave his oaths to Conall under the edge of his set of arms, that he was a loved comrade to him for ever; and any one stroke he might strike that he would strike it with him, and that he would not strike a stroke for ever against him; and he left his life with the Avus Ormanach.

"Thou shalt have that woman whom thou art courting and making love to (a suridh 's a scircanachadh), the daughter of the King of Lochlann," said the Amhus Ormanach.

"Thou shalt have that woman for thyself," said Conall; "it is not her that I am courting and making love to."

The daughter of the King of Lochlann was right well pleased that he had left his life with the Avus Ormanach, so that it might be her own but what should she do but send for Conall.

What should the daughter of the King of Lochlann do but send word for Conall to pass the evening together with the Queen and with herself, and if it were his will that she would not give him the trouble of taking a step with his foot, but that she would take him up in a creel to the top of the castle. Conall thought that much reproach should not belong to one that was in the realm of Lochlann, against one that was in the realm of Eirinn, that he should go to do that. He went and he gave a spring from the small of his foot to the point of his palm, and from the point of his palm to the top of the castle, and he reached the woman where she was.

"If thou art now sore or hurt," said the daughter of the King of Lochlann, "there is a vessel of balsam (ballan fiochshlaint), wash thyself in it, and thou wilt be well after it."

He did not know that it was not bad stuff that was in the vessel. He put a little twig into the vessel, so that he might know what thing was in it. The twig came up full of sap (snodhach) as it went down. Then he thought that it was good stuff, and not bad stuff. He went and he washed himself in it, and he was as whole and healthy as he ever was. Then meat and drink went to them, that they might have pleasure of mind while passing the evening, and after that they went to rest; but he drew his cold sword between himself and the woman. He passed the night so, and in the morning he rose and went out of the castle. He clashed his shield without, and he shouted battle or else combat to be sent to him, or else Breast of Light, daughter of the King of Laidheann. It was battle and combat he should get, and not Breast of Light, for she was not there to give him.

Then the daughter of the King of Lochlann called out. "Art thou there, my brother?"

"I am," said her brother.

"Well," said she, "it is but little count that thou hadst of me. That man who has made me a woman of harrying and hurrying, to whom I fell as a wedded wife last night, not to bring me hither his head to my breakfast, when I am greatly thirsting for it."

"Faire! faire! watch, oh queen," said he, "if thou hadst asked it sooner thou hadst not got it slower. There are none of men, small or great, in Christendom, who will turn back my hand."

He went, and before he reached the door, he set earthquaking seven miles from him. At the first (mothar) growl he gave after he got out of the castle, there was no cow in calf, or mare in foal, or woman with child, but suffered for fear. He began himself and Conall at each other, and if there were not gasgich there at work it was a strange matter.

They drew the slender grey swords, and they'd kindle the tightening of grasp, from the rising of sun till the evening, when she would be wending west; and without knowing with which would be loss or winning. Duanach was singing iolladh to them, and when the sun was near about west.

Then the daughter of the King of Lochlann cried out for Duanach acha Draodh that he should go down to give the urging of a truewise bard to her brother, to bring her the head of the wretch to her breakfast, that she was thirsting greatly for it.

Duanach went, and if he did, it was not at the back of the King of Lochlann he went, but behind Conall.

"Oh, Conall," said he, "thou hast not told me yet if it be thou. When thou art not hastening thine hand, but making heavy thy blow! and level that wretch that ought to be in a land of holes, or in clefts of rock, or in otters' cairns! Though thou shouldst fall, there would be no wife or sweetheart crying for thee, and not so with him."

Conall thought that it was in good purpose the man was for him, and that it was not in bad purpose. He put his sword under the sword of the King of Lochlann, and he cast it to the skies; and then he gave a spring himself on his back, and he levelled him on the ground, and he began to take off his head.

"Still thy hand, Conall," said Duanach achaidh Draodh, "little is his little shambling head worth to thee. You are long enough at that game, throw away your swords and try another way." They threw away their swords, and they put the soft white fists in each other's breasts; but they were not struggling long till Conall gave the panting of his heart to the young King of Lochlann on the hard stones of the causeway.

Said Conall to Duanach, "Reach hither to me my sword, that I may take off his head."

"Not I, indeed," said Duanach. "It is better for thee to have his head for thyself as it is, than five hundred heads that thou mightest take out with strife. Make him promise that he will be (diles duit) a friend to thee."

Conall made the young King of Lochlann promise with words and heavy vows that he would be a friend to Conall Guilbeanach, the son of the King of Eirinn, in each strait or extremity that might come upon him, whether the matter should come with right or unright; and that Conall should have the realm of Lochlann under cess.

When the King of Lochlann had given these promises, Conall let him up, and they caught each other by the hand, and they made peace and they ceased.

And the young King of Lochlann gave a bidding to Conall that he should come in with him to his great house, to dine with him; and the young king set a double watch upon each place, so that none should come to disturb himself or the young son of the King of Eirinn, while they were at their feast.

A churchman was got, and the Amhas Ormanach was married to the daughter of the King of Laidheann.

When each thing was ready the royal ones sat at the great board; they laid down lament, and they raised up music, with rejoicing and great joy, and they were in great pleasure of mind. Meat was set in the place for eating drink in the drinking place, music in the place for hearing; and they were plying the feast with great sport in the dining-room of the King of Lochlann, and they so liking and loving about each, taking their feast.

The soldiers were without watching, to guard the big house of the king, and they saw a great tasbarltach coming the way; they had such fear before him that they thought they could see the great world between his legs. As he was coming nearer, the watch were fleeing till they reached the great house, and into the passage, and from the passage into the room where were the young King of Lochlann and the Young son of the King of Eirinn, at their feast; and the great raw bones that came began to fetter and bind the men, and to cast them behind him till he had bound every one of them; and till he reached the young King of Lochlann, and he and the big man wrestled with each other.

He drew his fist and he struck the King of Lochlann between the mouth and nose, and he drove out three front teeth, and he caught them on the back of his fist; but the end for them was, that the young King of Lochlann was bound and laid under fetters, and thrown behind together with the rest; and the big man gave a dark leap and he seized the bride, and he took her with him.

Conall gazed on all the company that was within, to try if he could see any man rising to stand by the king. When he saw no living man arising, he arose himself.

"Let that woman go," said he; "thou hast no business with her." That he would not do.

He gave a spring, he caught the slender black man between the two sides of the door (bhith), and he levelled him; and when he had levelled him, he let the weight of his knee on his chest.

"Has death ever gone so near thee as that?" said Conall.

"It has gone nearer than that," said the slender black man.

He let the weight more on him. "Has he gone as near as that to thee?"

"Oh, he has not gone; let thy knee be lightened, and I will tell thee the time that he went nearest to me."

"I will let thee; stand up so long as thou art telling it," said Conall.

Conall loosed the young King of Lochlann and his men from their bonds and from their fetters, and he sat himself and the young King of Lochlann at the board, and they took their feast; and the big man was cast in under the board. Again when they were at supper the king's sister was with them, and every word she said she was trying to make the friendship greater and greater between her brother and Conall. The big man was lying under the board, and Conall said to him, "Thou man that art beneath, wert thou ever before in strait or extremity as great as to be lying under the great board, under the drippings of the waxen torches of the King of Lochlann and mine?"

Said he, "If I were above, a comrade of meat and cup to thee, I would tell thee a tale on that."

At the end of a while after that, when the drink was taking Conall a little, he was willing to hear the tale of the man who was beneath the board, and he said to him, "Thou that art beneath the board, if I had thy name it is that I would call thee; wert thou ever in strait or extremity like that?"

And he answered as before.

Said Conall, "If thou wilt promise to be peaceable when thou gettest up, I will let thee come up; and if thou art not peaceable, the two hands that put thee down before will put thee down again."

Conall loosed the man who was beneath, and he rose up aloft and he sat at the other side of the board, opposite to Conall; and Conall said,

"Aha! thou art on high now, thou man that wert beneath. If I had thy name it is that I would call thee. What strait or extremity wert thou ever in that was harder than to be laid under the board of the young king of Lochlann, and mine?"

Part II

When Garna Sgiathlais had finished his tale, he said to Conall, "Now, thou man that art yonder, I should like to have thy tale, thy name, thy land, and what is the reason of thy journey to Lochlann." And Conall said, "My name is Conall Guilbeannach, son of the king of Eirinn." And he told his own tale.

The sister of the king of Lochlann was listening; she grew sorrowful, and the drops rained from her eyes when she understood that Conall had another sweetheart. She arose, and she left the room, and she was heavy and sad. Duanach followed her to console her, and put her in order as best he might. She took a ring from her finger, and she sent it to Conall by Duanach.

Conall turned Duanach back with it to herself again. He said that he had a ring from another on his finger already, since he had got no gift (tabhartas) to give it to her, as eiric.

She sent Duanach back again with the ring to Conall, and she asked him to wear it for her. Conall took the ring and put it upon his finger.

"Thou must go with me," said Conall to Garna Sgiathlais, "in search of that woman Breast of Light."

"It is easier for me to bear death than to go to meet that man anymore."

"Thou wilt find death where thou art, then," said Conall.

"It is certain that if I am to suffer death where I am that I will go with thee," said the slender black man.

"The young king of Lochlann said that he would go too." Said Conall. "Who will be a guide to us to take us the shortest way?"

Said Duanach, "I will make a guide for you."

Conall and his warriors made ready. The king of Lochlann's sister wished Duanach to stay with her till the rest should come back, but Duanach would not stay.

Away went Conall, and he rigged a ship, and when the ship was rigged he took with him the slender black man, Duanach acha Draodh, the king of Lochlann, and the Amhus Ormanach; they sailed, and crew enough with them, and they reached the realm of the Sorcha.

When they reached, Duanach went into the house of Mac-a-Moir, and he said, "Hospitality from thee, A Mhic-a-Mhoir."

"Thou shalt have that, A Dhraoth aoith."

"Champions to fight from thee, great warrior."

"Thou shalt have that, thou Druid."

"A sight of Breast of Light," said Duanach.

"Thou shalt have that, Druid," said Mac-a-Moir.

Duanach got a sight of Breast of Light, and he told her that Conall had come with his warriors to take her from Mac-a-Moir, and Breast of Light was pleased, for she was tired of being kept there.

Duanach came out, and he told it to Conall, and the next day Conall came to the landmark of Mac-a-Moir. He clashed his shield – "Yielding or battle upon the field."

"Yielding thou gettest not in this town," said Mac-a Moir; "though it were but speech it was a mark to Mac-a-Moir to come out to try a combat with Conall."

"I should go up to seek the thing I want," said Conall.

"Well, indeed, thou shalt not. There promised to fall first none but me," said the slender black man. I will go up before thee, and I will come to thee with word how the place is up before thee."

The slender black man went up, and he shouted battle or combat, or else Breast of Light, daughter of the King of Laidhean, to be sent out. That he should have battle and combat, but not Breast of Light, daughter of the King of Laidhean.

They stood, Conall, the young King of Lochlann, and Garna Sgiathlais, opposite to the house of Mac-a-Moir, and they clashed their shields for battle. Mac-a-Moir sent out the three best warriors that were in his realm to battle with them. They drew their slender grey swords, and they went to meet each other, but the combat did not last long till the three heroes were slain.

On the next day Mac-a-Moir sent the Ridire Leidire, the knight, the mangler, his brother, out to try a combat with any one of Conall's warriors who had the heart to try against him.

"Who will go to battle with this hero of exploits today?" said Conall.

"Myself," said Garna Sgiathlais," because of how his brother threw me into the nest of the dreagan."

They went to meet each other; they drew their slender grey swords, and the two battled with each other; but long before the sun went west, the Ridire Leidire was slain.

Garna Sgiathlais took off the head, and he opened the mouth, and he cut the tongue out, and he split the tongue, and he struck it three slaps against himself; and he said to Mac-a-Moir –

"There, that is for thee, for how thou didst cast me into the dreagan's nest."

At night Duanach went into the house of Mac-a-Moir, and he said –

"Hospitality from thee, Vic-a-Voir."

"Thou shalt get that, thou Druid."

"Warriors to combat Conall tomorrow, Vic-a-Voir. Thou shalt get that, thou Druid."

"A sight of Breast of Light," said Duanach.

"Thou shalt get that, thou Druid," said Mac-a-Moir.

Duanach got a sight of Breast of Light, and he told her each thing as it was going on outside of the dun, and she was sorrowful that so much blood was being spilt for her; and Duanach came out, and he gave the tale of Breast of Light to Conall.

On the next day Mac-a-Moir himself came out to try a combat with anyone who had the heart to go to try him.

"Who will go to battle with the hero of exploits today?" said Conall.

"Myself," said Garna Sgiathlais, "for the day that he cast me down the rock to the dreagan's nest."

They came in front of each other; they drew their slender grey swords, and they kindled a fire of fists with their swords, from the rising of the sun till she was going west; but at last it went with Mac-a-Moir to level Garna Sgiathlais, to bind him and fetter him, and he took him with him, and he cast him into a den of lions that he kept for pastime for himself, and Mac-a-Moir would not come out again till the end of two days.

When the night came, Duanach went into the house of Mac-a-Moir, and he said –

"Hospitality from thee, Vic-a-Voir."

"Thou shalt get that, thou Druid."

"A sight of Breast of Light," said Duanach.

"Thou shalt not get that," said Mac-a-Moir; and then Breast of Light was put into a dark chamber, where she could not hear voice of friend, and where she could not see light of sun.

When the battle-day of Mac-a-Moir came, he came out, and he clashed his shield.

"Who will go to battle with the hero of exploits today?" said Conall.

"Myself," said the Young King of Lochlann.

They came in front of each other; they drew their hard thin swords, and they went to battle with each other. But long before the sun went west, the young King of Lochlann was levelled, bound, and fettered, and taken away, and cast into the den of lions, where Garna Sgiathlais was; and Mac-a-Moir would not come out anymore to hold battle till the end or five days. Duanach went in every night of these to seek food, and he got it; and on a night of these nights he asked for warriors to hold battle against Conall.

"Thou shalt get that, thou Druid," said Mac-a-Moir. A hundred full heroes were got in order before the great house on the next day.

It seemed strange to Conall to see the host going into order at the front of the big house; and he asked if there was any knowing what was the meaning of that host going into order, in ranks, at the front of the big house this day.

Said Duanach, "I thought thou wert finding the time long here, not doing anything, and I asked for warriors to combat with thee."

"I have no wish myself to be slaying men without knowing why; and, besides, how should I contend against a hundred full heroes, and I alone?" said Conall.

"So many as thou dost not slay with thy sword I will kill with my tongue," said Duanach.

They went to meet Conall. The smooth lad looked from one to two; and where they were thickest, there they were thinnest; and where they were thinnest, there were none at all there. He struck them under, and over, through, and throughout; and those who were thinnest, were most ill scattered; and as many as were dead of them were lying down; and as many as were hurt, they sat; and the rest that were alive of them ran away.

And when the five days of delay that Mac-a-Moir had were gone past, Conall went to the fence of his house.

Mac-a-Moir had a bell on the top of his house, and he was a warrior, anyone who could strike a blow on the bell; and when a blow was struck on the bell, unless Mac-a-Moir should come out, then he was a dastard (cladhaire). Then when Mac-a-Moir was eating his breakfast, Conall went up upon the top of the house, and he struck a blow on the bell, and he drove the tongue out of the bell; and the tongue fell down through the house, and down through the board at which Mac-a-Moir was taking his food; and Mac-a-Moir said, "Ha, ha! comrade, it was easier to hold battle against thee on the day of Bein Eidinn than on this day."

Mac-a-Moir came out to hold battle. Conall clashed his shield, and he said, "Yielding, or battle on the field."

"Yielding thou gettest not in this town," said Mac-a-Moir. Though it was but speech, it was a sign for Mac-a-Moir to come out, to try a battle with Conall.

They drew their slender grey swords, and they kindled a fire of fists, from the rising of the sun till the evening, when she would be going west; without knowing with which of them the victory would be.

Duanach was singing "iolla" to them, and he said, "You are long enough at this play; throw from you your swords, and try it another way." They threw from them their swords, and they put their soft white fists in each other's breasts, and they wrestled, but they did not take long at the wrestling, till Conall gave the panting of his heart to Mac-a-Moir on the hard stones of the causeway. "Stretch hither my sword," said Conall, "until I reap the head off him."

"I will not stretch it," said Duanach. It is better for thee that thou shouldst have his head for thyself as it is, than five hundred heads that thou mightest take out with strife," said Duanach; "take a pledge of him that he will be faithful to thee."

Conall made him promise that he would be faithful to Conall Guilbeanach, son of the King of Eirinn, whether the matter should come under right or unright; and that the realm of Scorcha should be under cess to the realm of Eirinn; and Mac-a-Moir gave these pledges to Conall, and he bound himself with words, and with weighty vows. Conall let him aloft; they caught hold of each other's hands, and they made peace with great friendship, and they were quiet.

Then the first thing that Conall did was to go to the den of lions, to see if his two comrades were alive, and they were; for it is as left with the lions that they will not touch, and that they will not do any hurt to kings, or to the clan of kings.

And Conall took Garna Sgiathlais and the young King of Lochlann out of the lion's den, and he loosed each bond and fetter that was upon them, and they were free and whole.

The next thing that Conall did was to take Breast of Light out of the dark place in which she was, and she was pleased and joyful coming out.

Mac-a-Moir gave a bidding to Conall, and to Breast of Light, to the King of Iospainde, and the young King of Lochlann, to come into his house to take a feast. They went there. They raised music, and they hid sorrow; word was sent for a priest, and Conall was wedded to Breast of Light, and they made a wedding that lasted for the six days of the week, and the last day was no worse than the first, and that was the wedding that was cheery. Meat was set in the place for using, and drink in the drinking place, and music in the place for hearing. They plied the feast and the company with joy, and pleasure of mind, and long was there mind of the wedding of Conall and Breast of Light.

But there was much envy (farnaite) with the young King of Lochlann, Garna Sgiathlais, and Mac-a-Moir at Conall, to see him married to one so beautiful, modest, and learned, and that they themselves should be wifeless, and they thought her like was not to be found. Each one of them was as anxious as the rest that her like should be his as a wife, and they left it to Breast of Light to say who was the other one that would come nearest to herself in look, learning, and modesty. She said that there was Aillidh, daughter of the King of Greece, but it was by mighty deeds that she would be got (sar ghaisge).

The three kings made it up that they would go to seek Aillidh, daughter of the King of Greece. Breast of Light was unwilling that Conall should go with the rest, but the rest would not go without him, and when she saw that she consented.

It was left to Conall to say which of them was to get Aillidh, and Conall said, "Since the King of Lochlann was the first king who had come under cess to him, that he was the first for whom he would get a wife." Duanach wished to go with them, but Conall left him to be a king, and to take care of Breast of Light till he should come back.

Away went Conall, young son of the King of Eirinn, Mac-a-Moir, son of the King of Sorcha, and Garna Sgiathlais, King of the Hispainde, to get Aillee (Beauty), daughter of the King of the Greyke (Greece), for the young King of Lochlann to wife, and they reached Greece.

An old man met them that was their guide. He gave them a tale about the realm of Greece, the desire of the hosts, the battle; the form of the arms, and the customs of the country (miann sloidh, feachd, 's rian nan arm, agus cleachdanan na ducha), and he told them the tale of the King of Greece, and how his daughter was kept in the dun, and that no one at all was to get Beauty, daughter of the King of Greece, to marry, but one who could bring her out by great valour; and the old man told them about the wall that was for a bulwark (daingneach) round about the dun, how many heroes and soldiers there were in the inside of the ramparts; and besides, that there was no way to get Beauty but by strong battle, brave deeds, and ruse (feachd làdir, sàr ghaisge, agus seoltachd). Conall went, and the three other kings, aloft up a mountain that was above the dun of the big town of the kin so that they might see what was going on below beneath them. They lighted upon hunting bothys (bothain sheilg) in the mountain, and they went in into them, and they were there all night, and on the next day they found old clothes in the hunting huts.

Conall put on some of the old clothes which they found, to go in the semblance of a poor lad, to try if he could get to the inside of the gates (cachlaidhean) of the dun of the king's town, and he said to the other kings if they should hear on the third day a hunting cry, or any terror (faoghaid na fuathas), that they should run swiftly to help him. He went, and he reached one of the gates (geata) of the dungeon (daingneach), and he was as a shy boy, ill-looking, without the look of a man, without the port of a lad, or a dress of armour (mar bhallach moitire mi sgiamhach, gun aogosg duine gun dreach gille, na culaidh armachd).

He reached the gate-keeper (fear gleidh a gheata), but that one would not let him in. He asked him what he sought, and Conall said that he had come to see if he could get teaching in feats of arms, nimbleness, and soldier-craft (ionnsach an iomairt arm, luth chleas, 's gaisge). The gate-keeper sent word for the ruler of the fort (fear riaghladh an duin), and he came and he asked Conall whence he was. Conall said that he had come from the neighbourhood (iomal) that was farthest off of the realm. The high ruler asked him what customs the people of that place had, and if they tried to do any feats.

Conall said that they used to try casting the stone of force (clach neart) and hurling the hammer.

The high ruler asked Conall to come in, and he set some to try putting the stone against Conall. Conall could throw the stone further than any of them, and they saw that he had no want of strength if there were enough of courage in him.

A stick sword was given him, and they were teaching him swordsmanship, and Conall was coming on well. But it was little they knew about the teaching that Conall had got from the Gruagach of Beinn Eidinn before then. Conall made himself acquainted with the keeper of the arms, and he was exceedingly anxious to get a sight of their arms-house, but the armourer said that could not be done, for fear of the high ruler of the dun. But on the morning of the third day, when the governor was eating his breakfast, the armourer said to Conall that if he were able enough now, that he might act a sight of the armoury before the high man who ruled the dun should come out from his morning meal.

Conall went with him swiftly, and the man who was keeping the arms opened the armoury (taisg airm). Conall went in and he looked amongst the arms, and he spied great glaives at the furthest off end of the armoury. He went where they were, and he began to try them, he would raise them in his hand, and brandish them, and some he would shake out of their hilts, and others he would break. The man who had the care of the arms began to shout to him that he should come out, but Conall was pretending that he heard him not. Conall would look at the swords, and some were rusted, and some were not. At last he found a sword that pleased him.

He was going the way of the door of the arms-house with it, and the man who had the care of the arms was begging him to put it from him, but Conall gave him no heed, and the man who had charge of the armoury said –

"If the high governor of the dun comes he will take the head off me for letting thee in."

When Conall was at the door the governor came in, and he desired Conall to put away that sword. If he knew the name of the man who had had that sword that he would not be long putting it from him that; his name was Mor ghaisge na mor ghleadh. Great valour of the great tricks.

"You may give it that name still," said Conall.

The high governor said that he would drive the head off the man who had the care of the arms for letting Conall into the armoury, and off Conall for taking the sword out.

"Take thou care that it is not thine own head that will be down first, comrade."

The high governor called for his men. Conall struck the head off the high Governor, and he gave a hunting whistle (fead fhaoghaid), and the people gathered with their arms about Conall.

He struck them, under them, over them, through and throughout them; where they were thickest there they were thinnest; where they were thinnest they were most scattered.

The king came out, and he said to Conall, "Thou man that came on us a-new; hold on thy hand, and thy blade.

The three other kings came to the gate, but they were not getting in. Conall ran to the gate, and he struck it a kick, and he drove it into splinters. Then came the King of Lochlann, and the King of Light, and the King of the Hispainde, in with their arms. The people of Greece fled back, and the King of Greece said –

"Oubh bhoubh ouv vouv! What a wonderful turn has come on the matters! It was in the prophecies that a son of a king of Eirinn would come, and that he would lay the realm of Greece under cess, and instead of that is an awkward fellow of an ill-looking boy, that came and put the realm under cess."

Said Conall, with a high voice, "Thou King of Greece, take not thou each man according to his seeming. I am Conall Guilbeinich, son of the King of Eirinn, but it is not to put the realm of Greece under cess I am come, but to take out Beauty, thy daughter."

Said the King of Greece, "Thou shalt have Beauty, my daughter, and two-thirds of my realm while I myself am alive, and the whole after my death."

Conall asked that Aillidh should be brought out, and she came, and she was right willing to wed Conall, but Conall told her he was married already to Breast of Light, daughter of the King of Laidhean; and the King of Greece said –

"If thou hast got Breast of Light, it is no wonder though thou shouldst not take my daughter."

Conall told Beauty that she had her two choices, to take the King of Lochlann, or be without a husband; and she preferred to marry the young King of Lochlann.

And word was sent for a priest; and Aillidh, daughter of the King of Greece, was wedded to the young King of Lochlann, and they made a wedding that lasted for the six days of the week, and the last day was no worse than the first day.

And when they were at the wedding, they asked Aillidh, the bride of Lochlann's King, who was the next one that was nearest to her in beauty and comeliness, virtue and learning. And she said that there was Cuimir, daughter of the King of Na Frainge (the Franks).

Conall asked Garna Sgiathlais if we were willing to take that one as a wife, and he said that he was. Conall asked Aillidh where Cuimir was dwelling, and Beauty told that she was in the great royal house, and that there was a great fortress wall about the great house, and that there was a lion on either side of the gate, that was in through the wall, and that there was the house of the Tamhaisg, the best warriors that the King of France had, a little further on; and the Tamhaisg were proud and merciless to any over whom they might gain victory.

The valiant kings made ready to go to France, but Aillidh was not willing to part with her new married husband, but the other warriors would not part from him; he must needs go with them, till they should put an end to all the valorous deeds they had to do, before they could get wives for Garda Sgiathlais, King of Hispania, and Mac-a-Moir, son of the King of Scorcha.

The four valorous kings put each matter in order in Greece as best they might, and they left Beauty in the care of her father till the King of Lochlann should come back. They went to France, and when they reached France they took a tale from each traveller that met them by the way, and so they got guidance to the great royal house, and when they reached the gate that was without in the fortress wall, there was a great lion at either side of the gate, but that put neither fear nor sorrow upon them, because it is as a charge left with lions that they will not injure kings or the clan of kings. And Conall went on past the lions, and no one of them stirred his head at him. He reached on forward to where the Tamhaisg were, and they began gnashing their teeth, making ready to spring upon him. He took sure notice of them, for the thick-knobbiest one and the thin-shankiest of them. He compassed them, under them, over them, through and throughout them; and he seized on the two shanks of the thin-shankiest one amongst them, and he was driving out the brains of the rest, with the knob of that one, and the brains of that one with the knobs of the rest, till the part that was thickest of them was thinnest, and the lot that was thinnest they were the most ill scattered.

The King of France came out, and he said to Conall –

"Thou man that hast come on us from a strange land, withhold thy blade and thine hand; slay not my warriors wholly; these are the Tamhaisg, the best warriors I have to guard the great royal house; but they are but as reeds in the front of a meadow before thee. How camest thou past the lions?"

"Thou and thy lions!" said Conall. "I will go down past thy lions, and I will come up past thy lions, and they will not touch me; and I will bring up three other warriors that are down here, and the lions will not touch them."

Garna Sgiathlais Mac-a-Moir and the King of Lochlann came up past the lions, kings were they, and a clan from kings all together, and the lions did not stir their tongues against them.

The King of France asked whence they were, and Conall told that he was Conall Guilbeanach, son of the King of Eirinn, and he shewed the young King of Lochlann, and

Mac-a-Moir, son of the King of Sorcha, and Garna Sgiathlais, king of Hispania; and he told him that it was not to disturb France they had come, but to take out Cuimir, daughter of the King of France, to be wife to Garna Sgiathlais King of Hispania.

Said the King of France, "He shall get that."

Cuimir was brought out, and the matter was hidden, and it was Conall she would rather take, for it was he that had done the bravest deeds; but Conall told her that he was wedded already to Breast of Light, daughter of the King of Laidhean, and that the young King of Lochlann was wedded to Aillidh daughter of the King of Greece, and that it was Garna Sgiathlais, King of Hispania, she was to have. Cuimir was willing to take the King of Hispania, so that she might be a queen in a realm that was near the realm of her father. Word was sent for a priest, and the wedding was done, and they made a wedding that lasted for the six days of the week, and the last day was no worse than the first day.

When they were at the wedding they were talking about who they should get for a wife for Mac-a-Moir; and they left it to be said by Cuimir, the young Queen of Spain, who was the one that was fittest, in her esteem, to be a wife to Mac-a-Moir. And she said that there was Deo Greine nighean righ an Eilean Uaine. They asked her if that one was to be got. She said that she was not, but by exceeding valour; that there was a fortress wall round about the dun of the king, and that it discomfited the heroes; that Deo Greine would be in a turret that was on the top of the dun, and that none but a valiant warrior could get her; but if Mac-a-Moir should get her, that he had no cause to regret that he was the last of the kings who had got a wife.

Mac-a-Moir was longing to begone in pursuit of Deo Greine, and the rest were as willing and well pleased as himself. When they were at the feast, the King of France was setting a ship in order for them. Cuimir, daughter of the King of France, was not willing to let her new married husband, Garna Sgiathlais, away with the rest, but when the rest saw that, they would not go without him. When Cuimir understood that, she agreed to let him go with them.

The King of France set his slender ship in order for them, with a crew of disciplined, active, strong, hardy men, and the four honourable kings went on board, and the Frenchmen sailed with them to the shore of the Green Island.

They brought the ship to port, and they put Mac-a-Moir and the three gallant kings who were with him on shore, and they themselves sailed back home to France.

They went on forwards to the dun of the town of the King of the Green Island, taking a tale from each traveller and journeyer that might fall in with them. They got on till they reached the fortress gate of the dun of the king's town. Conall struck at the gate, and the gate-keeper asked what they sought. Conall answered that they came to seek Sunbeam, daughter of the King of the Green Isle, to be wife to one of them. Word was sent for the high Governor of the dun, and he came, and he asked them who they were, and what they sought. Conall told him that they were kings, and they had come to seek Sunbeam as a wife to one of them. The high Governor said that they should not get her but by exceeding valour; that they must hold a battle against the warriors of the dun, and gain victory over them.

Conall asked who was the sturdy hero that would go first to battle against the warriors of the dun.

"Myself," said Mac-a-Moir. "If I am to get the daughter of the King of the Green Island as a wife, I will shew that I am worthy to have her."

They were asked in, and they went.

Warriors were got to combat Mac-a-Moir, son of the King of Sorcha. They drew their blades, and Conall, and Garna Sgiatlais, and the young King of Lochlann were singing "iolla" to them. But they had not taken long of the contest, when Mac-a-Moir struck the head off the champion of the Green Isle.

Said Mac-a-Moir to the Governor, "Pick up the champion's head, and get me another one."

Another was got; but they had not taken long at the combat when Mac-a-Moir struck the head off that one too. He asked for another, and another was got, but it was not long till the head went off that one in like manner.

The King of the Green Isle was taking sport at them, and he said –

"I see, my hero, that thou wouldst slay my men altogether, one after another, if thou hadst chance of arms. I am not for spilling more blood; I will try it another way.

My daughter is in a turret, that is at the top of the dun, and the man that can take her out shall get two-thirds of my realm while I live, and the whole of my realm when I die; I am but an old man, and it is not likely that I will be long alive now, at all events.

The way was shewn them to the turret, in which was the king's daughter, at the top of the dun.

"Who is the first man that will try to take the king's daughter out of the turret?" said Conall.

"Myself," said Mac-a-Moir.

The turret was aloft, on the top of three carraghan ard (lofty pillars).

Mac-a-Moir went, and he did his very best, but he could not get aloft; he thrust the pillars hither and thither; he tried every way he knew, but it discomfited him.

"Who will try it again?" said Conall.

"Myself," said the young King of Lochlann. He went, and tried as well as he could, but he could not level one of the posts that was beneath the turret, but it beat him.

Said the King of the Green Isle, "I perceive, my men, that it will not go with you to take my daughter out of the turret. Many a man has striven to take her out, but it went with none of them, and I see that it will not go with you anymore; you may be off home."

"Well, then, if it does not go with us to bring her out, it is a great disgrace to us," said Conall.

He went and he struck a kick on one of the posts that was keeping the turret aloft, and the post broke, and the turret fell, but Conall caught it between his hands before it reached the ground. A door opened, the Sunbeam came out, the daughter of the King of the Green Isle, and she clasped her two arms about the neck of Conall, and Conall put his two arms about Sunbeam, and he bore her into the great house, and he said to the King of the Green Isle, "Thy daughter is won."

Sunbeam was very willing to stick to Conall, but Conall told her that he was married already to Breast of Light, daughter of the King of Laidheann, and the King of Lochlann was wedded to Beauty, daughter of the King of Greece, and that Garna Sgiathlais, King of Hispania, was married to Comely, daughter of the King of France, and that Great Hero, son of the King of the Light, was the only one of them that was unmarried.

The King of the Green Isle was pleased when he understood that they were honourable kings altogether, and that his daughter had been taken out with honour; and he said that he would give two-thirds of his realm while he was alive, and the whole after his death, to the one that his daughter should have, and that he was an old man, and that he would not be long alive altogether. Every one of them was married but Mac-a-Moir, and he was the most unblemished amongst them. Though Mac-a-Moir was not so handsome as the rest, he was a stately, comely, personable man; and Sunbeam said that he was the husband she would have, and word was sent for a priest, and Sunbeam, the daughter of the King of the Green Island, was wedded to Mac-a-Moir, son of the King of Light, and they made a wedding that lasted for the six days of the week, and the last day was no worse than the first day, and if there were better there were, and if not let them be.

When the other heroes found that Mac-a-Moir was married, they were in great haste to go home to see their own wives.

The King of the Green Isle set in order a great high masted white-sailed ship. There was a pilot in her prow, and a steersman in the stern, and men managing the rigging-ropes in the middle. Each meat and each drink as seemly for kings was put on board.

When each thing was ready, and each matter arranged as it ought to be, Conall, son of the King of Eirinn, Garna Sgiathlais, King of Hispania, and the King of Lochlann left a blessing with the King of the Green Isle, with Mac-a-Moir, and Deo Greine, and they went on board of the ship. The shipmen sailed with the ship, and they sailed to the realm of Sorcha with Conall, the son of the King of Eirinn. Conall reached the dun of the big town of Sorcha, came to Breast of Light and Duanach, without their having hopes of him, and they rejoiced with great joy to see him. Conall and Breast of Light were a while merry, and joyously, and fondly about each other, and Duanach was blithely and cheerily with them, and when Conall had spent a while cheerily, joyously with Breast of Light and Duanach, he began to think it long that he was not hearing from the realm of Iubhar how the fight was coming on between his mother's brother and the Turks, or if his father or brothers were yet alive. He thought that he would go to the realm of the Iubhar to see. He wished to leave Duanach, as he was before, to take care of Breast of Light and the realm, but Duanach would not stay. If Conall would go the realm of Iubhar, Duanach would go with him. Breast of Light wished Conall to go first to Eirinn to see if each thing were right in Eirinn, but his own counsel was best with Conall, and he wished Duanach to stay. But this is what Duanach said: "If thou goest, Conall, to the realm of Iubhar thou wilt fight, and I will be needful enough for thee."

And so it was agreed that Conall should take Duanach as a servant and counsellor. Breast of Light, and Conall, and Duanach, went away. Then he took with him the woman on board of the ship, and when he and his men were returning he was running out of provisions. There was an island here which they called Eilean na h-Otolia. The man who was over the island was (so) that if he was for giving food it could be got for money, and if he were not he had three big dogs, and he would let them out, and they would kill them all.

Said the slender dark man to Conall, "I would rather myself thou wouldst stay out of it, than go into it."

"I myself would not rather stay than go, I will go and I will get it; but if you see that he is not willing to give it to me, you will leave me the front, and you will stay behind me, if so be that he hounds the dogs at us," said Conall.

He went up to the house, and he asked if he could get food. He said that they should not, that plenty were asking for it who were more likely to get it than he.

He let out the dogs. Every one of the company stood at the back of Conall, and he himself went to the front; he caught a napkin and put it about his fist. Each one as he came, he was seeing his liver down through his mouth, from the rage that he had towards the men. He thrust his hand into the mouths of the dogs, one after another, and he took the heart and the liver out of them, and he killed them.

"Come now and you shall get food," said the man who was over the island.

"Thou mayest give that now, but I will not give thee one sgillinn for it; unless thou thyself hadst been a Trusdar, a stingy filthy wretch, thou hadst got payment; but since thou wert so dirty, thou shalt not get payment, and we shall get meat in spite of thee."

"That is easy enough for you now," said he. "But hast thou heard how it has befallen the King of Eirinn and the King of Laidhean? They were fighting the Turk."

"Well then I have heard how it has befallen these doubtless; the battle went with the Turk, and all the company that the King of Eirinn, and the King of Laidhean had, have been slain; and the Great Turk has the King of Eirinn, and the King of Laidhean bound back to back, under cats, and dogs, and men's spittle, and with shame and insult on themselves and on their hosts, that came to give battle and could not do it."

"That story is sad for me to hear, but though it is, keep thou this woman for me till I come back from these men."

"Well, then," said he, "I will not keep her, I have no way of keeping her. The thing that I had myself for that, thou thyself hast put me in want of it."

"Unless thou hadst been such a Trusdar of a man as thou wert, I had not put thee in want of it, but thou must keep this woman, or else there will not be much of the world for thee, after letting her go," said Conall.

He went and he left the woman, and when they reached the realm of Iubhar, the fighting was going on; Conall and Duanach did not go to the house of the king but to a hostelry. They got their supper that night and they went to bed. On the next morning Conall's waking was to hear shouts of hosts and clash of armour; heroes starting, commanders arraying soldiers to go to give a day of battle to the Turks. Conall arose and Duanach, they put on them their army and their armour of battle, and they went to the fight on the side of the people of the Iubhar. The fighting began and Conall was mowing down the Turks as though it were a man who was cutting down sow-thistles. There was one big man amongst the Turks, and he was mowing down the people of the Iubhar in the same way. It was not going with anyone to slay him, and they thought that no arms could touch him. He and Conall met each other in the fight. They tried their nimble feats upon each other, and Conall slew the big Turk. When the Turks saw that their champion was slain, they fled; and the people of the Iubhar followed the rout, and they thought that they had not left many of the Turks alive. In the night the people of Iubhar returned back, and they thought they would have peace on the next day and no one of them could understand who he was, the hero that had slain the big Turk, that had done them so much skaith.

As on the other days Conall and Duanach went to the hostelry where they were the former night, they got food and bed, and they thought, by the number of Turks that had been killed, that the war was at an end, and they went to sleep.

The King of the Iubhar had never seen Conall before; but it seemed to him, by the look of his face, that he was of the people of Eirinn. They went to rest that night full of joy, thinking that the Turks would not bring any more trouble upon them. But no matter. What they got in the morning was the tale of horror that the Turks were coming forward as numerous as they ever were. They had for it but that they must arise, and put men in their harness, to go to give a day of battle to the Turks again; and

Conall's morning waking was to hear the shout of the chiefs calling out their soldiers to give a day of combat to the Turks.

Conall sprang out of his bed and he put on his array and armour, and he went with the host of the Iubhar to battle against the Turks. When the two hosts met each other, Conall saw the big Turk that he had slain the day before coming forward that day again and mowing down the people of the Iubhar as he used to do.

Conall was mowing down the Turks till he and the big Turk met each other, and tried their agile valour upon each other that day again; and the big Turk was killed again that day by Conall. When the Turks saw that their champion had been slain, they fled, and the people of Iubhar followed the rout, and killed so many of the Turks, that it seemed to them there were not many of them to the fore, and they returned joyfully, cheerily, thinking that there was an end of the war. When Conall returned to the hostelry, he ate his supper and lay down to sleep.

It seemed to the King of Iubhar, that the man who had done the great feats of valour was his sister's son Conall, and he went to inquire about him. He heard that it was in the hostelry that the gallant man was dwelling, and the king reached the inn.

Duanach knew him, and the king asked Duanach if his master were in.

"He is," said Duanach, "but he is in his sleep, and I will not wake him."

"I am anxious to see him," said the king.

"If thou choosest thyself to go to wake him," said Duanach, "thou mayest, but I will not wake him."

"What is thy country?" said the king.

"It is," said Duanach, "the country from which my master came."

"What is the country whence came thy master?"

"That," said Duanach, "is the realm whence came the King of Eirinn."

"What is his name?" said the king.

"It is," said Duanach, "Conall Guilbeanach Mac do Righ Eirinn."

"Tell Conall, when he wakes, that his mother's brother came to visit him, and that he wishes to see him at the house of the King of Iubhar tomorrow."

"I will do that," said Duanach.

On the next day the Turks were coming on to drive the battle as they used, against the host of Iubhar; and it was rustling of plumes, and shouting of hosts, that awoke Conall. Then there were chiefs setting soldiers in order to go to bold battle against the Turks. Conall arose and put on his armour, and as soon as he could, and he went with the people of Iubhar to the battle. Conall saw the big Turk coming opposite to him the third time; and Conall killed the big Turk the third time, and the rout went over the Turks. The people of Iubhar followed them, and they slew the Turks with a great battle; and when no more of the Turks were to be seen, the host of Iubhar returned.

It seemed to Conall that there was something that was to be understood going on in the field of battle in the night; and he ordered Duanach to go to the hostelry to take his sleep, and that he himself would stay to watch the slain. Duanach went a little way from Conall, and he stayed to watch Conall.

When the night grew dark there came a great Turkish Carlin, and she had a white glaive of light with which she could see seven miles behind her and seven miles before her; and she had a flask of balsam carrying it.

And when she would reach a corpse, she would put three drops of the balsam in his mouth; she would strike three slaps on their hurdies, and she would say, "Get up, and go home; thy kail will be cold," and they would rise and go.

She was going from one to one, and bringing them alive, and they would be ready to come to fight again on the next day. At last she came where Conall was himself; she put three drops of balsam into his mouth, and hit him three slaps, and she said, "Get up, and go home, thy kail will be cold."

Conall sprang up suddenly, and she knew that he was not of the dead Turks, by his sudden rising, and she fled. Conall stretched out after her; she threw away the flask of balsam that she had, and the white glaive of light, but Conall ran till he was up with her; he gave a stroke of his sword, and he made two halves of her. He turned back, and he found the white glaive of light, but he could not find the flask of balsam. He was seeking it back and forwards, and hither and thither, and at last he saw Duanach, and he shouted –

"Is that thou, Duanach?"

"It is I," said Duanach; "and it well for thee that I am here."

"Hast thou got the flask of balsam?" said Conall.

"I have," said Duanach.

Duanach took the flask of balsam where Conall was, and Conall gave the white glaive of light to Duanach to lead the Turks who had been brought alive out of the field, and Conall went to sleep since he could do no more good till he should sleep; and he put the flask of balsam under his head, and he slept. Duanach went away with the sword, and he led the Turks out of the field; he led them through mosses and bogs, and when he found that they were in a dangerous place he would put the sword out of sight, and the Turks could not see, and they would fall into holes, and they would go down into marshes (criathraichean), and into well-eyes (suiltean-cruthaich), and they would be drowned. And again, he would bring the sword in sight, and the sword would shine, and the Turks that had not been drowned would follow, and Duanach would lead them through places where there were many scaurs, and Duanach would put a covering on the white glaive of light, and darkness would come, and many of the Turks would fall amongst the scaurs; and when they were out of that peril Duanach would bring the white glaive of light into sight to let them see, and he would lead them amongst crags; and he would hide the sword, and the Turks would lose their way, and they would go over the crags. It was thus that Duanach followed on till be had put an end to all the Turks by leading them over crags, and through scaurs, and amongst bogs. Then Duanach turned back to where Conall was, and he staid near him till he had got his sleep over. When Conall awoke, Duanach told him how he had done with the Turks, and Conall was pleased that the war was over.

Then Conall brought the people that were slain to life with the balsam. He went about the field, and he found one of his brothers there levelled, and he said to Garna Sgiathlais, "Come thou and take this one with thee, and take care of him till I come back." He looked, and he searched about, and he found another of his brothers, and he put him on the back of the King of Lochlann, and he asked him to take him with him.

He went in where his father was, and the Great Turk came out on his hands and knees. He found his father and the King of Laidheann bound. He loosed his father and the King of Laidheann, and he seized nobles as honourable as there were within, and he bound them instead of his father and the King of Laidheann.

Then he asked what death the Great Turk was threatening for his father and the King of Laidheann. They said that he was threatening to bang them to an oaken beam that was within, and to thrust two iron darts through the bodies of each one of them. "The very death with which he threatened you I will give to him," said Conall.

He seized the Great Turk and he hanged him, and he thrust the darts through his body, and he did the very same to another great noble.

The King of Eirinn was right well pleased, and that day they had peace. The King of Eirinn took Conall before the King of the Iubhar. The King made great rejoicings at seeing Conall, and because Conall had given peace to the realm of the Iubhar. No less would suffice the brother of Conall's mother than that Conall should be crowned King of the realm of Iubhar. The nobles of the realm (flathan na Rioghachd) were gathered, a great feast was made, and Conall was crowned King over the Iubhair; but though he was he did not stay in that realm. He was in haste to see Breast of Light.

He took his father with him and the King of Laidheann and they sailed to the island (na h-Otolia). They took Breast of Light on board out of that realm and they put the young King of Lochlann on shore in a fitting place for going to Greece, and Garna Sgiathlais on shore in France.

They sailed to Eirinn, and they sent a gille on foot, and a gille upon the top of a horse, and another gille swifter than that, to tell the Queen of Eirinn that the king was coming home, and that Conall was married, and that he and his wife were coming home with the king. When the message came to the Queen of Eirinn, that was the joyful tale for her. She made a great preparation that she might have a feast ready for them, and a cheery company gathered to give them a royal welcome, and when the King of Eirinn, Conall, and Breast of Light came home, there were there to welcome them, Duncan MacBrian, Murdoch MacBrian, Frenzy, and Whitebelly, red men from Mull, boatmen from Lorn, the brave blinding band of the King of Eirinn, and the great gentles of the realm, together as many as there were of them at the time.

They had a hearty feast, with joy and solace; they raised music, and laid down lament, and each one was content, they never saw such rejoicing before; and when the people thought the time fitting to go home, each one went to his own place, and there was peace and quiet in Eirinn.

Conall and Breast of Light thought that they would go to the realm of Laidheann to see her father. They made ready a ship, they went on board, and they sailed; they reached the realm of Laidheann, and the king had no hope or expectation of them at the time, but he saluted them, and made them welcome. Each thing was set in order to make Conall and Breast of Light happy and merry.

And Conall and Breast of Light stayed in the realm of Laidheann till they had their first son, and they were happy and pleased together, but that she had had a cut-slicing tongue at odd times, as happed to many of the women, and sure am I that Duanoch Achaidh Draodh stuck to Conall, and that his counsel was ever truly wise and truly moderate.

And again, their son was crowned Emperor of Eirinn, and King over the realm of Laidheann, and over the realm of Iubhar, and he had the realm of Lochlann, the realm of Sorcha, the realm of Greece, France, and Hispania, under cess, and so be they left.

Osgar, the Son of Oisein

WHEN OSGAR WAS A BOY he was sent to a school. When they used to get out at the mid-day, they used to go to play shinny on to a strand that was there. At the time when he was sixteen years of age, there would be a like number of the lads working on each side, and the side on which Osgar might be, that was the side which would hold.

He became exceedingly big, so that there was no one of his contemporaries that he was not twice as much as he. At last there used to be two divisions against him, and one division with him. At last there would be no man with him but himself, and the rest altogether against him.

They were there on a day of these days playing shinny, and they saw a boat coming in, and one man in her, and they never saw a man equal to him. The scholars took great fear before the man when they saw him coming, and they gathered about Osgar, every begotten one of them, to make a protector of him, and this wild man that was here came down where they were, and not a bit of him to be seen but the eyes, with blue-green scales of hardening upon him.

He came towards them, and everyone on whom he would strike his palm he would level him on the strand. He struck Osgar and put him in a faint. It was but scarcely that he could rise; but he thought that it was best for him to lie still; if he should get up again that he would slay him utterly.

Then he seized on Osgar, and he put him on the end of a withy, and sixteen of the scholars on top of him, he put the withy on his shoulder, and he betook himself to the boat with it. He put in the withy, "and it's I that was under altogether," said Osgar.

"I am saying to you," said Osgar, "that was as sore a blow as I have had, when he struck my ribs against the boat's floor, and the rest on top of me." Then he rowed the boat away for the length of a time, and he reached an island, and then he caught hold of the withy again, and he put it out. Then he took with him the withy on his shoulder, and I below. He reached a castle, and he went in. He left the withy there, and he went up to the end of the house, and there was a fine woman there. He said to her that he was going to take a nap, and when he should wake that the best hero who was there should be cooked before him."

"She went where the withy was, and she began to feel them. And I was the biggest there. I caught her by the hand, and said to her to let me be for the present. She went and she took with her the best one she found of the others. She put the roasting stake through him, and she roasted him on the fire. Then he got up, and he asked if she had got him cooked. She said that he was. Then he said, "There was a better boy than this there; I am going to sleep, and unless thou hast him cooked when I awake, I will have thyself in his place."

She went down then again and said, "I must take thee with me now."

"That is not best for thee, but leave me alive. Art thou his wife?"

"Not I. It is (so) that he stole me here seven years ago, and I in dread that he will slay me every day. Do thou help me, and I will help thee, and may be that we might put an end to the monster. Put thou the poker in the fire, and when it is red give me notice."

She did this, and when it was red she gave him notice. Osgar went up then when she loosed him, and he took the poker with him to where he was in his sleep. There was no part of his face bare, with scales of hardness, but his two eyes. He put the poker down through his eye to the ground; and she caught hold of his sword, and she struck off his head.

They went away then, and they took with them silver and gold enough, and Osgar hit upon the spot where they had left the little boat. He did not know to what side he should turn her prow, but they began to row, and they reached the very spot from which they had gone, on the strand. Then he reached the king of the Finne. They took exceeding good care of the woman that was there.

The heroes of the Finne went one day to the hunting-hill, and they parted from each other. They went to a glen that was there, and they did not know that they had ever been in the glen before. They hit upon a kind of burgh there, and a great wild savage of a giant in the upper end of the house.

"What's the news of the warriors of the Finne?" said he.

"Well, then, we have the news that we had no knowledge of ever having been in this place before."

He arose, and he put a cauldron on the fire, and a stag of a deer in it.

"Sit," said he, "and burn (fuel) beneath that cauldron, but unless the deer be cooked when I awake, you shall have but what you can take off his head, and by all you have ever seen do not take out the head."

They were tormented by hunger, and they did not know what they should do. They saw a little shaggy man coming down from the mountain. "Ye are in extremity," said he, himself. "Why are ye not tasting what is in the cauldron?"

"We are not," said they, "fear will not let us."

They took the lid out of the end of the cauldron, when they thought it was boiled, and so it was that there was frozen ice came upon it.

The old carle got up so wildly, and when he saw the little shaggy man, he laid the one great grasp upon him.

The carle went down, and he asked battle or combat from them. Caolite rose in front of him, and they began upon each other. He was about to have got Caolite under him now, and the little shaggy man got up, and he shook himself.

"Take notice that I am here," said he to the giant. He took to the tuft of (fell upon) the giant, and he kept back Caolite. They arose against each other now, and the little shaggy man slew the giant.

"Go now, and be going home." They went, and they were going before them, but they were not hitting upon the proper road. They saw the very finest man they had ever seen coming to meet them, and he met them, and he asked what was their wish.

They told him that they were seeking (to get) home to the Finne.

"It were right for me, Osgar, son of Fionn," said he, "to tell the way to thee. I am the ugly man whom ye saw coming through the mountain, and that slew the giant. He has had me under spells for eight years there, and I should have been there for ever, unless thou hadst come to help me to kill him. I am the son of the King of Greece, and it was a sister of mine that thou tookest from the other giant in the island."

They reached the Fhinn, and the son of the King of Greece and his sister knew each other. He kissed her, and he himself and she herself went, and Fionn, and Osgar, to Greece; and before they came back, Osgar married her.

Manus

THERE WAS A KING OF LOCHLANN, and he married, and two sons were born to him. Oireal was the name of one, and Iarlaid of the other. Their father and mother died. A "Parlamaid" sat to put "Cileadearachd," a regency, on the realm, till the children should come to age, and till they should take the vows of the realm on themselves. They sent word for the lads, and Oireal was a feeble man, and Iarlaid was the bigger. Oireal said to the Parlamaid that he would not have anything to do with the realm as yet.

"Clod of it you shall not have," said the Parliament, "unless you take it this day."

Said Iarlaid to Oireal, "Take thou the one half, and I will take the other half."

"Well, then," said Oireal, "I will do that."

The realm was written upon the lads. In a few years Iarlaid married the daughter of the King of Greece, and Oireal married the daughter of King Sgiath Sgial, King of the Arcuinn.

Sgiath Sgial gave six maids of honour with his daughter, and the King of Greece gave the very like with his own daughter.

Three quarters from that night the ailment of children struck the daughter of the King of Greece; and besides, the ailment of children struck the daughter of Sgiath Sgial, and sons were born to them, and twelve sons were born to the maids of honour. Manus was given (as a name) to the son of Oireal, and Eochaidh to the son of Iarlaid. The sons began to come on; Manus was growing big, and Eochaidh was but little. They were sent to school, and his own foster brethren were together with each one of them.

They were playing shinny on the field, coming from school, and Manus drove the ball against Eochaidh.

"I will have my own father's realm," said Manus.

Said the daughter of the King of Greece, "It were my wish to put an end to Manus, of murdering and spoiling and slaying."

"Well, then, that were the great pity to put that (end) to the son of our brother," said the king.

"If thou wilt not do it, I will do it," said she.

She went in, and gave a slight box on the ear (Leideag) to her own son, and she drove him out of the house.

"Begone," said she, "and betake thyself to the four brown boundaries of the world, and let me not see thy sole on the same land as long as the world is set. I will take Manus with me, and he shall be a son for myself."

She took Manus in with herself, and she set her own son on a beautiful sunny single-stemmed hill, where he could see every man, and no man him.

Manus was within with her, and he was not getting to see his mother at all. Then his mother said that she would go where her muime was, and that she would take her counsel.

At the end of a year she sent word for Manus. And in a few years the wife of his father's brother sent word for Manus.

"What, oh Manus!" said the daughter of the King of Greece, "art thou thinking of doing this day? If thou wilt marry, thou wilt get the third part of the realm; land, corn-land, and treasure."

"Well, then, I am not of age to marry at all," said he.

"Thou needst not (say) that," said she. "There is one man on my own land that will suit thee. Thou shalt go to ask his daughter, and thou shalt marry her. He is the Earl of Fiughaidh; thou shalt marry the daughter of the Earl of Fiughaidh."

She went away, and she took with her high families, and she would take with her five hundred men. She reached the house of the Earl of Fiughaidh, to give her to Manus to marry.

Said the wife of the Earl of the Fiughaidh to her, "My daughter is not of age to marry yet, and Manus is not of age to marry."

"Well," said the daughter of the King of Greece, "house or heap thou shalt not have upon my land unless thou givest thy daughter to him."

The man thought that there was no good for him to refuse her, and Manus and the daughter of the Earl of the Fiughaidh were married to each other.

They lay that night in the house of his father's brother.

"Is it thou that art here, Manus, mighty son, and bad man? dost thou know what wife yonder one gave to her own son, Eochaidh? She gave him the swift March wind. It was not to a worldly wife she married him, so that he might take the head off thee. Thou with a wife on thy bed at this time of night! Thou wilt be going back every day, and thou wilt not hold battle against him."

"Is it thus it is?" said Manus.

He went where she was.

"Be leaving the realm," said the wife of his father's brother to him, "or else thou wilt have but what thou takest to its end."

"Clod thou shalt not have here," said she. "Thy share is under stones and rough mountains in the old Bergen."

"Well, then, since thou art putting me away, give me the six foster brothers of Eochaidh, that I may have twelve."

He got that; he went away, and he betook himself to the old Bergen.

When he reached the old Bergen, no man dared to come near his castle. There were sheep in the old Bergen, and sheep of Corrachar is what they were called.

They fell to making pits in the earth; the sheep were going into the pits, and they were catching them and they were killing them, and keeping themselves in flesh thus in the old Bergen.

"Be it from me! be it from me!" said Manus. "It is a year since I saw my muime; I had better go and see her."

"It were not my advice to thee to go there," said they; "but if thou art going, thou hast twelve foster brothers, and take them with thee."

"They were no sorry company for me to be with me," said he.

He went. The daughter of the King of Greece was looking out of a window, and she perceived Manus coming. She went down to where his father's brother was.

"The son of thy brother is coming here," said she, "with costly coloured belts on his left side, with which might be got the love of a young woman, and the liking of maidens" – that it were for her pleasure to put an end to him, of murdering, and misusing, and slaying.

His father's brother said that were a great pity, and that he would not be to the fore to do that to him.

"If thou wilt not do it, I will do it," said she.

She went out of the house, and she took his twelve foster brethren from him, and she swore them to herself. He went back to the Old Bergen by himself, gloomy, tearful, sorrowful, and it was late. What should he see but a man in a red vesture.

"It is thou that art here, Manus?" said he.

"It is I," said Manus.

"I think if thou hadst bad or good arms that thou would'st get to be King over Lochlann."

"I have not that," said he.

"Well," said he of the red vesture, "if thou would'st give me a promise I would give thee arms."

"What promise shall I give thee? I have not a jot to give thee."

"Well, I will not ask thee much. I was the armourer of thy grandfather, and thy great-grandfather, if thou wouldst give me a promise that I should be armourer with thee I would give thee arms this night."

"I will give thee that (promise), if so be that I am ever a king."

They went and they reached the house. The man of the red vesture took out a key, and he opened a door, and when he had opened it the house was full of arms, and not a jot in it but arms.

"Begin now and choose arms," said the man of the red vesture.

Manus seized a sword, and he broke it, and everyone he caught he was breaking it.

"Don't do that, Manus, don't be breaking the arms, in case thou mightest have need of them yet. When I was a young man thy grandsire had a war, and I had an old sword, an old helmet, and an old mail shirt on; try them," said the man of the red vesture.

Manus seized the sword, and it beat him to break it. He put the sword and the helmet on. What should he see but a cloth (hanging) down from the ridge of the house. "What is the use of that cloth?" said Manus.

"It is," said he, "that when thou spreadest it, to seek food and drink, thou wilt get as thou usest. There is another virtue in it. If a foe should meet thee, he would give a kiss to the back of thy fist."

He gave the cloth to Manus, and he folded the cloth in his oxter. What should he see but an iron chain (hanging) down from the ridge of the house.

"What is the good of that chain?" said Manus.

"There is no creature in the world that if yonder thing should be put about his neck the battle of a hundred men would not be upon him," said the man of the red vesture.

Manus took the chain with him. When he was going, what should he see but two lions, and a whelp with them. The lions came in front of him to eat him, and to put him to skaith. He spread the cloth, and the lions came, and they kissed the back of his fist, and they went past him. The lion whelp got in amongst the folds of the cloth, and he wrapped the cloth about him, and he lifted him with him to the old Bergen.

When he reached the old Bergen the daughter of the Earl of the Fiughaidh was within. He put the chain about the neck of the lion whelp. The lion whelp went, and he cleared the castle; he did not leave a creature or a monster alive in it. He set fire to the castle. He was there a year, and he had no want.

He went out one day, and he said he would go to see his muime.

He took the lion whelp with him, and he went away. She perceived him coming. There was a sword at his side that day. She came out to meet him, and she had a brown lapdog. He went to meet Manus with his mouth open, to put Manus to skaith, and to eat him. Away went the lion whelp, and he went before Manus, and he set his paw at the back of the throat of her "measan," and he let out his entrails on the earth.

"There, Manus," said she, "but put thy whelp in at the ridge of the lion's house."

He put the lion whelp in at the ridge of the house, and he put the chain about his neck, and he did not leave a lion under the ridge of the house unslain, and laid himself (down) stretched for dead along with them.

Manus went home without whelp, without man, that night. What work should his twelve foster brethren be set to, but to clear out the lion's house. When they were put out there was not a lion under the ridge of the house that had not his throat cut. The lion whelp was without a drop of sweat upon him, and the iron chain that Manus had put on him (was) about his neck. One of them said that the lion which was yonder seemed strange to him, without a drop of sweat upon him, unlike the rest.

"That is the lion whelp of the man of my love," said one of the company. "The lion whelp of Manus."

"Well, then," said one of them, "though we are sworn not to go out of the town, before he rises we might go, and give a message."

"There is no man who goes out of this town," said the rest, "after the coming of night that there is not the pain of seven years upon him afterwards."

They went to the window, and when they went to the window the lion's whelp opened his eyes, and he came alive.

She went where her husband was, and she said to him to put the rough traveller in order, and five hundred men in it.

He said that there would be the pain of seven years on any being who should go out after the falling of the night.

She said though there should be the pain of seventeen years in it, that they should go to seek the head of Manus.

The deaf haltman was what they used to call the man who was guarding the realm at that time, and he could not hear a jot till there should be nine nines shouting in his ear. He could kill nine nines backwards, and nine nines forwards with his sword. What should awake him but the stormy sound of the rough traveller coming, and he thought that it was a foe that was there. He arose upon the rough traveller, and he did not leave a mother's son of the five hundred alive, himself and the lion's whelp, and the twelve foster brothers of Manus went to the Old Bergen.

"Never thou mind," said she. "Though Manus did that to me. There is the Red Gruagach, son of the King of Greece, and he will take the head of Manus out of the Old Bergen."

Then went his mother here, and she sent a ship to Manus to the Old Bergen to take him away before the Red Gruagach should take the head off him. What should his muime do but put a sea thickening on the ocean, so that Manus might not get away. His mother sent a pilot in the ship, and what should the ship do but stop in the sea thickening.

"Is there a ship in the world that will take us out of this?" said Manus to the pilot.

"Indeed there is the speckled ship of the son of Valcan Smith," said the pilot.

They were on board, and they could not stir.

At the mouth of the night the lion whelp thrust his head under the arm of Manus, and he went out off the ship, and Manus on his back. He went and he reached a scaur. He left Manus on the scaur, and he himself made a spring down the other side of it. Manus fell asleep, and he would like as well to find death with the rest, rather than be left by himself on a rock. There came a voice to him, and it said to him, "Arise." He rose, and he saw a ship.

Who was here but the ship of MacBhalcan Smith, and the lion whelp in the shape of a pilot at the helm, and Mac-Vic-Valcan Smith and his twelve sailors dead on her deck. He reached the ship, and he put his twelve foster brethren and the daughter of the Earl of the Fiughaidh in the ship of MacBhalcan Smith. He fell to at sailing amongst the thickening. What should he see but land, and when he saw the land he saw the very finest castle he ever saw. He went on shore, and he put MacBhalcan Smith and his twelve sailors on shore on a point. He reached the castle, and he went in, and there was a fine woman there within, and twelve bald ruddy maidens. His twelve foster brothers sat beside the bald ruddy maidens, and they said that they would never go for ever till they should get them to marry.

It was not long till there came home the White Gruagach, son of the King of the Light, and a great auburn clumsy woman, his mother.

"Who is here," said he, "looking my twelve brown ruddy daughters in the front of the face? and that I never saw a man that might look at them that I would not take his head off against his throat."

"These are my twelve foster brothers, and they have taken love for thy bald ruddy daughters, and thou must give them to me to marry," said Manus.

"Well," said the White Gruagach, "the covenant on which I would do that, I am sure that thou wouldst not do it for me, that is, to put me in against my father, and that I am out from him for seven years."

"I will do that," said Manus, "but that thou thyself shouldst go with me."

On the morrow they went away, and they reached the King of the Light. The King of the Light came out, and he gave his right hand to his own son, and his left hand to Manus. The lion whelp went, and he seized him, and he levelled him.

"Choke off me the monster before he takes my life from off me," said the King of the Light.

"I will do that," said Manus, "but write with a drop of thy blood that thy son is thy beloved heir."

"Well, it's long since I would have done that, if he had come himself to ask it."

Then he went and he wrote, and they went away to come home. When they were coming the daughter of the Earl of the Fiughaidh was in a burn.

"O," said the White Gruagach, "I am dead."

"What ails thee?" said Manus.

"There is a stone," said he, "in the burn, and there are three trouts under the stone, and they are in thy wife's apron. As long as the trouts should be alive I would be alive, and thy wife has one of them now in the fire."

"Is there anything in the world," said Manus, "that would do thee good?"

"The King of the Great World has a horned venomous (creature), and if I could get his blood I would be as well as I ever was."

They reached the house, and the White Gruagach was dead.

Then Manus went, and the speckled ship was stolen from him, and there was no knowing who in the world had taken it from him.

One of his foster brothers said that Brodram, son of the King of the Great World, had taken it with him.

He went away to Brodram. He asked him what made him take that ship from him. He said that he had stolen her himself before, and that he had no right to her. He said that his father had a venomous horned (creature), and that while the Beannach Nimhe was alive that his father would be alive, and that if the Beannach Nimhe was slain that he would have the realm.

He went with Brodram, and the venomous horned beast was in a park. The lion whelp went into the park, and he put his paw into the hollow of the throat of the venomous horned beast. The venomous horned beast fell dead, and the king fell dead within.

Then Brodram was King over the Great World, and Manus got the blood, and he returned back, and with it he brought the White Gruagach to life.

"It may not be that thou wilt not go thyself with me now to put me in on the realm," said he to the White Gruagach.

The White Gruagach said that he would go. He reached Brodram, and he said that he would go with him.

Balcan and his twelve apprentices were working in the smithy, and he revived his twelve sailors. He asked him to go with him, and Balcan said that he would. There went Balcan, and the White Gruagach, and Brodram, and the Gruagach of the Tower, son of the King of Siginn, with him.

> They reached Lochlann,
> There met them a man in a red vesture;
> The White Gruagach, and the Red Gruagach began
> Fearfully, hatefully proudly,
> Three destructions they would drive off them.
> To the cloud flakes of aether and heaven.
> There gathered stag hounds, savage hounds,
> To take pleasure in the monsters.
> They would make the sea dry up,
> And the earth burst,
> And the stars fall.

The Red Gruagach was slain, and his head stuck on a stake, and Manus was crowned King over Lochlann, and he did not leave a living man in Lochlann.

Nighean Righ Fo Thuinn, the Daughter of King Under-Waves

THE FHINN WERE ONCE TOGETHER, on the side of Beinn Eudainn, on a wild night, and there was pouring rain and falling snow from the north. About midnight a creature of uncouth appearance struck at the door of Fionn. Her hair was down to her heels, and she cried to him to let her in under the border of his covering. Fionn raised up a corner of the covering, and he gazed at her. "Thou strange looking ugly creature," said he, "thy hair is down to thy heels, how shouldst thou ask me to let thee in?"

She went away, and she gave a scream. She reached Oisean, and she asked him to let her in under the border of his covering. Oisean lifted a corner of his covering, and he saw her.

"Thou strange, hideous creature, how canst thou ask me to let thee in?" said he.

"Thy hair is down to thy heels. Thou shalt not come in."

She went away, and she gave a shriek.

She reached Diarmaid, and she cried aloud to him to let her in under the border of his covering.

Diarmaid lifted a fold of his covering, and he saw her. "Thou art a strange, hideous creature. Thy hair is down to thy heels, but come in," said he. She came in under the border of his covering.

"Oh, Diarmaid," said she, "I have spent seven years travelling over ocean and sea, and of all that time I have not passed a night till this night, till thou hast let me in. Let me come in to the warmth of the fire."

"Come up," said Diarmaid.

When she came up, the people of the Fhinn began to flee, so hideous was she.

"Go to the further side," said Diarmaid, "and let the creature come to the warmth of the fire."

They went to the one side, and they let her be at the fire, but she had not been long at the fire, when she sought to be under the warmth of the blanket together with himself.

"Thou art growing too bold," said Diarmaid. "First thou didst ask to come under the border of the covering, then thou didst seek to come to the fire, and now thou seekest leave to come under the blanket with me; but come."

She went under the blanket, and he turned a fold of it between them. She was not long thus, when he gave a start, and he gazed at her, and he saw the finest drop of blood that ever was, from the beginning of the universe till the end of the world at his side. He shouted out to the rest to come over where he was, and he said to them:

"It is not often that men are unkind! Is not this the most beauteous woman that man ever saw!"

"She is," said they, as they covered her up, "the most beautiful woman that man ever saw."

Then she was asleep, and she did not know that they were looking at her. He let her sleep, and he did not awaken her, but a short time after that she awoke, and she said to him, "Art thou awake, Diarmaid?"

"I am awake," said Diarmaid.

"Where wouldst thou rather that the very finest castle thou hast ever seen should be built?"

"Up above Beinn Eudainn, if I had my choice," and Diarmaid slept, and she said no more to him.

"There went one out early, before the day, riding, and he saw a castle built up upon a hill. He cleared his sight to see if it was surely there; then he saw it, and he went home, and he did not say a word.

Another went out, and he saw it, and he did not say a word. Then the day was brightened, and two came in telling that the castle was most surely there.

Said she, as she rose up sitting, "Arise, Diarmaid, go up to thy castle, and be not stretched there any longer."

"If there was a castle to which I might go," said he.

"Look out, and see if there be a castle there."

He looked out, and he saw a castle, and he came in. "I will go up to the castle, if thou wilt go there together with me."

"I will do that, Diarmaid, but say not to me thrice how thou didst find me," said she.

"I will not say to thee for ever, how I found thee," said Diarmaid.

They went to the castle, the pair. That was a beautiful castle! There was not a shadow of thing, that was for the use of a castle that was not in it, even to a herd for the geese.

The meat was on the board, and there were maid servants, and men servants about it.

They spent three days in the castle together, and at the end of three days she said to him, "Thou art turning sorrowful, because thou art not together with the rest."

"Think that I am not feeling sorrow surely that I am not together with the Fhinn," said he.

"Thou hadst best go with the Fhinn, and thy meat and thy drink will be no worse than they are," said she.

"Who will take care of the greyhound bitch, and her three pups?" said Diarmaid.

"Oh," said she, "what fear is there for the greyhound, and for the three pups?"

He went away when he heard that. He left a blessing with her, and he reached the people of the Fhinn, and Fionn, the brother of his mother, and there was a chief's honour and welcome before Diarmaid when he arrived, and they had ill will to him, because the woman had come first to them, and that they had turned their backs to her, and that he had gone before her wishes, and the matter had turned out so well.

She was out after he had gone away, and what should she see but one coming in great haste. Then she thought of staying without till he should come, and who was there but Fionn. He hailed her, and caught her by the hand.

Thou art angry with me, damsel," said he.

"Oh, I am not at all, Fionn," said she. "Come in till thou take a draught from me."

"I will go if I get my request," said Fionn.

"What request might be here that thou shouldst not get?" said she.

"That is, one of the pups of the greyhound bitch."

"Oh, the request thou hast asked is not great," said she; "the one thou mayest choose take it with thee."

He got that, and he went away.

At the opening of the night came Diarmaid. The greyhound met him without, and she gave a yell.

"It is true, my lass, one of thy pups is gone. But if thou hadst mind of how I found thee, how thy hair was down to thy heels, thou hadst not let the pup go."

"Thou Diarmaid, what saidst thou so?"

"Oh," said Diarmaid, "I am asking pardon."

"Oh, thou shalt get that," said she, and he slept within that night, and his meat and drink were as usual.

On the morrow he went to where he was yesterday, and while he was gone she went out to take a stroll, and while she was strolling about, what should she see but a rider coming to where she was. She stayed without till he reached her.

Who reached her here but Oisean, son of Fionn.

They gave welcome and honour to each other. She told him to go in with her, and that he should take a draught from her, and he said that he would, if he might get his request.

"What request hast thou?" said she.

"One of the pups of the greyhound bitch."

"Thou shalt get that," said she, "take thy choice of them."

He took it with him, and he went away.

At the opening of the night came Diarmaid home, and the greyhound met him without, and she gave two yells.

"That is true, my lass," said Diarmaid, "another is taken from thee. But if she had mind of how I found her, she had not let one of thy pups go, when her hair was down to her heels."

"Diarmaid! What saidst thou?" said she.

"I am asking pardon," said Diarmaid.

"Thou shalt get that," said she, and they seized each other's hands, and they went home together, and there was meat and drink that night as there ever had been.

In the morning Diarmaid went away, and a while after he had gone she was without taking a stroll. She saw another rider coming today, and he was in great haste. She thought she would wait, and not go home till he should come forward. What was this but another of the Fhinn.

He went with civil words to the young damsel, and they gave welcome and honour to each other.

She told him to go home with her, and that he should take a draught from her. He said that he would go if he should get his request.

She asked that time what request that might be.

"One of the pups of the greyhound bitch," said he.

"Though it is a hard matter for me," said she, "I will give it to thee."

He went with her to the castle, he took a draught from her, he got the pup, and he went away.

At the opening of the night came Diarmaid. The greyhound met him, and she gave three yells, the most hideous that man ever heard.

"Yes, that is true, my lass, thou art without any this day," said Diarmaid, "but if she had mind of howl found her, she would not have let the pup go; when her hair was down to her heels, she would not have done that to me."

"Thou, Diarmaid, what saidst thou?"

"Oh, I am asking pardon," said Diarmaid. He went home, and he was without wife or bed beside him, as he ever had been. It was in a moss-hole he awoke on the morrow. There was no castle, nor a stone left of it on another. He began to weep, and he said to himself that he would not stay, head or foot, till he should find her.

Away he went, and what should he do but take his way across the glens. There was neither house nor ember in his way. He gave a glance over his shoulder, and what should he see but the greyhound just dead. He seized her by the tail, and he put her on his shoulder, and he would not part with her for the love that he bore her. He was going on, and what should he see above him but a herd.

"Didst thou see, this day or yesterday, a woman taking this way?" said Diarmaid to the herd.

"I saw a woman early in the morning yesterday, and she was walking hard," said the herd.

"What way didst thou see her going?"

"She went down yonder point to the strand, and I saw her no more."

He took the very road that she took, till there was no going any further. He saw a ship. He put the slender end of his spear under his chest, and he sprang into her, and he went to the other side. He laid himself down, stretched out on the side of a hill, and he slept, and when he awoke there was no ship to be seen. "A man to be pitied am I," said he, "I shall never get away from here, but there is no help for it."

He sat on a knoll, and he had not sat there long when he saw a boat coming, and one man in her, and he was rowing her.

He went down where she was, he grasped the greyhound by the tail, and he put her in, and he went in after her.

Then the boat went out over the sea, and she went down under, and he had but just gone down, when he saw ground, and a plain on which he could walk. He went on this land, and he went on.

He was but a short time walking, when he fell in with a gulp of blood. He lifted the blood, and he put it into a napkin, and he put it into his pouch. "It was the greyhound that lost this," said he.

He was a while walking, and he fell in with the next gulp, and he lifted it, and put it into his pouch. He fell in with the next one, and he did the like with it. What should he see a short space from him, after that, but a woman, as though she were crazed, gathering rushes. He went towards her, and he asked her what news she had. "I cannot tell till I gather the rushes," said she.

"Be telling it whilst thou art gathering," said Diarmaid.

"I am in great haste," said she.

"What place is here?" said he.

"There is here," said she, "Rioghachd Fo Thuinn, Realm Under-waves."

"Realm Under-waves!"

"Yes," said she.

"What use hast thou for rushes, when thou art gathering them?" said Diarmaid.

"The daughter of King Under-waves has come home, and she was seven years under spells, and she is ill, and the leeches of Christendom are gathered, and none are doing her good, and a bed of rushes is what she finds the wholesomest."

"Well then, I would be far in thy debt if thou wouldst see me where that woman is."

"Well then, I will see that. I will put thee into the sheaf of rushes, and I will put the rushes under thee and over thee, and I will take thee with me on my back."

That is a thing that thou canst not do," said Diarmaid.

"Be that upon me," said she.

She put Diarmaid into the bundle, and she took him on her back.

When she reached the chamber she let down the bundle.

"Oh! hasten that to me," said the daughter of King Under-waves.

He sprang out of the bundle, and he sprang to meet her, and they seized each other's hands, and there was joy then.

"Three parts of the ailment are gone, but I am not well, and I will not be. Every time I thought of thee when I was coming, I lost a gulp of the blood of my heart."

"Well then, I have got these three gulps of thy heart's blood, take thou them in a drink, and there will be nothing amiss."

"Well then, I will not take them," said she; "they will not do me a shade of good, since I cannot get one thing and I shall never get that in the world."

"What thing is that?" said he.

"There is no good in telling thee that; thou wilt not get it, nor any man in the world; it has discomfited them for long."

"If it be on the surface of the world I will get it, and do thou tell it," said Diarmaid.

"That is three draughts from the cup of Righ Magh an Ioghnaidh, the King of Plain of Wonder, and no man ever got that, and I shall not get it."

"Oh! said Diarmaid, "there are not on the surface of the world as many as will keep it from me. Tell me if that man be far from me."

"He is not; he is within a bound near my father, but a rivulet is there, and in it there is the sailing of a ship with the wind behind her, for a day and a year before thou reach it."

He went away, and he reached the rivulet, and he spent a good while walking at its side.

"I cannot cross over it; that was true for her," said Diarmaid.

Before he had let the word out of his mouth, there stood a little russet man in the midst of the rivulet.

"Diarmaid, son of Duibhne, thou art in straits," said he.

"I am in a strait just now," said Diarmaid.

What wouldst thou give to a man who would bring thee out of these straits? Come hither and put thy foot on my palm."

"Oh! my foot cannot go into thy palm," said Diarmaid.

"It can."

He went, and he put his foot on his palm. "Now, Diarmaid, it is to King Mag an Iunai that thou art going."

"It is indeed," said Diarmaid.

"It is to seek his cup thou art going."

"It is."

"I will go with thee myself."

"Thou shalt go," said Diarmaid.

Diarmaid reached the house of King Wonderplain. He shouted for the cup to be sent out, or battle, or combat; and it was not the cup.

There were sent out four hundred lugh ghaisgeach, and four hundred lan ghaisgeach, and in two hours he left not a man of them alive.

He shouted again for battle, or else combat, or the cup to be sent out.

That was the thing he should get, battle or else combat, and it was not the cup.

There were sent out eight hundred loo gaisgeach, and eight hundred lan gaisgeach, and in three hours he left not a man of them alive.

He shouted again for battle, or else combat, or else the cup to be sent out to him.

There were sent out nine hundred strong heroes, and nine hundred full heroes, and in four hours he left no man of them alive.

"Whence," said the king as he stood in his own great door, "came the man that has just brought my realm to ruin? If it be the pleasure of the hero, let him tell from whence he came."

"It is the pleasure of the hero; a hero of the people of the Fhinn am I. I am Diarmaid."

"Why didst thou not send in a message to say who it was, and I would not have spent my realm upon thee, for thou wouldst kill every man of them, for it was put down in the books seven years before thou wert born. What dost thou require?"

"That is the cup; it comes from thine own hand for healing."

"No man ever got my cup but thou, but it is easy for me to give thee a cup; but for healing there is but that I have myself about the board."

Diarmaid got the cup from King Wonderplain.

"I will now send a ship with thee, Diarmaid," said the king.

"Great thanks (Taing mhor) to thee, oh king. I am much in thy debt; but I have a ferry of my own."

Here the king and Diarmaid parted from each other. He remembered when he had parted from the king that he had never said a word at all, the day before about the little russet man, and that he had not taken him in. It was when he was coming near upon the rivulet that he thought of him; and he did not know how he should get over the burn.

"There is no help for it," said he. "I shall not now get over the ferry, and shame will not let me return to the king."

What should rise while the word was in his mouth but the little russet man out of the burn.

"Thou art in straits, Diarmaid."

"I am."

"It is this day that thou art in extremity."

"It is. I got the thing I desired, and I am not getting across."

"Though thou didst to me all that which thou hast done; though thou didst not say a word of me yesterday; put thy foot on my palm and I will take thee over the burn."

Diarmaid put his foot on his palm, and he took him over the burn.

"Thou wilt talk to me now, Diarmaid," said he.

"I will do it," said Diarmaid.

"Thou art going to heal the daughter of King Under-waves; she is the girl that thou likest best in the world."

"Oh! it is she."

"Thou shalt go to such and such a well. Thou wilt find a bottle at the side of the well, and thou shalt take it with thee full of the water. When thou reachest the damsel, thou shalt put the water in the cup, and a gulp of blood in it, and she will drink it. Thou shalt fill it again, and she will drink. Thou shalt fill it the third time, and thou shalt put the third gulp of blood into it, and she will drink it, and there will not be a whit ailing her that time. When thou hast given her the last, and she is well, she is the one for whom thou carest least that ever thou hast seen before thee."

"Oh! not she," said Diarmaid.

"She is; the king will know that thou hast taken a dislike to her. She will say, Diarmaid thou hast taken a dislike to me. Say thou that thou hast. Dost thou know what man is speaking to thee?" said the little russet man.

"Not I," said Diarmaid.

"In me there is the messenger of the other world, who helped thee; because thy heart is so warm to do good to another. King Under-waves will come, and he will offer thee much silver and gold for healing his daughter. Thou shalt not take a jot, but that the king should send a ship with thee to Eirinn, to the place from whence thou camest."

Diarmaid went; he reached the well; he got the bottle, and he filled it with water; he took it with him, and he reached the castle of King Under-waves. When he came in he was honoured and saluted.

"No man ever got that cup before," said she.

"I would have got it from all that there are on the surface of the world; there was no man to turn me back," said Diarmaid.

"I thought that thou wouldst not get it though thou shouldst go, but I see that thou hast it," said she.

He put a gulp of blood into the water in the cup, and she drank it. She drank the second one, and she drank the third one; and when she had drunk the third one there was not a jot ailing her. She was whole and healthy. When she was thus well, he took a dislike for her; scarcely could he bear to see her.

"Oh! Diarmaid," said she, "thou art taking a dislike for me."

"Oh! I am," said he.

Then the king sent word throughout the town that she was healed, and music was raised, and lament laid down. The king came where Diarmaid was, and he said to him,

"Now, thou shalt take so much by counting of silver for healing her, and thou shalt get herself to marry."

"I will not take the damsel; and I will not take anything but a ship to be sent with me to Eirinn, where the Fhinn are gathered."

A ship went with him, and he reached the Fhinn and the brother of his mother; and there was joy before him there, and pleasure that he had returned.

Tales of Magic & Fairy Folk

Introduction

WE LOOK IN VAIN to Scotland's fairy tales for pretty nymphs with butterfly wings and starry wands; even for engaging 'little people'. More typical is the grotesque gruagach in 'The Young King of Easaidh Ruadh'; the shape-shifting crow-man in 'The Tale of the Hoodie'; or the dark-dwelling marauders of 'The Page-Boy and the Silver Goblet'. Or, for that matter, the outwardly ordinary – yet, oddly, just as menacing – Woman of Peace who bothers the housewife in 'Sanntraigh'.

The 'brownie' is, incidentally, also sometimes referred to as a 'gruagach' (that word sometimes meaning a 'spectre of the class of Brownies to which the Highland dairymaids made frequent libations of milk' and 'rarely the chief of a place', but also a creature 'who did odd jobs about the house for the maids'). Brownies, while ugly and hairy, can at least be described as a kind of benevolent fairy, with their unerring drive to serve the family whose home they inhabit.

Really, though, what the fairy tradition and tales of magic represent in Scotland's folk tales is the permeability of the border between everyday reality and a life beyond that is mysterious and magical – albeit as often in a sinister way as in an agreeably 'enchanting' one.

The Brownie

THE SCOTTISH BROWNIE formed a class of being distinct in habit and disposition from the freakish and mischievous elves. He was meagre, shaggy, and wild in his appearance. In the day-time he lurked in remote recesses of the old houses which he delighted to haunt, and in the night sedulously employed himself in discharging any laborious task which he thought might be acceptable to the family to whose service he had devoted himself. But the Brownie does not drudge from the hope of recompense. On the contrary, so delicate is his attachment that the offer of reward, but particularly of food, infallibly occasions his disappearance for ever.

It is told of a Brownie, who haunted a border family now extinct, that the lady having fallen unexpectedly ill, and the servant, who was ordered to ride to Jedburgh for the *sage-femme*, showing no great alertness in setting out, the familiar spirit slipped on the greatcoat of the lingering domestic, rode to the town on the laird's best horse, and returned with the midwife *en croupe*. During the short space of his absence, the Tweed, which they must necessarily ford, rose to a dangerous height. Brownie, who transported his charge with all the rapidity of the ghostly lover of Lenore, was not to be stopped by the obstacle. He plunged in with the terrified old lady, and landed her in safety where her services were wanted. Having put the horse into the stable (where it was afterwards found in a woeful plight), he proceeded to the room of the servant, whose duty he had discharged, and finding him just in the act of drawing on his boots, he administered to him a most merciless drubbing with his own horsewhip. Such an important service excited the gratitude of the laird, who, understanding that Brownie had been heard to express a wish to have a green coat, ordered a vestment of the colour to be made, and left in his haunts. Brownie took away the green coat, but was never seen more. We may suppose that, tired of his domestic drudgery, he went in his new livery to join the fairies.

The last Brownie known in Ettrick Forest resided in Bodsbeck, a wild and solitary spot, near the head of Moffat Water, where he exercised his functions undisturbed, till the scrupulous devotion of an old lady induced her to "hire him away," as it was termed, by placing in his haunt a porringer of milk and a piece of money. After receiving this hint to depart, he was heard the whole night to howl and cry, "Farewell to bonnie Bodsbeck!" which he was compelled to abandon for ever.

The Young King of Easaidh Ruadh

THE YOUNG KING OF EASAIDH RUADH, after he got the heirship to himself, was at much merry making, looking out what would suit him, and what would come into his humour. There was a gruagach near his dwelling, who was called Gruagach carsalach donn (The brown curly long-haired one.)

He thought to himself that he would go to play a game with him. He went to the Seanagal (soothsayer) and he said to him – "I am made up that I will go to game with the Gruagach carsalach donn." "Aha!" said the Seanagal, "art thou such a man? Art thou so insolent that thou art going to play a game against the Gruagach carsalach donn? 'Twere my advice to thee to change thy nature and not to go there." "I wont do, that," said he. "'Twere my advice to thee, if thou shouldst win of the Gruagach carsalach donn, to get the cropped rough-skinned maid that is behind the door for the worth of thy gaming, and many a turn will he put off before thou gettest her." He lay down that night, and if it was early that the day came, 'twas earlier than that that the king arose to hold gaming against the Gruagach. He reached the Gruagach, he blessed the Gruagach, and the Gruagach blessed him. Said, the Gruagach to him, "Oh young king of Easaidh Ruadh, what brought thee to me today? Wilt thou game with me?" They began and they played the game. The king won. "Lift the stake of thy gaming so that I may get (leave) to be moving." "The stake of my gaming is to give me the cropped rough-skinned girl thou hast behind the door." "Many a fair woman have I within besides her," said the Gruagach. "I will take none but that one." "Blessing to thee and cursing to thy teacher of learning." They went to the house of the Gruagach, and the Gruagach set in order twenty young girls. "Lift now thy choice from amongst these." One was coming out after another, and every one that would come out she would say, "I am she; art thou not silly that art not taking me with thee?" But the Seanagal had asked him to take none but the last one that would come out. When the last one came out, he said, "This is mine." He went with her, and when they were a bit from the house, her form altered, and she is the loveliest woman that was on earth. The king was going home full of joy at getting such a charming woman.

He reached the house, and he went to rest. If it was early that the day arose, it was earlier than that that the king arose to go to game with the Gruagach. "I must absolutely go to game against the Gruagach today," said he to his wife. "Oh!" said she, "that's my father, and if thou goest to game with him, take nothing for the stake of thy play but the dun shaggy filly that has the stick saddle on her."

The king went to encounter the Gruagach, and surely the blessing of the two to each other was not beyond what it was before. "Yes!" said the Gruagach, "how did thy young bride please thee yesterday?" "She pleased fully." "Hast thou come to game with me today?" "I came." They began at the gaming, and the king won from the Gruagach on that day. "Lift the stake of thy gaming, and be sharp about it." "The stake of my gaming is the dun shag filly on which is the stick saddle."

They went away together. They reached the dun shaggy filly. He took her out from the stable, and the king put his leg over her and she was the swift heroine! He went home. His wife had her hands spread before him, and they were cheery together that night. "I would rather myself," said his wife, "that thou shouldest not go to game with the Gruagach any more, for if he wins he will put trouble on thy head." "I won't do that," said he, "I will go to play with him today."

He went to play with the Gruagach. When he arrived, he thought the Gruagach was seized with joy. "Hast thou come?" he said. "I came." They played the game, and, as a cursed victory for the king, the Gruagach won that day. "Lift the stake of thy game," said the young king of Easaidh Ruadh, "and be not heavy on me, for I cannot stand to it." "The stake of my play is," said he, "that I lay it as crosses and as spells on thee, and as the defect of the year, that the cropped rough-skinned creature, more uncouth and unworthy than thou thyself, should take thy head, and thy neck, and thy life's look off, if thou dost not get for me the Glaive of Light of the king of the oak windows." The king went home, heavily, poorly, gloomily. The young queen came meeting him, and she said to him, "Mohrooai! my pity! there is nothing with thee tonight." Her face and her splendour gave some pleasure to the king when he looked on her brow, but when he sat on a chair to draw her towards him, his heart was so heavy that the chair broke under him.

"What ails thee, or what should ail thee, that thou mightest not tell it to me?" said the queen. The king told how it happened. "Ha!" said she, "what should'st thou mind, and that thou hast the best wife in Erin, and the second best horse in Erin. If thou takest my advice, thou wilt come (well) out of all these things yet."

If it was early that the day came, it was earlier than that that the queen arose, and she set order in everything, for the king was about to go on his journey. She set in order the dun shaggy filly, on which was the stick saddle, and though he saw it as wood, it was full of sparklings with gold and silver. He got on it; the queen kissed him, and she wished him victory of battlefields. "I need not be telling thee anything. Take thou the advice of thine own she comrade, the filly, and she will tell thee what thou shouldest do." He set out on his journey, and it was not dreary to be on the dun steed. She would catch the swift March wind that would be before, and the swift March wind would not catch her. They came at the mouth of dusk and lateness, to the court and castle of the king of the oak windows.

Said the dun shaggy filly to him, "We are at the end of the journey, and we have not to go any further; take my advice, and I will take thee where the sword of light of the king of the oak windows is, and if it comes with thee without scrape or creak, it is a good mark on our journey. The king is now at his dinner, and the sword of light is in his own chamber. There is a knob on its end, and when thou catchest the sword, draw it softly out of the window 'case.'" He came to the window where the sword was. He caught the sword and it came with him softly till it was at its point, and then it gave a sort of a "sgread." "We will now be going," said the filly. "It is no stopping time for us. I know the king has felt us taking the sword out." He kept his sword in his hand, and they went away, and when they were a bit forward, the filly said, "We will stop now, and look thou whom thou seest behind thee." "I see" said he, "a swarm of brown horses coming madly." "We are swifter ourselves than these yet," said the filly. They went, and when they were a good distance forward, "Look now," said she; "whom seest thou coming?" "I see a swarm of black horses, and. one white-faced black horse, and he is coming and coming in madness, and a man on him." "That is the best horse in Erin; it is my brother, and he got three months more nursing than I, and he will come past me with a whirr, and try if thou wilt be so ready, that when he comes past me, thou wilt take the head off the man who is on him; for in the time of passing he will look at thee, and there is no sword in his court wilt take off his head but the very sword that is in thy hand." When this man was going past, he gave his head a turn to look at him, he drew the sword and he took his head off, and the shaggy dun filly caught it in her mouth.

This was the king of the oak windows. "Leap on the black horse," said she, "and leave the carcass there, and be going home as fast as he will take thee home, and I will be coming as best I may after thee." He leaped on the black horse, and, "Moirë!" he was the swift hero, and they reached the house long before day. The queen was without rest till he arrived. They raised music, and they laid down woe. On the morrow, he said, "I am obliged to go to see the Gruagach today, to try if my spells will be loose." "Mind that it is not as usual the Gruagach will meet thee. He will meet thee furiously, wildly, and he will say to thee, didst thou get the sword? and say thou that thou hast got it; he will say, how didst thou get it? and thou shalt say, if it were not the knob that was on its end I had not got it. He will ask thee again, how didst thou get the sword? and thou wilt say, if it were not the knob that was on its end, I had not got it. Then he will give himself a lift to look what knob is on the sword, and thou wilt see a mole on the right side of his neck, and stab the point of the sword in the mole; and if thou dost not hit the mole, thou and I are done. His brother was the king of the oak windows, and he knows that till the other had lost his life, he would not part with the sword. The death of the two is in the sword, but there is no other sword that will touch them but it." The queen kissed him, and she called on victory of battlefields (to be) with him, and he went away.

The Gruagach met him in the very same place where he was before. "Didst thou get the sword?" "I got the sword." "How didst thou get the sword?" "If it were not the knob that was on its end I had not got it," said he. "Let me see the sword." "It was not laid on me to let thee see it." "How didst thou get the sword?" "If it were not the knob that was on its end, I got it not." The Gruagach gave his head a lift to look at the sword; he saw the mole; he was sharp and quick, and he thrust the sword into the mole, and the Gruagach fell down dead.

He returned home, and when he returned home, he found his set of keepers and watchers tied back to back, without wife, or horse, or sweetheart of his, but was taken away.

When he loosed them, they said to him, "A great giant came and he took away thy wife and thy two horses." "Sleep will not come on mine eyes nor rest on mine head till I get my wife and my two horses back." In saying this, he went on his journey. He took the side that the track of the horses was, and he followed them diligently. The dusk and lateness were coming on him, and no stop did he make until he reached the side of the green wood. He saw where there was the forming of the site of a fire, and he thought that he would put fire upon it, and thus he would put the night past there.

He was not long here at the fire, when 'Cu Seang' of the green wood came on him.

He blessed the dog, and the dog blessed him.

"Oov! oov!" said the dog, "Bad was the plight of thy wife and thy two horses here last night with the big giant." "It is that which has set me so pained and pitiful on their track tonight; but there is no help for it." "Oh! king," said the dog, "thou must not be without meat." The dog went into the wood. He brought out creatures, and they made them meat contentedly. "I rather think myself," said the king, "that I may turn home; that I cannot go near that giant." "Don't do that," said the dog. "There's no fear of thee, king. Thy matter will grow with thee. Thou must not be here without sleeping." "Fear will not let me sleep without a warranty." "Sleep thou," said the dog, "and I will warrant thee." The king let himself down, stretched out at the side of the fire, and he slept. When the watch broke, the dog said to him, "Rise up, king, till thou gettest a morsel of meat that will strengthen thee, till thou wilt be going on thy journey. Now," said the dog, "if hardship or difficulty comes on thee, ask my aid, and I will be with thee in an instant." They left a blessing with each other, and he went away. In the time of dusk and lateness, he came to a great precipice of rock, and there was the forming of the site of a fire.

He thought he would gather dry fuel, and that he would set on fire. He began to warm himself, and he was not long thus when the hoary hawk of the grey rock came on him. "Oov! oov!" said she, "Bad was the plight of thy wife and thy two horses last night with the big giant." "There is no help for it," said be. "I have got much of their trouble and little of their benefit myself." "Catch courage," said she. "Thou wilt get something of their benefit yet. Thou must not be without meat here," said she. There is no contrivance for getting meat," said he. "We will not be long getting meat," said the falcon. She went, and she was not long when she came with three ducks and eight blackcocks in her mouth. They set their meat in order, and they took it. "Thou must not be without sleep," said the falcon. "How shall I sleep without a warranty over me, to keep me from any one evil that is here." "Sleep thou, king, and I will warrant thee." He let himself down, stretched out, and he slept.

In the morning, the falcon set him on foot. "Hardship or difficulty that comes on thee, mind, at any time, that thou wilt get my help." He went swiftly, sturdily. The night was coming, and the little birds of the forest of branching bushy trees, were talking about the briar roots and the twig tops; and if they were, it was stillness, not peace for him, till he came to the side of a great river that was there, and at the bank of the river there was the forming of the site of a fire. The king blew a heavy, little spark of fire. He was not long here when there came as company for him the brown otter of the river. "Och! och!" said the otter, "Bad was the plight of thy wife and thy two horses last night with the giant." "There is no help for it. I got much of their trouble and little of their benefit." "Catch courage, before mid-day tomorrow thou wilt see thy wife. Oh! king, thou must not be without meat," said the otter. "How is meat to be got here?" said the king. The otter went through the river, and she came and three salmon with her, that were splendid. They made meat, and they took it. Said the otter to the king, "Thou must sleep." How can I sleep without any warranty over me? Sleep thou, and I will warrant thee." The king slept. In the morning, the otter said to him, "Thou wilt be this night in presence of thy wife." He left blessing with the otter. "Now," said the otter, "if difficulty be on thee, ask my aid and thou shalt get it." The king went till he reached a rock, and he looked down into a chasm that was in the rock, and at the bottom he saw his wife and his two horses, and he did not know how be should get where they were. He went round till he came to the foot of the rock, and there was a fine road for going in. He went in, and if he went it was then she began crying. "Ud! ud!" said he, "this is bad! If thou art crying now when I myself have got so much trouble coming about thee." "Oo!" said the horses, "set him in front of us, and there is no fear for him, till we leave this." She made meat for him, and she set him to rights, and when they were a while together, she put him in front of the horses. When the giant came, he said, "The smell of the stranger is within." Says she, "My treasure! My joy and my cattle! there is nothing but the smell of the litter of the horses." At the end of a while he went to give meat to the horses, and the horses began at him, and they all but killed him, and he hardly crawled from them. "Dear thing," said she, "they are like to kill thee." "If I myself had my soul to keep, it's long since they had killed me," said he. "Where, dear, is thy soul? By the books I will take care of it." "It is," said he, "in the Bonnach stone." When he went on the morrow, she set the Bonnach stone in order exceedingly. In the time of dusk and lateness, the giant came home. She set her man in front of the horses. The giant went to give the horses meat and they mangled him more and more. "What made thee set the Bonnach stone in order like that?" said he. "Because thy soul is in it." "I perceive that if thou didst know where my soul is, thou wouldst give it much respect." "I would give (that)," said she. "It is not there," said he, "my soul is; it is in the threshold." She set in order the threshold finely on the morrow. When the giant returned, he went to give meat to the horses, and the horses mangled him more and more. "What brought thee to set the threshold in order like that?" "Because thy soul is in it." "I perceive if thou knewest where my soul is, that thou wouldst take care of it." "I would take that," said she. "It is not there that my soul is," said he. "There is a great flagstone under the threshold. There is a wether under the flag.

There is a duck in the wether's belly, and an egg in the belly of the duck, and it is in the egg that my soul is." When the giant went away on the morrow's day, they raised the flagstone and out went the wether. "If I had the slim dog of the greenwood, he would not be long bringing the wether to me." The slim dog of the greenwood came with the wether in his mouth. When they opened the wether, out was the duck on the wing with the other ducks. "If I had the Hoary Hawk of the grey rock, she would not be long bringing the duck to me." The Hoary Hawk of the grey rock came with the duck in her mouth; when they split the duck to take the egg from her belly, out went the egg into the depth of the ocean. "If I had the brown otter of the river, he would not be long bringing the egg to me." The brown otter came and the ego, in her mouth, and the queen caught the egg, and she crushed it between her two hands. The giant was coming in the lateness, and when she crushed the egg, he fell down dead, and he has never yet moved out of that. They took with them a great deal of his gold and silver. They passed a cheery night with the brown otter of the river, a night with the hoary falcon of the grey rock, and a night with the slim dog of the greenwood. They came home and they set in order "a Cuirm Curaidh Cridheil," a hearty hero's feast, and they were lucky and well pleased after that.

The Tale of the Hoodie

THERE WAS ERE NOW A FARMER, and he had three daughters. They were waulking clothes at a river. A hoodie came round and he said to the eldest one, 'M-pos-u-mi, "Wilt thou wed me, farmer's daughter?" "I won't wed thee, thou ugly brute. An ugly brute is the hoodie," said she. He came to the second one on the morrow, and he said to her, "M-pos-u-mi, wilt thou wed me?" "Not I, indeed," said she; "an ugly brute is the hoodie." The third day he said to the youngest, M-pos-u-mi, "Wilt thou wed me, farmer's daughter?," "I will wed thee," said she; "a pretty creature is the hoodie," and on the morrow they married.

The hoodie said to her, "Whether wouldst thou rather that I should be a hoodie by day, and a man at night; or be a hoodie at night, and a man by day?" "I would rather that thou wert a man by day, and a hoodie at night," says she. After this he was a splendid fellow by day, and a hoodie at night. A few days after they married he took her with him to his own house.

At the end of three quarters they had a son. In the night there came the very finest music that ever was heard about the house. Every man slept, and the child was taken away. Her father came to the door in the morning, and he asked how were all there. He was very sorrowful that the child should be taken away, for fear that he should be blamed for it himself.

At the end of three quarters again they had another son. A watch was set on the house. The finest of music came, as it came before, about the house; every man slept, and the child was taken away. Her father came to the door in the morning. He asked if every thing was safe; but the child was taken away, and he did not know what to do for sorrow.

Again, at the end of three quarters they had another son. A watch was set on the house as usual. Music came about the house as it came before; every one slept, and the child was taken away. When they rose on the morrow they went to another place of rest that they had, himself and his wife, and his sister-in-law. He said to them by the way, "See that you have not forgotten any thing." The wife said, "I forgot my coarse comb." The coach in which they were fell a withered faggot, and he went away as a hoodie.

Her two sisters returned home, and she followed after him. When he would be on a hill top, she would follow to try and catch him; and when she would reach the top of a hill, he would be in the hollow on the other side. When night came, and she was tired, she had no place of rest or dwelling; she saw a little house of light far from her, and though far from her she was not long in reaching it.

When she reached the house she stood deserted at the door. She saw a little laddie about the house, and she yearned to him exceedingly. The housewife told her to come up, that she knew her cheer and travel. She laid down, and no sooner did the day come than she rose. She went out, and when she was out, she was going from hill to hill to try if she could see a hoodie. She saw a hoodie on a hill, and when she would get on the hill the hoodie would be in the hollow, when she would go to the hollow, the hoodie would be on another hill. When the night came she had no place of rest or dwelling. She saw a little house of light far from her, and if far from her she, was not long reaching it. She went to the door. She saw a laddie on the floor to whom she yearned right much. The, housewife laid her to rest. No earlier came the day than she took out as she used. She passed this day as the other days. When the night came she reached a house. The housewife told her to come up, that she knew her cheer and travel, that her man had but left the house a little while, that she should be clever, that this was the last night she would see him, and not to sleep, but to strive to seize him. She slept, he came where she was, and he let fall a ring on her right hand. Now when she awoke she tried to catch hold of him, and she caught a feather of his wing. He left the feather with her, and he went away. When she rose in the morning she did not know what she should do. The housewife said that he had gone over a hill of poison over which she could not go without horseshoes on her hands and feet. She gave her man's clothes, and she told her to go to learn smithying till she should be able to make horse shoes for herself.

She learned smithying so well that she made horseshoes for her hands and feet. She went over the hill of poison. That same day after she had gone over the hill of poison, her man was to be married to the daughter of a great gentleman that was in the town.

There was a race in the town that day, and every one was to be at the race but the stranger that had come over to poison hill. The cook came to her, and he said to her, Would she go in his place to make the wedding meal, and that he might get to the race.

She said she would go. She was always watching where the bridegroom would be sitting.

She let fall the ring and the feather in the broth that was before him. With the first spoon he took up the ring, with the next he took up the feather. When the minister came to the fore to make the marriage, he would not marry till he should find out who had made ready the meal. They brought up the cook of the gentleman, and he said that this was not the cook who made ready the meal.

They brought up now the one who had made ready the meal. He said, "That now was his married wife." The spells went off him. They turned back over the hill of poison, she throwing the horse shoes behind her to him, as she went a little bit forward, and he following her. When they came, back over the hill, they went to the three houses in which she had been. These were the houses of his sisters, and they took with them the three sons, and they came home to their own house, and they were happy.

The Girl and the Dead Man

THERE WAS BEFORE NOW a poor woman, and she had a leash of daughters. Said the eldest one of them to her mother, "I had better go myself and seek for fortune." "I had better," said her mother, "bake a bannock for thee." When the bannock was ready, her mother said to her, "Whether wouldst thou like best the bit and my blessing, or the big bit and my curse?" "I would rather," said she, "the big bit and thy curse." She went away, and when the night was wreathing round her, she sat at the foot of a wall to eat the bannock. There gathered the sreath chuileanach and her twelve puppies, and the little birds of the air about her, for a part of the bannock. "Wilt thou give us a part of the bannock," said they. "I won't give it, you ugly brutes; I have not much for myself." "My curse will be thine, and the curse of my twelve birds; and thy mother's curse is the worst of all."

She rose and she went away, and she had not half enough with the bit of the bannock. She saw a little house a long way from her; and if a long way from her, she was not long reaching it. She struck in the door. "Who's there?" "A good maid seeking a master." "We want that," said they, and she got in. She had now a peck of gold and a peck of silver to get; and she was to be awake every night to watch a dead man, brother of the housewife, who was under spells. She had besides, of nuts as she broke, of needles as she lost, of thimbles as she pierced, of thread as she used, of candles as she burned, a bed of green silk over her, a bed of green silk under her, sleeping by day and watching by night. The first night when she was watching she fell asleep; the mistress came in, she struck the magic club on her, she fell down dead, and she threw her out at the back of the midden.

Said the middle one to her mother, "I had better go seek fortune and follow my sister." Her mother baked her a bannock; and she chose the big half and her mother's curse, as her elder sister did, and it happened to her as it happened to her sister.

Said the youngest one to her mother, "I had better myself go to seek fortune too, and follow my sisters." "I had better bake a bannock," said her mother. "Whether wouldst thou rather the little bit and my blessing, or the big bit and my curse?

"I would rather the little bit and your blessing." She went, and the night was wreathing round her, and she sat at the foot of a wall to eat the bannock. There gathered the sreath chuileanach and the twelve puppies, and the little birds of the air about her. "Wilt thou give us some of that?" "I will give, you pretty creatures, if you will keep me company." She gave them some of the bannock; they ate and they had plenty, and she had enough. They clapped their wings about her till she was snug with the warmth. She went, she saw a little house a long way from her; and if it was a long way from her, she was not long reaching it. She struck in the door. "Who's there?" "A good maid seeking a master." "We have need of that." The wages she had were a peck of gold and a peck of silver; of nuts as she broke, of needles as she lost, of thimbles as she pierced, of thread as she used, of candles as she burned, a bed of the green silk over her, and a bed of the green silk under her. She sat to watch the dead man, and she was sewing; on the middle of night he rose up, and screwed up a grin. "If thou dost not lie down properly, I will give thee the one leathering with a stick." He lay down. At the end of a while, he rose on one elbow, and screwed up a grin; and the third time he rose and screwed up a grin. When he rose the third time, she struck him a lounder of the stick; the stick stuck to the dead man, and the hand stuck to the stick; and out they were. They went forward till they were going through a wood; when it was low for her it was high for him; and when it was high for him it was low for her. The nuts were knocking their eyes out, and the sloes taking their ears off, till they got through the wood. After going through the wood they returned home. She got a peck of gold and a peck of silver, and the vessel of cordial. She rubbed the vessel of cordial to her two sisters, and brought them alive. They returned home; they left me sitting here, and if they were well, 'tis well; and if they were not, let them be.

Sanntraigh

THERE WAS A HERD'S WIFE in the island of Sanntraigh, and she had a kettle. A woman of peace (fairy) would come every day to seek the kettle. She would not say a word when she came, but she would catch hold of the kettle. When she would catch the kettle, the woman of the house would say –

> *A smith is able to make*
> *Cold iron hot with coal.*
> *The due of a kettle is bones,*
> *And to bring it back again whole.*

The woman of peace would come back every day with the kettle and flesh and bones in it. On a day that was there, the housewife was for going over the ferry to Baile a Chaisteil, and she said to her man, "If thou wilt say to the woman of peace as I say, I will go to Baile Castle." "Oo! I will say it. Surely it's I that will say it." He was spinning a heather rope to be set on the house. He saw a woman coming and a shadow from her feet, and he took fear of her. He shut the door. He stopped his work. When she came to the door she did not find the door open, and he did not open it for her. She went above a hole that was in the house. The kettle gave two jumps, and at the third leap it went out at the ridge of the house. The night came, and the kettle came not. The wife came back over the ferry, and she did not see a bit of the kettle within, and she asked, "Where was the kettle?" "Well then I don't care where it is," said the man; "I never took such a fright as I took at it. I shut the door, and she did not come any more with it." "Good-for-nothing wretch, what didst thou do? There are two that will be ill off – thyself and I." "She will come tomorrow with it." "She will not come."

She hasted herself and she went away. She reached the knoll, and there was no man within. It was after dinner, and they were out in the mouth of the night. She went in. She saw the kettle, and she lifted it with her. It was heavy for her with the remnants that they left in it. When the old carle that was within saw her going out, he said,

> *Silent wife, silent wife,*
> *That came on us from the land of chase,*
> *Thou man on the surface of the "Bruth,"*
> *Loose the black, and slip the Fierce.*

The two dogs were let loose; and she was not long away when she heard the clatter of the dogs coming. She kept the remnant that was in the kettle, so that if she could get it with her, well, and if the dogs should come that she might throw it at them. She perceived the dogs coming. She put her hand in the kettle. She took the board out of it, and she threw at them a quarter of what was in it. They noticed it there for a while. She perceived them again, and she threw another piece at them when they closed upon her. She went away walking as well as she might; when she came near the farm, she threw the mouth of the pot downwards, and there she left them all that was in it. The dogs of the town struck (up) a barking when they saw the dogs of peace stopping. The woman of peace never came more to seek the kettle.

Cailliach Mhor Chlibhrich

THIS CELEBRATED WITCH WAS ACCUSED of having enchanted the deer of the Reay forest, so that they avoided pursuit. Lord Reay was exceedingly angry, but at a loss how to remedy the evil. His man, William (the same who braved the witch and sat down in her hut) promised to find out if this was the case.

He watched her for a whole night, and by some counter enchantments managed to be present when in the early morning she was busy milking the hinds. They were standing all about the door of the hut till one of them ate a hank of blue worsted hanging from a nail in it. The witch struck the animal, and said, "The spell is off you; and Lord Reay's bullet will be your death today." William repeated this to his master to confirm the tale of his having passed the night in the hut of the great hag, which no one would believe. And the event justified it, for a fine yellow hind was killed that day, and the hank of blue yarn was found in its stomach.

The Smith and the Fairies

YEARS AGO THERE LIVED in Crossbrig a smith of the name of MacEachern. This man had an only child, a boy of about thirteen or fourteen years of age, cheerful, strong, and healthy. All of a sudden he fell ill; took to his bed and moped whole days away. No one could tell what was the matter with him, and the boy himself could not, or would not, tell how he felt. He was wasting away fast; getting thin, old, and yellow; and his father and all his friends were afraid that he would die.

At last one day, after the boy had been lying in this condition for a long time, getting neither better nor worse, always confined to bed, but with an extraordinary appetite, – one day, while sadly revolving these things, and standing idly at his forge, with no heart to work, the smith was agreeably surprised to see an old man, well known to him for his sagacity and knowledge of out-of-the-way things, walk into his workshop. Forthwith he told him the occurrence which had clouded his life.

The old man looked grave as he listened; and after sitting a long time pondering over all he had heard, gave his opinion thus – "It is not your son you have got. The boy has been carried away by the 'Daoine Sith,' and they have left a Sibhreach in his place." "Alas! and what then am I to do?" said the smith. "How am I ever to see my own son again?" "I will tell you how," answered the old man. "But, first, to make sure that it is not your own son you have got, take as many empty egg shells as you can get, go with them into the room, spread them out carefully before his sight, then proceed to draw water with them, carrying them two and two in your hands as if they were a great weight, and arrange when full, with every sort of earnestness round the fire." The smith accordingly gathered as many broken egg-shells as he could get, went into the room, and proceeded to carry out all his instructions.

He had not been long at work before there arose from the bed a shout of laughter, and the voice of the seeming sick boy exclaimed, "I am now 800 years of age, and I have never seen the like of that before."

The smith returned and told the old man. "Well, now," said the sage to him, "did I not tell you that it was not your son you had: your son is in Brorra-cheill in a digh there (that is, a round green hill frequented by fairies). Get rid as soon as possible of this intruder, and I think I may promise you your son."

"You must light a very large and bright fire before the bed on which this stranger is lying. He will ask you 'What is the use of such a fire as that?' Answer him at once, 'You will see that presently!' and then seize him, and throw him into the middle of it. If it is your own son you have got, he will call out to save him; but if not, this thing will fly through the roof."

The smith again followed the old man's advice, kindled a large fire, answered the question put to him as he had been directed to do, and seizing the child flung him in without hesitation. The 'Sibhreach' gave an awful yell, and sprung through the roof, where a hole was left to let the smoke out.

On a certain night the old man told him the green round hill, where the fairies kept the boy, would be open. And on that night the smith, having provided himself with a bible, a dirk, and a crowing cock, was to proceed to the hill. He would hear singing and dancing and much merriment going on, but he was to advance boldly; the bible he carried would be a certain safeguard to him against any danger from the fairies. On entering the hill he was to stick the dirk in the threshold, to prevent the hill from closing upon him; "and then," continued the old man, "on entering you will see a spacious apartment before you, beautifully clean, and there, standing far within, working at a forge, you will also see your own son. When you are questioned, say you come to seek him, and will not go without him."

Not long after this, the time came round, and the smith sallied forth, prepared as instructed. Sure enough as he approached the hill, there was a light where light was seldom seen before. Soon after a sound of piping, dancing, and joyous merriment reached the anxious father on the night wind.

Overcoming every impulse to fear, the smith approached the threshold steadily, stuck the dirk into it as directed, and entered. Protected by the bible he carried on his breast, the fairies could not touch him; but they asked him, with a good deal of displeasure, what he wanted there. He answered, "I want my son, whom I see down there, and I will not go without him."

Upon hearing this, the whole company before him gave a loud laugh, which wakened up the cock he carried dozing in his arms, who at once leaped up on his shoulders, clapped his wings lustily, and crowed loud and long.

The fairies, incensed, seized the smith and his son, and throwing them out of the hill, flung the dirk after them, "and in an instant a' was dark."

For a year and a day the boy never did a turn of work, and hardly ever spoke a word; but at last one day, sitting by his father and watching him finishing a sword he was making for some chief, and which he was very particular about, he suddenly exclaimed, "That is not the way to do it;" and taking the tools from his father's hands he set to work himself in his place, and soon fashioned a sword, the like of which was never seen in the country before.

From that day the young man wrought constantly with his father, and became the inventor of a peculiarly fine and well-tempered weapon, the making of which kept the two smiths, father and son, in constant employment, spread their fame far and wide, and gave them the means in abundance, as they before had the disposition to live content with all the world and very happily with one another.

Man

THE MANKS FAIRY CREED is the same as elsewhere in Scotland. Such beings are supposed to exist, and are known by the name of Ferish, which a Manksman assured me was a genuine Manks word. If so, fairy may be old Celtic, and derived from the same root as Peri, instead of being derived from it.

The fairies in the Isle of Man are believed to be spirits. They are not supposed to throw arrows as they are said still to do in the Highlands. None of the old peasants seemed to take the least interest in 'elf shots,' the flint arrows, which generally lead to a story when shown elsewhere. One old man said, "The ferish have no body, no bones and scorned the arrow heads. It is stated in Train's history, that no flint-arrow heads have ever been found in the Isle of Man; but as there are numerous barrows, flint weapons may yet be discovered when some one looks for them.

Still these Manks fairies are much the same as their neighbours on the main land. They go into mills at night and grind stolen corn; they steal milk from the cattle; they live in green mounds; in short, they axe like little mortals invested with supernatural power, thus: There was a man who lived not long ago near Port Erin, who had a Lhiannan Rhee. "He was like other people, but he had a fairy sweetheart; but he noticed her, and they do not like being noticed, the fairies, and so he lost his mind. Well, he was quite quiet like other people, but at night he slept in the barn; and they used to hear him talking to his sweetheart, and scolding her sometimes; but if any one made a noise he would be quiet at once."

Now, the truth of this story is clear enough; the man went mad; but this madness took the form of the popular belief, and that again attributed his madness to the fairy mistress. I am convinced that this was believed to be a case of genuine fairy intercourse; and it shows that the fairy creed still survives in the Isle of Man.

Thomas the Rhymer

OF ALL THE YOUNG GALLANTS in Scotland in the thirteenth century, there was none more gracious and debonair than Thomas Learmont, Laird of the Castle of Ercildoune, in Berwickshire.

He loved books, poetry, and music, which were uncommon tastes in those days; and, above all, he loved to study nature, and to watch the habits of the beasts and birds that made their abode in the fields and woods round about his home.

Now it chanced that, one sunny May morning, Thomas left his Tower of Ercildoune, and went wandering into the woods that lay about the Huntly Burn, a little stream that came rushing down from the slopes of the Eildon Hills. It was a lovely morning – fresh, and bright, and warm, and everything was so beautiful that it looked as Paradise might look.

The tender leaves were bursting out of their sheaths, and covering all the trees with a fresh soft mantle of green; and amongst the carpet of moss under the young man's feet, yellow primroses and starry anemones were turning up their faces to the morning sky.

The little birds were singing like to burst their throats, and hundreds of insects were flying backwards and forwards in the sunshine; while down by the burnside the bright-eyed water-rats were poking their noses out of their holes, as if they knew that summer had come, and wanted to have a share in all that was going on.

Thomas felt so happy with the gladness of it all, that he threw himself down at the root of a tree, to watch the living things around him.

As he was lying there, he heard the trampling of a horse's hooves, as it forced its way through the bushes; and, looking up, he saw the most beautiful lady that he had ever seen coming riding towards him on a grey palfrey.

She wore a hunting dress of glistening silk, the colour of the fresh spring grass; and from her shoulders hung a velvet mantle, which matched the riding-skirt exactly. Her yellow hair, like rippling gold, hung loosely round her shoulders, and on her head sparkled a diadem of precious stones, which flashed like fire in the sunlight.

Her saddle was of pure ivory, and her saddle-cloth of blood-red satin, while her saddle girths were of corded silk and her stirrups of cut crystal. Her horse's reins were of beaten gold, all hung with little silver bells, so that, as she rode along, she made a sound like fairy music.

Apparently she was bent on the chase, for she carried a hunting-horn and a sheaf of arrows; and she led seven greyhounds along in a leash, while as many scenting hounds ran loose at her horse's side.

As she rode down the glen, she lilted a bit of an old Scotch song; and she carried herself with such a queenly air, and her dress was so magnificent, that Thomas was like to kneel by the side of the path and worship her, for he thought that it must be the Blessed Virgin herself.

But when the rider came to where he was, and understood his thoughts, she shook her head sadly.

"I am not that Blessed Lady, as thou thinkest," she said. "Men call me Queen, but it is of a far other country; for I am the Queen of Fairy-land, and not the Queen of Heaven."

And certainly it seemed as if what she said were true; for, from that moment, it was as if a spell were cast over Thomas, making him forget prudence, and caution, and common-sense itself.

For he knew that it was dangerous for mortals to meddle with Fairies, yet he was so entranced with the Lady's beauty that he begged her to give him a kiss. This was just what she wanted, for she knew that if she once kissed him she had him in her power.

And, to the young man's horror, as soon as their lips had met, an awful change came over her. For her beautiful mantle and riding-skirt of silk seemed to fade away, leaving her clad in a long grey garment, which was just the colour of ashes. Her beauty seemed to fade away also, and she grew old and wan; and, worst of all, half of her abundant yellow hair went grey before his very eyes. She saw the poor man's astonishment and terror, and she burst into a mocking laugh.

"I am not so fair to look on now as I was at first," she said, "but that matters little, for thou hast sold thyself, Thomas, to be my servant for seven long years. For whoso kisseth the Fairy Queen must e'en go with her to Fairy-land, and serve her there till that time is past."

When he heard these words poor Thomas fell on his knees and begged for mercy. But mercy he could not obtain. The Elfin Queen only laughed in his face, and brought her dapple-grey palfrey close up to where he was standing.

"No, no," she said, in answer to his entreaties. "Thou didst ask the kiss, and now thou must pay the price. So dally no longer, but mount behind me, for it is full time that I was gone."

So Thomas, with many a sigh and groan of terror, mounted behind her; and as soon as he had done so, she shook her bridle rein, and the grey steed galloped off.

On and on they went, going swifter than the wind; till they left the land of the living behind, and came to the edge of a great desert, which stretched before them, dry, and bare, and desolate, to the edge of the far horizon.

At least, so it seemed to the weary eyes of Thomas of Ercildoune, and he wondered if he and his strange companion had to cross this desert; and, if so, if there were any chance of reaching the other side of it alive.

But the Fairy Queen suddenly tightened her rein, and the grey palfrey stopped short in its wild career.

"Now must thou descend to earth, Thomas," said the Lady, glancing over her shoulder at her unhappy captive, "and lout down, and lay thy head on my knee, and I will show thee hidden things, which cannot be seen by mortal eyes."

So Thomas dismounted, and louted down, and rested his head on the Fairy Queen's knee; and lo, as he looked once more over the desert, everything seemed changed. For he saw three roads leading across it now, which he had not noticed before, and each of these three roads was different.

One of them was broad, and level, and even, and it ran straight on across the sand, so that no one who was travelling by it could possibly lose his way.

And the second road was as different from the first as it well could be. It was narrow, and winding, and long; and there was a thorn hedge on one side of it, and a briar hedge on the other; and those hedges grew so high, and their branches were so wild and tangled, that those who were travelling along that road would have some difficulty in persevering on their journey at all.

And the third road was unlike any of the others. It was a bonnie, bonnie road, winding up a hillside among brackens, and heather, and golden-yellow whins, and it looked as if it would be pleasant travelling, to pass that way.

"Now," said the Fairy Queen, "an' thou wilt, I shall tell thee where these three roads lead to. The first road, as thou seest, is broad, and even, and easy, and there be many that choose it to travel on. But though it be a good road, it leadeth to a bad end, and the folk that choose it repent their choice for ever.

"And as for the narrow road, all hampered and hindered by the thorns and the briars, there be few that be troubled to ask where that leadeth to. But did they ask, perchance more of them might be stirred up to set out along it. For that is the Road of Righteousness; and, although it be hard and irksome, yet it endeth in a glorious City, which is called the City of the Great King.

"And the third road – the bonnie road – that runs up the brae among the ferns, and leadeth no mortal kens whither, but I ken where it leadeth, Thomas – for it leadeth unto fair Elf-land; and that road take we.

"And, mark 'ee, Thomas, if ever thou hopest to see thine own Tower of Ercildoune again, take care of thy tongue when we reach our journey's end, and speak no single word to anyone save me – for the mortal who openeth his lips rashly in Fairy-land must bide there for ever."

Then she bade him mount her palfrey again, and they rode on. The ferny road was not so bonnie all the way as it had been at first, however. For they had not ridden along it very far before it led them into a narrow ravine, which seemed to go right down under the earth, where there was no ray of light to guide them, and where the air was dank and heavy. There was a sound of rushing water everywhere, and at last the grey palfrey plunged right into it; and it crept up, cold and chill, first over Thomas's feet, and then over his knees.

His courage had been slowly ebbing ever since he had been parted from the daylight, but now he gave himself up for lost; for it seemed to him certain that his strange companion and he would never come safe to their journey's end.

He fell forward in a kind of swoon; and, if it had not been that he had tight hold of the Fairy's ash-grey gown, I warrant he had fallen from his seat, and had been drowned.

But all things, be they good or bad, pass in time, and at last the darkness began to lighten, and the light grew stronger, until they were back in broad sunshine.

Then Thomas took courage, and looked up; and lo, they were riding through a beautiful orchard, where apples and pears, dates and figs and wine-berries grew in great abundance. And his tongue was so parched and dry, and he felt so faint, that he longed for some of the fruit to restore him.

He stretched out his hand to pluck some of it; but his companion turned in her saddle and forbade him.

"There is nothing safe for thee to eat here," she said, "save an apple, which I will give thee presently. If thou touch aught else thou art bound to remain in Fairy-land for ever."

So poor Thomas had to restrain himself as best he could; and they rode slowly on, until they came to a tiny tree all covered with red apples. The Fairy Queen bent down and plucked one, and handed it to her companion.

"This I can give thee," she said, "and I do it gladly, for these apples are the Apples of Truth; and whoso eateth them gaineth this reward, that his lips will never more be able to frame a lie."

Thomas took the apple, and ate it; and for evermore the Grace of Truth rested on his lips; and that is why, in after years, men called him 'True Thomas.'

They had only a little way to go after this, before they came in sight of a magnificent Castle standing on a hillside.

"Yonder is my abode," said the Queen, pointing to it proudly. "There dwelleth my Lord and all the Nobles of his court; and, as my Lord hath an uncertain temper and shows no liking for any strange gallant whom he sees in my company, I pray thee, both for thy sake and mine, to utter no word to anyone who speaketh to thee; and, if anyone should ask me who and what thou art, I will tell them that thou art dumb. So wilt thou pass unnoticed in the crowd."

With these words the Lady raised her hunting-horn, and blew a loud and piercing blast; and, as she did so, a marvellous change came over her again; for her ugly ash-covered gown dropped off her, and the grey in her hair vanished, and she appeared once more in her green riding-skirt and mantle, and her face grew young and fair.

And a wonderful change passed over Thomas also; for, as he chanced to glance downwards, he found that his rough country clothes had been transformed into a suit of fine brown cloth, and that on his feet he wore satin shoon.

Immediately the sound of the horn rang out, the doors of the Castle flew open, and the King hurried out to meet the Queen, accompanied by such a number of Knights and Ladies, Minstrels and Page-boys, that Thomas, who had slid from his palfrey, had no difficulty in obeying her wishes and passing into the Castle unobserved.

Everyone seemed very glad to see the Queen back again, and they crowded into the Great Hall in her train, and she spoke to them all graciously, and allowed them to kiss her hand. Then she passed, with her husband, to a dais at the far end of the huge apartment, where two thrones stood, on which the Royal pair seated themselves to watch the revels which now began.

Poor Thomas, meanwhile, stood far away at the other end of the Hall, feeling very lonely, yet fascinated by the extraordinary scene on which he was gazing.

For, although all the fine Ladies, and Courtiers, and Knights were dancing in one part of the Hall, there were huntsmen coming and going in another part, carrying in great antlered deer, which apparently they had killed in the chase, and throwing them down in heaps on the floor. And there were rows of cooks standing beside the dead animals, cutting them up into joints, and bearing away the joints to be cooked.

Altogether it was such a strange, fantastic scene that Thomas took no heed of how the time flew, but stood and gazed, and gazed, never speaking a word to anybody. This went on for three long days, then the Queen rose from her throne, and, stepping from the dais, crossed the Hall to where he was standing.

"'Tis time to mount and ride, Thomas," she said, "if thou wouldst ever see the fair Castle of Ercildoune again."

Thomas looked at her in amazement. "Thou spokest of seven long years, Lady," he exclaimed, "and I have been here but three days."

The Queen smiled. "Time passeth quickly in Fairy-land, my friend," she replied. "Thou thinkest that thou hast been here but three days. 'Tis seven years since we two met. And now it is time for thee to go. I would fain have had thy presence with me longer, but I dare not, for thine own sake. For every seventh year an Evil Spirit cometh from the Regions of Darkness, and carrieth back with him one of our followers, whomsoever he chanceth to choose. And, as thou art a goodly fellow, I fear that he might choose thee.

"So, as I would be loth to let harm befall thee, I will take thee back to thine own country this very night."

Once more the grey palfrey was brought, and Thomas and the Queen mounted it; and, as they had come, so they returned to the Eildon Tree near the Huntly Burn.

Then the Queen bade Thomas farewell; and, as a parting gift, he asked her to give him something that would let people know that he had really been to Fairy-land.

"I have already given thee the Gift of Truth," she replied. "I will now give thee the Gifts of Prophecy and Poesie; so that thou wilt be able to foretell the future, and also to write wondrous verses. And, besides these unseen gifts, here is something that mortals can see with their own eyes – a Harp that was fashioned in Fairy-land. Fare thee well, my friend. Some day, perchance, I will return for thee again."

With these words the Lady vanished, and Thomas was left alone, feeling a little sorry, if the truth must be told, at parting with such a radiant Being and coming back to the ordinary haunts of men.

After this he lived for many a long year in his Castle of Ercildoune, and the fame of his poetry and of his prophecies spread all over the country, so that people named him True Thomas, and Thomas the Rhymer.

I cannot write down for you all the prophecies which Thomas uttered, and which most surely came to pass, but I will tell you one or two.

He foretold the Battle of Bannockburn in these words:

> *"The Burn of Breid*
> *Shall rin fou reid,"*

which came to pass on that terrible day when the waters of the little Bannockburn were reddened by the blood of the defeated English.

He also foretold the Union of the Crowns of England and Scotland, under a Prince who was the son of a French Queen, and who yet bore the blood of Bruce in his veins.

> *"A French Quen shall bearre the Sonne;*
> *Shall rule all Britainne to the sea,*
> *As neere as is the ninth degree,"*

which thing came true in 1603, when King James, son of Mary, Queen of Scots, became Monarch of both countries.

Fourteen long years went by, and people were beginning to forget that Thomas the Rhymer had ever been in Fairy-land; but at last a day came when Scotland was at war with England, and the Scottish army was resting by the banks of the Tweed, not far from the Tower of Ercildoune.

And the Master of the Tower determined to make a feast, and invite all the Nobles and Barons who were leading the army to sup with him.

That feast was long remembered.

For the Laird of Ercildoune took care that everything was as magnificent as it could possibly be; and when the meal was ended he rose in his place, and, taking his Elfin Harp, he sang to his assembled guests song after song of the days of long ago.

The guests listened breathlessly, for they felt that they would never hear such wonderful music again. And so it fell out.

For that very night, after all the Nobles had gone back to their tents, a soldier on guard saw, in the moonlight, a snow-white Hart and Hind moving slowly down the road that ran past the camp.

There was something so unusual about the animals that he called to his officer to come and look at them. And the officer called to his brother officers, and soon there was quite a crowd softly following the dumb creatures, who paced solemnly on, as if they were keeping time to music unheard by mortal ears.

"There is something uncanny about this," said one soldier at last. "Let us send for Thomas of Ercildoune, perchance he may be able to tell us if it be an omen or no."

"Ay, send for Thomas of Ercildoune," cried every one at once. So a little page was sent in haste to the old Tower to rouse the Rhymer from his slumbers.

When he heard the boy's message, the Seer's face grew grave and wrapt.

"'Tis a summons," he said softly, "a summons from the Queen of Fairy-land. I have waited long for it, and it hath come at last."

And when he went out, instead of joining the little company of waiting men, he walked straight up to the snow-white Hart and Hind. As soon as he reached them they paused for a moment as if to greet him. Then all three moved slowly down a steep bank that sloped to the little river Leader, and disappeared in its foaming waters, for the stream was in full flood.

And, although a careful search was made, no trace of Thomas of Ercildoune was found; and to this day the country folk believe that the Hart and the Hind were messengers from the Elfin Queen, and that he went back to Fairy-land with them.

The Page-Boy and the Silver Goblet

THERE WAS ONCE a little page-boy, who was in service in a stately Castle. He was a very good-natured little fellow, and did his duties so willingly and well that everybody liked him, from the great Earl whom he served every day on bended knee, to the fat old butler whose errands he ran.

Now the Castle stood on the edge of a cliff overlooking the sea, and although the walls at that side were very thick, in them there was a little postern door, which opened on to a narrow flight of steps that led down the face of the cliff to the sea shore, so that anyone who liked could go down there in the pleasant summer mornings and bathe in the shimmering sea.

On the other side of the Castle were gardens and pleasure grounds, opening on to a long stretch of heather-covered moorland, which, at last, met a distant range of hills.

The little page-boy was very fond of going out on this moor when his work was done, for then he could run about as much as he liked, chasing bumble-bees, and catching butterflies, and looking for birds' nests when it was nesting time.

So one night, when everyone else was asleep, he crept out of the Castle by the little postern door, and stole down the stone steps, and along the sea shore, and up on to the moor, and went straight to the Fairy Knowe.

To his delight he found that what everyone said was true. The top of the Knowe was tipped up, and from the opening that was thus made, rays of light came streaming out.

His heart was beating fast with excitement, but, gathering his courage, he stooped down and slipped inside the Knowe.

He found himself in a large room lit by numberless tiny candles, and there, seated round a polished table, were scores of the Tiny Folk, Fairies, and Elves, and Gnomes, dressed in green, and yellow, and pink; blue, and lilac, and scarlet; in all the colours, in fact, that you can think of.

He stood in a dark corner watching the busy scene in wonder, thinking how strange it was that there should be such a number of these tiny beings living their own lives all unknown to men, at such a little distance from them, when suddenly someone – he could not tell who it was – gave an order.

"Fetch the Cup," cried the owner of the unknown voice, and instantly two little Fairy pages, dressed all in scarlet livery, darted from the table to a tiny cupboard in the rock, and returned staggering under the weight of a most beautiful silver cup, richly embossed and lined inside with gold.

He placed it in the middle of the table, and, amid clapping of hands and shouts of joy, all the Fairies began to drink out of it in turn. And the page could see, from where he stood, that no one poured wine into it, and yet it was always full, and that the wine that was in it was not always the same kind, but that each Fairy, when he grasped its stem, wished for the wine that he loved best, and lo! in a moment the cup was full of it.

"'Twould be a fine thing if I could take that cup home with me," thought the page. "No one will believe that I have been here except I have something to show for it." So he bided his time, and watched.

Presently the Fairies noticed him, and, instead of being angry at his boldness in entering their abode, as he expected that they would be, they seemed very pleased to see him, and invited him to a seat at the table. But by and by they grew rude and insolent, and jeered at him for being content to serve mere mortals, telling him that they saw everything that went on at the Castle, and making fun of the old butler, whom the page loved with all his heart. And they laughed at the food he ate, saying that it was only fit for animals; and when any fresh dainty was set on the table by the scarlet-clad pages, they would push the dish across to him, saying: "Taste it, for you will not have the chance of tasting such things at the Castle."

At last he could stand their teasing remarks no longer; besides, he knew that if he wanted to secure the cup he must lose no time in doing so.

So he suddenly stood up, and grasped the stem of it tightly in his hand. "I'll drink to you all in water," he cried, and instantly the ruby wine was turned to clear cold water.

He raised the cup to his lips, but he did not drink from it. With a sudden jerk he threw the water over the candles, and instantly the room was in darkness. Then, clasping the precious cup tightly in his arms, he sprang to the opening of the Knowe, through which he could see the stars glimmering clearly.

He was just in time, for it fell to with a crash behind him; and soon he was speeding along the wet, dew-spangled moor, with the whole troop of Fairies at his heels.

They were wild with rage, and from the shrill shouts of fury which they uttered, the page knew well that, if they overtook him, he need expect no mercy at their hands.

And his heart began to sink, for, fleet of foot though he was, he was no match for the Fairy Folk, who gained on him steadily.

All seemed lost, when a mysterious voice sounded out of the darkness:

> "If thou wouldst gain the Castle door,
> Keep to the black stones on the shore."

It was the voice of some poor mortal, who, for some reason or other, had been taken prisoner by the Fairies – who were really very malicious Little Folk – and who did not want a like fate to befall the adventurous page-boy; but the little fellow did not know this.

He had once heard that if anyone walked on the wet sands, where the waves had come over them, the Fairies could not touch him, and this mysterious sentence brought the saying into his mind.

So he turned, and dashed panting down to the shore. His feet sank in the dry sand, his breath came in little gasps, and he felt as if he must give up the struggle; but he persevered, and at last, just as the foremost Fairies were about to lay hands on him, he jumped across the water-mark on to the firm, wet sand, from which the waves had just receded, and then he knew that he was safe.

For the Little Folk could go no step further, but stood on the dry sand uttering cries of rage and disappointment, while the triumphant page-boy ran safely along the shore, his precious cup in his arms, and climbed lightly up the steps in the rock and disappeared through the postern. And for many years after, long after the little page-boy had grown up and become a stately butler, who trained other little page-boys to follow in his footsteps, the beautiful cup remained in the Castle as a witness of his adventure.

The Elfin Knight

THERE IS A LONE MOOR in Scotland, which, in times past, was said to be haunted by an Elfin Knight. This Knight was only seen at rare intervals, once in every seven years or so, but the fear of him lay on all the country round, for every now and then someone would set out to cross the moor and would never be heard of again.

And although men might search every inch of the ground, no trace of him would be found, and with a thrill of horror the searching party would go home again, shaking their heads and whispering to one another that he had fallen into the hands of the dreaded Knight.

So, as a rule, the moor was deserted, for nobody dare pass that way, much less live there; and by and by it became the haunt of all sorts of wild animals, which made their lairs there, as they found that they never were disturbed by mortal huntsmen.

Now in that same region lived two young earls, Earl St Clair and Earl Gregory, who were such friends that they rode, and hunted, and fought together, if need be.

And as they were both very fond of the chase, Earl Gregory suggested one day that they should go a-hunting on the haunted moor, in spite of the Elfin King.

"Certes, I hardly believe in him at all," cried the young man, with a laugh. "Methinks 'tis but an old wife's tale to frighten the bairns withal, lest they go straying amongst the heather and lose themselves. And 'tis pity that such fine sport should be lost because we – two bearded men – pay heed to such gossip."

But Earl St Clair looked grave. "'Tis ill meddling with unchancy things," he answered, "and 'tis no bairn's tale that travellers have set out to cross that moor who have vanished bodily, and never mair been heard of; but it is, as thou sayest, a pity that so much good sport be lost, all because an Elfin Knight choosest to claim the land as his, and make us mortals pay toll for the privilege of planting a foot upon it.

"I have heard tell, however, that one is safe from any power that the Knight may have if one wearest the Sign of the Blessed Trinity. So let us bind That on our arm and ride forth without fear."

Sir Gregory burst into a loud laugh at these words. "Dost thou think that I am one of the bairns," he said, "'first to be frightened by an idle tale, and then to think that a leaf of clover will protect me? No, no, carry that Sign if thou wilt; I will trust to my good bow and arrow."

But Earl St Clair did not heed his companion's words, for he remembered how his mother had told him, when he was a little lad at her knee that whoso carried the Sign of the Blessed Trinity need never fear any spell that might be thrown over him by Warlock or Witch, Elf or Demon.

So he went out to the meadow and plucked a leaf of clover, which he bound on his arm with a silken scarf; then he mounted his horse and rode with Earl Gregory to the desolate and lonely moorland.

For some hours all went well; and in the heat of the chase the young men forgot their fears. Then suddenly both of them reined in their steeds and sat gazing in front of them with affrighted faces.

For a horseman had crossed their track, and they both would fain have known who he was and whence he came.

"By my troth, but he rideth in haste, whoever he may be," said Earl Gregory at last, "and tho' I always thought that no steed on earth could match mine for swiftness, I reckon that for every league that mine goeth, his would go seven. Let us follow him, and see from what part of the world he cometh."

"The Lord forbid that thou shouldst stir thy horse's feet to follow him," said Earl St Clair devoutly. "Why, man, 'tis the Elfin Knight! Canst thou not see that he doth not ride on the solid ground, but flieth through the air, and that, although he rideth on what seemeth a mortal steed, he is really carried by mighty pinions, which cleave the air like those of a bird? Follow him forsooth! It will be an evil day for thee when thou seekest to do that."

But Earl St Clair forgot that he carried a Talisman which his companion lacked, that enabled him to see things as they really were, while the other's eyes were holden, and he was startled and amazed when Earl Gregory said sharply, "Thy mind hath gone mad over this Elfin King. I tell thee he who passed was a goodly Knight, clad in a green vesture, and riding on a great black jennet. And because I love a gallant horseman, and would fain learn his name and degree, I will follow him till I find him, even if it be at the world's end."

And without another word he put spurs to his horse and galloped off in the direction which the mysterious stranger had taken, leaving Earl St Clair alone upon the moorland, his fingers touching the sacred Sign and his trembling lips muttering prayers for protection.

For he knew that his friend had been bewitched, and he made up his mind, brave gentleman that he was, that he would follow him to the world's end, if need be, and try to deliver him from the spell that had been cast over him.

Meanwhile Earl Gregory rode on and on, ever following in the wake of the Knight in green, over moor, and burn, and moss, till he came to the most desolate region that he had ever been in in his life; where the wind blew cold, as if from snow-fields, and where the hoar-frost lay thick and white on the withered grass at his feet.

And there, in front of him, was a sight from which mortal man might well shrink back in awe and dread. For he saw an enormous Ring marked out on the ground, inside of which the grass, instead of being withered and frozen, was lush, and rank, and green, where hundreds of shadowy Elfin figures were dancing, clad in loose transparent robes of dull blue, which seemed to curl and twist round their wearers like snaky wreaths of smoke.

These weird Goblins were shouting and singing as they danced, and waving their arms above their heads, and throwing themselves about on the ground, for all the world as if they had gone mad; and when they saw Earl Gregory halt on his horse just outside the Ring they beckoned to him with their skinny fingers.

"Come hither, come hither," they shouted; "come tread a measure with us, and afterwards we will drink to thee out of our Monarch's loving cup."

And, strange as it may seem, the spell that had been cast over the young Earl was so powerful that, in spite of his fear, he felt that he must obey the eldrich summons, and he threw his bridle on his horse's neck and prepared to join them.

But just then an old and grizzled Goblin stepped out from among his companions and approached him.

Apparently he dare not leave the charmed Circle, for he stopped at the edge of it; then, stooping down and pretending to pick up something, he whispered in a hoarse whisper:

"I know not whom thou art, nor from whence thou comest, Sir Knight, but if thou lovest thy life, see to it that thou comest not within this Ring, nor joinest with us in our feast. Else wilt thou be for ever undone."

But Earl Gregory only laughed. "I vowed that I would follow the Green Knight," he replied, "and I will carry out my vow, even if the venture leadeth me close to the nethermost world."

And with these words he stepped over the edge of the Circle, right in amongst the ghostly dancers.

At his coming they shouted louder than ever, and danced more madly, and sang more lustily; then, all at once, a silence fell upon them, and they parted into two companies, leaving a way through their midst, up which they signed to the Earl to pass.

He walked through their ranks till he came to the middle of the Circle; and there, seated at a table of red marble, was the Knight whom he had come so far to seek, clad in his grass-green robes. And before him, on the table, stood a wondrous goblet, fashioned from an emerald, and set round the rim with blood-red rubies.

And this cup was filled with heather ale, which foamed up over the brim; and when the Knight saw Sir Gregory, he lifted it from the table, and handed it to him with a stately bow, and Sir Gregory, being very thirsty, drank.

And as he drank he noticed that the ale in the goblet never grew less, but ever foamed up to the edge; and for the first time his heart misgave him, and he wished that he had never set out on this strange adventure.

But, alas! the time for regrets had passed, for already a strange numbness was stealing over his limbs, and a chill pallor was creeping over his face, and before he could utter a single cry for help the goblet dropped from his nerveless fingers, and he fell down before the Elfin King like a dead man.

Then a great shout of triumph went up from all the company; for if there was one thing which filled their hearts with joy, it was to entice some unwary mortal into their Ring and throw their uncanny spell over him, so that he must needs spend long years in their company.

But soon their shouts of triumphs began to die away, and they muttered and whispered to each other with looks of something like fear on their faces.

For their keen ears heard a sound which filled their hearts with dread. It was the sound of human footsteps, which were so free and untrammelled that they knew at once that the stranger, whoever he was, was as yet untouched by any charm. And if this were so he might work them ill, and rescue their captive from them.

And what they dreaded was true; for it was the brave Earl St Clair who approached, fearless and strong because of the Holy Sign he bore.

And as soon as he saw the charmed Ring and the eldrich dancers, he was about to step over its magic border, when the little grizzled Goblin who had whispered to Earl Gregory, came and whispered to him also.

"Alas! alas!" he exclaimed, with a look of sorrow on his wrinkled face, "hast thou come, as thy companion came, to pay thy toll of years to the Elfin King? Oh! if thou hast wife or child behind thee, I beseech thee, by all that thou holdest sacred, to turn back ere it be too late."

"Who art thou, and from whence hast thou come?" asked the Earl, looking kindly down at the little creature in front of him.

"I came from the country that thou hast come from," wailed the Goblin. "For I was once a mortal man, even as thou. But I set out over the enchanted moor, and the Elfin King appeared in the guise of a beauteous Knight, and he looked so brave, and noble, and generous that I followed him hither, and drank of his heather ale, and now I am doomed to bide here till seven long years be spent.

"As for thy friend, Sir Earl, he, too, hath drunk of the accursed draught, and he now lieth as dead at our lawful Monarch's feet. He will wake up, 'tis true, but it will be in such a guise as I wear, and to the bondage with which I am bound."

"Is there naught that I can do to rescue him!" cried Earl St Clair eagerly, "ere he taketh on him the Elfin shape? I have no fear of the spell of his cruel captor, for I bear the Sign of One Who is stronger than he. Speak speedily, little man, for time presseth."

"There is something that thou couldst do, Sir Earl," whispered the Goblin, "but to essay it were a desperate attempt. For if thou failest, then could not even the Power of the Blessed Sign save thee."

"And what is that?" asked the Earl impatiently.

"Thou must remain motionless," answered the old man, "in the cold and frost till dawn break and the hour cometh when they sing Matins in the Holy Church. Then must thou walk slowly nine times round the edge of the enchanted Circle, and after that thou must walk boldly across it to the red marble table where sits the Elfin King. On it thou wilt see an emerald goblet studded with rubies and filled with heather ale. That must thou secure and carry away; but whilst thou art doing so let no word cross thy lips. For this enchanted ground whereon we dance may look solid to mortal eyes, but in reality it is not so. 'Tis but a quaking bog, and under it is a great lake, wherein dwelleth a fearsome Monster, and if thou so much as utter a word while thy foot resteth upon it, thou wilt fall through the bog and perish in the waters beneath."

So saying the Grisly Goblin stepped back among his companions, leaving Earl St Clair standing alone on the outskirts of the charmed Ring.

There he waited, shivering with cold, through the long, dark hours, till the grey dawn began to break over the hill tops, and, with its coming, the Elfin forms before him seemed to dwindle and fade away.

And at the hour when the sound of the Matin Bell came softly pealing from across the moor, he began his solemn walk. Round and round the Ring he paced, keeping steadily on his way, although loud murmurs of anger, like distant thunder, rose from the Elfin Shades, and even the very ground seemed to heave and quiver, as if it would shake this bold intruder from its surface.

But through the power of the Blessed Sign on his arm Earl St Clair went on unhurt.

When he had finished pacing round the Ring he stepped boldly on to the enchanted ground, and walked across it; and what was his astonishment to find that all the ghostly Elves and Goblins whom he had seen, were lying frozen into tiny blocks of ice, so that he was sore put to it to walk amongst them without treading upon them.

And as he approached the marble table the very hairs rose on his head at the sight of the Elfin King sitting behind it, stiff and stark like his followers; while in front of him lay the form of Earl Gregory, who had shared the same fate.

Nothing stirred, save two coal-black ravens, who sat, one on each side of the table, as if to guard the emerald goblet, flapping their wings, and croaking hoarsely.

When Earl St Clair lifted the precious cup, they rose in the air and circled round his head, screaming with rage, and threatening to dash it from his hands with their claws;

while the frozen Elves, and even their mighty King himself stirred in their sleep, and half sat up, as if to lay hands on this presumptuous intruder. But the Power of the Holy Sign restrained them, else had Earl St Clair been foiled in his quest.

As he retraced his steps, awesome and terrible were the sounds that he heard around him. The ravens shrieked, and the frozen Goblins screamed; and up from the hidden lake below came the sound of the deep breathing of the awful Monster who was lurking there, eager for prey.

But the brave Earl heeded none of these things, but kept steadily onwards, trusting in the Might of the Sign he bore. And it carried him safely through all the dangers; and just as the sound of the Matin Bell was dying away in the morning air he stepped on to solid ground once more, and flung the enchanted goblet from him.

And lo! every one of the frozen Elves vanished, along with their King and his marble table, and nothing was left on the rank green grass save Earl Gregory, who slowly woke from his enchanted slumber, and stretched himself, and stood up, shaking in every limb. He gazed vaguely round him, as if he scarce remembered where he was.

And when, after Earl St Clair had run to him and had held him in his arms till his senses returned and the warm blood coursed through his veins, the two friends returned to the spot where Earl St Clair had thrown down the wondrous goblet, they found nothing but a piece of rough grey whinstone, with a drop of dew hidden in a little crevice which was hollowed in its side.

The Witch of Fife

IN THE KINGDOM OF FIFE, in the days of long ago, there lived an old man and his wife. The old man was a douce, quiet body, but the old woman was lightsome and flighty, and some of the neighbours were wont to look at her askance, and whisper to each other that they sorely feared that she was a Witch.

And her husband was afraid of it, too, for she had a curious habit of disappearing in the gloaming and staying out all night; and when she returned in the morning she looked quite white and tired, as if she had been travelling far, or working hard.

He used to try and watch her carefully, in order to find out where she went, or what she did, but he never managed to do so, for she always slipped out of the door when he was not looking, and before he could reach it to follow her, she had vanished utterly.

At last, one day, when he could stand the uncertainty no longer, he asked her to tell him straight out whether she were a Witch or no. And his blood ran cold when, without the slightest hesitation, she answered that she was; and if he would promise not to let anyone know, the next time that she went on one of her midnight expeditions she would tell him all about it.

The Goodman promised; for it seemed to him just as well that he should know all about his wife's cantrips.

He had not long to wait before he heard of them. For the very next week the moon was new, which is, as everybody knows, the time of all others when Witches like to stir abroad; and on the first night of the new moon his wife vanished. Nor did she return till daybreak next morning.

And when he asked her where she had been, she told him, in great glee, how she and four like-minded companions had met at the old Kirk on the moor and had mounted branches of the green bay tree and stalks of hemlock, which had instantly changed into horses, and how they had ridden, swift as the wind, over the country, hunting the foxes, and the weasels, and the owls; and how at last they had swam the Forth and come to the top of Bell Lomond. And how there they had dismounted from their horses, and drunk beer that had been brewed in no earthly brewery, out of horn cups that had been fashioned by no mortal hands.

And how, after that, a wee, wee man had jumped up from under a great mossy stone, with a tiny set of bagpipes under his arm, and how he had piped such wonderful music, that, at the sound of it, the very trouts jumped out of the Loch below, and the stoats crept out of their holes, and the corby crows and the herons came and sat on the trees in the darkness, to listen. And how all the Witches danced until they were so weary that, when the time came for them to mount their steeds again, if they would be home before cockcrow, they could scarce sit on them for fatigue.

The Goodman listened to this long story in silence, shaking his head meanwhile, and, when it was finished, all that he answered was: "And what the better are ye for all your dancing? Ye'd have been a deal more comfortable at home."

At the next new moon the old wife went off again for the night; and when she returned in the morning she told her husband how, on this occasion, she and her friends had taken cockle-shells for boats, and had sailed away over the stormy sea till they reached Norway. And there they had mounted invisible horses of wind, and had ridden and ridden, over mountains and glens, and glaciers, till they reached the land of the Lapps lying under its mantle of snow.

And here all the Elves, and Fairies, and Mermaids of the North were holding festival with Warlocks, and Brownies, and Pixies, and even the Phantom Hunters themselves, who are never looked upon by mortal eyes. And the Witches from Fife held festival with them, and danced, and feasted, and sang with them, and, what was of more consequence, they learned from them certain wonderful words, which, when they uttered them, would bear them through the air, and would undo all bolts and bars, and so gain them admittance to any place soever where they wanted to be. And after that they had come home again, delighted with the knowledge which they had acquired.

"What took ye to siccan a land as that?" asked the old man, with a contemptuous grunt. "Ye would hae been a sight warmer in your bed."

But when his wife returned from her next adventure, he showed a little more interest in her doings.

For she told him how she and her friends had met in the cottage of one of their number, and how, having heard that the Lord Bishop of Carlisle had some very rare wine in his cellar, they had placed their feet on the crook from which the pot hung, and had pronounced the magic words which they had learned from the Elves of Lappland. And, lo and behold! they flew up the chimney like whiffs of smoke, and sailed through the air like little wreathes of cloud, and in less time than it takes to tell they landed at the Bishop's Palace at Carlisle.

And the bolts and the bars flew loose before them, and they went down to his cellar and sampled his wine, and were back in Fife, fine, sober, old women by cock-crow.

When he heard this, the old man started from his chair in right earnest, for he loved good wine above all things, and it was but seldom that it came his way.

"By my troth, but thou art a wife to be proud of!" he cried. "Tell me the words, Woman! and I will e'en go and sample his Lordship's wine for myself."

But the Goodwife shook her head. "Na, na! I cannot do that," she said, "for if I did, an' ye told it over again, 'twould turn the whole world upside down. For everybody would be leaving their own lawful work, and flying about the world after other folk's business and other folk's dainties. So just bide content, Goodman. Ye get on fine with the knowledge ye already possess."

And although the old man tried to persuade her with all the soft words he could think of, she would not tell him her secret.

But he was a sly old man, and the thought of the Bishop's wine gave him no rest. So night after night he went and hid in the old woman's cottage, in the hope that his wife and her friends would meet there; and although for a long time it was all in vain, at last his trouble was rewarded. For one evening the whole five old women assembled, and in low tones and with chuckles of laughter they recounted all that had befallen them in Lappland. Then, running to the fireplace, they, one after another, climbed on a chair and put their feet on the sooty crook. Then they repeated the magic words, and, hey, presto! they were up the lum and away before the old man could draw his breath.

"I can do that, too," he said to himself; and he crawled out of his hiding-place and ran to the fire. He put his foot on the crook and repeated the words, and up the chimney he went, and flew through the air after his wife and her companions, as if he had been a Warlock born.

And, as Witches are not in the habit of looking over their shoulders, they never noticed that he was following them, until they reached the Bishop's Palace and went down into his cellar, then, when they found that he was among them, they were not too well pleased.

However, there was no help for it, and they settled down to enjoy themselves. They tapped this cask of wine, and they tapped that, drinking a little of each, but not too much; for they were cautious old women, and they knew that if they wanted to get home before cock-crow it behoved them to keep their heads clear.

But the old man was not so wise, for he sipped, and he sipped, until at last he became quite drowsy, and lay down on the floor and fell fast asleep.

And his wife, seeing this, thought that she would teach him a lesson not to be so curious in the future. So, when she and her four friends thought that it was time to be gone, she departed without waking him.

He slept peacefully for some hours, until two of the Bishop's servants, coming down to the cellar to draw wine for their Master's table, almost fell over him in the darkness. Greatly astonished at his presence there, for the cellar door was fast locked, they dragged him up to the light and shook him, and cuffed him, and asked him how he came to be there.

And the poor old man was so confused at being awakened in this rough way, and his head seemed to whirl round so fast, that all he could stammer out was, "that he came from Fife, and that he had travelled on the midnight wind."

As soon as they heard that, the men servants cried out that he was a Warlock, and they dragged him before the Bishop, and, as Bishops in those days had a holy horror of Warlocks and Witches, he ordered him to be burned alive.

When the sentence was pronounced, you may be very sure that the poor old man wished with all his heart that he had stayed quietly at home in bed, and never hankered after the Bishop's wine.

But it was too late to wish that now, for the servants dragged him out into the courtyard, and put a chain round his waist, and fastened it to a great iron stake, and they piled faggots of wood round his feet and set them alight.

As the first tiny little tongue of flame crept up, the poor old man thought that his last hour had come. But when he thought that, he forgot completely that his wife was a Witch.

For, just as the little tongue of flame began to singe his breeches, there was a swish and a flutter in the air, and a great Grey Bird, with outstretched wings, appeared in the sky, and swooped down suddenly, and perched for a moment on the old man's shoulder.

And in this Grey Bird's mouth was a little red pirnie, which, to everyone's amazement, it popped on to the prisoner's head. Then it gave one fierce croak, and flew away again, but to the old man's ears that croak was the sweetest music that he had ever heard.

For to him it was the croak of no earthly bird, but the voice of his wife whispering words of magic to him. And when he heard them he jumped for joy, for he knew that they were words of deliverance, and he shouted them aloud, and his chains fell off, and he mounted in the air – up and up – while the onlookers watched him in awestruck silence.

He flew right away to the Kingdom of Fife, without as much as saying good-bye to them; and when he found himself once more safely at home, you may be very sure that he never tried to find out his wife's secrets again, but left her alone to her own devices.

Farquhar MacNeill

ONCE UPON A TIME there was a young man named Farquhar MacNeill. He had just gone to a new situation, and the very first night after he went to it his mistress asked him if he would go over the hill to the house of a neighbour and borrow a sieve, for her own was all in holes, and she wanted to sift some meal.

Farquhar agreed to do so, for he was a willing lad, and he set out at once upon his errand, after the farmer's wife had pointed out to him the path that he was to follow, and told him that he would have no difficulty in finding the house, even though it was strange to him, for he would be sure to see the light in the window.

He had not gone very far, however, before he saw what he took to be the light from a cottage window on his left hand, some distance from the path, and, forgetting his Mistress's instructions that he was to follow the path right over the hill, he left it, and walked towards the light.

It seemed to him that he had almost reached it when his foot tripped, and he fell down, down, down, into a Fairy Parlour, far under the ground.

It was full of Fairies, who were engaged in different occupations.

Close by the door, or rather the hole down which he had so unceremoniously tumbled, two little elderly women, in black aprons and white mutches, were busily engaged in grinding corn between two flat millstones. Other two Fairies, younger women, in blue print gowns and white kerchiefs, were gathering up the freshly ground meal, and baking it into bannocks, which they were toasting on a girdle over a peat fire, which was burning slowly in a corner.

In the centre of the large apartment a great troop of Fairies, Elves, and Sprites were dancing reels as hard as they could to the music of a tiny set of bagpipes which were being played by a brown-faced Gnome, who sat on a ledge of rock far above their heads.

They all stopped their various employments when Farquhar came suddenly down in their midst, and looked at him in alarm; but when they saw that he was not hurt, they bowed gravely and bade him be seated. Then they went on with their work and with their play as if nothing had happened.

But Farquhar, being very fond of dancing, and being in no wise anxious to be seated, thought that he would like to have a reel first, so he asked the Fairies if he might join them. And they, although they looked surprised at his request, allowed him to do so, and in a few minutes the young man was dancing away as gaily as any of them.

And as he danced a strange change came over him. He forgot his errand, he forgot his home, he forgot everything that had ever happened to him, he only knew that he wanted to remain with the Fairies all the rest of his life.

And he did remain with them – for a magic spell had been cast over him, and he became like one of themselves, and could come and go at nights without being seen, and could sip the dew from the grass and honey from the flowers as daintily and noiselessly as if he had been a Fairy born.

Time passed by, and one night he and a band of merry companions set out for a long journey through the air. They started early, for they intended to pay a visit to the Man in the Moon and be back again before cock-crow.

All would have gone well if Farquhar had only looked where he was going, but he did not, being deeply engaged in making love to a young Fairy Maiden by his side, so he never saw a cottage that was standing right in his way, till he struck against the chimney and stuck fast in the thatch.

His companions sped merrily on, not noticing what had befallen him, and he was left to disentangle himself as best he could.

As he was doing so he chanced to glance down the wide chimney, and in the cottage kitchen he saw a comely young woman dandling a rosy-cheeked baby.

Now, when Farquhar had been in his mortal state, he had been very fond of children, and a word of blessing rose to his lips.

"God shield thee," he said, as he looked at the mother and child, little guessing what the result of his words would be.

For scarce had the Holy Name crossed his lips than the spell which had held him so long was broken, and he became as he had been before.

Instantly his thoughts flew to his friends at home, and to the new Mistress whom he had left waiting for her sieve; for he felt sure that some weeks must have elapsed since he set out to fetch it. So he made haste to go to the farm.

When he arrived in the neighbourhood everything seemed strange. There were woods where no woods used to be, and walls where no walls used to be. To his amazement, he could not find his way to the farm, and, worst of all, in the place where he expected to find his father's house he found nothing but a crop of rank green nettles.

In great distress he looked about for someone to tell him what it all meant, and at last he found an old man thatching the roof of a cottage.

This old man was so thin and grey that at first Farquhar took him for a patch of mist, but as he went nearer he saw that he was a human being, and, going close up to the wall and shouting with all his might, for he felt sure that such an ancient man would be deaf, he asked him if he could tell him where his friends had gone to, and what had happened to his father's dwelling.

The old man listened, then he shook his head. "I never heard of him," he answered slowly; "but perhaps my father might be able to tell you."

"Your father!" said Farquhar, in great surprise. "Is it possible that your father is alive?"

"Aye he is," answered the old man, with a little laugh. "If you go into the house you'll find him sitting in the arm-chair by the fire."

Farquhar did as he was bid, and on entering the cottage found another old man, who was so thin and withered and bent that he looked as if he must at least be a hundred years old. He was feebly twisting ropes to bind the thatch on the roof.

"Can ye tell me aught of my friends, or where my father's cottage is?" asked Farquhar again, hardly expecting that this second old man would be able to answer him.

"I cannot," mumbled this ancient person; "but perhaps my father can tell you."

"Your father!" exclaimed Farquhar, more astonished than ever. "But surely he must be dead long ago."

The old man shook his head with a weird grimace.

"Look there," he said, and pointed with a twisted finger, to a leathern purse, or sporran, which was hanging to one of the posts of a wooden bedstead in the corner.

Farquhar approached it, and was almost frightened out of his wits by seeing a tiny shrivelled face crowned by a red pirnie, looking over the edge of the sporran.

"Tak' him out; he'll no touch ye," chuckled the old man by the fire.

So Farquhar took the little creature out carefully between his finger and thumb, and set him on the palm of his left hand. He was so shrivelled with age that he looked just like a mummy.

"Dost know anything of my friends, or where my father's cottage is gone to?" asked Farquhar for the third time, hardly expecting to get an answer.

"They were all dead long before I was born," piped out the tiny figure. "I never saw any of them, but I have heard my father speak of them."

"Then I must be older than you!" cried Farquhar, in great dismay. And he got such a shock at the thought that his bones suddenly dissolved into dust, and he fell, a heap of grey ashes, on the floor.

The Minister and the Fairy

NOT LONG SINCE, a pious clergyman was returning home, after administering spiritual consolation to a dying member of his flock. It was late of the night, and he had to pass through a good deal of uncanny land. He was, however, a good and a conscientious minister of the Gospel, and feared not all the spirits in the country.

On his reaching the end of a lake which stretched along the roadside for some distance, he was a good deal surprised at hearing the most melodious strains of music. Overcome by pleasure and curiosity, the minister coolly sat down to listen to the harmonious sounds, and try what new discoveries he could make with regard to their nature and source. He had not sat many minutes before he could distinguish the approach of the music, and also observe a light in the direction from whence it proceeded gliding across the lake towards him. Instead of taking to his heels, as any faithless wight would have done, the pastor fearlessly determined to await the issue of the phenomenon. As the light and music drew near, the clergyman could at length distinguish an object resembling a human being walking on the surface of the water, attended by a group of diminutive musicians, some of them bearing lights, and others instruments of music, from which they continued to evoke those melodious strains which first attracted his attention. The leader of the band dismissed his attendants, landed on the beach, and afforded the minister the amplest opportunities of examining his appearance. He was a little primitive-looking grey-headed man, clad in the most grotesque habit the clergyman had ever seen, and such as led him at once to suspect his real character. He walked up to the minister, whom he saluted with great grace, offering an apology for his intrusion. The pastor returned his compliments, and, without further explanation, invited the mysterious stranger to sit down by his side. The invitation was complied with, upon which the minister proposed the following question: – "Who art thou, stranger, and from whence?"

To this question the fairy, with downcast eye, replied that he was one of those sometimes called Doane Shee, or men of peace, or good men, though the reverse of this title was a more fit appellation for them. Originally angelic in his nature and attributes, and once a sharer of the indescribable joys of the regions of light, he was seduced by Satan to join him in his mad conspiracies; and, as a punishment for his transgression, he was cast down from those regions of bliss, and was now doomed, along with millions of fellow-sufferers, to wander through seas and mountains, until the coming of the Great Day. What their fate would be then they could not divine, but they apprehended the worst. "And," continued he, turning to the minister, with great anxiety, "the object of my present intrusion on you is to learn your opinion, as an eminent divine, as to our final condition on that dreadful day." Here the venerable pastor entered upon a long conversation with the fairy, touching the principles of faith and repentance. Receiving rather unsatisfactory answers to his questions, the minister desired the "sheech" to repeat after him the Paternoster, in attempting to do which, it was not a little remarkable that he could not repeat the word "art," but said "wert," in heaven. Inferring from every circumstance that their fate was extremely precarious, the minister resolved not to puff the fairies up with presumptuous, and, perhaps, groundless expectations. Accordingly, addressing himself to the unhappy fairy, who was all anxiety to know the nature of his sentiments, the reverend gentleman told him that he could not take it upon him to give them any hopes of pardon, as their crime was of so deep a hue as scarcely to admit of it. On this the unhappy fairy uttered a shriek of despair, plunged headlong into the loch, and the minister resumed his course to his home.

Habetrot the Spinstress

IN BYGONE DAYS, in an old farmhouse which stood by a river, there lived a beautiful girl called Maisie. She was tall and straight, with auburn hair and blue eyes, and she was the prettiest girl in all the valley. And one would have thought that she would have been the pride of her mother's heart.

But, instead of this, her mother used to sigh and shake her head whenever she looked at her. And why?

Because, in those days, all men were sensible; and instead of looking out for pretty girls to be their wives, they looked out for girls who could cook and spin, and who gave promise of becoming notable housewives.

Maisie's mother had been an industrious spinster; but, alas! to her sore grief and disappointment, her daughter did not take after her.

The girl loved to be out of doors, chasing butterflies and plucking wild flowers, far better than sitting at her spinning-wheel. So when her mother saw one after another of Maisie's companions, who were not nearly so pretty as she was, getting rich husbands, she sighed and said:

"Woe's me, child, for methinks no brave wooer will ever pause at our door while they see thee so idle and thoughtless." But Maisie only laughed.

At last her mother grew really angry, and one bright Spring morning she laid down three heads of lint on the table, saying sharply, "I will have no more of this dallying. People will say that it is my blame that no wooer comes to seek thee. I cannot have thee left on my hands to be laughed at, as the idle maid who would not marry. So now thou must work; and if thou hast not these heads of lint spun into seven hanks of thread in three days, I will e'en speak to the Mother at St Mary's Convent, and thou wilt go there and learn to be a nun."

Now, though Maisie was an idle girl, she had no wish to be shut up in a nunnery; so she tried not to think of the sunshine outside, but sat down soberly with her distaff.

But, alas! she was so little accustomed to work that she made but slow progress; and although she sat at the spinning-wheel all day, and never once went out of doors, she found at night that she had only spun half a hank of yarn.

The next day it was even worse, for her arms ached so much she could only work very slowly. That night she cried herself to sleep; and next morning, seeing that it was quite hopeless to expect to get her task finished, she threw down her distaff in despair, and ran out of doors.

Near the house was a deep dell, through which ran a tiny stream. Maisie loved this dell, the flowers grew so abundantly there.

This morning she ran down to the edge of the stream, and seated herself on a large stone. It was a glorious morning, the hazel trees were newly covered with leaves, and the branches nodded over her head, and showed like delicate tracery against the blue sky. The primroses and sweet-scented violets peeped out from among the grass, and a little water wagtail came and perched on a stone in the middle of the stream, and bobbed up and down, till it seemed as if he were nodding to Maisie, and as if he were trying to say to her, "Never mind, cheer up."

But the poor girl was in no mood that morning to enjoy the flowers and the birds. Instead of watching them, as she generally did, she hid her face in her hands, and wondered what would become of her. She rocked herself to and fro, as she thought how terrible it would be if her mother fulfilled her threat and shut her up in the Convent of St Mary, with the grave, solemn-faced sisters, who seemed as if they had completely forgotten what it was like to be young, and run about in the sunshine, and laugh, and pick the fresh Spring flowers.

"Oh, I could not do it, I could not do it," she cried at last. "It would kill me to be a nun."

"And who wants to make a pretty wench like thee into a nun?" asked a queer, cracked voice quite close to her.

Maisie jumped up, and stood staring in front of her as if she had been moonstruck. For, just across the stream from where she had been sitting, there was a curious boulder, with a round hole in the middle of it – for all the world like a big apple with the core taken out.

Maisie knew it well; she had often sat upon it, and wondered how the funny hole came to be there.

It was no wonder that she stared, for, seated on this stone, was the queerest little old woman that she had ever seen in her life. Indeed, had it not been for her silver hair, and the white mutch with the big frill that she wore on her head, Maisie would have taken her for a little girl, she wore such a very short skirt, only reaching down to her knees.

Her face, inside the frill of her cap, was round, and her cheeks were rosy, and she had little black eyes, which twinkled merrily as she looked at the startled maiden. On her shoulders was a black and white checked shawl, and on her legs, which she dangled over the edge of the boulder, she wore black silk stockings and the neatest little shoes, with great silver buckles.

In fact, she would have been quite a pretty old lady had it not been for her lips, which were very long and very thick, and made her look quite ugly in spite of her rosy cheeks and black eyes. Maisie stood and looked at her for such a long time in silence that she repeated her question.

"And who wants to make a pretty wench like thee into a nun? More likely that some gallant gentleman should want to make a bride of thee."

"Oh, no," answered Maisie, "my mother says no gentleman would look at me because I cannot spin."

"Nonsense," said the tiny woman. "Spinning is all very well for old folks like me – my lips, as thou seest, are long and ugly because I have spun so much, for I always wet my fingers with them, the easier to draw the thread from the distaff. No, no, take care of thy beauty, child; do not waste it over the spinning-wheel, nor yet in a nunnery."

"If my mother only thought as thou dost," replied the girl sadly; and, encouraged by the old woman's kindly face, she told her the whole story.

"Well," said the old Dame, "I do not like to see pretty girls weep; what if I were able to help thee, and spin the lint for thee?"

Maisie thought that this offer was too good to be true; but her new friend bade her run home and fetch the lint; and I need not tell you that she required no second bidding.

When she returned she handed the bundle to the little lady, and was about to ask her where she should meet her in order to get the thread from her when it was spun, when a sudden noise behind her made her look round.

She saw nothing; but what was her horror and surprise when she turned back again, to find that the old woman had vanished entirely, lint and all.

She rubbed her eyes, and looked all round, but she was nowhere to be seen. The girl was utterly bewildered. She wondered if she could have been dreaming, but no that could not be, there were her footprints leading up the bank and down again, where she had gone for the lint, and brought it back, and there was the mark of her foot, wet with dew, on a stone in the middle of the stream, where she had stood when she had handed the lint up to the mysterious little stranger.

What was she to do now? What would her mother say when, in addition to not having finished the task that had been given her, she had to confess to having lost the greater part of the lint also? She ran up and down the little dell, hunting amongst the bushes, and peeping into every nook and cranny of the bank where the little old woman might have hidden herself. It was all in vain; and at last, tired out with the search, she sat down on the stone once more, and presently fell fast asleep.

When she awoke it was evening. The sun had set, and the yellow glow on the western horizon was fast giving place to the silvery light of the moon. She was sitting thinking of the curious events of the day, and gazing at the great boulder opposite, when it seemed to her as if a distant murmur of voices came from it.

With one bound she crossed the stream, and clambered on to the stone. She was right.

Someone was talking underneath it, far down in the ground. She put her ear close to the stone, and listened.

The voice of the queer little old woman came up through the hole. "Ho, ho, my pretty little wench little knows that my name is Habetrot."

Full of curiosity, Maisie put her eye to the opening, and the strangest sight that she had ever seen met her gaze. She seemed to be looking through a telescope into a wonderful little valley. The trees there were brighter and greener than any that she had ever seen before and there were beautiful flowers, quite different from the flowers that grew in her country. The little valley was carpeted with the most exquisite moss, and up and down it walked her tiny friend, busily engaged in spinning.

She was not alone, for round her were a circle of other little old women, who were seated on large white stones, and they were all spinning away as fast as they could.

Occasionally one would look up, and then Maisie saw that they all seemed to have the same long, thick lips that her friend had. She really felt very sorry, as they all looked exceedingly kind, and might have been pretty had it not been for this defect.

One of the Spinstresses sat by herself, and was engaged in winding the thread, which the others had spun, into hanks. Maisie did not think that this little lady looked so nice as the others. She was dressed entirely in grey, and had a big hooked nose, and great horn spectacles. She seemed to be called Slantlie Mab, for Maisie heard Habetrot address her by that name, telling her to make haste and tie up all the thread, for it was getting late, and it was time that the young girl had it to carry home to her mother.

Maisie did not quite know what to do, or how she was to get the thread, for she did not like to shout down the hole in case the queer little old woman should be angry at being watched.

However, Habetrot, as she had called herself, suddenly appeared on the path beside her, with the hanks of thread in her hand.

"Oh, thank you, thank you," cried Maisie. "What can I do to show you how thankful I am?"

"Nothing," answered the Fairy. "For I do not work for reward. Only do not tell your mother who span the thread for thee."

It was now late, and Maisie lost no time in running home with the precious thread upon her shoulder. When she walked into the kitchen she found that her mother had gone to bed. She seemed to have had a busy day, for there, hanging up in the wide chimney, in order to dry, were seven large black puddings.

The fire was low, but bright and clear; and the sight of it and the sight of the puddings suggested to Maisie that she was very hungry, and that fried black puddings were very good.

Flinging the thread down on the table, she hastily pulled off her shoes, so as not to make a noise and awake her mother; and, getting down the frying-pan from the wall, she took one of the black puddings from the chimney, and fried it, and ate it.

Still she felt hungry, so she took another, and then another, till they were all gone. Then she crept upstairs to her little bed and fell fast asleep.

Next morning her mother came downstairs before Maisie was awake. In fact, she had not been able to sleep much for thinking of her daughter's careless ways, and had been sorrowfully making up her mind that she must lose no time in speaking to the Abbess of St Mary's about this idle girl of hers.

What was her surprise to see on the table the seven beautiful hanks of thread, while, on going to the chimney to take down a black pudding to fry for breakfast, she found that every one of them had been eaten. She did not know whether to laugh for joy that her daughter had been so industrious, or to cry for vexation because all her lovely black puddings – which she had expected would last for a week at least – were gone. In her bewilderment she sang out:

"My daughter's spun se'en, se'en, se'en,
My daughter's eaten se'en, se'en, se'en,
And all before daylight."

Now I forgot to tell you that, about half a mile from where the old farmhouse stood, there was a beautiful Castle, where a very rich young nobleman lived. He was both good and brave, as well as rich; and all the mothers who had pretty daughters used to wish that he would come their way, some day, and fall in love with one of them. But he had never done so, and everyone said, "He is too grand to marry any country girl. One day he will go away to London Town and marry a Duke's daughter."

Well, this fine spring morning it chanced that this young nobleman's favourite horse had lost a shoe, and he was so afraid that any of the grooms might ride it along the hard road, and not on the soft grass at the side, that he said that he would take it to the smithy himself.

So it happened that he was riding along by Maisie's garden gate as her mother came into the garden singing these strange lines.

He stopped his horse, and said good-naturedly, "Good day, Madam; and may I ask why you sing such a strange song?"

Maisie's mother made no answer, but turned and walked into the house; and the young nobleman, being very anxious to know what it all meant, hung his bridle over the garden gate, and followed her.

She pointed to the seven hanks of thread lying on the table, and said, "This hath my daughter done before breakfast."

Then the young man asked to see the Maiden who was so industrious, and her mother went and pulled Maisie from behind the door, where she had hidden herself when the stranger came in; for she had come downstairs while her mother was in the garden.

She looked so lovely in her fresh morning gown of blue gingham, with her auburn hair curling softly round her brow, and her face all over blushes at the sight of such a gallant young man, that he quite lost his heart, and fell in love with her on the spot.

"Ah," said he, "my dear mother always told me to try and find a wife who was both pretty and useful, and I have succeeded beyond my expectations. Do not let our marriage, I pray thee, good Dame, be too long deferred."

Maisie's mother was overjoyed, as you may imagine, at this piece of unexpected good fortune, and busied herself in getting everything ready for the wedding; but Maisie herself was a little perplexed.

She was afraid that she would be expected to spin a great deal when she was married and lived at the Castle, and if that were so, her husband was sure to find out that she was not really such a good spinstress as he thought she was.

In her trouble she went down, the night before her wedding, to the great boulder by the stream in the glen, and, climbing up on it, she laid her head against the stone, and called softly down the hole, "Habetrot, dear Habetrot."

The little old woman soon appeared, and, with twinkling eyes, asked her what was troubling her so much just when she should have been so happy. And Maisie told her.

"Trouble not thy pretty head about that," answered the Fairy, "but come here with thy bridegroom next week, when the moon is full, and I warrant that he will never ask thee to sit at a spinning-wheel again."

Accordingly, after all the wedding festivities were over and the couple had settled down at the Castle, on the appointed evening Maisie suggested to her husband that they should take a walk together in the moonlight.

She was very anxious to see what the little Fairy would do to help her; for that very day he had been showing her all over her new home, and he had pointed out to her the beautiful new spinning-wheel made of ebony, which had belonged to his mother, saying proudly, "Tomorrow, little one, I shall bring some lint from the town, and then the maids will see what clever little fingers my wife has."

Maisie had blushed as red as a rose as she bent over the lovely wheel, and then felt quite sick, as she wondered whatever she would do if Habetrot did not help her.

So on this particular evening, after they had walked in the garden, she said that she should like to go down to the little dell and see how the stream looked by moonlight. So to the dell they went.

As soon as they came to the boulder Maisie put her head against it and whispered, "Habetrot, dear Habetrot"; and in an instant the little old woman appeared.

She bowed in a stately way, as if they were both strangers to her, and said, "Welcome, Sir and Madam, to the Spinsters' Dell." And then she tapped on the root of a great oak tree with a tiny wand which she held in her hand, and a green door, which Maisie never remembered having noticed before, flew open, and they followed the Fairy through it into the other valley which Maisie had seen through the hole in the great stone.

All the little old women were sitting on their white chucky stones busy at work, only they seemed far uglier than they had seemed at first; and Maisie noticed that the reason for this was, that, instead of wearing red skirts and white mutches as they had done before, they now wore caps and dresses of dull grey, and instead of looking happy, they all seemed to be trying who could look most miserable, and who could push out their long lips furthest, as they wet their fingers to draw the thread from their distaffs.

"Save us and help us! What a lot of hideous old witches," exclaimed her husband. "Whatever could this funny old woman mean by bringing a pretty child like thee to look at them? Thou wilt dream of them for a week and a day. Just look at their lips"; and, pushing Maisie behind him, he went up to one of them and asked her what had made her mouth grow so ugly.

She tried to tell him, but all the sound that he could hear was something that sounded like spin-n-n.

He asked another one, and her answer sounded like this: span-n-n. He tried a third, and hers sounded like spun-n-n.

He seized Maisie by the hand and hurried her through the green door. "By my troth," he said, "my mother's spinning-wheel may turn to gold ere I let thee touch it, if this is what spinning leads to. Rather than that thy pretty face should be spoilt, the linen chests at the Castle may get empty, and remain so for ever!"

So it came to pass that Maisie could be out of doors all day wandering about with her husband, and laughing and singing to her heart's content. And whenever there was lint at the Castle to be spun, it was carried down to the big boulder in the dell and left there, and Habetrot and her companions spun it, and there was no more trouble about the matter.

The Fairy Boy of Leith

"ABOUT FIFTEEN YEARS SINCE, having business that detained me for some time at Leith, which is near Edinburgh, in the kingdom of Scotland, I often met some of my acquaintance at a certain house there, where we used to drink a glass of wine for our refection. The woman which kept the house was of honest reputation among the neighbours, which made me give the more attention to what she told me one day about a fairy boy (as they called him) who lived about that town. She had given me so strange an account of him, that I desired her I might see him the first opportunity, which she promised; and not long after, passing that way, she told me there was the fairy boy, but a little before I came by; and, casting her eye into the street, said, 'Look you, sir, yonder he is, at play with those other boys'; and pointing him out to me, I went, and by smooth words, and a piece of money, got him to come into the house with me; where, in the presence of divers people, I demanded of him several astrological questions, which he answered with great subtlety; and, through all his discourse, carried it with a cunning much above his years, which seemed not to exceed ten or eleven.

"He seemed to make a motion like drumming upon the table with his fingers, upon which I asked him whether he could beat a drum? To which he replied, 'Yes, sir, as well as any man in Scotland; for every Thursday night I beat all points to a sort of people that used to meet under yonder hill' (pointing to the great hill between Edinburgh and Leith). 'How, boy?' quoth I, 'what company have you there?' 'There are, sir,' said he, 'a great company both of men and women, and they are entertained with many sorts of music besides my drum; they have, besides, plenty of variety of meats and wine, and many times we are carried into France or Holland in the night, and return again, and whilst we are there, we enjoy all the pleasures the country doth afford.' I demanded of him how they got under that hill? To which he replied that there was a great pair of gates that opened to them, though they were invisible to others, and that within there were brave large rooms, as well accommodated as most in Scotland. I then asked him how I should know what he said to be true? Upon which he told me he would read my fortune, saying, I should have two wives, and that he saw the forms of them over my shoulders; and both would be very handsome women.

"The woman of the house told me that all the people in Scotland could not keep him from the rendezvous on Thursday night; upon which, by promising him some more money, I got a promise of him to meet me at the same place in the afternoon, the Thursday following, and so dismissed him at that time. The boy came again at the place and time appointed, and I had prevailed with some friends to continue with me (if possible) to prevent his moving that night. He was placed between us, and answered many questions, until, about eleven of the clock, he was got away unperceived by the company; but I, suddenly missing him, hastened to the door, and took hold of him, and so returned him into the same room. We all watched him, and, of a sudden, he was again got out of doors; I followed him close, and he made a noise in the street, as if he had been set upon, and from that time I could never see him."

The Fairies and Donald Duaghal Mackay

THE CELTS ARE CREDITED with originating the fairy superstition, though it is unknown from what cause. In Scotland and other countries in which Celtic traditions predominate, the fairies were regarded on the whole as little given to malevolence; on the contrary, ready to help mankind at times, though when offended they exhibited an admixture of the malignant spirit of the elf and the dwarf of the Scandinavian, who introduced the belief in them to the Celts. Most spirits were supposed to have the attribute of enlarging or contracting their bulk at will; the fairy alone was regarded as essentially diminutive in size, the miniature of a human being, perfect in form, clad in pure green, brilliant and rich beyond conception, inhabiting subterranean palaces of indescribable splendour, and innumerable in numbers. They were represented as continually feasting, dancing, and making merry, or moving in procession amongst the shady green grass and verdant lawns of earth, entertained with the most harmonious and melodious music that mortal ear ever listened to, observant of the doings of mankind, and not unwilling to help them to overcome such unusual or extraordinary difficulties, if called upon, as my story tells.

The Story

Donald Duaghal, having returned from the wars in Germany to his own country, where his fame preceded him, was a great hero, in the estimation of his retainers. His extraordinary valour, his feats of daring, his fearless conduct, his escaping comparatively scatheless of wounds out of all the skirmishes, sieges, and battles in which he took a leading share; all this, magnified by the stories related of him by the few retainers who survived and returned home with him into the Reay country, threw around the man a halo of romance that gave rise to the belief that he must have had a charmed life, and, it might be, some occult relations with the "Droch Spiorad" and the "black art" in his travels abroad. "Nach robh e san Edailt for an d'iunnsaich e an sgoil dubh?" – Italy being the country above all others in which the "black art" was to be acquired. But Donald was never in Italy. It did not matter to Clann Mhic Aoidh. They did not trouble themselves much about correct geography; their chief was abroad; he might have been in Italy; and that was sufficient for the unsophisticated and unlettered people surrounding their beloved chief who had seen much in his travels and campaigns in Norway, Sweden, Germany, and Poland.

He had crossed rivers and estuaries, and transported his soldiers over them by bridges of boats constructed by Swedish and Danish military engineers in very little time, even while his soldiers were taking a hasty meal, Donald himself urging on the work and lending a hand – all this was related in Tongue, much to the astonishment of the natives around, who could not believe it. They could not understand how an estuary like the Kyle of Tongue could be bridged in half an hour. The feat was too marvellous to be true, and if true there must have been some supernatural assistance. But could he not do anything? Did he not learn the "black art" in Italy? Rumour went and was magnified, till in the long run it was believed that nothing was impossible to Donald. It was rumoured that he intended to throw a bridge over the estuary from Tongue to Melness. This report got wings and was believed. The knowing ones were incredulous, but the credulous had no doubt he could and would do it. Has he not the "black art?" besides, can he not send to the "Cailleach Mhor" in Dornoch? get her to send him the fairies, and the bridge will be built before morning.

This was so much talked about that it became a received opinion that Donald Duaghal was supposed to have actually attempted the feat. He sent his Gille to Dornoch to the Cailleach requesting her as a special favour to send him fairies to construct a bridge across the Kyle of Tongue. The Cailleach Mhor consulted the fairy queen, and she, willing to do anything for so brave a man as Donald Duaghal, gave the Cailleach a box to be conveyed to Donald. The Cailleach gave the box to the Gille with strict and peremptory injunctions not to open it till he had delivered it into his master's hands. Alas! for weak humanity, always prying into secrets, always doing the forbidden – the greater the restriction, the greater the temptation to disobey. In an unlucky moment, going over the Crask, he opened the box, when lo! in an instant, around him and about him on all sides were myriads of tiny creatures, hammer in hand, shrilly clamouring, "Obair, obair, obair" (Work, work, work). Nonplussed with the extraordinary sight, confounded for a moment with the effect of his disobedience of orders, Mackay's man was equal to the occasion. Rapidly recovering his presence of mind and appreciating his position, he ordered his importunate companions to set to work and pluck up the heather off the whole hillside upon which they were. No sooner ordered than it was done, and the same clamour was resumed of "Obair, obair, obair". Driven by this almost to desperation he ordered his little companions to fly away to Dornoch Firth opposite Tain, and there build a bridge for the accommodation of the lieges of Dornoch and Baile Dhuthaich. Instantly they went, and commenced operations, throwing up the sand in clouds to form an embankment, but as ill-luck would have it, some person passing the way about cock-crowing time, hearing the noise and uproar, exclaimed, "Dhia beannaich mis, ciod e an obair tha'n so" (God bless me, what work is this). Work was instantly suspended, never to be resumed, in consequence of God's name being mentioned, and a blessing asked on the work; and well would it have been, had it never been commenced, for the sand accumulated by the fairies in that night's work forms the dangerous shoals between Dornoch and Tain to this day, the sea roaring over them at every tide, and the noise of the waves heard at the distance of many a mile, portends to the natives the advent of foul weather. To this day the place is called Drochaid na h'Aogh, or the Elfin Bridge.

The Brownie o' Ferne-Den

THERE HAVE BEEN many Brownies known in Scotland; and stories have been written about the Brownie o' Bodsbeck and the Brownie o' Blednock, but about neither of them has a prettier story been told than that which I am going to tell you about the Brownie o' Ferne-Den.

Now, Ferne-Den was a farmhouse, which got its name from the glen, or "den," on the edge of which it stood, and through which anyone who wished to reach the dwelling had to pass.

And this glen was believed to be the abode of a Brownie, who never appeared to anyone in the daytime, but who, it was said, was sometimes seen at night, stealing about, like an ungainly shadow, from tree to tree, trying to keep from observation, and never, by any chance, harming anybody.

Indeed, like all Brownies that are properly treated and let alone, so far was he from harming anybody that he was always on the lookout to do a good turn to those who needed his assistance. The farmer often said that he did not know what he would do without him; for if there was any work to be finished in a hurry at the farm – corn to thrash, or winnow, or tie up into bags, turnips to cut, clothes to wash, a kirn to be kirned, a garden to be weeded – all that the farmer and his wife had to do was to leave the door of the barn, or the turnip shed, or the milk house open when they went to bed, and put down a bowl of new milk on the doorstep for the Brownie's supper, and when they woke the next morning the bowl would be empty, and the job finished better than if it had been done by mortal hands.

In spite of all this, however, which might have proved to them how gentle and kindly the Creature really was, everyone about the place was afraid of him, and would rather go a couple of miles round about in the dark, when they were coming home from Kirk or Market, than pass through the glen, and run the risk of catching a glimpse of him.

I said that they were all afraid of him, but that was not true, for the farmer's wife was so good and gentle that she was not afraid of anything on God's earth, and when the

Brownie's supper had to be left outside, she always filled his bowl with the richest milk, and added a good spoonful of cream to it, for, said she, "He works so hard for us, and asks no wages; he well deserves the very best meal that we can give him."

One night this gentle lady was taken very ill, and everyone was afraid that she was going to die. Of course, her husband was greatly distressed, and so were her servants, for she had been such a good Mistress to them that they loved her as if she had been their mother. But they were all young, and none of them knew very much about illness, and everyone agreed that it would be better to send off for an old woman who lived about seven miles away on the other side of the river, who was known to be a very skilful nurse.

But who was to go? That was the question. For it was black midnight, and the way to the old woman's house lay straight through the glen. And whoever travelled that road ran the risk of meeting the dreaded Brownie.

The farmer would have gone only too willingly, but he dare not leave his wife alone; and the servants stood in groups about the kitchen, each one telling the other that he ought to go, yet no one offering to go themselves.

Little did they think that the cause of all their terror, a queer, wee, misshapen little man, all covered with hair, with a long beard, red-rimmed eyes, broad, flat feet, just like the feet of a paddock, and enormous long arms that touched the ground, even when he stood upright, was within a yard or two of them, listening to their talk, with an anxious face, behind the kitchen door.

For he had come up as usual, from his hiding-place in the glen, to see if there were any work for him to do, and to look for his bowl of milk. And he had seen, from the open door and lit-up windows, that there was something wrong inside the farmhouse, which at that hour was wont to be dark, and still, and silent; and he had crept into the entry to try and find out what the matter was.

When he gathered from the servants' talk that the Mistress, whom he loved so dearly, and who had been so kind to him, was ill, his heart sank within him; and when he heard that the silly servants were so taken up with their own fears that they dared not set out to fetch a nurse for her, his contempt and anger knew no bounds.

"Fools, idiots, dolts!" he muttered to himself, stamping his queer, misshapen feet on the floor. "They speak as if a body were ready to take a bite off them as soon as ever he met them. If they only knew the bother it gives me to keep out of their road they wouldna be so silly. But, by my troth, if they go on like this, the bonnie lady will die amongst their fingers. So it strikes me that Brownie must e'en gang himself."

So saying, he reached up his hand, and took down a dark cloak which belonged to the farmer, which was hanging on a peg on the wall, and, throwing it over his head and shoulders, or as somewhat to hide his ungainly form, he hurried away to the stable, and saddled and bridled the fleetest-footed horse that stood there.

When the last buckle was fastened, he led it to the door and scrambled on its back. "Now, if ever thou travelledst fleetly, travel fleetly now," he said; and it was as if the creature understood him, for it gave a little whinny and pricked up its ears; then it darted out into the darkness like an arrow from the bow.

In less time than the distance had ever been ridden in before, the Brownie drew rein at the old woman's cottage.

She was in bed, fast asleep; but he rapped sharply on the window, and when she rose and put her old face, framed in its white mutch, close to the pane to ask who was there, he bent forward and told her his errand.

"Thou must come with me, Goodwife, and that quickly," he commanded, in his deep, harsh voice, "if the Lady of Ferne-Den's life is to be saved; for there is no one to nurse her up-bye at the farm there, save a lot of empty-headed servant wenches."

"But how am I to get there? Have they sent a cart for me?" asked the old woman anxiously; for, as far as she could see, there was nothing at the door save a horse and its rider.

"No, they have sent no cart," replied the Brownie, shortly. "So you must just climb up behind me on the saddle, and hang on tight to my waist, and I'll promise to land ye at Ferne-Den safe and sound."

His voice was so masterful that the old woman dare not refuse to do as she was bid; besides, she had often ridden pillion-wise when she was a lassie, so she made haste to dress herself, and when she was ready she unlocked her door, and, mounting the louping-on stane that stood beside it, she was soon seated behind the dark-cloaked stranger, with her arms clasped tightly round him.

Not a word was spoken till they approached the dreaded glen, then the old woman felt her courage giving way. "Do ye think that there will be any chance of meeting the Brownie?" she asked timidly. "I would fain not run the risk, for folk say that he is an unchancy creature."

Her companion gave a curious laugh. "Keep up your heart, and dinna talk havers," he said, "for I promise ye ye'll see naught uglier this night than the man whom ye ride behind."

"Oh, then, I'm fine and safe," replied the old woman, with a sigh of relief; "for although I havena' seen your face, I warrant that ye are a true man, for the care you have taken of a poor old woman."

She relapsed into silence again till the glen was passed and the good horse had turned into the farmyard. Then the horseman slid to the ground, and, turning round, lifted her carefully down in his long, strong arms. As he did so the cloak slipped off him, revealing his short, broad body and his misshapen limbs.

"In a' the world, what kind o' man are ye?" she asked, peering into his face in the grey morning light, which was just dawning. "What makes your eyes so big? And what have ye done to your feet? They are more like paddock's webs than aught else."

The queer little man laughed again. "I've wandered many a mile in my time without a horse to help me, and I've heard it said that ower much walking makes the feet unshapely," he replied. "But waste no time in talking, good Dame. Go thy way into the house; and hark'ee, if anyone asks thee who brought thee hither so quickly, tell them that there was a lack of men, so thou hadst e'en to be content to ride behind the Brownie o' Ferne-Den."

The Fairies of Merlin's Crag

ABOUT TWO HUNDRED YEARS AGO there was a poor man working as a labourer on a farm in Lanarkshire. He was what is known as an "Orra Man"; that is, he had no special work mapped out for him to do, but he was expected to undertake odd jobs of any kind that happened to turn up.

One day his master sent him out to cast peats on a piece of moorland that lay on a certain part of the farm. Now this strip of moorland ran up at one end to a curiously shaped crag, known as Merlin's Crag, because, so the country folk said, that famous Enchanter had once taken up his abode there.

The man obeyed, and, being a willing fellow, when he arrived at the moor he set to work with all his might and main. He had lifted quite a quantity of peat from near the Crag, when he was startled by the appearance of the very smallest woman that he had ever seen in his life. She was only about two feet high, and she was dressed in a green gown and red stockings, and her long yellow hair was not bound by any ribbon, but hung loosely round her shoulders.

She was such a dainty little creature that the astonished countryman stopped working, stuck his spade into the ground, and gazed at her in wonder.

His wonder increased when she held up one of her tiny fingers and addressed him in these words: "What wouldst thou think if I were to send my husband to uncover thy house? You mortals think that you can do aught that pleaseth you."

Then, stamping her tiny foot, she added in a voice of command, "Put back that turf instantly, or thou shalt rue this day."

Now the poor man had often heard of the Fairy Folk and of the harm that they could work to unthinking mortals who offended them, so in fear and trembling he set to work to undo all his labour, and to place every divot in the exact spot from which he had taken it.

When he was finished he looked round for his strange visitor, but she had vanished completely; he could not tell how, nor where. Putting up his spade, he wended his way homewards, and going straight to his master, he told him the whole story, and suggested that in future the peats should be taken from the other end of the moor.

But the master only laughed. He was a strong, hearty man, and had no belief in Ghosts, or Elves, or Fairies, or any other creature that he could not see; but although he laughed, he was vexed that his servant should believe in such things, so to cure him, as he thought, of his superstition, he ordered him to take a horse and cart and go back at once, and lift all the peats and bring them to dry in the farm steading.

The poor man obeyed with much reluctance; and was greatly relieved, as weeks went on, to find that, in spite of his having done so, no harm befell him.

In fact, he began to think that his master was right, and that the whole thing must have been a dream.

So matters went smoothly on. Winter passed, and spring, and summer, until autumn came round once more, and the very day arrived on which the peats had been lifted the year before.

That day, as the sun went down, the orra man left the farm to go home to his cottage, and as his master was pleased with him because he had been working very hard lately, he had given him a little can of milk as a present to carry home to his wife.

So he was feeling very happy, and as he walked along he was humming a tune to himself. His road took him by the foot of Merlin's Crag, and as he approached it he was astonished to find himself growing strangely tired. His eyelids dropped over his eyes as if he were going to sleep, and his feet grew as heavy as lead.

"I will sit down and take a rest for a few minutes," he said to himself; "the road home never seemed so long as it does today."

So he sat down on a tuft of grass right under the shadow of the Crag, and before he knew where he was he had fallen into a deep and heavy slumber.

When he awoke it was near midnight, and the moon had risen on the Crag. And he rubbed his eyes, when by its soft light he became aware of a large band of Fairies who were dancing round and round him, singing and laughing, pointing their tiny fingers at him, and shaking their wee fists in his face.

The bewildered man rose and tried to walk away from them, but turn in whichever direction he would, the Fairies accompanied him, encircling him in a magic ring, out of which he could in no wise go.

At last they stopped, and, with shrieks of elfin laughter, led the prettiest and daintiest of their companions up to him, and cried, "Tread a measure, tread a measure, Oh, Man! Then wilt thou not be so eager to escape from our company."

Now the poor labourer was but a clumsy dancer, and he held back with a shamefaced air; but the Fairy who had been chosen to be his partner reached up and seized his hands, and lo! some strange magic seemed to enter into his veins, for in a moment he found himself waltzing and whirling, sliding and bowing, as if he had done nothing else but dance all his life.

And, strangest thing of all! he forgot about his home and his children; and he felt so happy that he had no longer the slightest desire to leave the Fairies' company.

All night long the merriment went on. The Little Folk danced and danced as if they were mad, and the farm man danced with them, until at last a shrill sound came over the moor. It was the cock from the farmyard crowing its loudest to welcome the dawn.

In an instant the revelry ceased, and the Fairies, with cries of alarm, crowded together and rushed towards the Crag, dragging the countryman along in their midst. As they reached the rock, a mysterious door, which he never remembered having seen before, opened in it of its own accord, and shut again with a crash as soon as the Fairy Host had all trooped through.

The door led into a large, dimly lighted hall full of tiny couches, and here the Little Folk sank to rest, tired out with their exertions, while the good man sat down on a piece of rock in the corner, wondering what would happen next.

But there seemed to be some kind of spell thrown over his senses, for even when the Fairies awoke and began to go about their household occupations, and to carry out certain curious practices which he had never seen before, and which, as you will hear, he was forbidden to speak of afterwards, he was content to sit and watch them, without in any way attempting to escape.

As it drew toward evening someone touched his elbow, and he turned round with a start to see the little woman with the green dress and scarlet stockings, who had remonstrated with him for lifting the turf the year before, standing by his side.

"The divots which thou took'st from the roof of my house have grown once more," she said, "and once more it is covered with grass; so thou canst go home again, for justice is satisfied – thy punishment hath lasted long enough. But first must thou take thy solemn oath never to tell to mortal ears what thou hast seen whilst thou hast dwelt among us."

The countryman promised gladly, and took the oath with all due solemnity. Then the door was opened, and he was at liberty to depart.

His can of milk was standing on the green, just where he had laid it down when he went to sleep; and it seemed to him as if it were only yesternight that the farmer had given it to him.

But when he reached his home he was speedily undeceived. For his wife looked at him as if he were a ghost, and the children whom he had left wee, toddling things were now well-grown boys and girls, who stared at him as if he had been an utter stranger.

"Where hast thou been these long, long years?" cried his wife when she had gathered her wits and seen that it was really he, and not a spirit. "And how couldst thou find it in thy heart to leave the bairns and me alone?"

And then he knew that the one day he had passed in Fairyland had lasted seven whole years, and he realised how heavy the punishment had been which the Wee Folk had laid upon him.

Fairy Friends

IT IS A GOOD THING to befriend the fairies, as the following stories show:

There have been from time immemorial at Hawick, during the two or three last weeks of the year, markets once a week, for the disposal of sheep for slaughter, at which the greater number of people, both in the middle and poorer classes of life, have been accustomed to provide themselves with their *marts*. A poor man from Jedburgh who was on his way to Hawick for the purpose of attending one of these markets, as he was passing over that side of Rubislaw which is nearest the Teviot, was suddenly alarmed by a frightful and unaccountable noise. The sound, as he supposed, proceeded from an immense number of female voices, but no objects whence it could come were visible. Amidst howling and wailing were mixed shouts of mirth and jollity, but he could gather nothing articulate except the following words:

"O there's a bairn born, but there's naething to pit on 't."

The occasion of this elfish concert, it seemed, was the birth of a fairy child, at which the fairies, with the exception of two or three who were discomposed at having nothing to cover the little innocent with, were enjoying themselves with that joviality usually characteristic of such an event. The astonished rustic finding himself amongst a host of invisible beings, in a wild moorland place, and far from any human assistance, should assistance be required, full of the greatest consternation, immediately on hearing this expression again and again vociferated, stripped off his plaid, and threw it on the ground. It was instantly snatched up by an invisible hand, and the wailings immediately ceased, but the shouts of mirth were continued with increased vigour. Being of opinion that what he had done had satisfied his invisible friends, he lost no time in making off, and proceeded on his road to Hawick, musing on his singular adventure. He purchased a sheep, which turned out a remarkably good bargain, and returned to Jedburgh. He had no cause to regret his generosity in bestowing his plaid on the fairies, for every day afterwards his wealth multiplied, and he continued till the day of his death a rich and prosperous man.

* * *

About the beginning of harvest, there having been a want of meal for *shearers'* bread in the farmhouse of Bedrule, a small quantity of barley (being all that was yet ripe) was cut down and converted into meal. Mrs. Buckham, the farmer's wife, rose early in the morning to bake the bread, and, while she was engaged in baking, a little woman in green costume came in, and, with much politeness, asked for a loan of a capful of meal. Mrs. Buckham thought it prudent to comply with her request. In a short time afterwards the woman in green returned with an equal quantity of meal, which Mrs. Buckham put into the *meal-ark*. This meal had such a lasting quality, that from it alone the gudewife of Bedrule baked as much bread as served her own family and the reapers throughout the harvest, and when harvest was over it was not exhausted.

Rory MacGillivray

ONCE UPON A TIME a tenant in the neighbourhood of Cairngorm, in Strathspey, emigrated with his family and cattle to the forest of Glenavon, which is well known to be inhabited by many fairies as well as ghosts. Two of his sons being out late one night in search of some of their sheep which had strayed, had occasion to pass a fairy turret, or dwelling, of very large dimensions; and what was their astonishment on observing streams of the most refulgent light shining forth through innumerable crevices in the rock – crevices which the sharpest eye in the country had never seen before. Curiosity led them towards the turret, when they were charmed by the most exquisite sounds ever emitted by a fiddle-string, which, joined to the sportive mirth and glee accompanying it, reconciled them in a great measure to the scene, although they knew well enough the inhabitants of the nook were fairies.

Nay, overpowered by the enchanting jigs played by the fiddler, one of the brothers had even the hardihood to propose that they should pay the occupants of the turret a short visit. To this motion the other brother, fond as he was of dancing, and animated as he was by the music, would by no means consent, and he earnestly desired his brother to restrain his curiosity. But every new jig that was played, and every new reel that was danced, inspired the adventurous brother with additional ardour, and at length, completely fascinated by the enchanting revelry, leaving all prudence behind, at one leap he entered the "Shian". The poor forlorn brother was now left in a most uncomfortable situation. His grief for the loss of a brother whom he dearly loved suggested to him more than once the desperate idea of sharing his fate by following his example. But, on the other hand, when he coolly considered the possibility of sharing very different entertainment from that which rang upon his ears, and remembered, too, the comforts and convenience of his father's fireside, the idea immediately appeared to him anything but prudent.

After a long and disagreeable altercation between his affection for his brother and his regard for himself, he came to the resolution to take a middle course, that is, to shout in at the window a few remonstrances to his brother, which, if he did not attend to, let the consequences be upon his own head. Accordingly, taking his station at one of the crevices, and calling upon his brother three several times by name, as use is, he uttered the most moving pieces of elocution he could think of, imploring him, as he valued his poor parents' life and blessing, to come forth and go home with him, Donald MacGillivray, his thrice affectionate and unhappy brother. But whether it was the dancer could not hear this eloquent harangue, or, what is more probable, that he did not choose to attend to it, certain it is that it proved totally ineffectual to accomplish its object, and the consequence was that Donald MacGillivray found it equally his duty and his interest to return home to his family with the melancholy tale of poor Rory's fate. All the prescribed ceremonies calculated to rescue him from the fairy dominion were resorted to by his mourning relatives without effect, and Rory was supposed lost for ever, when a "wise man" of the day, having learned the circumstance, discovered to his friends a plan by which they might deliver him at the end of twelve months from his entry.

"Return," says the *Duin Glichd* to Donald, "to the place where you lost your brother a year and a day from the time. You will insert in your garment a *Rowan Cross*, which will protect you from the fairies' interposition. Enter the turret boldly and resolutely in the name of the Highest, claim your brother, and, if he does not accompany you voluntarily, seize him and carry him off by force – none dare interfere with you."

The experiment appeared to the cautious contemplative brother as one that was fraught with no ordinary danger, and he would have most willingly declined the prominent character allotted to him in the performance but for the importunate entreaty of his friends, who implored him, as he valued their blessing, not to slight such excellent advice. Their entreaties, together with his confidence in the virtues of the *Rowan Cross*, overcame his scruples, and he at length agreed to put the experiment in practice, whatever the result might be.

Well, then, the important day arrived, when the father of the two sons was destined either to recover his lost son, or to lose the only son he had, and, anxious as the father felt, Donald MacGillivray, the intended adventurer, felt no less so on the occasion. The hour of midnight approached when the drama was to be acted, and Donald MacGillivray, loaded with all the charms and benedictions in his country, took mournful leave of his friends, and proceeded to the scene of his intended enterprise. On approaching the well-known turret, a repetition of that mirth and those ravishing sounds, that had been the source of so much sorrow to himself and family, once more attracted his attention, without at all creating in his mind any extraordinary feelings of satisfaction. On the contrary, he abhorred the sounds most heartily, and felt much greater inclination to recede than to advance. But what was to be done? Courage, character, and everything dear to him were at stake, so that to advance was his only alternative. In short, he reached the "Shian," and, after twenty fruitless attempts, he at length entered the place with trembling footsteps, and amidst the brilliant and jovial scene the not least gratifying spectacle which presented itself to Donald was his brother Rory earnestly engaged at the Highland fling on the floor, at which, as might have been expected, he had greatly improved. Without losing much time in satisfying his curiosity by examining the quality of the company, Donald ran to his brother, repeating, most vehemently, the words prescribed to him by the "wise man," seized him by the collar, and insisted on his immediately accompanying him home to his poor afflicted parents. Rory assented, provided he would allow him to finish his single reel, assuring Donald, very earnestly, that he had not been half an hour in the house. In vain did the latter assure him that, instead of half an hour, he had actually remained twelve months. Nor would he have believed his overjoyed friends when his brother at length got him home, did not the calves, now grown into stots, and the new-born babes, now travelling the house, at length convince him that in his single reel he had danced for a twelvemonth and a day.

Horse and Hattock

THE POWER OF THE FAIRIES was not confined to unchristened children alone; it was supposed frequently to be extended to full-grown people, especially such as in an unlucky hour were devoted to the devil by the execrations of parents and of masters; or those who were found asleep under a rock, or on a green hill, belonging to the fairies, after sunset, or, finally, to those who unwarily joined their orgies.

A tradition existed, during the seventeenth century, concerning an ancestor of the noble family of Duffers, who, "walking abroad in the fields near to his own house, was suddenly carried away, and found the next day at Paris, in the French king's cellar, with a silver cup in his hand. Being brought into the king's presence, and questioned by him who he was, and how he came thither, he told his name, his country, and the place of his residence, and that on such a day of the month, which proved to be the day immediately preceding, being in the fields, he heard a noise of a whirlwind, and of voices crying 'Horse and hattock!' (this is the word which the fairies are said to use when they remove from any place), whereupon he cried 'Horse and hattock!' also, and was immediately caught up and transported through the air by the fairies to that place, where, after he had drunk heartily, he fell asleep, and before he woke the rest of the company were gone, and had left him in the posture wherein he was found. It is said the king gave him a cup which was found in his hand, and dismissed him."

The narrator affirms "that the cup was still preserved, and known by the name of the fairy cup." He adds that Mr. Steward, tutor to the then Lord Duffers, had informed him that, "when a boy at the school of Forres, he and his school-fellows were once upon a time whipping their tops in the churchyard, before the door of the church, when, though the day was calm, they heard a noise of a wind, and at some distance saw the small dust begin to rise and turn round, which motion continued advancing till it came to the place where they were, whereupon they began to bless themselves; but one of their number being, it seems, a little more bold and confident than his companion, said, 'Horse and hattock with my top!' and immediately they all saw the top lifted up from the ground, but could not see which way it was carried, by reason of a cloud of dust which was raised at the same time. They sought for the top all about the place where it was taken up, but in vain; and it was found afterwards in the churchyard, on the other side of the church."

Whippety-Stourie

I AM GOING TO TELL YOU A STORY about a poor young widow woman, who lived in a house called Kittlerumpit, though whereabouts in Scotland the house of Kittlerumpit stood nobody knows.

Some folk think that it stood in the neighbourhood of the Debateable Land, which, as all the world knows, was on the Borders, where the old Border Reivers were constantly coming and going; the Scotch stealing from the English, and the English from the Scotch. Be that as it may, the widowed Mistress of Kittlerumpit was sorely to be pitied.

For she had lost her husband, and no one quite knew what had become of him. He had gone to a fair one day, and had never come back again, and although everybody believed that he was dead, no one knew how he died.

Some people said that he had been persuaded to enlist, and had been killed in the wars; others, that he had been taken away to serve as a sailor by the press-gang, and had been drowned at sea.

At any rate, his poor young wife was sorely to be pitied, for she was left with a little baby boy to bring up, and, as times were bad, she had not much to live on.

But she loved her baby dearly, and worked all day amongst her cows, and pigs, and hens, in order to earn enough money to buy food and clothes for both herself and him.

Now, on the morning of which I am speaking, she rose very early and went out to feed her pigs, for rent-day was coming on, and she intended to take one of them, a great, big, fat creature, to the market that very day, as she thought that the price that it would fetch would go a long way towards paying her rent.

And because she thought so, her heart was light, and she hummed a little song to herself as she crossed the yard with her bucket on one arm and her baby boy on the other.

But the song was quickly changed into a cry of despair when she reached the pig-stye, for there lay her cherished pig on its back, with its legs in the air and its eyes shut, just as if it were going to breathe its last breath.

"What shall I do? What shall I do?" cried the poor woman, sitting down on a big stone and clasping her boy to her breast, heedless of the fact that she had dropped her bucket, and that the pig's-meat was running out, and that the hens were eating it.

"First I lost my husband, and now I am going to lose my finest pig. The pig that I hoped would fetch a deal of money."

Now I must explain to you that the house of Kittlerumpit stood on a hillside, with a great fir wood behind it, and the ground sloping down steeply in front.

And as the poor young thing, after having a good cry to herself, was drying her eyes, she chanced to look down the hill, and who should she see coming up it but an Old Woman, who looked like a lady born.

She was dressed all in green, with a white apron, and she wore a black velvet hood on her head, and a steeple-crowned beaver hat over that, something like those, as I have heard tell, that the women wear in Wales. She walked very slowly, leaning on a long staff, and she gave a bit hirple now and then, as if she were lame.

As she drew near, the young widow felt it was becoming to rise and curtsey to the Gentlewoman, for such she saw her to be.

"Madam," she said, with a sob in her voice, "I bid you welcome to the house of Kittlerumpit, although you find its Mistress one of the most unfortunate women in the world."

"Hout-tout," answered the old Lady, in such a harsh voice that the young woman started and grasped her baby tighter in her arms. "Ye have little need to say that. Ye have lost your husband, I grant ye, but there were waur losses at Shirra-Muir. And now your pig is like to die – I could, maybe, remedy that. But I must first hear how much ye wad gie me if I cured him."

"Anything that your Ladyship's Madam likes to ask," replied the widow, too much delighted at having the animal's life saved to think that she was making rather a rash promise.

"Very good," said the old Dame, and without wasting any more words she walked straight into the pig-stye.

She stood and looked at the dying creature for some minutes, rocking to and fro and muttering to herself in words which the widow could not understand; at least, she could only understand four of them, and they sounded something like this:

> "Pitter-patter,
> Haly water."

Then she put her hand into her pocket and drew out a tiny bottle with a liquid that looked like oil in it. She took the cork out, and dropped one of her long lady-like fingers into it; then she touched the pig on the snout and on his ears, and on the tip of his curly tail.

No sooner had she done so than up the beast jumped, and, with a grunt of contentment, ran off to its trough to look for its breakfast.

A joyful woman was the Mistress of Kittlerumpit when she saw it do this, for she felt that her rent was safe; and in her relief and gratitude she would have kissed the hem of the strange Lady's green gown, if she would have allowed it, but she would not.

"No, no," said she, and her voice sounded harsher than ever. "Let us have no fine meanderings, but let us stick to our bargain. I have done my part, and mended the pig; now ye must do yours, and give me what I like to ask – your son."

Then the poor widow gave a piteous cry, for she knew now what she had not guessed before – that the Green-clad Lady was a Fairy, and a Wicked Fairy too, else had she not asked such a terrible thing.

It was too late now, however, to pray, and beseech, and beg for mercy; the Fairy stood her ground, hard and cruel.

"Ye promised me what I liked to ask, and I have asked your son; and your son I will have," she replied, "so it is useless making such a din about it. But one thing I may tell you, for I know well that the knowledge will not help you. By the laws of Fairyland, I cannot take the bairn till the third day after this, and if by that time you have found out my name I cannot take him even then. But ye will not be able to find it out, of that I am certain. So I will call back for the boy in three days."

And with that she disappeared round the back of the pig-stye, and the poor mother fell down in a dead faint beside the stone.

All that day, and all the next, she did nothing but sit in her kitchen and cry, and hug her baby tighter in her arms; but on the day before that on which the Fairy said that she was coming back, she felt as if she must get a little breath of fresh air, so she went for a walk in the fir wood behind the house.

Now, in this fir wood there was an old quarry hole, in the bottom of which was a bonnie spring well, the water of which was always sweet and pure. The young widow was walking near this quarry hole, when, to her astonishment, she heard the whirr of a spinning-wheel and the sound of a voice lilting a song. At first she could not think where the sound came from; then, remembering the quarry, she laid down her child at a tree root, and crept noiselessly through the bushes on her hands and knees to the edge of the hole and peeped over.

She could hardly believe her eyes! For there, far below her, at the bottom of the quarry, beside the spring well, sat the cruel Fairy, dressed in her green frock and tall felt hat, spinning away as fast as she could at a tiny spinning-wheel.

And what should she be singing but –

> *"Little kens our guid dame at hame,*
> *Whippety-Stourie is my name."*

The widow woman almost cried aloud for joy, for now she had learned the Fairy's secret, and her child was safe. But she dare not, in case the wicked old Dame heard her and threw some other spell over her.

So she crept softly back to the place where she had left her child; then, catching him up in her arms, she ran through the wood to her house, laughing, and singing, and tossing him in the air in such a state of delight that, if anyone had met her, they would have been in danger of thinking that she was mad.

Now this young woman had been a merry-hearted maiden, and would have been merry-hearted still, if, since her marriage, she had not had so much trouble that it had made her grow old and sober-minded before her time; and she began to think what fun it would be to tease the Fairy for a few minutes before she let her know that she had found out her name.

So next day, at the appointed time, she went out with her boy in her arms, and seated herself on the big stone where she had sat before; and when she saw the old Dame coming up the hill, she crumpled up her nice clean cap, and screwed up her face, and pretended to be in great distress and to be crying bitterly.

The Fairy took no notice of this, however, but came close up to her, and said, in her harsh, merciless voice, "Good wife of Kittlerumpit, ye ken the reason of my coming; give me the bairn."

Then the young mother pretended to be in sorer distress than ever, and fell on her knees before the wicked old woman and begged for mercy.

"Oh, sweet Madam Mistress," she cried, "spare me my bairn, and take, an' thou wilt, the pig instead."

"We have no need of bacon where I come from," answered the Fairy coldly; "so give me the laddie and let me begone – I have no time to waste in this wise."

"Oh, dear Lady mine," pleaded the Goodwife, "if thou wilt not have the pig, wilt thou not spare my poor bairn and take me myself?"

The Fairy stepped back a little, as if in astonishment. "Art thou mad, woman," she cried contemptuously, "that thou proposest such a thing? Who in all the world would care to take a plain-looking, red-eyed, dowdy wife like thee with them?"

Now the young Mistress of Kittlerumpit knew that she was no beauty, and the knowledge had never vexed her; but something in the Fairy's tone made her feel so angry that she could contain herself no longer.

"In troth, fair Madam, I might have had the wit to know that the like of me is not fit to tie the shoe-string of the High and Mighty Princess, WHIPPETY-STOURIE!"

If there had been a charge of gunpowder buried in the ground, and if it had suddenly exploded beneath her feet, the Wicked Fairy could not have jumped higher into the air.

And when she came down again she simply turned round and ran down the brae, shrieking with rage and disappointment, for all the world, as an old book says, "like an owl chased by witches."

The Black Bull of Norroway

IN BYGONE DAYS, long centuries ago, there lived a widowed Queen who had three daughters. And this widowed Queen was so poor, and had fallen upon such evil days, that she and her daughters had often much ado to get enough to eat.

So the eldest Princess determined that she would set out into the world to seek her fortune. And her mother was quite willing that she should do so. "For," said she, "'tis better to work abroad than to starve at home."

But as there was an old hen-wife living near the Castle who was said to be a witch, and to be able to foretell the future, the Queen sent the Princess to her cottage, before she set out on her travels, to ask her in which of the Four Airts she ought to go, in order to find the best fortune.

"Thou needst gang nae farther than my back door, hinnie," answered the old Dame, who had always felt very sorry for the Queen and her pretty daughters, and was glad to do them a good turn.

So the Princess ran through the passage to the hen-wife's back door and peeped out, and what should she see but a magnificent coach, drawn by six beautiful cream-coloured horses, coming along the road.

Greatly excited at this unusual sight, she hurried back to the kitchen, and told the hen-wife what she had seen.

"Aweel, aweel, ye've seen your fortune," said the old woman, in a tone of satisfaction, "for that coach-and-six is coming for thee."

Sure enough, the coach-and-six stopped at the gate of the Castle, and the second Princess came running down to the cottage to tell her sister to make haste, because it was waiting for her. Delighted beyond measure at the wonderful luck that had come to her, she hurried home, and, saying farewell to her mother and sisters, took her seat within, and the horses galloped off immediately.

And I've heard tell that they drew her to the Palace of a great and wealthy Prince, who married her; but that is outside my story.

A few weeks afterwards, the second Princess thought that she would do as her sister had done, and go down to the hen-wife's cottage, and tell her that she, too, was going out into the world to seek her fortune. And, of course, in her heart of hearts she hoped that what had happened to her sister would happen to her also.

And, curious to say, it did. For the old hen-wife sent her to look out at her back door, and she went, and, lo and behold! another coach-and-six was coming along the road. And when she went and told the old woman, she smiled upon her kindly, and told her to hurry home, for the coach-and-six was her fortune also, and that it had come for her.

So she, too, ran home, and got into her grand carriage, and was driven away. And, of course, after all these lucky happenings, the youngest Princess was anxious to try what her fortune might be; so the very night, in high good humour, she tripped away down to the old witch's cottage.

She, too, was told to look out at the back door, and she was only too glad to do so; for she fully expected to see a third coach-and-six coming rolling along the high road, straight for the Castle door.

But, alas and alack! no such sight greeted her eager eyes, for the high road was quite deserted, and in great disappointment she ran back to the hen-wife to tell her so.

"Then it is clear that thy fortune is not coming to meet thee this day," said the old Dame, "so thou must e'en come back tomorrow."

So the little Princess went home again, and next day she turned up once more at the old wife's cottage.

But once more she was disappointed, for although she looked out long and eagerly, no glad sight of a coach-and-six, or of any other coach, greeted her eyes. On the third day, however, what should she see but a great Black Bull coming rushing along the road, bellowing as it came, and tossing its head fiercely in the air.

In great alarm, the little Princess shut the door, and ran to the hen-wife to tell her about the furious animal that was approaching.

"Hech, hinnie," cried the old woman, holding up her hands in dismay, "and who would have thocht that the Black Bull of Norroway wad be your fate!"

At the words, the poor little maiden grew pale. She had come out to seek her fortune, but it had never dawned upon her that her fortune could be anything so terrible as this.

"But the Bull cannot be my fortune," she cried in terror. "I cannot go away with a bull."

"But ye'll need tae," replied the hen-wife calmly. "For you lookit out of my door with the intent of meeting your fortune; and when your fortune has come tae ye, you must just thole it."

And when the poor Princess ran weeping to her mother, to beg to be allowed to stay at home, she found her mother of the same mind as the Wise Woman; and so she had to allow herself to be lifted up on to the back of the enormous Black Bull that had come up to the door of the Castle, and was now standing there quietly enough. And when she was settled, he set off again on his wild career, while she sobbed and trembled with terror, and clung to his horns with all her might.

On and on they went, until at last the poor maiden was so faint with fear and hunger that she could scarce keep her seat.

Just as she was losing her hold of the great beast's horns, however, and feeling that she must fall to the ground, he turned his massive head round a little, and, speaking in a wonderfully soft and gentle voice, said, "Eat out of my right ear, and drink out of my left ear, so wilt thou be refreshed for thy journey."

So the Princess put a trembling hand into the Bull's right ear, and drew out some bread and meat, which, in spite of her terror, she was glad to swallow; then she put her hand into his left ear, and found there a tiny flagon of wine, and when she had drunk that, her strength returned to her in a wonderful way.

Long they went, and sore they rode, till, just as it seemed to the Princess that they must be getting near the World's End, they came in sight of a magnificent Castle.

"That's where we maun bide this night," said the Black Bull of Norroway, "for that is the house of one of my brothers."

The Princess was greatly surprised at these words; but by this time she was too tired to wonder very much at anything, so she did not answer, but sat still where she was, until the Bull ran into the courtyard of the Castle and knocked his great head against the door.

The door was opened at once by a very splendid footman, who treated the Black Bull with great respect, and helped the Princess to alight from his back. Then he ushered her into a magnificent hall, where the Lord of the Castle, and his Lady, and a great and noble company were assembled; while the Black Bull trotted off quite contentedly to the grassy park which stretched all round the building, to spend the night there.

The Lord and his Lady were very kind to the Princess, and gave her her supper, and led her to a richly furnished bedroom, all hung round with golden mirrors, and left her to rest there; and in the morning, just as the Black Bull came trotting up to the front door, they handed her a beautiful apple, telling her not to break it, but to put it in her pocket, and keep it till she was in the greatest strait that mortal could be in. Then she was to break it, and it would bring her out of it.

So she put the apple in her pocket, and they lifted her once more on to the Black Bull's back, and she and her strange companion continued on their journey.

All that day they travelled, far further than I can tell you, and at night they came in sight of another Castle, which was even bigger and grander than the first.

"That's where we maun bide this night," said the Black Bull, "for that is the home of another of my brothers."

And here the Princess rested for the night in a very fine bedroom indeed, all hung with silken curtains; and the Lord and Lady of the Castle did everything to please her and make her comfortable.

And in the morning, before she left, they presented her with the largest pear that she had ever seen, and warned her that she must not break it until she was in the direst strait that she had ever been in, and then, if she broke it, it would bring her out of it.

The third day was the same as the other two had been. The Princess and the Black Bull of Norroway rode many a weary mile, and at sundown they came to another Castle, more splendid by far than the other two.

This Castle belonged to the Black Bull's youngest brother, and here the Princess abode all night; while the Bull, as usual, lay outside in the park. And this time, when they departed, the Princess received a most lovely plum, with the warning not to break it till she was in the greatest strait that mortal could be in. Then she was to break it, and it would set her free.

On the fourth day, however, things were changed. For there was no fine Castle waiting for them at the end of their journey; on the contrary, as the shadows began to lengthen, they came to a dark, deep glen, which was so gloomy and so awesome looking that the poor Princess felt her courage sinking as they approached it.

At the entrance the Black Bull stopped. "Light down here, Lady," he said, "for in this glen a deadly conflict awaits me, which I must face unaided and alone. For the dark and gloomy region that lies before us is the abode of a great Spirit of Darkness, who worketh much ill in the world. I would fain fight with him and overcome him; and, by my troth, I have good hope that I shall do so. As for thee, thou must seat thyself on this stone, and stir neither hand, nor foot, nor tongue till I return. For, if thou but so much as move, then the Evil Spirit of the Glen will have thee in his power."

"But how shall I know what is happening to thee?" asked the Princess anxiously, for she was beginning to grow quite fond of the huge black creature that had carried her so gallantly these last four days, "if I have neither to move hand nor foot, nor yet to speak."

"Thou wilt know by the signs around thee," answered the Bull. "For if everything about thee turn blue, then thou wilt know that I have vanquished the Evil Spirit; but if everything about thee turn red, then the Evil Spirit hath vanquished me."

With these words he departed, and was soon lost to sight in the dark recesses of the glen, leaving the little Princess sitting motionless on her stone, afraid to move so much as her little finger, in case some unknown evil fell upon her.

At last, when she had sat there for well-nigh an hour, a curious change began to pass over the landscape. First it turned grey, and then it turned a deep azure blue, as if the sky had descended on the earth.

"The Bull hath conquered," thought the Princess. "Oh! what a noble animal he is!" And in her relief and delight she moved her position and crossed one leg over the other.

Oh, woe-a-day! In a moment a mystic spell fell upon her, which caused her to become invisible to the eyes of the Prince of Norroway, who, having vanquished the Evil Spirit, was loosed from the spell which had lain over him, and had transformed him into the likeness of a great Black Bull, and who returned in haste down the glen to present himself, in his rightful form, to the maiden whom he loved, and whom he hoped to win for his bride.

Long, long he sought, but he could not find her, while all the time she was sitting patiently waiting on the stone; but the spell was on her eyes also, and hindered her seeing him, as it hindered him seeing her.

So she sat on and on, till at last she became so wearied, and lonely, and frightened, that she burst out crying, and cried herself to sleep; and when she woke in the morning she felt that it was no use sitting there any longer, so she rose and took her way, hardly knowing whither she was going.

And she went, and she went, till at last she came to a great hill made all of glass, which blocked her way and prevented her going any further. She tried time after time to climb it, but it was all of no avail, for the surface of the hill was so slippery that she only managed to climb up a few feet, to slide down again the next moment.

So she began to walk round the bottom of the hill, in the hope of finding some path that would lead her over it, but the hill was so big, and she was so tired, that it seemed almost a hopeless quest, and her spirit died completely within her. And as she went slowly along, sobbing with despair, she felt that if help did not come soon she must lie down and die.

About mid-day, however, she came to a little cottage, and beside the cottage there was a smithy, where an old smith was working at his anvil.

She entered, and asked him if he could tell her of any path that would lead her over the mountain. The old man laid down his hammer and looked at her, slowly shaking his head as he did so.

"Na, na, lassie," he said, "there is no easy road over the Mountain of Glass. Folk maun either walk round it, which is not an easy thing to do, for the foot of it stretches out for hundreds of miles, and the folk who try to do so are almost sure to lose their way; or they maun walk over the top of it, and that can only be done by those who are shod with iron shoon."

"And how am I to get these iron shoon?" cried the Princess eagerly. "Couldst thou fashion me a pair, good man? I would gladly pay thee for them." Then she stopped suddenly, for she remembered that she had no money.

"These shoon cannot be made for siller," said the old man solemnly. "They can only be earned by service. I alone can make them, and I make them for those who are willing to serve me."

"And how long must I serve thee ere thou makest them for me?" asked the Princess faintly.

"Seven years," replied the old man, "for they be magic shoon, and that is the magic number."

So, as there seemed nothing else for it, the Princess hired herself to the smith for seven long years: to clean his house, and cook his food, and make and mend his clothes.

At the end of that time he fashioned her a pair of iron shoon, with which she climbed the Mountain of Glass with as much ease as if it had been covered with fresh green turf.

When she had reached the summit, and descended to the other side, the first house that she came to was the house of an old washerwoman, who lived there with her only daughter. And as the Princess was now very tired, she went up to the door, and knocked, and asked if she might be allowed to rest there for the night.

The washerwoman, who was old and ugly, with a sly and evil face, said that she might – on one condition – and that was that she should try to wash a white mantle that the Black Knight of Norroway had brought to her to wash, as he had got it stained in a deadly fight.

"Yestreen I spent the lee-long day washing it," went on the old Dame, "and I might as well have let it lie on the table. For at night, when I took it out of the wash-tub, the stains were there as dark as ever. Peradventure, maiden, if thou wouldst try thy hand upon it thou mightest be more successful. For I am loth to disappoint the Black Knight of Norroway, who is an exceeding great and powerful Prince."

"Is he in any way connected with the Black Bull of Norroway?" asked the Princess; for at the name her heart had leaped for joy, for it seemed that mayhap she was going to find once more him whom she had lost.

The old woman looked at her suspiciously. "The two are one," she answered; "for the Black Knight chanced to have a spell thrown over him, which turned him into a Black Bull, and which could not be lifted until he had fought with, and overcome, a mighty Spirit of Evil that lived in a dark glen. He fought with the Spirit and overcame it, and once more regained his true form; but 'tis said that his mind is somewhat clouded at times, for he speaketh ever of a maiden whom he would fain have wedded, and whom he hath lost. Though who, or what she was, no living person kens. But this story can have no interest to a stranger like thee," she added slowly, as if she were sorry for having said so much. "I have no more time to waste in talking. But if thou wilt try and wash the mantle, thou art welcome to a night's lodging; and if not, I must ask thee to go on thy way."

Needless to say, the Princess said that she would try to wash the mantle; and it seemed as if her fingers had some magic power in them, for as soon as she put it into water the stains vanished, and it became as white and clean as when it was new.

Of course, the old woman was delighted, but she was very suspicious also, for it appeared to her that there must be some mysterious link between the maiden and the Knight, if his mantle became clean so easily when she washed it, when it had remained soiled and stained in spite of all the labour which she and her daughter had bestowed upon it.

So, as she knew that the young Gallant intended returning for it that very night, and as she wanted her daughter to get the credit of washing it, she advised the Princess to go to bed early, in order to get a good night's rest after all her labours. And the Princess followed her advice, and thus it came about that she was sound asleep, safely hidden in the big box-bed in the corner, when the Black Knight of Norroway came to the cottage to claim his white mantle.

Now you must know that the young man had carried about this mantle with him for the last seven years – ever since his encounter with the Evil Spirit of the Glen – always trying to find someone who could wash it for him, and never succeeding.

For it had been revealed to him by a wise woman that she who could make it white and clean was destined to be his wife – be she bonnie or ugly, old or young. And that, moreover, she would prove a loving, a faithful, and a true helpmeet.

So when he came to the washerwoman's cottage, and received back his mantle white as the driven snow, and heard that it was the washerwoman's daughter who had wrought this wondrous change, he said at once that he would marry her, and that the very next day.

When the Princess awoke in the morning and heard all that had befallen, and how the Black Knight had come to the cottage while she was asleep, and had received his mantle, and had promised to marry the washerwoman's daughter that very day, her heart was like to break. For now she felt that she never would have the chance of speaking to him and telling him who she really was.

And in her sore distress she suddenly remembered the beautiful fruit which she had received on her journey seven long years before, and which she had carried with her ever since.

"Surely I will never be in a sorer strait than I am now," she said to herself; and she drew out the apple and broke it. And, lo and behold! it was filled with the most beautiful precious stones that she had ever seen; and at the sight of them a plan came suddenly into her head.

She took the precious stones out of the apple, and, putting them into a corner of her kerchief, carried them to the washerwoman.

"See," said she, "I am richer than mayhap thou thoughtest I was. And if thou wilt, all these riches may be thine."

"And how could that come about?" asked the old woman eagerly, for she had never seen so many precious stones in her life before, and she had a great desire to become the possessor of them.

"Only put off thy daughter's wedding for one day," replied the Princess, "and let me watch beside the Black Knight as he sleeps this night, for I have long had a great desire to see him."

To her astonishment the washerwoman agreed to this request; for the wily old woman was very anxious to get the jewels, which would make her rich for life, and it did not seem to her that there was any harm in the Princess's request; for she had made up her mind that she would give the Black Knight a sleeping-draught, which would effectually prevent him as much as speaking to this strange maiden.

So she took the jewels and locked them up in her kist, and the wedding was put off, and that night the little Princess slipped into the Black Knight's apartment when he was asleep, and watched all through the long hours by his bedside, singing this song to him in the hope that he would awake and hear it:

"Seven lang years I served for thee,
The glassy hill I clamb for thee.
The mantle white I washed for thee,
And wilt thou no waken, and turn to me?"

But although she sang it over and over again, as if her heart would burst, he neither listened nor stirred, for the old washerwoman's potion had made sure of that.

Next morning, in her great trouble, the little Princess broke open the pear, hoping that its contents would help her better than the contents of the apple had done. But in it she found just what she had found before – a heap of precious stones; only they were richer and more valuable than the others had been.

So, as it seemed the only thing to do, she carried them to the old woman, and bribed her to put the wedding off for yet another day, and allow her to watch that night also by the Black Prince's bedside.

And the washerwoman did so; "for," said she, as she locked away the stones, "I shall soon grow quite rich at this rate."

But, alas! it was all in vain that the Princess spent the long hours singing with all her might:

"Seven lang years I served for thee,
The glassy hill I clamb for thee,
The mantle white I washed for thee,
And wilt thou no waken, and turn to me?"

for the young Prince whom she watched so tenderly, remained deaf and motionless as a stone.

By the morning she had almost lost hope, for there was only the plum remaining now, and if that failed, her last chance had gone. With trembling fingers she broke it open, and found inside another collection of precious stones, richer and rarer than all the others.

She ran with these to the washerwoman, and, throwing them into her lap, told her she could keep them all and welcome if she would put off the wedding once again, and let her watch by the Prince for one more night. And, greatly wondering, the old woman consented.

Now it chanced that the Black Knight, tired with waiting for his wedding, went out hunting that day with all his attendants behind him. And as the servants rode they talked together about something that had puzzled them sorely these two nights gone by. At last an old huntsman rode up to the Knight, with a question upon his lips.

"Master," he said, "we would fain ken who the sweet singer is who singeth through the night in thy chamber?"

"Singer!" he repeated. "There is no singer. My chamber hath been as quiet as the grave, and I have slept a dreamless sleep ever since I came to live at the cottage."

The old huntsman shook his head. "Taste not the old wife's draught this night, Master," he said earnestly; "then wilt thou hear what other ears have heard."

At other times the Black Knight would have laughed at his words, but today the man spoke with such earnestness that he could not but listen to them. So that evening, when the washerwoman, as was her wont, brought his sleeping-draught of spiced ale to his bedside, he told her that it was not sweet enough for his liking. And when she turned and went to the kitchen to fetch some honey to sweeten it, he jumped out of bed and poured it all out of the window, and when she came back he pretended that he had drunk it.

So it came to pass that he lay awake that night and heard the Princess enter his room, and listened to her plaintive little song, sung in a voice that was full of sobs:

> *"Seven lang years I served for thee,*
> *The glassy hill I clamb for thee,*
> *The mantle white I washed for thee,*
> *And wilt thou no waken, and turn to me?"*

And when he heard it, he understood it all; and he sprang up and took her in his arms and kissed her, and asked her to tell him the whole story.

And when he heard it, he was so angry with the old washerwoman and her deceitful daughter that he ordered them to leave the country at once; and he married the little Princess, and they lived happily all their days.

The Laird o' Co'

IT WAS A FINE SUMMER MORNING, and the Laird o' Co' was having a dander on the green turf outside the Castle walls. His real name was the Laird o' Colzean, and his descendants today bear the proud title of Marquises of Ailsa, but all up and down Ayrshire nobody called him anything else than the Laird o' Co'; because of the Co's, or caves, which were to be found in the rock on which his Castle was built.

He was a kind man, and courteous, always ready to be interested in the affairs of his poorer neighbours, and willing to listen to any tale of woe.

So when a little boy came across the green, carrying a small can in his hand, and, pulling his forelock, asked him if he might go to the Castle and get a little ale for his sick mother, the Laird gave his consent at once, and, patting the little fellow on the head, told him to go to the kitchen and ask for the butler, and tell him that he, the Laird, had given orders that his can was to be filled with the best ale that was in the cellar.

Away the boy went, and found the old butler, who, after listening to his message, took him down into the cellar, and proceeded to carry out his Master's orders.

There was one cask of particularly fine ale, which was kept entirely for the Laird's own use, which had been opened some time before, and which was now about half full.

"I will fill the bairn's can out o' this," thought the old man to himself. "'Tis both nourishing and light – the very thing for sick folk." So, taking the can from the child's hand, he proceeded to draw the ale.

But what was his astonishment to find that, although the ale flowed freely enough from the barrel, the little can, which could not have held more than a quarter of a gallon, remained always just half full.

The ale poured into it in a clear amber stream, until the big cask was quite empty, and still the quantity that was in the little can did not seem to increase.

The butler could not understand it. He looked at the cask, and then he looked at the can; then he looked down at the floor at his feet to see if he had not spilt any.

No, the ale had not disappeared in that way, for the cellar floor was as white, and dry, and clean, as possible.

"Plague on the can; it must be bewitched," thought the old man, and his short, stubby hair stood up like porcupine quills round his bald head, for if there was anything on earth of which he had a mortal dread, it was Warlocks, and Witches, and such like Bogles.

"I'm not going to broach another barrel," he said gruffly, handing back the half-filled can to the little lad. "So ye may just go home with what is there; the Laird's ale is too good to waste on a smatchet like thee."

But the boy stoutly held his ground. A promise was a promise, and the Laird had both promised, and sent orders to the butler that the can was to be filled, and he would not go home till it was filled.

It was in vain that the old man first argued, and then grew angry – the boy would not stir a step.

"The Laird had said that he was to get the ale, and the ale he must have."

At last the perturbed butler left him standing there, and hurried off to his master to tell him he was convinced that the can was bewitched, for it had swallowed up a whole half cask of ale, and after doing so it was only half full; and to ask if he would come down himself, and order the lad off the premises.

"Not I," said the genial Laird, "for the little fellow is quite right. I promised that he should have his can full of ale to take home to his sick mother, and he shall have it if it takes all the barrels in my cellar to fill it. So haste thee to the house again, and open another cask."

The butler dare not disobey; so he reluctantly retraced his steps, but, as he went, he shook his head sadly, for it seemed to him that not only the boy with the can, but his master also, was bewitched.

When he reached the cellar he found the bairn waiting patiently where he had left him, and, without wasting further words, he took the can from his hand and broached another barrel.

If he had been astonished before, he was more astonished now. Scarce had a couple of drops fallen from the tap, than the can was full to the brim.

"Take it, laddie, and begone, with all the speed thou canst," he said, glad to get the can out of his fingers; and the boy did not wait for a second bidding. Thanking the butler most earnestly for his trouble, and paying no attention to the fact that the old man had not been so civil to him as he might have been, he departed. Nor, though the butler took pains to ask all round the countryside, could he ever hear of him again, nor of anyone who knew anything about him, or anything about his sick mother.

Years passed by, and sore trouble fell upon the House o' Co'. For the Laird went to fight in the wars in Flanders, and, chancing to be taken prisoner, he was shut up in prison, and condemned to death. Alone, in a foreign country, he had no friends to speak for him, and escape seemed hopeless.

It was the night before his execution, and he was sitting in his lonely cell, thinking sadly of his wife and children, whom he never expected to see again. At the thought of them the picture of his home rose clearly in his mind – the grand old Castle standing on its rock, and the bonnie daisy-spangled stretch of greensward which lay before its gates, where he had been wont to take a dander in the sweet summer mornings. Then, all unbidden, a vision of the little lad carrying the can, who had come to beg ale for his sick mother, and whom he had long ago forgotten, rose up before him.

The vision was so clear and distinct that he felt almost as if he were acting the scene over again, and he rubbed his eyes to get rid of it, feeling that, if he had to die tomorrow, it was time that he turned his thoughts to better things.

But as he did so the door of his cell flew noiselessly open, and there, on the threshold, stood the self-same little lad, looking not a day older, with his finger on his lip, and a mysterious smile upon his face.

> *"Laird o' Co',*
> *Rise and go!"*

he whispered, beckoning to him to follow him. Needless to say, the Laird did so, too much amazed to think of asking questions.

Through the long passages of the prison the little lad went, the Laird close at his heels; and whenever he came to a locked door, he had but to touch it, and it opened before them, so that in no long time they were safe outside the walls.

The overjoyed Laird would have overwhelmed his little deliverer with words of thanks had not the boy held up his hand to stop him. "Get on my back," he said shortly, "for thou art not safe till thou art out of this country."

The Laird did as he was bid, and, marvellous as it seems, the boy was quite able to bear his weight. As soon as he was comfortably seated the pair set off, over sea and land, and never stopped till, in almost less time than it takes to tell it, the boy set him down, in the early dawn, on the daisy-spangled green in front of his Castle, just where he had spoken first to him so many years before.

Then he turned, and laid his little hand on the Laird's big one:

> *"Ae gude turn deserves anither,*
> *Tak' ye that for being sae kind to my auld mither,"*

he said, and vanished.

And from that day to this he has never been seen again.

Katherine Crackernuts

THERE WAS ONCE A KING whose wife died, leaving him with an only daughter, whom he dearly loved. The little Princess's name was Velvet-Cheek, and she was so good, and bonnie, and kind-hearted that all her father's subjects loved her. But as the King was generally engaged in transacting the business of the State, the poor little maiden had rather a lonely life, and often wished that she had a sister with whom she could play, and who would be a companion to her.

The King, hearing this, made up his mind to marry a middle-aged Countess, whom he had met at a neighbouring Court, who had one daughter, named Katherine, who was just a little younger than the Princess Velvet-Cheek, and who, he thought, would make a nice play-fellow for her.

He did so, and in one way the arrangement turned out very well, for the two girls loved one another dearly, and had everything in common, just as if they had really been sisters.

But in another way it turned out very badly, for the new Queen was a cruel and ambitious woman, and she wanted her own daughter to do as she had done, and make a grand marriage, and perhaps even become a Queen. And when she saw that Princess Velvet-Cheek was growing into a very beautiful young woman – more beautiful by far than her own daughter – she began to hate her, and to wish that in some way she would lose her good looks.

"For," thought she, "what suitor will heed my daughter as long as her stepsister is by her side?"

Now, among the servants and retainers at her husband's Castle there was an old hen-wife, who, men said, was in league with the Evil Spirits of the air, and who was skilled in the knowledge of charms, and philtres, and love potions.

"Perhaps she could help me to do what I seek to do," said the wicked Queen; and one night, when it was growing dusk, she wrapped a cloak round her, and set out to this old hen-wife's cottage.

"Send the lassie to me tomorrow morning ere she hath broken her fast," replied the old Dame when she heard what her visitor had to say. "I will find out a way to mar her beauty." And the wicked Queen went home content.

Next morning she went to the Princess's room while she was dressing, and told her to go out before breakfast and get the eggs that the hen-wife had gathered. "And see," added she, "that thou dost not eat anything ere thou goest, for there is nothing that maketh the roses bloom on a young maiden's cheeks like going out fasting in the fresh morning air."

Princess Velvet-Cheek promised to do as she was bid, and go and fetch the eggs; but as she was not fond of going out of doors before she had had something to eat, and as, moreover, she suspected that her stepmother had some hidden reason for giving her such an unusual order, and she did not trust her stepmother's hidden reasons, she slipped into the pantry as she went downstairs and helped herself to a large slice of cake. Then, after she had eaten it, she went straight to the hen-wife's cottage and asked for the eggs.

"Lift the lid of that pot there, your Highness, and you will see them," said the old woman, pointing to the big pot standing in the corner in which she boiled her hens' meat.

The Princess did so, and found a heap of eggs lying inside, which she lifted into her basket, while the old woman watched her with a curious smile.

"Go home to your Lady Mother, Hinny," she said at last, "and tell her from me to keep the press door better snibbit."

The Princess went home, and gave this extraordinary message to her stepmother, wondering to herself the while what it meant.

But if she did not understand the hen-wife's words, the Queen understood them only too well. For from them she gathered that the Princess had in some way prevented the old Witch's spell doing what she intended it to do.

So next morning, when she sent her stepdaughter once more on the same errand, she accompanied her to the door of the Castle herself, so that the poor girl had no chance of paying a visit to the pantry. But as she went along the road that led to the cottage, she felt so hungry that, when she passed a party of country-folk picking peas by the roadside, she asked them to give her a handful.

They did so, and she ate the peas; and so it came about that the same thing happened that had happened yesterday.

The hen-wife sent her to look for the eggs; but she could work no spell upon her, because she had broken her fast. So the old woman bade her go home again and give the same message to the Queen.

The Queen was very angry when she heard it, for she felt that she was being outwitted by this slip of a girl, and she determined that, although she was not fond of getting up early, she would accompany her next day herself, and make sure that she had nothing to eat as she went.

So next morning she walked with the Princess to the hen-wife's cottage, and, as had happened twice before, the old woman sent the royal maiden to lift the lid off the pot in the corner in order to get the eggs.

And the moment that the Princess did so, off jumped her own pretty head, and on jumped that of a sheep.

Then the wicked Queen thanked the cruel old Witch for the service that she had rendered to her, and went home quite delighted with the success of her scheme; while the poor Princess picked up her own head and put it into her basket along with the eggs, and went home crying, keeping behind the hedge all the way, for she felt so ashamed of her sheep's head that she was afraid that anyone saw her.

Now, as I told you, the Princess's stepsister Katherine loved her dearly, and when she saw what a cruel deed had been wrought on her she was so angry that she declared that she would not remain another hour in the Castle. "For," said she, "if my Lady Mother can order one such deed to be done, who can hinder her ordering another? So, methinks, 'twere better for us both to be where she cannot reach us."

So she wrapped a fine shawl round her poor stepsister's head, so that none could tell what it was like, and, putting the real head in the basket, she took her by the hand, and the two set out to seek their fortunes.

They walked and they walked, till they reached a splendid Palace, and when they came to it Katherine made as though she would go boldly up and knock at the door.

"I may perchance find work here," she explained, "and earn enough money to keep us both in comfort."

But the poor Princess would fain have pulled her back. "They will have nothing to do with thee," she whispered, "when they see that thou hast a sister with a sheep's head."

"And who is to know that thou hast a sheep's head," asked Katherine. "if thou hold thy tongue, and keep the shawl well round thy face, and leave the rest to me?"

So up she went and knocked at the kitchen door, and when the housekeeper came to answer it, she asked her if there was any work that she could give her to do. "For," said she, "I have a sick sister, who is sore troubled with the migraine in her head, and I would fain find a quiet lodging for her where she could rest for the night."

"Dost thou know aught of sickness?" asked the housekeeper, who was greatly struck by Katherine's soft voice and gentle ways.

"Ay, do I," replied Katherine, "for when one's sister is troubled with the migraine, one has to learn to go about softly and not to make a noise."

Now it chanced that the King's eldest son, the Crown Prince, was lying ill in the Palace of a strange disease, which seemed to have touched his brain. For he was so restless, especially at nights, that someone had always to be with him to watch that he did himself no harm; and this state of things had gone on so long that everyone was quite worn out.

And the old housekeeper thought that it would be a good chance to get a quiet night's sleep if this capable-looking stranger could be trusted to sit up with the Prince.

So she left her at the door, and went and consulted the King; and the King came out and spoke to Katherine and he, too, was so pleased with her voice and her appearance that he gave orders that a room should be set apart in the Castle for her sick sister and herself, and he promised that, if she would sit up that night with the Prince, and see that no harm befell him, she would have, as her reward, a bag of silver Pennies in the morning.

Katherine agreed to the bargain readily, "for," thought she, "'twill always be a night's lodging for the Princess; and, forbye that, a bag of silver Pennies is not to be got every day."

So the Princess went to bed in the comfortable chamber that was set apart for her, and Katherine went to watch by the sick Prince.

He was a handsome, comely young man, who seemed to be in some sort of fever, for his brain was not quite clear, and he tossed and tumbled from side to side, gazing anxiously in front of him, and stretching out his hands as if he were in search of something.

And at twelve o'clock at night, just when Katherine thought that he was going to fall into a refreshing sleep, what was her horror to see him rise from his bed, dress himself hastily, open the door, and slip downstairs, as if he were going to look for somebody.

"There be something strange in this," said the girl to herself. "Methinks I had better follow him and see what happens."

So she stole out of the room after the Prince and followed him safely downstairs; and what was her astonishment to find that apparently he was going some distance, for he put on his hat and riding-coat, and, unlocking the door, crossed the courtyard to the stable, and began to saddle his horse.

When he had done so, he led it out, and mounted, and, whistling softly to a hound which lay asleep in a corner, he prepared to ride away.

"I must go too, and see the end of this," said Katherine bravely; "for methinks he is bewitched. These be not the actions of a sick man."

So, just as the horse was about to start, she jumped lightly on its back, and settled herself comfortably behind its rider, all unnoticed by him.

Then this strange pair rode away through the woods, and, as they went, Katherine pulled the hazelnuts that nodded in great clusters in her face. "For," said she to herself, "Dear only knows where next I may get anything to eat."

On and on they rode, till they left the greenwood far behind them and came out on an open moor. Soon they reached a hillock, and here the Prince drew rein, and, stooping down, cried in a strange, uncanny whisper, "Open, open, Green Hill, and let the Prince, and his horse, and his hound enter."

"And," whispered Katherine quickly, "let his lady enter behind him."

Instantly, to her great astonishment, the top of the knoll seemed to tip up, leaving an aperture large enough for the little company to enter; then it closed gently behind them again.

They found themselves in a magnificent hall, brilliantly lighted by hundreds of candles stuck in sconces round the walls. In the centre of this apartment was a group of the most beautiful maidens that Katherine had ever seen, all dressed in shimmering ballgowns, with wreaths of roses and violets in their hair. And there were sprightly gallants also, who had been treading a measure with these beauteous damsels to the strains of fairy music.

When the maidens saw the Prince, they ran to him, and led him away to join their revels. And at the touch of their hands all his languor seemed to disappear, and he became the gayest of all the throng, and laughed, and danced, and sang as if he had never known what it was to be ill.

As no one took any notice of Katherine, she sat down quietly on a bit of rock to watch what would befall. And as she watched, she became aware of a wee, wee bairnie, playing with a tiny wand, quite close to her feet.

He was a bonnie bit bairn, and she was just thinking of trying to make friends with him when one of the beautiful maidens passed, and, looking at the wand, said to her partner, in a meaning tone, "Three strokes of that wand would give Katherine's sister back her pretty face."

Here was news indeed! Katherine's breath came thick and fast; and with trembling fingers she drew some of the nuts out of her pocket, and began rolling them carelessly towards the child. Apparently he did not get nuts very often, for he dropped his little wand at once, and stretched out his tiny hands to pick them up.

This was just what she wanted; and she slipped down from her seat to the ground, and drew a little nearer to him. Then she threw one or two more nuts in his way, and, when he was picking these up, she managed to lift the wand unobserved, and to hide it under her apron. After this, she crept cautiously back to her seat again; and not a moment too soon, for just then a cock crew, and at the sound the whole of the dancers vanished – all but the Prince, who ran to mount his horse, and was in such a hurry to be gone that Katherine had much ado to get up behind him before the hillock opened, and he rode swiftly into the outer world once more.

But she managed it, and, as they rode homewards in the grey morning light, she sat and cracked her nuts and ate them as fast as she could, for her adventures had made her marvellously hungry.

When she and her strange patient had once more reached the Castle, she just waited to see him go back to bed, and begin to toss and tumble as he had done before; then she ran to her stepsister's room, and, finding her asleep, with her poor misshapen head lying peacefully on the pillow, she gave it three sharp little strokes with the fairy wand and, lo and behold! the sheep's head vanished, and the Princess's own pretty one took its place.

In the morning the King and the old housekeeper came to inquire what kind of night the Prince had had. Katherine answered that he had had a very good night; for she was very anxious to stay with him longer, for now that she had found out that the Elfin Maidens who dwelt in the Green Hill had thrown a spell over him, she was resolved to find out also how that spell could be loosed.

And Fortune favoured her; for the King was so pleased to think that such a suitable nurse had been found for the Prince, and he was also so charmed with the looks of her stepsister, who came out of her chamber as bright and bonnie as in the old days, declaring that her migraine was all gone, and that she was now able to do any work that the housekeeper might find for her, that he begged Katherine to stay with his son a little longer, adding that if she would do so, he would give her a bag of gold Bonnet Pieces.

So Katherine agreed readily; and that night she watched by the Prince as she had done the night before. And at twelve o'clock he rose and dressed himself, and rode to the Fairy Hill, just as she had expected him to do, for she was quite certain that the poor young man was bewitched, and not suffering from a fever, as everyone thought he was.

And you may be sure that she accompanied him, riding behind him all unnoticed, and filling her pockets with nuts as she rode.

When they reached the Fairy Hill, he spoke the same words that he had spoken the night before. "Open, open, Green Hill, and let the young Prince in with his horse and his hound." And when the Green Hill opened, Katherine added softly, "And his lady behind him." So they all passed in together.

Katherine seated herself on a stone, and looked around her. The same revels were going on as yesternight, and the Prince was soon in the thick of them, dancing and laughing madly. The girl watched him narrowly, wondering if she would ever be able to find out what would restore him to his right mind; and, as she was watching him, the same little bairn who had played with the magic wand came up to her again. Only this time he was playing with a little bird.

And as he played, one of the dancers passed by, and, turning to her partner, said lightly, "Three bites of that birdie would lift the Prince's sickness, and make him as well as he ever was." Then she joined in the dance again, leaving Katherine sitting upright on her stone quivering with excitement.

If only she could get that bird, the Prince might be cured! Very carefully she began to shake some nuts out of her pocket and roll them across the floor towards the child.

He picked them up eagerly, letting go the bird as he did so; and, in an instant, Katherine caught it, and hid it under her apron.

In no long time after that the cock crew, and the Prince and she set out on their homeward ride. But this morning, instead of cracking nuts, she killed and plucked the bird, scattering its feathers all along the road; and the instant she gained the Prince's room, and had seen him safely into bed, she put it on a spit in front of the fire and began to roast it.

And soon it began to frizzle, and get brown, and smell deliciously, and the Prince, in his bed in the corner, opened his eyes and murmured faintly, "How I wish I had a bite of that birdie."

When she heard the words Katherine's heart jumped for joy, and as soon as the bird was roasted she cut a little piece from its breast and popped it into the Prince's mouth.

When he had eaten it his strength seemed to come back somewhat, for he rose on his elbow and looked at his nurse. "Oh! if I had but another bite of that birdie!" he said. And his voice was certainly stronger.

So Katherine gave him another piece, and when he had eaten that he sat right up in bed.

"Oh! if I had but a third bite o' that birdie!" he cried. And now the colour was coming back into his face, and his eyes were shining.

This time Katherine brought him the whole of the rest of the bird; and he ate it up greedily, picking the bones quite clean with his fingers; and when it was finished, he sprang out of bed and dressed himself, and sat down by the fire.

And when the King came in the morning, with his old housekeeper at his back, to see how the Prince was, he found him sitting cracking nuts with his nurse, for Katherine had brought home quite a lot in her apron pocket.

The King was so delighted to find his son cured that he gave all the credit to Katherine Crackernuts, as he called her, and he gave orders at once that the Prince should marry her. "For," said he, "a maiden who is such a good nurse is sure to make a good Queen."

The Prince was quite willing to do as his father bade him; and, while they were talking together, his younger brother came in, leading Princess Velvet-Cheek by the hand, whose acquaintance he had made but yesterday, declaring that he had fallen in love with her, and that he wanted to marry her immediately.

So it all fell out very well, and everybody was quite pleased; and the two weddings took place at once, and, unless they be dead sinsyne, the young couples are living yet.

The Tale of the Queen Who Sought a Drink from a Certain Well

THERE WAS BEFORE NOW, a queen who was sick, and she had three daughters. Said she to the one who was eldest, "Go to the well of true water, and bring to me a drink to heal me."

The daughter went, and she reached the well. A losgann (frog or toad) came up to ask her if she would wed him, if she should get a drink for her mother. "I will not wed thee, hideous creature, on any account!" said she. "Well then," said he, "thou shalt not get the water."

She went away home, and her mother sent away her sister that was nearest to her, to seek a drink of the water. She reached the well; and the toad came up and asked her if she would marry him if she should get the water. "I won't marry thee, hideous creature!" said she. "Thou shalt not get the water, then," said he.

She went home, and her sister that was youngest went to seek the water. When she reached the well the toad came up as he used, and asked her if she would marry him if she should get the water. "If I have no other way to get healing for my mother, I will marry thee," said she; and she got the water, and she healed her mother.

They had betaken themselves to rest in the night when the toad came to the door saying:

"*A chaomhag, a chaomhag,*
An cuimhneach leat
An gealladh beag
A thug thu aig
An tobar dhomh,
A ghaoil, a ghaoil."

("Gentle one, gentle one,
Rememberest thou
The little pledge
Thou gavest me
Beside the well,
My love, my love.")

When he was ceaselessly saying this, the girl rose and took him in, and put him behind the door, and she went to bed; but she was not long laid down, when he began again saying, everlastingly:

"A hàovaig, a hàovaig,
An cuineach leat
An geallug beag
A hoog oo aig
An tobar gaw,
A géule, a géule."

Then she got up and she put him under a noggin; that kept him quiet a while; but she was not long laid down when he began again, saying:

"A hàovaig, a hàovaig,
An cuineach leat
An geallug beag
A hoog oo aig
An tobar gaw,
A géule, a géule."

She rose again, and she made him a little bed at the fireside; but he was not pleased, and he began again saying:

"A chaomhag, a chaomhag,
An cuimhneach leat
An gealladh beag
A thug thu aig
An tobar dhomh,
A ghaoil, a ghaoil."

But she took no notice of his complaining, till he said to her, "There is an old rusted glave behind thy bed, with which thou hadst better take off my head, than be holding me longer in torture."

She took the glave and cut the head off him. When the steel touched him, he grew a handsome youth; and he gave many thanks to the young wife, who had been the means of putting off him the spells, under which he had endured for a long time. Then he got his kingdom, for he was a king; and he married the princess, and they were long alive and merry together.

The Widow's Son

THERE WAS A POOR FISHER'S WIDOW in Eirinn, and she had one son; and one day he left his mother with a lump of a horse, and a man met him with a gun, a dog, and a falcon (gunna cu agus seobhag); and he said, "Wilt thou sell me the horse, son of the fisher in Eirinn?" and he said, "What wilt thou give me? Wilt thou give me thy gun and thy dog, and thy falcon?" And he said, "I will give them;" and the bargain was struck; and Iain, the fisher's son, went home. When his mother saw him she was enraged, and she beat him; and in the night he took the gun and went away to be a hunter. He went and he went till he reached the house of a farmer, who was sitting there with his old wife. The farmer said, "It was fortune sent thee here with thy gun; there is a deer that comes every night to eat my corn, and she will not leave a straw." And they engaged Iain the fisherman's son to stay with them, and shoot the deer; and so he stayed; and on the morrow's day he went out, and when he saw the deer he put the gun to his eye to shoot her, and the lock was up; but when he would have fired, he saw the finest woman he ever saw before him, and he held his hand, and let down the gun, and let down the lock, and there was the deer eating the corn again.

Three times he did this, and then he ran after the deer to try to catch her.

The deer ran away, and he followed till they came to a house thatched with heather; and then the deer leaped on the house, and she said, "Go in now, thou fisher's son, and eat thy fill." He went in and there was a table spread with every kind of meat and drink, and no one within; for this was a robber's house, and they were away lifting spoil.

So the fisher's son went in, and as the deer had told him, he sat him down, and ate and drank; and when he had enough he went under a togsaid (hogshead).

He had not been long there when the twenty-four robbers came home, and they knew that someone had been at their food, and they began to grumble and dispute. Then the leader said, "Why will you dispute and quarrel? the man that has done this is here under the mouth of this hogshead, take him now, and let four of you go out and kill him."

So they took out Iain, the fisher's son, and four of them killed him; and then they had their food and slept, and in the morning they went out as usual.

When they had gone, the deer came where Iain was, and she shook sol (wax) from her ear on the dead man, and he was alive and whole as he was before. "Now," said she, "trust me, go in and eat as thou didst yesterday."

So Iain, the fisher's son, went in and ate and drank as he had done; and when he had enough he went in under the mouth of the hogshead; and when the robbers came home, there was more of their food eaten than on the day before, and they had a worse dispute. Then the captain said, "The man that did it is there, go out now with him, four of you, and kill him; and let those who went last night be killed also, because he is now alive." So the four robbers were slain, and Iain was killed again; and the rest of the robbers ate and drank, and slept; and on the morrow before dawn they were off again. Then the deer came, and she shook sol from her right ear on Iain the fisher's son, and he was alive as well as before, in a burst of sweat.

That day Iain ate and drank, and hid as before; and when the robbers came home, the captain ordered the four who had gone out to be slain; and now there were eight dead; and four more killed Iain the fisher's son, and left him there. On the morrow the deer came as before, and Iain was brought alive; and the next day the robbers all killed each other.

On that day the deer came, and Iain followed her to the white house of a window, where there lived an old hag, and Gille Caol dubh, a slender dark lad, her son, and the deer said, "Meet me tomorrow at eleven in yonder church," and she left him there.

On the morrow he went, but the carlin stuck a bior nimh (spike of hurt) in the outside of the door post; and when he came to the church he fell asleep, and the black lad was watching him. Then they heard the sweetest music they ever heard coming, and the finest lady that ever was came and tried to waken him; and when she could not, she wrote her name under his arm, Nighean Righ Rioghachd Baille Fo' Thuinn, the daughter of the king of the kingdom of the town under waves; and she said that she would come tomorrow, and she went away. When she was gone, he awoke, and the slim black lad told him what had happened, but did not tell him that her name was written under his arm.

On the next day it was the same, the sweetest of music was heard, and the lady came, and she laid his head on her knee and dressed his hair; and when she could not awaken him, she put a snuff-box in his pocket, and cried, and went away.

On the third day she said she would never come again, and she went away home; and when she was gone he awoke.

When the lad awoke, bha e falbh gus an robh dubhadh air a bhonan, toladh air a chasan, neoil dubha doracha na oidhche a tighinn neoil sithe seamh an latha ga fhagail gus an robh eoin bhega an t-shleibh a gabhail an am bun gach preas a b'fhaisge dhaibh na chéile (he was going till there was blackening on his soles, holes in his feet, the dark black clouds of the night coming, the quiet peaceful clouds of day leaving him, till the little mountain birds were betaking themselves about the root of each bush that was nearest to them).

And he went till he reached the house of a wife, who said, "All hail! son of the great fisher in Eirinn, I know thy journey and thine errand; come in and I will do what I can for thee." So he went in, and on the morrow she said, "I have a sister who dwells on the road; it is a walk of a year and a day, but here are a pair of old brown shoes with holes in them; put them on and thou wilt be there in an instant; and when thou art there, turn their toes to the known, and their heels to the unknown, and they will come home; and so he did.

The second sister did the very same; but she said, "I have a third sister, and she has a son, who is herd to the birds of the air, and sets them asleep; perhaps he can help thee." And then she gave him another pair of shoes, and he went to the third sister.

The third said she did not know how to help him farther, but perhaps her son might, when he came home; and he, when he came, proposed that the cow should be killed; and after some talk, that was done, and the meat was cooked, and a bag made of the hide, red side out; and John, the fisher's son, was put in with his son, but he left the dog and the falcon. He had not been long in the bag when the Creveenach came, for she had a nest in an island, and she raised the red bag; but she had not gone far when she dropped it in the sea. Then the other one came, and she gripped to it firmly with her claws; and at last they left the bag on the island, where all the birds of the air were wont to sleep. He came out of the bag; and he was for a day and year living on what he had, and on the birds which he killed with his gun; but at last there was nothing more to eat, and he thought he would die there. Then he searched his pockets for food, and found the box which the lady had put there; he opened it, and three came out, and they said, "Eege gu djeege, Master, good, what shall we do?" And he said, "Take me to the realm of the king under the waves;" and in a moment there he was.

He went up to the house of a weaver; and after he had been there for some time, the weaver came home with flesh, and other things from the great town; and he gave him both meat and lodging.

On the morrow the weaver told him that there was to be a horse race in the town; and he bethought him of the box, and opened it; and three came out and said, "Eege gu djeege, Master, good, what shall we do?" And he said, "Bring me the finest horse that ever was seen, and the grandest dress, and glass shoes;" and he had them all in a minute. Now he who won the races was to have the king's daughter to wife. Then he went, and won, and the king's daughter saw him; but he never stayed; he went back to the weaver, and threw three "mam" handsfull of gold into his apron, and said that a great gentleman, who won the race, had given him the gold; and then he broke the weaver's loom, and tore the cloth to bits.

Next day there was a dog race; and he got a finer dress, and a splendid dog, by the help of the box, and won, and threw handsfull of gold to the weaver, and did more mischief in his house.

On the third day it was a falcon race, and he did the very same; and he was the man who was to marry the princess, but he was nowhere to be found when the race was over.

Then the whole kingdom was gathered, and the winner of the prize was nowhere to be found. At last they came to the weaver's house, and the hunter's beard was grown over his face, and he was dirty and travel-stained; and he had given all the gold to the weaver, and smashed everything; and he was so dirty and ugly, and good for nothing, that he was to be hanged. But when he was under the gallows, he was to make the gallows speech, searmoin na croiche; and he put up his arm, and the king's daughter saw the name which she had written there, and knew him; and she called out, "Hold your hands, for everyone in the kingdom shall die if that man is hurt." And then she took him by the hand, and they were to be married.

Then she dressed him grandly, and asked how he had found her out; and he told her; and she asked where he had found the box; and he said, when he was in extremity in the island; and then she took him by the hand before her father, and all the kings, and she said she would marry the fisher's son, for he it was who had freed her from spells.

"Oh kings," said she, "if one of you were killed today, the rest would fly; but this man put his trust in me, and had his head cut off three times. Because he has done so much for me, I will marry him rather than any one of the great men who have come to marry me; for many kings have tried to free me from the spells, and none could do it but Iain here, the fisher's son."

Then a great war ship was fitted up and sent for the old carlin who had done all the evil, and for her black slim son; and seven fiery furnaces were set in order, and they were burnt, and the ashes were let fly with the wind; and a great wedding was made, and "I left them in the realm."

The Daughter of the Skies

THERE WAS THERE BEFORE NOW A FARMER, and he had a leash of daughters, and much cattle and sheep. He went on a day to see them, and none of them were to be found; and he took the length of the day to search for them. He saw, in the lateness, coming home, a little doggy running about a park.

The doggy came where he was – "What wilt thou give me," said he, "if I get thy lot of cattle and sheep for thee?" "I don't know myself, thou ugly thing; what wilt thou be asking, and I will give it to thee of anything I have?" "Wilt thou give me," said the doggy, "thy big daughter to marry?" "I will give her to thee," said he, "if she will take thee herself."

They went home, himself and the doggy. Her father said to the eldest daughter, would she take him? and she said she would not. He said to the second one, would she marry him? and she said, she would not marry him, though the cattle should not be got for ever. He said to the youngest one, would she marry him? and she said, that she would marry him. They married, and her sisters were mocking her because she had married him.

He took her with him home to his own place. When he came to his own dwelling-place, he grew into a splendid man. They were together a great time, and she said she had better go see her father. He said to her to take care that she should not stay till she should have children, for then she expected one. She said she would not stay. He gave her a steed, and he told her as soon as she reached the house, to take the bridle from her head and let her away; and when she wished to come home, that she had but to shake the bridle, and that the steed would come, and that she would put her head into it.

She did as he asked her; she was not long at her father's house when she fell ill, and a child was born. That night men were together at the fire to watch. There came the very prettiest music that ever was heard about the town; and everyone within slept but she. He came in and he took the child from her. He took himself out, and he went away. The music stopped, and each one awoke; and there was no knowing to what side the child had gone.

She did not tell anything, but so soon as she rose she took with her the bridle, and she shook it, and the steed came, and she put her head into it. She took herself off riding, and the steed took to going home; and the swift March wind that would be before her, she would catch; and the swift March wind that would be after her, could not catch her.

She arrived. "Thou art come," said he. "I came," said she. He noticed nothing to her; and no more did she notice anything to him. Near to the end of three quarters again she said, "I had better go see my father." He said to her on this journey as he had said before. She took with her the steed, and she went away; and when she arrived she took the bridle from the steed's head, and she set her home.

That very night a child was born. He came as he did before, with music; everyone slept, and he took with him the child. When the music stopped they all awoke. Her father was before her face, saying to her that she must tell what was the reason of the matter. She would not tell anything. When she grew well, and when she rose, she took with her the bridle, she shook it, and the steed came and put her head into it. She took herself away home. When she arrived he said, "Thou art come." "I came," said she. He noticed nothing to her; no more did she notice anything to him. Again at the end of three quarters, she said, "I had better go to see my father." "Do," said he, "but take care thou dost not as thou didst on the other two journeys." "I will not," said she. He gave her the steed and she went away.

She reached her father's house, and that very night a child was born. The music came as was usual, and the child was taken away. Then her father was before her face; and he was going to kill her, if she would not tell what was happening to the children; or what sort of man she had. With the fright he gave her, she told it to him. When she grew well she took the bridle with her to a hill that was opposite to her, and she began shaking the bridle, to try if the steed would come, or if she would put her head into it; and though she were shaking still, the steed would not come. When she saw that she was not coming, she went out on foot.

When she arrived, no one was within but the crone that was his mother. "Thou art without a houseman today," said the crone; "and if thou art quick thou wilt catch him yet." She went away, and she was going till the night came on her. She saw then a light a long way from her; and if it was a long way from her, she was not long in reaching it. When she went in, the floor was ready swept before her, and the housewife spinning up in the end of the house. "Come up," said the housewife, "I know of thy cheer and travel. Thou art going to try if thou canst catch thy man; he is going to marry the daughter of the King of the Skies." "He is!" said she. The housewife rose; she made meat for her; she set on water to wash her feet, and she laid her down. If the day came quickly, it was quicker than that that the housewife rose, and that she made meat for her. She set her on foot then for going; and she gave her shears that would cut alone; and she said to her, "Thou wilt be in the house of my middle sister tonight." She was going, and going, till the night came on her. She saw a light a long way from her; and if it was a long way from her, she was not long in reaching it. When she went in the house was ready swept, a fire on the middle of the floor, and the housewife spinning at the end of the fire. "Come up," said the housewife, "I know thy cheer and travel." She made meat for her, she set on water, she washed her feet, and she laid her down.

No sooner came the day than the housewife set her on foot, and made meat for her. She said she had better go; and she gave her a needle would sew by itself. "Thou wilt be in the house of my youngest sister tonight," said she. She was going, and going, till the end of day and the mouth of lateness. She saw a light a long way from her; and if it was a long way from her, she was not long in reaching it. She went in, the house was swept, and the housewife spinning at the end of the fire. "Come up," said she, "I know of thy cheer and travel." She made meat for her, she set on water, she washed her feet, and she laid her down. If the day came quickly, it was quicker than that that the housewife rose; she set her on foot, and she made her meat; she gave her a clue of thread, and the thread would go into the needle by itself and as the shears would cut, and the needle sew, the thread would keep up with them.

"Thou wilt be in the town tonight." She reached the town about evening, and she went into the house of the king's hen-wife, to lay down her weariness, and she was warming herself at the fire. She said to the crone to give her work, that she would rather be working than be still. "No man is doing a turn in this town today," says the hen-wife; "the king's daughter has a wedding." "Ud!" said she to the crone, "give me cloth to sew, or a shirt that will keep my hands going." She gave her shirts to make; she took the shears from her pocket, and she set it to work; she set the needle to work after it; as the shears would cut, the needle would sew, and the thread would go into the needle by itself. One of the king's servant maids came in; she was looking at her, and it caused her great wonder how she made the shears and the needle work by themselves. She went home and she told the king's daughter that one was in the house of the hen-wife, and that she had shears and a needle that could work of themselves. "If there is," said the king's daughter, "go thou over in the morning, and say to her, what will she take for the shears." In the morning she went over, and she said to her that the king's daughter was asking what would she take for the shears. "Nothing I asked," said she, "but leave to lie where she lay last night." "Go thou over," said the king's daughter, "and say to her that she will get that." She gave the shears to the king's daughter. When they were going to lie down, the king's daughter gave him a sleep drink, so that he might not wake. He did not wake the length of the night; and no sooner came the day, than the king's daughter came where she was, and set her on foot and put her out.

On the morrow she was working with the needle and cutting with other shears. The king's daughter sent the maid servant over, and she asked, what would she take for the needle? She said she would not take anything, but leave to lie where she lay last night. The maid servant told this to the king's daughter. "She will get that," said the king's daughter. The maid servant told that she would get that, and she got the needle. When they were going to lie down, the king's daughter gave him a sleep drink, and he did not wake that night. The eldest son he had was lying in a bed beside them; and he was hearing her speaking to him through the night, and saying to him that she was the mother of his three children. His father and he himself was taking a walk out, and he told his father what he was hearing. This day the king's daughter sent the servant maid to ask what she would take for the clue; and she said she would ask but leave to lie where she lay last night. "She will get that," said the king's daughter. This night when he got the sleep drink, he emptied it, and he did not drink it at all. Through the night she said to him that he was the father of her three sons; and he said that he was. In the morning, when the king's daughter came down, he said to her to go up, that she was his wife who was with him. When they rose they went away to go home. They came home; the spells went off him, they planted together and I left them, and they left me.

The Spell of Cadboll

IN OLDEN DAYS THE EAST COAST OF SCOTLAND was studded with fortresses, which, like a crescent chain of sentinels, watched carefully for the protection of their owners and their dependents. The ruins remain and raise their hoary heads over valley and stream, by riverbank and seashore, along which nobles, and knights, and followers "boden in effeyre-weir" went gallantly to their fates; and where in the Highlands many a weary drove followed from the foray, in which they had been driven far from Lowland pastures or distant glens, with whose inhabitants a feud existed. Could the bearded warriors, who once thronged these halls, awake, they would witness many a wonderful change since the half-forgotten days when they lived and loved, revelled and fought, conquered or sustained defeat. Where the bearer of the Crann-taraidh or fiery cross once rushed along on his hasty errand, the lightning of heaven now flashes, by telegraphic wires, to the farthest corners of the land. Through the craggy passes, and along the level plains, marked centuries ago with scarce a bridle path, the mighty steam horse now thunders over its iron road; and where seaward once swam the skin curach, or the crazy fleets of diminutive war galleys, and tiny merchant vessels with their fantastic prows and sterns, and carved mast-heads, the huge hull of the steam-propelled ship now breasts the waves that dash against the rugged headlands, or floats like a miniature volcano, with its attendant clouds of smoke obscuring the horizon.

The parish of Fearn, in Easter Ross, contains several antiquities of very distant date. One of these shattered relics, Castle Cadboll, deserves notice on account of a singular tradition regarding it, once implicitly credited by the people – namely, that although inhabited for ages, no person ever died within its walls. Its magical quality did not, however, prevent its dwellers from the suffering of disease, or the still more grievous evils attending on debility and old age. Hence many of the denizens of the castle became weary of life, particularly the Lady May, who lived there centuries ago, and who, being long ailing, and longing for death, requested to be carried out of the building to die. Her importunity at length prevailed; and, according to the tradition, no sooner did she leave it than she expired.

Castle Cadboll is situated on the seashore, looking over the broad ocean towards Norway. From that country, in the early ages of Scottish history, came many a powerful Jarl, or daring Viking, to the coasts, which, in comparison with their own land, seemed fertile and wealthy. There is a tradition of a Highland clan having sprung from one of those adventurers, who with his brother agreed that whoever should first touch the land would possess it by right.

The foremost was the ultimate ancestor of the tribe; his boat was almost on shore, when the other, by a vigorous stroke, shot ahead of him; but ere he could disembark, the disappointed competitor, with an exclamation of rage, cut off his left hand with his hatchet, and flinging the bloody trophy on the rocks, became, by thus "first touching Scottish ground," the owner of the country, and founder of the clan. The perfect accuracy of this story cannot now be vouched for; but it is an undeniable fact that the Clan Macleod have successfully traced their origin to a Norwegian source; and there is a probability that the claim is correct from the manifestly Norwegian names borne by the founders of the Clan Tormod and Torquil, hence the Siol Tormod – the race of Tormod – the Macleods of Harris; and the Siol Torquil, the race of Torquil – Macleods of Lewis – of whom came the Macleods of Assynt, one of whom betrayed Montrose in 1650, and from whom the estates passed away in the end of the seventeenth century to the Mackenzies.

The Macleods of Cadboll are cadets of the house of Assynt, but to what branch the Lady May of the legend belonged, it is difficult to decide, so many changes having occurred among Highland proprietors.

The cliffs of this part of Ross-shire are wild and precipitous, sinking with a sheer descent of two hundred feet to the ocean. The scenery is more rugged than beautiful – little verdure and less foliage. Trees are stunted by the bitter eastern blast, and the soil is poor. Alders are, however, plentiful, and from them the parish has derived its name of Fearn. There is a number of caves in the cliffs along the shore towards Tarbat, where the promontory is bold, and crowned with a lighthouse, whose flickering rays are now the only substitute for the wonderful gem which was said of yore to sparkle on the brow of one of these eastern cliffs – a bountiful provision of nature for the succour of the wave-tossed mariner.

During the reign of one of the early Stuart kings – which is of little moment – Roderick Macleod ruled with a high and lordly hand within the feudal stronghold of Cadboll. He was a stout and stern knight, whose life had been spent amidst the turmoil of national warfare and clan strife.

Many a battle had he fought, and many a wound received since first he buckled on his father's sword for deadly combat. Amid the conflicting interests which actuated each neighbouring clan – disagreement on any one of which rendered an immediate appeal to arms the readiest mode of solving the difficulty – it is not to be wondered at that Cadboll, as a matter of prudence, endeavoured to attach to himself, by every means in his power, those who were most likely to be serviceable and true. Macleod had married late in life, and his wife dying soon after, while on a visit to her mother, left behind her an only daughter, who was dear as the apple of his eye to the old warrior, but, at the same time, he had no idea of anyone connected with him having any freedom of will or exercise of opinion, save what he allowed; nor did he believe women's hearts were less elastic than his own, which he could bend to any needful expedient. About the period our story commences, the Lady May was nearly eighteen years of age, a beautiful and gentle girl, whose hand was sought by many a young chief of the neighbouring clans; but all unsuccessfully, for the truth was she already loved, and was beloved, in secret, by young Hugh Munro from the side of Ben-Wyvis.

The favoured of the daughter was not the choice of her father, simply because he was desirous to secure the aid of the Macraes, a tribe occupying Glenshiel, remarkable for great size and courage, and known in history as "the wild Macraes." The chief – Macrae of Inverinate – readily fell in with the views of Macleod, and as the time fixed for his marriage with the lovely Lady May drew nigh, gratified triumph over his rival Munro, and hate intense as a being of such fierce passions could feel, glowed like a gleaming light in his fierce grey eyes.

"Once more," he said, "I will to the mountains to find him before the bridal. There shall be no chance of a leman crossing my married life, and none to divide the love Inverinate shall possess entire. By my father's soul, but the boy shall rue the hour he dared to cross my designs. Yes, rue it, for I swear to bring him bound to witness my marriage, and then hang him like a skulking wild-cat on Inverinate green."

It was nightfall as he spoke thus. Little he knew that at the same moment Hugh Munro was sitting beneath the dark shadows of the alder trees, which grew under the window of the little chamber where May Macleod was weeping bitterly over the sad fate from which she could see no way of escape. As she sat thus, the soft cry of the cushat fell upon her ears. Intently she listened for a few moments, and when it was repeated she stepped to the window and opened it cautiously, leaning forth upon the sill. Again the sound stole from among the foliage, and May peered down into the gloom, but nothing met her gaze save the shadows of the waving branches upon the tower wall.

"It is his signal," she whispered to herself as the sound was repeated once more. "Ah me! I fear he will get himself into danger on account of these visits, and yet I cannot, I cannot bid him stay away."

She muffled herself in a dark plaid, moved towards the door, opened it cautiously, and, listening with dread, timidly ventured down to meet her lover.

"I must and will beg him tonight to stay away in future," continued she, as she tripped cautiously down the narrow winding stair; "and yet to stay away? Ah me! it is to leave me to my misery; but it must be done, unkind as it may be, otherwise he will assuredly be captured and slain, for I fear Macrae suspects our meetings are not confined to the day and my father's presence."

After stealing through many dark passages, corridors, and staircases in out-of-the-way nooks, she emerged into the open air, through a neglected postern shadowed by a large alder, opposite the spot from which the sound proceeded.

Again she gazed into the shadow, and there leaning against a tree, growing on the edge of the crag, she saw a tall slender figure. Well she knew the outlines of that form, and fondly her heart throbbed at the sound of the voice which now addressed her.

"Dearest," said the young Munro in a low tone, "I thought thou wouldst never come. I have been standing here like a statue against the trunk of this tree for the last half-hour watching for one blink of light from thy casement. But it seems that thou preferest darkness. Ah May, dear May, cease to indulge in gloomy forebodings."

"Would that I could, Hugh," she answered sadly. "What thoughts but gloomy ones can fill my mind when I am ever thinking of the danger you incur by coming here so often, and thinking, too, of the woeful fate to which we are both destined?"

"Think no more of it," said her lover in a cheerful tone. "We have hope yet."

"Alas, there is no hope. Even this day my father hath fixed the time for, to me, this dreaded wedding! And now, Hugh, let this be our last meeting – *Mar tha mi!* our last in the world. Wert thou caught by Inverinate, he so hates thee, he would have thy life by the foulest means."

"Fear not for that, dearest. And this bridal! Listen, May; before that happens the eagle will swoop down and bear thee away to his free mountains, amid their sunny glens and bosky wood, to love thee, darling, as no other mortal, and certainly none of the Clan-'ic-Rath mhearlaich has heart to do."

"Ah me!" sighed May, "would that it could be so. I cannot leave my father until all other hope is gone, and yet I fear if I do not, we are fated to be parted. Even this may be the last time we may meet. I warn thee, Hugh, I am well watched, and I beg you will be careful. Hush! was that a footfall in the grove below the crag?" and she pointed to a clump of trees at some distance under where they were standing, and on the path by which he would return.

"By my troth it may be so," said he. "Better, dear May, retire to your chamber, and I shall remain here till you bid me good-night from your window."

Again they listened, and again the rustling met their ears distinctly. It ceased, and the maiden, bidding her mountain lover a fond good-night, ascended to her chamber, while he, disdaining to be frightened away by sound, moved to his former position below the alder tree. Seating himself at its root, with his eyes fixed on the window, in a voice low but distinct, he sang to one of the sweet sad lays of long ago a ditty to his mistress, of which the following paraphrase will convey an idea:

> "O darling May, my promised bride,
> List to my love – come fly with me,
> Where down the dark Ben Wyvis side
> The torrent dashes wild and free.
> O'er sunny glen and forest brake;

O'er meadow green and mountain grand;
O'er rocky gorge and gleaming lake –
Come – reign, the lady of the land.
"Come cheer my lonely mountain home,
Where gleams the lake, where rills dance bright;
Where flowers bloom fair – come, dearest, come,
And light my dark and starless night.
One witching gleam from thy bright eye
Can change to halls of joy my home!
One song, one softly-uttered sigh,
Can cheer my lone heart – dearest, come."

The moment the song ceased, the fair form of May Macleod appeared at the casement overhead, she waved a fond farewell to her mountain minstrel, and closed the window; but the light, deprived of her fair face, had no charm for him – he gazed once more at the pane through which it beamed like a solitary star, amid the masses of foliage, and was turning away when he found a heavy hand laid on his shoulder.

"Stay," exclaimed the intruder in a deep stern voice, whose tone the young chief knew but too well, "Thou hast a small reckoning to discharge ere thou go, my good boy. I am Macrae."

"And I," answered the other, "am Hugh Munro, what seekst thou from me?"

"That thou shalt soon know, thou skulking hill cat," answered Macrae, throwing his unbuckled sword, belt, and scabbard on the ground, and advancing with extended weapon.

"Indeed! then beware of the wild-cat's spring," Munro promptly replied, giving a sudden bound which placed him inside the guard of his antagonist, whose waist he instantly encircled with his sinewy arms with the design of hurling him over the crag on which they stood. The struggle was momentary. Munro, struck to the heart with Macrae's dagger, fell with May's loved name on his lips, while Macrae, staggering over the height, in the act of falling so wounded himself by his own weapon as to render his future life one of helpless manhood and bitter mental regret.

Macleod was soon after slain in one of the many quarrels of the time, while his daughter May, the sorrowing heiress of the broad lands of Cadboll, lived on for fifty years one long unrelieved day of suffering.

Fifty years! alas for the mourner – spring succeeded winter, and summer spring, but no change of season lightened May Macleod's burden! Fifty years! year by year passing away only brought changes to those who lived under her gentle sway, and among the dependents of her home; youth passed into age, young men and maidens filled the places of the valued attendants of her girlhood; and the lady, solitary, still a mourner, in her feudal tower grew old and bent, thin and wan, but still in her heart the love of her youth bloomed fresh for her betrothed.

And then disease laid hold of her limbs – paralyzed, unable to move, she would fain have died, but the spell of Cadboll was on her, death could not enter within its walls.

Sickness and pain, care and grief, disappointment, trust betrayed, treachery, and all the ills which life is heir to, all might and did enter there. Death alone was barred without.

Sadly her maidens listened to her heart-breaking appeals to the spirit of Munro, her unwed husband, the murdered bridegroom of her young life, to come to her aid from the land of shadows and of silence. They knew her story of the fifty years of long ago, and they pitied and grieved with her, wondering at the constancy of her woman's heart.

Still more sadly did they listen to her appeals to be carried out from the castle to the edge of the precipice, where the power of the spell ceased, there to look for, meet and welcome death; but they knew not the story of the spell, and they deemed her mad with grief.

Terrified at last by her appeals to the dead, with whom she seemed to hold continual conversation, and who seemed to be present in the chamber with them, though unseen, and partly, at length, worn out with her unceasing importunities, and partly to gratify the whim, as they considered it, of the sufferer, tremblingly they agreed to obey her requests and to carry her forth to the edge of the cliff. A frightened band, they bore the Lady May, lying on her couch, smiling with hope and blessing them for thus consenting. Over the threshold, over the drawbridge, her eyes, fixed on the heavens, brightened as they proceeded. Hope flushed with hectic glow upon her pale suffering face, grateful thanks broke from her lips. Hastening their steps, they passed through the gate, wound along the hill side, and as the broad expanse of ocean, with the fresh wind curling it into wavelets, burst upon the sight, a flash of rapture beamed on her countenance, a cry of joy rushed from her pallid lips – their feeble burden grew heavier; a murmur of welcoming delight was uttered to some glorious presence, unseen by the maidens, and all became hushed eternally. The Lady May lay on her couch a stiffening corpse. The spell of Cadboll had been broken at last. A Macleod inhabited it no more, and decay and ruin seized on the hoary pile of which now scarcely a vestige remains to tell of the former extent and feudal strength of Castle Cadboll.

Spirits, Monsters & Ghostly Tales

Introduction

TOURISTS TODAY are drawn to the 'Dark Sky Park' of deepest Galloway to experience its spectacular show of stars. In past centuries, though, Scotland's nights were frightening. Huddled anxiously around their hearths, people could not but be conscious of how tiny their lives were against the vast unknown of the universe.

What terrors did the darkness hold? We see that clearly in stories of the cruel kelpie, like 'The Doomed Rider', the mischievous spectres of the 'Bogle' stories, or the kind of monstrous giant we find in 'Peerifool'. But such stories could be more subtle, too, exploring the limits of what mortal love could hope to attain, as we see in the haunting tale of 'The Mermaid Wife'.

The Fisherman and the Merman

OF MERMEN AND MERWOMEN many strange stories are told in the Shetland Isles. Beneath the depths of the ocean, according to these stories, an atmosphere exists adapted to the respiratory organs of certain beings, resembling, in form, the human race, possessed of surpassing beauty, of limited supernatural powers, and liable to the incident of death. They dwell in a wide territory of the globe, far below the region of fishes, over which the sea, like the cloudy canopy of our sky, loftily rolls, and they possess habitations constructed of the pearl and coral productions of the ocean. Having lungs not adapted to a watery medium, but to the nature of atmospheric air, it would be impossible for them to pass through the volume of waters that intervenes between the submarine and supramarine world, if it were not for the extraordinary power they inherit of entering the skin of some animal capable of existing in the sea, which they are enabled to occupy by a sort of demoniacal possession. One shape they put on is that of an animal human above the waist, yet terminating below in the tail and fins of a fish, but the most favourite form is that of the larger seal or Haaf-fish; for, in possessing an amphibious nature, they are enabled not only to exist in the ocean, but to land on some rock, where they frequently lighten themselves of their sea-dress, resume their proper shape, and with much curiosity examine the nature of the upper world belonging to the human race. Unfortunately, however, each merman or merwoman possesses but one skin, enabling the individual to ascend the seas, and if, on visiting the abode of man, the garb be lost, the hapless being must unavoidably become an inhabitant of the earth.

A story is told of a boat's crew who landed for the purpose of attacking the seals lying in the hollows of the crags at one of the stacks. The men stunned a number of the animals, and while they were in this state stripped them of their skins, with the fat attached to them. Leaving the carcasses on the rock, the crew were about to set off for the shore of Papa Stour, when such a tremendous swell arose that everyone flew quickly to the boat. All succeeded in entering it except one man, who had imprudently lingered behind. The crew were unwilling to leave a companion to perish on the skerries, but the surge increased so fast, that after many unsuccessful attempts to bring the boat close in to the stack, the unfortunate wight was left to his fate. A stormy night came on, and the deserted Shetlander saw no prospect before him but that of perishing from cold and hunger, or of being washed into the sea by the breakers which threatened to dash over the rocks. At length, he perceived many of the seals, who, in their flight had escaped the attack of the boatmen, approach the skerry, disrobe themselves of their amphibious hides, and resume the shape of the sons and daughters of the ocean. Their first object was to assist in the recovery of their friends, who, having been stunned by clubs, had, while in that state, been deprived of their skins. When the flayed animals had regained their sensibility, they assumed their proper form of mermen or merwomen, and began to lament in a mournful lay, wildly accompanied by the storm that was raging around, the loss of their sea-dress, which would prevent them from again enjoying their native azure atmosphere, and coral mansions that lay below the deep waters of the Atlantic. But their chief lamentation was for Ollavitinus, the son of Gioga, who, having been stripped of his seal's skin, would be for ever parted from his mates, and condemned to become an outcast inhabitant of the upper world. Their song was at length broken off, by observing one of their enemies viewing, with shivering limbs and looks of comfortless despair, the wild waves that dashed over the stack. Gioga immediately conceived the idea of rendering subservient to the advantage of the son the perilous situation of the man.

She addressed him with mildness, proposing to carry him safe on her back across the sea to Papa Stour, on condition of receiving the seal-skin of Ollavitinus. A bargain was struck, and Gioga clad herself in her amphibious garb; but the Shetlander, alarmed at the sight of the stormy main that he was to ride through, prudently begged leave of the matron, for his better preservation, that he might be allowed to cut a few holes in her shoulders and flanks, in order to procure, between the skin and the flesh, a better fastening for his hands and feet. The request being complied with, the man grasped the neck of the seal, and committing himself to her care, she landed him safely at Acres Gio in Papa Stour; from which place he immediately repaired to a skeo at Hamna Voe, where the skin was deposited, and honourably fulfilled his part of the contract, by affording Gioga the means whereby her son could again revisit the ethereal space over which the sea spread its green mantle.

The Mermaid Wife

A STORY IS TOLD of an inhabitant of Unst, who, in walking on the sandy margin of a voe, saw a number of mermen and mermaids dancing by moonlight, and several seal-skins strewed beside them on the ground.

At his approach they immediately fled to secure their garbs, and, taking upon themselves the form of seals, plunged immediately into the sea. But as the Shetlander perceived that one skin lay close to his feet, he snatched it up, bore it swiftly away, and placed it in concealment. On returning to the shore he met the fairest damsel that was ever gazed upon by mortal eyes, lamenting the robbery, by which she had become an exile from her submarine friends, and a tenant of the upper world. Vainly she implored the restitution of her property; the man had drunk deeply of love, and was inexorable; but he offered her protection beneath his roof as his betrothed spouse. The merlady, perceiving that she must become an inhabitant of the earth, found that she could not do better than accept of the offer. This strange attachment subsisted for many years, and the couple had several children. The Shetlander's love for his merwife was unbounded, but his affection was coldly returned. The lady would often steal alone to the desert strand, and, on a signal being given, a large seal would make his appearance, with whom she would hold, in an unknown tongue, an anxious conference. Years had thus glided away, when it happened that one of the children, in the course of his play, found concealed beneath a stack of corn a seal's skin; and, delighted with the prize, he ran with it to his mother. Her eyes glistened with rapture – she gazed upon it as her own – as the means by which she could pass through the ocean that led to her native home. She burst forth into an ecstasy of joy, which was only moderated when she beheld her children, whom she was now about to leave; and, after hastily embracing them, she fled with all speed towards the sea-side. The husband immediately returned, learned the discovery that had taken place, ran to overtake his wife, but only arrived in time to see her transformation of shape completed – to see her, in the form of a seal, bound from the ledge of a rock into the sea. The large animal of the same kind with whom she had held a secret converse soon appeared, and evidently congratulated her, in the most tender manner, on her escape. But before she dived to unknown depths, she cast a parting glance at the wretched Shetlander, whose despairing looks excited in her breast a few transient feelings of commiseration.

"Farewell!" said she to him, "and may all good attend you. I loved you very well when I resided upon earth, but I always loved my first husband much better."

The Seal Catcher and the Merman

ONCE UPON A TIME there was a man who lived not very far from John o' Groat's house, which, as everyone knows, is in the very north of Scotland. He lived in a little cottage by the seashore, and made his living by catching seals and selling their fur, which is very valuable.

He earned a good deal of money in this way, for these creatures used to come out of the sea in large numbers, and lie on the rocks near his house basking in the sunshine, so that it was not difficult to creep up behind them and kill them.

Some of those seals were larger than others, and the country people used to call them "Roane," and whisper that they were not seals at all, but Mermen and Merwomen, who came from a country of their own, far down under the ocean, who assumed this strange disguise in order that they might pass through the water, and come up to breathe the air of this earth of ours.

But the seal catcher only laughed at them, and said that those seals were most worth killing, for their skins were so big that he got an extra price for them.

Now it chanced one day, when he was pursuing his calling, that he stabbed a seal with his hunting-knife, and whether the stroke had not been sure enough or not, I cannot say, but with a loud cry of pain the creature slipped off the rock into the sea, and disappeared under the water, carrying the knife along with it.

The seal catcher, much annoyed at his clumsiness, and also at the loss of his knife, went home to dinner in a very downcast frame of mind. On his way he met a horseman, who was so tall and so strange-looking and who rode on such a gigantic horse, that he stopped and looked at him in astonishment, wondering who he was, and from what country he came.

The stranger stopped also and asked him his trade, and on hearing that he was a seal catcher, he immediately ordered a great number of seal skins. The seal catcher was delighted, for such an order meant a large sum of money to him. But his face fell when the horseman added that it was absolutely necessary that the skins should be delivered that evening.

"I cannot do it," he said in a disappointed voice, "for the seals will not come back to the rocks again until tomorrow morning."

"I can take you to a place where there are any number of seals," answered the stranger, "if you will mount behind me on my horse and come with me."

The seal catcher agreed to this, and climbed up behind the rider, who shook his bridle rein, and off the great horse galloped at such a pace that he had much ado to keep his seat.

On and on they went, flying like the wind, until at last they came to the edge of a huge precipice, the face of which went sheer down to the sea. Here the mysterious horseman pulled up his steed with a jerk.

"Get off now," he said shortly.

The seal catcher did as he was bid, and when he found himself safe on the ground, he peeped cautiously over the edge of the cliff, to see if there were any seals lying on the rocks below.

To his astonishment he saw no rocks, only the blue sea, which came right up to the foot of the cliff.

"Where are the seals that you spoke of?" he asked anxiously, wishing that he had never set out on such a rash adventure.

"You will see presently," answered the stranger, who was attending to his horse's bridle.

The seal catcher was now thoroughly frightened, for he felt sure that some evil was about to befall him, and in such a lonely place he knew that it would be useless to cry out for help.

And it seemed as if his fears would prove only too true, for the next moment the stranger's hand was laid upon his shoulder, and he felt himself being hurled bodily over the cliff, and then he fell with a splash into the sea.

He thought that his last hour had come, and he wondered how anyone could work such a deed of wrong upon an innocent man.

But, to his astonishment, he found that some change must have passed over him, for instead of being choked by the water, he could breathe quite easily, and he and his companion, who was still close at his side, seemed to be sinking as quickly down through the sea as they had flown through the air.

Down and down they went, nobody knows how far, till at last they came to a huge arched door, which appeared to be made of pink coral, studded over with cockle-shells. It opened of its own accord, and when they entered they found themselves in a huge hall, the walls of which were formed of mother-of-pearl, and the floor of which was of sea-sand, smooth, and firm, and yellow.

The hall was crowded with occupants, but they were seals, not men, and when the seal catcher turned to his companion to ask him what it all meant, he was aghast to find that he, too, had assumed the form of a seal. He was still more aghast when he caught sight of himself in a large mirror that hung on the wall, and saw that he also no longer bore the likeness of a man, but was transformed into a nice, hairy, brown seal.

"Ah, woe to me," he said to himself, "for no fault of mine own this artful stranger hath laid some baneful charm upon me, and in this awful guise will I remain for the rest of my natural life."

At first none of the huge creatures spoke to him. For some reason or other they seemed to be very sad, and moved gently about the hall, talking quietly and mournfully to one another, or lay sadly upon the sandy floor, wiping big tears from their eyes with their soft furry fins.

But presently they began to notice him, and to whisper to one another, and presently his guide moved away from him, and disappeared through a door at the end of the hall. When he returned he held a huge knife in his hand.

"Didst thou ever see this before?" he asked, holding it out to the unfortunate seal catcher, who, to his horror, recognised his own hunting knife with which he had struck the seal in the morning, and which had been carried off by the wounded animal.

At the sight of it he fell upon his face and begged for mercy, for he at once came to the conclusion that the inhabitants of the cavern, enraged at the harm which had been wrought upon their comrade, had, in some magic way, contrived to capture him, and to bring him down to their subterranean abode, in order to wreak their vengeance upon him by killing him.

But, instead of doing so, they crowded round him, rubbing their soft noses against his fur to show their sympathy, and implored him not to put himself about, for no harm would befall him, and they would love him all their lives long if he would only do what they asked him.

"Tell me what it is," said the seal catcher, "and I will do it, if it lies within my power."

"Follow me," answered his guide, and he led the way to the door through which he had disappeared when he went to seek the knife.

The seal catcher followed him. And there, in a smaller room, he found a great brown seal lying on a bed of pale pink seaweed, with a gaping wound in his side.

"That is my father," said his guide, "whom thou wounded this morning, thinking that he was one of the common seals who live in the sea, instead of a Merman who hath speech, and understanding, as you mortals have. I brought thee hither to bind up his wounds, for no other hand than thine can heal him."

"I have no skill in the art of healing," said the seal catcher, astonished at the forbearance of these strange creatures, whom he had so unwittingly wronged; "but I will bind up the wound to the best of my power, and I am only sorry that it was my hands that caused it."

He went over to the bed, and, stooping over the wounded Merman, washed and dressed the hurt as well as he could; and the touch of his hands appeared to work like magic, for no sooner had he finished than the wound seemed to deaden and die, leaving only the scar, and the old seal sprang up, as well as ever.

Then there was great rejoicing throughout the whole Palace of the Seals. They laughed, and they talked, and they embraced each other in their own strange way, crowding round their comrade, and rubbing their noses against his, as if to show him how delighted they were at his recovery.

But all this while the seal catcher stood alone in a corner, with his mind filled with dark thoughts, for although he saw now that they had no intention of killing him, he did not relish the prospect of spending the rest of his life in the guise of a seal, fathoms deep under the ocean.

But presently, to his great joy, his guide approached him, and said, "Now you are at liberty to return home to your wife and children. I will take you to them, but only on one condition."

"And what is that?" asked the seal catcher eagerly, overjoyed at the prospect of being restored safely to the upper world, and to his family.

"That you will take a solemn oath never to wound a seal again."

"That will I do right gladly," he replied, for although the promise meant giving up his means of livelihood, he felt that if only he regained his proper shape he could always turn his hand to something else.

So he took the required oath with all due solemnity, holding up his fin as he swore, and all the other seals crowded round him as witnesses.

And a sigh of relief went through the halls when the words were spoken, for he was the most noted seal catcher in the North.

Then he bade the strange company farewell, and, accompanied by his guide, passed once more through the outer doors of coral, and up, and up, and up, through the shadowy green water, until it began to grow lighter and lighter, and at last they emerged into the sunshine of earth.

Then, with one spring, they reached the top of the cliff, where the great black horse was waiting for them, quietly nibbling the green turf.

When they left the water their strange disguise dropped from them, and they were now as they had been before, a plain seal catcher and a tall, well-dressed gentleman in riding clothes.

"Get up behind me," said the latter, as he swung himself into his saddle. The seal catcher did as he was bid, taking tight hold of his companion's coat, for he remembered how nearly he had fallen off on his previous journey.

Then it all happened as it happened before. The bridle was shaken, and the horse galloped off, and it was not long before the seal catcher found himself standing in safety before his own garden gate.

He held out his hand to say "good-bye," but as he did so the stranger pulled out a huge bag of gold and placed it in it.

"Thou hast done thy part of the bargain – we must do ours," he said. "Men shall never say that we took away an honest man's work without making reparation for it, and here is what will keep thee in comfort to thy life's end."

Then he vanished, and when the astonished seal catcher carried the bag into his cottage, and turned the gold out on the table, he found that what the stranger had said was true, and that he would be a rich man for the remainder of his days.

Peerifool

THERE WAS ONCE A KING and a Queen in Rousay who had three daughters. When the young Princesses were just grown up, the King died, and the Crown passed to a distant cousin, who had always hated him, and who paid no heed to the widowed Queen and her daughters.

So they were left very badly off, and they went to live in a tiny cottage, and did all the housework themselves. They had a kailyard in front of the cottage, and a little field behind it, and they had a cow that grazed in the field, and which they fed with the cabbages that grew in the kailyard. For everyone knows that to feed cows with cabbages makes them give a larger quantity of milk.

But they soon discovered that some one was coming at night and stealing the cabbages, and, of course, this annoyed them very much. For they knew that if they had not cabbages to give to the cow, they would not have enough milk to sell.

So the eldest Princess said she would take out a three-legged stool, and wrap herself in a blanket, and sit in the kailyard all night to see if she could catch the thief. And, although it was very cold and very dark, she did so.

At first it seemed as if all her trouble would be in vain, for hour after hour passed and nothing happened. But in the small hours of the morning, just as the clock was striking two, she heard a stealthy trampling in the field behind, as if some very heavy person were trying to tread very softly, and presently a mighty Giant stepped right over the wall into the kailyard.

He carried an enormous creel on his arm, and a large, sharp knife in his hand; and he began to cut the cabbages, and to throw them into the creel as fast as he could.

Now the Princess was no coward, so, although she had not expected to face a Giant, she gathered up her courage, and cried out sharply, "Who gave thee liberty to cut our cabbages? Leave off this minute, and go away."

The Giant paid no heed, but went on steadily with what he was doing.

"Dost thou not hear me?" cried the girl indignantly; for she was the Princess Royal, and had always been accustomed to be obeyed.

"If thou be not quiet I will take thee too," said the Giant grimly, pressing the cabbages down into the creel.

"I should like to see thee try," retorted the Princess, rising from her stool and stamping her foot; for she felt so angry that she forgot for a moment that she was only a weak maiden and he was a great and powerful Giant.

And, as if to show her how strong he was, he seized her by her arm and her leg, and put her in his creel on the top of the cabbages, and carried her away bodily.

When he reached his home, which was in a great square house on a lonely moor, he took her out, and set her down roughly on the floor.

"Thou wilt be my servant now," he said, "and keep my house, and do my errands for me. I have a cow, which thou must drive out every day to the hillside; and see, here is a bag of wool, when thou hast taken out the cow, thou must come back and settle thyself at home, as a good housewife should, and comb, and card it, and spin it into yarn, with which to weave a good thick cloth for my raiment. I am out most of the day, but when I come home I shall expect to find all this done, and a great bicker of porridge boiled besides for my supper."

The poor Princess was very dismayed when she heard these words, for she had never been accustomed to work hard, and she had always had her sisters to help her; but the Giant took no notice of her distress, but went out as soon as it was daylight, leaving her alone in the house to begin her work.

As soon as he had gone she drove the cow to the pasture, as he had told her to do; but she had a good long walk over the moor before she reached the hill, and by the time that she got back to the house she felt very tired.

So she thought that she would put on the porridge pot, and make herself some porridge before she began to card and comb the wool. She did so, and just as she was sitting down to sup them the door opened, and a crowd of wee, wee Peerie Folk came in.

They were the tiniest men and women that the Princess had ever seen; not one of them would have reached half-way to her knee; and they were dressed in dresses fashioned out of all the colours of the rainbow – scarlet and blue, green and yellow, orange and violet; and the funny thing was, that every one of them had a shock of straw-coloured yellow hair.

They were all talking and laughing with one another; and they hopped up, first on stools, then on chairs, till at last they reached the top of the table, where they clustered round the bowl, out of which the Princess was eating her porridge.

"We be hungry, we be hungry," they cried, in their tiny shrill voices. "Spare a little porridge for the Peerie Folk."

But the Princess was hungry also; and, besides being hungry, she was both tired and cross; so she shook her head and waved them impatiently away with her spoon,

"Little for one, and less for two,
And never a grain have I for you."

she said sharply, and, to her great delight, for she did not feel quite comfortable with all the Peerie Folk standing on the table looking at her, they vanished in a moment.

After this she finished her porridge in peace; then she took the wool out of the bag, and she set to work to comb and card it. But it seemed as if it were bewitched; it curled and twisted and coiled itself round her fingers so that, try as she would, she could not do anything with it. And when the Giant came home he found her sitting in despair with it all in confusion round her, and the porridge, which she had left for him in the pot, burned to a cinder.

As you may imagine, he was very angry, and raged, and stamped, and used the most dreadful words; and at last he took her by the heels, and beat her until all her back was skinned and bleeding; then he carried her out to the byre, and threw her up on the joists among the hens. And, although she was not dead, she was so stunned and bruised that she could only lie there motionless, looking down on the backs of the cows.

Time went on, and in the kailyard at home the cabbages were disappearing as fast as ever. So the second Princess said that she would do as her sister had done, and wrap herself in a blanket, and go and sit on a three-legged stool all night, to see what was becoming of them.

She did so, and exactly the same fate befell her that had befallen her elder sister. The Giant appeared with his creel, and he carried her off, and set her to mind the cow and the house, and to make his porridge and to spin; and the little yellow-headed Peerie Folk appeared and asked her for some supper, and she refused to give it to them; and after that, she could not comb or card her wool, and the Giant was angry, and he scolded her, and beat her, and threw her up, half dead, on the joists beside her sister and the hens.

Then the youngest Princess determined to sit out in the kailyard all night, not so much to see what was becoming of the cabbages, as to discover what had happened to her sisters.

And when the Giant came and carried her off, she was not at all sorry, but very glad, for she was a brave and loving little maiden; and now she felt that she had a chance of finding out where they were, and whether they were dead or alive.

So she was quite cheerful and happy, for she felt certain that she was clever enough to outwit the Giant, if only she were watchful and patient; so she lay quite quietly in her creel above the cabbages, but she kept her eyes very wide open to see by which road he was carrying her off.

And when he set her down in his kitchen, and told her all that he expected her to do, she did not look downcast like her sisters, but nodded her head brightly, and said that she felt sure that she could do it.

And she sang to herself as she drove the cow over the moor to pasture, and she ran the whole way back, so that she should have a good long afternoon to work at the wool, and, although she would not have told the Giant this, to search the house.

Before she set to work, however, she made herself some porridge, just as her sisters had done; and, just as she was going to sup them, all the little yellow-haired Peerie Folk trooped in, and climbed up on the table, and stood and stared at her.

"We be hungry, we be hungry," they cried. "Spare a little porridge for the Peerie Folk."

"With all my heart," replied the good-natured Princess. "If you can find dishes little enough for you to sup out of, I will fill them for you. But, methinks, if I were to give you all porringers, you would smother yourselves among the porridge."

At her words the Peerie Folk shouted with laughter, till their straw-coloured hair tumbled right over their faces; then they hopped on to the floor and ran out of the house, and presently they came trooping back holding cups of blue-bells, and foxgloves, and saucers of primroses and anemones in their hands; and the Princess put a tiny spoonful of porridge into each saucer, and a tiny drop of milk into each cup, and they ate it all up as daintily as possible with neat little grass spoons, which they had brought with them in their pockets.

When they had finished they all cried out, "Thank you! Thank you!" and ran out of the kitchen again, leaving the Princess alone. And, being alone, she went all over the house to look for her sisters, but, of course, she could not find them.

"Never mind, I will find them soon," she said to herself. "Tomorrow I will search the byre and the outhouses; in the meantime, I had better get on with my work." So she went back to the kitchen, and took out the bag of wool, which the Giant had told her to make into cloth.

But just as she was doing so the door opened once more, and a Yellow-Haired Peerie Boy entered. He was exactly like the other Peerie Folk who had eaten the Princess's porridge, only he was bigger, and he wore a very rich dress of grass-green velvet. He walked boldly into the middle of the kitchen and looked round him.

"Hast thou any work for me to do?" he asked. "I ken grand how to handle wool and turn it into fine thick cloth."

"I have plenty of work for anybody who asks it," replied the Princess; "but I have no money to pay for it, and there are but few folk in this world who will work without wages."

"All the wages that I ask is that thou wilt take the trouble to find out my name, for few folk ken it, and few folk care to ken. But if by any chance thou canst not find it out, then must thou pay toll of half of thy cloth."

The Princess thought that it would be quite an easy thing to find out the Boy's name, so she agreed to the bargain, and, putting all the wool back into the bag, she gave it to him, and he swung it over his shoulder and departed.

She ran to the door to see where he went, for she had made up her mind that she would follow him secretly to his home, and find out from the neighbours what his name was.

But, to her great dismay, though she looked this way and that, he had vanished completely, and she began to wonder what she should do if the Giant came back and found that she had allowed someone, whose name she did not even know, to carry off all the wool.

And, as the afternoon wore on, and she could think of no way of finding out who the boy was, or where he came from, she felt that she had made a great mistake, and she began to grow very frightened.

Just as the gloaming was beginning to fall a knock came at the door, and, when she opened it, she found an old woman standing outside, who begged for a night's lodging.

Now, as I have told you, the Princess was very kind-hearted, and she would fain have granted the poor old Dame's request, but she dared not, for she did not know what the Giant would say. So she told the old woman that she could not take her in for the night, as she was only a servant, and not the mistress of the house; but she made her sit down on a bench beside the door, and brought her out some bread and milk, and gave her some water to bathe her poor, tired feet.

She was so bonnie, and gentle, and kind, and she looked so sorry when she told her that she would need to turn her away, that the old woman gave her her blessing, and told her not to vex herself, as it was a fine, dry night, and now that she had had a meal she could easily sit down somewhere and sleep in the shelter of the outhouses.

And, when she had finished her bread and milk, she went and laid down by the side of a green knowe, which rose out of the moor not very far from the byre door.

And, strange to say, as she lay there she felt the earth beneath her getting warmer and warmer, until she was so hot that she was fain to crawl up the side of the hillock, in the hope of getting a mouthful of fresh air.

And as she got near the top she heard a voice, which seemed to come from somewhere beneath her, saying, "tease, teasens, tease; card, cardens, card; spin, spinners, spin; for Peerifool Peerifool, Peerifool is what men call me." And when she got to the very top, she found that there was a crack in the earth, through which rays of light were coming; and when she put her eye to the crack, what should she see down below her but a brilliantly lighted chamber, in which all the Peerie Folk were sitting in a circle, working away as hard as they could.

Some of them were carding wool, some of them were combing it, some of them were spinning it, constantly wetting their fingers with their lips, in order to twist the yarn fine as they drew it from the distaff, and some of them were spinning the yarn into cloth.

While round and round the circle, cracking a little whip, and urging them to work faster, was a Yellow-Haired Peerie Boy.

"This is a strange thing, and these be queer on-goings," said the old woman to herself, creeping hastily down to the bottom of the hillock again. "I must e'en go and tell the bonnie lassie in the house yonder. Maybe the knowledge of what I have seen will stand her in good stead some day. When there be Peerie Folk about, it is well to be on one's guard."

So she went back to the house and told the Princess all that she had seen and heard, and the Princess was so delighted with what she had told her that she risked the Giant's wrath and allowed her to go and sleep in the hayloft.

It was not very long after the old woman had gone to rest before the door opened, and the Peerie Boy appeared once more with a number of webs of cloth upon his shoulder. "Here is thy cloth," he said, with a sly smile, "and I will put it on the shelf for thee the moment that thou tellest me what my name is."

Then the Princess, who was a merry maiden, thought that she would tease the little fellow for a time ere she let him know that she had found out his secret.

So she mentioned first one name and then another, always pretending to think that she had hit upon the right one; and all the time the Peerie Boy jumped from side to side with delight, for he thought that she would never find out the right name, and that half of the cloth would be his.

But at last the Princess grew tired of joking, and she cried out, with a little laugh of triumph, "Dost thou by any chance ken anyone called Peerifool, little Mannikin?"

Then he knew that in some way she had found out what men called him, and he was so angry and disappointed that he flung the webs of cloth down in a heap on the floor, and ran out at the door, slamming it behind him.

Meanwhile the Giant was coming down the hill in the darkening, and, to his astonishment, he met a troop of little Peerie Folk toiling up it, looking as if they were so tired that they could hardly get along. Their eyes were dim and listless, their heads were hanging on their breasts, and their lips were so long and twisted that the poor little people looked quite hideous.

The Giant asked how this was, and they told him that they had to work so hard all day, spinning for their Master that they were quite exhausted; and that the reason why their lips were so distorted was that they used them constantly to wet their fingers, so that they might pull the wool in very fine strands from the distaff.

"I always thought a great deal of women who could spin," said the Giant, "and I looked out for a housewife that could do so. But after this I will be more careful, for the housewife that I have now is a bonnie little woman, and I would be loth to have her spoil her face in that manner."

And he hurried home in a great state of mind in case he should find that his new servant's pretty red lips had grown long and ugly in his absence.

Great was his relief to see her standing by the table, bonnie and winsome as ever, with all the webs of cloth in a pile in front of her.

"By my troth, thou art an industrious maiden," he said, in high good humour, "and, as a reward for working so diligently, I will restore thy sisters to thee." And he went out to the byre, and lifted the two other Princesses down from the rafters, and brought them in and laid them on the settle.

Their little sister nearly screamed aloud when she saw how ill they looked and how bruised their backs were, but, like a prudent maiden, she held her tongue, and busied herself with applying a cooling ointment to their wounds, and binding them up, and by and by her sisters revived, and, after the Giant had gone to bed, they told her all that had befallen them.

"I will be avenged on him for his cruelty," said the little Princess firmly; and when she spoke like that her sisters knew that she meant what she said.

So next morning, before the Giant was up, she fetched his creel, and put her eldest sister into it, and covered her with all the fine silken hangings and tapestry that she could find, and on the top of all she put a handful of grass, and when the Giant came downstairs she asked him, in her sweetest tone, if he would do her a favour.

And the Giant, who was very pleased with her because of the quantity of cloth which he thought she had spun, said that he would.

"Then carry that creelful of grass home to my mother's cottage for her cow to eat," said the Princess. "'Twill help to make up for all the cabbages which thou hast stolen from her kailyard."

And, wonderful to relate, the Giant did as he was bid, and carried the creel to the cottage.

Next morning she put her second sister into another creel, and covered her with all the fine napery she could find in the house, and put an armful of grass on the top of it, and at her bidding the Giant, who was really getting very fond of her, carried it also home to her mother.

The next morning the little Princess told him that she thought that she would go for a long walk after she had done her housework, and that she might not be in when he came home at night, but that she would have another creel of grass ready for him, if he would carry it to the cottage as he had done on the two previous evenings. He promised to do so; then, as usual, he went out for the day.

In the afternoon the clever little maiden went through the house, gathering together all the lace, and silver, and jewellery that she could find, and brought them and placed them beside the creel. Then she went out and cut an armful of grass, and brought it in and laid it beside them.

Then she crept into the creel herself, and pulled all the fine things in above her, and then she covered everything up with the grass, which was a very difficult thing to do, seeing she herself was at the bottom of the basket. Then she lay quite still and waited.

Presently the Giant came in, and, obedient to his promise, he lifted the creel and carried it off to the old Queen's cottage.

No one seemed to be at home, so he set it down in the entry, and turned to go away. But the little Princess had told her sisters what to do, and they had a great can of boiling water ready in one of the rooms upstairs, and when they heard his steps coming round that side of the house, they threw open the window and emptied it all over his head; and that was the end of him.

The Doomed Rider

"THE CONAN IS AS BONNY a river as we hae in a' the north country. There's mony a sweet sunny spot on its banks, an' mony a time an' aft hae I waded through its shallows, whan a boy, to set my little scautling-line for the trouts an' the eels, or to gather the big pearl-mussels that lie sae thick in the fords.

But its bonny wooded banks are places for enjoying the day in – no for passing the nicht. I kenna how it is; it's nane o' your wild streams that wander desolate through a desert country, like the Aven, or that come rushing down in foam and thunder, ower broken rocks, like the Foyers, or that wallow in darkness, deep, deep in the bowels o' the earth, like the fearfu' Auldgraunt; an' yet no ane o' these rivers has mair or frightfuller stories connected wi' it than the Conan. Ane can hardly saunter ower half-a-mile in its course, frae where it leaves Coutin till where it enters the sea, without passing ower the scene o' some frightful auld legend o' the kelpie or the waterwraith. And ane o' the most frightful looking o' these places is to be found among the woods of Conan House. Ye enter a swampy meadow that waves wi' flags an' rushes like a corn-field in harvest, an' see a hillock covered wi' willows rising like an island in the midst. There are thick mirk-woods on ilka side; the river, dark an' awesome, an' whirling round an' round in mossy eddies, sweeps away behind it; an' there is an auld burying-ground, wi' the broken ruins o' an auld Papist kirk, on the tap. Ane can see amang the rougher stanes the rose-wrought mullions of an arched window, an' the trough that ance held the holy water. About twa hunder years ago – a wee mair maybe, or a wee less, for ane canna be very sure o' the date o' thae old stories – the building was entire; an' a spot near it, whar the wood now grows thickest, was laid out in a corn-field. The marks o' the furrows may still be seen amang the trees.

"A party o' Highlanders were busily engaged, ae day in harvest, in cutting down the corn o' that field; an' just aboot noon, when the sun shone brightest an' they were busiest in the work, they heard a voice frae the river exclaim: 'The hour but not the man has come.' Sure enough, on looking round, there was the kelpie stan'in' in what they ca' a fause ford, just fornent the auld kirk. There is a deep black pool baith aboon an' below, but i' the ford there's a bonny ripple, that shows, as ane might think, but little depth o' water; an' just i' the middle o' that, in a place where a horse might swim, stood the kelpie. An' it again repeated its words: 'The hour but not the man has come,' an' then flashing through the water like a drake, it disappeared in the lower pool. When the folk stood wondering what the creature might mean, they saw a man on horseback come spurring down the hill in hot haste, making straight for the fause ford. They could then understand her words at ance; an' four o' the stoutest o' them sprang oot frae amang the corn to warn him o' his danger, an' keep him back. An' sae they tauld him what they had seen an' heard, an' urged him either to turn back an' tak' anither road, or stay for an hour or sae where he was. But he just wadna hear them, for he was baith unbelieving an' in haste, an' wauld hae taen the ford for a' they could say, hadna the Highlanders, determined on saving him whether he would or no, gathered round him an' pulled him frae his horse, an' then, to mak' sure o' him, locked him up in the auld kirk. Weel, when the hour had gone by – the fatal hour o' the kelpie – they flung open the door, an' cried to him that he might noo gang on his journey. Ah! but there was nae answer, though; an' sae they cried a second time, an' there was nae answer still; an' then they went in, an' found him lying stiff an' cauld on the floor, wi' his face buried in the water o' the very stone trough that we may still see amang the ruins.

His hour had come, an' he had fallen in a fit, as 'twould seem, head-foremost amang the water o' the trough, where he had been smothered, – an' sae ye see, the prophecy o' the kelpie availed naething."

Michael Scott

IN THE EARLY PART of Michael Scott's life he was in the habit of emigrating annually to the Scottish metropolis, for the purpose of being employed in his capacity of mason. One time as he and two companions were journeying to the place of their destination for a similar object, they had occasion to pass over a high hill, the name of which is not mentioned, but which is supposed to have been one of the Grampians, and being fatigued with climbing, they sat down to rest themselves. They had no sooner done so than they were warned to take to their heels by the hissing of a large serpent, which they observed revolving itself towards them with great velocity. Terrified at the sight, Michael's two companions fled, while he, on the contrary, resolved to encounter the reptile.

The appalling monster approached Michael Scott with distended mouth and forked tongue; and, throwing itself into a coil at his feet, was raising its head to inflict a mortal sting, when Michael, with one stroke of his stick, severed its body into three pieces. Having rejoined his affrighted comrades, they resumed their journey; and, on arriving at the next public-house, it being late, and the travellers being weary, they took up their quarters at it for the night. In the course of the night's conversation, reference was naturally made to Michael's recent exploit with the serpent, when the landlady of the house, who was remarkable for her 'arts,' happened to be present. Her curiosity appeared much excited by the conversation; and, after making some inquiries regarding the colour of the serpent, which she was told was white, she offered any of them that would procure her the middle piece such a tempting reward, as induced one of the party instantly to go for it. The distance was not very great; and on reaching the spot, he found the middle and tail piece in the place where Michael left them, but the head piece was gone.

The landlady on receiving the piece, which still vibrated with life, seemed highly gratified at her acquisition; and, over and above the promised reward, regaled her lodgers very plentifully with the choicest dainties in her house. Fired with curiosity to know the purpose for which the serpent was intended, the wily Michael Scott was immediately seized with a severe fit of indisposition, which caused him to prefer the request that he might be allowed to sleep beside the fire, the warmth of which, he affirmed, was in the highest degree beneficial to him.

Never suspecting Michael Scott's hypocrisy, and naturally supposing that a person so severely indisposed would feel very little curiosity about the contents of any cooking utensils which might lie around the fire, the landlady allowed his request. As soon as the other inmates of the house were retired to bed, the landlady resorted to her darling occupation; and, in his feigned state of indisposition, Michael had a favourable opportunity of watching most scrupulously all her actions through the keyhole of a door leading to the next apartment where she was. He could see the rites and ceremonies with which the serpent was put into the oven, along with many mysterious ingredients. After which the unsuspicious landlady placed the dish by the fireside, where lay the distressed traveller, to stove till the morning.

Once or twice in the course of the night the 'wife of the change-house,' under the pretence of inquiring for her sick lodger, and administering to him some renovating cordials, the beneficial effects of which he gratefully acknowledged, took occasion to dip her finger in her saucepan, upon which the cock, perched on his roost, crowed aloud. All Michael's sickness could not prevent him considering very inquisitively the landlady's cantrips, and particularly the influence of the sauce upon the crowing of the cock. Nor could he dissipate some inward desires he felt to follow her example. At the same time, he suspected that Satan had a hand in the pie, yet he thought he would like very much to be at the bottom of the concern; and thus his reason and his curiosity clashed against each other for the space of several hours. At length passion, as is too often the case, became the conqueror. Michael, too, dipped his finger in the sauce, and applied it to the tip of his tongue, and immediately the cock perched on the spardan announced the circumstance in a mournful clarion. Instantly his mind received a new light to which he was formerly a stranger, and the astonished dupe of a landlady now found it her interest to admit her sagacious lodger into a knowledge of the remainder of her secrets.

Endowed with the knowledge of 'good and evil,' and all the 'second sights' that can be acquired, Michael left his lodgings in the morning, with the philosopher's stone in his pocket. By daily perfecting his supernatural attainments, by new series of discoveries, he became more than a match for Satan himself. Having seduced some thousands of Satan's best workmen into his employment, he trained them up so successfully to the architective business, and inspired them with such industrious habits, that he was more than sufficient for all the architectural work of the empire. To establish this assertion, we need only refer to some remains of his workmanship still existing north of the Grampians, some of them, stupendous bridges built by him in one short night, with no other visible agents than two or three workmen.

On one occasion work was getting scarce, as might have been naturally expected, and his workmen, as they were wont, flocked to his doors, perpetually exclaiming, "Work! work! work!" Continually annoyed by their incessant entreaties, he called out to them in derision to go and make a dry road from Fortrose to Ardersier, over the Moray Firth. Immediately their cry ceased, and as Scott supposed it wholly impossible for them to execute his order, he retired to rest, laughing most heartily at the chimerical sort of employment he had given to his industrious workmen. Early in the morning, however, he got up and took a walk at the break of day down to the shore to divert himself at the fruitless labours of his zealous workmen. But on reaching the spot, what was his astonishment to find the formidable piece of work allotted to them only a few hours before already nearly finished. Seeing the great damage the commercial class of the community would sustain from the operation, he ordered the workmen to demolish the most part of their work; leaving, however, the point of Fortrose to show the traveller to this day the wonderful exploit of Michael Scott's fairies.

On being thus again thrown out of employment, their former clamour was resumed, nor could Michael Scott, with all his sagacity, devise a plan to keep them in innocent employment. He at length discovered one. "Go," says he, "and manufacture me ropes that will carry me to the back of the moon, of these materials – miller's-sudds and sea-sand." Michael Scott here obtained rest from his active operators; for, when other work failed them, he always despatched them to their rope manufactory. But though these agents could never make proper ropes of those materials, their efforts to that effect are far from being contemptible, for some of their ropes are seen by the sea-side to this day.

We shall close our notice of Michael Scott by reciting one anecdote of him in the latter part of his life.

In consequence of a violent quarrel which Michael Scott once had with a person whom he conceived to have caused him some injury, he resolved, as the highest punishment he could inflict upon him, to send his adversary to that evil place designed only for Satan and his black companions. He accordingly, by means of his supernatural machinations, sent the poor unfortunate man thither; and had he been sent by any other means than those of Michael Scott, he would no doubt have met with a warm reception. Out of pure spite to Michael, however, when Satan learned who was his billet-master, he would no more receive him than he would receive the Wife of Beth; and instead of treating the unfortunate man with the harshness characteristic of him, he showed him considerable civilities. Introducing him to his 'Ben Taigh,' he directed her to show the stranger any curiosities he might wish to see, hinting very significantly that he had provided some accommodation for their mutual friend, Michael Scott, the sight of which might afford him some gratification. The polite housekeeper accordingly conducted the stranger through the principal apartments in the house, where he saw fearful sights. But the bed of Michael Scott! – his greatest enemy could not but feel satiated with revenge at the sight of it. It was a place too horrid to be described, filled promiscuously with all the awful brutes imaginable. Toads and lions, lizards and leeches, and, amongst the rest, not the least conspicuous, a large serpent gaping for Michael Scott, with its mouth wide open. This last sight having satisfied the stranger's curiosity, he was led to the outer gate, and came away. He reached his friends, and, among other pieces of news touching his travels, he was not backward in relating the entertainment that awaited his friend Michael Scott, as soon as he would 'stretch his foot' for the other world. But Michael did not at all appear disconcerted at his friend's intelligence. He affirmed that he would disappoint all his enemies in their expectations – in proof of which he gave the following signs: "When I am just dead," says he, "open my breast and extract my heart. Carry it to some place where the public may see the result. You will then transfix it upon a long pole, and if Satan will have my soul, he will come in the likeness of a black raven and carry it off; and if my soul will be saved it will be carried off by a white dove."

His friends faithfully obeyed his instructions. Having exhibited his heart in the manner directed, a large black raven was observed to come from the east with great fleetness, while a white dove came from the west with equal velocity. The raven made a furious dash at the heart, missing which, it was unable to curb its force, till it was considerably past it; and the dove, reaching the spot at the same time, carried off the heart amidst the rejoicing and ejaculations of the spectators.

The Battle of the Birds

THERE WAS ONCE A TIME when every creature and bird was gathering to battle. The son of the king of Tethertown said, that he would go to see the battle, and that he would bring sure word home to his father the king, who would be king of the creatures this year. The battle was over before he arrived all but one (fight), between a great black raven and a snake, and it seemed as if the snake would get the victory over the raven. When the King's son saw this, he helped the raven, and with one blow takes the head off the snake. When the raven had taken breath, and saw that the snake was dead, he said, "For thy kindness to me this day, I will give thee a sight. Come up now on the root of my two wings." The king's son mounted upon the raven, and, before he stopped, he took him over seven Bens, and seven Glens, and seven Mountain Moors.

"Now," said the raven, "seest thou that house yonder? Go now to it. It is a sister of mine that makes her dwelling in it; and I will go bail that thou art welcome. And if she asks thee, Wert thou at the battle of the birds? say thou that thou wert. And if she asks, Didst thou see my likeness? say that thou sawest it. But be sure that thou meetest me tomorrow morning here, in this place." The king's son got good and right good treatment this night. Meat of each meat, drink of each drink, warm water to his feet, and a soft bed for his limbs.

On the next day the raven gave him the same sight over seven Bens, and seven Glens, and seven Mountain moors. They saw a bothy far off, but, though far off, they were soon there. He got good treatment this night, as before – plenty of meat and drink, and warm water to his feet, and a soft bed to his limbs – and on the next day it was the same thing.

On the third morning, instead of seeing the raven as at the other times, who should meet him but the handsomest lad he ever saw, with a bundle in his hand. The king's son asked this lad if he had seen a big black raven. Said the lad to him, "Thou wilt never see the raven again, for I am that raven. I was put under spells; it was meeting thee that loosed me, and for that thou art getting this bundle. Now," said the lad, "thou wilt turn back on the self-same steps, and thou wilt lie a night in each house, as thou wert before; but thy lot is not to lose the bundle which I gave thee, till thou art in the place where thou wouldst most wish to dwell."

The king's son turned his back to the lad, and his face to his father's house; and he got lodging from the raven's sisters, just as he got it when going forward. When he was nearing his father's house he was going through a close wood. It seemed to him that the bundle was growing heavy, and he thought be would look what was in it.

When he loosed the bundle, it was not without astonishing himself. In a twinkling he sees the very grandest place he ever saw. A great castle, and an orchard about the castle, in which was every kind of fruit and herb. He stood full of wonder and regret for having loosed the bundle – it was not in his power to put it back again – and he would have wished this pretty place to be in the pretty little green hollow that was opposite his father's house; but, at one glance, he sees a great giant coming towards him.

"Bad's the place where thou hast built thy house, king's son," says the giant. "Yes, but it is not here I would wish it to be, though it happened to be here by mishap," says the king's son. "What's the reward thou wouldst give me for putting it back in the bundle as it was before?" "What's the reward thou wouldst ask?" says the king's son. "If thou wilt give me the first son thou hast when he is seven years of age," says the giant. "Thou wilt get that if I have a son," said the king's son.

In a twinkling the giant put each garden, and orchard, and castle in the bundle as they were before. "Now," says the giant, "take thou thine own road, and I will take my road; but mind thy promise, and though thou shouldst forget, I will remember."

The king's son took to the road, and at the end of a few days he reached the place he was fondest of. He loosed the bundle, and the same place was just as it was before. And when he opened the castle-door he sees the handsomest maiden he ever cast eye upon. "Advance, king's son," said the pretty maid; "everything is in order for thee, if thou, wilt marry me this very night." "It's I am the man that is willing," said the king's son. And on the same night they married.

But at the end of a day and seven years, what great man is seen coming to the castle but the giant. The king's son minded his promise to the giant, and till now he had not told his promise to the queen. "Leave thou (the matter) between me and the giant," says the queen.

"Turn out thy son," says the giant; "mind your promise." "Thou wilt get that," says the king, "when his mother puts him in order for his journey." The queen arrayed the cook's son, and she gave him to the giant by the hand. The giant went away with him; but he had not gone far when he put a rod in the hand of the little laddie. The giant asked him – "If thy father had that rod what would he do with it?" "If my father had that rod he would beat the dogs and the cats, if they would be going near the king's meat," said the little laddie. "Thou'rt the cook's son," said the giant. He catches him by the two small ankles and knocks him – "Sgleog" – against the stone that was beside him. The giant turned back to the castle in rage and madness, and he said that if they did not turn out the king's son to him, the highest stone of the castle would be the lowest. Said the queen to the king, "we'll try it yet; the butler's son is of the same age as our son." She arrayed the butler's son, and she gives him to the giant by the hand. The giant had not gone far when he put the rod in his hand. "If thy father had that rod," says the giant, "what would he do with it?" "He would beat the dogs and the cats when they would be coming near the king's bottles and glasses." "Thou art the son of the butler," says the giant, and dashed his brains out too. The giant returned in very great rage and anger. The earth shook under the sole of his feet, and the castle shook and all that was in it. "Out here thy son," says the giant, "or in a twinkling the stone that is highest in the dwelling will be the lowest." So needs must they had to give the king's son to the giant.

The giant took him to his own house, and he reared him as his own son. On a day of days when the giant was from home, the lad heard the sweetest music he ever heard in a room at the top of the giant's house. At a glance he saw the finest face he had ever seen. She beckoned to him to come a bit nearer to her, and she told him to go this time, but to be sure to be at the same place about that dead midnight.

And as he promised he did. The giant's daughter was at his side in a twinkling, and she said, "Tomorrow thou wilt get the choice of my two sisters to marry; but say thou that thou wilt not take either, but me. My father wants me to marry the son of the king of the Green City, but I don't like him." On the morrow the giant took out his three daughters, and he said, "Now son of the king of Tethertown, thou hast not lost by living with me so long. Thou wilt get to wife one of the two eldest of my daughters, and with her leave to go home with her the day after the wedding." "If thou wilt give me this pretty little one," says the king's son, "I will take thee at thy word."

The giant's wrath kindled, and he said, "Before thou gett'st her thou must do the three things that I ask thee to do." "Say on," says the king's son. The giant took him to the byre. "Now," says the giant, "the dung of a hundred cattle is here, and it has not been cleansed for seven years. I am going from home today, and if this byre is not cleaned before night comes, so clean that a golden apple will run from end to end of it, not only thou shalt not get my daughter, but 'tis a drink of thy blood that will quench my thirst this night." He begins cleaning the byre, but it was just as well to keep baling the great ocean. After midday, when sweat was blinding him, the giant's young daughter came where he was, and she said to him, "Thou art being punished, king's son." "I am that," says the king's son. "Come over," says she, "and lay down thy weariness." "I will do that," says he, "there is but death awaiting me, at any rate." He sat down near her. He was so tired that he fell asleep beside her. When he awoke, the giant's daughter was not to be seen, but the byre was so well cleaned that a golden apple would run from end to end of it. In comes the giant, and he said, "Thou hast cleaned the byre, king's son?" "I have cleaned it," says he. "Somebody cleaned it," says the giant. "Thou didst not clean it, at all events," said the king's son. "Yes, yes!" says the giant, "since thou wert so active today, thou wilt get to this time tomorrow to thatch this byre with birds' down – birds with no two feathers of one colour." The king's son was on foot before the sun; he caught up his bow and his quiver of arrows to kill the birds. He took to the moors, but if he did, the birds were not so easy to take. He was running after them till the sweat was blinding him. About mid-day who should come but the giant's daughter. "Thou art exhausting thyself, king's son," says she. "I am," said he. "There fell but these two blackbirds, and both of one colour." "Come over and lay down thy weariness on this pretty hillock," says the giant's daughter. "It's I am willing," said he.

He thought she would aid him this time, too, and he sat down near her, and he was not long there till he fell asleep.

When he awoke, the giant's daughter was gone.

He thought he would go back to the house, and he sees the byre thatched with the feathers. When the giant came home, he said, "Thou hast thatched the byre, king's son?" "I thatched it," says he. "Somebody thatched it," says the giant. "Thou didst not thatch it," says the king's son. "Yes, yes!" says the giant. "Now," says the giant, "there is a fir-tree beside that loch down there, and there is a magpie's nest in its top. The eggs thou wilt find in the nest. I must have them for my first meal. Not one must be burst or broken, and there are five in the nest." Early in the morning the king's son went where the tree was, and that tree was not hard to hit upon. Its match was not in the whole wood. From the foot to the first branch was five hundred feet. The king's son was going all round the tree. She came who was always bringing help to him; "Thou art losing the skin of thy hands and feet." "Ach! I am," says he. "I am no sooner up than down." "This is no time for stopping," says the giant's daughter. She thrust finger after finger into the tree, till she made a ladder for the king's son to go up to the magpie's nest. When he was at the nest, she said, "Make haste now with the eggs, for my father's breath is burning my back." In his hurry she left her little finger in the top of the tree. "Now," says she, "thou wilt go home with the eggs quickly, and thou wilt get me to marry tonight if thou canst know me. I and my two sisters will be arrayed in the same garments, and made like each other, but look at me when my father says, Go to thy wife, king's son; and thou wilt see a hand without a, little finger." He gave the eggs to the giant. "Yes, yes!" says the giant, "be making ready for thy marriage."

Then indeed there was a wedding, and it was a wedding! Giants and gentlemen, and the son of the king of the Green City was in the midst of them. They were married, and the dancing began, and that was a dance? The giant's house was shaking from top to bottom. But bed time came, and the giant said, "It is time for thee to go to rest, son of the king of Tethertown; take thy bride with thee from amidst those."

She put out the hand off which the little finger was, and he caught her by the hand.

"Thou hast aimed well this time too; but there is no knowing but we may meet thee another way," said the giant.

But to rest they went. "Now," says she, "sleep not, or else thou diest. We must fly quick, quick, or for certain my father will kill thee."

Out they went, and on the blue gray filly in the stable they mounted. "Stop a while," says she, "and I will play a trick to the old hero." She jumped in, and cut an apple into nine shares, and she put two shares at the head of the bed, and two shares at the foot of the bed, and two shares at the door of the kitchen, and two shares at the big door, and one outside the house.

The giant awoke and called, "Are you asleep?" "We are not yet," said the apple that was at the head of the bed. At the end of a while he called again. "We are not yet," said the apple that was at the foot of the bed. A while after this he called again. "We are not yet," said the apple at the kitchen door. The giant called again. The apple that was at the big door answered "You are now going far from me," says the giant. "We are not yet," says the apple that was outside the house. "You are flying," says the giant.

The giant jumped on his feet, and to the bed he went, but it was cold – empty.

"My own daughter's tricks are trying me," said the giant. "Here's after them," says he.

In the mouth of day, the giant's daughter said that her father's breath was burning her back. "Put thy hand, quick," said she, "in the ear of the gray filly, and whatever thou findest in it, throw it behind thee." "There is a twig of sloe tree," said he. "Throw it behind thee," said she.

No sooner did he that, than there were twenty miles of black thorn wood, so thick that scarce a weasel could go through it. The giant came headlong, and there he is fleecing his head and neck in the thorns.

"My own daughter's tricks are here as before," said the giant; "but if I had my own big axe and wood knife here, I would not be long making a way through this." He went home for the big axe and the wood knife, and sure he was not long on his journey, and he was the boy behind the big axe. He was not long making a way through the black thorn. "I will leave the axe and the wood knife here till I return," says he.

"If thou leave them," said a Hoodie that was in a tree, "we will steal them."

"You will do that same," says the giant, "but I will set them home." He returned and left them at the house. At the heat of day the giant's daughter felt her father's breath burning her back.

"Put thy finger in the filly's ear, and throw behind thee whatever thou findest in it." He got a splinter of gray stone, and in a twinkling there were twenty miles, by breadth and height, of great gray rock behind them. The giant came full pelt, but past the rock he could not go.

"The tricks of my own daughter are the hardest things that ever met me," says the giant; "but if I had my lever and my mighty mattock, I would not be long making my way through this rock also." There was no help for it, but to turn the chase for them; and he was the boy to split the stones. He was not lone, making a road through the rock. "I will leave the tools here, and I will return no more." "If thou leave them," says the hoodie, "we will steal them." "Do that if thou wilt; there is no time too go back." At the time of breaking the watch, the giant's daughter said that she was feeling her father's breath burning her back. "Look in the filly's ear, king's son, or else we are lost." He did so, and it was a bladder of water that was in her ear this time. He threw it behind him and there was a fresh-water loch, twenty miles in length and breadth, behind them.

The giant came on, but with the speed he had on him, he was in the middle of the loch, and he went under, and he rose no more.

On the next day the young companions were come in sight of his father's house. "Now," said she, "my father is drowned, and he won't trouble us any more; but before we go further," says she, "go thou to thy father's house, and tell that thou hast the like of me but this is thy lot, let neither man nor creature kiss thee, for if thou dost thou wilt not remember that thou hast ever seen me." Every one he met was giving him welcome and luck, and he charged his father and mother not to kiss him; but as mishap was to be, an old greyhound was in and she knew him, and jumped up to his mouth, and after that he did not remember the giant's daughter.

She was sitting at the well's side as he left her, but the king's son was not coming. In the mouth of night she climbed up into a tree of oak that was beside the well, and she lay in the fork of the tree all that night. A shoemaker had a house near the well, and about mid-day on the morrow, the shoemaker asked his wife to go for a drink for him out of the well. When the shoemaker's wife reached the well, and when she saw the shadow of her that was in the tree, thinking of it that it was her own shadow – and she never thought till now that she was so handsome – she gave a cast to the dish that was in her hand, and it was broken on the ground, and she took herself to the house without vessel or water.

"Where is the water, wife?" said the shoemaker. "Thou shambling, contemptible old carle, without grace, I have stayed too long thy water and wood thrall." "I am thinking, wife, that thou hast turned crazy. Go thou, daughter, quickly, and fetch a drink for thy father." His daughter went, and in the same way so it happened to her. She never thought till now that she was so loveable, and she took herself home. "Up with the drink," said her father. "Thou hume-spun shoe carle, dost thou think that I am fit to be thy thrall." The poor shoemaker thought that they had taken a turn in their understandings, and he went himself to the well. He saw the shadow of the maiden in the well, and he looked up to the tree, and he sees the finest woman he ever saw. "Thy seat is wavering, but thy face is fair," said the shoemaker. "Come down, for there is need of thee for a short while at my house." The shoemaker understood that this was the shadow that had driven his people mad. The shoemaker took her to his house, and he said that he had but a poor bothy, but that she should get a share of all that was in it. At the end of a day or two came a leash of gentlemen lads to the shoemaker's house for shoes to be made them, for the king had come home, and he was going to marry. The glance the lads gave they saw the giant's daughter, and if they saw her, they never saw one so pretty as she. "'Tis thou hast the pretty daughter here," said the lads to the shoe-maker. "She is pretty, indeed," says the shoemaker, "but she is no daughter of mine." "St Nail!" said one of them, "I would give a hundred pounds to marry her." The two others said the very same. The poor shoemaker said that he had nothing to do with her. "But," said they, "ask her tonight, and send us word tomorrow." When the gentles went away, she asked the shoemaker – "What's that they were saying about me?" The shoemaker told her. "Go thou after them," said she; "I will marry one of them, and let him bring his purse with him." The youth returned, and he gave the shoemaker a hundred pounds for tocher. They went to rest, and when she had laid down, she asked the lad for a drink of water from a tumbler that was on the board on the further side of the chamber. He went; but out of that he could not come, as he held the vessel of water the length of the night. "Thou lad," said she, "why wilt thou not lie down?" but out of that he could not drag till the bright morrow's day was. The shoemaker came to the door of the chamber, and she asked him to take away that lubberly boy. This wooer went and betook himself to his home, but he did not tell the other two how it happened to him. Next came the second chap, and in the same way, – when she had gone to rest – "Look," she said, "if the latch is on the door." The latch laid hold of his hands, and out of that he could not come the length of the night, and out of that he did not come till the morrow's day was bright. He went, under shame and disgrace. No matter, he did not tell the other chap how it had happened, and on the third night he came. As it happened to the two others, so it happened to him. One foot stuck to the floor; he could neither come nor go, but so he was the length of the night. On the morrow, he took his soles out (of that), and he was not seen looking behind him. "Now," said the girl to the shoemaker, "thine is the sporran of gold; I have no need of it. It will better thee, and I am no worse for thy kindness to me." The shoemaker had the shoes ready, and on that very day the king was to be married. The shoemaker was going to the castle with the shoes of the young people, and the girl said to the shoemaker, "I would like to get a sight of the king's son before he marries." "Come with me," says the shoemaker, "I am well acquainted with the servants at the castle, and thou shalt get a sight of the king's son and all the company." And when the gentles saw the pretty woman that was here they took her to the wedding-room, and they filled for her a glass of wine. When she was going to drink what is in it, a flame went up out of the glass, and a golden pigeon and a silver pigeon sprung out of it, They were flying about when three grains of barley fell on the floor. The silver pigeon sprang, and he eats that. Said the golden pigeon to him, "If thou hadst mind when I cleared the byre, thou wouldst not eat that without giving me a share." Again fell three other grains of barley, and the silver pigeon sprang, and he eats that, as before. "If thou hadst mind when I thatched the byre, thou wouldst not eat that without giving me my share," says the golden pigeon. Three other grains fall, and the silver pigeon sprang, and he eats that. "If thou hadst mind when I harried the magpie's nest, thou wouldst not eat that without giving me my share," says the golden pigeon; "I lost my little finger bringing it down, and I want it still." The king's son minded, and he knew who it was he had got. He sprang where she was, and kissed her from hand to mouth. And when the priest came they married a second time. And there I left them.

The Sea-Maiden

THERE WAS ERE NOW a poor old fisher, but on this year he was not getting much fish. On a day of days, and he fishing, there rose a sea-maiden at the side of his boat, and she asked him if he was getting fish. The old man answered, and he said that he was not. "What reward wouldst thou give me for sending plenty of fish to thee?" "Ach!" said the old man, "I have not much to spare." "Wilt thou give me the first son thou hast?" said she. "It is I that would give thee that, if I were to have a son; there was not, and there will not be a son of mine," said he, "I and my wife are grown so old." "Name all thou hast." "I have but an old mare of a horse, an old dog, myself and my wife. There's for thee all the creatures of the great world that are mine." "Here, then, are three grains for thee that thou shalt give thy wife this very night, and three others to the dog, and these three to the mare, and these three likewise thou shalt plant behind thy house, and in their own time thy wife will have three sons, the mare three foals, and the dog three puppies, and there will grow three trees behind thy house, and the trees will be a sign, when one of the sons dies, one of the trees will wither. Now, take thyself home, and remember me when thy son is three years of age, and thou thyself wilt get plenty of fish after this."

Everything happened as the sea-maiden said, and he himself was getting plenty of fish; but when the end of the three years was nearing, the old man was growing sorrowful, heavy hearted, while he failed each day as it came. On the namesake of the day, he went to fish as he used, but he did not take his son with him.

The sea-maiden rose at the side of the boat, and asked, "Didst thou bring thy son with thee hither to me?" "Och! I did not bring him. I forgot that this was the day." "Yes! yes! then," said the sea-maiden; "thou shalt get four other years of him, to try if it be easier for thee to part from him. Here thou hast his like age," and she lifted up a big bouncing baby. "Is thy son as fine as this one?" He went home full of glee and delight, for that he had got four other years of his son, and he kept on fishing and getting plenty of fish, but at the end of the next four years sorrow and woe struck him, and he took not a meal, and he did not a turn, and his wife could not think what was ailing him. This time he did not know what to do, but he set it before him, that he would not take his son with him this time either.

He went to fish as at the former times, and the sea-maiden rose at the side of the boat, and she asked him, "Didst thou bring thy son hither to me?" "Och! I forgot him this time too," said the old man. "Go home then," said the sea-maiden, "and at the end of seven years after this, thou art sure to remember me, but then it will not be the easier for thee to part with him, but thou shalt get fish as thou used to do."

The old man went home full of joy; he had got seven other years of his son, and before seven years passed, the old man thought that he himself would be dead, and that he would see the sea-maiden no more. But no matter, the end of those seven years was nearing also, and if it was, the old man was not without care and trouble. He had rest neither day nor night. The eldest son asked his father one day if any one were troubling him? The old man said that some one was, but that belonged neither to him nor to any one else. The lad said he must know what it was. His father told him at last how the matter was between him and the sea-maiden. "Let not that put you in any trouble," said the son; "I will not oppose you." "Thou shalt not; thou shalt not go, my son, though I should not get fish for ever." "If you will not let me go with you, go to the smithy, and let the smith make me a great strong sword, and I will go to the end of fortune." His father went to the smithy, and the smith made a doughty sword for him. His father came home with the sword. The lad grasped it and gave it a shake or two, and it went in a hundred splinters. He asked his father to go to the smithy and get him another sword in which there should be twice as much weight; and so did his father, and so likewise it happened to the next sword – it broke in two halves. Back went the old man to the smithy; and the smith made a great sword, its like he never made before. "There's thy sword for thee," said the smith, "and the fist must be good that plays this blade." The old man gave the sword to his son, he gave it a shake or two. "This will do," said he; "it's high time now to travel on my way." On the next morning he put a saddle on the black horse that the mare had, and he put the world under his head, and his black dog was by his side. When he went on a bit, he fell in with the carcass of a sheep beside the road. At the carrion were a great dog, a falcon and an otter. He came down off the horse, and he divided the carcass amongst the three. Three third shares to the dog, two third shares to the otter, and a third share to the falcon. "For this," said the dog, "if swiftness of foot or sharpness of tooth will give thee aid, mind me, and I will be at thy side." Said the otter, "If the swimming of foot on the ground of a pool will loose thee, mind me, and I will be at thy side." Said the falcon, "if hardship comes on thee, where swiftness of wing or crook of a claw will do good, mind me, and I will be at thy side." On this he went onward till he reached a king's house, and he took service to be a herd, and his wages were to be according to the milk of the cattle. He went away with the cattle, and the grazing was but bare. When lateness came (in the evening), and when he took (them) home they had not much milk, the place was so bare, and his meat and drink was but spare this night.

On the next day he went on further with them; and at last he came to a place exceedingly grassy, in a green glen, of which he never saw the like.

But about the time when he should go behind the cattle, for taking homewards, who is seen coming but a great giant with his sword in his hand. "Hiu! Hau!! Hogaraich!!!" says the giant. "It is long since my teeth were rusted seeking thy flesh. The cattle are mine; they are on my march; and a dead man art thou." "I said, not that," says the herd; "there is no knowing, but that may be easier to say than to do."

To grips they go – himself and the giant. He saw that he was far from his friend, and near his foe. He drew the great clean-sweeping sword, and he neared the giant; and in the play of the battle the black dog leaped on the giant's back. The herd drew back his sword, and the head was off the giant in a twinkling. He leaped on the black horse, and he went to look for the giant's house. He reached a door, and in the haste that the giant made he had left each gate and door open. In went the herd, and that's the place where there was magnificence and money in plenty, and dresses of each kind on the wardrobe with gold and silver, and each thing finer than the other. At the mouth of night he took himself to the king's house, but he took not a thing from the giant's house. And when the cattle were milked this night there was milk. He got good feeding this night, meat and drink without stint, and the king was hugely pleased that he had caught such a herd. He went on for a time in this way, but at last the glen grew bare of grass, and the grazing was not so good.

But he thought he would go a little further forward in on the giant's land; and he sees a great park of grass. He returned for the cattle, and he puts them into the park.

They were but a short time grazing in the park when a great wild giant came full of rage and madness. "Hiu! Haw!! Hoagraich!!!" said the giant. "It is a drink of thy blood that quenches my thirst this night." "There is no knowing," said the herd, "but that's easier to say than to do." And at each other went the men. There was the shaking of blades! At length and at last it seemed as if the giant would get the victory over the herd. Then he called on his dog, and with one spring the black dog caught the giant by the neck, and swiftly the herd struck off his head.

He went home very tired this night, but it's a wonder if the king's cattle had not milk. The whole family was delighted that they had got such a herd.

He followed herding in this way for a time; but one night after he came home, instead of getting "all hail" and "good luck" from the dairymaid, all were at crying and woe.

He asked what cause of woe there was this night. The dairymaid said that a great beast with three heads was in the loch, and she was to get (some) one every year, and the lots had come this year on the king's daughter, "and in the middle of the day (tomorrow) she is to meet the Uile Bheist at the upper end of the loch, but there is a great suitor yonder who is going to rescue her."

"What suitor is that?" said the herd. "Oh, he is a great General of arms," said the dairymaid, "and when he kills the beast, he will marry the king's daughter, for the king has said, that he who could save his daughter should get her to marry."

But on the morrow when the time was nearing, the king's daughter and this hero of arms went to give a meeting to the beast, and they reached the black corrie at the upper end of the loch. They were but a short time there when the beast stirred in the midst of the loch; but on the general's seeing this terror of a beast with three heads, he took fright, and he slunk away, and he hid himself. And the king's daughter was under fear and under trembling with no one at all to save her. At a glance, she sees a doughty handsome youth, riding a black horse, and coming where she was. He was marvellously arrayed, and full armed, and his black dog moving after him. "There is gloom on thy face, girl," said the youth. "What dost thou here?" "Oh! that's no matter," said the king's daughter. "It's not long I'll be here at all events." "I said not that," said he. "A worthy fled as likely as thou, and not long since," said she. "He is a worthy who stands the war," said the youth. He lay down beside her, and he said to her, if he should fall asleep, she should rouse him when she should see the beast making for shore. "What is rousing for thee?" said she. "Rousing for me is to put the gold ring on thy finger on my little finger." They were not long there when she saw the beast making for shore. She took a ring off her finger, and put it on the little finger of the lad. He awoke, and to meet the beast he went with his sword and his dog. But there was the spluttering and splashing between himself and the beast. The dog was doing all he might, and the king's daughter was palsied by fear of the noise of the beast. They would now be under, and now above. But at last he cut one of the heads off her. She gave one roar Raivic, and the son of earth, Mactalla of the rocks (echo), called to her screech, and she drove the loch in spindrift from end to end, and in a twinkling she went out of sight. "Good luck and victory that were following thee, lad!" said the king's daughter. "I am safe for one night, but the beast will come again, and for ever, until the other two heads come off her." He caught the beast's head, and he drew a withy through it, and he told her to bring it with her there tomorrow. She went home with the head on her shoulder, and the herd betook himself to the cows, but she had not gone far when this great General saw her, and he said to her that he would kill her, if she would not say that 'twas he took the head off the beast. "Oh!" says she, "'tis I will say it. Who else took the head off the beast but thou!" They reached the king's house, and the head was on the General's shoulder. But here was rejoicing, that she should come home alive and whole, and this great captain with the beast's head full of blood in his hand. On the morrow they went away, and there was no question at all but that this hero would save the king's daughter.

They reached the same place, and they were not long there when the fearful Uile Bheist stirred in the midst of the loch, and the hero slunk away as he did on yesterday, but it was not long after this when the man of the black horse came, with another dress on. No matter, she knew that it was the very same lad. "It is I am pleased to see thee," said she. "I am in hopes thou wilt handle thy great sword today as thou didst yesterday. Come up and take breath." But they were not long there when they saw the beast steaming in the midst of the loch.

The lad lay down at the side of the king's daughter, and he said to her, "If I sleep before the beast comes, rouse me." "What is rousing for thee?" "Rousing for me is to put the ear-ring that is in thine ear in mine." He had not well fallen asleep when the king's daughter cried, "Rouse! Rouse!" but wake he would not; but she took the ear-ring out of her ear, and she put it in the ear of the lad. At once he woke, and to meet the beast he went, but there was Tloopersteich and Tlaperstich, rawceil s'taweeil, spluttering, splashing, raving and roaring on the beast! They kept on thus for a long time, and about the mouth of night, he cut another head off the beast. He put it on the withy, and he leaped on the black horse, and he betook himself to the herding. The king's daughter went home with the heads. The General met her, and took the heads from her, and he said to her, that she must tell that it was he who took the head off the beast this time also. "Who else took the head off the beast but thou?" said she. They reached the king's house with the heads. Then there was joy and gladness. If the king was hopeful the first night, he was now sure that this great hero would save his daughter, and there was no question at all but that the other head would be off the beast on the morrow.

About the same time on the morrow, the two went away. The officer bid himself as he usually did. The king's daughter betook herself to the bank of the loch. The hero of the black horse came, and he lay at her side. She woke the lad, and put another ear-ring in his other ear; and at the beast he went. But if rawceil and toiceil, roaring and raving were on the beast on the days that were passed, this day she was horrible. But no matter, he took the third head off the beast; and if he did, it was not without a struggle. He drew it through the withy, and she went home with the heads. When they reached the king's house, all were full of smiles, and the General was to marry the king's daughter the next day. The wedding was going on, and every one about the castle longing till the priest should come.

But when the priest came, she would marry but the one who could take the heads off the withy without cutting the withy. "Who should take the heads off the withy but the man that put the heads on?" said the king.

The General tried them, but he could not loose them; and at last there was no one about the house but had tried to take the heads off the withy, but they could not. The king asked if there were any one else about the house that would try to take the heads off the withy? They said that the herd had not tried them yet. Word went for the herd; and he was not long throwing them hither and thither. "But stop a bit, my lad," said the king's daughter, "the man that took the heads off the beast, he has my ring and my two ear-rings." The herd put his hand in his pocket, and he threw them on the board. "Thou art my man," said the king's daughter. The king was not so pleased when he saw that it was a herd who was to marry his daughter, but he ordered that he should be put in a better dress; but his daughter spoke, and she said that he had a dress as fine as any that ever was in his castle; and thus it happened. The herd put on the giant's golden dress, and they married that same night.

They were now married, and everything going on well. They were one day sauntering by the side of the loch, and there came a beast more wonderfully terrible than the other, and takes him away to the loch without fear, or asking. The king's daughter was now mournful, tearful, blind-sorrowful for her married man; she was always with her eye on the loch. An old smith met her, and she told how it had befallen her married mate. The smith advised her to spread everything that was finer than another in the very same place where the beast took away her man; and so she did. The beast put up her nose, and she said, "Fine is thy jewellery, king's daughter." "Finer than that is the jewel that thou tookest from me," said she. "Give me one sight of my man, and thou shalt get any one thing of all these thou seest." The beast brought him up. "Deliver him to me, and thou shalt get all thou seest," said she. The beast did as she said. She threw him alive and whole on the bank of the loch.

A short time after this, when they were walking at the side of the loch, the same beast took away the king's daughter. Sorrowful was each one that was in the town on this night. Her man was mournful, tearful, wandering down and up about the banks of the loch, by day and night. The old smith met him. The smith told him that there was no way of killing the Uille Bheist but the one way, and this is it – "In the island that is in the midst of the loch is Eillid Chaisfhion – the white footed hind, of the slenderest legs, and the swiftest step, and though she should be caught, there would spring a hoodie out of her, and though the hoodie should be caught, there would spring a trout out of her, but there is an egg in the mouth of the trout, and the soul of the beast is in the egg, and if the egg breaks, the beast is dead."

Now, there was no way of getting to this island, for the beast would sink each boat and raft that would go on the loch. He thought he would try to leap the strait with the black horse, and even so he did. The black horse leaped the strait, and the black dog with one bound after him. He saw the Eillid, and he let the black dog after her, but when the black dog would be on one side of the island, the Eillid would be on the other side. "Oh! good were now the great dog of the carcass of flesh here!" No sooner spoke he the word than the generous dog was at his side; and after the Eillid he took, and the worthies were not long in bringing her to earth. But he no sooner caught her than a hoodie sprang out of her. "'Tis now, were good the falcon grey, of sharpest eye and swiftest wing!" No sooner said he this than the falcon was after the hoodie, and she was not long putting her to earth;

and as the hoodie fell on the bank of the loch, out of her jumps the trout. "Oh, that thou wert by me now, oh otter!" No sooner said than the otter was at his side, and out on the loch she leaped, and brings the trout from the midst of the loch; but no sooner was the otter on shore with the trout than the egg came from his mouth. He sprang and he put his foot on it. 'Twas then the beast let out a roar, and she said, "Break not the egg, and thou gettest all thou askest." "Deliver to me my wife?" In the wink of an eye she was by his side. When he got hold of her hand in both his hands he let his foot (down) on the egg and the beast died.

The beast was dead now, and now was the sight to be seen. She was horrible to look upon. The three heads were off her doubtless, but if they were, there were heads under and heads over head on her, and eyes, and five hundred feet. But no matter, they left her there, and they went home, and there was delight and smiling in the king's house that night. And till now he had not told the king how he killed the giants. The king put great honour on him, and he was a great man with the king.

Himself and his wife were walking one day, when he noticed a little castle beside the loch in a wood; he asked his wife who was dwelling in it? She said that no one would be going near that castle, for that no one had yet come back to tell the tale, who had gone there.

"The matter must not be so," said he; "this very night I will see who is dwelling in it." "Go not, go not," said she; "there never went man to this castle that returned." "Be that as it pleases," says he. He went; he betakes himself to the castle. When he reached the door, a little flattering crone met him standing in the door. "All hail and good luck to thee, fisher's son; 'tis I myself am pleased to see thee; great is the honour for this kingdom, thy like to be come into it – thy coming in is fame for this little bothy; go in first; honour to the gentles; go on, and take breath." In he went, but as he was going up, she drew the Slachdan druidhach on him, on the back of his head, and at once – there he fell.

On this night there was woe in the king's castle, and on the morrow there was a wail in the fisher's house. The tree is seen withering, and the fisher's middle son said that his brother was dead, and he made a vow and oath, that he would go, and that he would know where the corpse of his brother was lying. He put saddle on a black horse, and rode after his black dog; (for the three sons of the fisher had a black horse and a black dog), and without going hither or thither he followed on his brother's step till he reached the king's house.

This one was so like his elder brother, that the king's daughter thought it was her own man. He stayed in the castle. They told him how it befell his brother; and to the little castle of the crone, go he must – happen hard or soft as it might. To the castle he went; and just as befell the eldest brother, so in each way it befell the middle son, and with one blow of the Slachdan druidhach, the crone felled him stretched beside his brother.

On seeing the second tree withering, the fisher's youngest son said that now his two brothers were dead, and that he must know what death had come on them. On the black horse he went, and he followed the dog as his brothers did, and he hit the king's house before he stopped. 'Twas the king who was pleased to see him; but to the black castle (for that was its name) they would not let him go. But to the castle he must go; and so he reached the castle. "All hail and good luck to thyself, fisher's son: 'tis I am pleased to see thee; go in and take breath," said she (the crone). "In before me thou crone: I don't like flattery out of doors; go in and let's hear thy speech." In went the crone, and when her back was to him he drew his sword and whips her head off; but the sword flew out of his hand. And swift the crone gripped her head with both hands, and puts it on her neck as it was before. The dog sprung on the crone, and she struck the generous dog with the club of magic; and there he lay. But this went not to make the youth more sluggish. To grips with the crone he goes; he got a hold of the Slachan druidhach, and with one blow on the top of the head, she was on earth in the wink of an eye. He went forward, up a little, and he sees his two brothers lying side by side. He gave a blow to each one with the Slachdan druidhach and on foot they were, and there was the spoil! Gold and silver, and each thing more precious than another, in the crone's castle. They came back to the king's house, and then there was rejoicing! The king was growing old. The eldest son of the fisherman was crowned king, and the pair of brothers stayed a day and a year in the king's house, and then the two went on their journey home, with the gold and silver of the crone, and each other grand thing which the king gave them; and if they have not died since then, they are alive to this very day.

The Draiglin' Hogney

THERE WAS ONCE A MAN who had three sons, and very little money to provide for them. So, when the eldest had grown into a lad, and saw that there was no means of making a livelihood at home, he went to his father and said to him:

"Father, if thou wilt give me a horse to ride on, a hound to hunt with, and a hawk to fly, I will go out into the wide world and seek my fortune."

His father gave him what he asked for; and he set out on his travels. He rode and he rode, over mountain and glen, until, just at nightfall, he came to a thick, dark wood. He entered it, thinking that he might find a path that would lead him through it; but no path was visible, and after wandering up and down for some time, he was obliged to acknowledge to himself that he was completely lost.

There seemed to be nothing for it but to tie his horse to a tree, and make a bed of leaves for himself on the ground; but just as he was about to do so he saw a light glimmering in the distance, and, riding on in the direction in which it was, he soon came to a clearing in the wood, in which stood a magnificent Castle.

The windows were all lit up, but the great door was barred; and, after he had ridden up to it, and knocked, and received no answer, the young man raised his hunting horn to his lips and blew a loud blast in the hope of letting the inmates know that he was without.

Instantly the door flew open of its own accord, and the young man entered, wondering very much what this strange thing would mean. And he wondered still more when he passed from room to room, and found that, although fires were burning brightly everywhere, and there was a plentiful meal laid out on the table in the great hall, there did not seem to be a single person in the whole of the vast building.

However, as he was cold, and tired, and wet, he put his horse in one of the stalls of the enormous stable, and taking his hawk and hound along with him, went into the hall and ate a hearty supper. After which he sat down by the side of the fire, and began to dry his clothes.

By this time it had grown late, and he was just thinking of retiring to one of the bedrooms which he had seen upstairs and going to bed, when a clock which was hanging on the wall struck twelve.

Instantly the door of the huge apartment opened, and a most awful-looking Draiglin' Hogney entered. His hair was matted and his beard was long, and his eyes shone like stars of fire from under his bushy eyebrows, and in his hands he carried a queerly shaped club.

He did not seem at all astonished to see his unbidden guest; but, coming across the hall, he sat down upon the opposite side of the fireplace, and, resting his chin on his hands, gazed fixedly at him.

"Doth thy horse ever kick any?" he said at last, in a harsh, rough voice.

"Ay, doth he," replied the young man; for the only steed that his father had been able to give him was a wild and unbroken colt.

"I have some skill in taming horses," went on the Draiglin' Hogney, "and I will give thee something to tame thine withal. Throw this over him" – and he pulled one of the long, coarse hairs out of his head and gave it to the young man. And there was something so commanding in the Hogney's voice that he did as he was bid, and went out to the stable and threw the hair over the horse.

Then he returned to the hall, and sat down again by the fire. The moment that he was seated the Draiglin' Hogney asked another question.

"Doth thy hound ever bite any?"

"Ay, verily," answered the youth; for his hound was so fierce-tempered that no man, save his master, dare lay a hand on him.

"I can cure the wildest tempered dog in Christendom," replied the Draiglin' Hogney. "Take that, and throw it over him." And he pulled another hair out of his head and gave it to the young man, who lost no time in flinging it over his hound.

There was still a third question to follow. "Doth ever thy hawk peck any?"

The young man laughed. "I have ever to keep a bandage over her eyes, save when she is ready to fly," said he; "else were nothing safe within her reach."

"Things will be safe now," said the Hogney, grimly. "Throw that over her." And for the third time he pulled a hair from his head and handed it to his companion. And as the other hairs had been thrown over the horse and the hound, so this one was thrown over the hawk.

Then, before the young man could draw breath, the fiercesome Draiglin' Hogney had given him such a clout on the side of his head with his queer-shaped club that he fell down in a heap on the floor.

And very soon his hawk and his hound tumbled down still and motionless beside him; and, out in the stable, his horse became stark and stiff, as if turned to stone. For the Draiglin's words had meant more than at first appeared when he said that he could make all unruly animals quiet.

Some time afterwards the second of the three sons came to his father in the old home with the same request that his brother had made. That he should be provided with a horse, a hawk, and a hound, and be allowed to go out to seek his fortune. And his father listened to him, and gave him what he asked, as he had given his brother.

And the young man set out, and in due time came to the wood, and lost himself in it, just as his brother had done; then he saw the light, and came to the Castle, and went in, and had supper, and dried his clothes, just as it all had happened before.

And the Draiglin' Hogney came in, and asked him the three questions, and he gave the same three answers, and received three hairs – one to throw over his horse, one to throw over his hound, and one to throw over his hawk; then the Hogney killed him, just as he had killed his brother.

Time passed, and the youngest son, finding that his two elder brothers never returned, asked his father for a horse, a hawk, and a hound, in order that he might go and look for them. And the poor old man, who was feeling very desolate in his old age, gladly gave them to him.

So he set out on his quest, and at nightfall he came, as the others had done, to the thick wood and the Castle. But, being a wise and cautious youth, he liked not the way in which he found things. He liked not the empty house; he liked not the spread-out feast; and, most of all, he liked not the look of the Draiglin' Hogney when he saw him. And he determined to be very careful what he said or did as long as he was in his company.

So when the Draiglin' Hogney asked him if his horse kicked, he replied that it did, in very few words; and when he got one of the Hogney's hairs to throw over him, he went out to the stable, and pretended to do so, but he brought it back, hidden in his hand, and, when his unchancy companion was not looking, he threw it into the fire. It fizzled up like a tongue of flame with a little hissing sound like that of a serpent.

"What's that fizzling?" asked the Giant suspiciously.

"'Tis but the sap of the green wood," replied the young man carelessly, as he turned to caress his hound.

The answer satisfied the Draiglin' Hogney, and he paid no heed to the sound which the hair that should have been thrown over the hound, or the sound which the hair that should have been thrown over the hawk, made, when the young man threw them into the fire; and they fizzled up in the same way that the first had done.

Then, thinking that he had the stranger in his power, he whisked across the hearthstone to strike him with his club, as he had struck his brothers; but the young man was on the outlook, and when he saw him coming he gave a shrill whistle. And his horse, which loved him dearly, came galloping in from the stable, and his hound sprang up from the hearthstone where he had been sleeping; and his hawk, who was sitting on his shoulder, ruffled up her feathers and screamed harshly; and they all fell on the Draiglin' Hogney at once, and he found out only too well how the horse kicked, and the hound bit, and the hawk pecked; for they kicked him, and bit him, and pecked him, till he was as dead as a door nail.

When the young man saw that he was dead, he took his little club from his hand, and, armed with that, he set out to explore the Castle.

As he expected, he found that there were dark and dreary dungeons under it, and in one of them he found his two brothers, lying cold and stiff side by side. He touched them with the club, and instantly they came to life again, and sprang to their feet as well as ever.

Then he went into another dungeon; and there were the two horses, and the two hawks, and the two hounds, lying as if dead, exactly as their Masters had lain. He touched them with his magic club, and they, too, came to life again.

Then he called to his two brothers, and the three young men searched the other dungeons, and they found great stores of gold and silver hidden in them, enough to make them rich for life.

So they buried the Draiglin' Hogney, and took possession of the Castle; and two of them went home and brought their old father back with them, and they all were as prosperous and happy as they could be; and, for aught that I know, they are living there still.

The Ghosts of Craig-Aulnaic

TWO CELEBRATED GHOSTS EXISTED, once on a time, in the wilds of Craig-Aulnaic, a romantic place in the district of Strathdown, Banffshire. The one was a male and the other a female. The male was called Fhuna Mhoir Ben Baynac, after one of the mountains of Glenavon, where at one time he resided; and the female was called Clashnichd Aulnaic, from her having had her abode in Craig-Aulnaic. But although the great ghost of Ben Baynac was bound by the common ties of nature and of honour to protect and cherish his weaker companion, Clashnichd Aulnaic, yet he often treated her in the most cruel and unfeeling manner. In the dead of night, when the surrounding hamlets were buried in deep repose, and when nothing else disturbed the solemn stillness of the midnight scene, oft would the shrill shrieks of poor Clashnichd burst upon the slumberer's ears, and awake him to anything but pleasant reflections.

But of all those who were incommoded by the noisy and unseemly quarrels of these two ghosts, James Owre or Gray, the tenant of the farm of Balbig of Delnabo, was the greatest sufferer. From the proximity of his abode to their haunts, it was the misfortune of himself and family to be the nightly audience of Clashnichd's cries and lamentations, which they considered anything but agreeable entertainment.

One day as James Gray was on his rounds looking after his sheep, he happened to fall in with Clashnichd, the ghost of Aulnaic, with whom he entered into a long conversation. In the course of it he took occasion to remonstrate with her on the very disagreeable disturbance she caused himself and family by her wild and unearthly cries – cries which, he said, few mortals could relish in the dreary hours of midnight. Poor Clashnichd, by way of apology for her conduct, gave James Gray a sad account of her usage, detailing at full length the series of cruelties committed upon her by Ben Baynac. From this account, it appeared that her living with the latter was by no means a matter of choice with Clashnichd; on the contrary, it seemed that she had, for a long time, lived apart with much comfort, residing in a snug dwelling, as already mentioned, in the wilds of Craig-Aulnaic; but Ben Baynac having unfortunately taken into his head to pay her a visit, took a fancy, not to herself, but her dwelling, of which, in his own name and authority, he took immediate possession, and soon after he expelled poor Clashnichd, with many stripes, from her natural inheritance. Not satisfied with invading and depriving her of her just rights, he was in the habit of following her into her private haunts, not with the view of offering her any endearments, but for the purpose of inflicting on her person every torment which his brain could invent.

Such a moving relation could not fail to affect the generous heart of James Gray, who determined from that moment to risk life and limb in order to vindicate the rights and avenge the wrongs of poor Clashnichd, the ghost of Craig-Aulnaic. He, therefore, took good care to interrogate his new protégée touching the nature of her oppressor's constitution, whether he was of that killable species of ghost that could be shot with a silver sixpence, or if there was any other weapon that could possibly accomplish his annihilation. Clashnichd informed him that she had occasion to know that Ben Baynac was wholly invulnerable to all the weapons of man, with the exception of a large mole on his left breast, which was no doubt penetrable by silver or steel; but that, from the specimens she had of his personal prowess and strength, it were vain for mere man to attempt to combat him. Confiding, however, in his expertness as an archer – for he was allowed to be the best marksman of the age – James Gray told Clashnichd he did not fear him with all his might, – that he was a man; and desired her, moreover, next time the ghost chose to repeat his incivilities to her, to apply to him, James Gray, for redress.

It was not long ere he had an opportunity of fulfilling his promises. Ben Baynac having one night, in the want of better amusement, entertained himself by inflicting an inhuman castigation on Clashnichd, she lost no time in waiting on James Gray, with a full and particular account of it. She found him smoking his cutty, for it was night when she came to him; but, notwithstanding the inconvenience of the hour, James needed no great persuasion to induce him to proceed directly along with Clashnichd to hold a communing with their friend, Ben Baynac, the great ghost. Clashnichd was stout and sturdy, and understood the knack of travelling much better than our women do. She expressed a wish that, for the sake of expedition, James Gray would suffer her to bear him along, a motion to which the latter agreed; and a few minutes brought them close to the scene of Ben Baynac's residence. As they approached his haunt, he came forth to meet them, with looks and gestures which did not at all indicate a cordial welcome. It was a fine moonlight night, and they could easily observe his actions. Poor Clashnichd was now sorely afraid of the great ghost. Apprehending instant destruction from his fury, she exclaimed to James Gray that they would be both dead people, and that immediately, unless James Gray hit with an arrow the mole which covered Ben Baynac's heart. This was not so difficult a task as James had hitherto apprehended it. The mole was as large as a common bonnet, and yet nowise disproportioned to the natural size of the ghost's body, for he certainly was a great and a mighty ghost. Ben Baynac cried out to James Gray that he would soon make eagle's meat of him; and certain it is, such was his intention, had not the shepherd so effectually stopped him from the execution of it. Raising his bow to his eye when within a few yards of Ben Baynac, he took deliberate aim; the arrow flew – it hit – a yell from Ben Baynac announced the result. A hideous howl re-echoed from the surrounding mountains, responsive to the groans of a thousand ghosts; and Ben Baynac, like the smoke of a shot, vanished into air.

Clashnichd, the ghost of Aulnaic, now found herself emancipated from the most abject state of slavery, and restored to freedom and liberty, through the invincible courage of James Gray. Overpowered with gratitude, she fell at his feet, and vowed to devote the whole of her time and talents towards his service and prosperity. Meanwhile, being anxious to have her remaining goods and furniture removed to her former dwelling, whence she had been so iniquitously expelled by Ben Baynac, the great ghost, she requested of her new master the use of his horses to remove them. James observing on the adjacent hill a flock of deer, and wishing to have a trial of his new servant's sagacity or expertness, told her those were his horses – she was welcome to the use of them; desiring that when she had done with them, she would inclose them in his stable. Clashnichd then proceeded to make use of the horses, and James Gray returned home to enjoy his night's rest.

Scarce had he reached his arm-chair, and reclined his cheek on his hand, to ruminate over the bold adventure of the night, when Clashnichd entered, with her "breath in her throat," and venting the bitterest complaints at the unruliness of his horses, which had broken one-half of her furniture, and caused her more trouble in the stabling of them than their services were worth.

"Oh! they are stabled, then?" inquired James Gray. Clashnichd replied in the affirmative. "Very well," rejoined James, "they shall be tame enough tomorrow."

From this specimen of Clashnichd, the ghost of Craig-Aulnaic's expertness, it will be seen what a valuable acquisition her service proved to James Gray and his young family. They were, however, speedily deprived of her assistance by a most unfortunate accident. From the sequel of the story, from which the foregoing is an extract, it appears that poor Clashnichd was deeply addicted to propensities which at that time rendered her kin so obnoxious to their human neighbours. She was constantly in the habit of visiting her friends much oftener than she was invited, and, in the course of such visits, was never very scrupulous in making free with any eatables which fell within the circle of her observation.

One day, while engaged on a foraging expedition of this description, she happened to enter the Mill of Delnabo, which was inhabited in those days by the miller's family. She found his wife engaged in roasting a large gridiron of fine savoury fish, the agreeable smell proceeding from which perhaps occasioned her visit. With the usual inquiries after the health of the miller and his family, Clashnichd proceeded with the greatest familiarity and good-humour to make herself comfortable at their expense. But the miller's wife, enraged at the loss of her fish, and not relishing such unwelcome familiarity, punished the unfortunate Clashnichd rather too severely for her freedom. It happened that there was at the time a large caldron of boiling water suspended over the fire, and this caldron the enraged wife overturned in Clashnichd's bosom!

Scalded beyond recovery, she fled up the wilds of Craig-Aulnaic, uttering the most melancholy lamentations, nor has she been ever heard of since.

The Fiddler and the Bogle of Bogandoran

"LATE ONE NIGHT, as my grand-uncle, Lachlan Dhu Macpherson, who was well known as the best fiddler of his day, was returning home from a ball, at which he had acted as a musician, he had occasion to pass through the once-haunted Bog of Torrans.

Now, it happened at that time that the bog was frequented by a huge bogle or ghost, who was of a most mischievous disposition, and took particular pleasure in abusing every traveller who had occasion to pass through the place betwixt the twilight at night and cock-crowing in the morning. Suspecting much that he would also come in for a share of his abuse, my grand-uncle made up his mind, in the course of his progress, to return the ghost any civilities which he might think meet to offer him. On arriving on the spot, he found his suspicions were too well grounded; for whom did he see but the ghost of Bogandoran apparently ready waiting him, and seeming by his ghastly grin not a little overjoyed at the meeting. Marching up to my grand-uncle, the bogle clapped a huge club into his hand, and furnishing himself with one of the same dimensions, he put a spittle in his hand, and deliberately commenced the combat. My grand-uncle returned the salute with equal spirit, and so ably did both parties ply their batons that for a while the issue of the combat was extremely doubtful. At length, however, the fiddler could easily discover that his opponent's vigour was much in the fagging order. Picking up renewed courage in consequence, he plied the ghost with renewed force, and after a stout resistance, in the course of which both parties were seriously handled, the ghost of Bogandoran thought it prudent to give up the night.

"At the same time, filled no doubt with great indignation at this signal defeat, it seems the ghost resolved to re-engage my grand-uncle on some other occasion, under more favourable circumstances. Not long after, as my grand-uncle was returning home quite unattended from another ball in the Braes of the country, he had just entered the hollow of Auldichoish, well known for its 'eerie' properties, when, lo! who presented himself to his view on the adjacent eminence but his old friend of Bogandoran, advancing as large as the gable of a house, and putting himself in the most threatening and fighting attitudes.

"Looking at the very dangerous nature of the ground where they had met, and feeling no anxiety for a second encounter with a combatant of his weight, in a situation so little desirable, the fiddler would have willingly deferred the settlement of their differences till a more convenient season. He, accordingly, assuming the most submissive aspect in the world, endeavoured to pass by his champion in peace, but in vain. Longing, no doubt, to retrieve the disgrace of his late discomfiture, the bogle instantly seized the fiddler, and attempted with all his might to pull the latter down the precipice, with the diabolical intention, it is supposed, of drowning him in the river Avon below. In this pious design the bogle was happily frustrated by the intervention of some trees which grew on the precipice, and to which my unhappy grand-uncle clung with the zeal of a drowning man. The enraged ghost, finding it impossible to extricate him from those friendly trees, and resolving, at all events, to be revenged upon him, fell upon maltreating the fiddler with his hands and feet in the most inhuman manner.

"Such gross indignities my worthy grand-uncle was not accustomed to, and being incensed beyond all measure at the liberties taken by Bogandoran, he resolved again to try his mettle, whether life or death should be the consequence.Having no other weapon wherewith to defend himself but his biodag, which, considering the nature of his opponent's constitution, he suspected much would be of little avail to him – I say, in the absence of any other weapon, he sheathed the biodag three times in the ghost of

Bogandoran's body. And what was the consequence? Why, to the great astonishment of my courageous forefather, the ghost fell down cold dead at his feet, and was never more seen or heard of."

The Bogle

THIS IS A FREAKISH SPIRIT who delights rather to perplex and frighten mankind than either to serve or seriously hurt them. The Esprit Follet of the French, Shakespeare's Puck, or Robin Goodfellow, and Shellycoat, a spirit who resides in the waters, and has given his name to many a rock and stone on the Scottish coast, belong to the class of bogles.

One of Shellycoat's pranks is thus narrated: Two men in a very dark night, approaching the banks of the Ettrick, heard a doleful voice from its waves repeatedly exclaim, "Lost! lost!" They followed the sound, which seemed to be the voice of a drowning person, and, to their astonishment, found that it ascended the river; still they continued to follow the cry of the malicious sprite, and, arriving before dawn at the very sources of the river, the voice was now heard descending the opposite side of the mountain in which they arise. The fatigued and deluded travellers now relinquished the pursuit, and had no sooner done so, than they heard Shellycoat applauding, in loud bursts of laughter, his successful roguery.

The Death "Bree"

THERE WAS ONCE A WOMAN, who lived in the Camp-del-more of Strathavon, whose cattle were seized with a murrain, or some such fell disease, which ravaged the neighbourhood at the time, carrying off great numbers of them daily. All the forlorn fires and hallowed waters failed of their customary effects; and she was at length told by the wise people, whom she consulted on the occasion, that it was evidently the effect of some infernal agency, the power of which could not be destroyed by any other means than the never-failing specific – the juice of a dead head from the churchyard, a nostrum certainly very difficult to be procured, considering that the head must needs be abstracted from the grave at the hour of midnight. Being, however, a woman of a stout heart and strong faith, native feelings of delicacy towards the sanctuary of the dead had more weight than had fear in restraining her for some time from resorting to this desperate remedy.

At length, seeing that her stock would soon be annihilated by the destructive career of the disease, the wife of Camp-del-more resolved to put the experiment in practice, whatever the result might be. Accordingly, having with considerable difficulty engaged a neighbouring woman as her companion in this hazardous expedition, they set out a little before midnight for the parish churchyard, distant about a mile and a half from her residence, to execute her determination.

On arriving at the churchyard her companion, whose courage was not so notable, appalled by the gloomy prospect before her, refused to enter among the habitations of the dead. She, however, agreed to remain at the gate till her friend's business was accomplished. This circumstance, however, did not stagger the wife's resolution. She, with the greatest coolness and intrepidity, proceeded towards what she supposed an old grave, took down her spade, and commenced her operations. After a good deal of toil she arrived at the object of her labour. Raising the first head, or rather skull, that came in her way, she was about to make it her own property, when a hollow, wild, sepulchral voice exclaimed, "That is my head; let it alone!" Not wishing to dispute the claimant's title to this head, and supposing she could be otherwise provided, she very good-naturedly returned it and took up another. "That is my father's head," bellowed the same voice. Wishing, if possible, to avoid disputes, the wife of Camp-del-more took up another head, when the same voice instantly started a claim to it as his grandfather's head. "Well," replied the wife, nettled at her disappointments, "although it were your grandmother's head, you shan't get it till I am done with it." "What do you say, you limmer?" says the ghost, starting up in his awry habiliments. "What do you say, you limmer?" repeated he in a great rage. "By the great oath, you had better leave my grandfather's head." Upon matters coming this length, the wily wife of Camp-del-more thought it proper to assume a more conciliatory aspect. Telling the claimant the whole particulars of the predicament in which she was placed, she promised faithfully that if his honour would only allow her to carry off his grandfather's skull or head in a peaceable manner, she would restore it again when done with. Here, after some communing, they came to an understanding; and she was allowed to take the head along with her, on condition that she should restore it before cock-crowing, under the heaviest penalties.

On coming out of the churchyard and looking for her companion, she had the mortification to find her "without a mouthful of breath in her body"; for, on hearing the dispute between her friend and the guardian of the grave, and suspecting much that she was likely to share the unpleasant punishments with which he threatened her friend, at the bare recital of them she fell down in a faint, from which it was no easy matter to recover her. This proved no small inconvenience to Camp-del-more's wife, as there were not above two hours to elapse ere she had to return the head according to the terms of her agreement. Taking her friend upon her back, she carried her up a steep acclivity to the nearest adjoining house, where she left her for the night; then repaired home with the utmost speed, made the 'death bree' (broth) from the head ere the appointed time had expired, restored the skull to its guardian, and placed the grave in its former condition. It is needless to add that, as a reward for her exemplary courage, the 'bree' had its desired effect. The cattle speedily recovered, and, so long as she retained any of it, all sorts of diseases were of short duration.

The Haunted Ships

"Though my mind's not
Hoodwinked with rustic marvels, I do think
There are more things in the grove, the air, the flood,
Yea, and the charnelled earth, than what wise man,
Who walks so proud as if his form alone
Filled the wide temple of the universe,
Will let a frail mind say. I'd write i' the creed
O' the sagest head alive, that fearful forms,
Holy or reprobate, do page men's heels;
That shapes, too horrid for our gaze, stand o'er
The murderer's dust, and for revenge glare up,
Even till the stars weep fire for very pity."

ALONG THE SEA OF SOLWAY, romantic on the Scottish side, with its woodland, its bays, its cliffs, and headlands; and interesting on the English side, with its many beautiful towns with their shadows on the water, rich pastures, safe harbours, and numerous ships, there still linger many traditional stories of a maritime nature, most of them connected with superstitions singularly wild and unusual. To the curious these tales afford a rich fund of entertainment, from the many diversities of the same story; some dry and barren, and stripped of all the embellishments of poetry; others dressed out in all the riches of a superstitious belief and haunted imagination. In this they resemble the inland traditions of the peasants; but many of the oral treasures of the Galwegian or the Cumbrian coast have the stamp of the Dane and the Norseman upon them, and claim but a remote or faint affinity with the legitimate legends of Caledonia. Something like a rude prosaic outline of several of the most noted of the northern ballads, the adventures and depredations of the old ocean kings, still lends life to the evening tale; and, among others, the story of the Haunted Ships is still popular among the maritime peasantry.

One fine harvest evening I went on board the shallop of Richard Faulder, of Allanbay, and, committing ourselves to the waters, we allowed a gentle wind from the east to waft us at its pleasure towards the Scottish coast. We passed the sharp promontory of Siddick, and, skirting the land within a stonecast, glided along the shore till we came within sight of the ruined Abbey of Sweetheart. The green mountain of Criffel ascended beside us; and the bleat of the flocks from its summit, together with the winding of the evening horn of the reapers, came softened into something like music over land and sea. We pushed our shallop into a deep and wooded bay, and sat silently looking on the serene beauty of the place. The moon glimmered in her rising through the tall shafts of the pines of Caerlaverock; and the sky, with scarce a cloud, showered down on wood and headland and bay the twinkling beams of a thousand stars, rendering every object visible. The tide, too, was coming with that swift and silent swell observable when the wind is gentle; the woody curves along the land were filling with the flood, till it touched the green branches of the drooping trees; while in the centre current the roll and the plunge of a thousand pellocks told to the experienced fisherman that salmon were abundant.

As we looked, we saw an old man emerging from a path that wound to the shore through a grove of doddered hazel; he carried a halve-net on his back, while behind him came a girl, bearing a small harpoon, with which the fishers are remarkably dexterous in striking their prey. The senior seated himself on a large grey stone, which overlooked the bay, laid aside his bonnet, and submitted his bosom and neck to the refreshing sea breeze, and, taking his harpoon from his attendant, sat with the gravity and composure of a spirit of the flood, with his ministering nymph behind him. We pushed our shallop to the shore, and soon stood at their side.

"This is old Mark Macmoran the mariner, with his granddaughter Barbara," said Richard Faulder, in a whisper that had something of fear in it; "he knows every creek and cavern and quicksand in Solway; has seen the Spectre Hound that haunts the Isle of Man; has heard him bark, and at every bark has seen a ship sink; and he has seen, too, the Haunted Ships in full sail; and, if all tales be true, he has sailed in them himself – he's an awful person."

Though I perceived in the communication of my friend something of the superstition of the sailor, I could not help thinking that common rumour had made a happy choice in singling out old Mark to maintain her intercourse with the invisible world. His hair, which seemed to have refused all intercourse with the comb, hung matted upon his shoulders; a kind of mantle, or rather blanket, pinned with a wooden skewer round his neck, fell mid-leg down, concealing all his nether garments as far as a pair of hose, darned with yarn of all conceivable colours, and a pair of shoes, patched and repaired till nothing of the original structure remained, and clasped on his feet with two massy silver buckles. If the dress of the old man was rude and sordid, that of his granddaughter was gay, and even rich. She wore a bodice of fine wool, wrought round the bosom with alternate leaf and lily, and a kirtle of the same fabric, which, almost touching her white and delicate ankle, showed her snowy feet, so fairy-light and round that they scarcely seemed to touch the grass where she stood. Her hair, a natural ornament which woman seeks much to improve, was of bright glossy brown, and encumbered rather than adorned with a snood, set thick with marine productions, among which the small clear pearl found in the Solway was conspicuous. Nature had not trusted to a handsome shape and a sylph-like air for young Barbara's influence over the heart of man, but had bestowed a pair of large bright blue eyes, swimming in liquid light, so full of love and gentleness and joy, that all the sailors from Annanwater to far Saint Bees acknowledged their power, and sang songs about the bonnie lass of Mark Macmoran. She stood holding a small gaff-hook of polished steel in her hand, and seemed not dissatisfied with the glances I bestowed on her from time to time, and which I held more than requited by a single glance of those eyes which retained so many capricious hearts in subjection.

The tide, though rapidly augmenting, had not yet filled the bay at our feet. The moon now streamed fairly over the tops of Caerlaverock pines, and showed the expanse of ocean dimpling and swelling, on which sloops and shallops came dancing, and displaying at every turn their extent of white sail against the beam of the moon. I looked on old Mark the mariner, who, seated motionless on his grey stone, kept his eye fixed on the increasing waters with a look of seriousness and sorrow, in which I saw little of the calculating spirit of a mere fisherman. Though he looked on the coming tide, his eyes seemed to dwell particularly on the black and decayed hulls of two vessels, which, half immersed in the quicksand, still addressed to every heart a tale of shipwreck and desolation. The tide wheeled and foamed around them, and, creeping inch by inch up the side, at last fairly threw its waters over the top, and a long and hollow eddy showed the resistance which the liquid element received.

The moment they were fairly buried in the water, the old man clasped his hands together, and said, "Blessed be the tide that will break over and bury ye for ever! Sad to mariners, and sorrowful to maids and mothers, has the time been you have choked up this deep and bonnie bay. For evil were you sent, and for evil have you continued. Every season finds from you its song of sorrow and wail, its funeral processions, and its shrouded corpses. Woe to the land where the wood grew that made ye! Cursed be the axe that hewed ye on the mountains, the hands that joined ye together, the bay that ye first swam in, and the wind that wafted ye here! Seven times have ye put my life in peril, three fair sons have ye swept from my side, and two bonnie grand-bairns; and now, even now, your waters foam and flash for my destruction, did I venture my infirm limbs in quest of food in your deadly bay. I see by that ripple and that foam, and hear by the sound and singing of your surge, that ye yearn for another victim; but it shall not be me nor mine."

Even as the old mariner addressed himself to the wrecked ships, a young man appeared at the southern extremity of the bay, holding his halve-net in his hand, and hastening into the current. Mark rose and shouted, and waved him back from a place which, to a person unacquainted with the dangers of the bay, real and superstitious, seemed sufficiently perilous; his granddaughter, too, added her voice to his, and waved her white hands; but the more they strove, the faster advanced the peasant, till he stood to his middle in the water, while the tide increased every moment in depth and strength. "Andrew, Andrew," cried the young woman, in a voice quavering with emotion, "turn, turn, I tell you! O the Ships, the Haunted Ships!" But the appearance of a fine run of fish had more influence with the peasant than the voice of bonnie Barbara, and forward he dashed, net in hand. In a moment he was borne off his feet, and mingled like foam with the water, and hurried towards the fatal eddies which whirled and roared round the sunken ships. But he was a powerful young man, and an expert swimmer; he seized on one of the projecting ribs of the nearest hulk, and, clinging to it with the grasp of despair, uttered yell after yell, sustaining himself against the prodigious rush of the current.

From a shealing of turf and straw, within the pitch of a bar from the spot where we stood, came out an old woman bent with age, and leaning on a crutch. "I heard the voice of that lad Andrew Lammie; can the chield be drowning that he skirls sae uncannily?" said the old woman, seating herself on the ground, and looking earnestly at the water. "Ou, ay," she continued, "he's doomed, he's doomed; heart and hand can never save him; boats, ropes, and man's strength and wit, all vain! vain! – he's doomed, he's doomed!"

By this time I had thrown myself into the shallop, followed reluctantly by Richard Faulder, over whose courage and kindness of heart superstition had great power, and with one push from the shore, and some exertion in sculling, we came within a quoitcast of the unfortunate fisherman. He stayed not to profit by our aid; for, when he perceived us near, he uttered a piercing shriek of joy, and bounded towards us through the agitated element the full length of an oar. I saw him for a second on the surface of the water, but the eddying current sucked him down; and all I ever beheld of him again was his hand held above the flood, and clutching in agony at some imaginary aid. I sat gazing in horror on the vacant sea before us; but a breathing-time before, a human being, full of youth and strength and hope, was there; his cries were still ringing in my ears, and echoing in the woods; and now nothing was seen or heard save the turbulent expanse of water, and the sound of its chafing on the shores. We pushed back our shallop, and resumed our station on the cliff beside the old mariner and his descendant.

"Wherefore sought ye to peril your own lives fruitlessly," said Mark, "in attempting to save the doomed? Whoso touches those infernal ships never survives to tell the tale. Woe to the man who is found nigh them at midnight when the tide has subsided, and they arise in their former beauty, with forecastle, and deck, and sail, and pennon, and shroud! Then is seen the streaming of lights along the water from their cabin windows, and then is heard the sound of mirth and the clamour of tongues, and the infernal whoop and halloo and song, ringing far and wide. Woe to the man who comes nigh them!"

To all this my Allanbay companion listened with a breathless attention. I felt something touched with a superstition to which I partly believed I had seen one victim offered up; and I inquired of the old mariner, "How and when came these Haunted Ships there? To me they seem but the melancholy relics of some unhappy voyagers, and much more likely to warn people to shun destruction than entice and delude them to it."

"And so," said the old man with a smile, which had more of sorrow in it than of mirth; "and so, young man, these black and shattered hulks seem to the eye of the multitude. But things are not what they seem: that water, a kind and convenient servant to the wants of man, which seems so smooth and so dimpling and so gentle, has swallowed up a human soul even now; and the place which it covers, so fair and so level, is a faithless quicksand, out of which none escape. Things are otherwise than they seem. Had you lived as long as I have had the sorrow to live; had you seen the storms, and braved the perils, and endured the distresses which have befallen me; had you sat gazing out on the dreary ocean at midnight on a haunted coast; had you seen comrade after comrade, brother after brother, and son after son, swept away by the merciless ocean from your very side; had you seen the shapes of friends, doomed to the wave and the quicksand, appearing to you in the dreams and visions of the night, then would your mind have been prepared for crediting the maritime legends of mariners; and the two haunted Danish ships would have had their terrors for you, as they have for all who sojourn on this coast.

"Of the time and the cause of their destruction," continued the old man, "I know nothing certain; they have stood as you have seen them for uncounted time; and while all other ships wrecked on this unhappy coast have gone to pieces, and rotted and sunk away in a few years, these two haunted hulks have neither sunk in the quicksand, nor has a single spar or board been displaced. Maritime legend says that two ships of Denmark having had permission, for a time, to work deeds of darkness and dolor on the deep, were at last condemned to the whirlpool and the sunken rock, and were wrecked in this bonnie bay, as a sign to seamen to be gentle and devout. The night when they were lost was a harvest evening of uncommon mildness and beauty: the sun had newly set; the moon came brighter and brighter out; and the reapers, laying their sickles at the root of the standing corn, stood on rock and bank, looking at the increasing magnitude of the waters, for sea and land were visible from Saint Bees to Barnhourie. The sails of two vessels were soon seen bent for the Scottish coast; and, with a speed outrunning the swiftest ship, they approached the dangerous quicksands and headland of Borranpoint. On the deck of the foremost ship not a living soul was seen, or shape, unless something in darkness and form, resembling a human shadow could be called a shape, which flitted from extremity to extremity of the ship, with the appearance of trimming the sails, and directing the vessel's course. But the decks of its companion were crowded with human shapes; the captain and mate, and sailor and cabin-boy all seemed there; and from them the sound of mirth and minstrelsy echoed over land and water. The coast which they skirted along was one of extreme danger, and the reapers shouted to warn them to beware of sandbank and rock; but of this friendly counsel no notice was taken, except that a large and famished dog, which sat on the prow, answered every shout with a long, loud, and melancholy howl. The deep sandbank of Carsethorn was expected to arrest the career of these desperate navigators; but they passed, with the celerity of water-fowl, over an obstruction which had wrecked many pretty ships.

"Old men shook their heads and departed, saying, 'We have seen the fiend sailing in a bottomless ship; let us go home and pray;' but one young and wilful man said, 'Fiend! I'll warrant it's nae fiend, but douce Janet Withershins the witch, holding a carouse with some of her Cumberland cummers, and mickle red wine will be spilt atween them. Dod I would gladly have a toothfu'! I'll warrant it's nane o' your cauld sour slae-water like a bottle of Bailie Skrinkie's port, but right drap-o'-my-heart's-blood stuff, that would waken a body out of their last linen. I wonder where the cummers will anchor their craft?' 'And I'll vow,' said another rustic, 'the wine they quaff is none of your visionary drink, such as a drouthie body has dished out to his lips in a dream; nor is it shadowy and unsubstantial, like the vessels they sail in, which are made out of a cockel-shell or a cast-off slipper, or the paring of a seaman's right thumb-nail. I once got a hansel out of a witch's quaigh myself – auld Marion Mathers, of Dustiefoot, whom they tried to bury in the old kirkyard of Dunscore; but the cummer raise as fast as they laid her down, and naewhere else would she lie but in the bonnie green kirkyard of Kier, among douce and sponsible fowk. So I'll vow that the wine of a witch's cup is as fell liquor as ever did a kindly turn to a poor man's heart; and be they fiends, or be they witches, if they have red wine asteer, I'll risk a drouket sark for ae glorious tout on't.'

"'Silence, ye sinners,' said the minister's son of a neighbouring parish, who united in his own person his father's lack of devotion with his mother's love of liquor. 'Whist! – speak as if ye had the fear of something holy before ye. Let the vessels run their own way to destruction: who can stay the eastern wind, and the current of the Solway sea? I can find ye Scripture warrant for that; so let them try their strength on Blawhooly rocks, and their might on the broad quicksand. There's a surf running there would knock the ribs together of a galley built by the imps of the pit, and commanded by the Prince of Darkness. Bonnily and bravely they sail away there, but before the blast blows by they'll be wrecked; and red wine and strong brandy will be as rife as dyke-water, and we'll drink the health of bonnie Bell Blackness out of her left-foot slipper.'

"The speech of the young profligate was applauded by several of his companions, and away they flew to the bay of Blawhooly, from whence they never returned. The two vessels were observed all at once to stop in the bosom of the bay, on the spot where their hulls now appear; the mirth and the minstrelsy waxed louder than ever, and the forms of maidens, with instruments of music and wine-cups in their hands, thronged the decks. A boat was lowered; and the same shadowy pilot who conducted the ships made it start towards the shore with the rapidity of lightning, and its head knocked against the bank where the four young men stood who longed for the unblest drink. They leaped in with a laugh, and with a laugh were they welcomed on deck; wine-cups were given to each, and as they raised them to their lips the vessels melted away beneath their feet, and one loud shriek, mingled with laughter still louder, was heard over land and water for many miles. Nothing more was heard or seen till the morning, when the crowd who came to the beach saw with fear and wonder the two Haunted Ships, such as they now seem, masts and tackle gone; nor mark, nor sign, by which their name, country, or destination could be known, was left remaining. Such is the tradition of the mariners; and its truth has been attested by many families whose sons and whose fathers have been drowned in the haunted bay of Blawhooly."

"And trow ye," said the old woman, who, attracted from her hut by the drowning cries of the young fisherman, had remained an auditor of the mariner's legend. "And trow ye, Mark Macmoran, that the tale of the Haunted Ships is done? I can say no to that. Mickle have mine ears heard; but more mine eyes have witnessed since I came to dwell in this humble home by the side of the deep sea. I mind the night weel; it was on Hallowmas Eve; the nuts were cracked, and the apples were eaten, and spell and charm were tried at my fireside; till, wearied with diving into the dark waves of futurity, the lads and lasses fairly took to the more visible blessings of kind words, tender clasps, and gentle courtship. Soft words in a maiden's ear, and a kindly kiss o' her lip were old-world matters to me, Mark Macmoran; though I mean not to say that I have been free of the folly of daunering and daffin with a youth in my day, and keeping tryst with him in dark and lonely places. However, as I say, these times of enjoyment were passed and gone with me – the mair's the pity that pleasure should fly sae fast away – and as I couldna make sport I thought I should not mar any; so out I sauntered into the fresh cold air, and sat down behind that old oak, and looked abroad on the wide sea. I had my ain sad thoughts, ye may think, at the time: it was in that very bay my blythe good-man perished, with seven more in his company; and on that very bank where ye see the waves leaping and foaming, I saw seven stately corses streeked, but the dearest was the eighth. It was a woful sight to me, a widow, with four bonnie boys, with nought to support them but these twa hands, and God's blessing, and a cow's grass. I have never liked to live out of sight of this bay since that time; and mony's the moonlight night I sit looking on these watery mountains and these waste shores; it does my heart good, whatever it may do to my head. So ye see it was Hallowmas Night, and looking on sea and land sat I; and my heart wandering to other thoughts soon made me forget my youthful company at hame. It might be near the howe hour of the night. The tide was making, and its singing brought strange old-world stories with it, and I thought on the dangers that sailors endure, the fates they meet with, and the fearful forms they see. My own blythe goodman had seen sights that made him grave enough at times, though he aye tried to laugh them away.

"Aweel, atween that very rock aneath us and the coming tide, I saw, or thought I saw – for the tale is so dreamlike that the whole might pass for a vision of the night – I saw the form of a man; his plaid was grey, his face was grey; and his hair, which hung low down till it nearly came to the middle of his back, was as white as the white sea-foam. He began to howk and dig under the bank; an' God be near me, thought I, this maun be the unblessed spirit of auld Adam Gowdgowpin the miser, who is doomed to dig for shipwrecked treasure, and count how many millions are hidden for ever from man's enjoyment. The form found something which in shape and hue seemed a left-foot slipper of brass; so down to the tide he marched, and, placing it on the water, whirled it thrice round, and the infernal slipper dilated at every turn, till it became a bonnie barge with its sails bent, and on board leaped the form, and scudded swiftly away. He came to one of the Haunted Ships, and striking it with his oar, a fair ship, with mast and canvas and mariners, started up; he touched the other Haunted Ship, and produced the like transformation; and away the three spectre ships bounded, leaving a track of fire behind them on the billows which was long unextinguished. Now wasna that a bonnie and fearful sight to see beneath the light of the Hallowmas moon? But the tale is far frae finished, for mariners say that once a year, on a certain night, if ye stand on the Borran Point, ye will see the infernal shallops coming snoring through the Solway; ye will hear the same laugh and song and mirth and minstrelsy which our ancestors heard; see them bound over the sandbanks and sunken rocks like sea-gulls, cast their anchor in Blawhooly Bay, while the shadowy figure lowers down the boat, and augments their numbers with the four unhappy mortals to whose memory a stone stands in the kirkyard, with a sinking ship and a shoreless sea cut upon it. Then the spectre ships vanish, and the drowning shriek of mortals and the rejoicing laugh of fiends are heard, and the old hulls are left as a memorial that the old spiritual kingdom has not departed from the earth. But I maun away, and trim my little cottage fire, and make it burn and blaze up bonnie, to warm the crickets and my cold and crazy bones that maun soon be laid aneath the green sod in the eerie kirkyard." And away the old dame tottered to her cottage, secured the door on the inside, and soon the hearth-flame was seen to glimmer and gleam through the keyhole and window.

"I'll tell ye what," said the old mariner, in a subdued tone, and with a shrewd and suspicious glance of his eye after the old sibyl, "it's a word that may not very well be uttered, but there are many mistakes made in evening stories if old Moll Moray there, where she lives, knows not mickle more than she is willing to tell of the Haunted Ships and their unhallowed mariners. She lives cannily and quietly; no one knows how she is fed or supported; but her dress is aye whole, her cottage ever smokes, and her table lacks neither of wine, white and red, nor of fowl and fish, and white bread and brown. It was a dear scoff to Jock Matheson, when he called old Moll the uncanny carline of Blawhooly: his boat ran round and round in the centre of the Solway – everybody said it was enchanted – and down it went head foremost; and hadna Jock been a swimmer equal to a sheldrake, he would have fed the fish. But I'll warrant it sobered the lad's speech; and he never reckoned himself safe till he made old Moll the present of a new kirtle and a stone of cheese."

"O father!" said his granddaughter Barbara, "ye surely wrong poor old Mary Moray; what use could it be to an old woman like her, who has no wrongs to redress, no malice to work out against mankind, and nothing to seek of enjoyment save a canny hour and a quiet grave – what use could the fellowship of fiends and the communion of evil spirits be to her? I know Jenny Primrose puts rowan-tree above the door-head when she sees old Mary coming; I know the good-wife of Kittlenaket wears rowan-berry leaves in the headband of her blue kirtle, and all for the sake of averting the unsonsie glance of Mary's right ee; and I know that the auld Laird of Burntroutwater drives his seven cows to their pasture with a wand of witch-tree, to keep Mary from milking them. But what has all that to do with haunted shallops, visionary mariners, and bottomless boats? I have heard myself as pleasant a tale about the Haunted Ships and their unworldly crews as anyone would wish to hear in a winter evening. It was told me by young Benjie Macharg, one summer night, sitting on Arbigland-bank: the lad intended a sort of love meeting; but all that he could talk of was about smearing sheep and shearing sheep, and of the wife which the Norway elves of the Haunted Ships made for his uncle Sandie Macharg. And I shall tell ye the tale as the honest lad told it to me.

"Alexander Macharg, besides being the laird of three acres of peatmoss, two kale gardens, and the owner of seven good milch cows, a pair of horses, and six pet sheep, was the husband of one of the handsomest women in seven parishes. Many a lad sighed the day he was brided; and a Nithsdale laird and two Annandale moorland farmers drank themselves to their last linen, as well as their last shilling, through sorrow for her loss.

But married was the dame; and home she was carried, to bear rule over her home and her husband, as an honest woman should. Now ye maun ken that though the flesh-and-blood lovers of Alexander's bonnie wife all ceased to love and to sue her after she became another's, there were certain admirers who did not consider their claim at all abated, or their hopes lessened by the kirk's famous obstacle of matrimony. Ye have heard how the devout minister of Tinwald had a fair son carried away, and wedded against his liking to an unchristened bride, whom the elves and the fairies provided; ye have heard how the bonnie bride of the drunken Laird of Soukitup was stolen by the fairies out at the back-window of the bridal chamber, the time the bridegroom was groping his way to the chamber door; and ye have heard – but why need I multiply cases? Such things in the ancient days were as common as candle-light. So ye'll no hinder certain water elves and sea fairies, who sometimes keep festival and summer mirth in these old haunted hulks, from falling in love with the weel-faured wife of Laird Macharg; and to their plots and contrivances they went how they might accomplish to sunder man and wife; and sundering such a man and such a wife was like sundering the green leaf from the summer, or the fragrance from the flower.

"So it fell on a time that Laird Macharg took his halve-net on his back, and his steel spear in his hand, and down to Blawhooly Bay gaed he, and into the water he went right between the two haunted hulks, and placing his net awaited the coming of the tide. The night, ye maun ken, was mirk, and the wind lowne, and the singing of the increasing waters among the shells and the peebles was heard for sundry miles. All at once light began to glance and twinkle on board the two Haunted Ships from every hole and seam, and presently the sound as of a hatchet employed in squaring timber echoed far and wide. But if the toil of these unearthly workmen amazed the laird, how much more was his amazement increased when a sharp shrill voice called out, 'Ho, brother! what are you doing now?' A voice still shriller responded from the other haunted ship, 'I'm making a wife to Sandie Macharg!' And a loud quavering laugh running from ship to ship, and from bank to bank, told the joy they expected from their labour.

"Now the laird, besides being a devout and a God-fearing man, was shrewd and bold; and in plot and contrivance, and skill in conducting his designs, was fairly an overmatch for any dozen land elves; but the water elves are far more subtle; besides their haunts and their dwellings being in the great deep, pursuit and detection is hopeless if they succeed in carrying their prey to the waves. But ye shall hear. Home flew the laird, collected his family around the hearth, spoke of the signs and the sins of the times, and talked of mortification and prayer for averting calamity; and, finally, taking his father's Bible, brass clasps, black print, and covered with calf-skin, from the shelf, he proceeded without let or stint to perform domestic worship. I should have told ye that he bolted and locked the door, shut up all inlet to the house, threw salt into the fire, and proceeded in every way like a man skilful in guarding against the plots of fairies and fiends. His wife looked on all this with wonder; but she saw something in her husband's looks that hindered her from intruding either question or advice, and a wise woman was she.

"Near the mid-hour of the night the rush of a horse's feet was heard, and the sound of a rider leaping from its back, and a heavy knock came to the door, accompanied by a voice, saying, 'The cummer drink's hot, and the knave bairn is expected at Laird Laurie's tonight; sae mount, good-wife, and come.'

"'Preserve me!' said the wife of Sandie Macharg, 'that's news indeed; who could have thought it? The laird has been heirless for seventeen years! Now, Sandie, my man, fetch me my skirt and hood.'

"But he laid his arm round his wife's neck, and said, 'If all the lairds in Galloway go heirless, over this door threshold shall you not stir tonight; and I have said, and I have sworn it; seek not to know why or wherefore – but, Lord, send us thy blessed mornlight.' The wife looked for a moment in her husband's eyes, and desisted from further entreaty.

"'But let us send a civil message to the gossips, Sandy; and hadna ye better say I am sair laid with a sudden sickness? though it's sinful-like to send the poor messenger a mile agate with a lie in his mouth without a glass of brandy.'

"'To such a messenger, and to those who sent him, no apology is needed,' said the austere laird; 'so let him depart.' And the clatter of a horse's hoofs was heard, and the muttered imprecations of its rider on the churlish treatment he had experienced.

"'Now, Sandie, my lad,' said his wife, laying an arm particularly white and round about his neck as she spoke, 'are you not a queer man and a stern? I have been your wedded wife now these three years; and, beside my dower, have brought you three as bonnie bairns as ever smiled aneath a summer sun. O man, you a douce man, and fitter to be an elder than even Willie Greer himself, I have the minister's ain word for 't, to put on these hard-hearted looks, and gang waving your arms that way, as if ye said, "I winna take the counsel of sic a hempie as you;" I'm your ain leal wife, and will and maun have an explanation.'

"To all this Sandie Macharg replied, 'It is written, "Wives, obey your husbands"; but we have been stayed in our devotion, so let us pray;' and down he knelt: his wife knelt also, for she was as devout as bonnie; and beside them knelt their household, and all lights were extinguished.

"'Now this beats a',' muttered his wife to herself; 'however, I shall be obedient for a time; but if I dinna ken what all this is for before the morn by sunket-time, my tongue is nae langer a tongue, nor my hands worth wearing.'

"The voice of her husband in prayer interrupted this mental soliloquy; and ardently did he beseech to be preserved from the wiles of the fiends and the snares of Satan; from witches, ghosts, goblins, elves, fairies, spunkies, and water-kelpies; from the spectre shallop of Solway; from spirits visible and invisible; from the Haunted Ships and their unearthly tenants; from maritime spirits that plotted against godly men, and fell in love with their wives—"

"'Nay, but His presence be near us!' said his wife, in a low tone of dismay. 'God guide my gudeman's wits: I never heard such a prayer from human lips before. But, Sandie, my man, Lord's sake, rise. What fearful light is this? Barn and byre and stable maun be in a blaze; and Hawkie, and Hurley, Doddie, and Cherrie, and Damsonplum will be smoored with reek, and scorched with flame.'

"And a flood of light, but not so gross as a common fire, which ascended to heaven and filled all the court before the house, amply justified the good-wife's suspicions. But to the terrors of fire Sandie was as immovable as he was to the imaginary groans of the barren wife of Laird Laurie; and he held his wife, and threatened the weight of his right hand – and it was a heavy one – to all who ventured abroad, or even unbolted the door. The neighing and prancing of horses, and the bellowing of cows, augmented the horrors of the night; and to anyone who only heard the din, it seemed that the whole onstead was in a blaze, and horses and cattle perishing in the flame. All wiles, common or extraordinary, were put in practice to entice or force the honest farmer and his wife to open the door; and when the like success attended every new stratagem, silence for a little while ensued, and a long, loud, and shrilling laugh wound up the dramatic efforts of the night. In the morning, when Laird Macharg went to the door, he found standing against one of the pilasters a piece of black ship oak, rudely fashioned into something like human form, and which skilful people declared would have been clothed with seeming flesh and blood, and palmed upon him by elfin adroitness for his wife, had he admitted his visitants. A synod of wise men and women sat upon the woman of timber, and she was finally ordered to be devoured by fire, and that in the open air. A fire was soon made, and into it the elfin sculpture was tossed from the prongs of two pairs of pitchforks. The blaze that arose was awful to behold; and hissings and burstings and loud cracklings and strange noises were heard in the midst of the flame; and when the whole sank into ashes, a drinking-cup of some precious metal was found; and this cup, fashioned no doubt by elfin skill, but rendered harmless by the purification with fire, the sons and daughters of Sandie Macharg and his wife drink out of to this very day. Bless all bold men, say I, and obedient wives!"

Ewen of the Little Head

ABOUT THREE HUNDRED YEARS AGO, Ewen Maclaine of Lochbuy, in the island of Mull, having been engaged in a quarrel with a neighbouring chief, a day was fixed for determining the affair by the sword. Lochbuy, before the day arrived, consulted a celebrated witch as to the result of the feud. The witch declared that if Lochbuy's wife should on the morning of that day give him and his men food unasked, he would be victorious, but if not, the result would be the reverse. This was a disheartening response for the unhappy votary, his wife being a noted shrew.

The fatal morning arrived, and the hour for meeting the enemy approached, but there appeared no symptoms of refreshment for Lochbuy and his men. At length the unfortunate man was compelled to ask his wife to supply them with food. She set down before them curds, but without spoons. When the husband inquired how they were to eat them, she replied they should assume the bills of hens. The men ate the curds, as well as they could, with their hands; but Lochbuy himself ate none. After behaving with the greatest bravery in the bloody conflict which ensued, he fell covered with wounds, leaving his wife to the execration of the people. She is still known in that district under the appellation of Corr-dhu, or the Black Crane.

But the miseries brought on the luckless Lochbuy by his wife did not end with his life, for he died fasting, and his ghost is frequently seen to this day riding the very horse on which he was mounted when he was killed. It was a small, but very neat and active pony, dun or mouse-coloured, to which the Laird was much attached, and on which he had ridden for many years before his death. Its appearance is as accurately described in the island of Mull as any steed is at Newmarket. The prints of its shoes are discerned by connoisseurs, and the rattling of its curb is recognised in the darkest night. It is not particular with regard to roads, for it goes up hill and down dale with equal velocity. Its hard-fated rider still wears the same green cloak which covered him in his last battle; and he is particularly distinguished by the small size of his head, a peculiarity which, we suspect, the learned disciples of Spurzheim have never yet had the sagacity to discover as indicative of an extraordinary talent and incomparable perseverance in horsemanship.

It is now above three hundred years since Ewen-a-chin-vig (*Anglice*, Hugh of the Little Head) fell in the field of honour; but neither the vigour of the horse nor of the rider is yet diminished. His mournful duty has always been to attend the dying moments of every member of his own tribe, and to escort the departed spirit on its long and arduous journey. He has been seen in the remotest of the Hebrides; and he has found his way to Ireland on these occasions long before steam navigation was invented. About a century ago he took a fancy for a young man of his own race, and frequently did him the honour of placing him behind himself on horseback. He entered into conversation with him, and foretold many circumstances connected with the fate of his successors, which have undoubtedly since come to pass.

Many a long winter night have I listened to the feats of Ewen-a-chin-vig, the faithful and indefatigable guardian of his ancient family, in the hour of their last and greatest trial, affording an example worthy the imitation of every chief – perhaps not beneath the notice of Glengarry himself.

About a dozen years since some symptoms of Ewen's decay gave very general alarm to his friends. He accosted one of his own people (indeed he never has been known to notice any other), and, shaking him cordially by the hand, he attempted to place him on the saddle behind him, but the uncourteous dog declined the honour. Ewen struggled hard, but the clown was a great, strong, clumsy fellow, and stuck to the earth with all his might. He candidly acknowledged, however, that his chief would have prevailed, had it not been for a birch-tree which stood by, and which he got within the fold of his left arm. The contest became very warm indeed, and the tree was certainly twisted like an osier, as thousands can testify who saw it as well as myself. At length, however, Ewen lost his seat for the first time, and the instant the pony found he was his own master, he set off with the fleetness of lightning. Ewen immediately pursued his steed, and the wearied rustic sped his way homeward. It was the general opinion that Ewen found considerable difficulty in catching the horse; but I am happy to learn that he has been lately seen riding the old mouse-coloured pony without the least change in either the horse or the rider. Long may he continue to do so!

Those who from motives of piety or curiosity have visited the sacred island of Iona, must remember to have seen the guide point out the tomb of Ewen, with his figure on horseback, very elegantly sculptured in alto-relievo, and many of the above facts are on such occasions related.

The Dracae

THESE ARE A SORT OF WATER-SPIRITS who inveigle women and children into the recesses which they inhabit, beneath lakes and rivers, by floating past them, on the surface of the water, in the shape of gold rings or cups. The women thus seized are employed as nurses, and after seven years are permitted to revisit earth. Gervase mentions one woman in particular who had been allured by observing a wooden dish, or cup, float by her, while she was washing clothes in the river. Being seized as soon as she reached the depths, she was conducted into one of the subterranean recesses, which she described as very magnificent, and employed as nurse to one of the brood of the hag who had allured her. During her residence in this capacity, having accidentally touched one of her eyes with an ointment of serpent's grease, she perceived, at her return to the world, that she had acquired the faculty of seeing the *Dracae*, when they intermingle themselves with men. Of this power she was, however, deprived by the touch of her ghostly mistress, whom she had one day incautiously addressed. It is a curious fact that this story, in almost all its parts, is current in both the Highlands and Lowlands of Scotland, with no other variation than the substitution of Fairies for Dracae, and the cavern of a hill for that of a river. Indeed many of the vulgar account it extremely dangerous to touch anything which they may happen to find without saining (blessing) it, the snares of the enemy being notorious and well-attested. A pool-woman of Teviotdale having been fortunate enough, as she thought herself, to find a wooden beetle, at the very time when she needed such an implement, seized it without pronouncing a proper blessing, and, carrying it home, laid it above her bed to be ready for employment in the morning. At midnight the window of her cottage opened, and a loud voice was heard calling up someone within by a strange and uncouth name. The terrified cottager ejaculated a prayer, which, we may suppose, ensured her personal safety; while the enchanted implement of housewifery, tumbling from the bedstead, departed by the window with no small noise and precipitation. In a humorous fugitive tract, Dr. Johnson has been introduced as disputing the authenticity of an apparition, merely because the spirit assumed the shape of a teapot and a shoulder of mutton. No doubt, a case so much in point as that we have now quoted would have removed his incredulity.

The Red-Etin

THERE WERE ONCE TWO WIDOWS who lived in two cottages which stood not very far from one another. And each of those widows possessed a piece of land on which she grazed a cow and a few sheep, and in this way she made her living.

One of these poor widows had two sons, the other had one; and as these three boys were always together, it was natural that they should become great friends.

At last the time arrived when the eldest son of the widow who had two sons, must leave home and go out into the world to seek his fortune. And the night before he went away his mother told him to take a can and go to the well and bring back some water, and she would bake a cake for him to carry with him.

"But remember," she added, "the size of the cake will depend on the quantity of water that thou bringest back. If thou bringest much, then will it be large; and, if thou bringest little, then will it be small. But, big or little, it is all that I have to give thee."

The lad took the can and went off to the well, and filled it with water, and came home again. But he never noticed that the can had a hole in it, and was running out; so that, by the time that he arrived at home, there was very little water left. So his mother could only bake him a very little cake.

But, small as it was, she asked him, as she gave it to him, to choose one of two things. Either to take the half of it with her blessing, or the whole of it with her malison. "For," said she, "thou canst not have both the whole cake and a blessing along with it."

The lad looked at the cake and hesitated. It would have been pleasant to have left home with his mother's blessing upon him; but he had far to go, and the cake was little; the half of it would be a mere mouthful, and he did not know when he would get any more food. So at last he made up his mind to take the whole of it, even if he had to bear his mother's malison.

Then he took his younger brother aside, and gave him his hunting-knife, saying, "Keep this by thee, and look at it every morning. For as long as the blade remains clear and bright, thou wilt know that it is well with me; but should it grow dim and rusty, then know thou that some evil hath befallen me."

After this he embraced them both and set out on his travels. He journeyed all that day, and all the next, and on the afternoon of the third day he came to where an old shepherd was sitting beside a flock of sheep.

"I will ask the old man whose sheep they are," he said to himself, "for mayhap his master might engage me also as a shepherd." So he went up to the old man, and asked him to whom the sheep belonged. And this was all the answer he got:

> *"The Red-Etin of Ireland*
> *Ance lived in Ballygan,*
> *And stole King Malcolm's daughter,*
> *The King of fair Scotland.*
> *He beats her, he binds her,*
> *He lays her on a band,*
> *And every day he dings her*
> *With a bright silver wand.*
> *Like Julian the Roman,*
> *He's one that fears no man.*
> *"It's said there's ane predestinate*
> *To be his mortal foe,*
> *But that man is yet unborn,*
> *And lang may it be so."*

"That does not tell me much; but somehow I do not fancy this Red-Etin for a master," thought the youth, and he went on his way.

He had not gone very far, however, when he saw another old man, with snow-white hair, herding a flock of swine; and as he wondered to whom the swine belonged, and if there was any chance of him getting a situation as a swineherd, he went up to the countryman, and asked who was the owner of the animals.

He got the same answer from the swineherd that he had got from the shepherd:

> *"The Red-Etin of Ireland*
> *Ance lived in Ballygan,*
> *And stole King Malcolm's daughter,*

The King of fair Scotland.
He beats her, he binds her,
He lays her on a band,
And every day he dings her
With a bright silver wand.
Like Julian the Roman,
He's one that fears no man.
"It's said there's ane predestinate
To be his mortal foe,
But that man is yet unborn,
And lang may it be so."

"Plague on this old Red-Etin; I wonder when I will get out of his domains," he muttered to himself; and he journeyed still further.

Presently he came to a very, very old man – so old, indeed, that he was quite bent with age – and he was herding a flock of goats.

Once more the traveller asked to whom the animals belonged, and once more he got the same answer:

"The Red-Etin of Ireland
Ance lived in Ballygan,
And stole King Malcolm's daughter,
The King of fair Scotland.
He beats her, he binds her,
He lays her on a band,
And every day he dings her
With a bright silver wand.
Like Julian the Roman,
He's one that fears no man.
"It's said there's ane predestinate
To be his mortal foe,
But that man is yet unborn,
And lang may it be so."

But this ancient goatherd added a piece of advice at the end of his rhyme. "Beware, stranger," he said, "of the next herd of beasts that ye shall meet. Sheep, and swine, and goats will harm nobody; but the creatures ye shall now encounter are of a sort that ye have never met before, and *they* are not harmless."

The young man thanked him for his counsel, and went on his way, and he had not gone very far before he met a herd of very dreadful creatures, unlike anything that he had ever dreamed of in all his life.

For each of them had three heads, and on each of its three heads it had four horns; and when he saw them he was so frightened that he turned and ran away from them as fast as he could.

Up hill and down dale he ran, until he was well-nigh exhausted; and, just when he was beginning to feel that his legs would not carry him any further, he saw a great Castle in front of him, the door of which was standing wide open.

He was so tired that he went straight in, and after wandering through some magnificent halls, which appeared to be quite deserted, he reached the kitchen, where an old woman was sitting by the fire.

He asked her if he might have a night's lodging, as he had come a long and weary journey, and would be glad of somewhere to rest.

"You can rest here, and welcome, for me," said the old Dame, "but for your own sake I warn you that this is an ill house to bide in; for it is the Castle of the Red-Etin, who is a fierce and terrible Monster with three heads, and he spareth neither man nor woman, if he can get hold of them."

Tired as he was, the young man would have made an effort to escape from such a dangerous abode had he not remembered the strange and awful beasts from which he had just been fleeing, and he was afraid that, as it was growing dark, if he set out again he might chance to walk right into their midst. So he begged the old woman to hide him in some dark corner, and not to tell the Red-Etin that he was in the Castle.

"For," thought he, "if I can only get shelter until the morning, I will then be able to avoid these terrible creatures and go on my way in peace."

So the old Dame hid him in a press under the back stairs, and, as there was plenty of room in it, he settled down quite comfortably for the night.

But just as he was going off to sleep he heard an awful roaring and trampling overhead. The Red-Etin had come home, and it was plain that he was searching for something.

And the terrified youth soon found out what the "Something" was, for very soon the horrible Monster came into the kitchen, crying out in a voice like thunder:

> *"Seek but, and seek ben,*
> *I smell the smell of an earthly man!*
> *Be he living, or be he dead,*
> *His heart this night I shall eat with my bread."*

And it was not very long before he discovered the poor young man's hiding-place and pulled him roughly out of it.

Of course, the lad begged that his life might be spared, but the Monster only laughed at him.

"It will be spared if thou canst answer three questions," he said; "if not, it is forfeited."

The first of these three questions was, "Whether Ireland or Scotland was first inhabited?"

The second, "How old was the world when Adam was made?"

And the third, "Whether men or beasts were created first?"

The lad was not skilled in such matters, having had but little book-learning, and he could not answer the questions. So the Monster struck him on the head with a queer little hammer which he carried, and turned him into a piece of stone.

Now every morning since he had left home his younger brother had done as he had promised, and had carefully examined his hunting-knife.

On the first two mornings it was bright and clear, but on the third morning he was very much distressed to find that it was dull and rusty. He looked at it for a few moments in great dismay; then he ran straight to his mother, and held it out to her.

"By this token I know that some mischief hath befallen my brother," he said, "so I must set out at once to see what evil hath come upon him."

"First must thou go to the well and fetch me some water," said his mother, "that I may bake thee a cake to carry with thee, as I baked a cake for him who is gone. And I will say to thee what I said to him. That the cake will be large or small according as thou bringest much or little water back with thee."

So the lad took the can, as his brother had done, and went off to the well, and it seemed as if some evil spirit directed him to follow his example in all things, for he brought home little water, and he chose the whole cake and his mother's malison, instead of the half and her blessing, and he set out and met the shepherd, and the swineherd, and the goatherd, and they all gave the same answers to him which they had given to his brother. And he also encountered the same fierce beasts, and ran from them in terror, and took shelter from them in the Castle; and the old woman hid him, and the Red-Etin found him, and, because he could not answer the three questions, he, too, was turned into a pillar of stone.

And no more would ever have been heard of these two youths had not a kind Fairy, who had seen all that had happened, appeared to the other widow and her son, as they were sitting at supper one night in the gloaming, and told them the whole story, and how their two poor young neighbours had been turned into pillars of stone by a cruel enchanter called Red-Etin.

Now the third young man was both brave and strong, and he determined to set out to see if he could in anywise help his two friends. And, from the very first moment that he had made up his mind to do so, things went differently with him than they had with them. I think, perhaps, that this was because he was much more loving and thoughtful than they were.

For, when his mother sent him to fetch water from the well so that she might bake a cake for him, just as the other mother had done for her sons, a raven, flying above his head, croaked out that his can was leaking, and he, wishing to please his mother by bringing her a good supply of water, patched up the hole with clay, and so came home with the can quite full.

Then, when his mother had baked a big bannock for him, and giving him his choice between the whole cake and her malison, or half of it and her blessing, he chose the latter, "for," said he, throwing his arms round her neck, "I may light on other cakes to eat, but I will never light on another blessing such as thine."

And the curious thing was that, after he had said this, the half cake which he had chosen seemed to spread itself out, and widen, and broaden, till it was bigger by far than it had been at first.

Then he started on his journey, and, after he had gone a good way he began to feel hungry. So he pulled it out of his pocket and began to eat it.

Just then he met an old woman, who seemed to be very poor, for her clothing was thin, and worn, and old, and she stopped and spoke to him.

"Of thy charity, kind Master," she said, stretching out one of her withered hands, "spare me a bit of the cake that thou art eating."

Now the youth was very hungry, and he could have eaten it all himself, but his kind heart was touched by the woman's pinched face, so he broke it in two, and gave her half of it.

Instantly she was changed into the Fairy who had appeared to his mother and himself as they had sat at supper the night before, and she smiled graciously at the generous lad, and held out a little wand to him.

"Though thou knowest it not, thy mother's blessing and thy kindness to an old and poor woman hath gained thee many blessings, brave boy," he said. "Keep that as thy reward; thou wilt need it ere thy errand be done." Then, bidding him sit down on the grass beside her, she told him all the dangers that he would meet on his travels, and the way in which he could overcome them, and then, in a moment, before he could thank her, she vanished out of his sight.

But with the little wand, and all the instructions that she had given him, he felt that he could face fearlessly any danger that he might be called on to meet, so he rose from the grass and went his way, full of a cheerful courage.

After he had walked for many miles further, he came, as each of his friends had done, to the old shepherd herding his sheep. And, like them, he asked to whom the sheep belonged. And this time the old man answered:

> "The Red-Etin of Ireland
> Ance lived in Ballygan,
> And stole King Malcolm's daughter,
> The King of fair Scotland.
> He beats her, he binds her,
> He lays her on a band,
> And every day he dings her
> With a bright silver wand.
> Like Julian the Roman,
> He's one that fears no man.
> "But now I fear his end is near,
> And destiny at hand;
> And you're to be, I plainly see,
> The heir of all his land."

Then the young man went on, and he came to the swineherd, and to the goatherd; and each of them in turn repeated the same words to him.

And, when he came to where the droves of monstrous beasts were, he was not afraid of them, and when one came running up to him with its mouth wide open to devour him, he just struck it with his wand, and it dropped down dead at his feet.

At last he arrived at the Red-Etin's Castle, and he knocked boldly at the door. The old woman answered his knock, and, when he had told her his errand, warned him gravely not to enter.

"Thy two friends came here before thee," she said, "and they are now turned into two pillars of stone; what advantage is it to thee to lose thy life also?"

But the young man only laughed. "I have knowledge of an art of which they knew nothing," he said. "And methinks I can fight the Red-Etin with his own weapons."

So, much against her will, the old woman let him in, and hid him where she had hid his friends.

It was not long before the Monster arrived, and, as on former occasions, he came into the kitchen in a furious rage, crying:

> "Seek but, and seek ben,
> I smell the smell of an earthly man!

> *Be he living, or be he dead,*
> *His heart this night I shall eat with my bread."*

Then he peered into the young man's hiding-place, and called to him to come out. And after he had come out, he put to him the three questions, never dreaming that he could answer them; but the Fairy had told the youth what to say, and he gave the answers as pat as any book.

Then the Red-Etin's heart sank within him for fear, for he knew that someone had betrayed him, and that his power was gone.

And gone in very truth it was. For when the youth took an axe and began to fight with him, he had no strength to resist, and, before he knew where he was, his heads were cut off. And that was the end of the Red-Etin.

As soon as he saw that his enemy was really dead, the young man asked the old woman if what the shepherd, and the swineherd, and the goatherd had told him were true, and if King Malcolm's daughter were really a prisoner in the Castle.

The old woman nodded. "Even with the Monster lying dead at my feet, I am almost afraid to speak of it," she said. "But come with me, my gallant gentleman, and thou wilt see what dule and misery the Red-Etin hath caused to many a home."

She took a huge bunch of keys, and led him up a long flight of stairs, which ended in a passage with a great many doors on each side of it. She unlocked these doors with her keys, and, as she opened them, she put her head into every room and said, "Ye have naught to fear now, Madam, the Predestinated Deliverer hath come, and the Red-Etin is dead."

And behold, with a cry of joy, out of every room came a beautiful lady who had been stolen from her home, and shut up there, by the Red-Etin.

Among them was one who was more beautiful and stately than the rest, and all the others bowed down to her and treated her with such great reverence that it was clear to see that she was the Royal Princess, King Malcolm's daughter.

And when the youth stepped forward and did reverence to her also, she spoke so sweetly to him, and greeted him so gladly, and called him her Deliverer, in such a low, clear voice, that his heart was taken captive at once.

But, for all that, he did not forget his friends. He asked the old woman where they were, and she took him into a room at the end of the passage, which was so dark that one could scarcely see in it, and so low that one could scarcely stand upright.

In this dismal chamber stood two blocks of stone.

"One can unlock doors, young Master," said the old woman, shaking her head forebodingly, "but 'tis hard work to try to turn cauld stane back to flesh and blood."

"Nevertheless, I will do it," said the youth, and, lifting his little wand, he touched each of the stone pillars lightly on the top.

Instantly the hard stone seemed to soften and melt away, and the two brothers started into life and form again. Their gratitude to their friend, who had risked so much to save them, knew no bounds, while he, on his part, was delighted to think that his efforts had been successful.

The next thing to do was to convey the Princess and the other ladies (who were all noblemen's daughters) back to the King's Court, and this they did next day.

King Malcolm was so overjoyed to see his dearly loved daughter, whom he had given up for dead, safe and sound, and so grateful to her deliverer, that he said that he should become his son-in-law and marry the Princess, and come and live with them at Court. Which all came to pass in due time; while as for the two other young men, they married noblemen's daughters, and the two old mothers came to live near their sons, and everyone was as happy as they could possibly be.

Assipattle and the Mester Stoorworm

IN FAR BYGONE DAYS, in the North, there lived a well-to-do farmer, who had seven sons and one daughter. And the youngest of these seven sons bore a very curious name; for men called him Assipattle, which means, "He who grovels among the ashes."

Perhaps Assipattle deserved his name, for he was rather a lazy boy, who never did any work on the farm as his brothers did, but ran about the doors with ragged clothes and unkempt hair, and whose mind was ever filled with wondrous stories of Trolls and Giants, Elves and Goblins.

When the sun was hot in the long summer afternoons, when the bees droned drowsily and even the tiny insects seemed almost asleep, the boy was content to throw himself down on the ash-heap amongst the ashes, and lie there, lazily letting them run through his fingers, as one might play with sand on the sea-shore, basking in the sunshine and telling stories to himself.

And his brothers, working hard in the fields, would point to him with mocking fingers, and laugh, and say to each other how well the name suited him, and of how little use he was in the world.

And when they came home from their work, they would push him about and tease him, and even his mother would make him sweep the floor, and draw water from the well, and fetch peats from the peat-stack, and do all the little odd jobs that nobody else would do.

So poor Assipattle had rather a hard life of it, and he would often have been very miserable had it not been for his sister, who loved him dearly, and who would listen quite patiently to all the stories that he had to tell; who never laughed at him or told him that he was telling lies, as his brothers did.

But one day a very sad thing happened – at least, it was a sad thing for poor Assipattle.

For it chanced that the King of these parts had one only daughter, the Princess Gemdelovely, whom he loved dearly, and to whom he denied nothing. And Princess Gemdelovely was in want of a waiting-maid, and as she had seen Assipattle's sister standing by the garden gate as she was riding by one day, and had taken a fancy to her, she asked her father if she might ask her to come and live at the Castle and serve her.

Her father agreed at once, as he always did agree to any of her wishes; and sent a messenger in haste to the farmer's house to ask if his daughter would come to the Castle to be the Princess's waiting-maid.

And, of course, the farmer was very pleased at the piece of good fortune which had befallen the girl, and so was her mother, and so were her six brothers, all except poor

Assipattle, who looked with wistful eyes after his sister as she rode away, proud of her new clothes and of the rivlins which her father had made her out of cowhide, which she was to wear in the Palace when she waited on the Princess, for at home she always ran barefoot.

Time passed, and one day a rider rode in hot haste through the country bearing the most terrible tidings. For the evening before, some fishermen, out in their boats, had caught sight of the Mester Stoorworm, which, as everyone knows, was the largest, and the first, and the greatest of all Sea-Serpents. It was that beast which, in the Good Book, is called the Leviathan, and if it had been measured in our day, its tail would have touched Iceland, while its snout rested on the North Cape.

And the fishermen had noticed that this fearsome Monster had its head turned towards the mainland, and that it opened its mouth and yawned horribly, as if to show that it was hungry, and that, if it were not fed, it would kill every living thing upon the land, both man and beast, bird and creeping thing.

For 'twas well known that its breath was so poisonous that it consumed as with a burning fire everything that it lighted on. So that, if it pleased the awful creature to lift its head and put forth its breath, like noxious vapour, over the country, in a few weeks the fair land would be turned into a region of desolation.

As you may imagine, everyone was almost paralysed with terror at this awful calamity which threatened them; and the King called a solemn meeting of all his Counsellors, and asked them if they could devise any way of warding off the danger.

And for three whole days they sat in Council, these grave, bearded men, and many were the suggestions which were made, and many the words of wisdom which were spoken; but, alas! no one was wise enough to think of a way by which the Mester Stoorworm might be driven back.

At last, at the end of the third day, when everyone had given up hope of finding a remedy, the door of the Council Chamber opened and the Queen appeared.

Now the Queen was the King's second wife, and she was not a favourite in the Kingdom, for she was a proud, insolent woman, who did not behave kindly to her stepdaughter, the Princess Gemdelovely, and who spent much more of her time in the company of a great Sorcerer, whom everyone feared and dreaded, than she did in that of the King, her husband.

So the sober Counsellors looked at her disapprovingly as she came boldly into the Council Chamber and stood up beside the King's Chair of State, and, speaking in a loud, clear voice, addressed them thus:

"Ye think that ye are brave men and strong, oh, ye Elders, and fit to be the Protectors of the People. And so it may be, when it is mortals that ye are called on to face. But ye be no match for the foe that now threatens our land. Before him your weapons be but as straw. 'Tis not through strength of arm, but through sorcery, that he will be overcome. So listen to my words, even though they be but those of a woman, and take counsel with the great Sorcerer, from whom nothing is hid, but who knoweth all the mysteries of the earth, and of the air, and of the sea."

Now the King and his Counsellors liked not this advice, for they hated the Sorcerer, who had, as they thought, too much influence with the Queen; but they were at their wits' end, and knew not to whom to turn for help, so they were fain to do as she said and summon the Wizard before them.

And when he obeyed the summons and appeared in their midst, they liked him none the better for his looks. For he was long, and thin, and awesome, with a beard that came down to his knee, and hair that wrapped him about like a mantle, and his face was the colour of mortar, as if he had always lived in darkness, and had been afraid to look on the sun.

But there was no help to be found in any other man, so they laid the case before him, and asked him what they should do. And he answered coldly that he would think over the matter, and come again to the Assembly the following day and give them his advice.

And his advice, when they heard it, was like to turn their hair white with horror.

For he said that the only way to satisfy the Monster, and to make it spare the land, was to feed it every Saturday with seven young maidens, who must be the fairest who could be found; and if, after this remedy had been tried once or twice, it did not succeed in mollifying the Stoorworm and inducing him to depart, there was but one other measure that he could suggest, but that was so horrible and dreadful that he would not rend their hearts by mentioning it in the meantime.

And as, although they hated him, they feared him also, the Council had e'en to abide by his words, and pronounced the awful doom.

And so it came about that, every Saturday, seven bonnie, innocent maidens were bound hand and foot and laid on a rock which ran into the sea, and the Monster stretched out his long, jagged tongue, and swept them into his mouth; while all the rest of the folk looked on from the top of a high hill – or, at least, the men looked – with cold, set faces, while the women hid theirs in their aprons and wept aloud.

"Is there no other way," they cried, "no other way than this, to save the land?"

But the men only groaned and shook their heads. "No other way," they answered; "no other way."

Then suddenly a boy's indignant voice rang out among the crowd. "Is there no grown man who would fight that Monster, and kill him, and save the lassies alive? I would do it; I am not feared for the Mester Stoorworm."

It was the boy Assipattle who spoke, and everyone looked at him in amazement as he stood staring at the great Sea Serpent, his fingers twitching with rage, and his great blue eyes glowing with pity and indignation.

"The poor bairn's mad; the sight hath turned his head," they whispered one to another; and they would have crowded round him to pet and comfort him, but his elder brother came and gave him a heavy clout on the side of his head.

"Thou fight the Stoorworm!" he cried contemptuously. "A likely story! Go home to thy ash-pit, and stop speaking havers;" and, taking his arm, he drew him to the place where his other brothers were waiting, and they all went home together.

But all the time Assipattle kept on saying that he meant to kill the Stoorworm; and at last his brothers became so angry at what they thought was mere bragging, that they picked up stones and pelted him so hard with them that at last he took to his heels and ran away from them.

That evening the six brothers were threshing corn in the barn, and Assipattle, as usual, was lying among the ashes thinking his own thoughts, when his mother came out and bade him run and tell the others to come in for their supper.

The boy did as he was bid, for he was a willing enough little fellow; but when he entered the barn his brothers, in revenge for his having run away from them in the afternoon, set on him and pulled him down, and piled so much straw on top of him that, had his father not come from the house to see what they were all waiting for, he would, of a surety, have been smothered.

But when, at suppertime, his mother was quarrelling with the other lads for what they had done, and saying to them that it was only cowards who set on bairns littler and younger than themselves, Assipattle looked up from the bicker of porridge which he was supping.

"Vex not thyself, Mother," he said, "for I could have fought them all if I liked; ay, and beaten them, too."

"Why didst thou not essay it then?" cried everybody at once.

"Because I knew that I would need all my strength when I go to fight the Giant Stoorworm," replied Assipattle gravely.

And, as you may fancy, the others laughed louder than before.

Time passed, and every Saturday seven lassies were thrown to the Stoorworm, until at last it was felt that this state of things could not be allowed to go on any longer; for if it did, there would soon be no maidens at all left in the country.

So the Elders met once more, and, after long consultation, it was agreed that the Sorcerer should be summoned, and asked what his other remedy was. "For, by our troth," said they, "it cannot be worse than that which we are practising now."

But, had they known it, the new remedy was even more dreadful than the old. For the cruel Queen hated her stepdaughter, Gemdelovely, and the wicked Sorcerer knew that she did, and that she would not be sorry to get rid of her, and, things being as they were, he thought that he saw a way to please the Queen. So he stood up in the Council, and, pretending to be very sorry, said that the only other thing that could be done was to give the Princess Gemdelovely to the Stoorworm, then would it of a surety depart.

When they heard this sentence a terrible stillness fell upon the Council, and everyone covered his face with his hands, for no man dare look at the King.

But although his dear daughter was as the apple of his eye, he was a just and righteous Monarch, and he felt that it was not right that other fathers should have been forced to part with their daughters, in order to try and save the country, if his child was to be spared.

So, after he had had speech with the Princess, he stood up before the Elders, and declared, with trembling voice, that both he and she were ready to make the sacrifice.

"She is my only child," he said, "and the last of her race. Yet it seemeth good to both of us that she should lay down her life, if by so doing she may save the land that she loves so well."

Salt tears ran down the faces of the great bearded men as they heard their King's words, for they all knew how dear the Princess Gemdelovely was to him. But it was felt that what he said was wise and true, and that the thing was just and right; for 'twere better, surely, that one maiden should die, even although she were of Royal blood, than that bands of other maidens should go to their death week by week, and all to no purpose.

So, amid heavy sobs, the aged Lawman – he who was the chief man of the Council – rose up to pronounce the Princess's doom. But, ere he did so, the King's Kemper – or Fighting-man – stepped forward.

"Nature teaches us that it is fitting that each beast hath a tail," he said; "and this Doom, which our Lawman is about to pronounce, is in very sooth a venomous beast. And, if I had my way, the tail which it would bear after it is this, that if the Mester Stoorworm doth not depart, and that right speedily, after he have devoured the Princess, the next thing that is offered to him be no tender young maiden, but that tough, lean old Sorcerer."

And at his words there was such a great shout of approval that the wicked Sorcerer seemed to shrink within himself, and his pale face grew paler than it was before.

Now, three weeks were allowed between the time that the Doom was pronounced upon the Princess and the time that it was carried out, so that the King might send Ambassadors to all the neighbouring Kingdoms to issue proclamations that, if any Champion would come forward who was able to drive away the Stoorworm and save the Princess, he should have her for his wife.

And with her he should have the Kingdom, as well as a very famous sword that was now in the King's possession, but which had belonged to the great god Odin, with which he had fought and vanquished all his foes.

The sword bore the name of Sickersnapper, and no man had any power against it.

The news of all these things spread over the length and breadth of the land, and everyone mourned for the fate that was like to befall the Princess Gemdelovely. And the farmer, and his wife, and their six sons mourned also – all but Assipattle, who sat amongst the ashes and said nothing.

When the King's Proclamation was made known throughout the neighbouring Kingdoms, there was a fine stir among all the young Gallants, for it seemed but a little thing to slay a Sea-Monster; and a beautiful wife, a fertile Kingdom, and a trusty sword are not to be won every day.

So six-and-thirty Champions arrived at the King's Palace, each hoping to gain the prize.

But the King sent them all out to look at the Giant Stoorworm lying in the sea with its enormous mouth open, and when they saw it, twelve of them were seized with sudden illness, and twelve of them were so afraid that they took to their heels and ran, and never stopped till they reached their own countries; and so only twelve returned to the King's Palace, and as for them, they were so downcast at the thought of the task that they had undertaken that they had no spirit left in them at all.

And none of them dare try to kill the Stoorworm; so the three weeks passed slowly by, until the night before the day on which the Princess was to be sacrificed. On that night the King, feeling that he must do something to entertain his guests, made a great supper for them.

But, as you may think, it was a dreary feast, for everyone was thinking so much about the terrible thing that was to happen on the morrow, that no one could eat or drink.

And when it was all over, and everybody had retired to rest, save the King and his old Kemperman, the King returned to the great hall, and went slowly up to his Chair of State, high up on the dais. It was not like the Chairs of State that we know nowadays; it was nothing but a massive Kist, in which he kept all the things which he treasured most.

The old Monarch undid the iron bolts with trembling fingers, and lifted the lid, and took out the wondrous sword Sickersnapper, which had belonged to the great god Odin.

His trusty Kemperman, who had stood by him in a hundred fights, watched him with pitying eyes.

"Why lift ye out the sword," he said softly, "when thy fighting days are done? Right nobly hast thou fought thy battles in the past, oh, my Lord! when thine arm was strong and sure. But when folk's years number four score and sixteen, as thine do, 'tis time to leave such work to other and younger men."

The old King turned on him angrily, with something of the old fire in his eyes. "Wheest," he cried, "else will I turn this sword on thee. Dost thou think that I can see my only bairn devoured by a Monster, and not lift a finger to try and save her when no other man will? I tell thee – and I will swear it with my two thumbs crossed on Sickersnapper – that both the sword and I will be destroyed before so much as one of her hairs be touched. So go, an' thou love me, my old comrade, and order my boat to be ready, with the sail set and the prow pointed out to sea. I will go myself and fight the Stoorworm; and if I do not return, I will lay it on thee to guard my cherished daughter. Peradventure, my life may redeem hers."

Now that night everybody at the farm went to bed betimes, for next morning the whole family was to set out early, to go to the top of the hill near the sea, to see the Princess eaten by the Stoorworm. All except Assipattle, who was to be left at home to herd the geese.

The lad was so vexed at this – for he had great schemes in his head – that he could not sleep. And as he lay tossing and tumbling about in his corner among the ashes, he heard his father and mother talking in the great box-bed. And, as he listened, he found that they were having an argument.

"'Tis such a long way to the hill overlooking the sea, I fear me I shall never walk it," said his mother. "I think I had better bide at home."

"Nay," replied her husband, "that would be a bonny-like thing, when all the country-side is to be there. Thou shalt ride behind me on my good mare Go-Swift."

"I do not care to trouble thee to take me behind thee," said his wife, "for methinks thou dost not love me as thou wert wont to do."

"The woman's havering," cried the Goodman of the house impatiently. "What makes thee think that I have ceased to love thee?"

"Because thou wilt no longer tell me thy secrets," answered his wife. "To go no further, think of this very horse, Go-Swift. For five long years I have been begging thee to tell me how it is that, when thou ridest her, she flies faster than the wind, while if any other man mount her, she hirples along like a broken-down nag."

The Goodman laughed. "'Twas not for lack of love, Goodwife," he said, "though it might be lack of trust. For women's tongues wag but loosely; and I did not want other folk to ken my secret. But since my silence hath vexed thy heart, I will e'en tell it thee.

"When I want Go-Swift to stand, I give her one clap on the left shoulder. When I would have her go like any other horse, I give her two claps on the right. But when I want her to fly like the wind, I whistle through the windpipe of a goose. And, as I never ken when I want her to gallop like that, I aye keep the bird's thrapple in the left-hand pocket of my coat."

"So that is how thou managest the beast," said the farmer's wife, in a satisfied tone; "and that is what becomes of all my goose thrapples. Oh! but thou art a clever fellow, Goodman; and now that I ken the way of it I may go to sleep."

Assipattle was not tumbling about in the ashes now; he was sitting up in the darkness, with glowing cheeks and sparkling eyes.

His opportunity had come at last, and he knew it.

He waited patiently till their heavy breathing told him that his parents were asleep; then he crept over to where his father's clothes were, and took the goose's windpipe out of the pocket of his coat, and slipped noiselessly out of the house. Once he was out of it, he ran like lightning to the stable. He saddled and bridled Go-Swift, and threw a halter round her neck, and led her to the stable door.

The good mare, unaccustomed to her new groom, pranced, and reared, and plunged; but Assipattle, knowing his father's secret, clapped her once on the left shoulder, and she stood as still as a stone. Then he mounted her, and gave her two claps on the right shoulder, and the good horse trotted off briskly, giving a loud neigh as she did so.

The unwonted sound, ringing out in the stillness of the night, roused the household, and the Goodman and his six sons came tumbling down the wooden stairs, shouting to one another in confusion that someone was stealing Go-Swift.

The farmer was the first to reach the door; and when he saw, in the starlight, the vanishing form of his favourite steed, he cried at the top of his voice:

"Stop thief, ho!
Go-Swift, whoa!"

And when Go-Swift heard that she pulled up in a moment. All seemed lost, for the farmer and his sons could run very fast indeed, and it seemed to Assipattle, sitting motionless on Go-Swift's back, that they would very soon make up on him.

But, luckily, he remembered the goose's thrapple, and he pulled it out of his pocket and whistled through it. In an instant the good mare bounded forward, swift as the wind, and was over the hill and out of reach of its pursuers before they had taken ten steps more.

Day was dawning when the lad came within sight of the sea; and there, in front of him, in the water, lay the enormous Monster whom he had come so far to slay. Anyone would have said that he was mad even to dream of making such an attempt, for he was but a slim, unarmed youth, and the Mester Stoorworm was so big that men said it would reach the fourth part round the world. And its tongue was jagged at the end like a fork, and with this fork it could sweep whatever it chose into its mouth, and devour it at its leisure.

For all this, Assipattle was not afraid, for he had the heart of a hero underneath his tattered garments. "I must be cautious," he said to himself, "and do by my wits what I cannot do by my strength."

He climbed down from his seat on Go-Swift's back, and tethered the good steed to a tree, and walked on, looking well about him, till he came to a little cottage on the edge of a wood.

The door was not locked, so he entered, and found its occupant, an old woman, fast asleep in bed. He did not disturb her, but he took down an iron pot from the shelf, and examined it closely.

"This will serve my purpose," he said; "and surely the old dame would not grudge it if she knew 'twas to save the Princess's life."

Then he lifted a live peat from the smouldering fire, and went his way.

Down at the water's edge he found the King's boat lying, guarded by a single boatman, with its sails set and its prow turned in the direction of the Mester Stoorworm.

"It's a cold morning," said Assipattle. "Art thou not well-nigh frozen sitting there? If thou wilt come on shore, and run about, and warm thyself, I will get into the boat and guard it till thou returnest."

"A likely story," replied the man. "And what would the King say if he were to come, as I expect every moment he will do, and find me playing myself on the sand, and his good boat left to a smatchet like thee? 'Twould be as much as my head is worth."

"As thou wilt," answered Assipattle carelessly, beginning to search among the rocks. "In the meantime, I must be looking for a wheen mussels to roast for my breakfast." And after he had gathered the mussels, he began to make a hole in the sand to put the live peat in. The boatman watched him curiously, for he, too, was beginning to feel hungry.

Presently the lad gave a wild shriek, and jumped high in the air. "Gold, gold!" he cried. "By the name of Thor, who would have looked to find gold here?"

This was too much for the boatman. Forgetting all about his head and the King, he jumped out of the boat, and, pushing Assipattle aside, began to scrape among the sand with all his might.

While he was doing so, Assipattle seized his pot, jumped into the boat, pushed her off, and was half a mile out to sea before the outwitted man, who, needless to say, could find no gold, noticed what he was about.

And, of course, he was very angry, and the old King was more angry still when he came down to the shore, attended by his Nobles and carrying the great sword Sickersnapper, in the vain hope that he, poor feeble old man that he was, might be able in some way to defeat the Monster and save his daughter.

But to make such an attempt was beyond his power now that his boat was gone. So he could only stand on the shore, along with the fast assembling crowd of his subjects, and watch what would befall.

And this was what befell!

Assipattle, sailing slowly over the sea, and watching the Mester Stoorworm intently, noticed that the terrible Monster yawned occasionally, as if longing for his weekly feast. And as it yawned a great flood of seawater went down its throat, and came out again at its huge gills.

So the brave lad took down his sail, and pointed the prow of his boat straight at the Monster's mouth, and the next time it yawned he and his boat were sucked right in, and, like Jonah, went straight down its throat into the dark regions inside its body. On and on the boat floated; but as it went the water grew less, pouring out of the Stoorworm's gills, till at last it stuck, as it were, on dry land. And Assipattle jumped out, his pot in his hand, and began to explore.

Presently he came to the huge creature's liver, and, having heard that the liver of a fish is full of oil, he made a hole in it and put in the live peat.

Woe's me! but there was a conflagration! And Assipattle just got back to his boat in time; for the Mester Stoorworm, in its convulsions, threw the boat right out of its mouth again, and it was flung up, high and dry, on the bare land.

The commotion in the sea was so terrible that the King and his daughter – who by this time had come down to the shore dressed like a bride, in white, ready to be thrown to the Monster – and all his Courtiers, and all the country-folk, were fain to take refuge on the hilltop, out of harm's way, and stand and see what happened next.

And this was what happened next.

The poor, distressed creature – for it was now to be pitied, even although it was a great, cruel, awful Mester Stoorworm – tossed itself to and fro, twisting and writhing.

And as it tossed its awful head out of the water, its tongue fell out, and struck the earth with such force that it made a great dent in it, into which the sea rushed. And that dent formed the crooked Straits which now divide Denmark from Norway and Sweden.

Then some of its teeth fell out and rested in the sea, and became the Islands that we now call the Orkney Isles; and a little afterwards some more teeth dropped out, and they became what we now call the Shetland Isles.

After that the creature twisted itself into a great lump and died; and this lump became the Island of Iceland; and the fire which Assipattle had kindled with his live peat still burns on underneath it, and that is why there are mountains which throw out fire in that chilly land.

When at last it was plainly seen that the Mester Stoorworm was dead, the King could scarce contain himself with joy. He put his arms round Assipattle's neck, and kissed him, and called him his son. And he took off his own Royal Mantle and put it on the lad, and girded his good sword Sickersnapper round his waist. And he called his daughter, the Princess Gemdelovely, to him, and put her hand in his, and declared that when the right time came she should be his wife, and that he should be ruler over all the Kingdom.

Then the whole company mounted their horses again, and Assipattle rode on Go-Swift by the Princess's side; and so they returned, with great joy, to the King's Palace.

But as they were nearing the gate, Assipattle's sister, she who was the Princess's maid, ran out to meet him, and signed to the Princess to lout down, and whispered something in her ear.

The Princess's face grew dark, and she turned her horse's head and rode back to where her father was, with his Nobles. She told him the words that the maiden had spoken; and when he heard them his face, too, grew as black as thunder.

For the matter was this: the cruel Queen, full of joy at the thought that she was to be rid, once for all, of her stepdaughter, had been making love to the wicked Sorcerer all the morning in the old King's absence.

"He shall be killed at once," cried the Monarch. "Such behaviour cannot be overlooked."

"Thou wilt have much ado to find him, your Majesty," said the girl, "for 'tis more than an hour since he and the Queen fled together on the fleetest horses that they could find in the stables."

"But I can find him," cried Assipattle; and he went off like the wind on his good horse Go-Swift.

It was not long before he came within sight of the fugitives, and he drew his sword and shouted to them to stop.

They heard the shout, and turned round, and they both laughed aloud in derision when they saw that it was only the boy who grovelled in the ashes who pursued them.

"The insolent brat! I will cut off his head for him! I will teach him a lesson!" cried the Sorcerer; and he rode boldly back to meet Assipattle. For although he was no fighter, he knew that no ordinary weapon could harm his enchanted body; therefore he was not afraid.

But he did not count on Assipattle having the Sword of the great god Odin, with which he had slain all his enemies; and before this magic weapon he was powerless. And, at one thrust, the young lad ran it through his body as easily as if he had been any ordinary man, and he fell from his horse, dead.

Then the Courtiers of the King, who had also set off in pursuit, but whose steeds were less fleet of foot than Go-Swift, came up, and seized the bridle of the Queen's horse, and led it and its rider back to the Palace.

She was brought before the Council, and judged, and condemned to be shut up in a high tower for the remainder of her life. Which thing surely came to pass.

As for Assipattle, when the proper time came, he was married to the Princess Gemdelovely, with great feasting and rejoicing. And when the old King died, they ruled the Kingdom for many a long year.

The Brollachan

IN THE MILL OF THE GLENS, Muilinn na Gleannan, lived long ago a cripple of the name of Murray, better known as "Ally" na Muilinn. He was maintained by the charity of the miller and his neighbours, who, when they removed their meal, put each a handful into the lamiter's bag. The lad slept usually at the mill; and it came to pass that one night, who should enter but the Brollachan, son of the Fuath.

Now the Brollachan had eyes and a mouth, and can say two words only, mi-fhein, myself, and thu-fhein, thyself; besides that, he has no speech, and alas no shape. He lay all his lubber-length by the dying fire; and Murray threw a fresh peat on the embers, which made them fly about red hot, and Brollachan was severely burnt. So he screamed in an awful way, and soon comes the "Vough," very fierce, crying, "Och, my Brollachan, who then burnt you?" but all he could say was "mee!" and then he said "oo!" (me and thou, mi thu) and she replied, "Were it any other, wouldn't I be revenged."

Murray slipped the peck measure over himself, and hid among the machinery, so as to look as like a sack as possible, ejaculating at times, "May the Lord preserve me," so he escaped unhurt; and the "Vough" and her Brollachan left the mill. That same night a woman, going by the place, was chased by the still furious parent, and could have been saved had she not been nimble to reach her own door in time, to leave nothing for the "Vough" to catch but her heel; this heel was torn off, and the woman went lame all the rest of her days.

ANIMALS & FABLES

Introduction

ANIMALS HAVE BEEN a storyteller's staple in just about every culture. Even where, as with the sheep who stars in 'The Story of the White Pet', not much appears to be made of the creature's animal nature, the very fact that it is playing a quasi-human part gives a sense of the extraordinary in itself.

Sometimes, as in 'The Tulman', animals act as instruments of enchantment, intermediaries between the fairy and the human realm. Frequently they facilitate what are essentially human actions, like the great goggle-eyed frog who helps the heroine of 'The Well of the World's End'. If kindness to animals is repaid in such stories; cruelty is punished, as in 'The Burgh'. In some fables, animals stand in for particular temperaments and talents, as the tale of 'The Fox and the Wolf' pits the former's cunning against the latter's strength. In others, animals don't appear but instead moral messages are portrayed through the actions of human characters.

The Well of the World's End

ONCE UPON A TIME, and a very good time it was, though it wasn't in my time, nor in your time, nor any one else's time, there was a girl whose mother had died, and her father had married again. And her stepmother hated her because she was more beautiful than herself, and she was very cruel to her. She used to make her do all the servant's work, and never let her have any peace. At last, one day, the stepmother thought to get rid of her altogether; so she handed her a sieve and said to her: "Go, fill it at the Well of the World's End and bring it home to me full, or woe betide you." For she thought she would never be able to find the Well of the World's End, and, if she did, how could she bring home a sieve full of water?

Well, the girl started off, and asked every one she met to tell her where was the Well of the World's End. But nobody knew, and she didn't know what to do, when a queer little old woman, all bent double, told her where it was, and how she could get to it.

So she did what the old woman told her, and at last arrived at the Well of the World's End. But when she dipped the sieve in the cold, cold water, it all ran out again. She tried and she tried again, but every time it was the same; and at last she sate down and cried as if her heart would break.

Suddenly she heard a croaking voice, and she looked up and saw a great frog with goggle eyes looking at her and speaking to her.

"What's the matter, dearie?" it said.

"Oh, dear, oh dear," she said, "my stepmother has sent me all this long way to fill this sieve with water from the Well of the World's End, and I can't fill it no how at all."

"Well," said the frog, "if you promise me to do whatever I bid you for a whole night long, I'll tell you how to fill it."

So the girl agreed, and then the frog said:

> *"Stop it with moss and daub it with clay,*
> *And then it will carry the water away;"*

and then it gave a hop, skip and jump, and went flop into the Well of the World's End.

So the girl looked about for some moss, and lined the bottom of the sieve with it, and over that she put some clay, and then she dipped it once again into the Well of the World's End; and this time, the water didn't run out, and she turned to go away.

Just then the frog popped up its head out of the Well of the World's End, and said: "Remember your promise."

"All right," said the girl; for thought she, "what harm can a frog do me?"

So she went back to her stepmother, and brought the sieve full of water from the Well of the World's End. The stepmother was fine and angry, but she said nothing at all.

That very evening they heard something tap tapping at the door low down, and a voice cried out:

"Open the door, my hinny, my heart,
Open the door, my own darling;
Mind you the words that you and I spoke,
Down in the meadow, at the World's End Well."

"Whatever can that be?" cried out the stepmother, and the girl had to tell her all about it, and what she had promised the frog.

"Girls must keep their promises," said the stepmother. "Go and open the door this instant." For she was glad the girl would have to obey a nasty frog.

So the girl went and opened the door, and there was the frog from the Well of the World's End. And it hopped, and it skipped, and it jumped, till it reached the girl, and then it said:

"Lift me to your knee, my hinny, my heart;
Lift me to your knee, my own darling;
Remember the words you and I spoke,
Down in the meadow by the World's End Well."

But the girl didn't like to, till her stepmother said "Lift it up this instant, you hussy! Girls must keep their promises!"

So at last she lifted the frog up on to her lap, and it lay there for a time, till at last it said:

"Give me some supper, my hinny, my heart,
Give me some supper, my darling;
Remember the words you and I spake,
In the meadow, by the Well of the World's End."

Well, she didn't mind doing that, so she got it a bowl of milk and bread, and fed it well. And when the frog had finished, it said:

"Go with me to bed, my hinny, my heart,
Go with me to bed, my own darling;
Mind you the words you spake to me,
Down by the cold well, so weary."

But that the girl wouldn't do, till her stepmother said: "Do what you promised, girl; girls must keep their promises. Do what you're bid, or out you go, you and your froggie."

So the girl took the frog with her to bed, and kept it as far away from her as she could. Well, just as the day was beginning to break what should the frog say but:

"Chop off my head, my hinny, my heart,
Chop off my head, my own darling;
Remember the promise you made to me,
Down by the cold well so weary."

At first the girl wouldn't, for she thought of what the frog had done for her at the Well of the World's End. But when the frog said the words over again, she went and took an axe and chopped off its head, and lo! and behold, there stood before her a handsome young prince, who told her that he had been enchanted by a wicked magician, and he could never be unspelled till some girl would do his bidding for a whole night, and chop off his head at the end of it.

The stepmother was that surprised when she found the young prince instead of the nasty frog, and she wasn't best pleased, you may be sure, when the prince told her that he was going to marry her stepdaughter because she had unspelled him. So they were married and went away to live in the castle of the king, his father, and all the stepmother had to console her was, that it was all through her that her stepdaughter was married to a prince.

The Wedding of Robin Redbreast and Jenny Wren

THERE WAS ONCE AN OLD grey Pussy Baudrons, and she went out for a stroll one Christmas morning to see what she could see. And as she was walking down the burnside she saw a little Robin Redbreast hopping up and down on the branches of a briar bush.

"What a tasty breakfast he would make," thought she to herself. "I must try to catch him."

So, "Good morning, Robin Redbreast," quoth she, sitting down on her tail at the foot of the briar bush and looking up at him. "And where mayest thou be going so early on this cold winter's day?"

"I'm on my road to the King's Palace," answered Robin cheerily, "to sing him a song this merry Yule morning."

"That's a pious errand to be travelling on, and I wish you good success," replied Pussy slyly; "but just hop down a minute before thou goest, and I will show thee what a bonnie white ring I have round my neck. 'Tis few cats that are marked like me."

Then Robin cocked his head on one side, and looked down on Pussy Baudrons with a twinkle in his eye. "Ha, ha! grey Pussy Baudrons," he said. "Ha, ha! for I saw thee worry the little grey mouse, and I have no wish that thou shouldst worry me."

And with that he spread his wings and flew away. And he flew, and he flew, till he lighted on an old sod dyke; and there he saw a greedy old gled sitting, with all his feathers ruffled up as if he felt cold.

"Good morning, Robin Redbreast," cried the greedy old gled, who had had no food since yesterday, and was therefore very hungry. "And where mayest thou be going to, this cold winter's day?"

"I'm on my road to the King's Palace," answered Robin, "to sing to him a song this merry Yule morning." And he hopped away a yard or two from the gled, for there was a look in his eye that he did not quite like.

"Thou art a friendly little fellow," remarked the gled sweetly, "and I wish thee good luck on thine errand; but ere thou go on, come nearer me, I prith'ee, and I will show thee what a curious feather I have in my wing. 'Tis said that no other gled in the country-side hath one like it."

"Like enough," rejoined Robin, hopping still further away; "but I will take thy word for it, without seeing it. For I saw thee pluck the feathers from the wee lintie, and I have no wish that thou shouldst pluck the feathers from me. So I will bid thee good day, and go on my journey."

The next place on which he rested was a piece of rock that overhung a dark, deep glen, and here he saw a sly old fox looking out of his hole not two yards below him.

"Good morning, Robin Redbreast," said the sly old fox, who had tried to steal a fat duck from a farmyard the night before, and had barely escaped with his life. "And where mayest thou be going so early on this cold winter's day?"

"I'm on my road to the King's Palace, to sing him a song this merry Yule morning," answered Robin, giving the same answer that he had given to the grey Pussy Baudrons and the greedy gled.

"Thou wilt get a right good welcome, for His Majesty is fond of music," said the wily fox. "But ere thou go, just come down and have a look at a black spot which I have on the end of my tail. 'Tis said that there is not a fox 'twixt here and the Border that hath a spot on his tail like mine."

"Very like, very like," replied Robin; "but I chanced to see thee worrying the wee lambie up on the braeside yonder, and I have no wish that thou shouldst try thy teeth on me. So I will e'en go on my way to the King's Palace, and thou canst show the spot on thy tail to the next passer-by."

So the little Robin Redbreast flew away once more, and never rested till he came to a bonnie valley with a little burn running through it, and there he saw a rosy-cheeked boy sitting on a log eating a piece of bread and butter. And he perched on a branch and watched him.

"Good morning, Robin Redbreast; and where mayest thou be going so early on this cold winter's day?" asked the boy eagerly; for he was making a collection of stuffed birds, and he had still to get a Robin Redbreast.

"I'm on my way to the King's Palace to sing him a song this merry Yule morning," answered Robin, hopping down to the ground, and keeping one eye fixed on the bread and butter.

"Come a bit nearer, Robin," said the boy, "and I will give thee some crumbs."

"Na, na, my wee man," chirped the cautious little bird; "for I saw thee catch the goldfinch, and I have no wish to give thee the chance to catch me."

At last he came to the King's Palace and lighted on the window-sill, and there he sat and sang the very sweetest song that he could sing; for he felt so happy because it was the Blessed Yuletide, that he wanted everyone else to be happy too. And the King and the Queen were so delighted with his song, as he peeped in at them at their open window, that they asked each other what they could give him as a reward for his kind thought in coming so far to greet them.

"We can give him a wife," replied the Queen, "who will go home with him and help him to build his nest."

"And who wilt thou give him for a bride?" asked the King. "Methinks 'twould need to be a very tiny lady to match his size."

"Why, Jenny Wren, of course," answered the Queen. "She hath looked somewhat dowie of late, this will be the very thing to brighten her up."

Then the King clapped his hands, and praised his wife for her happy thought, and wondered that the idea had not struck him before.

So Robin Redbreast and Jenny Wren were married, amid great rejoicings, at the King's Palace; and the King and Queen and all the fine Nobles and Court Ladies danced at their wedding. Then they flew away home to Robin's own country-side, and built their nest in the roots of the briar bush, where he had spoken to Pussy Baudrons. And you will be glad to hear that Jenny Wren proved the best little housewife in the world.

The Fox and the Wolf

THERE WAS ONCE A FOX and a Wolf, who set up house together in a cave near the sea-shore. Although you may not think so, they got on very well for a time, for they went out hunting all day, and when they came back at night they were generally too tired to do anything but to eat their supper and go to bed.

They might have lived together always had it not been for the slyness and greediness of the Fox, who tried to over-reach his companion, who was not nearly so clever as he was.

And this was how it came about.

It chanced, one dark December night, that there was a dreadful storm at sea, and in the morning the beach was all strewn with wreckage. So as soon as it was daylight the two friends went down to the shore to see if they could find anything to eat.

They had the good fortune to light on a great Keg of Butter, which had been washed overboard from some ship on its way home from Ireland, where, as all the world knows, folk are famous for their butter.

The simple Wolf danced with joy when he saw it. "Marrowbones and trotters! but we will have a good supper this night," cried he, licking his lips. "Let us set to work at once and roll it up to the cave."

But the wily Fox was fond of butter, and he made up his mind that he would have it all to himself. So he put on his wisest look, and shook his head gravely.

"Thou hast no prudence, my friend," he said reproachfully, "else wouldst thou not talk of breaking up a Keg of Butter at this time of year, when the stackyards are full of good grain, which can be had for the eating, and the farmyards are stocked with nice fat ducks and poultry. No, no. It behoveth us to have foresight, and to lay up in store for the spring, when the grain is all threshed, and the stackyards are bare, and the poultry have gone to market. So we will e'en bury the Keg, and dig it up when we have need of it."

Very reluctantly, for he was thinner and hungrier than the Fox, the Wolf agreed to this proposal. So a hole was dug, and the Keg was buried, and the two animals went off hunting as usual.

About a week passed by: then one day the Fox came into the cave, and flung himself down on the ground as if he were very much exhausted. But if anyone had looked at him closely they would have seen a sly twinkle in his eye.

"Oh, dear, oh, dear!" he sighed. "Life is a heavy burden."

"What hath befallen thee?" asked the Wolf, who was ever kind and soft-hearted.

"Some friends of mine, who live over the hills yonder, are wanting me to go to a christening tonight. Just think of the distance that I must travel."

"But needst thou go?" asked the Wolf. "Canst thou not send an excuse?"

"I doubt that no excuse would be accepted," answered the Fox, "for they asked me to stand god-father. Therefore it behoveth me to do my duty, and pay no heed to my own feelings."

So that evening the Fox was absent, and the Wolf was alone in the cave. But it was not to a christening that the sly Fox went; it was to the Keg of Butter that was buried in the sand. About midnight he returned, looking fat and sleek, and well pleased with himself.

The Wolf had been dozing, but he looked up drowsily as his companion entered. "Well, how did they name the bairn?" he asked.

"They gave it a queer name," answered the Fox. "One of the queerest names that I ever heard."

"And what was that?" questioned the Wolf.

"Nothing less than 'Blaisean' (Let-me-taste)," replied the Fox, throwing himself down in his corner. And if the Wolf could have seen him in the darkness he would have noticed that he was laughing to himself.

Some days afterwards the same thing happened. The Fox was asked to another christening; this time at a place some twenty-five miles along the shore. And as he had grumbled before, so he grumbled again; but he declared that it was his duty to go, and he went.

At midnight he came back, smiling to himself and with no appetite for his supper. And when the Wolf asked him the name of the child, he answered that it was a more extraordinary name than the other – 'Be na Inheadnon' (Be in its middle).

The very next week, much to the Wolf's wonder, the Fox was asked to yet another christening. And this time the name of the child was 'Sgriot an Clar' (Scrape the staves). After that the invitations ceased.

Time went on, and the hungry spring came, and the Fox and the Wolf had their larder bare, for food was scarce, and the weather was bleak and cold.

"Let us go and dig up the Keg of Butter," said the Wolf. "Methinks that now is the time we need it."

The Fox agreed – having made up his mind how he would act – and the two set out to the place where the Keg had been hidden. They scraped away the sand, and uncovered it; but, needless to say, they found it empty.

"This is thy work," said the Fox angrily, turning to the poor, innocent Wolf. "Thou hast crept along here while I was at the christenings, and eaten it up by stealth."

"Not I," replied the Wolf. "I have never been near the spot since the day that we buried it together."

"But I tell thee it must have been thou," insisted the Fox, "for no other creature knew it was there except ourselves. And, besides, I can see by the sleekness of thy fur that thou hast fared well of late."

Which last sentence was both unjust and untrue, for the poor Wolf looked as lean and badly nourished as he could possibly be.

So back they both went to the cave, arguing all the way. The Fox declaring that the Wolf must have been the thief, and the Wolf protesting his innocence.

"Art thou ready to swear to it?" said the Fox at last; though why he asked such a question, dear only knows.

"Yes, I am," replied the Wolf firmly; and, standing in the middle of the cave, and holding one paw up solemnly he swore this awful oath:

> *"If it be that I stole the butter; if it be, if it be –*
> *May a fateful, fell disease fall on me, fall on me."*

When he was finished, he put down his paw and, turning to the Fox, looked at him keenly; for all at once it struck him that his fur looked sleek and fine.

"It is thy turn now," he said. "I have sworn, and thou must do so also."

The Fox's face fell at these words, for although he was both untruthful and dishonest now, he had been well brought up in his youth, and he knew that it was a terrible thing to perjure oneself and swear falsely.

So he made one excuse after another, but the Wolf, who was getting more and more suspicious every moment, would not listen to him.

So, as he had not courage to tell the truth, he was forced at last to swear an oath also, and this was what he swore:

> *"If it be that I stole the butter; if it be, if it be –*
> *Then let some most deadly punishment fall on me, fall on me –*
> *Whirrum wheeckam, whirrum wheeckam,*
> *Whirram whee, whirram whee!"*

After he had heard him swear this terrible oath, the Wolf thought that his suspicions must be groundless, and he would have let the matter rest; but the Fox, having an uneasy conscience, could not do so. So he suggested that as it was clear that one of them must have eaten the Keg of Butter, they should both stand near the fire; so that when they became hot, the butter would ooze out of the skin of whichever of them was guilty. And he took care that the Wolf should stand in the hottest place.

But the fire was big and the cave was small; and while the poor lean Wolf showed no sign of discomfort, he himself, being nice and fat and comfortable, soon began to get unpleasantly warm.

As this did not suit him at all, he next proposed that they should go for a walk, "for," said he, "it is now quite plain that neither of us can have taken the butter. It must have been some stranger who hath found out our secret."

But the Wolf had seen the Fox beginning to grow greasy, and he knew now what had happened, and he determined to have his revenge. So he waited until they came to a smithy which stood at the side of the road, where a horse was waiting just outside the door to be shod.

Then, keeping at a safe distance, he said to his companion, "There is writing on that smithy door, which I cannot read, as my eyes are failing; do thou try to read it, for perchance it may be something 'twere good for us to know."

And the silly Fox, who was very vain, and did not like to confess that his eyes were no better than those of his friend, went close up to the door to try and read the writing. And he chanced to touch the horse's fetlock, and, it being a restive beast, lifted its foot and struck out at once, and killed the Fox as dead as a door-nail.

And so, you see, the old saying in the Good Book came true after all: "Be sure your sin will find you out."

The Story of the White Pet

THERE WAS A FARMER before now who had a White Pet (sheep), and when Christmas was drawing near, he thought that he would kill the White Pet. The White Pet heard that, and he thought he would run away; and that is what he did.

He had not gone far when a bull met him. Said the bull to him, "All hail! White Pet, where art thou going?" "I," said the White Pet, "am going to seek my fortune; they were going to kill me for Christmas, and I thought I had better run away."

"It is better for me," said the bull, "to go with thee, for they were going to do the very same with me."

"I am willing," said the White Pet; "the larger the party the better the fun."

They went forward till they fell in with a dog.

"All hail! White Pet," said the dog. "All hail! thou dog." "Where art thou going?" said the dog.

"I am running away, for I heard that they were threatening to kill me for Christmas."

"They were going to do the very same to me," said the dog, "and I will go with you." "Come, then," said the White Pet.

They went then, till a cat joined them, "All hail! White Pet!" said the cat. "All hail! oh cat."

"Where art thou going?" said the cat. "I am going to seek my fortune," said the White Pet, "because they were going to kill me at Christmas."

"They were talking about killing me too," said the cat, "and I had better go with you."

"Come on then," said the White Pet.

Then they went forward till a cock met them. "All hail! White Pet," said the cock. "All hail to thyself! oh cock," said the White Pet. "Where," said the cock, "art thou going?" "I," said the White Pet, "am going (away), for they were threatening my death at Christmas."

"They were going to kill me at the very same time," said the cock, "and I will go with you."

"Come, then," said the White Pet.

They went forward till they fell in with a goose.

"All hail! White Pet," said the goose. "All hail to thyself! oh goose," said the White Pet. "Where art thou going?" said the goose.

"I," said the White Pet, "am running away because they were going to kill me at Christmas."

"They were going to do that to me too," said the goose, "and I will go with you."

The party went forward till the night was drawing on them, and they saw a little light far away; and though far off, they were not long getting there. When they reached the house, they said to each other that they would look in at the window to see who was in the house, and they saw thieves counting money; and the White Pet said, "Let every one of us call his own call. I will call my own call; and let the bull call his own call; let the dog call his own call; and the cat her own call, and the cock his own call; and the goose his own call." With that they gave out one shout – Gaire!

When the thieves heard the shouting that was without, they thought the mischief was there; and they fled out, and they went to a wood that was near them. When the White

Pet and his company saw that the house was empty, they went in and they got the money that the thieves had been counting, and they divided it amongst themselves; and then they thought that they would settle to rest. Said the White Pet, "Where wilt thou sleep tonight, oh bull?" "I will sleep," said the bull, "behind the door where I used" (to be). "Where wilt thou sleep thyself, White Pet?" "I will sleep," said the White Pet, "in the middle of the floor where I used" (to be). "Where wilt thou sleep, oh dog?" said the White Pet. "I will sleep beside the fire where I used" (to be), said the dog. "Where wilt thou sleep, oh cat?" "I will sleep," said the cat, "in the candle press, where I like to be." "Where wilt thou sleep, oh cock?" said the White Pet. "I," said the cock, "will sleep on the rafters where I used" (to be). "Where wilt thou sleep, oh goose?" "I will sleep," said the goose, "on the midden, where I was accustomed to be."

They were not long settled to rest, when one of the thieves returned to look in to see if he could perceive if any one at all was in the house. All things were still, and he went on forward to the candle press for a candle, that he might kindle to make him a light; but when he put his hand in the box the cat thrust her claws into his hand, but he took a candle with him, and he tried to light it. Then the dog got up, and he stuck his tail into a pot of water that was beside the fire; he shook his tail and put out the candle. Then the thief thought that the mischief was in the house, and he fled; but when he was passing the White Pet, he gave him a blow; before he got past the bull, he gave him a kick; and the cock began to crow; and when he went out, the goose began to belabour him with his wings about the shanks.

He went to the wood where his comrades were, as fast as was in his legs. They asked him how it had gone with him. "It went," said he, "but middling; when I went to the candle press, there was a man in it who thrust ten knives into my hand; and when I went to the fireside to light the candle, there was a big black man lying there, who was sprinkling water on it to put it out; and when I tried to go out, there was a big man in the middle of the floor, who gave me a shove; and another man behind the door who pushed me out; and there was a little brat on the loft calling out Cuir-anees-an-shaw-ay-s-foni-mi-hayn-da – Send him up here and I'll do for him; and there was a Gree-as-ich-e, shoemaker, out on the midden, belabouring me about the shanks with his apron."

When the thieves heard that, they did not return to seek their lot of money; and the White Pet and his comrades got it to themselves; and it kept them peaceably as long as they lived.

The Burgh

FOUR WERE WATCHING CATTLE in Baileburgh (Burgh Farm). They were in a fold. The four were Domhnull MacGhilleathain, Domhnull Mac-an-t-Saoir, Calum MacNill, and Domhnull Domhnullach. They saw a dog. Calum MacNill said that they should strike the dog. Said Domhnull MacGhilleathain, "We will not strike. If thou strikest him thou wilt repent it."

Calum MacNill struck the dog, and his hand and his arm lost their power. He felt a great pain in his hand and his arm, and one of the other lads carried his stick home; he could not carry it himself. He was lamenting his hand, and he went where there was an old woman, Nic a Phi, to get knowledge about his hand. She said to him that he would be so till the end of a day and a year; and at the end of a day and year, to go to the knoll and say to it, "If thou dost not let with me the strength of my hand, I or my race will leave neither stick nor stone of thee that we will not drive to pieces."

At the end of a day and year his comrades said, "There is now a day and year since thou hast lost the power of thy hand, come to the knoll till thy hand get its power, as the woman said." He went himself and his comrades. They reached the hill. He drew his stick, and he said to the knoll, "If thou dost not let with me the strength of my hand, I myself or my race will leave neither stick nor stone of thee that we will not drive to pieces." And he got the power of his hand.

The Tulman

THERE WAS A WOMAN in Baile Thangusdail, and she was out seeking a couple of calves; and the night and lateness caught her, and there came rain and tempest, and she was seeking shelter. She went to a knoll with the couple of calves, and she was striking a tether-peg into it. The knoll opened. She heard a gleegashing as if a pot-hook were clashing beside a pot. She took wonder, and she stopped striking the tether-peg.

A woman put out her head and all above her middle, and she said, "What business hast thou to be troubling this tulman in which I make my dwelling?" "I am taking care of this couple of calves, and I am but weak. Where shall I go with them?" "Thou shalt go with them to that breast down yonder. Thou wilt see a tuft of grass. If thy couple of calves eat that tuft of grass, thou wilt not be a day without a milk cow as long as thou art alive, because thou hast taken my counsel."

As she said, she never was without a milk cow after that, and she was alive fourscore and fifteen years after the night that was there.

Osean After the Feen

OISEAN WAS AN OLD MAN after the (time of the) Feen, and he (was) dwelling in the house of his daughter. He was blind, deaf, and limping, and there were nine oaken skewers in his belly, and he ate the tribute that Padraig had over Eirinn. They were then writing the old histories that he was telling them.

They killed a right big stag; they stripped the shank, and brought him the bone. "Didst thou ever see a shank that was thicker than that in the Feen?" "I saw a bone of the black bird's chick in which it would go round about." – "In that there are but lies." When he heard this, he caught hold of the books with rage, and he set them in the fire. His daughter took them out and quenched them, and she kept them. Oisean asked, with wailing, that the worst lad and dog in the Feen should lay weight on his chest. He felt a weight on his chest. "What's this?" – "I MacRuaghadh" (son of the red, or auburn one). "What is that weight which I feel at my feet?" "There is MacBuidheig" (the son of the little yellow). They stayed as they were till the day came. They arose. He asked the lad to take him to such a glen. The lad reached the glen with him. He took out a whistle from his pocket, and he played it. "Seest thou anything going past on yonder mountain?" – "I see deer on it." – "What sort dost thou see on it "I see some slender and grey on it." – "Those are the seed of the Lon Luath, swift elk; let them pass." – "What kind seest thou now?" – "I see some gaunt and grizzled." – "Those are the seed of Dearg dasdanach, the red Fierce: let them pass." – "What kind seest thou now?" – "I see some heavy and sleek." – "Let the dog at them Vic Vuiaig!" MacBhuieig went. "Is he dragging down plenty?" – "He is." – "Now, when thou seest that he has a dozen thou shalt check him." When he thought he had them, he played the whistle, and he checked the dog. "Now if the pup is sated with chase, he will come quietly, gently; if not, he will come with his gape open." He was coming with his gape open, and his tongue out of his mouth. "Bad is the thing which thou hast done to cheek the pup unsated with chase." – "When he comes, catch my hand, and try to put it in his gape, or he will have us." He put the hand of Oisean in his gape, and he shook his throat out. "Come, gather the stags to that knoll of rushes." He went, and that is done; and it was nine stags that were there, and that was but enough for Oisean alone; the lad's share was lost. "Put my two hands about the rushy knoll that is here;" he did that, and the great caldron that the Feen used to have was in it. "Now, make ready, and put the stags in the caldron, and set fire under it." The lad did that. When they were here ready to take it, Oisean said to him, "Touch thou them not till I take my fill first." Oisean began upon them, and as he ate each one, he took one of the skewers out of his belly. When Oisean had six eaten, the lad had three taken from him. "Hast thou done this to me?" said Oisean. "I did it," said he I would need a few when thou thyself hadst so many of them." – "Try if thou wilt take me to such a rock." He went down there, and he brought out the chick of a blackbird out of the rock. "Let us come to be going home." The lad caught him under the arm, and they went away. When be thought that they were nearing the house, he said, "Are we very near the house?" "We are," said the lad. "Would the shout of a man reach the house where we are just now?" – "It would reach it." – "Set my front straight on the house." The lad did thus. When he was coming on the house, he caught the lad, and he put his hand in his throat, and he killed him. "Now," said he, "neither thou nor another will tell tales of me." He went home with his hands on the wall, and he left the blackbird's chick within. They were asking him where he had been since the day came; he said he had been where he had often passed pleasant happy days. "How didst thou go there when thou art blind?" – "I got a chance to go there this day at all events. There is a little pet yonder that I brought home, and bring it in." They went out to look, and if they went, there did not go out so many as could bring it home. He himself arose, and he brought it in. He asked for a knife. He caught the shank, he stripped it, and then took the flesh off it. He broke the two ends of the bone. "Get now the shank of the dun deer that you said I never saw the like of in the Feen." They got this for him, and he threw it out through the marrow hole. Now he was made truthful. They began to ask more tales from him, but it beat them ever to make him begin at them any more.

The Widow and Her Daughters

THERE WAS FORMERLY A POOR widow, and she had three daughters, and all she had to feed them was a kailyard. There was a great gray horse who was coming every day to the yard to eat the kail. Said the eldest of the daughters to her mother, "I will go to the yard today, and I will take the spinning-wheel with me, and I will keep the horse out of the kail." "Do," said her mother. She went out. The horse came; she took the distaff from the wheel and she struck him. The distaff stuck to the horse, and her hand stuck to the distaff. Away went the horse till, they reached a green hill, and he called out, "Open, open, oh green hill, and let in the king's son; open, open, oh green hill, and let in the widow's daughter." The hill opened, and they went in. He warmed water for her feet, and made a soft bed for her limbs, and she lay down that night.

Early on the morrow, when he rose, he was going to hunt. He gave her the keys of the whole house, and he said to her that she might open every chamber inside but the one. "By all she ever saw not to open that one." That she should have his dinner ready when he should come back, and that if she would be a good woman that he would marry her. When he went away she began to open the chambers. Every one, as she opened it, was getting finer and finer, till she came to the one that was forbidden. It seemed to her, "What might be in it that she might not open it too." She opened it, and it was full of dead gentle women, and she went down to the knee in blood. Then she came out, and she was cleansing her foot; and though she were cleaning it, still she could not take a bit of the blood off it. A tiny cat came where she was, and she said to her, "If she would give a little drop of milk that she would clean her foot as well as it was before. "Thou! ugly beast! be off before thee. Dost thou suppose that I won't clean them better than thou?" "Yes, yes, take thine own away. Thou wilt see what will happen to thee when himself comes home." He came home, and she set the dinner on the board, and they sat down at it. Before they ate a bit he said to her, "Wert thou a good woman today was," said she. "Let me see thy foot, and I will tell thee whether thou wert or wert not." She let him see the one that was clean. "Let me see the other one," said he. When he saw the blood, "Oh! ho!" said he. He rose and took the axe and took her head off, and he threw her into the chamber with the other dead people. He laid down that night, and early on the morrow he went to the widow's yard again. Said the second one of the widow's daughters to her mother – "I will go out today, and I will keep the gray horse out of the yard." She went out sewing. She struck the thing she was sewing on the horse. The cloth stuck to the horse, and her hand stuck to the cloth. They reached the hill. He called as usual to the hill; the hill opened, and they went in. He warmed water for her feet, and made a soft bed for her limbs, and they lay down that night. Early in the morning he was going to hunt, and he said to her that she should open every chamber inside but one, and "by all she ever saw" not to open that one. She opened every chamber till she came to the little one, and because she thought "What might be in that one more than the rest that she might not open it?" She opened it, and it was full of dead gentlewomen, and her own sister amongst them. She went down to the knee in blood. She came out, and as she was cleaning herself, and the little cat came round about, and she said to her, "If thou wilt give me a tiny drop of milk I will clean thy foot is well as it ever was." "Thou! ugly beast! begone. Dost thou think that I will not clean it myself better than thou?" "Thou wilt see," said the cat, "what will happen to thee when himself comes home." When he came she set down the dinner, and they sat at it. Said he – "Wert thou a good woman today?" "I was," said she. "Let me see thy foot, and I will tell thee whether thou wert or wert not." She let him see the foot that was clean. "Let me see the other one," said he. She let him see it. "Oh! ho!" said he, and he took the axe and took her head off. He lay down that night. Early on the morrow, said the youngest one to her mother, as she wove a stocking – "I will go out with my stocking today, and I will watch the gray horse. I will see what happened to my two sisters, and I will return to tell you." "Do," said her mother, "and see thou dost not stay away. She went out, and the horse came. She struck the stocking on the horse. The stocking stuck to the horse, and the hand stuck to the stocking. They went away, and they reached the green hill. He called out as usual, and they got in. He warmed water for her feet, and made a soft bed for her limbs, and they lay down that night. On the morrow he was going to hunt, and he said to her – "If she would behave herself as a good woman till he returned, that they would be married in a few days." He gave her the keys, and he said to her that she might open every chamber that was within but that little one, "but see that she should not open that one." She opened every one, and when she came to this one, because she thought "what might be in it that she might not open it more than the rest?" she opened it, and she saw her two sisters there dead, and she went down to the two knees in blood. She came out, and she was cleaning her feet, and she could not take a bit of the blood off them. The tiny cat came where she was, and she said to her – "Give me a tiny drop of milk, and I will clean thy feet as well as they were before." "I will give it thou creature; I will give thee thy desire of milk if thou will clean my feet." The cat licked her feet as well as they were before. Then the king came home, and they set down his dinner, and they sat at it. Before they ate a bit, he said to her, "Wert thou a good woman today?" "I was middlin," said she; "I have no boasting to make of myself." "Let me see thy feet," said he. She let him see her feet. "Thou wert a good woman," said he; "and if thou holdest on thus till the end of a few days, thyself and I will be married." On the morrow he went away to hunt. When he went away the little cat came where she was. "Now, I will tell thee in what way thou wilt be quickest married to him," said the cat. "There are," said she, "a lot of old chests within. Thou shalt take out three of them; thou shalt clean them. Thou shalt say to him next night, that he must leave these three chests, one about of them, in thy mother's house, as they are of no use here; that there are plenty here without them; thou shalt say to him that he must not open any of them on the road, or else, if he opens, that thou wilt leave him; that thou wilt go up into a tree top, and that thou wilt be looking, and that if he opens any of them that thou wilt see. Then when he goes hunting, thou shalt open the chamber, thou shalt bring out thy two sisters; thou shalt draw on them the magic club, and they will be as lively and whole as they were before; thou shalt clean them then, and thou shalt put one in each chest of them, and thou shalt go thyself into the third one. Thou shalt put of silver and of gold, as much in the chests as will keep thy mother and thy sisters right for their lives. When he leaves the chests in thy mother's house, and when he returns he will fly in a wild rage: he will then go to thy mother's house in this fury, and he will break in the door; be thou behind the door, and take off his head with the bar; and then he will be a king's son, as precious as he was before, and he will marry thee. Say to thy sisters, if he attempts the chests to open them by the way, to call out, 'I see thee, I see thee,' and that he wilt think that thou wilt be calling out in the tree." When he came home he went away with the chests, one after one, till he left them in her mother's house. When he came to a glen, where he thought she in the tree could not see him, he began to let the chest down to see what was in it; she that was in the chest called out, "I see thee, I see thee!"

"Good luck be on thy pretty little head," said he, "if thou canst not see a long way!"

This was the way with him each journey, till he left the chests altogether in her mother's house.

When he returned home on the last journey, and saw that she was not before him, he flew in a wild rage; he went back to the widow's house, and when he reached the door he drove it in before him. She was standing behind the door, and she took his head off with the bar. Then he grew a king's son, as precious as ever came; there he was within and they were in great gladness, She and himself married, and they left with her mother and sisters, of gold and silver, as much as left them well for life.

The Sharp Grey Sheep

THERE WAS A KING and a queen, and they had a daughter, and the queen found death, and the king married another. And the last queen was bad to the daughter of the first queen, and she used to beat her and put her out of the door. She sent her to herd the sheep, and was not giving her what should suffice her. And there was a sharp (horned) grey sheep in the flock that was coming with meat to her.

The queen was taking wonder that she was keeping alive and that she was not getting meat enough from herself, and she told it to the henwife. The henwife thought that she would send her own daughter to watch how she was getting meat, and Ni Mhaol Charach, the henwife's daughter, went to herd the sheep with the queen's daughter. The sheep would not come to her so long as Ni Mhaol Charach was there, and Ni Mhaol Charach was staying all the day with her. The queen's daughter was longing for her meat, and she said – "Set thy head on my knee and I will dress thy hair." And Ni Mhaol Charach set her head on the knee of the queen's daughter, and she slept.

The sheep came with meat to the queen's daughter, but the eye that was in the back of the head of the bald black-skinned girl, the henwife's daughter, was open, and she saw all that went on, and when she awoke she went home and told it to her mother, and the henwife told it to the queen, and when the queen understood how the girl was getting meat, nothing at all would serve her but that the sheep should be killed.

The sheep came to the queen's daughter and said to her –

"They are going to kill me, but steal thou my skin and gather my bones and roll them in my skin, and I will come alive again, and I will come to thee again."

The sheep was killed, and the queen's daughter stole her skin, and she gathered her bones and her hoofs and she rolled them in the skin; but she forgot the little hoofs. The sheep came alive again, but she was lame. She came to the king's daughter with a halting step, and she said, "Thou didst as I desired thee, but thou hast forgotten the little hoofs."

And she was keeping her in meat after that.

There was a young prince who was hunting and coming often past her, and he saw how pretty she was, and he asked, "Who's she?" And they told him, and he took love for her, and he was often coming the way; but the bald black-skinned girl, the henwife's daughter, took notice of him, and she told it to her mother, and the henwife told it to the queen.

The queen was wishful to get knowledge what man it was, and the henwife sought till she found out who he (was), and she told the queen. When the queen heard who it was she was wishful to send her own daughter in his way, and she brought in the first queen's daughter, and she sent her own daughter to herd in her place, and she was making the daughter of the first queen do the cooking and every service about the house.

The first queen's daughter was out a turn, and the prince met her, and he gave her a pair of golden shoes. And he was wishful to see her at the sermon, but her muime would not let her go there.

But when the rest would go she would make ready, and she would go after them, and she would sit where he might see her, but she would rise and go before the people would scatter, and she would be at the house and everything in order before her muime would come. But the third time she was there the prince was wishful to go with her, and he sat near to the door, and when she went he was keeping an eye on her, and he rose and went after her. She was running home, and she lost one of her shoes in the mud; and he got the shoe, and because he could not see her he said that the one who had the foot that would fit the shoe was the wife that would be his.

The queen was wishful that the shoe would fit her own daughter, and she put the daughter of the first queen in hiding, so that she should not be seen till she should try if the shoe should fit her own daughter.

When the prince came to try the shoe on her, her foot was too big, but she was very anxious that the shoe should fit her, and she spoke to the henwife about it. The henwife cut the points of her toes off that the shoe might fit her, and the shoe went on her when the points of the toes were cut.

When the wedding-day came the daughter of the first queen was set in hiding in a nook that was behind the fire.

When the people were all gathered together, a bird came to the window, and he cried –

"The blood's in the shoe, and the pretty foot's in the nook at the back of the fire."

One of them said, "What is that creature saying?"

And the queen said – "It's no matter what that creature is saying; it is but a nasty, beaky, lying creature." The bird came again to the window; and the third time he came, the prince said – "We will go and see what he is saying."

And he rose and he went out, and the bird cried – "The blood's in the shoe, and the pretty foot's in the nook that is at the back of the fire."

He returned in, and he ordered the nook at the back of the fire to be searched. And they searched it, and they found the first queen's daughter there, and the golden shoe on the one foot. They cleaned the blood out of the other shoe, and they tried it on her, and the shoe fitted her, and its like was on the other foot. The prince left the daughter of the last queen, and he married the daughter of the first queen, and he took her from them with him, and she was rich and lucky after that.

The Fox and the Little Bonnach

THE FOX WAS ONCE GOING over a loch, and there met him a little bonnach, and the fox asked him where he was going.

The little bonnach told him he was going to such a place.

"And whence camest thou?" said the fox.

"I came from Geeogan, and I came from Cooaigean, and I came from the slab of the bonnach stone, and I came from the eye of the quern, and I will come from thee if I may," quoth the little bonnach.

"Well, I myself will take thee over on my back," said the fox.

"Thou'lt eat me, thou'lt eat me," quoth the little bonnach.

"Come then on the tip of my tail," said the fox.

"Oh! I will not; thou wilt eat me," said the little bonnach.

"Come into my ear," said the fox.

"I will not go; thou wilt eat me," said the little bonnach.

"Come into my mouth," said the fox.

"Thou wilt eat me that time at all events," said the little bonnach.

"Oh, I will not eat thee," said the fox. "At the time when I am swimming I cannot eat anything at all."

He went into his mouth.

"Oh! ho!" said the fox, "I may do my own pleasure to thee now. It is long since it was heard that a hard morsel is good in the mouth of the stomach."

The fox ate the little bonnach.

Then he went to the house of a gentleman, and he went to a loch, and he caught hold of a duck that was in it, and he ate that.

He went up to a hill side, and he began to stroke his sides on the hill.

"Oh king! how finely the bullet would spank upon my belly just now."

Who was listening but a hunter.

"It will be tried upon thee directly," said the hunter.

"Bad luck to the place that is here," quoth the fox, "in which a creature dares not say a word in fun that is not taken in earnest."

The hunter put a bullet in his gun, and he fired at him and killed him.

How the Cock Took a Turn Out of the Fox

THE RUSSET DOG came to a house, and he caught hold of a cock. He went away with the cock, and the people of the town-land went away after him.

"Are they not silly!" quoth the cock, "going after thee, and that they cannot catch thee at any rate." The cock was for that he should open his mouth that he might spring out.

When the fox saw that the cock was so willing to go along with himself, he was so pleased.

"Oh! musician, wilt thou not say, 'It is my own cock that is here', and they will turn back," said the cock.

The fox said, "Shê-mo-haolach-hay-n-a-han;" and when the fox opened his mouth the cock sprung away.

The Hen

THERE WAS A WOMAN before now, and she bore a hen in rock by the shore, after she had been driven into banishment in some way or other.

The hen grew big, and she used to be going to the king's house every day to try if she could get something that she might give to her mother. The king came out on a day of these days, and he said to her,

"What, thou nasty little creature, art thou doing standing there upon my door?"

"Well, then, though I be little, and even nasty, I can do a thing that the fine big queen thou hast cannot do," said she.

"What canst thou do?" quoth the king.

"I can spring from spar to spar, with the tongs and the hook for hanging the pot trailing after me."

He went in and he told that to the queen. The hen was tried, and she did it; they tied the pot-hook and the tongs to her, and she sprang over three spars (rafters), and she came down on the ground.

Then they tied the pot-hook and the tongs to the queen, and she went and she took a spring out of herself, and she cut the edge of her two shanks, and she fell, and the brain went out of her.

He had four queens, and the hen put them all out with this work.

"It would be better for you to marry my mother," quoth the hen; "she is a very fine woman."

"Avoid me," said the king; "thou hast caused me loss enough already, thou nasty creature."

"Well, then, that is not what is best for thee, but to marry her," said the hen.

"Send down thy mother so that we may see her," said the king.

She went where her mother was, and she said to her, "The king is seeking you, mother; I was asking him to marry you."

She went up, and she herself and the king married.

Then there was a Sunday, and they were going to sermon, the king and the queen; and they left within but the hen and the son of the first wife. The hen went when they went away, and she went to a chamber, and she cast off her the husk that was upon her, and the lad went into the room, and he saw the husk that was upon her. He caught hold of it, and he put it into the hot middle of the fire. She came down and she had no tale of the "cochall".

She came where the lad was, and she had a naked sword, and she said to him,

"Get for me my husk, or else I will take the head off thee, against the throat."

The lad took much fear, and he could not say a word to her.

"Thou nasty creature," said she, "it is much for me that thy death should be on my hands; I don't know what I shall do now; if I get another cochall they will think that I am a witch, and I had better stay as I am."

When the king came home he saw that fine woman within, going about the house, and he had no knowledge what had put her there, and the king must know what sort of a woman she was. She told every whit. She herself and the king's son married, and a great wedding was made for them.

The Keg of Butter

THE RUSSET DOG AND THE WILD DOG, the fox and the wolf, were going together; and they went round about the seashore, and they found a keg of butter, and they buried it.

On the morrow the fox went out, and when he returned in he said that a man had come to ask him to a baptism. The fox went and he arrayed himself in excellent attire, and he went away, and where should he go but to the butter keg; and when he came home the wolf asked him what name was on the child; and he said that there was Foveeal (under its mouth).

On the morrow he said that a man had sent to ask him to a baptism, and he reached the keg and he took out about half. The wolf asked when he came home what name was on the child.

"Well," said he, "there is a queer name that I myself would not give to my man child, if I had him; there is Moolay Moolay" (about half and half).

On the morrow he said that there was a man there came to ask him to a baptism again; and he went and he reached the keg, and he ate it all up. When he came home the wolf asked him what name was on the child, and he said that there was Booill Eemlich (tackling, licking, or licking all up).

On the morrow he went and he said to the wolf that they ought to bring the keg home. They went, and, when they reached the keg – there was not a shadow of the butter in it.

"Well! thou wert not without coming to watch this, though I was without coming here," quoth the fox.

The other one swore that he had not come near it.

"Thou needst not be blessing that thou didst not come here – I know that thou didst come, and that it was thou that took it out; but I will know it from thee when thou goest home, if it was thou that ate the butter," said the fox.

He went, and when he went home he hung the wolf by his hind legs, with his head dangling below him, and he had a dab of the butter and he put it under his mouth, and if it was true, it was out of the wolf's belly that it came.

"Thou red thief!" said he, "I said before that it was thou ate the butter."

They slept that night as they were, and on the morrow when they rose the fox said,

"Well, then, it is silly for ourselves to be going to death in this way with great excess of sloth; we will reach such and such a town-land, and we will take a piece of land in it."

They reached the town-land, and the man to whom it belonged gave them a piece of land the worth of seven Saxon pounds.

It was oats that they set that year, and they reaped it, and they began to divide it.

"Well, then," said the fox, "whether wouldst thou rather have the root or the tip? Thou shalt have thy two choices."

"I'd rather the root," said the wolf.

Then the fox had fine oaten bread all the year, and the other one had fodder.

On the next year they set a crop; and it was tata root (potatoes) that they set, and the potatoes grew well.

"Which wouldst thou like best, the root or the crop this year?" said the fox.

"Indeed, thou shalt not take the twist out of me anymore; I will have the (top) crop this year," quoth the wolf.

"Good enough, my hero," said the fox.

Then the wolf had the potato tops again, and the fox the potatoes. Then the wolf used to keep stealing the potatoes from the fox.

"Thou hadst best go yonder, and read that name that I have in the hoofs of the grey mare," quoth the fox.

Away went the wolf, and he began to read the name; and on a time of these times the white mare drew her leg, and she cast the head off the wolf.

"Oh!" said the fox, "it is long since I heard it. I would rather be a clerk than be reading a book."

He went home, and the wolf was not putting trouble upon him anymore.

The Brown Bear of the Green Glen

THERE WAS A KING IN ERIN ONCE, who had a leash of sons. John was the name of the youngest one, and it was said that he was not wise enough; and this good worldly king lost the sight of his eyes, and the strength of his feet. The two eldest brothers said that they would go seek three bottles of the water of the green Isle that was about the heaps of the deep. And so it was that these two brothers went away. Now the fool said that he would not believe but that he himself would go also. And the first big town he reached in his father's kingdom, there he sees his two brothers there, the blackguards! "Oh! my boys," says the young one, "it is thus you are?" "With swiftness of foot," said they, "take thyself home, or we will have thy life." "Don't be afraid, lads. It is no thing to me to stay with you." Now John went away on his journey till he came to a great desert of a wood. "Hoo, hoo!" says John to himself, "It is not canny for me to walk this wood alone." The night was coming now, and growing pretty dark. John ties the cripple white horse that was under him to the root of a tree, and he went up in the top himself. He was but a very short time in the top, when he saw a bear coming with a fiery cinder in his mouth. "Come down, son of the king of Erin," says he. "Indeed, I won't come. I am thinking I am safer where I am." "But if thou wilt not come down, I will go up," said the bear. "Art thou, too, taking me for a fool?" says John. "A shaggy, shambling creature like thee, climbing a tree!" "But if thou wilt not come down, I will go up," says the bear, as he fell out of hand to climb the tree. "Lord! thou canst do that same?" said John; "keep back from the root of the tree, then, and I will go down to talk to thee." And when the son of Erin's king drew down, they came to chatting. The bear asked him if he was hungry. "Weel! by your leave," said John, "I am a little at this very same time." The bear took that wonderful watchful turn and he catches a roebuck. "Now, son of Erin's king," says the bear, "whether wouldst thou like thy share of the buck boiled or raw?" "The sort of meat I used to get would be kind of plotted boiled," says John; and thus it fell out. John got his share roasted. "Now," said the bear, "lie down between my paws, and thou hast no cause to fear cold or hunger till morning." Early in the morning the Mathon (bear) asked, "Art thou asleep, son of Erin's king?" "I am not very heavily," said he. "It is time for thee to be on thy soles then. Thy journey is long – two hundred miles; but art thou a good horseman, John?" "There are worse than me at times," said he. "Thou hadst best get on top of me, then." He did this, and at the first leap John was to earth.

"Foil! foil!" says John. "What! thou art not bad at the trade thyself. Thou hadst best come back till we try thee again." And with nails and teeth he fastened on the Mathon, till they reached the end of the two hundred miles and a giant's house. "Now, John," said the Mathon, "thou shalt go to pass the night in this giant's house; thou wilt find him pretty grumpy, but say thou that it was the brown bear of the green glen that set thee here for a night's share, and don't thou be afraid that thou wilt not get share and comfort." And he left the bear to go to the giant's house.

"Son of Ireland's King," says the giant, "thy coming was in the prophecy; but if I did not get thy Father, I have got his son. I don't know whether I will put thee in the earth with my feet, or in the sky with my breath." "Thou wilt do neither of either," said John, "for it is the brown bear of the green glen that sent me here." "Come in, son of Erin's king," said he, "and thou shalt be well taken to this night." And as he said, it was true, John got meat and drink without stint. But to make a long tale short, the bear took John day after day to the third giant. "Now," says the bear, "I have not much acquaintance with this giant, but thou wilt not be long in his house when thou must wrestle with him. And if he is too hard on thy back, say thou, 'If I had the brown bear of the green glen here, that was thy master.'" As soon as John went, in – "Ai! ai!! or ee! ee!!" says the giant, "If I did not, get thy father, I have got his son;" and to grips they go.

They would make the boggy bog of the rocky rock. In the hardest place they would sink to the knee; in the softest, up to the thighs; and they would bring wells of spring water from the face of every rock. The giant gave John a sore wrench or two. "Foil! foil!"

says he, "if I had here the brown bear of the green glen, thy leap would not be so hearty." And no sooner spoke he the word than the worthy bear was at his side. "Yes! yes!" says the giant, "son of Erin's king, now I know thy matter better than thou dost thyself." So it was that the giant ordered his shepherd to bring home the best wether he had in the hill, and to throw his carcass before the great door. "Now, John," says the giant, "an eagle will come, and she will settle on the carcass of this wether, and there is a wart on the ear of this eagle which thou must cut off her with this sword, but a drop of blood thou must not draw."

The eagle came, but she was not long eating when John drew close to her, and with one stroke he cut the wart off her without drawing one drop of blood. "Now," said the eagle, "come on the root of my two wings, for I know thy matter better than thou dost thyself." He did this; and they were now on sea, and now on land, and now on the wing, till they reached the Green Isle. "Now, John," says she, "be quick, and fill thy three bottles; remember that the black dogs are away just now." When he filled the bottles with the water out of the well, he sees a little house beside him. John said to himself that he would go in, and that he would see what was in it. And the first chamber he opened, he saw a full bottle. He filled a glass out of it, and he drank it; and when he was going, he gave a glance, and the bottle was as full as it was before. "I will have this bottle along with the bottles of water," says he.

Then he went into another chamber, and he saw a loaf; he took a slice out of it, but the loaf was as whole as it was before. "Ye gods! I won't leave thee," says John. He went on thus till he came to another chamber. He saw a great cheese; he took a slice off the cheese, but it was as whole as ever. "I will have this along with the rest," says he. Then he went to another chamber, and he saw laid there the very prettiest little jewel of a woman he ever saw. "It were a great pity not to kiss thy lips, my love," says John.

Soon after, John jumped on top of the eagle, and she took him on the self-same steps till they reached the house of the big giant, and they were paying rent to the giant, and there was the sight of tenants and giants and meat and drink. "Well! John," says the giant, "didst thou see such drink as this in thy father's house in Erin?" "Pooh," says John, "Hoo! my hero; thou other man, I have a drink that is unlike it." He gave the giant a glass out of the bottle, but the bottle was as full as it was before. "Well!" said the giant, "I will give thee myself two hundred notes, a bridle and a saddle for the bottle." "It is a bargain, then," says John, "but that the first sweetheart I ever had must get it if she comes the way." "She will get that," says the giant; but, to make the long story short, he left each loaf and cheese with the two other giants, with the same covenant that the first sweetheart he ever had should get them if she came the way.

Now John reached his father's big town in Erin and he sees his two brothers as he left them – the "blackguardan!" "You had best come with me, lads," says he, "and you will get a dress of cloth, and a horse and a saddle and bridle each." And so they did; but when they were near to their father's house, the brothers thought that they had better kill him, and so it was that they set on him. And when they thought he was dead, they threw him behind a dike; and they took from him the three bottles of water, and they went home. John was not too long here, when his father's smith came the way with a cartload of rusty iron. John called out, "Whoever the Christian is that is there, oh! that he should help him."

The smith caught him, and he threw John amongst the iron; and because the iron was so rusty, it went into each wound and sore that John had; and so it was that John became rough-skinned and bald. Here we will leave John, and we will go back to the pretty little jewel that John left in the Green Isle. She became pale and heavy; and at the end of three quarters, she had a fine lad son. "Oh! in all the great world," says she, "how did I find this?" "Foil! foil!" says the hen-wife, "don't let that set thee thinking. Here's for thee a bird, and as soon as he sees the father of thy son, he will hop on the top of his head." The Green Isle was gathered from end to end, and the people were put in at the back door and out at the front door; but the bird did not stir, and the babe's father was not found. Now here, she said she would go through the world altogether till she should find the father of the babe. Then she came to the house of the big giant and sees the bottle. "Ai! ai!!" said she, "who gave thee this bottle?" Said the giant, "It was young John, son of Erin's king, that left it." "Well, then, the bottle is mine," said she. But to make the long story short, she came to the house of each giant, and she took with her each bottle, and each loaf, and each cheese, till at length and at last she came to the house of the king of Erin. Then the five-fifths of Erin were gathered, and the bridge of nobles of the people; they were put in at the back door and out at the front door, but the bird did not stir. Then she asked if there was one other or anyone else at all in Erin, that had not been here. "I have a bald rough-skinned gillie in the smithy," said the smith, but – "Rough on or off, send him here," says she. No sooner did the bird see the head of the bald rough-skinned gillie, than he took a flight and settles on the bald top of the rough-skinned lad. She caught him and kissed him. "Thou art the father of my babe."

"But, John," says the great king of Erin, "It is thou that gottest the bottles of water for me?" "Indeed, 'twas I," says John. "Weel, then, what art thou willing to do to thy two brothers?" "The very thing they wished to do to me, do for them;" and that same was done. John married the daughter of the king of the Green Isle, and they made a great rich wedding that lasted seven days and seven years, and thou couldst but hear leeg, leeg, and beeg, beeg, solid sound and peg drawing. Gold a-crushing from the soles of their feet to the tips of their fingers, the length of seven years and seven days.

Nippit Fit and Clippit Fit

IN A COUNTRY, FAR ACROSS THE SEA, there once dwelt a great and mighty Prince. He lived in a grand Castle, which was full of beautiful furniture, and curious and rare ornaments. And among them was a lovely little glass shoe, which would only fit the tiniest foot imaginable.

And as the Prince was looking at it one day, it struck him what a dainty little lady she would need to be who wore such a very small shoe. And, as he liked dainty people, he made up his mind that he would never marry until he found a maiden who could wear the shoe, and that, when he found her, he would ask her to be his wife.

And he called all his Lords and Courtiers to him, and told them of the determination that he had come to, and asked them to help him in his quest.

And after they had taken counsel together they summoned a trusty Knight, and appointed him the Prince's Ambassador; and told him to take the slipper, and mount a fleet-footed horse, and ride up and down the whole of the Kingdom until he found a lady whom it would fit.

So the Ambassador put the little shoe carefully in his pocket and set out on his errand.

He rode, and he rode, and he rode, going to every town and castle that came in his way, and summoning all the ladies to appear before him to try on the shoe. And, as he caused a Proclamation to be made that whoever could wear it should be the Prince's Bride, I need not tell you that all the ladies in the countryside flocked to wherever the Ambassador chanced to be staying, and begged leave to try on the slipper.

But they were all disappointed, for not one of them, try as she would, could make her foot small enough to go into the Fairy Shoe; and there were many bitter tears shed in secret, when they returned home, by countless fair ladies who prided themselves on the smallness of their feet, and who had set out full of lively expectation that they would be the successful competitors.

At last the Ambassador arrived at a house where a well-to-do Laird had lived. But the Laird was dead now, and there was nobody left but his wife and two daughters, who had grown poor of late, and who had to work hard for their living.

One of the daughters was haughty and insolent; the other was little, and young, and modest, and sweet.

When the Ambassador rode into the courtyard of this house, and, holding out the shoe, asked if there were any fair ladies there who would like to try it on, the elder sister, who always thought a great deal of herself, ran forward, and said that she would do so, while the younger girl just shook her head and went on with her work. "For," said she to herself, "though my feet are so little that they might go into the slipper, what would I do as the wife of a great Prince? Folk would just laugh at me, and say that I was not fit for the position. No, no, I am far better to bide as I am."

So the Ambassador gave the glass shoe to the elder sister, who carried it away to her own room; and presently, to everyone's astonishment, came back wearing it on her foot.

It is true that her face was very white, and that she walked with a little limp; but no one noticed these things except her younger sister, and she only shook her wise little head, and said nothing.

The Prince's Ambassador was delighted that he had at last found a wife for his master, and he mounted his horse and rode off at full speed to tell him the good news.

When the Prince heard of the success of his errand, he ordered all his Courtiers to be ready to accompany him next day when he went to bring home his Bride.

You can fancy what excitement there was at the Laird's house when the gallant company arrived, with their Prince at their head, to greet the lady who was to be their Princess.

The old mother and the plain-looking maid-of-all-work ran hither and thither, fetching such meat and drink as the house could boast to set before their high-born visitors, while the bonnie little sister went and hid herself behind a great pot which stood in the corner of the courtyard, and which was used for boiling hen's meat.

She knew that her foot was the smallest in the house; and something told her that if the Prince once got a glimpse of her he would not be content till she had tried on the slipper.

Meanwhile, the selfish elder sister did not help at all, but ran up to her chamber, and decked herself out in all the fine clothes that she possessed before she came downstairs to meet the Prince.

And when all the Knights and Courtiers had drunk a stirrup-cup, and wished Good Luck to their Lord and his Bride, she was lifted up behind the Prince on his horse, and rode off so full of her own importance, that she even forgot to say good-bye to her mother and sister.

Alas! alas! pride must have a fall. For the cavalcade had not proceeded very far when a little bird which was perched on a branch of a bush by the roadside sang out:

> *"Nippit fit, and clippit fit, behind the King rides,*
> *But pretty fit, and little fit, ahint the caldron hides."*

"What is this that the birdie says?" cried the Prince, who, if the truth be told, did not feel altogether satisfied with the Bride whom fortune had bestowed upon him. "Hast thou another sister, Madam?"

"Only a little one," murmured the lady, who liked ill the way in which things seemed to be falling out.

"We will go back and find her," said the Prince firmly, "for when I sent out the slipper I had no mind that its wearer should nip her foot, and clip her foot, in order to get it on."

So the whole party turned back; and when they reached the Laird's house the Prince ordered a search to be made in the courtyard. And the bonnie little sister was soon discovered and brought out, all blushes and confusion, from her hiding-place behind the caldron.

"Give her the slipper, and let her try it on," said the Prince, and the eldest sister was forced to obey. And what was the horror of the bystanders, as she drew it off, to see that she had cut off the tops of her toes in order to get it on.

But it fitted her little sister's foot exactly, without either paring or clipping; and when the Prince saw that it was so, he lifted the elder sister down from his horse and lifted the little one up in her place, and carried her home to his Palace, where the wedding was celebrated with great rejoicing; and for the rest of their lives they were the happiest couple in the whole kingdom.

Mac Iain Direach

AT SOME TIME THERE WAS A KING and a queen, and they had one son; but the queen died, and the king married another wife. The name of the son that the first queen had was Iain Direach. He was a handsome lad; he was a hunter, and there was no bird at which he would cast his arrow, that he would not fell; and he would kill the deer and the roes at a great distance from him; there was no day that he would go out with his bow and his quiver, that he would not bring venison home.

He was one day in the hunting hill hunting, and he got no venison at all; but there came a blue falcon past him, and he let an arrow at her, but he did but drive a feather from her wing. He raised the feather and he put it into his hunting bag, and he took it home; and when he came home his muime said to him, "Where is thy game today?" and he put his hand into the hunting bag, and he took out the feather and he gave it to her. And his muime took the feather in her hand, and she said, "I am setting it as crosses, and as spells, and as the decay of the year on thee; that thou be not without a pool in thy shoe, and that thou be wet, cold, and soiled, until thou gettest for me the bird from which that feather came."

And he said to his muime, "I am setting it as crosses and as spells, and as the decay of the year on thee; that thou be standing with the one foot on the great house, and the other foot on the castle; and that thy face be to the tempest whatever wind blows, until I return back."

And MacIain Direach went away as fast as he could to seek the bird from which the feather came, and his muime was standing with the one foot on the castle, and the other on the great house, till he should come back, and her front was to the face of the tempest, however long he might be without coming.

MacIain Direach was gone, travelling the waste to see if he could see the falcon, but the falcon he could not see; and much less than that, he could not get her; and he was going by himself through the waste, and it was coming near to the night. The little fluttering birds were going from the bush tops, from tuft to tuft, and to the briar roots, going to rest; and though they were, he was not going there, till the night came blind and dark; and he went and crouched at the root of a briar; and who came the way but An Gille Mairtean, the fox; and he said to him, "Thou'rt down in the mouth a Mhic Iain Direach; thou camest on a bad night; I have myself but one wether's trotter and a sheep's cheek, but needs must do with it."

They kindled a fire, and they roasted flesh, and they ate the wether's trotter and the sheep's cheek; and in the morning Gille Mairtean said to the king's son, "Oh son of Iain Direach, the falcon thou seekest is by the great giant of the Five Heads, and the Five Humps, and the Five Throttles, and I will shew thee where his house is; and it is my advice to thee to go to be as his servant, and that thou be nimble and ready to do each thing, that is asked of thee, and each thing that is trusted thee; and be very good to his birds, and it well may be that he will trust thee with the falcon to feed, and when thou gettest the falcon to feed be right good to her, till thou gettest a chance; at the time when the giant is not at home, run away with her, but take care that so much as one feather of her does not touch any one thing that is within the house, or if it touches, it will not go (well) with thee."

MacIain Direach said that he would take care of that; and he went to the giant's house; he arrived, and he struck at the door.

The giant shouted, "Who is there?"

"It is me," said MacIain Direach, "one coming to see if thou hast need of a lad."

"What work canst thou do?" said the giant.

"It is (this)," said MacIain Direach. "I can feed birds and swine, and feed and milk a cow, or goats or sheep."

"It is the like of thee that I want," said the giant.

The giant came out and he settled wages on MacIain Direach; and he was taking right good care of everything that the giant had, and he was very kind to the hens and to the ducks; and the giant took notice how well he was doing; and he said that his table was so good since MacIain Direach had come, by what it was before, that he had rather one hen of those which he got now, than two of those he used to get before. "My lad is so good that I begin to think I may trust him the falcon to feed;" and the giant gave the falcon to MacIain Direach to feed, and he took exceeding care of the falcon; and when the giant saw how well MacIain Direach was taking care of the falcon, he thought that he might trust her to him when he was (away) from the house; and the giant gave him the falcon to keep, and he was taking exceeding care of the falcon.

The giant thought each thing was going right, and he went from the house one day; and MacIain Direach thought that was the time to run away with the falcon, and he seized the falcon to go away with her; and when he opened the door and the falcon saw the light, she spread her wings to spring, and the point of one of the feathers of one of her wings touched one of the posts of the door, and the door post let out a screech. The giant came home running, and he caught MacIain Direach, and he took the falcon from him; and he said to him, "I would not give thee my falcon, unless thou shouldst get for me the White Glave of Light that the Big Women of Dhiurradh have;" and the giant sent MacIain away.

MacIain Direach went out again and through the waste, and the Gille Mairtean met with him, and he said –

"Thou art down in the mouth MacIain Direach; thou didst not, and thou wilt not do as I tell thee; bad is the night on which thou hast come; I have but one wether's trotter and one sheep's cheek, but needs must do with that."

They roused a fire, and they made ready the wether's trotter and the sheep's cheek, and they took their meat and sleep; and on the next day the Gille Mairtean said, "We will go to the side of the ocean."

They went and they reached the side of the ocean, and the Gille Mairtean said, "I will grow into a boat, and go thou on board of her, and I will take thee over to Dhiurradh; and go to the seven great women of Dhurrah and ask service, that thou be a servant with them; and when they ask thee what thou canst do, say to them that thou art good at brightening iron and steel, gold and silver, and that thou canst make them bright, clear, and shiny; and take exceeding care that thou dost each thing right, till they trust thee the White Glave of Light; and when thou gettest a chance, run away with it, but take care that the sheath does not touch a thing on the inner side of the house, or it will make a screech, and thy matter will not go with thee."

The Gille Mairtean grew into a boat, and MacIain Direach went on board of her, and he came on shore at Creagan nan Deargan, on the northern side of Dhiurradh, and MacIain Direach leaped on shore, and he went to take service with the Seven Big Women of Dhiurradh. He reached, and he struck at the door; the Seven Big Women came out, and they asked what he was seeking. He said, "He could brighten, or make clear, white and shiny, gold and silver, or iron or steel." They said, "We have need of thy like;" and set wages on him. And he was right diligent for six weeks, and put everything in exceeding order; and the Big Women noticed it; and they kept saying to each other, "This is the best lad we have ever had; we may trust him the White Glave of Light."

They gave him the White Glave of Light to keep in order; and he was taking exceeding care of the White Glave of Light, till one day that the Big Women were not at the house; he thought that was the time for him to run away with the White Glave of Light. He put it into the sheath, and he raised it on his shoulder; but when he was going out at the door, the point of the sheath touched the lintel, and the lintel made a screech; and the Big Women ran home, and took the sword from him; and they said to him, "We would not give thee our White Glave of Light, unless thou shouldst get for us the Yellow (Bay) Filly of the King of Eirinn."

MacIain Direach went to the side of the ocean and the Gille Mairtean met him, and he said to him, "Thou'rt down in the mouth, MacIain Direach; thou didst not, and thou wilt not do as I ask thee; I have tonight but one wether's trotter and one sheep's cheek, but needs must do with it."

They kindled a fire, and they roasted flesh, and they were satisfied. On the next day the Gille Mairtean said to MacIain Direach, "I will grow into a barque, and go thou on board of her, and I will go to Eirinn with thee; and when we reach Eirinn go thou to the house of the king, and ask service to be a stable lad with him; and when thou gettest that, be nimble and ready to do each thing that is to be done, and keep the horses and the harness in right good order, till the king trusts the Yellow (Bay) Filly to thee; and when thou gettest a chance, run away with her; but take care when thou art taking her out that no bit of her touches anything that is on the inner side of the gate, except the soles of her feet; or else thy matter will not prosper with thee."

And then the Gille Mairtean put himself into the form of a barque, MacIain Direach went on board, and the barque sailed with him to Eirinn. When they reached the shore of Eirinn, MacIain Direach leaped on land, and he went to the house of the king; and when he reached the gate, the gatekeeper asked where he was going; and he said that he was going to see if the king had need of a stable lad; and the gate-keeper let him past, and he reached the king's house; he struck at the door and the king came out; and the king said, "What art thou seeking here?"

Said he, "With your leave, I came to see if you had need of a stable lad."

The king asked, "What canst thou do?"

Said he, "I can clean and feed the horses, and clean the silver work, and the steel work, and make them shiny."

The king settled wages on him, and he went to the stable; and he put each thing in good order; he took good care of the horses, he fed them well, and he kept them clean, and their skin was looking sliom, sleek; and the silver work and the steel work shiny to look at; and the king never saw them so well in order before. And he said, "This is the best stable lad I have ever had, I may trust the Yellow (Bay) Filly to him."

The king gave the Yellow (Bay) Filly to MacIain Direach to keep; and MacIain Direach took very great care of the Yellow (Bay) Filly; and he kept her clean, till her skin was so sleek and slippery, and she so swift, that she would leave the one wind and catch the other. The king never saw her so good.

The king went one day to the hunting hill, and MacIain Direach thought that was the time to run away with the Yellow Bay Filly; and he set her in what belonged to her, with a bridle and saddle; and when he took her out of the stable and was taking her through the gate, she gave a switch, sguaise, with her tail, and the point of her tail touched the post of the gate, and it let out a screech.

The king came running, and he took the filly from MacIain Direach; and he said to him, "I would not give thee the Yellow (Bay) Filly, unless thou shouldst get for me the daughter of the king of the Frainge.

And MacIain Direach needs must go; and when he was within a little of the side of the sea, the Gille Mairtean met him; and he said to him, "Thou art down in the mouth, oh son of Iain Direach; thou didst not, and thou wilt not do as I ask thee; we must now go to France, I will make myself a ship, and go thou on board, and I will not be long till I take thee to France."

The Gille Mairtean put himself in the shape of a ship, and MacIain Direach went on board of her, and the Gille Mairtean sailed to France with him, and he ran himself on high up the face of a rock, on dry land; and he said to MacIain Direach, to go up to the king's house and to ask help, and to say that his skipper had been lost, and his ship thrown on shore.

MacIain Direach went to the king's house, and he struck at the door; one came out to see who was there; he told his tale and he was taken into the fort. The king asked him whence he was, and what he was doing here.

He told them the tale of misery; that a great storm had come on him, and the skipper he had was lost; and the ship he had thrown on dry land, and she was there, driven up on the face of a rock by the waves, and that he did not know how he should get her out.

The king and the queen, and the family together, went to the shore to see the ship; and when they were looking at the ship, exceeding sweet music began on board; and the King of France's daughter went on board to see the musical instrument, together with MacIain Direach; and when they were in one chamber, the music would be in another chamber; but at last they heard the music on the upper deck of the ship, and they went above on the upper deck of the ship, and (so) it was that the ship was out on the ocean, and out of sight of land.

And the King of France's daughter said, "Bad is the trick thou hast done to me. Where art thou for going with me?"

"I am," said MacIain Direach, "going with thee to Eirinn, to give thee as a wife to the King of Eirinn, so that I may get from him his Yellow (Bay) Filly, to give her to the Big Women of Dhiurradh, that I may get from them their White Glave of Light, to give it to the Great Giant of the Five Heads, and Five Humps, and Five Throttles, that I may get from him his Blue Falcon, to take her home to my muime, that I may be free from my crosses, and from my spells, and from the bad diseases of the year."

And the King of France's daughter said, "I had rather be as a wife to thyself."

And when they came to shore in Eirinn, the Gille Mairtean put himself in the shape of a fine woman, and he said to MacIain Direach, "Leave thou the King of France's daughter here till we return, and I will go with thee to the King of Eirinn; I will give him enough of a wife."

MacIain Direach went with the Gille Mairtean in the form of a fine maiden, with his hand in the oxter of MacIain Direach. When the King of Eirinn saw them coming, he came to meet them; he took out the Yellow (Bay) Filly and a golden saddle on her back, and a silver bridle on her head.

MacIain Direach went with the filly where the King of France's daughter was. The King of Eirinn was right well pleased with the young wife he had got; but little did the King of Eirinn know that he had got Gille Mairtean; and they had not long been gone to rest, when the Gille Mairtean sprung on the king, and he did not leave a morsel of flesh between the back of his neck and his haunch that he did not take off him. And the Gille Mairtean left the King of Eirinn a pitiful wounded cripple; and he went running where MacIain Direach was, and the King of France's daughter, and the Yellow (Bay) Filly.

Said the Gille Mairtean, "I will go into the form of a ship, and go you on board of her, and I will take you to Diurradh; he grew into the form of a ship; and MacIain Direach put in the Yellow (Bay) Filly first, and he himself and the King of France's daughter went in after her; and the Gille Mairtean sailed with them to Diurradh, and they went on shore at Creagan nan deargan, at Cilla-mhoire, at the northern end of Diurradh; and when they went on shore, the Gille Mairtean said, "Leave thou the Yellow (Bay) Filly here, and the king's daughter, till thou return; and I will go in the form of a filly, and I will go with thee to the Big Women of Diurradh, and I will give them enough of filly-ing."

The Gille Mairtean went into the form of a filly, MacIain Direach put the golden saddle on his back, and the silver bridle on his head, and he went to the Seven Big Women of Diurradh with him. When the Seven Big Women saw him coming, they came to meet him with the White Glave of Light, and they gave it to him. MacIain Direach took the golden saddle off the back of the Gille Mairtean, and the silver bridle out of his head, and he left him with them: and he went away himself with the White Glave of Light, and he went where he left the King of France's daughter, and the Yellow Bay Filly which he got from the King of Eirinn; and the Big Women of Diurradh thought that it was the Yellow Bay Filly of the King of Eirinn that they had got, and they were in great haste to ride. They put a saddle on her back, and they bridled her head, and one of them went up on her back to ride her, another went up at the back of that one, and another at the back of that one, and there was always room for another one there, till one after one, the Seven Big Women went up on the back of the Gille Mairtean, thinking that they had got the Yellow Bay Filly.

One of them gave a blow of a rod to the Gille Mairtean; and if she gave, he ran, and he raced backwards and forwards with them through the mountain moors; and at last he went bounding on high to the top of the Monadh mountain of Duirradh, and he reached the top of the face of the great crag that is there, and he moved his front to the crag, and he put his two forefeet to the front of the crag, and he threw his aftermost end on high, and he threw the Seven Big women over the crag, and he went away laughing; and he reached where were MacIain Direach and the King of France's daughter, with the Yellow Bay Filly, and the White Glave of Light.

Said the Gille Mairtean, "I will put myself in the form of a boat, and go thyself, and the daughter of the King of France on board, and take with you the Yellow Baby Filly and the White Glave of Light, and I will take you to mainland."

The Gille Mairtean put himself in the shape of a boat; MacIain Direach put the White Glave of Light and the Yellow Bay Filly on board, and he went himself, and the King of France's daughter, in on board after them; and the Gille Mairtean went with them to the mainland. When they reached shore, the Gille Mairtean put himself into his own shape, and he said to MacIain Direach –

"Leave thou the King of France's daughter, the Yellow Bay Filly from the King of Eirinn, and the White Glave of Light there, and I will go into the shape of a White Glave of Light; and take thou me to the giant and give thou me to him for the falcon, and I will give him enough of swords."

The Gille Mairtean put himself into the form of a sword, and MacIain Direach took him to the giant; and when the giant saw him coming, he put the blue falcon into a muirlag, and he gave it to MacIain Direach, and he went away with it to where he had left the King of France's daughter, the Yellow (Bay) Filly, and the White Glave of Light.

The giant went in with the Gille Mairtean in his hand, himself thinking that it was the White Glave of Light of the Big Women of Diurradh that he had, and he began at fionnsaireach, fencing, and at sguaiseal, slashing with it; but at last the Gille Mairtean bent himself, and he swept the five heads off the giant, and he went where MacIain Direach was, and he said to him, "Son of John the Upright, put the saddle of gold on the filly, and the silver bridle in her head, and go thyself riding her, and take the King of France's daughter at thy back, and the White Glave of Light with its back against thy nose; or else if thou be not so, when thy muime sees thee, she has a glance that is so deadly that she will bewitch thee, and thou wilt fall a faggot of firewood; but if the back of the sword is against thy nose, and its edge to her, when she tries to bewitch thee, she will fall down herself as a faggot of sticks.

MacIain Direach did as the Gille Mairtean asked him; and when he came in sight of the house, and his muime looked at him with a deadly bewitching eye, she fell as a faggot of sticks, and MacIain Direach set fire to her, and then he was free from fear; and he had got the best wife in Albainn; and the Yellow (Bay) Filly was so swift that she could leave the one wind and she would catch the other wind, and the Blue Falcon would keep him in plenty of game, and the White Glave of Light would keep off each foe; and MacIain Direach was steadily, luckily off.

Said MacIain Direach to the Gille Mairtean, "Thou art welcome, thou Lad of March, to go through my ground, and to take any beast thou dost desire thyself to take with thee; and I will give word to my servants that they do not let an arrow at thee, and that they do not kill thee, nor any of thy race, whatever one of the flock thou takest with thee."

Said the Gille Mairtean, "Keep thou thy herds to thyself; there is many a one who has wethers and sheep as well as thou hast, and I will get plenty of flesh in another place without coming to put trouble on thee; and the fox gave a blessing to the son of Upright John, and he went away; and the tale was spent.

The Three Questions

THERE WAS ONCE, LONG AGO, a scholar; and when he had done learning, his master said that he must now answer three questions, or have his head taken off. The scholar was to have time to make ready, and being in a great fright, he went to a miller who was the master's brother, and asked his aid.

The miller disguised himself and went instead of the scholar, and the first question put to him was this: "How many ladders would reach the sky?"

"Now," said the narrator, "can *you* answer that?"

"One, if it were long enough."

"That's right." The second was: "Where is the middle of the world?"

So the miller laid down a rod, and he said: "Here, set a hoop about the world, and thou will find the middle here."

The third was: "What is the world's worth?"

"Well," said the miller, "the Saviour was sold for thirty pieces of silver, I am sure the world is worth no more."

"Oh," said the brother who was riding beside us, "that's not the way I have heard it.

The second was: "How long will it take to go round the world?"

And the miller said: "If I were as swift as the sun and moon, I would run it in twenty-four hours."

And the third was: "What is my thought?"

And the miller answered: "I can tell: Thou thinkest that I am thy scholar, but I am thy brother, the miller."

The Master and His Man

THERE WERE AT SOME TIME ere now bad times, and there were many servants seeking places, and there were not many places for them.

There was a farmer there, and he would not take any servant but one who would stay with him till the end of seven years, and who would not ask for wages, but what he could catch in his mouth of the seed corn, when he should be thrashing corn in the barn.

None were taking (service) with him. At last he said that he would let them plant their seed in the best ground that he might have, and they should get his own horses and plough to make the thraive, and his own horses to harrow it.

There was a young lad there, and he said, "I will take wages with thee," and the farmer set wages on that lad, and the bargain that they made was that the wages which the lad was to have were to be as many grains of seed as he could catch in his mouth when they were beating sheaves in the barn, and he was to get (leave) to plant that seed in the best land that the farmer had, and he was to keep as much as grew on that seed, and to put with it what seed soever he might catch in his mouth when he was thrashing the corn, and to plant that in the best land which the farmer had on the next year. He was to have horses, and plough, or any other "gairios" he might want for planting or reaping from his master, and so on to the end of the seven years. That he should have seen winters in the barn thrashing, seven springs to plant, seven summers of growth for the crop, and seven autumns of reaping, and whatsoever were the outcoming that might be in the lad's seed, that was the wage that he was to have when he should go away.

The lad went home to his master, and always when he was thrashing in the barn his master was thrashing with him, and he caught but three grains of seed in his mouth on that winter; and he kept these carefully till the spring came, and he planted them in the best land the carle had.

There grew out of these three ears, and there were on each ear threescore good grains of seed. The lad kept these carefully, and what grains soever he caught he put them together with them. He planted these again in the spring, and in the autumn again he had as good as he had the year before that.

The lad put his seed bye carefully, and anything he caught in his mouth when he was thrashing in the next winter he put it with the other lot; and so with the lad from year to year, till at last, to make a long story short, the lad planted on the last year every (bit of) ploughing land that the carle had, and he had more seed to set, and the carle was almost harried. He had to pay rent to the farmer who was nearest to him, for land in which the lad might set the excess of seed which he had, and to sell part of his cattle for want of ground on which they might browse, and he would not make a bargain in the same way with a servant for ever after.

The Wee Bannock

"Some tell about their sweethearts,
How they tirled them to the winnock,
But I'll tell you a bonnie tale
About a guid oatmeal bannock."

THERE WAS ONCE an old man and his wife, who lived in a dear little cottage by the side of a burn. They were a very canty and contented couple, for they had enough to live on, and enough to do. Indeed, they considered themselves quite rich, for, besides their cottage and their garden, they possessed two sleek cows, five hens and a cock, an old cat, and two kittens.

The old man spent his time looking after the cows, and the hens, and the garden; while the old woman kept herself busy spinning.

One day, just after breakfast, the old woman thought that she would like an oatmeal bannock for her supper that evening, so she took down her bakeboard, and put on her girdle, and baked a couple of fine cakes, and when they were ready she put them down before the fire to harden.

While they were toasting, her husband came in from the byre, and sat down to take a rest in his great armchair. Presently his eyes fell on the bannocks, and, as they looked very good, he broke one through the middle and began to eat it.

When the other bannock saw this, it determined that it should not have the same fate, so it ran across the kitchen and out of the door as fast as it could. And when the old woman saw it disappearing, she ran after it as fast as her legs would carry her, holding her spindle in one hand and her distaff in the other.

But she was old, and the bannock was young, and it ran faster than she did, and escaped over the hill behind the house. It ran, and it ran, and it ran, until it came to a large newly thatched cottage, and, as the door was open, it took refuge inside, and ran right across the floor to a blazing fire, which was burning in the first room that it came to.

Now, it chanced that this house belonged to a tailor, and he and his two apprentices were sitting cross-legged on the top of a big table by the window, sewing away with all their might, while the tailor's wife was sitting beside the fire carding lint.

When the wee bannock came trundling across the floor, all three tailors got such a fright that they jumped down from the table and hid behind the Master Tailor's wife.

"Hoot," she said, "what a set of cowards ye be! 'Tis but a nice wee bannock. Get hold of it and divide it between you, and I'll fetch you all a drink of milk."

So she jumped up with her lint and her lint cards, and the tailor jumped up with his great shears, and one apprentice grasped the line measure, while another took up the saucer full of pins; and they all tried to catch the wee bannock. But it dodged them round and round the fire, and at last it got safely out of the door and ran down the road, with one of the apprentices after it, who tried to snip it in two with his shears.

It ran too quickly for him, however, and at last he stopped and went back to the house, while the wee bannock ran on until it came to a tiny cottage by the roadside. It trundled in at the door, and there was a weaver sitting at his loom, with his wife beside him, winding a clue of yarn.

"What's that, Tibby?" said the weaver, with a start as the little cake flew past him.

"Oh!" cried she in delight, jumping to her feet, "'tis a wee bannock. I wonder where it came from?"

"Dinna bother your head about that, Tibby," said her man, "but grip it, my woman, grip it."

But it was not so easy to get hold of the wee bannock. It was in vain that the Goodwife threw her clue at it, and that the Goodman tried to chase it into a corner and knock it down with his shuttle. It dodged, and turned, and twisted, like a thing bewitched, till at last it flew out at the door again, and vanished down the hill, "for all the world," as the old woman said, "like a new tarred sheep, or a daft cow."

In the next house that it came to it found the Goodwife in the kitchen, kirning. She had just filled her kirn, and there was still some cream standing in the bottom of her cream jar.

"Come away, little bannock," she cried when she saw it. "Thou art come in just the nick of time, for I am beginning to feel hungry, and I'll have cakes and cream for my dinner."

But the wee bannock hopped round to the other side of the kirn, and the Goodwife after it. And she was in such a hurry that she nearly upset the kirn; and by the time that she had put it right again, the wee bannock was out at the door and half-way down the brae to the mill.

The miller was sifting meal in the trough, but he straightened himself up when he saw the little cake.

"It's a sign of plenty when bannocks are running about with no one to look after them," he said; "but I like bannocks and cheese, so just come in, and I will give thee a night's lodging."

But the little bannock had no wish to be eaten up by the miller, so it turned and ran out of the mill, and the miller was so busy that he did not trouble himself to run after it.

After this it ran on, and on, and on, till it came to the smithy, and it popped in there to see what it could see.

The smith was busy at the anvil making horseshoe nails, but he looked up as the wee bannock entered.

"If there be one thing I am fond of, it is a glass of ale and a well-toasted cake," he cried. "So come in by here, and welcome to ye."

But as soon as the little bannock heard of the ale, it turned and ran out of the smithy as fast as it could, and the disappointed smith picked up his hammer and ran after it. And when he saw that he could not catch it, he flung his heavy hammer at it, in the hope of knocking it down, but, luckily for the little cake, he missed his aim.

After this the bannock came to a farmhouse, with a great stack of peats standing at the back of it. In it went, and ran to the fireside. In this house the master had all the lint spread out on the floor, and was cloving it with an iron rod, while the mistress was heckling what he had already cloven.

"Oh, Janet," cried the Goodman in surprise, "here comes in a little bannock. It looks rare and good to eat. I'll have one half of it."

"And I'll have the other half," cried the Goodwife. "Hit it over the back with your cloving-stick, Sandy, and knock it down. Quick, or it will be out at the door again."

But the bannock played "jook-about," and dodged behind a chair. "Hoot!" cried Janet contemptuously, for she thought that her husband might easily have hit it, and she threw her heckle at it.

But the heckle missed it, just as her husband's cloving-rod had done, for it played "jook-about" again, and flew out of the house.

This time it ran up a burnside till it came to a little cottage standing among the heather.

Here the Goodwife was making porridge for the supper in a pot over the fire, and her husband was sitting in a corner plaiting ropes of straw with which to tie up the cow.

"Oh, Jock! come here, come here," cried the Goodwife. "Thou art aye crying for a little bannock for thy supper; come here, histie, quick, and help me to catch it."

"Ay, ay," assented Jock, jumping to his feet and hurrying across the little room. "But where is it? I cannot see it."

"There, man, there," cried his wife, "under that chair. Run thou to that side; I will keep to this."

So Jock ran into the dark corner behind the chair; but, in his hurry, he tripped and fell, and the wee bannock jumped over him and flew laughing out at the door.

Through the whins and up the hillside it ran, and over the top of the hill, to a shepherd's cottage on the other side.

The inmates were just sitting down to their porridge, and the Goodwife was scraping the pan.

"Save us and help us," she exclaimed, stopping with the spoon half-way to her mouth. "There's a wee bannock come in to warm itself at our fireside."

"Sneck the door," cried the husband, "and we'll try to catch it. It would come in handy after the porridge."

But the bannock did not wait until the door was sneckit. It turned and ran as fast as it could, and the shepherd and his wife and all the bairns ran after it, with their spoons in their hands, in hopes of catching it.

And when the shepherd saw that it could run faster than they could, he threw his bonnet at it, and almost struck it; but it escaped all these dangers, and soon it came to another house, where the folk were just going to bed.

The Goodman was half undressed, and the Goodwife was raking the cinders carefully out of the fire.

"What's that?" said he, "for the bowl of brose that I had at supper-time wasna' very big."

"Catch it, then," answered his wife, "and I'll have a bit, too. Quick! quick! Throw your coat over it or it will be away."

So the Goodman threw his coat right on the top of the little bannock, and almost managed to smother it; but it struggled bravely, and got out, breathless and hot, from under it. Then it ran out into the grey light again, for night was beginning to fall, and the Goodman ran out after it, without his coat. He chased it and chased it through the stackyard and across a field, and in amongst a fine patch of whins. Then he lost it; and, as he was feeling cold without his coat, he went home.

As for the poor little bannock, it thought that it would creep under a whin bush and lie there till morning, but it was so dark that it never saw that there was a fox's hole there. So it fell down the fox's hole, and the fox was very glad to see it, for he had had no food for two days.

"Oh, welcome, welcome," he cried; and he snapped it through the middle with his teeth, and that was the end of the poor wee bannock.

And if a moral be wanted for this tale, here it is: That people should never be too uplifted or too cast down over anything, for all the good folk in the story thought that they were going to get the bannock, and, lo and behold! the fox got it after all.

Historical Legend

Introduction

AMONG THE MOST important functions of myth is explaining where a particular country and its culture come from. 'The Origin of Loch Ness' recounts how this famous feature was formed, in the most fanciful – but at the same time the most literal and matter-of-fact – of terms.

More subtly, though, myths may offer an account of a nation's history that seems satisfying to it emotionally – however sceptical scholarly historians may be. 'Young Glengarry, the Black Raven' makes of a real historical figure an emblem of youth and daring – and loyalty. As for the figure formerly known as 'Bonnie Prince Charlie', historians have not been forgiving. Charles Edward Stuart's bid to win the British throne in 1745 was criminally incompetent in both conception and execution. As we see in 'Allan Donn and Annie Campbell' and 'Prince Charlie and Mary Macleod', however, he became a focus for stories of romantic patriotism.

The Inheritance

THERE WAS ONCE A FARMER, and he was well off. He had three sons. When he was on the bed of death he called them to him, and he said, "My sons, I am going to leave you: let there be no disputing when I am gone. In a certain drawer, in a dresser in the inner chamber, you will find a sum of gold; divide it fairly and honestly amongst you, work the farm, and live together as you have done with me;" and shortly after the old man went away. The sons buried him; and when all was over, they went to the drawer, and when they drew it out there was nothing in it.

They stood for a while without speaking a word. Then the youngest spoke, and he said – "There is no knowing if there ever was any money at all;" the second said – "There was money surely, wherever it is now;" and the eldest said – "Our father never told a lie, There was money certainly, though I cannot understand the matter." "Come," said the eldest, "let us go to such an old man; he was our father's friend; he knew him well; he was at school with him; and no man knew so much of his affairs. Let us go to consult him."

So the brothers went to the house of the old man, and they told him all that had happened. "Stay with me," said the old man, "and I will think over this matter. I cannot understand it; but, as you know, your father and I were very great with each other. When he had children I had sponsorship, and when I had children he had gostji. I know that your father never told a lie." And he kept them there, and he gave them meat and drink for ten days.

Then he sent for the three young lads, and he made them sit down beside him, and he said –

"There was once a young lad, and he was poor; and he took love for the daughter of a rich neighbour, and she took love for him; but because he was so poor there could be no wedding. So at last they pledged themselves to each other, and the young man went away, and stayed in his own house. After a time there came another suitor, and because he was well off, the girl's father made her promise to marry him, and after a time they were married. But when the bridegroom came to her, he found her weeping and bewailing; and he said, 'What ails thee?' The bride would say nothing for a long time; but at last she told him all about it, and how she was pledged to another man. 'Dress thyself,' said the man, 'and follow me.' So she dressed herself in the wedding clothes, and he took the horse, and put her behind him, and rode to the house of the other man, and when he got there, he struck in the door, and he called out, 'Is there man within?' and when the other answered, he left the bride there within the door, and he said nothing, but he returned home. Then the man got up, and got a light, and who was there but the bride in her wedding dress.

"'What brought thee here?' said he. 'Such a man,' said the bride. 'I was married to him today, and when I told him of the promise we had made, he brought me here himself and left me.'

"'Sit thou there,' said the man; 'art thou not married?' So he took the horse, and he rode to the priest, and he brought him to the house, and before the priest he loosed the woman from the pledge she had given, and he gave her a line of writing that she was free, and he set her on the horse, and said, 'Now return to thy husband.'

"So the bride rode away in the darkness in her wedding dress. She had not gone far when she came to a thick wood where three robbers stopped and seized her. 'Aha!' said one, 'we have waited long, and we have got nothing, but now we have got the bride herself.' 'Oh,' said she, 'let me go: let me go to my husband; the man that I was pledged to has let me go. Here are ten pounds in gold – take them, and let me go on my journey.' And so she begged and prayed for a long time, and told what had happened to her. At last one of the robbers, who was of a better nature than the rest, said, 'Come, as the others have done this, I will take you home myself.' 'Take thou the money,' said she. 'I will not take a penny,' said the robber; but the other two said, 'Give us the money,' and they took the ten pounds. The woman rode home, and the robber left her at her husband's door, and she went in, and showed him the line – the writing that the other had given her before the priest, and they were well pleased."

"Now," said the old man, "which of all these do you think did best?" So the eldest son said, "I think the man that sent the woman to him to whom she was pledged, was the honest, generous man: he did well." The second said, "Yes, but the man to whom she was pledged did still better, when he sent her to her husband." "Then," said the youngest, "I don't know myself; but perhaps the wisest of all were the robbers who got the money." Then the old man rose up, and he said, "Thou hast thy father's gold and silver. I have kept you here for ten days; I have watched you well. I know your father never told a lie, and thou hast stolen the money." And so the youngest son had to confess the fact, and the money was got and divided.

Castle Urquhart and the Fugitive Lovers

GLEN-URQUHART, WHERE CASTLE URQUHART is situated, is one of the most beautiful of our Highland valleys, distant from Inverness some fourteen miles, and expands first from the waters of Loch-Ness into a semi-circular plain, divided into fields by hedgerows, and having its hill-sides beautifully diversified by woods and cultivated grounds. The valley then runs upwards some ten miles to Corriemonie, through a tract of haugh-land beautifully cultivated, and leading to a rocky pass or gorge half-way upwards or thereabouts, which, on turning, an inland valley, as it were, is attained, almost circular, and containing Loch-Meiglie, a beautiful small sheet of water, the edges of which are studded with houses, green lawns, and cultivated grounds.

Over a heathy ridge beyond these, two or three miles, we reach the flat of Corriemonie, adorned by some very large ash and beech trees, where the land is highly cultivated, at an elevation of eight or nine hundred feet above, and twenty-five miles distant from, the sea. At the base of Mealfourvonie, a small circular lake, of a few acres in extent, exists, which was once thought to be unfathomable, and to have a subterranean communication with Loch-Ness. From it flows the Aultsigh Burn, a streamlet which, tumbling down a rocky channel, at the base of one of the grandest frontlets of rock in the Highlands, nearly fifteen hundred feet high, empties itself into Loch-Ness within three miles of Glenmoriston. Besides the magnificent and rocky scenery to be seen in the course of this burn, it displays, at its mouth, an unusually beautiful waterfall, and another about two miles further up, shaded with foliage of the richest colour. A tributary of the Coiltie, called the Dhivach, amid beautiful and dense groves of birch, displays a waterfall as high and picturesque as that of Foyers; and near the source of the Enneric River, which flows from Corriemonie into the still waters of Loch-Meiglie, another small, though highly picturesque cascade, called the Fall of Moral, is to be seen. Near it is a cave large enough to receive sixteen or twenty persons. Several of the principal gentlemen of the district concealed themselves here from the Hanoverian troops during the troubles of the '45.

On the southern promontory of Urquhart Bay are the ruins of the Castle, rising over the dark waters of the Loch, which, off this point, is 125 fathoms in depth. The castle has the appearance of having been a strong and extensive building. The mouldings of the corbel table which remain are as sharp as on the day they were first carved, and indicate a date about the beginning of the 14th century. The antiquary will notice a peculiar arrangement in the windows, for pouring molten lead on the heads of the assailants. It overhangs the lake, and is built on a detached rock separated from the adjoining hill, at the base of which it lies, by a moat of about twenty-five feet deep and sixteen feet broad. The rock is crowned by the remains of a high wall or curtain, surrounding the building, the principal part of which, a strong square keep of three storeys, is still standing, surmounted by four square hanging turrets. This outward wall encloses a spacious yard, and is in some places terraced. In the angles were platforms for the convenience of the defending soldiery. The entrance was by a spacious gateway between two guard rooms, projected beyond the general line of the walls, and was guarded by more than one massive portal and huge portcullis to make security doubly sure. These entrance towers were much in the style of architecture peculiar to the Castles of Edward I of England, and in front of them lay the drawbridge across the outer moat. The whole works were extensive and strong, and the masonry was better finished than is common in the generality of Scottish strongholds.

The first siege Urquhart Castle is known to have sustained was in the year 1303, when it was taken by the officers of Edward I who were sent forward by him, to subdue the country, from Kildrummie, near Nairn, beyond which he did not advance in person, and of all the strongholds in the North, it was that which longest resisted his arms.

Alexander de Bois, the brave governor, and his garrison, were put to the sword. Sir Robert Lauder of Quarrelwood, in Morayshire, governor of the Castle in A.D. 1332, maintained it against the Baliol faction. His daughter, marrying the Earl of Strathglass, the offspring of their union, Sir Robert Chisholm of that Ilk, became Laird of Quarrelwood in right of his grandfather. After this period it is known to have been a Royal fort or garrison; but it is very likely it was so also at the commencement of the 14th century, and existed as such in the reigns of the Alexanders and other Scottish sovereigns, and formed one of a chain of fortresses erected for national defence, and for insuring internal peace. In 1359 the barony and the Castle of Urquhart were disponed by David II to William, Earl of Sutherland, and his son John. In 1509 it fell into the hands of the chief of the Clan Grant, and in that family's possession it has continued to this day.

How it came into the possession of John Grant, the 10th Laird, surnamed the 'Bard,' is not known; but it was not won by the broadsword, from Huntly, the Lieutenant-General of the King. It has been the boast of the chiefs of the Clan Grant that no dark deeds of rapine and blood have been transmitted to posterity by any of their race. Their history is unique among Highland clans, in that, down to the period of the disarming after Culloden, the broadswords of the Grants were as spotless as a lady's bodkin. True it is, there were some dark deeds enacted between the Grants of Carron and Ballindalloch, and at the battles of Cromdale and Culloden the Grants of Glenmoriston were present; but far otherwise was the boast of the Grants of Strathspey – a gifted ancestry seemed to transmit hereditary virtues, and each successive scion of the house seemed to emulate the peaceful habits of his predecessor. That this amiable life did not conceal craven hearts is abundantly evident from the history of our country. There is a continual record of gallant deeds and noble bearing in their records down to the present time, and there are few families whose names, like the Napiers and the Grants, are more conspicuous in our military annals. But their rise into a powerful clan was due to the more peaceful gifts, of 'fortunate alliances' and 'royal bounties.'

It is much to be regretted that so little has been transmitted to posterity of the history of this splendid ruin of Castle Urquhart.

The probability is that it is connected with many a dark event over which the turbulence of the intervening period and the obscurity of its situation have cast a shade of oblivion.

The most prominent part of the present mass, the fine square tower at the north-eastern extremity of the building, is supposed to have been the keep, and is still pretty entire. From this point, the view is superb. It commands Loch-Ness from one end to the other, and is an object on which the traveller fixes an admiring gaze as the steamer paddles her merry way along the mountain-shadowed water. On a calm day the dashing echo of the Fall of Foyers bursts fitfully across the Loch, and when the meridian sun lights up the green earth after a midsummer shower, a glimpse of the distant cataract may be occasionally caught, slipping like a gloriously spangled avalanche to the dark depths below. The story in which the castle was the principal scene of action is quite characteristic of the times referred to. A gentleman of rank, who had been out with the Prince and had been wounded at Culloden, found himself on the evening of that disastrous day on the banks of the River Farigaig, opposite Urquhart Castle. He had been helped so far by two faithful retainers, one of whom, a fox-hunter, was a native of the vale of Urquhart. This man, perceiving the gentleman was unable to proceed further, and seeing a boat moored to the shore, proposed that they should cross to the old Castle, in a vault of which, known only to a few of the country people, they might remain secure from all pursuit. The hint was readily complied with, and in less than a couple of hours they found themselves entombed in the ruins of Urquhart Castle, where sleep shortly over-powered them, and the sun was high in the heavens next day ere any of them awoke. The gentleman's wound having been partially dressed, the fox-hunter's comrade yawningly observed "that a bit of something to eat would be a Godsend." "By my troth it would," said the fox-hunter, "and if my little Mary knew aught of poor Eoghainn Brocair's (Ewan the fox-hunter) plight, she would endeavour to relieve him though Sassenach bullets were flying about her ears." "By heaven! our lurking-place is discovered!" whispered the gentleman, "do you not observe a shadow hovering about the entrance." "'Tis the shadow of a friend," replied the Brocair; and in an instant a long-bodied, short-legged Highland terrier sprung into the vault. "Craicean, a dhuine bhochd," said the overjoyed fox-hunter, hugging the faithful animal to his bosom, "this is the kindest visit you ever paid me." As soon as the shades of evening had darkened their retreat, Eoghainn untied his garter, and binding it round the dog's neck, caressed him, and pointing up the Glen, bade him go and bring the Brocair some food. The poor terrier looked wistfully in his face, and with a shake of his tail, quietly took his departure. In about four hours 'Craicean' reappeared, and endeavoured by every imaginable sign to make Eoghainn follow him outside. With this the Brocair complied, but in a few seconds he re-entered, accompanied by another person. Eoghainn having covered the only entrance to the cave with their plaids, struck a light and introduced to his astonished friends his betrothed, young Mary Maclauchlan. The poor girl had understood by the garter which bound the terrier's neck, and which she herself had woven, that her Eoghainn was in the neighbourhood, and hastened to his relief with all the ready provisions she could procure; and not least, in the estimation of at least two of the fugitives, the feeling maiden had brought them a sip of unblemished whisky. In this manner they had been supplied with aliment for some time, when one night their fair visitor failed to come as usual. This, though it created no immediate alarm, somewhat astonished them; but when the second night came and neither Mary nor her shaggy companion appeared, Eoghainn's uneasiness on Mary's account overcame every other feeling, and, in spite of all remonstrance, he ventured forth to ascertain the cause of her delay. The night was dark and squally, and Eoghainn was proceeding up his native glen like one who felt that the very sound of his tread might betray him to death. With a beating heart he had walked upwards of two miles, when his ears were saluted with the distant report of a musket. Springing aside, he concealed himself in a thicket which overhung the river. Here he remained but a very short time when he was joined by the Craicean dragging after him a cord several yards in length. This circumstance brought the cold sweat from the brow of the Brocair. He knew that their enemies were in pursuit of them, that the cord had been affixed to the dog's neck in order that he might lead to their place of concealment; and alas! Eoghainn feared much that his betrothed was at the mercy of his pursuers. What was to be done? The moment was big with fate, but he was determined to meet it like a man. Cutting the cord and whispering to the terrier, "cul mo chois" (back of my heel) he again ventured to the road and moved warily onward. On arriving at an old wicker-wrought barn, he saw a light streaming from it, when creeping towards it, he observed a party of the enemy surrounding poor Mary Maclauchlan, who was, at the moment, undergoing a close examination by their officer. "Come girl," said he "though that blind rascal has let your dog, who would certainly have introduced us to the rebels, escape, you will surely consult your own safety by guiding me to the spot; nay, I know you will, here is my purse in token of my future friendship, and in order to conceal your share in the transaction you and I shall walk together to a place where you may point me out the lurking place of these fellows, and leave the rest to me; and do you," continued he, turning to his party, "remain all ready until you hear a whistle, when instantly make for the spot." The Brocair crouched, as many a time he did, but never before did his heart beat at such a rate. As the officer and his passive guide took the road to the old Castle, Eoghainn followed close in their wake, and, when they had proceeded about a mile from the barn, they came upon the old hill road when Mary made a dead halt, as if quite at a loss how to act. "Proceed, girl," thundered the officer, "I care not one farthing for my own life, and if you do not instantly conduct me to the spot where the bloody rebels are concealed, this weapon," drawing his sword, "shall within two minutes penetrate your cunning heart." The poor girl trembled and staggered as the officer pointed the sword at her bosom, when the voice of Eoghainn fell on his ear like the knell of death, "Turn your weapon this way, brave sir," said the Brocair, "Turn it this way," and in a moment the officer and his shivered sword lay at his feet. "Oh, for heaven's sake," screamed the fainting girl, "meddle not with his life." "No, no, Mary; I shall not dirty my hands in his blood. I have only given him the weight of my oak sapling, so that he may sleep soundly till we are safe from the fangs of his bloodhounds." That very night the fugitives left Urquhart Castle and got safe to the forests of Badenoch, where they skulked about with Lochiel and his few followers until the gentleman escaped to France, when Eoghainn Brocair and his companion ventured once more, as they themselves expressed it, 'to the communion of Christians.' The offspring of the Brocair and Mary Maclauchlan are still in Lochaber.

Young Glengarry, the Black Raven

ONCE UPON A TIME old Glengarry was very unpopular with all the northern chiefs, in consequence of his many raids and creachs among the surrounding tribes, but although he was now advanced in years and unable to lead his clan in person, none of the neighbouring chiefs could muster courage to beard him in his den single-handed. There was never much love lost between him and the chief of the Mackenzies, and about this time some special offence was given to the latter by the Macdonells, which the chief of Eilean Donan swore would have to be revenged; and the insult must be wiped out at whatever cost. His clan was at that time very much subdivided, and he felt himself quite unable to cope with Glengarry in arms. Mackenzie, however, far excelled his enemy in ready invention, and possessed a degree of subtlety which usually more than made up for his enemy's superior physical power.

'Kintail' managed to impress his neighbouring chiefs with the belief that Glengarry proposed, and was making arrangements, to take them all by surprise and annihilate them by one fell swoop, and that in these circumstances it was imperative, for their mutual safety, to make arrangements forthwith by which the danger would be obviated and the hateful author of such a diabolical scheme extinguished root and branch. By this means he managed to produce the most bitter prejudice against Glengarry and his clan; but all of them being convinced of the folly and futility of meeting the 'Black Raven,' as he was called, man to man and clan to clan, Mackenzie invited them to meet him at a great council in Eilean Donan Castle, the following week, to discuss the best means of protecting their mutual interests, and to enter into a solemn league, and swear on the 'raven's cross' to exterminate the hated Glengarry and his race, and to raze, burn, and plunder everything belonging to them.

Old Glengarry, whom the ravages of war had already reduced to one son out of several, and he only a youth of immature years, heard of the confederacy formed against him with great and serious concern. He well knew the impossibility of holding out against the combined influence and power of the Western Chiefs. His whole affections were concentrated on his only surviving son, and on realizing the common danger, he bedewed him with tears, and strongly urged upon him the dire necessity of fleeing from the land of his fathers to some foreign land until the danger had passed away. He, at the same time, called his clan together, absolved them from their allegiance, and implored them also to save themselves by flight; and to their honour be it said, one and all spurned the idea of leaving their chief in his old age alone to his fate, exclaiming – "that death itself was preferable to shame and dishonour." To the surprise of all, however, the son, dressed in his best garb, and armed to the teeth, after taking a formal and affectionate farewell of his father, took to the hills amidst the contemptuous sneers of his brave retainers. But he was no sooner out of sight than he directed his course to Lochduich, determined to attend the great council at Eilean Donan Castle, at which his father's fate was to be sealed. He arrived in the district on the appointed day, and carefully habilitating himself in a fine Mackenzie tartan plaid, with which he had provided himself, he made for the stronghold and passed the outer gate with the usual salutation – "Who is welcome here?" and passed by unheeded, the guard replying in the most unsuspicious manner – "Any, any but a Macdonell." On being admitted to the great hall he carefully scanned the brilliant assembly. The Mackenzie plaid had put the company completely off their guard; for in those days no one would ever dream of wearing the tartan of any but that of his own leader. The chiefs had already, as they entered the great hall, drawn their dirks and stuck them in the tables before them as an earnest of their unswerving resolution to rid the world of their hated enemy. The brave and intrepid stranger coolly walked up to the head of the table, where the Chief of Kintail presided over the great council, threw off his disguise, seized Mackenzie by the throat, drew out his glittering dagger, held it against his enemy's heart, and exclaimed with a voice and a determination which struck terror into every breast – "Mackenzie, if you or any of your assembled guests make the slightest movement, as I live, by the great Creator of the universe, I will instantly pierce you to the heart." Mackenzie well knew by the appearance of the youth, and the commanding tone of his voice, that the threat would be instantly executed if any movement was made, and he tremulously exclaimed – "My friends, for the love of God, stir not, lest I perish at the hands of my inveterate foe at my own table." The appeal was hardly necessary, for all were terror-stricken and confused, sitting with open mouths, gazing vacantly, at each other. "Now," said the young hero, "lift up your hands to heaven and swear by the Long, am Bradan, agus an Lamh Dhearg (the ship, the salmon, and the bloody hand), that you will never again molest my father or any of his clan." "I do now swear as you request" answered the confused chief. "Swear now," continued the dauntless youth, "you, and all ye round this table, that I will depart from here and be permitted to go home unmolested by you or any of your retainers." All, with uplifted hands, repeated the oath. Young Glengarry released his hold on Mackenzie's throat sheathed his dirk and prepared to take his departure, but was, curious to relate, prevailed upon to remain at the feast and spend the night with the sworn enemies of his race and kindred, and the following morning they parted the best of friends. And thus, by the daring of a stripling, was Glengarry saved the fearful doom that awaited him. The youth ultimately became famous as one of the most courageous warriors of his race. He fought many a single combat with powerful combatants, and invariably came off victorious. He invaded and laid waste Glenmoriston, Urquhart, and Caithness. His life had been one scene of varied havoc, victory, ruin, and bloodshed. He entered into a fierce encounter with one of the Munros of Fowlis, but ultimately met the same fate at the hands of the 'grim tyrant' as the greatest coward in the land, and his body lies buried in the churchyard of Tuiteam-tarbhach.

A Legend of Invershin

LONG AGES AGO THERE STOOD in the vicinity of Invershin a strong massive castle, built and inhabited by a foreign knight – a stern, haughty man – of whose antecedents nothing could be learned with certainty, although there were plenty of rumours concerning him; the most generally received one being that he had fled from his own country on account of treason, or some other crime. Be that as it may, he had plenty of wealth, built a splendid castle, and kept a great number of retainers. He was extremely fond of fishing, and spent the greater part of his time in the pursuit of the gentle craft. He invented a peculiar kind of cruive, so ingeniously constructed that the salmon on entering it set in motion some springs to which bells were attached: thus they literally tolled their own funeral knell. He was accompanied in his exile by his daughter Bona, and his niece Oykel, both alike beautiful in face and figure, but very dissimilar in disposition. Bona was a fair, gentle being, who seemed formed to love and be loved. Oykel was a dark beauty, handsome, proud, and vindictive.

Among their numerous household there was one who, without being a relative, seemed on terms of intimacy and equality. He was called Prince Shin of Norway, and was supposed to have retired to this northern part of the kingdom for the same reason as his host. He was young, handsome, and brave, and, as a matter of course, the two young ladies fell violently in love with him. For a while he wavered between the two, but at last he fixed his affections upon the gentle Bona, and sought her hand in marriage. The old knight gave his consent, and the future looked bright and full of happiness for the young lovers.

The proud Oykel was deeply mortified at the prince for choosing her cousin in preference to herself, and the daily sight of their mutual attachment drove her into a perfect frenzy of jealousy and wounded pride, until at length nothing would satisfy her but the death of her rival. She accordingly bribed one of her uncle's unscrupulous retainers to murder her cousin Bona, vainly hoping that in time the prince would transfer his love to herself. The ruffian carried out his cruel order, and concealed the body in a disused dungeon of the castle.

Great was the consternation and dismay caused by the sudden and mysterious disappearance of the lovely Bona; hill and dale, mountain and strath, corrie and burn, were searched in vain; river and loch were dragged to no purpose. Prince Shin was inconsolable; he exerted himself to the utmost in the fruitless search, then, wearied in mind and body, he wandered listless and sad through the flowery fields of Inveran until he reached the birchen groves of Achany, the quiet solitude of which suited better his desolate state. Here, with no prying eyes to see his misery, nor babbling tongues to repeat his sighs and exclamations, he gave himself up for a while to the luxury of grief. Then arose in the breast of the father the agonizing suspicion of foul play; but upon whom could his suspicions fall? Who could have the slightest reason or incentive to injure the kind and gentle Bona?

He pondered and mused in gloomy solitude until the terrible idea grew in his mind that it must have been her lover and affianced husband who had thus so cruelly betrayed

373

her trustful love. "Yes," he muttered, "it must be Prince Shin who has committed this diabolical crime; he has tired of her, and took this way to release himself from his solemn contract with her and me, but the villain shall not escape; his punishment shall be as sudden and as great as his crime."

Having thus settled his conviction of the Prince's guilt, he caused him to be seized during the night, and thrown into the same dungeon in which, unknown to him, lay the body of his beloved daughter.

The accusation and his seizure was so sudden and unexpected, that for a time Shin lay in his dungeon totally overwhelmed with grief and indignation – grief at the loss of his bride, and indignation at the suspicion and treatment of himself. He was at length aroused and startled by hearing a faint moan somewhere near him, as if from some one in great pain. He strained his eyes to pierce the gloomy darkness that surrounded him; at last, guided by the sound being repeated, he discovered at the other end of the dungeon a recumbent figure, so still and motionless, that it might have been lifeless, but for the occasional faint, unconscious moan. "Alas!" exclaimed he, "this is another victim of treachery and cruelty, who is even worse off than I, but who can it be? I have missed no one from the castle, except my adored and lamented Bona." While thus speaking, he knelt down to examine the figure more closely, and as he began to get used to the gloom, he could see a little better, when to his inexpressible horror, dismay, and astonishment, he discovered it to be no other than his lost bride, whose young life was fast ebbing away through a frightful stab in her snow-white bosom.

Nearly frantic with grief, he strove with trembling hand to staunch the blood and bind up the wound, at the same time calling her by every endearing name that love could suggest. Again and again he kissed her cold lips, and pressed her tenderly to his heart, trying in vain to infuse life and warmth to the inanimate form of her he loved so well. He was interrupted in his melancholy task by the heavy door of the dungeon creaking on its rusty hinges, as it slowly opened to admit a man-at-arms, whom Shin recognised as one of the foreign retainers of the old knight.

"Ah! Randolph, is it thou they have sent to murder me? Well, do thy work quickly, death has lost its terrors for me, now that it has seized on my Bona; but yet I would that another hand than thine should strike the fatal blow, for I remember, tho' perhaps thou forgettest, the day when stricken down in the battle-field thou wert a dead man, had not I interposed my shield, and saved thy life at the risk of my own." So saying, he looked the man calmly but sadly in the face.

Randolph had, on first entering, seemed thunder-struck at seeing the prince, and looked, during the delivery of his speech, more like a victim than an executioner; he changed colour, trembled, and finally, throwing himself at the feet of the prince, faltered out with broken voice, "Oh! my lord; indeed, indeed, you do me wrong. I knew not that you were here; never would I raise an arm to injure you, my benefactor, my preserver? No, I came to – to—" Then glancing from the prince to the lady Bona, he hid his face in his hands and groaned out, "I knew not you loved her, or I would rather have died than—"

A sudden light broke in on the mind of Shin, he sprang like a tiger at the trembling man, and seizing him by the throat, thundered out, "Accursed villain, is it thou who hast done this foul deed? thy life shall be the forfeit." Then changing his mind, he loosened his deadly grasp, and flinging the man from him as though he were a dog, muttered between his close-set-teeth, "I will not soil my hands with the blood of such a dastard, he is only the base tool of another." Then raising his voice, he continued, "Tell me, thou double-dyed traitor, who set thee on to do this most horrible deed? and for what reason? See that thou tellest me the truth, villain, or by the bones of my father, I will dash thy brains out on the stones beneath our feet."

The trembling Randolph then explained how he, being absent from the castle on a foraging expedition, knew nothing of the betrothal of Prince Shin and the lady Bona, that on his return he was sent for by Oykel, who, in a private interview, told him she was engaged to the prince, and that Bona, through jealousy, was trying all she could to set the old knight against Shin, and had even laid a plot to poison both her and the prince, and that he (Randolph), believing this specious story, and being greatly attached to the prince, was easily prevailed upon by Oykel to murder her cousin; that he had temporarily hidden her body in the dungeon, and was now come to remove it, and was astonished and horrified to find she was still alive. He then went on to say, that he thought he saw a way to undo some of the mischief he had been the means of doing, and that was to assist Shin to escape, and to carry the lady Bona to a place of safety, until it was seen whether she would recover, and what turn affairs might take at the castle. The prince gladly availed himself of his assistance. They made their escape, and remained in concealment for some time until Bona had somewhat recovered her strength.

In the meantime Oykel, driven to distraction at the disappearance of Shin, seeing the utter fruitlessness of her crime, stung by remorse, and rendered reckless by the pangs of unrequited love, threw herself into the river, which has ever since been called by her name, and which, it is said, is still haunted by her restless, weary spirit. Bona is commemorated in Bonar.

Prince Shin and Bona now came from their concealment, and being fully reconciled to the old knight, were married with great pomp, and shortly afterwards sailed away to Norway, where they lived long and died happy.

Allan Donn and Annie Campbell

DONALD CAMPBELL OF SCALPAY, HARRIS – whose name is on record in connection with Prince Charles, when a refugee in the Western Isles after his defeat at Culloden – had a very beautiful daughter, who was so modest, pleasant, and affectionate, that she had few equals in the Isles. The charming Annie was for some considerable time, previous to the year 1768, loved by Allan Morrison, son of Roderick Morrison, of Stornoway, a ship captain. Being a gallant, and withal a comely young man, his affection was reciprocated by the fair Annie.

Captain Allan – he was seldom called Morrison – traded with his vessel principally between Stornoway and the Isle of Man, but he frequently went to Spain. Like many other lovers, Captain Allan, when he returned from abroad, presented the object of his affections with small presents of silk and linen – rare articles in the Highlands in those days. The more Allan saw of his Annie, the more he loved her, and he ardently longed for the day when they should be united in wedlock. This day was at length fixed; but before the happy event could take place, a voyage to the Isle of Man and back had to be accomplished. It was arranged, however, that the preliminary ceremony – the 'contract' – should be gone through prior to setting out on the voyage, on the evening before setting sail. For this purpose, one afternoon in the spring of 1768, Captain Allan left Stornoway for Scalpay with his vessel. Besides having a select number of relatives on board, who were to be present at the ceremony, he was accompanied by another ship, commanded by his brother, Captain Roderick. It was a fine day, with a nice breeze of fair wind, when they set sail. They did not proceed far, however, when the wind, which veered round to the south, rose suddenly to a perfect hurricane. To make matters worse, a blinding sleet shortly afterwards set in. Nobly, but in vain, did both the ships strive to bear up against the furious onsets of the rolling Minch; but notwithstanding their brave efforts to reach Scalpay before nightfall, they had barely got as far as the Shiant Isles when it was pitch dark, and thus their already dangerous situation became more perilous still. That each vessel might know the position of the other, a red light, in addition to the usual white one, was exhibited on the masts of both, and the brothers, being determined to arrive at their destination that night, if possible, continued to battle against the mighty billows, which now dashed themselves with fearful force against the creaking planks of the vessels, and anon broke over them with a deafening noise. This did not continue long when it became apparent that they could not possibly hold out much longer together. This was at least part of Captain Roderick's surmises, when he suddenly heard loud cries proceeding from his brother's ship. Being slightly in advance of Captain Allan at the time, and supposing that the shouts were intended as a sign for him to keep up his courage, he paid very little attention to the matter, for under the circumstances there was no possibility of rendering the least aid, should such be required. Above the sound of the raging tempest, the shouts from Allan's ship continued to be distinctly heard for a few seconds, when lo! all of a sudden, the screaming ceased, and the lights on the mast suddenly disappeared. It was then, and only then, that Captain Roderick understood the real meaning of the shouts which came from his brother's crew, whose ship had been sinking, and had now evidently gone to the bottom. Although there was but little hope of his being able much longer to keep his own ship afloat, Captain Roderick, like a brave sailor and an affectionate brother, directly made for the spot where the lights of his brother's ship were last observed, but nothing, alas! was seen or heard of the ship or crew. The deep wail which now rose from Captain Roderick's crew was truly heart-rending. From that day till now nothing has been seen of Captain Allan's crew or his ship.

Soon after the foundering of the gallant ship the gale moderated so much that Captain Roderick was able to reach the north harbour of Scalpay early next morning. Being expected there the previous night, none of the Campbells – who were, as might be supposed, greatly concerned for Captain Allan's safety, knowing, as they did, that his non-arrival arose from the furious tempest – went to bed that night. They were, therefore, by early dawn on the top of the hill which flanked their house, which is still standing, and from which they secured a view of the Minch in all directions. From this position they early descried Captain Roderick's ship making for the island. As the brave vessel passed up through the narrow Sound of Scalpay, the Campbells, and chief among them the fair Annie, some relatives and friends, stood on the north-east point of the island, and, thinking it was Captain Allan's ship, welcomed her with waving handkerchiefs. But their gay signs of joy were but of short duration, for presently a small flag was observed half-mast-high, and the next moment a sharp scream burst from the lovely Annie, exclaiming that Allan Donn was gone! Captain Roderick's ship soon cast anchor; in a few minutes he landed, and conveyed the sad tidings of his brother's and relatives' untimely end, as above described.

We will not attempt to describe the effect which this melancholy intelligence had upon the fair Annie, whose grief at that moment knew no bounds – her heart broke for him whom she would never see again. Refusing to be comforted, she might be seen at early dawn, mid-day, and twilight, wandering sorrowfully on the shore, looking for her "dear Allan's body," and crying "Allain Duinn Shiubhlainn leat." She continued thus while she lived, which was only a few days, her heart having, it is said, literally burst. It is even asserted that her pure white breast wasted to that extent that an aperture was formed opposite her heart. She composed a song or lament for her devoted lover each day afterwards while she lived.

The song composed by Annie Campbell on the day she received the tidings of her beloved's death, is entitled, 'Allain Duinn, Shiubhlainn leat.' It has a peculiarly touching air, and is still sung by many people on the Island of Harris, and it is now published in Part II of Mr Sinclair's 'Oranaiche.'

It was an oft expressed wish of the broken-hearted maiden that her body should be buried in the sea, that she might share her 'dear Allan's grave.' But whether her friends promised compliance with her request is not said. It is worthy of note, however, that his name was the last word she uttered. Surrounded by a crowded chamber of weeping friends, her gentle spirit took its flight to that brighter region which lies beyond the grave; and, though grief had wasted her body to a mere shadow, the same pleasant features which graced her in life continued to adorn her even when embraced in the cold arms of death. Her demise excited universal regret in the whole Outer Hebrides.

The respect and admiration in which Annie Campbell was held by her acquaintances in life were fully demonstrated at her death, for during the week in which her body lay in state at Scalpay, scores of people who could not, on account of the throng, obtain admission to the house of mourning, although kept open day and night, might be seen, with sad countenances and sorrowful hearts, standing around it from morn to eve, and eve to morn, and the respectful silence which prevailed among them was such that 'the fall of a pin might be heard.' Some people may be disposed to say that to devote a whole week to the ceremony called the 'leekwake,' was a needless waste of time. But, considering the great preparations which had to be made for the deceased lady's funeral, it must be confessed that it was short enough. Fifteen gallons of whisky, two or three large creelfuls of beef, mutton, and fowl, and a corresponding supply of newly-baked oaten cake, and cheese, were generally required at the interment of a common person in the Highlands in the olden times; and although they had neither pastry nor confections from Edinburgh, nor brandy from Cognac, at Annie's funeral, the expenditure was, nevertheless, most profuse. There was gin from Schiedam, wine from Oporto, and whisky from Berneray, in unlimited quantities; and as to the supply of oat and barley meal cakes, cheese, beef, mutton, and fowl, it was simply enormous.

Rodel, the place of interment, was only twelve miles from the island of Scalpay, but, on account of the large number of people which was to take part in the proceedings at Cille Chliaran (Rodel churchyard), which is supposed to have been built in the tenth century, and was dedicated to St Clement, three large galleys, or boats, were required for the funeral procession. One of the boats, which was manned by a select crew, was intended for the coffin and chief mourners; another was for the deceased's kinsfolk and friends, and the third for carrying the provisions. The day fixed for the funeral arrived – it was a Saturday in the year 1768 – a day which will be remembered in Harris while a Highlander breathes on its soil. On the morning of that day, the three boats left Scalpay for Rodel. In the foremost boat, Am Bata Caol Cannach, was the coffin, and the chief mourners were Kenneth Campbell, deceased's brother; Campbell of Marrig, Campbell of Strond, Macleod of Hushinish, Macleod of Luskintyre, and two or three other leading Harris-men. It also contained several casks of rum, gin, &c. The morning was so calm and pleasant, that the surface of the Minch seemed like a huge sheet of glass, so that the sails, which seamen depend so much upon, were useless; but, stripped to the shirts, the stalwart oarsmen pulled their respective galleys through the briny water with great speed. The little procession had hardly passed Rudha Reibinish when a smart head-wind began to blow. The horizon was soon afterwards darkened by a sheet of black clouds that betokened the approaching storm, which almost immediately set in. It soon blew a perfect hurricane, against which oars could make little headway. At the outset of the rising wind, the Bata Caol Cannach set sail, was thus carried far out to sea, and was in mid-channel when the tempest was at its height. The sails were torn to shreds, and the snow, which began to fall thick and fast, hid the land from view. They were now in a most critical position, for it was impossible for any boat to live long in such an awful sea, and the boat was half full of water. They gave up all hope of surviving many moments longer, and each began to pray earnestly for his soul's salvation, when to their still greater horror, the form of a female – Annie's phantom – was observed quite near them, following in the wake of their boat. This extraordinary circumstance was at once laid down as one of the direst omens. Nor need we wonder much if it did, when we consider the peculiar circumstances under which the figure appeared, and the superstitious beliefs which then, and to a certain extent still, prevail in the Highlands. Each time the phantom, which seemed to scowl angrily upon them, appeared, the Bata Caol Cannach shipped fearful seas. Life being sweet, the poor fellows used every means in their power to keep their vessel afloat. They used the wine and gin ankers, out of which they knocked the ends, spilling the liquor among the salt water, for bailing the boat. The phantom still followed, and was coming closer and closer to the boat's stern, when they recalled to mind Annie's oft expressed desire to be buried in the sea, that she might share Allan's grave; and they at once concluded that her spirit followed them, first in the storm, and now in visible shape, to enforce compliance with her last request. Some of them, therefore, advised that the coffin should be immediately committed to the deep; but to this proposal Kenneth Campbell, the deceased's brother, would not consent. He was sitting in the stern of the boat, and his late sister's spirit drew so near to him that she could put her hand on his shoulder. He chanced to have a bunch of keys in his pocket, to which some fabulous charm was attached, and he threw them to the phantom to appease her, but without effect. By this time some of the crew lay helplessly in the bottom of the boat, when one of the most courageous proposed that, to lighten the craft, the 'knocked up' men should be thrown overboard. "Not one," replied an elderly man, "of the living shall be put out, till the dead is put out first." He had hardly finished speaking, when a huge sea rolled over the boat, which almost swamped her, and the coffin, which was then floating in the boat, striking Kenneth Campbell on the chest, had almost pitched him overboard. He, thereupon, immediately ordered it to be thrown out, an order which, we need hardly say, was directly obeyed; but another tremendous sea again threw it into the water-logged boat. They managed, however, with great difficulty to unship it again, and knocking one of the ends out of it with their oars, all that remained of the fair Annie sank in a twinkling to the bottom of the sea, and the angry spirit immediately disappeared.

Meanwhile, the other two boats, which had never raised their sails at all, went ashore at Manish. Having landed, the men proceeded at once by land to Rodel, where they communicated the manner of their parting with the Bata Caol Cannach, as above described. All agreed that she had foundered, "for it was impossible," they said, "for any open, or other boat, to live in the Minch that day." This was a terrible circumstance – a calamity which plunged the whole country into an overwhelming grief. The deaths of Annie Campbell and Allan Donn were wholly absorbed by this extraordinary affair – an affair which seemed, to all appearance, to be nothing less than a judgment from God; for the flower of all the Harris gentlemen shared in one hour the same watery grave. The sorrow caused by this sad occurrence was so universal that a dry eye could not be found that evening from one end of Harris to the other; and this general grief continued for days and nights together, for all sympathised with the bereaved.

But to return to the Bata Caol Cannach, which we left water-logged, and about to sink in the middle of the Minch. It was a remarkable coincidence, that as soon as the cold clay of the fair maiden sank in the sea, the furious storm immediately abated, and the raging billows ceased their wild commotion. The Bata Caol Cannach was then bailed as quickly as possible, and one of the men – Malcolm Macleod – happening to have his plaid along with him, it was hoisted before the wind instead of a sail. The boat's stern was turned to the wind which drove it forward at a considerable rate, but, being pitch dark, none of them knew whither they were going. A new danger now began to alarm them – the danger of the boat being dashed to pieces on some shore. This fresh evil had only presented itself when the Bata Caol Cannach's keel struck the ground. The gratitude to an all-ruling Providence that filled their hearts at that moment none but those similarly situated can tell. They immediately leaped ashore, leaving the boat in the spot where it struck; and after wandering about for some time, stumbled upon a house, where they were kindly received and cared for. On entering this house, they discovered that one of their number was amissing, and, hungry and exhausted though they were, they immediately went to search for him, and found him lying insensible in the bows of the boat. He was at once carried to the house which they had just left, and with much care and attention he soon recovered. The place where the Bata Caol Cannach went ashore, and where the men were so hospitably entertained, was Snizort, in the Isle of Skye. It was some time before the Harris-men had thoroughly recovered from the hardships they underwent; but, as soon as they were able to undertake the journey, they returned home.

Kenneth Campbell, Annie's brother, was afterwards also drowned. He commanded a vessel, and being met by a French pirate, his ship, after being robbed, was sent to the bottom, every soul on board perishing. There are many other anecdotes connected with the men who composed the crew of the Bata Caol Cannach on the occasion referred to, but I must conclude, merely mentioning that the body of the unfortunate Allan Donn was found at the Shiant Isles shortly after the death of his sorrowing lover Annie, and was interred with befitting solemnities in the family sepulchre in Lewis. As an extraordinary coincidence, the body of the fair Annie Campbell was soon after Di-Sathairn an Fhuadaich also found at the Shiant Isle, and in the very spot where the body of her lover had been recovered. Whether it was placed in the same grave as Allan tradition does not record.

Malcolm Macleod, grandson of Malcolm Macleod, whose plaid was used as a sail in the Bata Caol Cannach, an elder in the Free Church at Tarbert, Harris, who only died about two years ago, repeatedly told me the above story. The Bata Caol Cannach was so called on account of having been purchased by the Campbells from a man in the island of Canna.

Coinnach Oer

COINNACH OER, WHICH MEANS dun Kenneth, was a celebrated man in his generation. He has been called the Isaiah of the North. The prophecies of this man are very frequently alluded to and quoted in various parts of the Highlands; although little is known of the man himself, except in Ross-shire. He was a small farmer in Strathpeffer, near Dingwall, and for many years of his life neither exhibited any talents, nor claimed any intelligence above his fellows. The manner in which he obtained the prophetic gift was told by himself in the following manner:

As he was one day at work in the hill casting (digging) peats, he heard a voice which seemed to call to him out of the air. It commanded him to dig under a little green knoll which was near, and to gather up the small white stones which he would discover beneath the turf. The voice informed him, at the same time, that while he kept these stones in his possession, he should be endued with the power of supernatural foreknowledge.

Kenneth, though greatly alarmed at this aerial conversation, followed the directions of his invisible instructor, and turning up the turf on the hillock, in a little time discovered the talismans. From that day forward, the mind of Kenneth was illuminated by gleams of unearthly light; and he made many predictions, of which the credulity of the people, and the coincidence of accident, often supplied confirmation; and he certainly became the most notable of the Highland prophets. The most remarkable and well known of his vaticinations is the following: "Whenever a M'Lean with long hands, a Fraser with a black spot on his face, a M'Gregor with a black knee, and a club-footed M'Leod of Raga, shall have existed; whenever there shall have been successively three M'Donalds of the name of John, and three M'Kinnons of the same Christian name, oppressors will appear in the country, and the people will change their own land for a strange one." All these personages have appeared since; and it is the common opinion of the peasantry, that the consummation of the prophecy was fulfilled, when the exaction of the exorbitant rents reduced the Highlanders to poverty, and the introduction of the sheep banished the people to America.

Whatever might have been the gift of Kenneth Oer, he does not appear to have used it with an extraordinary degree of discretion; and the last time he exercised it, he was very near paying dear for his divination.

On this occasion he happened to be at some high festival of the M'Kenzies at Castle Braan. One of the guests was so exhilarated by the scene of gaiety, that he could not forbear an eulogium on the gallantry of the feast, and the nobleness of the guests. Kenneth, it appears, had no regard for the M'Kenzies, and was so provoked by this sally in their praise, that he not only broke out into a severe satire against their whole race, but gave vent to the prophetic denunciation of wrath and confusion upon their posterity. The guests being informed (or having overheard a part) of this rhapsody, instantly rose up with one accord to punish the contumely of the prophet. Kenneth, though he foretold the fate of others, did not in any manner look into that of himself; for this reason, being doubtful of debating the propriety of his prediction upon such unequal terms, he fled with the greatest precipitation. The M'Kenzies followed with infinite zeal; and more than one ball had whistled over the head of the seer before he reached Loch Ousie. The consequences of this prediction so disgusted Kenneth with any further exercise of his prophetic calling, that, in the anguish of his flight, he solemnly renounced all communication with its power; and, as he ran along the margin of Loch Ousie, he took out the wonderful pebbles, and cast them in a fury into the water. Whether his evil genius had now forsaken him, or his condition was better than that of his pursuers, is unknown, but certain it is, Kenneth, after the sacrifice of the pebbles, outstripped his enraged enemies, and never, so far as I have heard, made any attempt at prophecy from the hour of his escape.

Kenneth Oer had a son, who was called Ian Dubh Mac Coinnach (Black John, the son of Kenneth), and lived in the village of Miltoun, near Dingwall. His chief occupation was brewing whisky; and he was killed in a fray at Miltoun, early in the present century. His exit would not have formed the catastrophe of an epic poem, and appears to have been one of those events of which his father had no intelligence, for it happened in the following manner:

Having fallen into a dispute with a man with whom he had previously been on friendly terms, they proceeded to blows; in the scuffle, the boy, the son of Ian's adversary, observing the two combatants locked in a close and firm gripe of eager contention, and being doubtful of the event, ran into the house and brought out the iron pot-crook, with which he saluted the head of the unfortunate Ian so severely, that he not only relinquished his combat, but departed this life on the ensuing morning.

The Dwarfie Stone

FAR UP IN A GREEN VALLEY in the Island of Hoy stands an immense boulder. It is hollow inside, and the natives of these northern islands call it the Dwarfie Stone, because long centuries ago, so the legend has it, Snorro the Dwarf lived there.

Nobody knew where Snorro came from, or how long he had dwelt in the dark chamber inside the Dwarfie Stone. All that they knew about him was that he was a little man, with a queer, twisted, deformed body and a face of marvellous beauty, which never seemed to look any older, but was always smiling and young.

Men said that this was because Snorro's father had been a Fairy, and not a denizen of earth, who had bequeathed to his son the gift of perpetual youth, but nobody knew whether this were true or not, for the Dwarf had inhabited the Dwarfie Stone long before the oldest man or woman in Hoy had been born.

One thing was certain, however: he had inherited from his mother, whom all men agreed had been mortal, the dangerous qualities of vanity and ambition. And the longer he lived the more vain and ambitious did he become, until at last he always carried a mirror of polished steel round his neck, into which he constantly looked in order to see the reflection of his handsome face.

And he would not attend to the country people who came to seek his help, unless they bowed themselves humbly before him and spoke to him as if he were a King.

I say that the country people sought his help, for he spent his time, or appeared to spend it, in collecting herbs and simples on the hillsides, which he carried home with him to his dark abode, and distilled medicines and potions from them, which he sold to his neighbours at wondrous high prices.

He was also the possessor of a wonderful leathern-covered book, clasped with clasps of brass, over which he would pore for hours together, and out of which he would tell the simple Islanders their fortunes, if they would.

For they feared the book almost as much as they feared Snorro himself, for it was whispered that it had once belonged to Odin, and they crossed themselves for protection as they named the mighty Enchanter.

But all the time they never guessed the real reason why Snorro chose to live in the Dwarfie Stone.

I will tell you why he did so. Not very far from the Stone there was a curious hill, shaped exactly like a wart. It was known as the Wart Hill of Hoy, and men said that somewhere in the side of it was hidden a wonderful carbuncle, which, when it was found, would bestow on its finder marvellous magic gifts – Health, Wealth, and Happiness. Everything, in fact, that a human being could desire.

And the curious thing about this carbuncle was, that it was said that it could be seen at certain times, if only the people who were looking for it were at the right spot at the right moment.

Now Snorro had made up his mind that he would find this wonderful stone, so, while he pretended to spend all his time in reading his great book or distilling medicines from his herbs, he was really keeping a keen look-out during his wanderings, noting every tuft of grass or piece of rock under which it might be hidden. And at night, when everyone else was asleep, he would creep out, with pickaxe and spade, to turn over the rocks or dig over the turf, in the hope of finding the long-sought-for treasure underneath them.

He was always accompanied on these occasions by an enormous grey-headed Raven, who lived in the cave along with him, and who was his bosom friend and companion. The Islanders feared this bird of ill omen as much, perhaps, as they feared its Master; for, although they went to consult Snorro in all their difficulties and perplexities, and bought medicines and love-potions from him, they always looked upon him with a certain dread, feeling that there was something weird and uncanny about him.

Now, at the time we are speaking of, Orkney was governed by two Earls, who were half-brothers. Paul, the elder, was a tall, handsome man, with dark hair, and eyes like sloes. All the country people loved him, for he was so skilled in knightly exercises, and had such a sweet and loving nature, that no one could help being fond of him. Old people's eyes would brighten at the sight of him, and the little children would run out to greet him as he rode by their mothers' doors.

And this was the more remarkable because, with all his winning manner, he had such a lack of conversation that men called him Paul the Silent, or Paul the Taciturn.

Harold, on the other hand, was as different from his brother as night is from day. He was fair-haired and blue-eyed, and he had gained for himself the name of Harold the Orator, because he was always free of speech and ready with his tongue.

But for all this he was not a favourite. For he was haughty, and jealous, and quick-tempered, and the old folks' eyes did not brighten at the sight of him, and the babes, instead of toddling out to greet him, hid their faces in their mothers' skirts when they saw him coming.

Harold could not help knowing that the people liked his silent brother best, and the knowledge made him jealous of him, so a coldness sprang up between them.

Now it chanced, one summer, that Earl Harold went on a visit to the King of Scotland, accompanied by his mother, the Countess Helga, and her sister, the Countess Fraukirk.

And while he was at Court he met a charming young Irish lady, the Lady Morna, who had come from Ireland to Scotland to attend upon the Scottish Queen. She was so sweet, and good, and gentle that Earl Harold's heart was won, and he made up his mind that she, and only she, should be his bride.

But although he had paid her much attention, Lady Morna had sometimes caught glimpses of his jealous temper; she had seen an evil expression in his eyes, and had heard him speak sharply to his servants, and she had no wish to marry him. So, to his great amazement, she refused the honour which he offered her, and told him that she would prefer to remain as she was.

Earl Harold ground his teeth in silent rage, but he saw that it was no use pressing his suit at that moment. So what he could not obtain by his own merits he determined to obtain by guile.

Accordingly he begged his mother to persuade the Lady Morna to go back with them on a visit, hoping that when she was alone with him in Orkney, he would be able to overcome her prejudice against him, and induce her to become his wife. And all the while he never remembered his brother Paul; or, if he did, he never thought it possible that he could be his rival.

But that was just the very thing that happened. The Lady Morna, thinking no evil, accepted the Countess Helga's invitation, and no sooner had the party arrived back in Orkney than Paul, charmed with the grace and beauty of the fair Irish Maiden, fell head over ears in love with her. And the Lady Morna, from the very first hour that she saw him, returned his love.

Of course this state of things could not long go on hidden, and when Harold realised what had happened his anger and jealousy knew no bounds. Seizing a dagger, he rushed up to the turret where his brother was sitting in his private apartments, and threatened to stab him to the heart if he did not promise to give up all thoughts of winning the lovely stranger.

But Paul met him with pleasant words.

"Calm thyself, Brother," he said. "It is true that I love the lady, but that is no proof that I shall win her. Is it likely that she will choose me, whom all men name Paul the Silent, when she hath the chance of marrying you, whose tongue moves so swiftly that to you is given the proud title of Harold the Orator?"

At these words Harold's vanity was flattered, and he thought that, after all, his step-brother was right, and that he had a very small chance, with his meagre gift of speech, of being successful in his suit. So he threw down his dagger, and, shaking hands with him, begged him to pardon his unkind thoughts, and went down the winding stair again in high good-humour with himself and all the world.

By this time it was coming near to the Feast of Yule, and at that Festival it was the custom for the Earl and his Court to leave Kirkwall for some weeks, and go to the great Palace of Orphir, nine miles distant. And in order to see that everything was ready, Earl Paul took his departure some days before the others.

The evening before he left he chanced to find the Lady Morna sitting alone in one of the deep windows of the great hall. She had been weeping, for she was full of sadness at the thought of his departure; and at the sight of her distress the kind-hearted young Earl could no longer contain himself, but, folding her in his arms, he whispered to her how much he loved her, and begged her to promise to be his wife.

She agreed willingly. Hiding her rosy face on his shoulder, she confessed that she had loved him from the very first day that she had seen him; and ever since that moment she had determined that, if she could not wed him, she would wed no other man.

For a little time they sat together, rejoicing in their new-found happiness. Then Earl Paul sprang to his feet.

"Let us go and tell the good news to my mother and my brother," he said. "Harold may be disappointed at first, for I know, Sweetheart, he would fain have had thee for his own. But his good heart will soon overcome all that, and he will rejoice with us also."

But the Lady Morna shook her head. She knew, better than her lover, what Earl Harold's feeling would be; and she would fain put off the evil hour.

"Let us hold our peace till after Yule," she pleaded. "It will be a joy to keep our secret to ourselves for a little space; there will be time enough then to let all the world know."

Rather reluctantly, Earl Paul agreed; and next day he set off for the Palace at Orphir, leaving his lady-love behind him.

Little he guessed the danger he was in! For, all unknown to him, his step-aunt, Countess Fraukirk, had chanced to be in the hall, the evening before, hidden behind a curtain, and she had overheard every word that Morna and he had spoken, and her heart was filled with black rage.

For she was a hard, ambitious woman, and she had always hated the young Earl, who was no blood-relation to her, and who stood in the way of his brother, her own nephew; for, if Paul were only dead, Harold would be the sole Earl of Orkney.

And now that he had stolen the heart of the Lady Morna, whom her own nephew loved, her hate and anger knew no bounds. She had hastened off to her sister's chamber as soon as the lovers had parted; and there the two women had remained talking together till the chilly dawn broke in the sky.

Next day a boat went speeding over the narrow channel of water that separates Pomona (on the mainland) from Hoy. In it sat a woman, but who she was, or what she was like, no one could say, for she was covered from head to foot with a black cloak, and her face was hidden behind a thick, dark veil.

Snorro the Dwarf knew her, even before she laid aside her trappings, for Countess Fraukirk was no stranger to him. In the course of her long life she had often had occasion to seek his aid to help her in her evil deeds, and she had always paid him well for his services in yellow gold. He therefore welcomed her gladly; but when he had heard the nature of her errand his smiling face grew grave again, and he shook his head.

"I have served thee well, Lady, in the past," he said, "but methinks that this thing goeth beyond my courage. For to compass an Earl's death is a weighty matter, especially when he is so well beloved as is the Earl Paul.

"Thou knowest why I have taken up my abode in this lonely spot – how I hope some day to light upon the magic carbuncle. Thou knowest also how the people fear me, and hate me too, forsooth. And if the young Earl died, and suspicion fell on me, I must needs fly the Island, for my life would not be worth a grain of sand. Then my chance of success would be gone. Nay! I cannot do it, Lady; I cannot do it."

But the wily Countess offered him much gold, and bribed him higher and higher, first with wealth, then with success, and lastly she promised to obtain for him a high post at the Court of the King of Scotland; and at that his ambition stirred within him, his determination gave way, and he consented to do what she asked.

"I will summon my magic loom," he said, "and weave a piece of cloth of finest texture and of marvellous beauty; and before I weave it I will so poison the thread with a magic potion that, when it is fashioned into a garment, whoever puts it on will die ere he hath worn it many minutes."

"Thou art a clever knave," answered the Countess, a cruel smile lighting up her evil face, "and thou shalt be rewarded. Let me have a couple of yards of this wonderful web, and I will make a bonnie waistcoat for my fine young Earl and give it to him as a Yuletide gift. Then I reckon that he will not see the year out."

"That will he not," said Dwarf Snorro, with a malicious grin; and the two parted, after arranging that the piece of cloth should be delivered at the Palace of Orphir on the day before Christmas Eve.

Now, when the Countess Fraukirk had been away upon her wicked errand, strange things were happening at the Castle at Kirkwall. For Harold, encouraged by his brother's absence, offered his heart and hand once more to the Lady Morna. Once more she refused him, and in order to make sure that the scene should not be repeated, she told him that she had plighted her troth to his brother. When he heard that this was so, rage and fury were like to devour him. Mad with anger, he rushed from her presence, flung himself upon his horse, and rode away in the direction of the sea shore.

While he was galloping wildly along, his eyes fell on the snow-clad hills of Hoy rising up across the strip of sea that divided the one island from the other. And his thoughts flew at once to Snorro the Dwarf, who he had had occasion, as well as his step-aunt, to visit in bygone days.

"I have it," he cried. "Stupid fool that I was not to think of it at once. I will go to Snorro, and buy from him a love-potion, which will make my Lady Morna hate my precious brother and turn her thoughts kindly towards me."

So he made haste to hire a boat, and soon he was speeding over the tossing waters on his way to the Island of Hoy. When he arrived there he hurried up the lonely valley to where the Dwarfie Stone stood, and he had no difficulty in finding its uncanny occupant, for Snorro was standing at the hole that served as a door, his raven on his shoulder, gazing placidly at the setting sun.

A curious smile crossed his face when, hearing the sound of approaching footsteps, he turned round and his eyes fell on the young noble.

"What bringeth thee here, Sir Earl?" he asked gaily, for he scented more gold.

"I come for a love-potion," said Harold; and without more ado he told the whole story to the Wizard. "I will pay thee for it," he added, "if thou wilt give it to me quickly."

Snorro looked at him from head to foot. "Blind must the maiden be, Sir Orator," he said, "who needeth a love-potion to make her fancy so gallant a Knight."

Earl Harold laughed angrily. "It is easier to catch a sunbeam than a woman's roving fancy," he replied. "I have no time for jesting. For, hearken, old man, there is a proverb that saith, 'Time and tide wait for no man,' so I need not expect the tide to wait for me. The potion I must have, and that instantly."

Snorro saw that he was in earnest, so without a word he entered his dwelling, and in a few minutes returned with a small phial in his hand, which was full of a rosy liquid.

"Pour the contents of this into the Lady Morna's wine-cup," he said, "and I warrant thee that before four-and-twenty hours have passed she will love thee better than thou lovest her now."

Then he waved his hand, as if to dismiss his visitor, and disappeared into his dwelling-place.

Earl Harold made all speed back to the Castle; but it was not until one or two days had elapsed that he found a chance to pour the love-potion into the Lady Morna's wine-cup. But at last, one night at supper, he found an opportunity of doing so, and, waving away the little page-boy, he handed it to her himself.

She raised it to her lips, but she only made a pretence at drinking, for she had seen the hated Earl fingering the cup, and she feared some deed of treachery. When he had gone back to his seat she managed to pour the whole of the wine on the floor, and smiled to herself at the look of satisfaction that came over Harold's face as she put down the empty cup.

His satisfaction increased, for from that moment she felt so afraid of him that she treated him with great kindness, hoping that by doing so she would keep in his good graces until the Court moved to Orphir, and her own true love could protect her.

Harold, on his side, was delighted with her graciousness, for he felt certain that the charm was beginning to work, and that his hopes would soon be fulfilled.

A week later the Court removed to the Royal Palace at Orphir, where Earl Paul had everything in readiness for the reception of his guests.

Of course he was overjoyed to meet Lady Morna again, and she was overjoyed to meet him, for she felt that she was now safe from the unwelcome attentions of Earl Harold.

But to Earl Harold the sight of their joy was as gall and bitterness, and he could scarcely contain himself, although he still trusted in the efficacy of Snorro the Dwarf's love-potion.

As for Countess Fraukirk and Countess Helga, they looked forward eagerly to the time when the magic web would arrive, out of which they hoped to fashion a fatal gift for Earl Paul.

At last, the day before Christmas Eve, the two wicked women were sitting in the Countess Helga's chamber talking of the time when Earl Harold would rule alone in Orkney, when a tap came to the window, and on looking round they saw Dwarf Snorro's grey-headed Raven perched on the sill, a sealed packet in its beak.

They opened the casement, and with a hoarse croak the creature let the packet drop on to the floor; then it flapped its great wings and rose slowly into the air again its head turned in the direction of Hoy.

With fingers that trembled with excitement they broke the seals and undid the packet. It contained a piece of the most beautiful material that anyone could possibly imagine, woven in all the colours of the rainbow, and sparkling with gold and jewels.

"'Twill make a bonnie waistcoat," exclaimed Countess Fraukirk, with an unholy laugh. "The Silent Earl will be a braw man when he gets it on."

Then, without more ado, they set to work to cut out and sew the garment. All that night they worked, and all next day, till, late in the afternoon, when they were putting in the last stitches, hurried footsteps were heard ascending the winding staircase, and Earl Harold burst open the door.

His cheeks were red with passion, and his eyes were bright, for he could not but notice that, now that she was safe at Orphir under her true love's protection, the Lady Morna's manner had grown cold and distant again, and he was beginning to lose faith in Snorro's charm.

Angry and disappointed, he had sought his mother's room to pour out his story of vexation to her.

He stopped short, however, when he saw the wonderful waistcoat lying on the table, all gold and silver and shining colours. It was like a fairy garment, and its beauty took his breath away.

"For whom hast thou purchased that?" he asked, hoping to hear that it was intended for him.

"'Tis a Christmas gift for thy brother Paul," answered his mother, and she would have gone on to tell him how deadly a thing it was, had he given her time to speak. But her words fanned his fury into madness, for it seemed to him that this hated brother of his was claiming everything.

"Everything is for Paul! I am sick of his very name," he cried. "By my troth, he shall not have this!" and he snatched the vest from the table.

It was in vain that his mother and his aunt threw themselves at his feet, begging him to lay it down, and warning him that there was not a thread in it which was not poisoned. He paid no heed to their words, but rushed from the room, and, drawing it on, ran downstairs with a reckless laugh, to show the Lady Morna how fine he was.

Alas! alas! Scarce had he gained the hall than he fell to the ground in great pain.

Everyone crowded round him, and the two Countesses, terrified now by what they had done, tried in vain to tear the magic vest from his body. But he felt that it was too late, the deadly poison had done its work, and, waving them aside, he turned to his brother, who, in great distress, had knelt down and taken him tenderly in his arms.

"I wronged thee, Paul," he gasped. "For thou hast ever been true and kind. Forgive me in thy thoughts, and," he added, gathering up his strength for one last effort, and pointing to the two wretched women who had wrought all this misery, "beware of those two women, for they seek to take thy life." Then his head sank back on his brother's shoulder, and, with one long sigh, he died.

When he learned what had happened, and understood where the waistcoat came from, and for what purpose it had been intended, the anger of the Silent Earl knew no bounds. He swore a great oath that he would be avenged, not only on Snorro the Dwarf, but also on his wicked step-mother and her cruel sister.

His vengeance was baulked, however, for in the panic and confusion that followed Harold's death, the two Countesses slipped out of the Palace and fled to the coast, and took boat in haste to Scotland, where they had great possessions, and where they were much looked up to, and where no one would believe a word against them.

But retribution fell on them in the end, as it always does fall, sooner or later, on everyone who is wicked, or selfish, or cruel; for the Norsemen invaded the land, and their Castle was set on fire, and they perished miserably in the flames.

When Earl Paul found that they had escaped, he set out in hot haste for the Island of Hoy, for he was determined that the Dwarf, at least, should not escape. But when he came to the Dwarfie Stone he found it silent and deserted, all trace of its uncanny occupants having disappeared.

No one knew what had become of them; a few people were inclined to think that the Dwarf and his Raven had accompanied the Countess Fraukirk and the Countess Helga on their flight, but the greater part of the Islanders held to the belief, which I think was the true one, that the Powers of the Air spirited Snorro away, and shut him up in some unknown place as a punishment for his wickedness, and that his Raven accompanied him.

At any rate, he was never seen again by any living person, and wherever he went, he lost all chance of finding the magic carbuncle.

As for the Silent Earl and his Irish Sweetheart, they were married as soon as Earl Harold's funeral was over; and for hundreds of years afterwards, when the inhabitants of the Orkney Isles wanted to express great happiness, they said, "As happy as Earl Paul and the Countess Morna."

Saint Columba

SOON AFTER SAINT COLUMBA established his residence in Iona, tradition says that he paid a visit to a great seminary of Druids, then in the vicinity, at a place called Camusnan Ceul, or Bay of Cells, in the district of Ardnamurchan. Several remains of Druidical circles are still to be seen there, and on that bay and the neighbourhood many places are still named after their rites and ceremonies; such as Ardintibert, the Mount of Sacrifice, and others. The fame of the Saint had been for some time well known to the people, and his intention of instructing them in the doctrines of Christianity was announced to them. The ancient priesthood made every exertion to dissuade the inhabitants from hearing the powerful eloquence of Columba, and in this they were seconded by the principal man then in that country, whose name was Donald, a son of Connal.

The Saint had no sooner made his appearance, however, than he was surrounded by a vast multitude, anxious to hear so celebrated a preacher; and after the sermon was ended, many persons expressed a desire to be baptized, in spite of the remonstrances of the Druids. Columba had made choice of an eminence centrally situated for performing worship; but there was no water near the spot, and the son of Connal threatened with punishment any who should dare to procure it for his purpose. The Saint stood with his back leaning on a rock; after a short prayer, he struck the rock with his foot, and a stream of water issued forth in great abundance. The miracle had a powerful effect on the minds of his hearers, and many became converts to the new religion. This fountain is still distinguished by the name of Columba, and is considered of superior efficacy in the cure of diseases. When the Catholic form of worship prevailed in that country it was greatly resorted to, and old persons yet remember to have seen offerings left at the fountain in gratitude for benefits received from the benignant influence of the Saint's blessing on the water. At length it is said that a daughter of Donald, the son of Connal, expressed a wish to be baptized, and the father restrained her by violence. He also, with the aid of the Druids, forced Columba to take refuge in his boat, and the holy man departed for Iona, after warning the inhospitable Caledonian to prepare for another world, as his life would soon terminate.

The Saint was at sea during the whole night, which was stormy; and when approaching the shores of his own sacred island the following morning, a vast number of ravens were observed flying over the boat, chasing another of extraordinary large size. The croaking of the ravens awoke the Saint, who had been sleeping; and he instantly exclaimed that the son of Connal had just expired, which was afterwards ascertained to be true.

A very large Christian establishment appears to have been afterwards formed in the Bay of Cells; and the remains of a chapel, dedicated to Saint Kiaran, are still to be seen there. It is the favourite place of interment among the Catholics of this day. Indeed, Columba and many of his successors seem to have adopted the policy of engrafting their institutions on those which had formerly existed in the country. Of this there are innumerable instances, at least we observe the ruins of both still visible in many places; even in Iona we find the burying-ground of the Druids known at the present day. This practice may have had advantages at the time, but it must have been ultimately productive of many corruptions; and, in a great measure, accounts for many superstitious and absurd customs which prevailed among that people to a very recent period, and which are not yet entirely extinct. In a very ancient family in that country two round balls of coarse glass have been carefully preserved from time immemorial, and to these have been ascribed many virtues – amongst others, the cure of any extraordinary disease among cattle. The balls were immersed in cold water for three days and nights, and the water was afterwards sprinkled over all the cattle; this was expected to cure those affected, and to prevent the disease in the rest. From the names and appearance of these balls, there is no doubt that they had been symbols used by the Archdruids.

Within a short distance of the Bay of Cells there is a cave very remarkable in its appearance, and still more so from the purposes to which it has been appropriated. Saint Columba, on one of his many voyages among the Hebrides, was benighted on this rocky coast, and the mariners were alarmed for their own safety. The Saint assured them that neither he nor his crew would ever be drowned. They unexpectedly discovered a light at no great distance, and to that they directed their course. Columba's boat consisted of a frame of osiers, which was covered with hides of leather, and it was received into a very narrow creek close to this cave. After returning thanks for their escape, the Saint and his people had great difficulty in climbing up to the cave, which is elevated considerably above sea. They at length got sight of the fire which had first attracted their attention. Several persons sat around it, and their appearance was not much calculated to please the holy man. Their aspects were fierce, and they had on the fire some flesh roasting over the coals. The Saint gave them his benediction; and he was invited to sit down among them and to share their hurried repast, with which he gladly complied. They were freebooters, who lived by plunder and robbery, and this Columba soon discovered. He advised them to forsake that course, and to be converted to his doctrines, to which they all assented, and in the morning they accompanied the Saint on his voyage homeward. This circumstance created a high veneration for the cave among the disciples and successors of Columba, and that veneration still continues, in some degree. In one side of it there was a cleft of the rock, where lay the water with which the freebooters had been baptized; and this was afterwards formed by art into a basin, which is supplied with water by drops from the roof of the cave. It is alleged never to be empty or to overflow, and the most salubrious qualities are ascribed to it. To obtain the benefit of it, however, the votaries must undergo a very severe ordeal. They must be in the cave before daylight; they stand on the spot where the Saint first landed his boat, and nine waves must dash over their heads; they must afterwards pass through nine openings in the walls of the cave; and, lastly, they must swallow nine mouthfuls out of the holy basin. After invoking the aid of the Saint, the votaries within three weeks are either relieved by death or by recovery. Offerings are left in a certain place appropriated for that purpose; and these are sometimes of considerable value, nor are they ever abstracted.

Strangers are always informed that a young man, who had wantonly taken away some of these not many years since, broke his leg before he got home, and this affords the property of the Saint ample protection.

The Origin of Loch Ness

WHERE LOCH NESS NOW IS, there was long ago a fine glen. A woman went one day to the well to fetch water, and she found the spring flowing so fast that she got frightened, and left her pitcher and ran for her life; she never stopped till she got to the top of a high hill; and when there, she turned about and saw the glen filled with water. Not a house or a field was to be seen! "Aha!" said she, "Tha Loch ann a nis." (Ha Loch an a neesh). There is a lake in it now; and so the lake was called Loch Ness (neesh).

Prince Charlie and Mary MacLeod

THE FATE OF THE CHEVALIER and his devoted Highlanders forms one of the most romantic and darkest themes in the history of Scotland, so rich in historical narrative, song, and tradition –

Still freshly streaming
When pride and pomp have passed away,
To mossy tomb and turret grey,
Like friendship clinging.

In the contemplation of their misfortunes, their faults and failings are forgotten, and now that the unfortunate Chevalier's name and memory have become 'such stuff as dreams are made of,' every heart throbs in sympathy with the pathetic lyric 'Oh! wae's me for Prince Charlie.'

In the present day, when it is not accounted disloyal to speak kindly of the Prince, or of those who espoused his cause – one cannot help indulging in admiration of the courage and cheerfulness with which he bore trials, dangers, and 'hairbreadth 'scapes by flood and field,' nor wonder at the devotedness of the poorer Highlanders; their affection to his person; the care with which they watched over him in his wanderings; and, above all, the incorruptible fidelity which scorned to betray him, though tempted by what, in their poverty, must have seemed inconceivable wealth.

The history of the rising, and particularly of what followed after Culloden, relating to Prince Charlie, although generally minute, gives but little idea of the wonderful dangers he incurred, and the escapes he made. One should, in order to form a moderately correct idea of his hardships, have listened to those who had been out with him, as they, in the late evening of their days, talked of the past, and of the "lad they looed sae dearly," or heard their descendants, who were proud of their forbears, having been out in the '45, when –

The story was told, as a legend old,
And by withered dame and sire,
When they sat secure from the winter's cold,
All around the evening fire.

His capabilities of enduring cold, hunger, and fatigue prove that his constitution was of a very high order, and not what might have been expected from the descendant of a hundred kings brought up in the enervating atmosphere of courts. The magnanimity was surprising with which he bore up under his adverse lot, and the very trying privations to which he was subjected. The buoyancy of spirit with which he encountered the toils that hemmed him round, seemed to gather fresh energy from each recurring escape while wandering about, a hunted fugitive.

His appearance when concealed in the cave of Achnacarry as described by Dr Cameron, who was for a time a companion of his wanderings, is not suggestive of much comfort, but rather of contentedly making the most of circumstances. "He was then," says Dr Cameron, "bare footed; he had an old black kilt and coat on, a plaid, philabeg, and waistcoat, a dirty shirt, and a long red beard, a gun in his hand, a pistol and dirk by his side. He was very cheerful and in good health, and, in my opinion, fatter than when he was at Inverness." His courage and patience during his wandering drew forth even the admiration of his enemies, while his friends regretted that one capable of so much was so wanting in decision of character when it was urgently required by his own affairs, and the fortunes and lives of those who had perilled all for his sake. His friends, rich and poor, "for a' that had come and gane," were staunch in his favour to the very death; while his enemies, hounded on by a scared and vindictive Government, and earnestly anxious to enrich themselves by obtaining the reward offered for his capture, left no means untried to secure his person.

Among the many who signalized themselves in these attempts was one Ferguson, who, in command of a small squadron, cruised round the coast in search of the Prince and his fugitive friends, but in reality sparing none on whom it was possible or not dangerous to vent those feelings of oppression and worse, which the cruel Cumberland had made a fashion as regards Highlanders and the Highlands, and a sure recommendation to the notice of Government.

Soon after Culloden, Ferguson appeared off the coast and dropped anchor in Loch-Cunnard. A party landed there and proceeded up the strath as far as the residence of Mackenzie of Langwell, who was married to a near relation of Earl George of Cromartie. Mackenzie got out of the way, but the lady was obliged to attend some of her children who were confined by small-pox. The house was ransacked, a trunk containing valuable papers, and among these a wadset of Langwell and Inchvennie from the Earl of Cromartie, was burnt before her eyes, and about fifty head of black cattle were mangled by their swords and driven away to their ships.

Similar depredations were committed in the neighbourhood, without discrimination of friends or enemies. So familiarized were the west Highlanders and Islanders with Captain Ferguson, his cutter and crew, that they were in the habit of jeering him and them by calling after them – "Tha sinn eolach air a h-uile car a tha na t'eaman" – (We are acquainted with every turn in your tail) – a source of great irritation to the annoyed commander, who knew well the fugitives were hiding on the West Coast of Inverness-shire, and consequently resolved to adopt every species of decoy to entrap the Prince and his companions. To deceive the inhabitants of this wild and extensive coast, Ferguson pretended to give over the search and leave for Ireland. The Highlanders, wondering what would be the next move, were not deceived, nor did they relax their watchful precautions. The dwellers at Samalaman, the most western point of Moidart, had been especially harassed, as it was suspected they were in the confidence of Prince Charles. The suspicion was correct, and therefore, although they went about their usual employments they kept many an anxious look towards the ocean – many a lonely watch and walk was taken for the protection of the hunted wanderers.

To those who are not oppressed by anxiety the look-out from this headland is of surpassing beauty. Few scenes are equal to that presented in a midnight walk by moonlight along the sea beach, the glossy sea sending from its surface a long stream of dancing and dazzling light, no sound to be heard save the small ripple of the idle wavelets or the scream of a sea bird watching the fry that swarms along the shores! In the short nights of summer the melancholy song of the throstle has scarcely ceased on the hillside when the merry carol of the lark commences, and the snipe and the plover sound their shrill pipe. Again, how glorious is the scene which presents itself from the summits of the hills when the great ocean is seen glowing with the last splendour of the setting sun, and the lofty hills of the farther isles rear their giant heads amid the purple blaze on the extreme verge of the horizon.

Nothing of all this, for they were sights and scenes of continual recurrence, did Mary Macleod feel. Mary was a bold, spirited, handsome girl, who, in company with her father and two brothers forming the boat's crew, knew well all ocean's moods, and often braved the storms so common on that coast, and so fatal to many toilers of the deep.

On the morning of the fifth day after the departure of Captain Ferguson, Mary arose as usual to prepare the food for the family, and in going outside for a basket of peat fuel was surprised to observe a strange looking little vessel at anchor in a dark creek in the opposite island of Shona which partly occupies the mouth of Loch-Moidart. Time was when a circumstance, so apparently trivial, would have created no wonder nor left in the mind any cause for suspicion; but now Mary carefully scanned the low long dark hull of the craft, and her tanned and patched sails, which ill agreed with the trimness about her, and which at once spoke against her being a fishing craft or smuggler. "Cuilean an t-seann mhadaidh" (cub of the old fox) sighed the girl as she returned to the house to communicate the circumstance to the rest of the family, each of whom on reconnoitring the vessel confirmed her opinion. "Well then," said Mary, "let us advise the neighbours to betake themselves to their daily employment without seeming to suspect the new comer, and above all let us warn the deer of the mountain that the bloodhounds have appeared."

As the Moidart men were about to go to sea they were visited by a couple of miserable looking men from the suspected craft. One of them who spoke in Irish made them understand that they had lately left the coast of France laden with tobacco and spirits, some of which they would gladly exchange for dried fish and other provisions of which they were much in want, having been pursued for the last three days by an armed cutter, from which they had escaped with difficulty, and from which they intended to conceal themselves for some days longer in their present secluded anchorage. The fishermen, pretending to commiserate their condition, replied that they had no provisions to spare, and left only more convinced that Mary's suspicions were well founded. Matters remained in this state for a few days, the craft lying quietly at anchor, and her six hands, being, it was said, the full complement of her crew, sneaking about in all directions, in pairs, on pretence of searching for provisions. At last, after an unusually fine day the sun sank suddenly behind a mountain mass of clouds which for some time before had been collecting into dense columns, whose tall and fantastic shapes threw an obscurity far over the western horizon.

The coming storm was so apparent that the fishermen of Samalaman secured their boats upon the beach just as some heavy drops, bursting from the region of the storm clouds, showed that the elemental war had begun.

The Atlantic rolled its enormous billows upon the coast, dashing them with inconceivable fury upon the headlands, and scouring the sands and creeks, which, from the number of shoals and sunken rocks in them, exhibited the magnificent spectacle of breakers white with foam extending for miles. The blast howled among the grim and desolate rocks. Still greater masses of black clouds advanced from the west, pouring forth torrents of rain and hail. A sudden flash illuminated the gloom, and was followed by the crash and roar of thunder which gradually became fainter until the dash of the waves upon the shore prevailed over it.

Far as the eye could reach the ocean boiled and heaved in one wide extended field of foam, the spray from the summits of the waves sweeping along its surface like drifting snow.

Seaward no sign of life was to be seen, save when a gull, labouring hard to bear itself against the breeze, hovered overhead, or shot across the gloom like a meteor. Long ranges of giant waves rushed in succession to the shore, chasing each other like monsters at play. The thunder of their shock echoed among the crevices and caves, the spray mounted along the face of the cliffs in columns, the rocks shook as if in terror, and the baffled wave returned to meet its advancing successor.

By-and-bye there came a pause like the sudden closing of a blast furnace, or as if the storm had retired within itself; but now and then, in fitful bursts, proclaiming that its power was but partially smothered. During the conflict of the elements Mary Macleod seemed to suffer the most acute agonies of mind; and no sooner did it abate than, wrapping herself in her plaid, she sallied out and proceeded towards the sea shore. There, straining her eyes over the dark and fearful deep, she thought she saw, by a broad flash of lightning, a small speck on the wild waters, pitching as if in dark uncertainty, about the mouth of Loch-Moidart. With the speed of frenzy away flew the maiden to the nearest cottage, and grasping a burning peat and a lapful of dried brushwood, she, with equal speed, retraced her steps to the shore. In an instant the beacon threw its crackling flame far over the loch, and in an instant more the small black craft at Shona had cut from her moorings and stood out to the entrance of the bay. Now rose the struggle in Mary's mind. There stood the maid of Moidart in the shade of the lurid beacon, listening to the fitful blast, like the angel of pity. Something was passing on in the troubled bosom of that dark loch over which she often looked, that drew forth all the energies of her soul; but what that something was, was as hidden to her as futurity. She was startled from this state of intense feeling by a momentary flash on the water, instantaneously followed by a crash among the rocks at her side, and then came booming on her ear a sound as if the island of Shona had burst from its centre. "A Dhia nan dùl bi maile ris" (God of the elements be with him) ejaculated Mary as she bent her trembling knees on the wet sand, and then, like a spring from life to death, a boat rushed ashore, grounding on the shingle at her feet. A band of armed men immediately sprung on land, one of whom, gently clasping the girl, pressed her to his heart. "Failte 'Phrions" faltered Mary, giving a momentary scope to the woman in her bosom, but instantly recollecting herself, she whispered, "Guide him some of you to the hut of Marsaly Buie in the copse of Cul-a-chnaud, and I shall meet you there when the sun of the morning shall show me the fate of the pursuer." By this time the intrepid girl was joined by the villagers, who extinguished all traces of the late fire, and carried the stranger's boat where none but a friend could find it. The storm had again broken from its restless slumber, and the rain and sickly sun of the following day showed the pretended smuggler scattered on the beach. She appeared to have been well armed, and the easily recognised body of Captain Ferguson's first mate was one of the twelve who were washed ashore.

The Rout of Moy

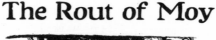

THE RIVER FINDHORN, WHICH RISES in the Monadh-liath Mountains, flows through the glen of Strathdearn. Its scenery passes from Alpine to Lowland, exhibits almost every variety of the picturesque, strikes the eye with force or delight all the way from the source to the sea, and is not excelled in aggregate richness by the scenery of any river or stream north of the Tay.

The river is remarkable for the rapidity with which it rises and falls, and for its swift torrent, which, when in flood, often takes a straight course at the cost of much injury to life and property. In 1829 Sir Thomas Dick Lauder, with powerful dramatic effect, told the story of the floods which then ravaged Morayshire along the courses of the rivers descending from the Monadh-liath and Cairngorm Mountains, notably the Findhorn and Spey, both of which rose to an unexampled height, in some parts of their course to fifty feet above their natural level.

The valley of Strathdearn will amply repay a visit. The Findhorn begins at the very head of the valley, and first issues forth through a remarkable rent in the rock called Clach Sgoilte, or the cloven stone. As it passes onwards it is joined by various small streams, proceeding from minor glens called shealings, into which the Highlanders were in the habit of driving their cattle to feed on abundance of the richest natural grass, sheltered from the scorching heat of the summer sun. There are, indeed, many lovely spots along the course of the river, and by the little rills among the hills, unknown now, save to the shepherd and the gamekeeper, servants of the sportsman who rents the district. There are the natural wood trees, 'the oak and the ash, and the bonnie elm tree,' the alder and the birch, the lady of the wood, and then the rivulets which drop from pool to pool, and anon hiding themselves among sandstone ledges deeply bedded in dark sedge and broad, bright burdoch leaves, and tall angelica, and tufts of king and crown and lady fern. Up the glens there are bits of boggy moor, all fragrant with the gold-tipped gale, and the turf is enamelled with the hectic marsh violet and the pink pimpernel, and the pale yellow-leaf stars of the butterwort, and the blue bells and green threads of the ivy-leaved campanula. And then to stop a few minutes and look around on the earth, like one great emerald, set round with heathery amethyst roofed with sapphire, in the distance the blue sea and blue mountains, and covering all the bright blue sky overhead; and under foot the wayside fringed with the purple vetch, the golden bed-straw, and the fragrant meadow-queen, while at intervals the wild rasp bushes, adorned with their crimson berries, offer a tempting refreshment to the passing bird, and the bare footed boy and girl ramblers. The time of the wild rose is past, but the hips and haws will soon put on their red, red coats, the coral beads are even now in cluster on the rowan tree, while the bramble trails over every ditch with its delicious load of juicy, purpling fruit. 'Eheu fugaces labuntur anni!' Well does the schoolboy love the rough skinned bramble, and often in the sunny days of boyhood do his fingers and lips know the stains of its luscious blobs:

> *"The bramble berries were our food,*
> *The water was our wine,*
> *And the linnet in the self same bush,*
> *Came after us to dine.*
> *And grow it in the woods sae green,*
> *Or grow it on the brae,*
> *We like to meet the bramble bush,*
> *Where'er our footsteps gae."*

As the ramble proceeds, the surrounding country becomes highly picturesque. Now we have a crag robed in lichen cropping upwards, and crowned with heather and tangled foliage; now we have a little runlet jinking among the seggans, and singing a sweet undersong as it steals down its tiny glen; and now a landscape all yellow with 'golden shields flung down from the sun,' in the foreground, and the glorious hills backing all behind. Verily, Strathdearn is a lovely glen.

About a mile from the church of Moy there is a singular hollow, called 'Ciste craig an eoin,' (the Chest of the craig of the bird), surrounded by high rocks, and accessible only through one narrow entrance. Situated close to the Pass called 'Starsach nan Gael' – the Doorstep of the Highlanders – it was used as a place of concealment for their wives and children by the Highlanders during their absence on predatory excursions into the low country. This is the scene of one of those romantic achievements which so marked the rebellion of '45.

Previous to the battle of Culloden, Prince Charlie was for some days at Moyhall, the guest of Colonel Ann, as Lady Mackintosh was called. The Chief himself, with a prudence to be commended, took the Royalist side, leaving what in this case was hardly the weaker vessel to espouse the cause of the Prince, for whom the distant clans were arming. Mackintosh himself was absent in Ross-shire, in the King's service, but his wife, who was a daughter of Farquharson of Invercauld, entertained the Prince, and was so enthusiastic in his cause that she afterwards raised a regiment of 400 of her husband's clan and followers to support him.

With these she joined Lord Strathallan, who had been left by Prince Charles at Perth, to collect troops and military stores, and these Mackintoshes afterwards fought at Culloden. Her ladyship was no favourer of half measures. At times she rode at the head of her regiment, with a man's hat on her head and pistols at her saddle-bow – hence her soubriquet of Colonel Ann.

That Prince Charles was at Moyhall, the guest of Lady Mackintosh, was well known to the Earl of Loudon, whose detachment of Royalist troops then occupied Inverness, about twelve miles distant. At breakfast his lordship, discussing his information with his officers, suddenly formed the decision to move on Moyhall in order to surprise the young Chevalier, gain the offered reward, and save the country from further bloodshed. A Highland lassie who waited at table in the 'Horns' overheard their plans, and at once, bare-footed and bare-headed, ran on to Moyhall to tell of the danger.

The tidings produced consternation and confusion, for there were no troops to defend the House of Moy, nor meet the coming foe. But Colonel Ann and the council of war she assembled were equal to the occasion. Donald Fraser, the Chief's blacksmith, afterwards known as 'Caiptin nan Cuignear,' the Captain of the Five, at once left his forge, and taking along with him five men whom she named, hurried off with sword and musket to repel the 1500 invading troops.

It was in the dusk of the evening when they reached the narrow pass of Craig an Eoin, two miles from the Hall, and there they waited the approach of the foe. There was a quantity of turf divots and peats set up to dry in small hillocks or stacks, and Donald and his men, in order the better to watch the motions of the troops, placed themselves a few hundred yards asunder among these heaps, concealed by the shadows of the hills rising on either side.

They were hardly in ambush when they became aware of the approach of the soldiers. It was the dusk of the evening. Now was the time for action. Fraser waited until the army was within 100 yards, when, starting up, the command was passed from Donald, and then from man to man, in a loud voice, along a distance of nearly a quarter of a mile – 'The Mackintoshes, the Macgillivrays, the Macbeans to form instantly the centre; the Macdonalds on the right, and the Frasers on the left.' All this in the hearing of the commander-in-chief of the Royal army, accompanied by the firing of the muskets of the concealed party. Macrimmon, the piper in the advanced guard of the Macleods, fell, and this, coupled with the fear that masses of Highlanders were ready to surround them, and cut them to pieces, caused the troops to flee back precipitately to Inverness, where Lord Loudon, not considering himself safe, continued his route to Sutherlandshire, a distance of seventy miles, where he took up his quarters.

Fraser returned quietly with the dirk of the fallen piper, and was locally promoted to the rank of captain. He fought afterwards bravely at Culloden, and his sword is still kept, with many another piece of rusty armour, at Tomatin House.

Thus ended what has been humorously called the Rout of Moy.

Cawdor Castle

ON THE BANKS OF A HIGHLAND BURN, which falls into the River Nairn some five miles from the town of Nairn, and fifteen from Inverness, stands Castle Cawdor, perhaps the best specimen extant of the baronial castle of the olden time. Its central tower is the oldest portion of the structure. On its east side, commanded by loop holes, is a small court, through which the visitor is ushered by an old drawbridge across a moat. The drawbridge, raised by chains attached to beams resting on the court wall, gives ingress through gateways secured by wooden bars. The staircase, the iron gate – brought from Lochindorb – the great baronial kitchen, partly hewn out of the rock, the massive tower walls, the ample stone mantlepieces, carved with quaint devices, the old furniture, and particularly the old mirrors and tapestry, carry one back many a long year into the social life of the past. Of the building of the castle there is a traditionary tale. In the dungeon of the castle there is the stem of a hawthorn tree, and tradition says that the noble builder was decided as to the position of his intended home by turning adrift an ass loaded with a chest full of gold, and noting the spot on which the animal rested, which was the third hawthorn tree from which he started. That tree is still in the dungeon, the chest itself is a part of the castle relics, and when friends wish prosperity to the family, they do so in the words, "Freshness to the hawthorn tree of Cawdor".

The tapestry on the walls was purchased in Arras in 1682, and brought by ship from Bruges to Dysart and Leith, and thence to Findhorn. It is curious to note that one of the grotesque figures on the mantlepiece, dated 1510, is that of a fox smoking, and that, too, a veritable cutty pipe, while the introduction of tobacco by Sir Walter Raleigh did not occur till 1585. After the battle of Culloden, the famous Lord Lovat was concealed in the roof of the castle, but finding his enemies becoming too numerous within the building, he let himself down over the wall by a rope, when he escaped, only to be taken in a hollow tree in an island (in Loch-Morar), was thereafter carried to London, tried, condemned, and beheaded on Tower Hill, on the 9th of April 1747, in the 80th year of his age.

Shakspeare's imperishable tragedy of Macbeth, founded upon a fictitious narrative which Hollinshed copied from Boece, has immortalized the name of Cawdor. Local tradition insisted on showing, until lately, the room in which the grooms were laid –

> *"Those of his chamber, as it seem'd had done't*
> *Their hands and faces were all badged with blood,*
> *So were their daggers, which unwiped we found*
> *Upon their pillows."*

The very blood-marks upon the woodwork were also shown as evidence of Duncan's assassination by Macbeth, and this, too, in the face of the fact that the licence was granted by James II to erect the tower in which the tragedy was supposed to have taken place.

The myth has now disappeared locally, a fire having taken place a few years ago, which destroyed the woodwork.

It is now an accredited piece of history that neither in Cawdor nor in Macbeth's Castle of Inverness, which once stood on the height called the Crown, but at Bothgowanan, near Elgin, the tragedy was accomplished. Macbeth by birth was Maormor of Ross, and – through his marriage with Lady Gruoch, grand-daughter of Kenneth – the fourth Thane of Cawdor. Her grandfather had been dethroned by Malcolm the Second, who also burned her first husband, murdered her brother, and slew the father of Macbeth. All these wrongs were avenged on Duncan, the grandson of Malcolm, whose presence in this part of the country was in order to compel his cousin, who had revolted, to pay tribute.

The castle was built by William, Thane of Cawdor, whose son, John, married Isabel Rose, the daughter of Hugh Rose of Kilravock. This John was a second son, and on him and his heirs was entailed the estate, because his elder brother, William, was lame, and inclined to enter the Church. John died in 1498, leaving two daughters, Janet and Muriel, born after his death. Janet died while an infant, and Muriel succeeded to the estate in virtue of the above-mentioned entail. The Laird of Kilravock designed the heiress for her own cousin, his grandson, but having joined with Mackintosh in a foray in the lands of Urquhart of Cromarty, he was pursued in a criminal process for robbery. Argyle, the then Justice General and Second Earl, had also his intentions regarding Muriel, and having made matters easy for Kilravock, in the matter of the law proceedings, induced the King, with her grandfather's consent, to award her in marriage to whomsoever he pleased.

Under pretence of sending the child to school, Campbell of Inverliver, in 1499, was sent with a party of sixty men to Kilravock to convey the child to Inveraray to be educated there in the family of Argyle.

The old lady of Kilravock, who did not quite approve of this mode of disposing of the hand of her grandchild, to which the pretended education tended, took good care to prevent the child being changed, a common trick of the times, by marking her on the hip with the key of her coffer, made red hot. That there was a necessity for this, may be imagined from the reply of Campbell of Auchinbeck, when asked what was to be done should the child die before she was marriageable: "She can never die," said he, "as long as a red-haired lassie can be found on either side of Loch-Awe." The child was, however, delivered to Campbell of Inverliver and his escort, but on arriving at Daltulich, in Strathnairn, he became aware that he was pursued by Alexander and Hugh Calder, the uncles of Muriel, who by no means agreed to the proceeding.

Inverliver faced about, with the largest portion of his party, to receive the Calders, and, to deceive them, kept one of his men in the rear, having a sheaf of oats wrapped in a plaid, as if it were the child, who, however, had been previously sent off with a smaller escort under charge of one of his sons, with strict instructions to proceed to Argyle's castle with all speed.

The conflict was a severe one, and many fell on both sides. It is said that in the heat of the skirmish, in his extremity, Inverliver gave utterance to the saying which has since passed into a proverb, "S fada glaodh o' Loch-Ou, 's fada cabhair o' Clann Dhuine" ('Tis a far cry to Loch-Awe, and a distant help to Clan Duine), signifying immediate danger and distant relief. When Macliver imagined she was safe, and at a considerable distance, he retreated, and, following her, conducted her to Inveraray, where she was educated, and, in 1510, married to Sir John Campbell, the third son of the Earl of Argyle. For his conduct in the affair, Macliver was rewarded by a gift of the twenty-pound land of Inverliver.

It was a sister of this Sir John Campbell who married Maclean of Duart, and who was exposed on a low rock between the islands of Mull and Lismore, that she might be drowned by the rising tide. The rock is still known by the name of the Lady's Rock. From this perilous situation she was rescued by a boat accidentally passing, and conveyed to her brother's house. Her relations, although much exasperated, smothered their resentment for a time, but only to break out afterwards with greater violence. Maclean of Duart, happening to be in Edinburgh, was surprised when in bed, and assassinated by Muriel's husband. Sir John Campbell died in 1546, but Muriel survived him until 1575.

Caol Reidhinn: Why the Name Was Given to It

ON A CERTAIN TIME, when the Feinn had come home from the chase to the house of Farabhuil, at the foot of Farabhein in Ardnamurchan, they were much astonished to find their wives so lusty, fair, and comely; for the chase was very scarce at the time with the Feinn.

The Feinn determined that they would know what their wives were getting to make them thus; and when they went away again to the chase, they left Conan, one of themselves, at the house, so that he might find this out.

Conan kept a watch, and the meat that they had was the hazel top boiled, and they were drinking the bree. It is said besides that they used to wash themselves with this.

The women understood that it was to watch them that Conan had been left at the house, and they were in a great fury.

In the night when Conan laid down to sleep, they tied his hair to two stakes which they drove into the earth on either side of his head. Then the women went out to the front of the house, and they struck their palms with a great lament, till they awoke Conan.

Conan sprang on foot with great haste, but he left part of his hair and of the hide of his head fast to the stakes.

When Conan got the women within, he set fire to heather and faggots in front of the house, so that he might kill the women with the smoke.

The Feinn were at this time opposite to the house of Farabheil on the other side of Caol Readhin (Kyle Ray), and when they saw the fire and the smoke rising up, they cried out loudly, striking their left hands on the front of their faces, with their eyes on the sky.

Then they ran to succour their set of wives, but the strait was between them; but with their blades they leaped the strait, (all) but one Mac an Reaidhinn (Ramsay). Mac an

Reaidhinn fell in the strait and he was drowned; and since then to this day's day, (the name of) Reaidhinn's Strait has stuck to the narrows.

> *Valour so swiftly for wives of the Feinn,*
> *And each one sprang on the point of his spear;*
> *And they left Mac an Reaidhinn in the strait.*

By good fortune the women all came through it but one or two of them, for the Feinn made mighty running to succour them. The Feinn were in great fury against Conan for what he had done, and they seized him to put him to death. Conan asked as a favour that the head should be taken off him with Mac an Luinne that would not leave a shred behind, the sword of Fionn MacDhuil (MacDuguld), and that his own son Garbh should smite him on the thigh of Fionn.

> *With earnest entreaty I would ask it*
> *And my soul's privation to seek it;*
> *The son of Luinne to reap my soul*
> *Upon the thigh of the sense of the Feinn.*

This was allowed him, but first seven grey hides and seven faggots of firewood, and seven "tiruin" of grey bark were laid about the thigh of Fionn.

Then the head of Conan was laid on that, and Garbh, his son, struck the head off him with Mac an Luinne –

> *And folds in the palm were not more plenteous*
> *Than severed thews in the thigh of Fionn.*

Then Garbh asked them where were the Feinn, for he had gone mad; and they said to him that they were below beneath him. Then he went down till he reached the sea, and he slashed at it till he drowned himself.

The Raid of Cilliechriost

THE ANCIENT CHAPEL OF CILLIECHRIOST, in the parish of Urray, in Ross-shire, was the scene of one of the bloodiest acts of ferocity and revenge that history has recorded. The original building has long since disappeared, but the lonely and beautifully situated burying-ground is still in use. The tragedy originated in the many quarrels which arose between two great chiefs of the North Highlands – Mackenzie of Kintail and Macdonell of Glengarry. As usual, the dispute was regarding land, but it is difficult to arrive at the degree of blame to which each party was entitled; enough that there was bad blood between these two paladins of the North.

Of course, the quarrel was not allowed to go to sleep for lack of action on the part of their friends and clansmen. The Macdonells having made several raids on the Mackenzie country, the Mackenzies retaliated by the spoiling of Morar with a large, overwhelming force. The Macdonells, taking advantage of Kenneth Mackenzie's visit to Mull with the view to influence Maclean to induce the former to peace, once more committed great devastation in the Mackenzie country, under the leadership of Glengarry's son, Angus. From Kintail and Lochalsh the clan Mackenzie gathered fast, but too late to prevent Macdonell from escaping to sea with his boats loaded with the foray. A portion of the Mackenzies ran to Eileandonan, while another portion sped to the narrow strait of the Kyle between Skye and the mainland, through which the Macdonells, on their return, of necessity must pass. At Eileandonan Lady Mackenzie furnished them with two boats, one ten-oared and one four-oared, also with arrows and ammunition. Though without their chief, the MacKenzies sallied forth, and rowing towards Kyleakin, lay in wait for the approach of the Macdonells. The first of the Glengarry boats they allowed to pass unchallenged, but the second, which was the thirty-two-oared galley of the chief, was furiously attacked. The unprepared Macdonells, rushing to the side of the heavily loaded boat, swamped the craft, and were all thrown into the sea, where they were dispatched in large numbers, and those who escaped to the land were destroyed "by the Kintail men, who killed them like sealchies."

Time passed on, Donald Gruamach, the old chief, died ere he could mature matters for adequate retaliation of the Kyle tragedy and the loss of his son Angus. The chief of the clan was an infant in whom the feelings of revenge could not be worked out by action; but there was one, his cousin, who was the captain or leader, in whom the bitterest thoughts exercised their fullest sway. It seems now impossible that such acts could have occurred, and it gives one a startling idea of the state of the country, when such a terrible instance of private vengeance could have been carried out so recently as the beginning of the seventeenth century, without any notice being taken of it, even in those days of general blood and rapine. Notwithstanding the hideousness of sacrilege and murder, which in magnitude of atrocity was scarcely ever equalled, there are many living, even in the immediate neighbourhood, who are ignorant of the cause of the act.

Macranuil of Lundi, captain of the clan, whose personal prowess was only equalled by his intense ferocity, made many incursions into the Mackenzie country, sweeping away their cattle and otherwise doing them serious injury; but these were but preludes to that sanguinary act on which his soul gloated, and by which he hoped effectually to avenge the loss of influence and property of which his clan was deprived by the Mackenzies, and more particularly to wash out the records of the death of his chief and clansman at Kyleakin. In order to form his plans more effectually, he wandered for some time as a mendicant among the Mackenzies, in order the more successfully to fix on the best means and place for his revenge. A solitary life offered up to expiate the manes of his relatives was not sufficient in his estimation, but the life's blood of such a number of his bitterest foemen, and an act at which the country should stand aghast was absolutely necessary.

Returning home, he gathered together a number of the most desperate of his clan, and by a forced march across the hills arrived at the Church of Cilliechriost on a Sunday forenoon, when it was filled by a crowd of worshippers of the clan Mackenzie. Without a moment's delay, without a single pang of remorse, and while the song of praise ascended to heaven from fathers, mothers, and children, he surrounded the church with his band, and with lighted torches set fire to the roof. The building was thatched, and while a gentle breeze from the east fanned the fire, the song of praise mingled with the crackling of the flames, until the imprisoned congregation, becoming conscious of their situation, rushed to the doors and windows, where they were met by a double row of bristling swords. Now, indeed, arose the wild wail of despair, the shrieks of women, the infuriated cries of men, and the helpless screaming of children; these, mingled with the roaring of the flames, appalled even the Macdonells, but not so Allan Dubh. "Thrust them back into the flames," cried he, "for he that suffers aught to escape alive from Cilliechriost shall be branded as a traitor to his clan;" and they were thrust back or mercilessly hewn down within the narrow porch, until the dead bodies, piled upon each other, opposed an unsurmountable barrier to the living. Anxious for the preservation of their young children, the scorching mothers threw them from the windows in the vain hope that the feelings of parents awakened in the breasts of the Macdonells would induce them to spare them, but not so. At the command of Allan of Lundi they were received on the points of the broadswords of men in whose breasts mercy had no place. It was a wild and fearful sight, only witnessed by a wild and fearful race. During the tragedy they listened with delight to the piper of the band, who, marching round the burning pile, played, to drown the screams of the victims, an extempore pibroch, which has ever since been distinguished as the war tune of Glengarry, under the title of "Cilliechriost." The flaming roof fell upon the burning victims; soon the screams ceased to be heard, a column of smoke and flame leapt into the air, the pibroch ceased, and the last smothering groan of existence ascended into the still sky of that Sabbath morning, whispering as it died away that the agonies of the congregation were over.

East, west, north, and south looked Allan Dubh Macranuil. Not a living soul met his eye. The fire he kindled had destroyed, like the spirit of desolation. Not a sound met his ear, and his own tiger soul sunk within him in dismay. The parish of Cilliechriost seemed swept of every living thing. The fearful silence that prevailed, in a quarter lately so thickly peopled, struck his followers with dread: for they had given in one hour the inhabitants of a whole parish one terrible grave. The desert which they had created filled them with dismay, heightened into terror by the howls of the masterless sheep dogs, and they turned to fly. Worn out with the suddenness of their long march from Glengarry, and with their late fiendish exertions, on their return they sat down to rest on the green face of Glenconvinth, which route they took in order to reach Lundi through the centre of Glenmoriston by Urquhart. Before they fled from Cilliechriost, Allan divided his party into two, one passing by Inverness and the other as already mentioned.

The Macdonells, however, were not allowed to escape, for the terrible deed had roused the Mackenzies as effectually as if the fiery cross had been sent through their territories. A youthful leader, a cadet of the family of Seaforth, in an incredibly short time, found himself surrounded by a determined band of Mackenzies eager for the fray; these were also divided into two bodies, one commanded by Murdoch Mackenzie of Redcastle, proceeded by Inverness, to follow the pursuit along the southern side of Loch-Ness. Another, headed by Alexander Mackenzie of Coul, struck across the country from Beauly, to follow the party of the Macdonells who fled along the northern side of Loch-Ness under their leader Allan Dubh Macranuil.

The party that fled by Inverness were surprised by Redcastle in a public-house at Torbreck, three miles to the west of the town, where they stopped to refresh themselves. The house was set on fire, and they all – thirty-seven in number – suffered the death which, in the earlier part of the day, they had so wantonly inflicted.

The Mackenzies, under Coul, after a few hours hard running, came up with the Macdonells as they sought a brief repose on the hills towards the burn of Aultsigh. There the Macdonells maintained an unequal conflict; but as guilt only brings faint hearts to its unfortunate votaries, they turned and again fled precipitately to the burn. Many, however, missed the ford, and, the channel being rough and rocky, several fell under the swords of the victorious Mackenzies. The remainder, with all the speed they could make, held on for miles, lighted by a splendid and cloudless moon, and when the rays of the morning burst upon them, Allan Dubh Macranuil and his party were seen ascending the southern ridge of Glen-Urquhart, with the Mackenzies close in their rear. Allan, casting an eye behind him and observing the superior numbers and determination of his pursuers, called upon his band to disperse, in order to confuse his pursuers, and so divert the chase from himself. This being done, he again set forward at the height of his speed, and after a long run, drew breath to reconnoitre, when, to his dismay, he found that the avenging Mackenzies were still on his track in one unbroken mass. Again he divided his men and bent his flight towards the shore of Loch-Ness, but still he saw the foe bearing down upon him with redoubled vigour. Becoming fearfully alive to his position, he cried to his few remaining companions again to disperse, until they left him, one by one, and he was alone. Allan, who as a mark of superiority and as Captain of the Glengarry Macdonells, always wore a red jacket, was thus easily distinguished from the rest of his clansmen, and the Mackenzies, being anxious for his capture, easily singled him out as the object of their joint and undivided pursuit. Perceiving the sword of vengeance ready to descend on his head, he took a resolution as desperate in its conception as it was unequalled in its accomplishment.

Taking a short course towards the fearful ravine of Aultsigh, he divested himself of his plaid and buckler, and, turning to the leader of the Mackenzies, who had nearly come up to him, beckoned him to follow, then, with a few yards of a run, he sprang over the yawning chasm, never before contemplated without a shudder. The agitation of his mind at the moment completely overshadowed the danger of the attempt, and being of an athletic frame, he succeeded in clearing the desperate leap. The young and reckless Mackenzie, full of ardour and determined at all hazards to capture the murderer, followed; but, being a stranger to the real width of the chasm, perhaps of less nerve than his adversary, and certainly not stimulated with the same feelings, he only touched the opposite brink with his toes, and slipping downwards, he clung by a slender shoot of hazel which grew over the tremendous abyss. Allan Dubh, looking round on his pursuer and observing the agitation of the hazel bush, immediately guessed the cause and, returning with the ferocity of a demon who had succeeded in getting his victim into his fangs, hoarsely whispered, "I have given much to your race this day, I shall give them this also; surely now the debt is paid;" then cutting the hazel twig with his sword, the intrepid youth was dashed from crag to crag until he reached the stream below, a bloody and misshapen mass.

Macranuil again commenced his flight, but one of the Mackenzies, who by this time had come up, sent a musket shot after him, by which he was wounded, and obliged to slacken his pace. None of his pursuers, however, on coming up to Aultsigh, dared or dreamt of taking a leap which had been so fatal to their youthful leader, and were therefore under the necessity of taking a circuitous route to gain the other side. This circumstance enabled Macranuil to increase the distance between him and his pursuers, but the loss of blood, occasioned by his wound, so weakened him that very soon he found his determined enemies were fast gaining on him. Like an infuriated wolf he hesitated whether to await the undivided attack of the Mackenzies or plunge into Loch-Ness and attempt to swim across its waters. The shouts of his approaching enemies soon decided him, and he sprung into its deep and dark wave. Refreshed by its invigorating coolness, he soon swam beyond the reach of their muskets; but in his weak and wounded state it is more than probable he would have sunk ere he had crossed half the breadth, had not the firing and the shouts of his enemies proved the means of saving his life. Fraser of Foyers, seeing a numerous band of armed men standing on the opposite bank of Loch-Ness, and observing a single swimmer struggling in the water, ordered his boat to be launched and, pulling hard to the individual, discovered him to be his friend Allan Dubh, with whose family Fraser was on terms of friendship. Macranuil, thus rescued, remained at the house of Foyers until he was cured of his wound. The influence and the Clan of the Macdonells subsequently declined, while that of the Mackenzies surely and steadily increased.

The heavy ridge between the vale of Urquhart and Aultsigh, where Allan Dubh Macranuil so often divided his men, is to this day called Monadh-an-leumanaich, or "the Moor of the Leaper".

A Legend of Loch-Maree

OF ALL THE MANY beautiful places in Scotland, none can surpass Loch-Maree (Loch-ma-righ, or the King's Loch), so called from the incidents related in the following legend:

Some centuries ago there lived near the loch an old woman and her son. Her husband and three elder sons had been slain, their humble home burnt, and their cattle driven off, during one of the fierce clan feuds which were only too common in those days. The poor woman had fled with her youngest son to this lonely secluded spot, where they found shelter, and after a while lived comfortably enough; for Kenneth grew a fine active lad and keen sportsman, and with his bow and arrow and fishing-rod supplied plenty food. They also possessed a small herd of goats, which rambled at will among the mountains surrounding the loch, returning to the widow's cottage at milking-time. Among them was a very beautiful dun-coloured one, which gave more milk than any of the others. This, together with her docile habits, made her a great favourite with the widow.

One evening Kenneth, returning home laden with the spoils of the chase, met his mother at the cottage door. The good woman was carrying the milk she had just taken from the goats, wearing a very dissatisfied look on her usually placid countenance. On her son asking what was the matter, she replied tartly, "Matter enough; see the small quantity of milk I have got tonight; the dun goat, who used to give more than any of the others, hardly gave a spoonful, and it has been the same the last two nights. I can't make out what ails the creature." Kenneth, tired after a long day's sport, answered lightly, that perhaps the goat was ill, or that she had not received food enough. His mother made no reply; she, however, gave the goat a double allowance of food that night, and saw that she took it well; but the next evening not a drop of milk did she give – indeed, it was evident she had been newly milked. The old woman was at her wits end; and directly her son came in, she began to complain loudly. "We must do something about that dun goat, Kenneth; not a drop of milk did she give again tonight; I am sure the fairies suck her, and if we don't stop it, I shant be able to make a single cheese to put by for the winter. You really must help me to find out all about it."

Kenneth, who began to miss his usual allowance of milk at suppertime, professed his willingness to assist his mother. "But," said he, "what can I do to prevent it? Would it not be better to tie the goat up?" "No, no, that would never do," replied his mother, "she has never been tethered, and would not stand it. The best thing for you to do will be to follow her tomorrow, and see where she goes." To this proposal Kenneth agreed, and early next morning started off after the dun goat, who soon separated herself from the rest of the herd, and made straight for a pass between two high rocks, bleating as she went. "Oh, oh!" said Kenneth to himself, "I shouldn't wonder if she has picked up some motherless fawn, which she suckles, for I have heard of such things before, and that is more likely than the fairies that mother talks about."

He found it, however, no easy matter to keep the goat in sight, and her colour being so peculiar, it was nearly impossible to see her at a little distance. Kenneth persevered manfully, springing from rock to rock almost as nimbly as the goat herself; but at last a sudden turn hid her for a minute from his sight, and try as he would, he could not again catch sight of her. So he had to own himself beaten; but he determined to wait until the usual time for milking, thinking he would be sure to see where she came from, so he waited patiently, but to no purpose. Not a glimpse did he get of her until he arrived at home, and saw her taking her food among the rest. His mother was anything but pleased at his non-success, more especially as she again did not get a single spoonful of milk from her. Terribly chagrined, Kenneth vowed he would solve the mystery if it took him a week to do so. Rising with the sun next morning, and taking some provisions and his bow and arrows with him, he started off in the same direction the goat had led him the day before. When he came to the place at which he lost sight of her, he concealed himself and waited. Before long he saw her pass, and immediately followed her, but the sagacious animal seemed to know that she was being traced, and redoubled her speed; so, in spite of Kenneth's utmost exertions, he again lost sight of her.

Heated and vexed, he threw himself on the ground, and exclaimed, "Confound the beast, I believe mother is right after all in saying the fairies have something to do with her. I'll give her up for this day." Having rested a while and taken some food, he strung his bow, for, said he, "'Twill never do to go home empty-handed a second day." He spent the day among the hills with fair success, and was turning towards home, when, endeavouring to recover a bird he had shot, he scrambled on to a small grass-covered platform in front of a natural cave in the rock, and much was his astonishment to see his lost goat standing at the entrance of the cave. He called her, and held out his hand, but instead of running to him and licking his hand as usual, she stamped with her feet, and, lowering her head, stood in a state of defence.

Convinced there was something in the cave, Kenneth tried to enter, but the goat stood firm, giving him some hard knocks with her horns. Finding she was so resolute, and not wishing to hurt her, he desisted for the present, marking the place well so as to find it easily again. The goat was again home before him, but not a drop of milk did she give. His mother was pleased he had discovered so much, and said, "Tomorrow I will go with you, and surely between us we shall manage to get a sight of the inside of the cave."

Next morning the old woman and her son started, taking a rope with them to secure the goat if she should prove unmanageable. When they arrived at the cave, the goat was standing at the entrance, evidently angry, and determined to oppose them. In vain the widow called her pet names, and held out sweet herbs; the stubborn animal would not budge an inch for all their entreaties or threats. "Well," said Kenneth, "it's no use standing here all day; I'll throw the rope over her, and drag her from the cave, and you shall go in, Mother, and see what she is hiding inside." No sooner said than done, and the poor goat was struggling on the ground, bleating loudly. As if in answer to her piteous cries, there issued from the cave, crawling on all fours, a beautiful boy about a year old, who scrambled at once to the goat, and, putting his little arms round the animal's neck, laid his face against its shaggy coat. She appeared delighted at the caress, and licked the hands and face of the child with evident affection.

At this unexpected sight, Kenneth and his mother were lost in astonishment and admiration. He at once satisfied himself, from the fairness and beauty of the child, and its being dressed in green, that it was indeed a veritable fairy, and his admiration for the goat was somewhat damped by a feeling of superstitious awe at being brought in such close proximity to one of "the good people". But the warm, motherly heart of the widow at once opened to the helpless infant, and, forgetting her natural fear of the supernatural, as well as her annoyance at the loss of her milk supply, she rushed forward and, catching the child in her arms, covered it with kisses, mingled with blessings on its beauty, and pity for its forlorn condition, vowing she would take it home, and cherish it as her own child.

Kenneth did not altogether approve of this proceeding, and exclaimed with some heat, "Mother! Mother! what are you saying; don't you see it is a fairy? Put it down, put it down, or perhaps you will get bewitched, and changed into some animal or other. How could a child like that, unless it was a fairy, live alone among these wild mountains, with no one to see after it? And where did it come from? No, no! Mother; it is nothing but a fairy, and we had better leave it alone, and the goat too, for she is also, no doubt, bewitched, and we shall only get ourselves into mischief by meddling with her; or, if you must needs have the goat, just hold the rope while I throw the fairy creature down the face of the rock, out of the animal's sight."

Before, however, Kenneth could lay hold of the child, he was arrested, and startled, by hearing a voice from the interior of the cave exclaiming, "Touch him if you dare! he is no fairy, but far better flesh and blood than you are." The next instant there rushed from the cave a young woman, scarcely out of her girlhood; fair enough, but with privation written in every feature of her face, while her torn dress and dishevelled hair told a tale of want and exposure. Withal, there was a certain dignity about her that made Kenneth and his mother give way when she approached to take possession of the child, who clung to her with every mark of affection.

With an air of respect, mingled with astonishment, the widow asked who she was, and how she came there.

The stranger explained how she had been menaced with great danger in her own country, and had fled with her child for concealment to this secluded spot, and should have perished from absolute want if it had not been for the good-natured goat, whom she had enticed to the cave, and on whose milk she and the child had subsisted for several days.

The kind-hearted widow at once offered them shelter and protection at her cottage, adding that she knew from sad experience what it was to be hunted from her own country like a wild animal.

Strange to say, Kenneth offered not the slightest objection to his mother's kind invitation. His dread of, and dislike to the fairies seemed to evaporate at the sight of a good-looking young girl. He offered no objection this time to the exercise of his mother's hospitality, which Flora gladly accepted, and they all wended their way to the widow's cottage, followed by the sagacious goat, who seemed to perfectly understand how matters stood.

Thus they for a time lived happily and safely, and the widow found her visitors no encumbrance; for Kenneth exerted himself with such good will in hunting and fishing that he supplied more than sufficient for them all. The boy grew a strong, sturdy fellow; and Flora, by good nourishment and mind at ease as to the safety of herself and charge, expanded into a most lovely woman, as amiable as she was beautiful, and assisted the widow in all her household duties, although it was very evident she belonged to a far higher class than that of her protectors.

Kenneth was the only one of the small circle who was not perfectly at ease. He who used to be one of the most happy and careless of mortals, with no higher ambition than to be a good sportsman, now became dissatisfied with himself and discontented with his lot in life. When out on the hills alone he would fall into moods of abstraction, building castles in the air, wishing he were a soldier – ah! if so, what wonderful feats of valour would he not perform; he would surpass all comrades in courage and dexterity; he would be rewarded with knighthood; and then he would have the right to mingle with the best and noblest of the land; and then – then there would flash across his mind a vision of a brave knight fighting to assert the lawful claims of a fair lady, of his being successful, of his being rewarded by the hand and heart of the beautiful heroine; and then – then poor Kenneth would find his fine castle crumbling away, and standing alone with empty game-bag. So, with a sigh, he would wake to the commonplace world, and hasten to redeem the idle time already wasted; and besides, did not Flora prefer one sort of game, which he must get, and did she not also admire a wildflower he had taken home yesterday, and he must scale the highest rocks to find more for her today. On his return home he would present the flowers shyly, blushing and stammering at the graceful thanks he received for them. He would scarcely taste his food, but sit quietly, following with his eyes every movement of the bewitching Flora, until little MacGabhar – for so they named the boy – would come and challenge him to a game of romps.

One day, when alone with his mother, Kenneth suddenly asked her if she thought Flora was really the mother of the boy. "Foolish boy," answered she, "do you think I have lived all these years and not know a maid from a wife? No, no; Flora is no more his mother than I am. And, son Kenneth, I wish to give you some advice: don't you go and fall in love with Flora – you might as well fall in love with the moon or the stars. Don't you see she is some great lady, perhaps a princess, although now obliged to live in concealment. I expect little MacGabhar is her brother, and heir to some great lord. What we must do is to treat her with respect and kindness, and perhaps some day, if she gets her rights, you may be her servant, if she will accept your services. Though she never told me who she was, she showed me a very handsome sword and a beautiful scarlet velvet mantle trimmed with fur, which she said belonged to the boy's father, and she was keeping them to prove his birth some day."

This sensible, though unpalatable, advice fell like lead upon Kenneth's heart, but still, thought he, "It will be something to be even her servant. I shall at least see her, and hear her voice."

Matters went on thus at the cottage for some time, until one day Kenneth came home hastily with the news that the Lord of Castle Donain, the chief of that part of the country, was come on a grand hunting expedition to the neighbourhood, and would probably call at the cottage, as he had done on former occasions. For themselves Kenneth had no fear, for although they did not belong to the chief's clan, he knew of their living on his estate, and had never offered any objection. It was only on Flora's account that he had hastened with the news. She, poor girl, seemed dreadfully agitated, and said that Lord Castle Donain was one of the last men she wished to know of her whereabouts, and suggested that she and MacGabhar should again take refuge in the cave until the danger was past; but, alas, it was too late. Already some of the foremost clansmen were in sight. In another minute the chief himself appeared, calling out to Kenneth to come as their guide, as he knew the ground so well. Kenneth hurried out, closing the door of the cottage after him. This, Lord Castle Donain noticed, as also the uneasiness of the young man's manner. "How now, Kenneth," he exclaimed, eyeing him suspiciously, "what have you in hiding there? Where is your mother? And why do you not ask me in to take a drink of milk as you used to do?" Kenneth confusedly muttered something about his mother not being well, and offered to fetch some milk for his lordship. The chief was now convinced that there was a secret, and determined to find it out. He entered the cottage without ceremony, exclaiming angrily, "What is the meaning of this, old dame? Do you not know you are only living on my estate on sufferance, and if you don't render me proper respect as your chief, I will soon pack you and your son off again." Then perceiving Flora, and being struck with her exceeding loveliness, he involuntarily altered his tone, and continued in a more gentle voice, "Ah! I now see the cause; you have a stranger with you. Who is she, Kenneth?"

Now this was a very puzzling question for poor Kenneth to answer, as he did not know himself, and being fearful of saying anything that might injure Flora. However, he answered as boldly as he could that she was his wife. "Your wife, Kenneth?" said the Chief. "Impossible, where did you get her from? I am sure she does not belong to this part of the country, or I should have noticed her before; however, I must claim the privileges of a chief, and give her a salute." But when he approached Flora, she waved him off with conscious dignity, saying he must excuse her, as it was not the custom in her country to kiss strangers. Her voice and manner, so different to what he expected from one in her seeming position, more than ever convinced the chief there was a mystery in the case, and when in answer to his inquiries she told him her name was Flora, he exclaimed, "Kenneth, I am sure you are deceiving me, she is not your wife; her voice, her manner, and, above all, her name, convince me that she is of high birth, and most probably of some hostile clan. Consequently she must return with me to Castle Donain until I fathom the mystery surrounding her, and you may think yourself lucky that I do not order you to be strung up on the nearest tree for a traitor."

This speech threw them all into the greatest consternation. In vain Flora pleaded to be left alone with her husband and child; in vain the widow and Kenneth asserted their innocence of wishing harm to the chief; he remained inexorable. To Castle Donain she must and should go. The widow, in the extremity of her grief, caught up the child, to whom she was greatly attached, and exclaimed, "Oh! little MacGabhar, what will become of you?"

On hearing this, Lord Castle Donain started as if an adder had stung him, and with agitated voice cried out, "MacGabhar! whence got he that name, for it is a fatal one to my family. Hundreds of years ago it was prophesied that –

"The son of the goat shall triumphantly bear
The mountain in flame; and the horns of the deer –
From forest of Loyne to the hill of Ben-Croshen –
From mountain to vale, and from ocean to ocean."

"So, little blue-eyed MacGabhar, you must come with me too, for I am sure you are a prize worth having."

Again poor Flora pleaded hard to be allowed to remain in her humble home, urging what a disgrace it would be for him to tear her and her child away from her husband and home; but all vain. The chief refused to believe the story of her being the wife of Kenneth, and insisted in no very measured terms on her at once accompanying him to the Castle of Islandonain.

Finding all her appeals and supplications of no avail, Flora began to grow desperate. Drawing the child to her, she faced the chief with a look as haughty as his own, and, producing a small, richly ornamented dirk, which she had concealed about her dress, vowed she would rather kill herself and the boy, too, than that they should be taken prisoners.

This bold mien and determined speech of Flora somewhat confused the chief, as he was far from wishing to offer any violence to one whom he was convinced was of high birth. It was consequently with a gentler voice and more respectful manner that he now addressed her, saying, "I do not wish to use any force towards you, and will therefore waive the question of you leaving your seclusion at present, but as I am thoroughly convinced there is a mystery about you, I will, as a precaution for my own safety, require to know more of your future movements." He accordingly directed one of his clansmen, Hector Dubh Mackenzie, to remain meantime as her guard; and then, to the great relief of the whole of the inmates, he retired from the cottage.

Though left unmolested for a time, poor Flora knew well that she was in the power of the Lord of Castle Donain, and her distress and perplexity of mind was extreme. She had the wit, however, to hide it from Hector, who was now a constant and unwelcome visitor at the cottage, and chatted and laughed with him and Kenneth, when they came home in the evening, as though she was quite careless and contented. Hers was not a nature to sit down quietly under danger. No, the greater the danger, the higher her courage seemed to rise, and she determined to effect her escape. She arranged with the widow that they should pack up a few necessaries, take the boy and the goat, and again have recourse to the cave for a present refuge. Unfortunately, however, she could find no opportunity to confide her plans to Kenneth, for the vigilance of Hector was so great that neither she nor his mother ever had a chance of speaking to him alone even for a moment. She was anxious to give him a clue, however slight, to their intended movements, so on the morning of the day they had fixed upon for the attempt, before the men went out, she carelessly said to him, "Oh Kenneth, I wish you would try to get me some more of these flowers, they are so beautiful," at the same time exhibiting a bit of a plant which Kenneth and herself well knew grew only in the neighbourhood of the cave. "But," she continued, "you need not trouble about it today, as you are going fishing; tomorrow, when you go to the hills, will be quite soon enough." These simple words, so frankly spoken, caused no suspicion to cross the mind of Hector, but to Kenneth, accompanied as they were with a quick expressive glance of her beautiful eyes, they were fraught with meaning, and he felt assured that she wished him to go to the neighbourhood of the cave on the morrow, though for what reason he could not surmise. As he promised to endeavour to procure the flowers, he gave her a look, intelligent as her own, which at once convinced her that he understood some plot was hatching.

That evening, when Kenneth and Hector returned from their day's fishing, they found no fire on the hearth, no supper ready, no voice to welcome them. Kenneth, from the hint he had received, was somewhat prepared for this unusual state of matters, but at the same time he echoed his companion's exclamations of astonishment; he tried to account for it to the satisfaction of his companion by suggesting that the women were out milking the goats, but, as if to contradict him, they heard a bleating outside the cottage, and, going out to ascertain the cause, they found the goats, tired of waiting, had actually come to the door themselves to be relieved of their milky treasure. Kenneth said nothing, but his quick eye at once detected the absence of the dun-coloured favourite which had nursed the boy. Hector, terribly chagrined and annoyed at finding himself thus outwitted, questioned and cross-questioned poor Kenneth until they both lost their temper, but failed to obtain any satisfactory information. They both passed a sleepless night, and at dawn of day Hector started, accompanied by Kenneth, in pursuit of the fugitives, feeling sure they could not have gone far in such a wild and rocky country. He kept a strict watch on Kenneth, who, notwithstanding, managed in the course of the day to get near the cave, and unseen by his companion gave a signal, which he was delighted to see answered. He now knew that his friends were safely lodged, and had no fear of their discovery by Hector, but how to communicate with them he could not imagine, for Hector kept the most jealous eye on his slightest movements.

The day was nearly spent; the men, fagged and wearied with their long and toilsome search among the mountains, lay down on the heather.

Hector, sulky, and deeply mortified at the trick played upon him, lay thinking of what excuse he could make to his chief, and how that high-spirited gentleman was likely to receive the news of Flora's escape. One thing was certain, he must at once acquaint his lord with the circumstances, whatever the consequences might be to himself; but the difficulty was, how to do so. He first thought of securing Kenneth, and taking him a prisoner along with him, but, glancing at the well-knit hardy figure and determined eyes of the young Highlander, he concluded it would be no easy task to secure him single-handed; and Hector, who, though brave, was also very prudent, saw no benefit likely to accrue from a combat between himself and Kenneth, which would probably end in the death of one, perhaps of both of them. At last he decided that the best plan for him would be to go off quickly and quietly, give information to his chief, and return with a sufficient number to trace and secure Kenneth and the runaways. The idea was no sooner conceived than executed. Seeing that Kenneth lay with his face covered, buried in thought, Hector rose and ran through the hills with the fleetness of a deer.

Kenneth lay for some time, revolving scheme after scheme, when, wondering at his companion's unwonted silence, he raised his head, and was astonished to find him gone. He jumped to his feet and looked eagerly around; at last he espied him at a distance, running as if for his life. This conduct somewhat puzzled him, and for a moment he was tempted to send an arrow after him, but recollecting he was now too far away, he dismissed the idea from his mind, and began to reflect how best to turn Hector's absence to his own benefit. The first thing he did was to hasten to the cave to inform its inmates of the strange and abrupt departure. Flora, with her usual intelligence, soon defined the reason, and a consultation was at once held as to what they had better do in the perplexing situation in which they now found themselves.

They could not stay in the cave for any length of time for want of provisions; the small stock they had brought with them would soon be exhausted; the goat's milk would not even be sufficient for little MacGabhar himself, and it would be unsafe for Kenneth to venture out to procure food for fear of their retreat being discovered, and they dreaded this might be the case even as it was, for if their enemies brought their slot hounds they would soon be tracked. Under all these circumstances, in about a week they concluded upon going down to the seashore, trusting fortune might favour them by sending a boat or vessel that way, in which they might make good their escape. This they did, taking the goat (which would not part from the boy) and their baggage along with them. As if in answer to their wishes, they no sooner arrived at the shore than they saw a large ship sailing towards them, and casting anchor at Poolewe. Shortly after they saw one of the ship's boats, with five or six men, rowing in their direction. Kenneth and Flora hastened forward to hail it and see if the men would take them on board. In their eagerness, they were nearly at the water's edge before they discovered that the principal figure in the boat was none other than Hector Dubh himself. With a scream of terror the affrighted Flora turned and fled, followed by Kenneth, back towards the child, for whose safety she had undergone so many hardships; but, alas, she was destined never to reach him, for in her haste she stumbled and fell. Kenneth stopped to raise her; the next moment they were surrounded, taken prisoners, and hurried to the boat.

Flora's anguish of mind at being thus cruelly separated from the boy was painful to witness. She prayed and entreated the men to return for him, promising that she would go quietly along with them if she only had the child. But all in vain, the men turned a deaf ear to her most vehement and impressive appeals, Hector saying, "No, no, my pretty madam, you have cheated me once already; I'll take care you shan't do it a second time. We can easily return for the boy if our lord desires us to do so, but we will make sure of you and Kenneth at any rate." So, in spite of Flora's tears and sobs, and the more violent expressions of Kenneth's anger (who was deeply grieved at leaving his mother in such a critical situation), the boat speedily bore them from the shore, and shortly after Hector had the satisfaction of handing them over to the custody of his chief.

The Lord of Castle Donain was very much put out at losing the boy, whose fate he felt was strangely interwoven with his own, and in proportion to his dread of what that fate might be was his anxiety to gain possession of MacGabhar. Many a long and fruitless search he caused to be made for him, many a sleepless night he passed in endeavouring to unravel the mystic meaning of the prophecy, and many an hour he spent in consulting his aged bard, who possessed the gift of second sight; but they could arrive at no satisfactory conclusion, save that MacGabhar should surely in the end become the possessor of the vast estates of Castle Donain, but whether it would be accomplished by victory in war, or by more peaceful means, whether in the lifetime of the present lord, or in that of his successors, was at present hidden from their vision.

Flora, who was kept in a kind of honourable captivity, would not afford him the slightest clue to her own identity, or the parentage of the boy, for whose loss she never ceased to grieve. On being perfectly satisfied that Kenneth was as ignorant as himself regarding Flora's antecedents, and being assured by her of Kenneth's absolute innocence of any design against him, the chief allowed the young man to go free.

Kenneth, however, was too devoted to the fair Flora to leave the place, while she was unwillingly detained there. He accordingly lingered about at a safe distance until a favourable opportunity occurred which enabled him to effect her escape, and of safely conducting her to another part of the country, out of the reach of the Lord of Castle Donain. Flora, finding herself alone and desolate, afraid of returning to her own country, and being deeply touched by Kenneth's unfailing devotion, at length consented to become his wife, a decision she never had cause to rue, but realized more every day the fact that

> *The rank is but the guinea stamp,*
> *The man's the gold for a' that.*

After this they wandered about in many places, where it is unnecessary to follow them, searching for the widow and the boy; but at length gave up their efforts as useless. They then went south, and Kenneth joined the army of the king, in which he speedily found favour, rose step by step, until the summit of his youthful ambition was attained, being knighted by the king for his distinguished gallantry on the battlefield.

When the poor widow saw her son and Flora so suddenly torn from her side, and herself and the child left desolate on the shore, she knew not what to do, nor where to turn for shelter. It was no use returning to the cave, for how could they subsist there? her cottage was not better now that Kenneth was gone. She, alone, would be totally unable to provide a livelihood. She had now only the one supreme idea of discovering and, if possible, rejoining her beloved and only son.

The kind and hospitable people of Poolewe supported her and her charge for several days, till at last they secured a passage for her on board a ship, the crew of which promised to take her to Castle Donain. The widow, like most old women, was rather garrulous; she told the captain all her troubles, and the strange story of the boy she found among the rocks of Loch-Maree sucking her favourite goat, showing him at the same time the velvet mantle and sword of state which belonged to little MacGabhar's father, to corroborate her statements. The captain, interested in the touching narrative, listened patiently, and condoled with the poor woman in her misfortunes; but, at the same time, feeling sure that the boy belonged to some family of note, he determined, instead of carrying them to the desired destination, taking his passengers to his own chief, Colin Gillespick, or Colin More, as he was generally called, a noted, brave, though rather unscrupulous chieftain.

Gillespick, on their arrival, was very glad to obtain possession of the boy, and on hearing the whole story, he decided on taking MacGabhar into his own family and bringing him up as one of his own sons. He also provided the widow with a small cottage near his castle, and allowed her enough to live upon very comfortably. She had liberty to see MacGabhar as often as she wished, and as she was very much attached to him, she would have been quite happy but for her grief at the loss of her son, which almost obliterated every other feeling. The boy was never tired of listening to her while she told and retold him all the incidents of his discovery in the cave with Flora, of their subsequent happy days at the cottage, and of their sad and sudden termination. As MacGabhar grew up, he became intensely anxious respecting his parentage, and many a pleasant converse he had with the old widow, who always maintained and taught him to believe that he came of noble blood. He would gaze on the mantle and sword by the hour together, trying to imagine what his father had been. The time thus spent was not altogether wasted, for these reveries made him feel that, if he was well born, it was necessary for him to conduct himself like a nobleman, which he accordingly strove to do, and soon excelled all his companions, as much by his skill and dexterity in the warlike games and manly accomplishments of the times, as in his fine athletic figure, handsome features, and dignified bearing.

When MacGabhar was about eighteen, his adopted father told him that he would now give him an opportunity of showing his prowess on the battlefield, as he had resolved to gather all his clan and retainers, and make a grand raid into a neighbouring territory, of which the people were at the time in a state of anarchy and confusion, which circumstance he had no doubt would greatly aid him in his intended project of subjugation. This was welcome news to the fiery youth, longing "to flesh his maiden sword", and he exerted himself with right good will in making the necessary preparations for the forthcoming foray.

When Flora married Kenneth, she, like a true wife, concealed no secret from him, but told him all her history – a strange and romantic one. She was of high birth, but, being an orphan, lived with her only sister, who had married and become the queen of the chief or king of a powerful neighbouring kingdom. They had an only child, a boy, named Ewen, to whom Flora was devotedly attached, being his companion and nurse by day and by night. When the child was about a year old, a revolt broke out in his domains, led by a natural brother of the king, who, being the elder, thought he had a better right. The rebels seized and murdered Ewen's father, their lawful sovereign, and took the queen prisoner.

Kenneth's blood ran cold as his wife continued, in graphic terms, to relate the horrors of that period; how the rebels, not satisfied with the death of their king, plotted to murder herself and the young heir during the night. Even in this trying emergency she did not lose her presence of mind, but courageously determined to defeat their wicked purpose by a counter-plot. She accordingly concealed her agitation during the day, and on some pretext persuaded the wife and child of one of the conspirators to change bedrooms with her; the latter were slain, while she made good her escape with her darling Ewen, but in such haste that she could make no preparations for her flight beyond carrying away the sword and mantle of the murdered king, as evidence, if ever opportunity occurred, to prove Ewen's high lineage and birth. After days of painful travel, she at last reached Loch-Maree, where she was happily found in the cave, succoured by the goat, by Kenneth and his devoted mother.

After Kenneth had been made a knight, and stood high in favour at court, his wife accidentally heard from a wandering minstrel that great changes had taken place in her native country. The usurper was dead, leaving no successor, and the people were divided and in a state of discord, some wishing to have the queen of the late rightful king restored, while others wished for a male ruler. Flora, on hearing this, at once expressed her desire once more to visit her sister, of whom she had heard nothing for so many years, and suggested to her husband that he might possibly help the queen to resume her rightful position. Sir Kenneth, ever ready for adventure, consented, provided he could get the king's consent for a time to withdraw from his service.

The kingdom being now at peace, the king readily granted him leave of absence, and also permission to take his immediate retainers along with him. They all started in high spirits, and arrived at their journey's end in safety, when Flora was overjoyed to find her sister alive and well. The queen, on meeting her, was no less delighted to find her long lost sister, and to hear of the wonderful preservation of her beloved son, though their joy was dampened by the uncertainty of his fate since Flora was separated from him. With the valuable assistance of Sir Kenneth and his brave men-at-arms, the queen was soon reinstated in her proper position. But no sooner was this accomplished than she was threatened with an immediate attack from the formidable and dreaded Colin More. Her subjects, however, rallied round her, and, forgetting their mutual quarrels, stood well together, and, led on by the brave Sir Kenneth, they rushed to meet the advancing foe with irresistible force, and gained a complete victory over him, taking several important prisoners, among whom were three of Gillespick's sons, and his adopted son Ewen MacGabhar.

Colin More's raid being so unjust, for there was no reason for it but the desire for plunder, it was decided that his punishment should be severe; consequently all the prisoners of any pretension to rank were ordered the morning after the battle to be publicly executed, beginning with the youngest. This happened to be Ewen MacGabhar, who determined to meet his fate without flinching, as befitted his birth, which he always felt was of noble origin. He accordingly dressed himself with care, and threw over all the scarlet velvet mantle he had preserved for so many years, and girded on the sword, with a sigh to think that he should never know the secret of his birth.

At the time appointed, the prisoners were brought out for execution before the queen and her court, according to the barbarous custom of the time. MacGabhar walked at their head with a stately step, his fine figure as erect, his fair head held as lofty, and his bright blue eye as fearless, as if he were a conqueror and not a captive. As he approached nearer where the queen sat, surrounded by her ladies, her sister Flora started violently, and, seizing her husband by the arm, exclaimed, "Oh Kenneth, see! see! that mantle, that sword; look at his fair hair, his blue eyes – it must, it must be he." Then, rushing toward Ewen, she cried out, "Your name, your name, young man; where did you get that sword and mantle? Speak, speak – I adjure you by all you hold sacred to tell the truth." Young Ewen, considerably surprised by this impassioned appeal, drew himself up, and answered firmly and respectfully, "Madam, these articles belong to my father, whom I never knew, and the name I am known by is Ewen MacGabhar, but I know not whether it is my right name or not." This answer, far from allaying the lady's agitation, only served to increase it, and, with an hysterical laugh, she screamed out, "MacGabhar! yes, yes, I was sure of it. Sister! husband! see, see, our lost darling – my own dear MacGabhar." Then, in the excess of her emotion, she threw her arms around him, and swooned away.

All was now confusion and perplexity. Sir Kenneth hastened to his wife's assistance. The queen rose and stood with an agitated face and out-stretched hands, looking earnestly at Ewen. The older chieftains, who remembered his father, began to remark the extraordinary likeness Ewen bore to the late king; clansmen caught up the excitement and began to shout "A MacCoinnich Mòr! A MacCoinnich Mòr!"

After a while, when the Lady Flora had regained consciousness, and some degree of order was restored, the queen began to closely question her sister as to the identity of Ewen; "For," she sagely remarked, "although that mantle and sword did indeed belong to my husband, that does not prove its present possessor to be his heir, and further, though I admit I perceive a great resemblance in that young man to the late king, yet he might be his son without being mine, and until I am persuaded that he is indeed my own lawful son, I will not yield up this honoured seat to him." This spirited speech was received with approval by the nobles, but still the common people kept up the cry of "A MacCoinnich Mòr! A MacCoinnich Mòr!"

"Stay, stay," exclaimed Kenneth, "I think I shall be able to decide if he is indeed MacGabhar; do you remember, Flora, the day when little Ewen was playing with my hunting knife and inflicted a severe cut on his arm? Now, if this young man has the mark of that wound, it will be conclusive. Approach then, and bare your left arm, MacGabhar."

Ewen stood forward, and amid the anxious, breathless attention of all, bared his muscular arm, when there plainly appeared a large cicatrice, evidently of many years standing.

All doubt was now removed; the queen embraced him and owned him her son. The chieftains crowded round to offer their congratulations, and the clansmen shouted loud and long.

MacGabhar bore himself throughout this strange and exciting scene with a dignity and composure of manner which greatly raised him in the estimation of his new-found friends. His first act was to beg the lives and liberty of his late fellow-prisoners, which was readily granted; and when he had explained to his mother how indebted he was to Gillespick for his kindness in bringing him up, and had also told Sir Kenneth how well treated his mother had been, their indignant feelings towards Gillespick gave way to more kindly emotions, and a firm and lasting peace was concluded between the two clans. Sir Kenneth hastened to fetch his mother, whose joy at being thus reunited to her beloved son, after so many years of separation and anxiety, was almost overpowering to the now aged woman. Sir Kenneth took up his abode in his wife's native country, and by his wise and sagacious council greatly assisted Ewen in the management of his kingdom, the queen, his mother, resigning all her authority in his favour. He ruled his people firmly and well, and by his courage in the field and wisdom in the council, he so raised the strength and increased the dimensions of his kingdom that it became the most prosperous and powerful in the Highlands. He married the only daughter of the Lord of Castle Donain, and by her inherited all that vast estate, in this way fulfilling the old prophecy which had caused so much uneasiness for years to his future father-in-law.

Mary Macleod and Her Lover

MARRIG HOUSE STANDS on a gentle declivity near the upper end of Loch-Seaforth, a bay some miles in length, in the Outer Hebrides. It was in olden times a structure of the most primitive description. Its walls, some six feet in thickness, and about four feet in height, were built of sods, earth, and mountain boulders; and its roof of pieces of wreckage found on the seashore, covered over with sods, ferns, and rushes. It had neither window nor chimney, save a rude opening at the top of the wall, and an old creel stuck into the ridge, which served the double purpose of admitting light and emitting the dense volumes of smoke which invariably darkened the interior. The fire was in the centre of the clay-made floor. The cooking utensils were suspended from the rafters by a heather rope. The partitions, made of boards, pieces of wreckage, and old sails, did not extend higher than the level of the walls.

Being on a portion of the estate of Harris – which was from time immemorial possessed by the branch of the Macleods known as Siol Thormaid – Marrig House was occupied by a Macleod; and not unfrequently did it afford temporary shelter and entertainment to the Chief of Siol Thormaid himself, when following the chase in the adjoining forests. It was from this house that Sir Rory Mor Macleod of Dunvegan and

Harris, while laid up with a bad leg, wrote, on the 2nd of September 1596, a letter to King James, acknowledging receipt of the King's charge, of the 18th of August, commanding him to be at Islay with all his forces on the second day thereafter, under pain of treason, and explaining that it was impossible to comply with His Majesty's orders, even "althocht my hail force haid beine togidder, and wund and widder serued one at eiverir airt." But the house which was then at Marrig has long since disappeared, and a more substantial and modern one now stands in its place. The tenant of Marrig was locally called "Fear Mharig", or the good man of Marrig, a term which was and still is applied in the Highlands to large tenants.

Marrig at the time of which we write was tenanted by a near relation of the Chief of Siol Thormaid, a brave, prudent, and upright man. He had an only daughter, his heiress, upon whom Nature had bestowed no small share of her favours; she was as modest and tender-hearted as she was beautiful. She was courted and sought after by all the young gentlemen of the island; but being devotedly attached to her father, whom she idolized, and on whose advice and counsel she invariably acted, their proffered suits were always rejected, until circumstances which took place in the neighbourhood of Glasgow at that time brought a new and more successful suitor on the scene.

It happened, while a son of the then Earl of Argyll was prosecuting his studies in the University of Glasgow, that a dispute arose between him and one of his fellow-students regarding the superiority of their respective clans. The quarrel ultimately assumed such proportions, that it was resolved to decide it by an appeal to arms. The weapons chosen were the broadsword and target, these being the common weapons of war in those days. At the proper time the combatants, with their seconds, appeared at the appointed place. A desperate combat immediately began, and continued with unabated fury for some time; and so well were the warriors matched that it became doubtful latterly which of them would carry the day. Campbell, however, ultimately made a clever and skilful stroke, which secured him the victory – having split his adversary's head almost in two. Campbell was thus, according to law, guilty of manslaughter, and being "wanted" for that offence, he and his second, a son of Macleod of Dunvegan and Harris, fled to the latter island for refuge.

Campbell was not long in the island when he became acquainted with Mary Macleod, the fair heiress of Marrig, and became deeply enamoured of her; and being a handsome man of prepossessing appearance, refined address, winning manners, and withal of an illustrious family, his love was soon warmly returned, and with the full concurrence of the young lady's father the day of their marriage was fixed for an early date. But it happened soon afterwards that the old gentleman casually received a full account of the reason which brought his daughter's affianced to Harris, and, his whole nature revolting at the idea of marrying his daughter to a man guilty of manslaughter, he at once resolved to break off the alliance. He well knew that this could not be accomplished without encountering some serious difficulty, possibly a bitter and deadly feud. Not that he apprehended any serious opposition on the part of his daughter, who, he was sure, would sacrifice almost anything to please him; but her suitor was a very different person. He was proud and easily irritated, and that he was of a violent disposition was sufficiently demonstrated from the fact that he had already fought a duel and had slain his opponent for the honour of his name. He belonged to a powerful family, whose chief might feign offence at his son's proffered suit and engagement being thus summarily rejected and violated, and who might come to make reprisals, or, peradventure, declare open war with the Siol Thormaid, the result of which might be disastrous. Carefully considering all these questions which operated strongly on his feelings, the good man of Marrig called his daughter to his presence, and told her in an affectionate and feeling manner what he had discovered of the history of her lover, and then, in a tone sufficiently firm to manifest that he meant what he said, he made known his resolution. "You must not," he said, "have any further communication with Campbell. Sorry, indeed, am I to be under the necessity of thwarting my dear Mary's affections, but ten times more would it pain me to see her wedded to a man whose past conduct my soul loathes. My darling Mary is still very young. Let her trust in Providence, and she will yet get a husband, in whom she may safely repose her trust, and whom her aged father can love as he loves his daughter."

"Never have I attempted to go against my father's commands," answered she, weeping bitterly, "nor shall I do so now; but as my heart bleeds for my beloved, I trust you have authentic information before you can act so harshly. Shall I, Oh! shall I be permitted to see him once more?"

"I have no reason to doubt the correctness of my information," replied he, "for I received it from young Macleod, who witnessed the duel. You may see Campbell once more, but once for all."

A meeting had previously been arranged between the lovers for the very evening of the day on which the above conversation took place between Mary Macleod and her father; and with buoyant spirits, and a step so light that it scarcely bent the purple heather, Campbell walked from Rodel to Marrig that day – a distance of between twenty-five and thirty miles – to meet his affianced Mary. Little, alas! did he think, while performing his journey, that she would greet him with such heart-rending words to both as "My dear, I must see you no more." The lovers embraced each other when they met. "How happy am I to meet you and see you, my darling Mary, once more," said Campbell, who was the first to speak; "but, thank God, we shall soon meet to part no more while we live."

"Happy, thrice happy would I be," sobbed the maiden, "if that were so; but, alas! it cannot be." And in broken accents she recapitulated all that her father said to her, adding with a groan, "I must never see you again."

"What?" exclaimed Campbell in great excitement. "Must I never see my dear, my own Mary again? It cannot be. The very thought would kill me. I will not part with my own, my darling Mary."

They both burst into tears, and continued to weep and sob for a time; but the young lady, who, on the whole, considering the trying nature of it, bore the ordeal with remarkable fortitude, remarked that as her father's word was inexorable as the laws of the Medes and Persians which altered not, they must be reconciled to their fate.

"If it must be so, then," Campbell replied, "I shall try to submit to it. But the island of Harris will henceforth have no attraction for me. I shall depart from it at once, and go to the seas, where I can muse in melancholy silence on the maid who first stole my heart and afterwards rejected me."

"Restrain thy plaint, my dear Archy," rejoined the maiden, as she proceeded to assure him that the step she had taken was entirely in obedience to the wishes of her father, without whose consent she would never marry while he lived; but she would faithfully promise that if he would wait for her until her father had paid the debt of nature, she would be only too happy to fulfil her engagement and become his wife. "And," she continued, "I shall never marry another while you live."

Campbell replied that since he found that her love to him was still unaltered, he would become more reconciled to his hard fate; that her kind and loving words had infused him with fresh hopes; that her father, in the natural course of things, before many years had passed away, would go to his fathers, and that till that event took place he would patiently wait for his loving Mary. He then handed her the ring which he intended to place on her finger on the day of her nuptials, saying, "Take this and keep it till we meet again."

She took the ring with mingled feelings of joy and sorrow – of joy, because she could look at it as a memento of their engagement; of sorrow, because it would remind her of an absent lover. After looking intensely at it for some time, she carefully placed it in her bosom, saying, "I, too, will give you a pledge of our betrothal; it was intended to be worn on your breast at our wedding," and she then handed him a knot of blue ribbon, made by herself, and having both their initials wrought in it with golden silk thread. Taking a parting embrace of each other, they wept long and bitterly, and with heavy hearts separated, it might be, for ever.

During this conversation they sat on the south side of an elevated spot overlooking Loch-Seaforth, and when they parted she went direct to Marrig House, while he went in the direction of Stornoway, with the view of procuring employment as a seaman on board some vessel. Many a look did he give towards Marrig, between Athline, at the head of Loch-Seaforth, and Araidh Bhruthaich, the Shealing of the Ascent, in Lochs, made famous in local tradition as the place where the Irish plunderers lifted Donald Cam Macaulay's cattle in his absence while he was away on business at the Flannel Isles, and for which act they paid with their lives; for Donald overtook them at Loch-Seaforth, and slew every one of them.

Stornoway is twenty-six miles north of Marrig; and though the evening was far advanced ere Campbell left, he arrived at the capital of the Lews before many of the good citizens had retired for the night. One would have thought that, after travelling upwards of fifty miles that day, he would have slept pretty soundly; but such was not the case. The thought of what had occurred at Marrig disquieted his mind so much, that it almost became unhinged. Sleep, usually the sweet and refreshing balm to the weary traveller, left him to writhe on a sleepless pillow. No wonder, then, that the first peep of daylight found him in the neighbourhood of the old castle of Stornoway – then the seat and stronghold of the once famous Chief of Siol Thorcuil – sauntering on the sandy beach, and peering out into the placid blue water of the bay, in the hope of descrying some ship to take him away from the scene of his present sorrow. He did not long look in vain, for he soon noticed a vessel lying some distance off; and presently a small boat coming for a supply of water left her for the shore. The ship, which had shortened her cable before the boat had put off, he found, was bound for Holland.

"Short of men?" exclaimed Campbell, as the boat touched the beach.

"Would ship one good hand," one of the sailors replied.

"All right; here he is," responded Campbell, who, as soon as the casks were full, accompanied the sailors to the vessel. He was engaged at once; the ship weighed anchor and proceeded to sea. Campbell having now left the Hebrides, we shall return to Harris and note affairs at Marrig.

Several years had passed away before Mary Macleod thoroughly recovered from the effects of the shock produced by her bitter disappointment. She mourned long and sorrowfully for her absent lover, and feared she would never see him more. Her lamentations were so pitiful, she grew so terribly thin and wan, that her father was sorely grieved that he could not undo what he had done. "Woe to me," he often exclaimed, "for killing my daughter. She is rapidly sinking to an untimely grave." Although some of Mary's former admirers returned with the full ardour of their love as soon as Campbell had left the island, and pressed their suits with renewed zeal, she politely but firmly rejected their proposals, with the saying, "I am not yet a widow."

Five years had now almost passed away since Mary Macleod and Archie Campbell parted, and still no tidings reached her of his whereabouts. She knew not whether he was dead or alive. At that time some of the sailors belonging to a large ship which came into Loch-Seaforth for shelter called one evening for milk at Marrig House; and in conversation with them it transpired that their vessel, then in Loch-Seaforth, was the identical ship in which Campbell sailed from Stornoway five years before; that he never left her until he was accidentally drowned in the Bay of Biscay four years afterwards; that, by his kind and obliging manner, he became a general favourite with all his comrades, all of whom deeply lamented his loss. This unexpected intelligence acted upon the forlorn and broken-hearted maiden as if struck by lightning. She uttered a wild and piercing scream, and fell fainting on the floor. During the excitement that followed, the sailors made their exit, and proceeded to their ship, which weighed anchor next morning and disappeared; so that the fair maiden had now lost further opportunity of obtaining any additional information she might desire about her lover. Sad and melancholy as she had been hitherto, she was now depressed and cheerless in the extreme. Refusing to be comforted, she moaned and sighed day and night for weeks and months together. Nothing apparently could rouse her spirits from the deep melancholy which had taken possession of her. She continued thus for nearly two years, during which time she was all but a hermit. She was often visited, it is true, during those solitary years by many admirers, who used all the fair words at their command to press their suit upon her, but she invariably answered that she did not yet tire of her widow's weeds. Eventually, however, she became gradually more cheerful, and took some pleasure in society; and ultimately went and sang and danced at local balls and other fashionable gatherings as in days long gone by.

Of all Mary Macleod's admirers, Macleod of Hushinish was her greatest favourite; and some three years after she obtained intelligence of Campbell's death, she consented to become his wife, with the full consent of the father and other relations, and the day of their espousal was fixed. The preparations for the wedding, which was to be on a grand scale, were necessarily extensive. The liquors consisted of whisky, rum, gin, and brandy. The marriage ceremony was, according to the usual custom, to be performed in her father's house, whither the officiating clergyman had been invited several days previously. For some days prior to the marriage a strong gale of wind blew from the south, and the barometer gave every indication of its continuance. This proved a fortunate circumstance for the bride's father, whose stock of gin and brandy had become somewhat limited at the very time when it was most required; for, two days previous to that of the marriage, a foreign vessel had put into Loch-Seaforth to shelter from the storm, and from this ship he procured an addition to the necessary supply of spirits. On account of the liberal terms on which the captain supplied him, Fear Mharig invited him and the first mate to the wedding. The captain – a middle-aged burly man, with a well-tanned face – was, as became his position, dressed in a suit corresponding to his rank; but the mate, who seemed about thirty years of age, with brown but well-fared face, of ordinary height and handsome figure, was dressed in the garb of an ordinary seaman.

The number of people collected at Marrig House was so large that the marriage ceremony had to be performed in the large barn, where as many as it could contain were requested to go and witness the proceedings. In the general rush the captain and his mate were left outside. But being the greatest strangers, and anxious that they should see the ritual, some of the leading Harris men gave up their own seats in favour of the sailors, who thus received front positions. They had scarcely occupied them when the bride and her maids entered, followed almost immediately by the bridegroom and his party. The bride, attired in her magnificent marriage robes, looking beautiful, and spotless as an angel, was greeted with vociferous cheering. This enthusiastic welcome over, and just when the minister was about to commence the service, the mate, who chanced to be exactly opposite to the bride, interrupted the proceedings by saying in the blunt but pointed manner peculiar to sailors, "I presume that all the ladies and gentlemen present have already presented the bride with their presents. I haven't yet had a proper opportunity of giving mine; and although it is but small, and apparently trifling, I trust the young lady will, nevertheless, accept and appreciate it as a token of my constant love and devoted affection."

He then handed to the bride a neatly folded paper parcel, about the size of a small-sized envelope. She nervously tore it open, and on examining the contents, she, to the great astonishment of the assembly, exclaimed, "Archy, Archy, my dear! my long absent Archy," and springing forward she embraced him again and again. It is almost needless to say that the sailor's gift was the identical knot of blue ribbon given by Mary Macleod to Archibald Campbell some eight years before. Mary and her betrothed, Archibald Campbell (for it was he), were for several minutes locked fast in each other's embrace, and she, after the commotion produced by this unexpected meeting had somewhat subsided, said, in an audible tone, that she was now ready to fulfil her original engagement to her first love, and that her father, she was quite sure, would now offer no objections to their marriage. Fear Mharig at once replied that he had already suffered quite enough of harrowed remorse for the part he had previously taken in their separation to offer any further objection. He would therefore give his full consent, for the whole matter seemed to him to have been arranged by Providence.

Young Macleod of Harris, Campbell's University companion, now stepped forward, and shook the sailor warmly by the hand, giving him a thousand welcomes, and congratulating him on coming so opportunely to claim the hand of Mary Macleod; and Fear Mharig suggested that, as all the arrangements were ready, and the clergyman standing there, the marriage ceremony had better be proceeded with; which proposal was acted upon, and Archibald Campbell and Mary Macleod were there and then made man and wife. During the proceedings, young Hushinish, the disappointed bridegroom, stood a silent spectator and quite dumbfounded.

The marriage ceremony over, Campbell entertained the company, relating his travels and all the peculiar incidents which occurred during the eight years that elapsed since he left Harris, one of which was how his ship came to Loch-Seaforth three years before, as already noticed, how that he himself formed one of the party of sailors who then called at Marrig House for milk, and personally reported that he had been drowned in the Bay of Biscay. His object in making this untrue statement was to test his Mary's affection; for finding that her father was still alive, he deemed it prudent not to make himself known.

He then solemnly assured them, corroborated by his Captain, that his coming to Loch-Seaforth two days ago, driven by the storm, was by the merest accident.

It need hardly be said that the vessel left Loch-Seaforth minus the first mate, who was from his marriage-day henceforth called Fear Mharig. From Mary Macleod and Archibald Campbell descended all the Campbells in Harris, Lews, Uist, and Skye, many of whom became famous in their day and generation.

Edinburgh Castle

WHILE ROBERT BRUCE was gradually getting possession of the country and driving out the English, Edinburgh, the principal town of Scotland, remained with its strong castle in possession of the invaders. Sir Thomas Randolph was extremely desirous to gain this important place, but the castle is situated on a very steep and lofty rock, so that it is difficult, or almost impossible even, to get up to the foot of the walls, much more to climb over them. So, while Randolph was considering what was to be done, there came to him a Scottish gentleman, named Francis, who had joined Bruce's standard, and asked to speak with him in private. He then told Randolph that in his youth he had lived in the castle of Edinburgh, and that his father had then been governor of the fortress.

It happened at that time that Francis was much in love with a lady who lived in a part of the town beneath the castle, which is called the Grass-Market. Now, as he could not get out of the castle by day to see his mistress, he had practiced a way of clambering by night down the castle crag on the steep side, and returning up at his pleasure; when he came to the foot of the wall he made use of a ladder to get over it, as it was not very high on that point, those who built it having trusted to the steepness of the crag. Francis had gone and come so frequently in this dangerous manner that, though it was now long ago, he told Randolph he knew the road so well that he would undertake to guide a small party of men by night to the bottom of the wall, and, as they might bring ladders with them, there would be no difficulty in scaling it. The great risk was that of their being discovered by the watchmen while in the act of ascending the cliff, in which case every man of them must perish.

Nevertheless, Randolph did not hesitate to attempt the adventure. He took with him only thirty men, and came one dark night to the foot of the crag, which they began to ascend under the guidance of Francis, who went before them, upon his hands and feet, where there was scarce room to support themselves. All the while these thirty men were obliged to follow in a line, one after the other, by a path that was fitter for a cat than for a man. The noise of a stone falling, or a word spoken from one to another, would have alarmed the watchmen. They were obliged, therefore, to move with the greatest precaution. When they were far up the crag, and near the foundation of the wall, they heard the guards going their rounds, to see that all was safe in and about the castle.

Randolph and his party had nothing for it but to lie close and quiet, each man under the crag, as he happened to be placed, and trust that the guards would pass by without noticing them. And while they were waiting in breathless alarm, they got a new cause of fright. One of the soldiers of the castle, willing to startle his comrades, suddenly threw a stone from the wall and cried out, "Aha! I see you well!" The stone came thundering down over the heads of Randolph and his men, who naturally thought themselves discovered. If they had stirred, or made the slightest noise, they would have been destroyed, for the soldiers above might have killed every man of them, merely by rolling down stones. But being courageous and chosen men, they remained quiet, and the English soldiers, who thought their comrade was merely playing them a trick (as indeed he was), passed on, without further examination.

Then Randolph and his men got up and came in haste to the foot of the wall, which was not above twice a man's height in that place. They planted the ladders they had brought, and Francis mounted first to show them the way; Sir Andrew Grey, a brave knight, followed him; and Randolph himself was the third man who got over. Then the rest followed. When once they were within the walls, there was not so much to do, for the garrison were asleep, and unarmed, excepting the watch, who were speedily destroyed. Thus was Edinburgh Castle taken, in the year 1312–13.

Scottish Strategy

THERE WAS A STRONG CASTLE near Linlithgow, where an English governor, with a powerful garrison, lay in readiness to support the English cause, and used to exercise much severity upon the Scotch in the neighbourhood. There lived, at no great distance from this stronghold, a farmer, a bold and stout man, whose name was Binnock, or, as it is now pronounced, Binning. This man saw with great joy the progress which the Scotch were making in recovering their country from the English, and resolved to do something to help his countrymen, by getting possession, if it were possible, of the Castle of Linlithgow. But the place was very strong, situated by the side of a lake, defended not only by gates, which were usually kept shut against strangers, but also by a portcullis. A portcullis is a sort of door formed of cross-bars of iron, like a gate. It has not hinges like a door, but is drawn up by pulleys, and let down when any danger approaches. It may be let go in a moment, and then falls down into the doorway, and, as it has great iron spikes at the bottom, it crushes all that it lights upon; and in case of a sudden alarm, a portcullis may be let suddenly fall, to defend the entrance when it is not possible to shut the gates. Binnock knew this very well, but he resolved to be provided against this risk also when he attempted to surprise the castle.

So he spoke with some bold, courageous countrymen, and engaged them in the enterprise, which he accomplished thus: Binnock had been accustomed to supply the garrison of Linlithgow with hay, and he had been ordered by the English governor to furnish some cartloads, of which they were in want. He promised to bring it accordingly;

but, in the night before he drove the hay to the castle, he stationed a party of his friends, as well-armed as possible, near the entrance, where they could not be seen by the garrison, and gave them directions that they should come to his assistance as soon as they should hear him give a signal, which was to be, "Call all, call all!" Then he loaded his cart, and placed eight strong men, well-armed, lying flat on their breasts, and covered over with hay, so that they could not be seen. He himself walked carelessly beside the wagon; and he chose the stoutest and bravest of his servants to be the driver, who carried at his belt a stout axe or hatchet.

In this way Binnock approached the castle early in the morning; and the watchman, who only saw two men, Binnock being one of them, with a cart of hay, which they expected, opened the gates, and raised up the portcullis to permit them to enter the castle. But as soon as the cart had got under the gateway, Binnock made a sign to his servant, who, with his axe suddenly cut asunder the soam (that is, the yoke which fastens the horses to the cart), and the horses, finding themselves free, naturally started forward, the cart remaining behind. At the same moment Binnock cried, as loud as he could, "Call all, call all!" and, drawing his sword, which he had under his country habit, he killed the porter. The armed men then jumped up from under the hay, where they lay concealed, and rushed on the English guard. The Englishmen tried to shut the gates, but they could not, because the cart of hay remained in the gateway, and prevented the folding-doors from being closed. The portcullis was also let fall, but the grating was caught on the cart, and so could not drop to the ground. The men who were in ambush near the gate, hearing the cry, "Call all, call all!" ran to assist those who had leaped out from among the hay; the castle was taken, and all the Englishmen killed or made prisoners. King Robert rewarded Binnock by bestowing on him an estate, which his posterity afterward enjoyed.

Castle Dangerous

ROXBURGH WAS THEN a very large castle, situated near where two fine rivers, the Tweed and the Teviot, join each other. Being within five or six miles of the border, the English were extremely desirous of retaining it, and the Scots equally so of obtaining possession of it.

It was upon the night of what is called Shrove-tide, a holiday, which Roman Catholics paid great respect to, and solemnized, with much gayety and feasting.

Most of the garrison of Roxburgh Castle were feasting and drinking, but still they had set watches on the battlements of the castle, in case of any sudden attack; for, as the Scots had succeeded in so many enterprises of the kind, and as Douglas was known to be in the neighbourhood, they thought themselves obliged to keep a very strict guard.

There was also an Englishwoman, the wife of one of the officers, who was sitting on the battlements with her child in her arms, and, looking out on the fields below, she saw some black objects, like a herd of cattle, straggling in near the foot of the wall, and approaching the ditch or moat of the castle. She pointed them out to the sentinel, and asked him what they were. "Pooh, pooh!" said the soldier, "it is Farmer Such-a-man's cattle" (naming a man whose farm lay near to the castle). "The good man is keeping a jolly Shrove-tide, and has forgot to shut up his bullocks in their yard; but if the Douglas come across them before morning, he is likely to rue his negligence."

Now, these creeping objects they saw from the castle were no real cattle, but Douglas himself and his soldiers, who had put black cloaks above their armour, and were creeping about on their hands and feet, in order, without being observed, to get so near to the foot of the castle wall as to be able to set ladders to it. The poor woman, who knew nothing of this, sat quietly on the wall, and began to sing to her child. You must know that the name of Douglas was become so terrible to the English, that the women used to frighten their children with it, and say to them, when they behaved ill, that they would make the Black Douglas take them. And this soldier's wife was singing to her child:

> *"Hush ye, hush ye, little pet ye;*
> *Hush ye, hush ye, do not fret ye;*
> *The Black Douglas shall not get thee."*

"You are not so sure of that!" said a voice close beside her. She felt at that moment a heavy hand, with an iron glove, laid on her shoulder, and when she looked round, she saw the very Black Douglas she had been singing about, standing close beside her, a tall, swarthy, strong man. At the same time another Scotsman was seen ascending the walls near to the sentinel. The soldier gave the alarm, and rushed at the Scotsman, whose name was Simon Ledehouse, with his lance; but Simon parried the blow, and, closing with the sentinel, struck him a deadly blow with his dagger.

The rest of the Scots followed to assist Douglas and Ledehouse, and the castle was taken. Many of the soldiers were put to death, but Douglas protected the woman and the child. I dare say she made no more songs about the Black Douglas.

Black Agnes

AMONG THE WARLIKE EXPLOITS of this period, we must not forget the defence of the Castle of Dunbar, by the celebrated Countess of March. Her lord had embraced the side of David Bruce, and had taken the field with the regent. The countess, who from her complexion was termed Black Agnes, by which name she is still familiarly remembered, was a high-spirited and courageous woman, the daughter of Thomas Randolph, Earl of Moray, and the heiress of his valour and patriotism. The Castle of Dunbar itself was very strong, being built upon a chain of rocks stretching into the sea, having only one passage to the mainland, which was well fortified. It was besieged by Montague, Earl of Salisbury, who employed to destroy its walls great military engines, constructed to throw huge stones, with which machines fortifications were attacked before the use of cannon.

Black Agnes set all his attempts at defiance, and showed herself with her maids on the walls of the castle, wiping the places where the huge stones fell with a clean towel, as if they could do no ill to her castle, save raising a little dust, which a napkin could wipe away. The Earl of Salisbury then commanded them to bring forward to the assault an engine of another kind, being a species of wooden shed, or house, rolled forward on wheels, with a roof of peculiar strength, which from resembling the ridge of a hog's back, occasioned the machine to be called a sow. This, according to the old mode of warfare, was thrust up to the walls of a besieged castle or city, and served to protect from the arrows and stones of the besieged a party of soldiers placed within the sow, who were in the meanwhile to undermine the wall, or break an entrance through it with pick-axes and mining-tools. When the Countess of March saw this engine advanced to the walls of the castle, she called out to the Earl of Salisbury in derision, and making a kind of rhyme –

> "Beware, Montagow,
> For farrow shall thy sow!"

At the same time she made a signal, and a huge fragment of rock, which hung prepared for the purpose, was dropped down from the wall upon the sow, whose roof was thus dashed to pieces. As the English soldiers who had been within it were running away as fast as they could to get out of the way of the arrows and stones from the wall, Black Agnes called out, "Behold the litters of English pigs!"

The Earl of Salisbury could jest also on such serious occasions. One day he rode near the walls with a knight dressed in armour of proof, having three folds of mail over an acton, or leathern jacket; notwithstanding which, one William Spens shot an arrow with such force that it penetrated all these defences and reached the heart of the wearer. "That is one of my lady's love-tokens," said the earl, as he saw the knight fall dead from his horse. "Black Agnes's love-shafts pierce to the heart!"

Upon another occasion, the Countess of March had well-nigh made the Earl of Salisbury her prisoner. She made one of her people enter into a treaty with the besiegers, pretending to betray the castle. Trusting to this agreement, the earl came at midnight before the gate, which he found open, and the portcullis drawn up. As Salisbury was about to enter, one John Copland, a squire of Northumberland, pressed on before him, and, as soon as he passed the threshold, the portcullis was dropped; and thus the Scots missed their principal prey, and made prisoner only a person of inferior condition.

At length, the Castle of Dunbar was relieved by Alexander Ramsay, of Dalwolsy, who brought the countess supplies by sea, both of men and provisions. The Earl of Salisbury, learning this, despaired of success, and raised the siege, which had lasted nineteen weeks. The minstrels made songs in praise of the perseverance and courage of Black Agnes. The following lines are nearly the sense of what is preserved:

> "She kept a stir in tower and trench,
> The brawling, boisterous Scottish wench;
> Came I early, came I late,
> I found Agnes at the gate."

How the Een Was Set Up

THERE WAS A KING on a time over Eirinn, to whom the cess which the Lochlanners had laid on Alba and on Eirinn was grevious. They were coming on his own realm, in harvest and summer, to feed themselves on his goods; and they were brave strong men, eating and spoiling as much as the Scotch and Irish (Albannaich and Eirionnaich; Alban-ians Eirin-ians) were making ready for another year.

He sent word for a counsellor that he had, and he told him all what was in his thought, that he wanted to find a way to keep the Scandinavians (Lochlannaich; Lochlan-ians) back. The counsellor said to him that this would not grow with him in a moment; but if he would take his counsel, that it would grow with him in time.

"Marry," said he, "the hundred biggest men and women in Eirinn to each other; marry that race to each other; marry the second race to each other again; and let the third kindred (ginealach) go to face the Lochlanners."

This was done, and when the third kindred came to man's estate they came over to Albainn, and Cumhall at their head.

It grew with them to rout the Lochlanners, and to drive them back. Cumhall made a king of himself in Alba that time with these men, and he would not let Lochlanner or Irelander to Alba but himself. This was a grief to the King of Lochlann, and he made up to the King of Alba, that there should be friendship between them, here and yonder, at that time. They settled together the three kings – the King of Lochlann, and the King of Alba, and the King of Eirinn – that they would have a great "*ball*" of dancing, and there should be friendship and truce amongst them.

There was a "*schame*" between the King of Eirinn and the King of Lochlann, to put the King of Scotland to death. Cumhall was so mighty that there was no contrivance for putting him to death, unless he was slain with his own sword when he was spoilt with drink, and love-making, and asleep.

He had his choice of a sweetheart amongst any of the women in the company; and it was the daughter of the King of Lochlann whom he chose.

When they went to rest, there was a man in the company, whose name was Black Arcan, whom they set apart to do the murder when they should be asleep. When they slept, Black Arcan got the sword of Cumhall, and he slew him with it. The murder was done, and everything was right. Alba was under the Lochlanners, and the Irelanders and the Black Arcan had the sword of Cumhall.

The King of Lochlann left his sister with the King of Eirinn, with an order that if she should have a babe son to slay him; but if it were a baby daughter, to keep her alive. A prophet had told that Fionn MacChumhail would come; and the sign that was for this was a river in Eirinn; that no trout should be killed on it till Fionn should come. That which came as the fruit of the wedding that was there, was that the daughter of the King of Lochlann bore a son and daughter to Cumhall. Fionn had no sister but this one, and she was the mother of Diarmaid. On the night they were born his muime (nurse) fled with the son, and she went to a desert place with him, and she was keeping him up there till she raised him as a stalwart goodly child.

She thought that it was sorry for her that he should be nameless with her. The thing which she did was to go with him to the town, to try if she could find means to give him a name. She saw the schoolboys of the town swimming on a fresh water loch.

"Go out together with these," said she to him, "and if thou gettest hold of one, put him under and drown him; and if thou gettest hold of two, put them under and drown them."

He went out on the loch, and he began drowning the children, and it happened that one of the bishops of the place was looking on.

"Who," said he "is that bluff fair son, with the eye of a king in his head, who is drowning the schoolboys?"

"May he steal his name!" said his muime, "Fionn, son of Cumhall, son of Finn, son of every eloquence, son of Art, son of Eirinn's high king, and it is my part to take myself away."

Then he came on shore, and she snatched him with her.

When the following were about to catch them, he leapt off his muime's back, and he seized her by the two ankles, and he put her about his neck. He went in through a wood with her, and when he came out of the wood he had but the two shanks. He met with a loch after he had come out of the wood, and he threw the two legs out on the loch, and it is Loch nan Lurgan, the lake of the shanks, that the loch was called after this. Two great monsters grew from the shanks of Fionn's muime. That is the kindred that he had with the two monsters of Loch nan Lurgan.

Then he went, and without meat or drink, to the great town. He met Black Arcan fishing on the river, and a hound in company with him. Bran MacBuidheig (black, or raven, son of the little yellow).

"Put out the rod for me," said he to the fisherman, "for I am hungry, to try if thou canst get a trout for me." The trout laid to him, and he killed the trout. He asked the trout from Black Arcan.

"Thou art the man!" said Black Arcan; "when thou wouldst ask a trout, and that I am fishing for years for the king, and that I am as yet without a trout for him."

He knew that it was Fionn he had. To put the tale on the short cut, he killed a trout for the king, and for his wife, and for his son, and for his daughter, before he gave any to Fionn. Then he gave him a trout.

Thou must, said Black Arcan, broil the trout on the further side of the river, and the fire on this side of it, before thou gettest a bit of it to eat; and thou shalt not have leave to set a stick that is in the wood to broil it. He did not know here what he should do. The thing that he fell in with was a mound of sawdust, and he set it on fire beyond the river. A wave of the flame came over, and it burned a spot on the trout, the thing that was on the crook. Then he put his finger on the black spot that came on the trout, and it burnt him, and then he put it into his mouth. Then he got knowledge that it was this Black Arcan who had slain his father, and unless he should slay Black Arcan in his sleep, that Black Arcan would slay him when he should awake. The thing that happened was that he killed the carle, and then he got a glaive and a hound, and the name of the hound was Bran MacBuidheig.

Then he thought that he would not stay any longer in Eirinn, but that he would come to Alba, to get the soldiers of his father. He came on shore in Farbaine. There he found a great clump of giants, men of stature. He understood that these were the soldiers that his father had, and they (were) as poor captives by the Lochlanners hunting for them, and not getting (aught) but the remnants of the land's increase for themselves. The Lochlanners took from the arms when war or anything should come, for fear they should rise with the foes. They had one special man for taking their arms, whose name was Ullamh Lamh fhaba. He gathered the arms and he took them with him altogether, and it fell out that the sword of Fionn was amongst them. Fionn went after him, asking for his own sword. When they came within sight of the armies of Lochlann, he said –

> *"Blood on man and man bloodless,*
> *Wind over hosts, 'tis pity without the son of Luin."*

"To what may that belong?" said Ulamh lamh fhada.

"It is to a little bit of a knife of a sword that I had," said Fionn. "You took it with you amongst the rest, and I am the worse for wanting it, and you are no better for having it."

"What is the best exploit thou wouldst do if thou hadst it?"

"I would quell the third part of the hosts that I see before me."

Oolav Longhand laid his hand on the arms. The most likely sword and the best that he found there he gave it to him. He seized it, and he shook it, and he cast it out of the wooden handle, and said he –

> *"It is one of the black-edged glaives,*
> *It was not Mac an Luin my blade;*
> *It was no hurt to draw from sheath,*
> *It would not take off the head of a lamb."*

Then he said the second time the same words.
He said the third time –

> *"Blood on man, and bloodless man,*
> *Wind o'er the people, 'tis pity without the son of Luin."*

"What wouldst thou do with it if thou shouldst get it?"

"I would do this, that I would quell utterly all I see."

He threw down the arms altogether on the ground. Then Fionn got his sword, and said he then –

"This is the one of thy right hand."

Then he returned to the people he had left. He got the ord Fiannta of the Fian, and he sounded it. There gathered all that were in the southern end of Alba of the Faintaichean to where he was. He went with these men, and they went to attack the Lochlanners, and those which he did not kill he swept them out of Alba.

Biographies & Sources

J.F. Campbell
Conall Cra Bhuidhe; The Young King of Easaidh Ruadh; The Battle of the Birds; and other stories appearing here
J.F. Campbell (1821–1885) was a Scottish author, folktale collector, and scholar of Celtic studies. Campbell, also known as Iain Òg Ìle, or Young John of Islay, was born on the island of Islay, in the Inner Hebrides. Throughout his life he travelled widely throughout Scotland recording traditional tales, anecdotes, and songs. He became known as an authority on the subjects of Celtic folklore and the Gaelic peoples. His best-known collection, Popular Tales of the West Highlands, was published in four volumes in 1890. He also published a collection of ballads entitled Leabhar na Feinne, which he self-published in 1872.

Elizabeth W. Grierson
Gold-Tree and Silver-Tree; Thomas the Rhymer; The Seal Catcher and the Merman; and other stories appearing here
Elizabeth W. Grierson (1869–1943) was born on a farm near Hawick, in the Scottish Borders. Throughout the course of her life she published more than thirty books, many of which covered the subjects of Scottish fairy tales and folklore. In addition to these, she also published travel guides for Edinburgh, Scotland, and Florence, Italy. Her best-known works are her collections The Scottish Fairy Book (1910) and Children's Tales from Scottish Ballads (1906).

Joseph Jacobs
The Well of the World's End
Joseph Jacobs (1854–1916) was a folklorist, author, translator, and historian. Jacobs was born in Sydney, Australia, and later moved to Cambridge, England, aged 18, to study at St John's College. Jacobs was known for his work of collecting and preserving English folklore, some of which was published in his collections English Fairy Tales (1890) and More English Fairy Tales (1893). Jacobs is most notable for popularising such English tales as 'Jack and the Beanstalk', 'The Three Little Pigs', and 'Goldilocks and the Three Bears', among others. He was a member of England's Folklore Society and was an editor of the journal Folklore.

James Johonnot
Edinburgh Castle; Scottish Strategy; Castle Dangerous; Black Agnes
James Johonnot (1823–1888) was an American educator and author. Born in Vermont, Johonnot studied at the New England Seminary, after which he became principal of Jefferson School in Syracuse, New York, in 1845. He later worked as an agent for the publisher D. Appleton & Company. He held various other principal roles in schools throughout America. His published works primarily focused on school- and education-related subjects, one of which was his collection entitled Stories of Heroic Deeds for Boys and Girls (1887).

Alexander Mackenzie

The Fairies and Donald Duaghal Mackay; The Spell of Cadboll; Castle Urquhart and the Fugitive Lovers; Young Glengarry, the Black Raven; A Legend of Invershin; Allan Donn and Annie Campbell; Prince Charlie and Mary MacLeod; The Rout of Moy; Cawdor Castle; The Raid of Cilliechriost; A Legend of Loch-Maree; Mary Macleod and Her Lover

Alexander Mackenzie (1838–1898) was a Scottish author, historian, politician, and magazine editor. Born in Gairloch, Scotland, Mackenzie worked as a labourer and ploughman before starting a business in the cloth trade. Later he became an editor and publisher of Celtic Magazine and Scottish Highlander. His best-known work is his collections entitled Historical Tales and Legends of the Highlands (1878). He also penned histories of a number of Scottish clans. He became a member of the Society of Antiquaries of Scotland and a founding member of the Gaelic Society of Inverness.

FLAME TREE PUBLISHING
Epic, Dark, Thrilling & Gothic

New & Classic Writing

**Flame Tree's Gothic Fantasy books offer a carefully curated series of new titles,
each with combinations of original and classic writing:**

*Chilling Horror • Chilling Ghost • Asian Ghost • Science Fiction • Murder Mayhem
Crime & Mystery • Swords & Steam • Dystopia Utopia • Supernatural Horror
Lost Worlds • Time Travel • Heroic Fantasy • Pirates & Ghosts • Agents & Spies
Endless Apocalypse • Alien Invasion • Robots & AI • Lost Souls • Haunted House
Cosy Crime • American Gothic • Urban Crime • Epic Fantasy • Detective Mysteries
Detective Thrillers • A Dying Planet • Footsteps in the Dark • Bodies in the Library
Strange Lands • Weird Horror • Lost Atlantis • Lovecraft Mythos • Terrifying Ghosts
Black Sci-Fi • Chilling Crime • Compelling Science Fiction • Christmas Gothic
First Peoples Shared Stories • Alternate History • Hidden Realms
Immigrant Sci-Fi • Spirits & Ghouls*

**Also, new companion titles offer rich collections of classic fiction, myths
and tales in the gothic fantasy tradition:**

*Charles Dickens Supernatural • George Orwell Visions of Dystopia • H.G. Wells
Sherlock Holmes • Edgar Allan Poe • Bram Stoker Horror • Mary Shelley Horror
Lovecraft • M.R. James Ghost Stories • Algernon Blackwood Horror Stories
Robert Louis Stevenson Collection • The Divine Comedy • The Age of Queen Victoria
Brothers Grimm Fairy Tales • Hans Christian Andersen Fairy Tales • Moby Dick
Alice's Adventures in Wonderland • King Arthur & The Knights of the Round Table
The Wonderful Wizard of Oz • Ramayana • The Odyssey and the Iliad • The Aeneid
Paradise Lost • The Decameron • One Thousand and One Arabian Nights
Persian Myths & Tales • African Myths & Tales • Celtic Myths & Tales
Greek Myths & Tales • Norse Myths & Tales • Chinese Myths & Tales • Japanese Myths & Tales
Native American Myths & Tales • Aztec Myths & Tales • Egyptian Myths & Tales
Irish Fairy Tales • Scottish Folk & Fairy Tales • Viking Folk & Fairy Tales
Heroes & Heroines Myths & Tales • Gods & Monsters Myths & Tales
Beasts & Creatures Myths & Tales • Witches, Wizards, Seers & Healers Myths & Tales*

Available from all good bookstores, worldwide, and online at
flametreepublishing.com

See our new fiction imprint
FLAME TREE PRESS | FICTION WITHOUT FRONTIERS
New and original writing in Horror, Crime, SF and Fantasy

And join our monthly newsletter with offers and more stories:
FLAME TREE FICTION NEWSLETTER
flametreepress.com

GOTHIC FANTASY

For our books, calendars, blog
and latest special offers please see:
flametreepublishing.com